THE COMPLETE
BROTHERS
GRIMM
FAIRY TALES

Hausmärchen

FAIRY TALES FOR THE HOUSEHOLD

The Complete Brothers Grimm Fairy Tales

Edited by Lily Owens

Illustrated

PORTLAND HOUSE

CONTENTS

CONTENTS.

THE CHILDREN'S LEGENDS

INTRODUCTION

The magic world of fairies, witches and goblins opens before us in Grimm's fairy tales. Cinderella and Rumpelstiltskin are known the world over, but many other memorable characters await the reader of this complete collection.

The stories can be as wild a mixture as "The Rich Man's Grave," where fantasy and religion combine, or as gruesome as "The Robber Bridegroom." Animals can talk—"The Cat Who Married a Mouse"— and objects go a-walking—"The Straw, the Coal, and the Bean." Some are full of humor and nonsense—"Clever Grethel" and "The Story of Schlauraffenland"—while the intent of others is to scare young ones into virtue—"The Widow's Two Daughters."

In the nineteenth century, Jakob and Wilhelm Grimm collected folk tales as part of a larger study of German culture. They believed that the tales were important as reflections of the popular mind. Though most authors had previously altered and embellished the stories to suit themselves and their audience, the Grimms were the first collectors to maintain strict allegiance to the original tales, believing that their true value and strength lay in their authenticity.

The brothers recorded oral tales from friends and neighbors, local storytellers and collections of old German myths and tales. Dorothea Wild, a neighbor who contributed a number of stories, later became Wilhelm's wife.

After six years of research, the first volume of *Nursery and Household Tales* was published in 1812. Though the stories received a cold reception from critics, who found them shocking and coarse, they were immediately and widely read.

Because the tales were meant for adults as well as young people, references to their being children's literature disgruntled the brothers. Images, emotions and beings we associate with the primitive or childlike mind abound: fairies, sorcerers and animated objects assail the adventurer. Magic and mystery, great joy and great fear are everyday experiences. But it was the Grimms' contention that these "primitive" expressions reflect the emotions, dreams and desires of every human being.

Many of the fairy tales' central themes and story elements recall the myths and tales of ancient cultures or cultures half a world away—

some of these tales were undoubtedly spread by travelers. Others express ways of seeing the world that are common to all people.

However high or low, exaggerated or outlandish, the emotions and experiences of fairy-tale characters have their real-life counterparts. Half the enjoyment of reading Grimm's fairy tales is recognizing our world in theirs. The other half, of course, is the simple pleasure of the stories in all their variety, with all their vitality.

LILY OWENS

GRIMM'S FAIRY TALES.

THE FROG PRINCE.

In olden times, when people could have all they wished for at once, lived a king who had many beautiful daughters; but the youngest was so lovely, that the sun himself would wonder whenever he shone on her face. Near to the king's castle lay a dark, gloomy forest, in the midst of which stood an old linden tree, shading with its foliage the pleasant waters of a fountain.

One day, when the weather was very hot, the king's daughter came into the forest, and seated herself on the side of the cool fountain, and when at last the silence became wearisome, she began to toss a golden ball in the air, and catch it again, as an amusement. Presently, however, the king's daughter failed to catch the golden ball in her hand, so that it fell on the ground, and rolled over the grass into the water.

The princess followed it with her eyes till it disappeared, for the water was so deep that she could not see the bottom.

Then she cried aloud, and began to weep bitterly for the loss of her golden ball. Presently she heard a voice exclaiming:

'Why do you weep, O king's daughter? Your tears could melt even the stones to pity you!'

She looked at the spot from whence the voice came, and saw a frog stretching his thick ugly head out of the water.

'Oh! there you are, old water-paddler,' she said. 'Well, then, I am crying for the loss of my golden ball that has fallen into the fountain.'

'Then weep no more,' answered the frog; 'I can get it for you. But what will you give me if I fetch your plaything?'

'Oh! anything you like, dear frog,' she replied. 'What will you have—my dresses, my pearls and jewels, or the golden crown I wear sometimes?'

'Neither,' answered the frog. 'Your clothes, your pearls and your jewels, or even your golden crown, are nothing to me. I want you to love me, and let me be your companion and playfellow. I should like to sit at your table, eat from your golden plate, and drink out of your cup, and sleep in your nice little bed. If you will promise me all this, then I will dive down into the water and bring up your pretty golden ball.'

'Oh yes!' she replied. 'I will promise you anything you like if you will only bring up my ball again.'

But she thought to herself that a silly, chattering frog as he was, living in the water with others like himself, and croaking, could not be fit to associate with mankind.

The frog, who believed in the promise of the king's daughter, dipped his head under the water, and sank down to the bottom, where he quickly found the ball, and seizing it in his mouth, carried it to the surface and threw it on the grass. When the king's daughter saw the beautiful plaything, she was full of joy, and, catching it up, ran away as fast as she could run.

'Wait, wait,' cried the frog, 'take me with you, I cannot run so fast as you can.' But the young princess would not listen to the frog's croaking; she got to the house as fast as she could, and soon forgot the poor frog, who was obliged to return to the fountain, and remain there.

The next day, however, while the princess was sitting with the king and his courtiers, and eating out of her own little golden plate, she heard a strange noise on the marble steps outside, splish, splash, splish, splash, and presently came a knock at the door, and a voice cried, 'Lovely princess, open the door for me.' So she rose and went to see who could be outside; but when she caught sight of the frog, she closed the door hastily and seated herself again at the table, looking quite pale. The king, seeing that his daughter was alarmed, said to her, 'My child, what is there at the door? is it a giant come to carry you away?'

'Oh no, my father!' she replied; 'it is no giant, only a great ugly frog.'

'A frog! What can he want with you, my daughter?'

'Ah, my dear father, I will tell you all about it. Yesterday, when I was playing with my golden ball by the fountain in the forest, I let it fall into the water, and because I cried, the frog fetched it out for me, and he made me promise that he should come to the castle and be my companion, for I thought he could not get out of the water to come to me, and now here he is.'

Just then came a second knock at the door, and a voice cried:

'King's daughter, king's daughter, open for me;
You promised that I your companion should be,
When you sat in the shade from the sun's bright beam,
And I fetched up your ball from the fountain's cool stream.'

THE FROG PRINCE

THE GOOD BARGAIN

'Then,' said the king, 'my daughter, you must keep your promise; go and let him in at once.' So she was obliged to go and open the door, and the frog hopped in after her close to her feet and quite up to her chair. But when she sat down he cried: 'Take me up by you.' She would not at first, till her father obliged her to lift the frog on the chair by her side. He was no sooner there than he jumped upon the table and said: 'Now, then, push your little golden plate nearer, and we will eat together.' The princess did as he told her, but everyone could see how much she disliked it. The frog seemed to relish his dinner very much, but he would give the princess half of all he took. At last he said: 'I have eaten and drank quite enough, and I feel very tired, so now carry me upstairs into your little bedroom, and make your silken bed ready, that we may sleep together.'

When the princess heard this, she began to weep, for she was really afraid of the cold frog: she could not even touch him, and now he actually wanted to sleep in her neat beautiful little bed.

But the king was displeased at her tears, and he said: 'He who helped you when you were in trouble must not be despised now.' So the young princess found she must obey. Then she took up the frog with two fingers, and holding him as far from her as possible, she carried him upstairs and placed him in a corner of her room.

In the evening, however, as soon as the princess was in bed, the frog crept out of his corner and said to her: 'I am so tired; lift me up, and let me sleep in your bed, or I will tell your father.'

On hearing this, the princess fell into a great passion, so seizing the frog in her hand, she dashed him with all her strength against the wall, saying: 'You will be quiet now, I hope, you ugly frog.'

But as he fell, how surprised she was to see the frog change into a handsome young prince, with beautiful friendly eyes, who afterwards became her constant companion, and at last her father gave his consent to their marriage.

Before it took place, however, the prince told them his history, how he had been changed into a frog by a wicked witch, and that she had condemned him to live in the fountains until a king's daughter should come and release him. No one else in the world had the power to do so.

After they were married, the young prince proposed that he should take his bride to his own kingdom. So on the wedding-day a splendid carriage drawn by eight white horses drove up to the door. They had white feathers on their heads and golden harness, and by the side of the carriage stood the prince's steward, the faithful Harry. This faithful Harry had been so unhappy when his master was changed into a frog, that he had fastened three iron bands round his heart, to prevent it from bursting with woe and sorrow.

The carriage with the prince and his bride soon drove away with Harry behind in his old place, and full of joy at the release of his master. They had not travelled far when they heard a loud crack—as if something had broken.

Now, the prince knew nothing of the iron bands round his servant's heart, so he cried out : 'Harry, is the carriage breaking?'

'No, sire,' he replied, 'only the iron bands which I bound round my heart for fear it should burst with sorrow while you were a frog confined to the fountain. They are breaking now because I am so happy to see my master restored to his own shape, and travelling to his kingdom with a beautiful bride.'

The prince and princess never forgot faithful Harry, who had loved his master so well while he was in trouble.

THE CAT WHO MARRIED A MOUSE.

ONCE upon a time, a cat made acquaintance with a mouse, and they were together so much that a great love and friendship arose between them, for the mouse was a clever little thing. At last they agreed to marry and dwell together in the same house and be very comfortable.

One day during summer, the cat said to his wife : 'My dear, we must take care to lay in a store for the winter, or we shall die with hunger; you, little Mousey, cannot venture to go about anywhere for fear you should be caught in a trap, but I had better go and see about it.'

This good advice was followed, and in a few days Tom came safely back with a large jar full of beautiful meat covered with fat, which he had found. They had a long talk about a place in which to hide this treasure ; but at last Tom said : 'I don't know a better place than the church—no one ever thinks of robbing a church ; so if we place the jar under the altar and take care not to touch it, then we shall have plenty to eat in winter.'

So the jar was carried to the church and put in a place of safety; but it did not remain there long.

Tom kept thinking of the contents of the jar, and longing so much for a taste, that at last he invented an excuse to get away from home.

'Mousey,' he said one day, 'I have had an invitation from one of my cousins, to be present at the christening of her little son, who was born a few weeks ago ; he is a beautiful kitten, she tells me, gray, with black stripes, and my cousin wishes me to be godfather.'

'Oh yes! go by all means,' replied the mouse; 'but when you are enjoying yourself think of me, and bring me a drop of the sweet red wine, if you can.' Tom promised to do as she asked him, and went off as if he were going to see his cousin. But after all it was not true. Tom had no cousin, nor had he been asked to be godfather.

No; he went right off to the church and slipped under the table where the jar of meat stood, and sat looking at it. He did not look for long, however, for presently he went close up and began licking and licking the fat on the top of the jar, till it was nearly all gone. Then he took a walk on the roofs of the houses in the town, and at last stretched himself out in the sun and stroked his whiskers as often as he thought of the delicious feast he had had. As soon as the evening closed in he returned home.

'Oh! here you are again,' said the mouse. 'Have you spent a pleasant day?'

'Yes, indeed,' he replied. 'Everything passed off very well.'

'And what name did they give the young kitten?' she asked.

'Top-off,' said Tom, quite coolly.

'Top-off!' cried the mouse; 'that is a curious and uncommon name! Is it a family name?'

'It is a very old name in our family,' replied the cat, 'and it is not worse than *Thieves*, as your ancestors were called.'

Poor little Mousey made no reply, and for awhile nothing more was said about Tom's cousins.

But Tom could not forget the jar of meat in the church, and the thought of it made him long so much, that he was obliged to invent another tale of a christening. So he told the little mouse that a lady cat, his aunt, had invited him this time, and that the kitten was a great beauty, all black, excepting a white ring round its neck, so he could not refuse to be present.

'For one day, dear Mousey,' he added, 'you will do me this kindness and keep house at home alone?'

The good little mouse willingly agreed, and Tom ran off; but as soon as he had reached the town, he jumped over the churchyard wall, and very quickly found his way to the place where the jar of meat was concealed. This time he feasted so greedily that when he had finished the jar was more than half empty.

'It tastes as nice as it smells,' said the cat, after his joyful day's work was over and he had had a nice nap. But as soon as he returned home the mouse asked what name had been given to the kitten this time.

Tom was a little puzzled to know what to say, but at last he said: 'Ah! I remember now: they named it "*Half-gone.*"'

'Half-gone! Why, Tom, what a queer name! I never heard of it before in my life, and I am sure it cannot be found in the "Register."'

The cat did not reply, and for a time all went on as usual till another longing fit made him rub his whiskers, and think of the jar of meat. 'Mousey,' said he one day, 'of all good things there are always three: do you know I have had a third invitation to be godfather? and this time the little kitten is quite black, without a single white hair on its whole body; such a thing has not happened in our family for many years, so you will let me go, won't you?'

'*Top-off* and *Half-gone* are such curious names, Tom,' replied the mouse, 'that they are enough to make one suspicious.'

'Oh, nonsense!' replied the cat; 'what can you know about names, staying at home here all day long in your gray coat and soft fur, with nothing to do but to catch crickets? you can know very little of what men do in the world.'

Poor little Mousey was silent, and she patiently remained at home during the absence of the greedy, deceitful cat, who this time feasted himself secretly till he had quite cleaned out the jar, and left it empty.

'When all is gone, then one can rest,' said he to himself, as he returned home at night quite fat and sleek.

'Well, Tom,' said the mouse, as soon as she saw him, 'and what is the name of this third child?'

'I hope you will be pleased at last,' he said; 'it is named *All-gone*.'

'All-gone!' cried the mouse, 'that is the most suspicious name yet; I can scarcely believe it; what does it mean?' Then she shook her head, rolled herself up, and went to sleep.

After this, Tom was not invited to any more christenings; but, as the winter came on, and in the night no provisions could be found, the mouse thought of the careful store they had laid up for the winter, and said to the cat, 'Come, Tom, let us fetch the jar of meat from the church; it will be such a nice relish for us.'

'Ah, yes,' he replied; 'it will be a nice relish to you, I dare say, when you stretch out your fine little tongue to taste it!' So he took himself out of the way, and Mousey went to the church by herself. But what was her vexation at finding the jar still standing in the same place, but quite empty.

Then she returned home, and found Tom looking as if he did not care, although he was at first rather ashamed to face her.

'I understand now,' said the little mouse quite gently; 'I can see what has happened; a fine friend you have been to me to deceive me in this manner. When you told me you were going to stand godfather to the three little kittens, you never visited your relations at all; but, instead of that, you went to the church three times, and ate up all the meat in the jar. I know, now, what you mean by *Top-off, Half-gone*——'

'Will you be quiet?' said the cat in a rage; 'if you say another word I will eat you.'

But the unfortunate mouse had *"All-gone"* on its lips, and hardly had it come out than the cat made a spring, seized the mouse, and gobbled it up.

Now, that's the way of the world, you see.

FAIRY TELL TRUE.

NEAR the opening to a large forest lived a woodcutter with his wife. They had only one child, a little maiden of three years old, and they were so very poor that they could scarcely find bread to eat from day to day.

One morning the woodcutter, full of sorrow, went into the wood to his work, and while he cut down trees with his axe, all at once a beautiful lady stood before him. She had a crown of glittering stars on her head, and diamonds sparkled in her hair. Then she spoke to the woodcutter: 'I am the good Fairy Tell True, and mother of all good children. You are poor and miserable: bring me your little child; I will be a mother to her, and provide for her with the greatest care.' The woodcutter was very glad to give up his little girl to such a good fairy, so he called her to him, and gave her to the beautiful lady, who carried her up to a delightful palace in the clouds.

Here she was very happy; she had sugared bread to eat, and sweet fresh milk to drink; her clothes were of silk and gold, and she played with the fairy's good children all day.

Here she remained till she reached the age of fourteen, and one day the good fairy called her to her side and said: 'Dear child, I have a long journey to take, and while I am absent I intend to leave the thirteen keys of the doors in my fairy palace in your care. You are free to open twelve of these doors and examine the wonderful things which the rooms contain, but the thirteenth, to which this little key belongs, you are forbidden to enter. If you do, great sorrow and misfortune will happen to you.'

The young girl promised faithfully to remember this injunction, and when the good fairy was gone, she began at once to examine the rooms of the palace. Each day she unlocked one, until she had opened all the twelve. In each room she saw a beautiful fairy surrounded with a clear and brilliant light, and so much brightness and glory, that she, as well as the good children who accompanied her, were full of joy.

Now the forbidden door still remained unopened; but such a longing desire arose in her heart to see what the room contained, that she said to her companions: 'I will just open this door a very little way, and peep in.'

'Oh no, don't!' said one of the good children; 'that would be wrong; the good fairy has forbidden you to do so, and something dreadful will happen if you do.'

The young girl was silent, but the longing desire in her heart would not be still, and day after day her curiosity increased so much that she could not rest.

At last, one day when all her young companions were absent, she thought to herself, ' Now I shall be able to go in and have a peep, and no one will ever know.'

So she fetched the keys, and taking the right one in her hand, placed it in the lock, and turned it round. The moment she did so, the door sprang open, and she saw three beautiful fairies seated on a throne of fire in a blaze of light. She stood for a while bewildered with astonishment. Then she moved forwards a little, and placed her finger in the glittering light; and when she drew it back, her finger was covered with gold. On seeing this, she was seized with a terrible fear, and shutting the door quickly, she ran away to another part of the palace. But she could not overcome her fear, and her heart beat violently when she found that the gold would not come off her finger, although she rubbed and washed it with all her might.

Not very long after this the good fairy returned home, and calling the maiden to her, requested her to give up the keys of the palace.

As she placed them in the fairy's hand, she looked earnestly into the young girl's eyes, and said : ' Have you opened the thirteenth door ?'

' No,' was the reply.

The good fairy laid her hand on the young girl's heart, and knew by its beating, which she felt, that she had been disobeyed, and that the door had been opened. Then she said again : ' Have you opened the thirteenth door ?'

' No,' was the reply for the second time.

Then the fairy caught sight of the maiden's finger which had become golden when she touched the fiery light, and knew by this that she was guilty. For a third time she asked the same question, but the young girl still answered, ' No.'

Then the good fairy said to the maiden : ' You have not attended to my commands, nor spoken the truth; you are therefore not fit to remain with good children in this beautiful palace in the clouds.' As the fairy spoke, the maiden fell into a deep sleep, and sunk down upon the earth.

When she awoke, she found herself alone in a great wilderness; and on attempting to cry out, her voice could no longer be heard, for she had been struck dumb. Then she sprang up, and attempted to force her way out of the wilderness, but wherever she turned the thick thorn bushes drove her back, and she could not pass through them. The enclosure in which she now found herself shut in was surrounded by hollow caves, and in one of these she determined to take up her abode; therefore, when night came on, she crept in and slept till morning, and during stormy or rainy weather it formed her only shelter. Her life now was indeed miserable, and whenever she thought of those happy days when she had lived in the beautiful palace, with good children for her companions, she wept bitterly.

Her food consisted of roots and wild berries, which she had to search for, and in autumn she collected all the dry leaves, and carried them to the hollow cave, to serve her for a bed. In winter the nuts were her food, and when the snow and ice came, she rolled herself like a poor animal in the leaves, and let her long hair fall round her like a mantle, for her clothes were all in rags. So one year after another passed, during which she endured the greatest want and misery.

One day in the spring, when the trees were decked in their fresh green leaves, the king of the country was hunting in the forest, and, while following a deer, he saw it disappear among the thick bushes which encircled the old hollow caves. To follow the deer, he alighted from his horse, and made a way for himself through the bushes with his sword.

When he had thus cleared a path, he saw a beautiful maiden seated under a tree, and clothed from head to foot in her own golden hair. He stood still at first in silent astonishment, and then he said: 'Who art thou, fair maiden, and why dost thou sit here in this lonely place?' But she could not answer him, for her lips were sealed.

Then the king spoke again: 'Will you go with me to my palace?' Then she nodded her head, and the king taking her in his arms, lifted her on his horse, and rode home with her.

As soon as they arrived at the castle, he gave her beautiful clothing and everything she wanted in abundance; and although she could not speak, she was so beautiful and graceful that the king fell in love with her, and in a very short time they were married.

In a year after, the young queen had a little son, and while she was lying on her bed during the night, the good fairy appeared to her, and said: 'Wilt thou now own the truth, that thou didst open the forbidden door? If thou wilt, I will restore to thee the power of speech; but if thou art still obstinate, and persist in denying thy sin, then I will take thy new-born babe with me.'

Then the power of speech was given to the queen, to enable her to answer; but she remained obdurate, and said: 'No, I did not open the forbidden door.'

On this the good fairy took the new-born baby in her arms and disappeared with it.

In the morning when the child could not be found, a murmur arose amongst the people; they declared that the queen had destroyed her baby. She heard all they said, but she could not explain; however, the king loved her too well to believe a word of evil against her.

In another year the queen had a second son born, and again the good fairy appeared to her and said: 'If thou wilt now confess that thou hast opened the forbidden door, I will restore to thee thy child and set thy tongue at liberty, but if thou wilt persist in thy denial, thou shalt still remain dumb, and I will take away from thee thy second baby also.' But the queen again replied: 'No, I did not open the forbidden door.' Then the fairy took up the second child and carried it away to her palace in the clouds. The next morning, when the second child also was missing, the people were loud in their complaints against the queen; they even said that they believed she was an ogress, and had eaten it. The king's counsellors also demanded that she should be brought to justice. But the king's love for her was so great that he believed nothing, and even threatened the counsellors, who, at the peril of their lives, did not dare to say a word against her.

But in the third year a little baby girl was born to the queen, and the good fairy came a third time and said to her 'Follow me.' Then she took her by the hand and carried her to the palace in the clouds. She led her in and showed her two beautiful boys, who were laughing and playing beyond the stars in the glorious sunlight. Great was the queen's joy at seeing her children, and the good fairy said to her : 'Is thy heart not yet softened ? Even now, if thou wilt confess that thou hast opened the forbidden door, I will restore to thee both thy two little sons.'

But the queen answered for the third time :

'No, I did not open the forbidden door.'

Then the good fairy allowed her to sink down again to earth, and took away from her the new-born daughter.

When the people discovered the next morning that the third child was missing, they became very angry, and said : 'Our queen is really an ogress ; she has eaten her children ; she must be condemned to die.' This time the king could not silence his counsellors. The queen was brought before the tribunal, and as she would not answer nor defend herself, she was condemned to be burnt alive. The funeral pile was formed, and she was fastened to the stake, but when the flames began to spread around, her pride was melted from her heart, and she repented ; the thought arose, 'Oh ! if I could only confess to the good fairy before I die, and tell her that I did open that door.' As she thought this her voice came back to her, and she cried : 'Oh ! good Fairy Tell True, I am guilty.'

As soon as the words were out of her mouth the rain began to pour down, and quickly put out the flames. A bright light surrounded her, and in it appeared the good fairy, leading by the hand the queen's dear, long-lost boys, and carrying in her arms the little baby girl. The fairy spoke kindly to her, and said : 'Now that thou hast confessed thy sin and art forgiven, I can restore to thee not only the power of speech, but also thy three dear children, and promise thee happiness and joy for the remainder of thy life. For,' she said, 'those who confess and forsake their sins shall find mercy.'

THE YOUTH WHO COULD NOT SHIVER AND SHAKE.

A FATHER had two sons, the eldest clever and sensible, but the younger was so stupid that he could neither learn nor understand anything, and people would say: 'What a burden that stupid boy must be to his father!'

Whatever the father wanted done, Jack, the eldest boy, was obliged to do, even to take messages, for his brother was too stupid to understand or remember. But Jack was a terrible coward, and if his father wished him to go anywhere late in the evening, and the road led through the churchyard, he would say: 'Oh no, father! I can't go there; it makes me tremble and shake so.'

Sometimes when they sat round the fire of an evening, while some one related tales that frightened him, he would say: 'Oh! please don't go on, it makes me shake all over.'

The youngest boy, seated in his corner among the listeners, would open his eyes quite wide and say: 'I can't think what he means by saying it makes him shiver and shake; it must be something very wonderful that could make me shiver and shake.'

At last one day the father spoke to his youngest son very plainly, and said: 'Listen, you there in the corner: you are growing tall and strong, you must learn very soon to earn your own living. See how your brother works, while you do nothing but run and jump about all day.'

'Well, father,' he replied, 'I am quite ready to earn my own living when you like, if I may only learn to shiver and shake, for I don't know how to do that at all.'

His brother laughed at this speech, and said to himself: 'What a simpleton my brother is! he will have to sweep the streets by-and-by, or else starve.'

His father sighed and said: 'You will never get your living by that, boy, but you will soon learn to shiver and shake, no doubt.'

Just at this moment the sexton of the church came in, and the father related the trouble he was in about his youngest son, who was so silly and unable to learn. 'What do you think he said to me when I told him he must learn to earn his own living?' asked the father.

'Something silly, I suppose,' answered the sexton.

'Silly, indeed! he said he wished he could learn to shiver and shake.'

'Oh!' cried the sexton, 'let him come to me, I'll soon manage that for him; he won't be long learning to shiver and shake if I have him with me.'

The father was delighted with this proposal; it was really a good beginning for his stupid son. So the sexton took the youth in hand at once, led him to the church-tower, and made him help to ring the bells. For the first two days he liked it very well, but on the third at midnight the sexton roused him out of his sleep to toll the passing bell, so he had to mount to the highest part of the church-tower and toll the bell.

'You will soon learn what it is to shiver and shake now, young man,' thought the sexton, but he did not go home, as we shall hear by-and-by. The youth walked through the churchyard and mounted the steps to the belfry without feeling the least fear, but just as he reached the bell-rope, he saw a figure in white standing on the steps.

'Who's there?' he cried. But the figure neither moved nor spoke. 'Answer me,' he said, 'or take yourself off; you have no business here.'

But the sexton, who had disguised himself to frighten the boy, remained immovable, for he wished to be taken for a ghost; but Hans was not to be frightened. He exclaimed, for the second time: 'What do you want here? Speak, if you are an honest man, or I will throw you down the steps.'

The sexton, thinking he could not intend to do anything so dreadful, answered not a word, but stood still, as if he were made of stone. 'Once more, I ask you what you want,' said Hans; and as there was still no answer, he sprung upon the sham ghost, and giving him a push, he rolled down ten steps, and falling into a corner, there remained.

Thereupon Hans went back to the bell, tolled it for the proper number of minutes, then went home, laid himself down without saying a word, and went fast asleep.

The sexton's wife waited a long time for her husband, and finding he did not come home she became alarmed, and going to Hans, woke him and said: 'Do you know why my husband is staying out so late—he was with you in the tower, I suppose?'

'There was some one standing on the top of the steps when I went into the belfry, dressed in white, and as he would not answer a word when I spoke to him, I took him for a thief and kicked him downstairs. We will go and see who it is; if it should be your husband, I shall be sorry, but, of course, I did not know.'

The wife ran out to the tower and found her husband lying in a corner groaning, for he had broken his leg. Then she went to the father of Hans with a loud outcry against the boy. 'Your son,' cried she, 'has brought bad luck to the house; he has thrown my husband down the steps and broken his leg; he shan't stay with us any longer; send for him home.'

Then the father was terribly vexed, sent for his son, and scolded him. 'What do you mean, you wretched boy,' he said, 'by these wicked tricks?'

'Father,' answered the boy, 'hear what I have to say. I never meant to do wrong, but when I saw a white figure standing there in the night, of course I thought it was there for some bad purpose. I did not know it was the sexton, and I warned him three times what I would do, if he did not answer.'

'Ah yes! you are the plague of my life,' said his father. 'Now go out of my sight, and never let me see you more.'

'Yes, father, I will go right willingly to-morrow; and then if I learn to shiver and shake, I shall acquire knowledge that will enable me to earn my living, at all events.'

'Learn what you like,' said his father, 'it's all the same to me. There are fifty crowns, take them and go out into the world when you please; but don't tell anyone where you come from, or who is your father, for I am ashamed to own you.'

'Father,' said Hans, 'I will do just as you tell me; your orders are very easy to perform.'

At daybreak the next morning, the youth put the fifty crowns into his pocket, and went out into the highroad, saying to himself as he walked on: 'When shall I learn to shiver and shake—when shall I learn to be afraid?'

Presently a man met him on the road, overheard what he said, and saw at once that the young man was fearless. He quickly joined him, and they walked a little way together till they came to a spot where they could see a gallows.

'Look,' he said, 'there is a tree where seven men have been married with the rope-maker's daughter, and have learnt how to swing; if you only sit down here and watch them till night comes on, I'll answer for it you will shiver and shake before morning.'

'I never had a better opportunity,' answered the youth. 'That is very easily done. You come to me again early to-morrow morning, and if it teaches me to shiver and shake, you shall have my fifty crowns.'

Then the young man went and seated himself under the gallows and waited till the evening, and feeling cold he lighted a fire; but at midnight the wind rose and blew so fiercely and chill, that even a large fire could not warm him.

The high wind, as well as being cold, made the bodies of the murderers swing to and fro, and he thought to himself, 'If I am so cold down here by the fire, they must be frozen up there;' and after pitying them for some time he climbed up, untied the ropes, and brought down all the seven bodies, stirred the fire into a blaze, and seated them round it so close that their clothes caught fire. Finding they did not move, he said to them: 'Sit farther back, will you, or I will hang you up again.' But the dead could not hear him; they only sat silent and let their rags burn.

Then Hans became angry, and said: 'If you will not move, there is no help for it; I must not let you burn, I must hang you up.' So he hung the seven bodies up again all in a row, then laid himself down by the fire and fell fast asleep.

In the morning the man came, according to his promise, hoping to get the fifty crowns. 'Well, I suppose you know now what it is to shiver and shake?' he said.

'No, indeed,' he replied. 'Why should I? those up there have not opened their mouths once; and when I seated them round the fire, they allowed their old rags to burn without moving, and if I had not hung the bodies up again, they would have been burned also.' The man looked quite scared when he heard this, and went away without attempting to ask for the fifty crowns.

Then Hans continued his journey, and again said aloud to himself: 'I wonder what this shivering and shaking can be.'

A waggoner walking along the road by his horses overtook him, and asked who he was.

'I don't know,' he replied.

The waggoner asked again: 'Why are you here?'

'I can't tell,' said Hans.

'Who is your father?'

'I dare not say.'

'What were you grumbling about just now, when I came up with you?'

'I want to learn to shiver and shake,' said Hans.

'Don't talk nonsense,' said the waggoner. 'Come with me, I will show you a little of the world, and find you something to do better than that.'

So the young man went with the waggoner, and about evening they arrived at an inn, where they put up for the night. No sooner, however, did Hans enter the room than he muttered to himself: 'Oh! if I could only learn to shiver and shake.'

The landlord heard him, and said with a laugh: 'If that is all you wish to learn, I can tell you of a splendid opportunity in this part of the world.'

'Ah! be silent now,' said the landlady. 'You know how many people have already lost their lives through their curiosity. It would be a pity for a nice young man like this, with such fine blue eyes, never to see daylight again.'

But Hans spoke for himself at once: 'If it is so bad as you say,' he cried, 'I should like to try as soon as possible; all I want is to learn how to shiver and shake, so tell me what I am to do.' And the youth gave the landlord no rest till he had explained the matter to him.

'Well,' he said at last, 'not far from here stands an enchanted castle, where you could easily learn to shiver and shake, if you remain in it. The king of the country has promised to give his daughter in marriage to anyone who will venture to sleep in the castle for three nights, and she is as beautiful a young lady as the sun ever shone upon. Rich and valuable treasures in the castle are watched over by wicked spirits, and anyone who could destroy these goblins and demons, and set free the treasures which are rotting in the castle, would be made a rich and lucky man. Numbers of persons have gone into the castle full of hope that they should succeed, but they have not been heard of since.'

Hans was not in the least alarmed by this account, and the next morning he started off early to visit the king.

When he was admitted to the palace, the king looked at him earnestly, and seemed much pleased with his appearance; then he said : ' Do you really wish to be allowed to remain for three nights in the enchanted castle ?'

' Yes,' replied Hans, ' I do request it.'

' You can take no living creature with you,' said the king; ' what else will you have ?'

' I only ask for a fire, a turning-lathe, a cutting-board, and a knife,' he replied.

To this the king readily agreed, and these articles he was permitted to take into the castle during the day. When night came, he took up his abode in one of the rooms, lighted a fire which soon burned brightly, placed the turning-lathe and the cutting-board near it, and sat down on the cutting-board, determined to make himself comfortable. Presently he exclaimed : ' Oh, when shall I learn to shiver and shake ? Not here, I am certain, for I am feeling too comfortable.'

But at midnight, just as he had stirred the fire into a blaze, he suddenly heard in a corner the cry of a cat—' Miou, miou; how cold it is.'

' What a fool you must be, then,' cried Hans, ' to stay out there in the cold ! Come and seat yourself by the fire, and get warm if you will.'

As he spoke, two very large black cats sprung forward furiously, seated themselves on each side of the fire, and stared at him with wild, fiery eyes. After a while, when the cats became thoroughly warm, they spoke, and said : ' Comrade, will you have a game of cards ?'

' With all my heart,' answered Hans ; ' but first stretch out your feet, and let me examine your claws.'

The cats stretched out their paws. ' Ah !' said he, what long nails you have, and now that I have seen your fingers, I would rather be excused from playing cards with you.'

Then he killed them both, and threw them out of the window into the moat. As soon as he had settled these two intruders, he seated himself again by the fire, hoping to have a little rest; but in a few moments there rushed out from every corner of the room black cats and black dogs in a fiery chain one after another, till there seemed no end of them. They mewed, and barked, and growled, and at length jumped on his fire and scattered it about the room, as if they wished to put it out.

For awhile he watched them in silence, till at last he got angry, and seizing his cutting-board, exclaimed : ' Be off ! you horrid creatures !' and then rushing after them, he chased them round the room. Some few escaped in the clamour, but the rest he killed with his cutting-board, and threw into the moat.

As soon as he had cleared the room, he rekindled his fire, by gathering the sparks together, and sat down to warm himself in the blaze.

After a time he began to feel so sleepy that his eyes would not keep open any longer; so he looked round the room and espied in a corner a large bed. 'That is the very place for me,' he said, rising, and laying himself upon it; but just as he was closing his eyes to sleep, the bed began to move about the room, and at last increased its speed, and went off at a gallop through the castle.

'All right,' cried Hans, 'now go on again.' At this the bed started off, as if six horses were harnessed to it, through the doorway, down the steps, to the great gates of the castle, against which it came with a great bump, and tumbled, legs uppermost, throwing all the pillows and blankets on Hans, who lay underneath, as if a mountain were upon him. He struggled out from the load, and said: 'Anyone may travel in that fashion who likes, but I don't.' So he laid himself down again by the fire, and slept till the daybreak.

In the morning the king came to the castle, and, as he caught sight of Hans lying by the fire asleep, he thought the evil spirits had killed him, and that he was dead. 'Alas!' said the king, 'I am very sorry; it is a great pity that such a fine youth should lose his life in this manner.'

But Hans, who heard, sprang up in a moment, and exclaimed: 'No, king, I am not dead yet.' The king, quite astonished and joyful at finding him unhurt, asked him how he had passed the night.

'Oh, very pleasantly indeed,' replied Hans; and then he related to the king all that had passed, which amused him very much.

On returning to the inn, the landlord stared at him with wide open eyes: 'I never expected to see you again alive; but I suppose you have learnt to shiver and shake by this time.'

'Not I,' he replied; 'I believe it is useless for me to try, for I never shall learn to be afraid.'

The second night came, and he again went up to the old castle, and seated himself by the fire, singing the burden of his old song, 'When shall I learn to shiver and shake?'

At midnight he heard a noise, as of something falling. It came nearer; then for a little while all was quiet; at last, with a tremendous scream, half the body of a man came tumbling down the chimney, and fell right in front of Hans.

'Holloa!' he cried, 'all that noise, and only half a man! where's the other half?' At this, the noise and tumult began again, and, amidst yellings and howlings, the other half of the man fell on the hearth.

'Wait,' said Hans, rising; 'I will stir the fire into a blaze first.' But when he turned to sit down again, he found that the two halves of the man had joined, and there sat an ugly looking object in his place. 'Stay,' cried the young man; 'I did not bargain for this: that seat is mine.'

The ugly man tried to push Hans away; but he was too quick for him, and putting out all his strength, he dislodged the creature from his seat, and placed himself again upon it.

Immediately there came tumbling down the chimney nine more of these horrid men, one after the other; each of them held a human thigh-bone in his hand, and the first who appeared brought out two skulls, and presently they set up the nine bones like skittles, and began to play, with the skulls for balls.

'Shall I play with you?' asked Hans, after he had looked on for some time.

'Yes, willingly,' they replied, 'if you have any money.'

'Plenty,' he said; 'but your balls are not quite round.' So he took the skulls and turned them on his lathe. 'Now they will roll better; come on, let us set to work.'

The strange men played with great spirit, and won a few of his dollars; but all at once the cock crew, and they vanished from his eyes. After they were gone he laid himself down and slept peacefully till the king arrived, and asked him what had happened, and how it had fared with him during the night.

'Well,' said Hans, 'I played a game of skittles with some horrid looking fellows who had bones and skulls for skittles and balls; I won sometimes, and I lost a couple of dollars.'

'Did you not shiver and shake?' asked the king, in surprise.

'Not I, indeed! I wish I could! Oh! if I only knew how to shiver and shake.'

The third night came, and found our hero once more seated on his bench by the fire, and saying quite mournfully: 'When shall I ever learn to shiver and shake?'

As he spoke there came into the room six tall men, bearing a coffin containing a dead man.

'Ah!' said Hans, 'I know what you have there; it is the body of my cousin. He has been dead two days.' Then he beckoned with his finger, and said: 'Come here, little cousin; I should like to see you!'

The men placed the coffin on the ground before him, and took off the lid. Hans touched the face, and it felt as cold as ice. 'Wait,' he said; 'I will soon warm it!' so he went to the fire, and, warming his hand, laid it on the face of the dead man, which remained as cold as ever.

At last he took him out of the coffin, carried him to the fire, and placed him on his lap, while he rubbed the hands and chest that he might cause the blood to circulate, but all to no purpose; the body remained as cold as before. Presently he remembered that when two lie in bed together they warm each other, so he placed the dead man in bed, covered him over, and lay down beside him. After awhile this seemed to produce warmth in the body, the blood began to circulate, and at last the dead man moved and spoke.

'There now, dear cousin,' said Hans; 'see, I have warmed you into life again, as I said I could.' But the dead man sprang up and cried: 'Yes, and now I will strangle you.'

'What!' cried Hans, 'is that your gratitude? then you may as well go back into your coffin again.' He leaped out of bed as he spoke, and, seizing the body, he threw it into the coffin and shut the lid down closely upon it.

Then the six tall men walked in, lifted up the coffin, and carried it away.

'That's over,' said Hans   'Oh! I am sure nothing will ever teach me to shiver and shake.'

As he spoke a man walked in who was taller and larger than any of the others, and the look of his eyes was frightful; he was old and wore a long white beard.

'You wretched creature,' cried the man, 'I will soon teach you what it is to shiver and shake, for you shall die.'

'Not so fast, friend,' answered Hans. 'You cannot kill me without my own consent.'

'I will soon have you on the ground,' replied the monster.

'Softly, softly, do not boast; you may be strong, but you will find that I am stronger than you.'

'That is to be proved,' said the old man; 'if you are stronger than I am, I will let you go.   Come, we will try.'

The old man, followed by Hans, led the way through long dark passages and cellars, till they saw the reflection of a smith's fire, and presently came to a forge.   Then the old man took an axe, and with one blow cut through the anvil right down to the ground.

'I can do better than that,' said Hans, taking up the axe and going towards another anvil.   The monster was so surprised at this daring on the part of Hans that he followed him closely, and as he leaned over to watch what the youth was going to do, his long white beard fell on the anvil.   Hans raised his axe, and split the anvil at one blow, wedging the old man's beard in the opening at the same time.

'Now I have got you, old fellow,' cried Hans; 'prepare for the death you deserve.'   Then he took up an iron bar and beat the old man till he cried for mercy, and promised to give him all the riches that were hidden in the castle.

At this Hans drew out the axe from the anvil, and set the old man's beard free, while he watched him closely.   He kept his word, however, and leading the young man back to the castle, pointed out to him a cellar in which were three immense chests full of gold.

'There is one for the poor,' said he; 'another for the king, and the third for yourself.'

Hans was about to thank him, when the cock crew, and the old man vanished, leaving the youth standing in the dark.

'I must find my way out of this place,' he said, after groping about for some time; but at last daylight penetrated into the vaults, and he succeeded in reaching his old room, and lying down by the fire, slept soundly till he was aroused by the king's arrival.

'Well,' he said in a glad voice, when he saw the young man alive, 'have you learnt to shiver and shake yet?'

'No,' replied Hans; 'what was there to make me fear?   My dead cousin came to see me, and a bearded old man tried to conquer me, but I managed him, and he has shown me where to find hidden treasures of gold, and how could I shiver and shake at these visitors?'

'Then,' said the king, 'you have released the castle from enchantment. I will give you, as I promised, my daughter in marriage.'

'That is good news,' cried Hans. 'But I have not learnt to shiver and shake after all.'

The gold was soon after brought away from the castle, and the marriage celebrated with great pomp. Young Prince Hans, as he was now called, did not seem quite happy after all. Not even the love of his bride could satisfy him. He was always saying: 'When shall I learn to shiver and shake?'

This troubled the princess very much, till her lady's-maid said: 'I will help you in this matter; I will show you how to make the prince shiver and shake, that you may depend upon.'

So the princess agreed to do what the lady's-maid advised.

First she went out to a brook that flowed through the gardens of the palace, and brought in a whole pailful of water, containing tiny fish, which she placed in the room.

'Remember,' said the lady's-maid, 'when the prince is asleep in bed, you must throw this pail of water over him; that will make him shiver and shake I am quite certain, and then he will be contented and happy.'

So that night, while Hans was in bed and asleep, the princess drew down the bedclothes gently, and threw the cold water with the gudgeons all over him. The little fish wriggled about as they fell on the bed, and the prince, waking suddenly, exclaimed: 'Oh dear! how I do shiver and shake; what can it be?' Then, seeing the princess standing by his bed, he guessed what she had done.

'Dear wife,' he said, 'now I am satisfied; you have taught me to shiver and shake at last;' and from that hour he lived happily and contented with his wife, for he had learnt to shiver and shake—but not to fear.

THE WOLF AND THE SEVEN YOUNG KIDS.

THERE was once an old goat who had seven young ones, and she loved them as much as any mother could love her children.

One day she wished to go into the forest and get food for them, so she assembled them round her and said: 'Dear children, I am going out into the wood; don't open the door while I am away, for if the wolf should get into our hut, the wicked deceitful creature will eat you up, even to the very hairs; you may easily know him by his rough voice and his large black feet.'

'Dear mother,' said the young kids, 'we will be very careful to keep out the wolf; you may leave us without the least anxiety.' So the old goat made herself quite comfortable and started on her way.

She had not been absent long, when there came a knock at the door, and a voice cried: 'Open the door, my dear children, I have brought something nice for each of you.'

But the young kids knew by the rough voice that it was the old wolf, and not their mother; so the eldest said: 'We shall not open the door, you are not our mother; she has a soft and gentle voice, and your voice is rough. You are only a wolf.'

Then the wolf ran away to a shop at some distance, and bought a great stick of white chalk, which he ate to make his voice soft. After he had eaten it, he went back to the goat's cottage and knocked again at the door and said, in a soft voice, which the little kids thought was their mother's: 'Open the door for me now, dear children; I am your mother, and I have something nice for each of you.'

But the wolf put his foot on the window-sill as he spoke, and looked into the room; the young kids saw it, and one of them said; 'No! we shall not open the door; our mother has no black feet like that; go away, you are the wolf.'

So the wolf went away again to a baker's, and said: 'Baker, I have crushed my foot; please to wrap it in dough, that will soon cure it.' And as soon as the baker had done this, he went off to the miller and asked him to cover his foot with flour. The miller was too frightened to refuse, so he floured the wolf's foot and sent him away. Such is the way of the world.

Now went the wicked animal for the third time to the house door, and said: 'Open the door, dear children, it is your mother this time; she has brought you something from the forest.'

'Show us your feet,' said the little kids, 'then we shall know if you really are our mother.' The wolf placed his white foot on the window, and when they all saw it was white, they believed that what he had said was all true, so they opened the door; but as soon as he entered the house they discovered that it was the wolf, and with screams of terror ran to hide themselves.

One hid under the table, another in the bed, the third in the oven, the fourth in the kitchen, the fifth in the cupboard, the sixth under the wash-tub, and the seventh in the clock-case. But the wolf found six, and, without much ceremony, gobbled them up one after the other, excepting the youngest, who was hidden in the clock-case.

After the wolf had satisfied his greedy appetite, he went out lazily and laid himself down in the green meadow under a tree and fell fast asleep.

Not long after the old goat returned home from the forest. Ah! what a scene it was for her. The house door wide open. Table, chairs, and stools upset. The wash-tub broken to pieces, the counterpanes and pillows dragged from the bed. She sought for her children in terror, but not one could she find. At last she heard a little voice cry: 'Dear mother, here I am, shut up in the clock-case.' The old goat helped her kid out, and then listened while she described the deceitful manner in which the wolf had managed to get into the hut and eat up all her brothers and sisters. We can guess how the poor mother mourned and wept for her children. At last she went out, and the little kid followed her. As they crossed the meadow, they saw the wolf lying under a tree and snoring so loud that the ground trembled.

The goat examined him on all sides, and saw a movement as if something were alive in his stomach. 'Ah!' thought she, 'if he only swallowed my dear children, they must be still alive.' So she sent the little kid into the house for a pair of scissors, a needle, and some thread, and very quickly began to cut open the monster's stomach. She had scarcely made one cut, when a little kid stretched out his head, and then a second, and a third sprang out as she cut farther, till the whole six were safe and alive, jumping around their mother for joy; the monster in his eagerness had swallowed them whole, and they were not hurt in the least.

Then their mother said to them: 'Go and fetch me some large pebbles from the brook, that we may fill the stomach of the dreadful creature while he still sleeps.' The seven little kids started off to the brook in great haste, and brought back as many large stones as they could carry; with these they filled the stomach of the wolf; then the old goat sewed it up again so gently and quietly that the wolf neither awoke nor moved.

As soon, however, as he had had his sleep out, he awoke, and stretching out his legs, felt himself very heavy and uncomfortable, and the great stones in his stomach made him feel so thirsty that he got up and went to the brook to drink. As he trotted along the stones rattled and knocked one against the other and against his sides in a most strange manner. Then he cried out:

> 'What a rattle and rumble!
> They cannot be bones
> Of those nice little kids,
> For they feel just like stones.'

But when he came to the brook and stooped over to drink, the weight of the stones in his stomach overbalanced him, so that he fell in and was drowned.

The little kids and their mother ran over towards the brook when they heard the splash and saw what happened. Then they danced round their mother for joy, crying out: 'The wolf is dead! The wolf is dead!' And this was the end of the greedy wolf.

FAITHFUL JOHN.

THERE was once a king who became so very ill that he felt sure he must be lying on his death-bed, so he said to those around him: 'Send Faithful John to me.' Now John was the king's favourite servant, who had lived with him for many years, and had always been faithful and true. As soon as the faithful servant appeared at the king's bedside, the king said to him:

'My trustworthy friend, I feel that my end is approaching, and I have no anxiety or care on my mind excepting for my son; he is still young, and does not always know how to guide himself. If you will promise to instruct him in all that he ought to know, and be to him a second father, then shall I close my eyes and sleep in peace.'

'I promise,' replied Faithful John. 'I will never leave him, and I will serve him faithfully always, though it should cost me my life.'

'Then,' said the king, 'now I can die in peace and in comfort. After my death you must take my son over the whole castle and show him all the rooms, the saloons, the vaults and the treasures that are concealed therein. But the last room at the end of the long gallery he must not enter, for it contains the statue of the "Princess of the Golden Dome." If he should see this, he will fall deeply in love, and will be placed in great and many dangers; it must be your duty to watch him carefully.'

Then Faithful John took the old king's hand and again promised to do all he wished. After this the king's mind became calm and peaceful, and he laid his head on his pillow and died.

As soon as the old king was laid in his grave, Faithful John related to the young monarch what his father had made him promise on his death-bed, and said: 'That promise I will firmly hold, and I will serve you as faithfully as I have served your father, even should it cost me my life.'

The days of mourning being over, John spoke to the young king again, and said: 'It is now time that you should go round the estate which has been left by your father, and I am ready to show you over the castle.' Then he led him all though the different saloons, and allowed him to see the beautiful rooms and the rich treasures. Only one chamber he did not open, in which the dangerous statue stood.

This figure was so wonderfully chiselled, that on opening the door it attracted the eye of a stranger at once, for the form and colour were more lovely and beautiful than anything else in the whole world.

The young king quickly perceived that Faithful John passed by this door without opening it, and said: ' Why do you not unlock this door for me?'

' There is something in that chamber too terrible for you to see, replied John.

But the king replied : ' I have seen all over the rest of the castle, and I will know what this room contains.'

He went forward as he spoke and tried to open the door by force. But John held him back, saying: ' I promised your father on his death-bed never to allow you to see the interior of this chamber, and I know that misfortune will be the result to both, if I break that promise.'

' Ah no !' he replied, ' on the contrary, if I go not into that room, it will be my certain ruin ; I shall have no rest day or night till I have seen it with mine eyes. Neither will I stir from this spot till you have unlocked the door.'

Then Faithful John saw that it was useless to resist any longer, so with a heavy heart and many sighs he separated the key from the rest and opened the door. As he did so he stepped in first and tried to hide the figure, but it was of no use. The king, standing on tiptoe, saw it over John's shoulder. But as soon as he caught sight of the beautiful statue of the young lady so gloriously bedecked with gold and jewels, he fainted and fell insensible upon the floor. Faithful John lifted him up and carried him to his room full of sorrow, saying to himself : ' The misfortune has commenced now. Oh ! what will become of us ?' Then he gave the young king some wine, and after a time he came to himself.

The first words he uttered were to ask whose beautiful image he had seen.

' That is "The Princess of the Golden Dome," ' answered Faithful John.

' Oh !' he replied, ' already is my love for her so great that if every leaf on every tree of the forest were a tongue, they could not express it. My life depends upon obtaining her hand. You are my faithful John, and you must help me.'

The faithful servant reflected for a long time on the best way to find the young princess for his master, or even to get a glimpse of her countenance. At last he thought of a plan, and spoke to the king about it. ' Everything surrounding the beautiful statue of the princess,' said Faithful John, ' is of gold—the tables, the chairs, the dishes, the cups, the goblets, and even the furniture. In the castle you have five tons of golden treasures. All these you must place in the hands of the gold-smith to be formed into various and beautiful articles, such as vases and curious ornaments in the forms of birds, beasts and wild animals. As soon as these are ready, we will set out on our travels and seek our fortunes.'

On hearing this, the king summoned all the goldsmiths in his kingdom, and desired them to work night and day to get the articles ready as quickly as possible.

The goldsmiths worked day and night to get these beautiful things finished, and Faithful John having engaged a ship, they were carried on board and stowed away carefully. The king and his faithful servant both arrayed themselves in the dress of a merchant that they might not be recognised. As soon as everything was ready they started, and, after a long and prosperous voyage, reached the city where 'The Princess of the Golden Dome' dwelt.

Faithful John left the king on board, and landed by himself, carrying with him in his pocket several beautiful little ornaments of gold. 'Very likely I shall bring the princess back with me to visit you on board ship,' he said, before he went. 'Have the golden vases placed where they can be seen, and let the ship be dressed with flags and banners as if for a grand fête.' The young king promised obedience, and then Faithful John went ashore and found his way to the castle in which the princess lived.

When he entered the courtyard of the palace, he saw, standing by a fountain, a beautiful maiden, who was drawing water in a golden vessel. As she turned to go with the sparkling water in her hands, she caught sight of a strange man, and inquired who he was. 'I am a merchant,' he replied, and opening his case he showed her some of its contents.

'Oh, what beautiful things!' she exclaimed, setting down her pitcher and examining them one by one. 'The princess must see these,' she continued; 'she is so fond of golden trinkets that I am sure she will buy them all!' Then she took him by the hand and led him into the castle, for she was the princess's maid.

As soon as the princess saw the beautiful merchandise, she was delighted, and said: 'The workmanship is so exquisite that I should like to buy all you have.'

But Faithful John replied: 'I am only the servant of a rich merchant who owns these articles, and these are nothing to what my master has with him on board ship; there you would see most costly golden trinkets and far more precious.'

'Can you not bring them to me?' she asked.

'Oh no,' he replied; 'it would occupy many days to do so, and there are more than your palace would hold.'

This only renewed her anxiety and wish to see them, so at last she said: 'Conduct me to the ship; I will go myself and see what your master's treasures really are.'

In a very short time Faithful John was joyfully leading the beautiful princess to the ship, and into the presence of the king, who, as soon as he beheld her, saw that her beauty was far greater than that of the beautiful statue of her in his own palace, and his heart bounded with joy. He offered her his hand to lead her on deck, and as soon as she was safely on board, Faithful John went over quietly to the captain and told him to weigh anchor and spread all sail immediately. His orders were obeyed, and in a few minutes the ship was flying before the wind like a bird.

Meanwhile the king was showing the beautiful princess in the cabin and all over the ship the various and rich cups and vessels, vases, and other wonderful things it contained. He was so kind and gentle to her, and the golden curiosities were so delightful, that she did not observe that the ship was leaving the shore. At last, after giving the supposed merchant a large order, and thanking him for his politeness, she requested to be put on shore. But when she reached the deck and saw that the ship in full sail had left the land and was far out at sea, she became terribly alarmed, and cried out: 'I am betrayed; I am in the power of a merchant who has carried me off; rather let me die.'

Then the king seized her by the hand, and said: 'No, I am not a merchant, I am a king, and as well born as yourself. Nothing but my great love for you would have induced me to carry you away by stratagem; indeed, it is so overpowering that when I first glanced at your statue, I fainted and fell to the earth before it.'

As the princess heard this, she gained courage, and in her heart was disposed to treat this bold young king graciously, and before the voyage was over she had consented to become the wife of such a handsome young prince. It was a very pleasant voyage, and the king, while sailing over the sea with the beautiful princess whom he loved so fondly, felt very happy. One evening, however, when they were seated together in the stern of the vessel, and Faithful John sat playing on the lute near them, three crows flew over the ship and rested for awhile on the rigging. Faithful John saw them, and stopped his playing to hear what they said to each other, for he understood their language well.

'Ah!' said one, 'there sails "The Princess of the Golden Dome" with the king who has carried her off.'

'Yes,' replied the second, 'but he will not marry her.'

'Well, but he has her by his side in the ship now,' said the third.

Then the first cried out quickly: 'What does that matter? as soon as they land, a chestnut horse will be brought to the king to mount, and if he does so, the horse will spring into the air and carry him out of sight, so that he will never see the princess more.'

'Can nothing be done to save him?' asked the second crow.

'Oh yes; if some one standing near would start forward quickly, snatch a pistol from the holster and shoot the horse dead, then the king might be saved.'

'But who knows this? and even if anyone did know it and speak of it, he would instantly be turned into stone from his feet to his knees.'

Then the second crow spoke again: 'I know something more; even should the king escape by the horse being killed, he will never marry his betrothed, for, as soon as they enter the palace, a splendid bridal robe will be presented to him on a silver salver, and it will appear as if woven of gold and silver thread, instead of which it will be made of sulphur and pitch, and the moment he puts it on it will burn him even to the marrow of his bones.'

'And is there a remedy for this also?' asked the third crow.

'Of course there is, for if anyone with gloves on will seize the robe and throw it into the fire, the robe will be burnt and the king saved. And should any person know this and speak of it, he would be turned into stone from his knees to his heart.'

'Ah! well,' cried the third crow, 'even supposing the king were saved from the burning robe, he would still lose his bride, for at the ball on the wedding night, while he is dancing with her, she will suddenly faint and fall down as if dead, and unless some one will immediately draw three drops of blood from her right shoulder and spit it out again, she will really die. And if anyone did know this, and spoke of it, he would be changed to stone from the crown of the head to the sole of the foot and become a statue.'

As soon as the crows had finished this conversation they flew away, but Faithful John had heard and understood it all, and remained for a long time still and sad.

At last he determined to be silent and not say a word to his master of what he had heard; besides, he knew that even to hint about it to the king would cost him his own life.

'Ah! well,' he said to himself, 'I will save my master, even if it should be my own ruin.'

As soon as they landed, John saw at once that what the crows had prophesied would take place.

There was the noble chesnut horse in readiness for the king to mount. 'Heyday,' said he, 'here is a splendid creature for me to ride to my castle; I will mount at once.' But Faithful John started forward, and, quickly drawing a pistol from the holster, shot the horse dead.

There was a great disturbance among the other servants, who were rather jealous of John. 'It was scandalous,' they said, 'to kill such a beautiful horse, just as it had been brought for the king to ride to the castle.'

But the king ordered them to be silent. 'Leave him to do as he likes,' he said; 'he is my faithful John, and knows what he is about.'

In a short time they arrived at the castle, and there in the saloon lay the splendid bridal robe on a salver. It looked exactly like a web of gold and silver, and the king went forward to touch it. Then John, who had already put on thick gloves, pushed him away, and, seizing the bridal robe, threw it into the fire and left it to burn.

The other servants murmured against John more than ever, and said: 'Why, he has actually burnt the king's bridal robe.' 'Never mind,' said the young king, 'he knows what he is about; leave him to himself, he is my faithful John.'

In a few days the wedding was celebrated, and at the ball in the evening the young queen danced. John, who watched her face with anxious care, saw her all at once turn pale and fall on the floor as if dead. Then he sprang hastily forward, lifted her up, bore her into another room, laid her again on the ground, then, kneeling by her side,

FAITHFUL JOHN SHOT THE HORSE DEAD.

he sucked three drops of blood from her right shoulder, and spat it out on the floor.

At the same instant she breathed again and raised herself from the ground; but the young king, who had seen all this with astonishment, could not in the least understand the conduct of his faithful servant, so he flew into a passion, and cried: 'Take him off to prison!'

Next morning John was brought before the judge and sentenced to death. As he stood in the king's presence, he said: 'Everyone who is about to die is allowed to speak for himself; shall I not also have that right?'

'Yes,' answered the king; 'I grant you permission.'

'Then,' said Faithful John, 'I have been unjustly condemned, for in every circumstance I have proved myself true and faithful to my king.' And then he related what he had heard of the conversation of the crows while at sea, and how all he had done had been necessary for the safety of the king and queen.

'Then,' cried the king, 'oh! my faithful John, pardon me, pardon me! Bring him here; he must be saved.' But it was too late, for by the last words the faithful servant had uttered in telling the king he had incurred the consequences spoken off by the crows: he fell lifeless and was turned into stone.

Then were the king and queen greatly troubled, and the king said: 'Ah! my faithful John, how badly have I repaid thy devotion;' and he commanded that the stone statue should be carried to his sleeping-room and placed near his bed, and whenever he looked at it, he said: 'Oh! if I could only restore thee to life again, my faithful John.'

And so time passed on, and the queen had twin sons, who, as they grew up, were the joy and delight of their parents. One day, while the queen was at church, the two children were amusing themselves in the room with their father; he cast his eyes on the statue, and, feeling full of sorrow, he sighed and said: 'Oh! if I could only restore thee to life, my most faithful John.'

Then the power of speech was given to the statue, and it replied, 'Thou canst restore me to life again if thou wilt give up for me what you love most.'

'Then,' cried the king, 'I would sacrifice all I have in the world for thee.'

'Well,' replied the statue, 'if thou wilt with thine own hand cut off the heads of thy two dear children, and smear me all over with their blood, I shall be restored to life.'

When the king heard this, he was at first stricken with horror; it was indeed dreadful that to save his faithful John, he must kill his two dear children. But when he recalled the great devotion of this faithful servant, who had died for his sake, he hesitated no longer: he drew his sword, and with his own hand cut off the heads of his dear boys, and smeared the statue with their blood. In an instant the statue received new life, and his faithful John stood safe and well before the king, and said:

'Thy devotion to me shall not remain unrewarded,' and as he spoke, he took up the heads of the two children, replaced them, and quickly healed the wounds by anointing them with their own blood. So completely was this done that the next moment they were skipping and jumping about the room as if nothing had happened.

Now indeed was the king's heart full of joy, and as soon as he heard that the queen had returned, he made John and the children hide themselves in a large cupboard. Presently she entered the room, and he said: 'Have you prayed at church?'

'Yes,' she replied, 'for I am constantly thinking of our faithful John and what he has endured for our sakes.'

'Dear wife,' he replied, 'we have the power to bring him back to life, but it would cost us both our dear little sons, whom we must sacrifice for him.'

The queen turned very pale and looked terrified, and her heart seemed to stand still, yet she said: 'We owe him even this sacrifice because of his great devotion to us.'

Then was the king glad to find that they both thought alike on the matter, and joyfully unlocking the cupboard, called out the children and Faithful John. 'See!' he said, 'Heaven be praised, John is set free, and our little sons we have still with us.'

Then he related to her how it had been brought about, and from that hour they lived in happiness and peace to the end of their lives.

THE GOOD BARGAIN.

A PEASANT had led his cow to the market and sold her for seven dollars. On his way home he had to pass a pond, but long before he reached it, he could hear the frogs crying: 'Akt, akt, akt, akt.'*

'Yes, I hear you,' he said, 'screaming out in your snug quarters; but it's seven I have received, not eight.' As soon as he reached the water he exclaimed: 'Stupid creatures that you are, don't you know better? seven dollars are not eight.'

The frogs, taking no heed, continued to cry: 'Akt, akt, akt.'

'Now,' said the peasant, 'if you do not believe me, I can count it out to you'; and he took the money out of his pocket and counted over the seven dollars in seventy-four groschens.

The frogs cared nothing for the peasant's reckoning, but went on croaking: 'Akt, akt, akt, akt.'

'Oh!' cried the peasant in a rage, 'do you know better how to count than I do?' and he threw the money into the water, right in the midst of them. Then he stood and waited till they were ready to return his property to him, but the frogs were constant to their first opinion and

---

* The word 'acht,' is German for eight.

screamed out still louder, ' Akt, akt, akt, akt,' and did not attempt to throw the money back again to him.

He waited for a good while till evening came on, and he knew he must go home. Then he abused the frogs, and cried: ' You water-plashers! you thickheads! you blind eyes! with your great jaws, you can scream enough to split one's ears, but you cannot count seven dollars; and do you think I am going to stay here and wait till you are ready?' Then he walked away very fast, but he heard the frogs still croaking ' Akt, akt,' for a long distance, and he arrived home quite out of humour.

After a time he bought another cow, which he slaughtered, and while reckoning how much he should get by the sale of the flesh, as well as the skin, he hoped to make a good bargain with profits, even with the loss caused by the obstinacy of the frogs.

So he started off to the town to sell his dead cow, but on arriving at the butcher's stall he saw a pack of hounds, who all surrounded him, barking and smelling at the meat. ' Wass, wass,'* they cried.

' Ah! yes,' said the peasant, ' it is all very well to say, ' What, what?' as if you wanted to know what I have got here, and you know it is meat all the while.'

There was no one to watch the butcher's shop but a large house-dog, and the countryman had often heard his master say how true and faithful he was. So he said to him, ' If I leave this meat here, will you answer for these friends of yours, that it shan't be touched?' ' Wass, wass,' cried the dog; while the others barked ' Wass, wass,' and sprang at the meat.

' Oh! well,' said the peasant to the butcher's dog, ' as you have pro-mised, I will leave the meat for your master to sell; but, remember, I must have the money in three days, and if he doesn't send it, I shall come for it.' Thereupon he laid the meat down on the counter, and turned to go. The dogs all ran round it barking ' Wass, wass,' and the peasant heard them for a long distance. ' Ah!' he said, ' they are all longing for a piece; but it's all right, the big one is answerable for them.'

Three days passed, and the countryman made himself quite com-fortable in the thought of what he was to receive. ' I shall have plenty of money in my pocket by to-morrow evening,' he said in a contented tone.

But the morrow came, and no money. He waited two days, and then said, ' I can't stand this; I must go and demand my money.' The butcher at first thought he was talking about a sparrow.

' Sparrow, indeed!' replied the peasant. ' I want my money for the meat I left under the care of your great dog three days ago—the flesh of a whole cow.'

---

* The German ' was ' is translated ' what.' It is used instead of ' bow-wow ' for the bark of a dog.

At this the butcher flew in a rage, and seizing a broom, laid it over the peasant's shoulders, and drove him out of the shop.

'Just wait,' cried the peasant, 'there is some justice after all left in the world.' And away he went to the castle, when, as it happened on that day, the king himself sat as chief magistrate, with his daughter by his side.

'What is your trouble?' asked the king.

'Alas! your majesty,' he replied, 'the frogs and the dogs have taken all I possess, and when I asked the butcher for my money, he beat me with a broomstick;' and then he related in a confused manner all that had occurred.

On hearing the countryman's story, the king's daughter burst into a fit of laughter, and laughed so loudly that for some minutes the king could not speak. At length he said, 'I cannot restore to you the money you have lost, but I can give you my daughter in marriage. She has never during her whole life laughed till now. I long ago promised her as a wife to the first man who could make her laugh, and you are that man, so you may thank Heaven for your good fortune.'

'Ah! my lord king,' replied the peasant, 'I cannot marry the princess; I have one wife at home already, and she is quite too much for me to manage; there is no room for another in our chimney-corner.'

Then was the king angry, and said, 'You are a rude clown.'

'Ah! my lord king,' he replied, 'what can you expect from a pig but a grunt?' and he turned to go.

'Stay!' cried the king, calling him back; 'I mean you to have some reward after all: five hundred times as much as you have lost shall be ready for you if you come here again in three days.'

The peasant looked so joyful as he passed out after hearing this, that the sentinel asked him the cause. 'You have made the princess laugh, I hear. What reward are you to have?'

'Five hundred dollars,' he replied.

'Why, what will you do with all that money?' asked the sentinel. 'You may as well give me some.'

'I will, if you like,' he said; 'and if you will go with me to the king in three days, he shall pay you two hundred dollars instead of me;' and away he went.

A money lender, who was standing near, overheard this promise, and, running after the peasant, pulled him by the sleeve, and said, 'You are a lucky fellow, friend, to have all that money promised you, but you must wait three days for it; would you not like to receive it at once, cash down?'

'I should, indeed,' replied the peasant. 'How can it be managed?'

'Oh! very easily! you shall give me an order to receive the three hundred dollars, and I will pay you the amount in silver and small coin.'

So the bill of exchange was drawn, and the money paid; but the money lender charged such enormous interest, and some of the coins were so bad, that the peasant did not get much after all. At the end of three days, the peasant went to the king, according to his command.

'You must open your pockets very wide, to receive all these dollars,' said the king.

'Ah! no,' cried the peasant, 'they do not belong to me. Two hundred I have promised to the sentinel, and I have given a money lender a bill to receive three hundred, as he gave me cash for it, so that I have justly nothing to receive.' While he spoke, in came the soldier and the money lender, who demanded what they had obtained from the peasant, and persisted that the money was justly theirs.

At first the king could not help laughing at the countryman's folly, and then he became angry at the conduct of the money lender and the soldier. 'So,' he said to the peasant, 'as you have been so foolish as to give up your money, before it even belonged to you, to strangers, I suppose I must make you some compensation. Go into that room opposite, and help yourself to as much money as your pockets will hold.' The countryman did not require to be told twice; he went, as he was told, and filled his wide pockets to overflowing.

Away he started to the inn to count his money, and the money lender sneaked after him, and heard him talking to himself. 'Now, if I had been a knave, and hidden all this from the king, he would never have allowed me to take this money. I wish I knew how much I had. Oh, if the king had only told me what amount I was to take. I'm so afraid I may have taken more than I ought.'

'Ah, ah!' muttered the money lender, 'he is grumbling even now, and speaking disrespectfully of my lord the king. Catch me quarrelling with such a sum of money because I couldn't count it.'

The money lender had spoken loud enough for the king to hear, and he called him, and desired him to fetch the ungrateful man again before his majesty. 'You must appear before the king immediately,' cried the money lender. 'There must be no excuse.'

'Indeed, I cannot,' he replied. 'Who ever heard of a man with such a heap of gold in his pockets as I have going before the king in such a ragged coat as this?'

The money lender, seeing that the peasant was determined, and fearing that the wrath of the king would cool, promised to lend him a coat, which was very good and nearly new. 'I lend it for you for true friendship's sake,' he said; 'and that is seldom done in the world.'

So the peasant put it on, and went into the king's presence. But when the king repeated what he had been told by the money lender, the peasant exclaimed, 'Your majesty, it is all false; there is never a

THE PEASANT'S JOYFUL RETURN.

true word out of that money lender's mouth. I dare say he will affirm that the coat I have on belongs to him.'

'What do you mean?' screamed the money lender. 'You know it is my coat; I lent it you out of pure friendship, that you might appear before the king.'

'Yes, of course, to hear your lies about me, and get punished by having the money taken from me,' replied the peasant. Then he repeated what he had really said at the inn; and the king dismissed them both, saying that the money lender's word was evidently not to be taken, and therefore the countryman might keep the coat as his own, as some recompense for the money lender's false accusation.

The peasant went home joyfully, to count the gold in his pockets and said to himself:

'This time, at least, I have made a good bargain.'

THE WONDERFUL FIDDLER.

A FIDDLER once set out on a journey, and on his way came to a forest, through which he must pass. 'I am very lonely all by myself,' he said; 'if I could only but meet with a companion besides my fiddle, I should be happier.' Then he slipped his violin from his shoulder and commenced playing so merrily that it echoed through the wood.

Before long a wolf came out of the thicket and trotted towards him. 'Ah! here comes a wolf,' he exclaimed; 'but I don't want him for a companion.'

But the wolf stepped nearer, and said, 'Dear fiddler, how beautifully you do play. I wish I could learn.'

'You could learn very quickly,' replied the fiddler, 'if you will do all I tell you.'

'Oh! indeed, I will listen and obey you in everything, as if I were your scholar and you my master.'

'Come along then,' said the fiddler, and they walked away together.

They had not gone far when they came to a hollow oak-tree, in which was a slit wide enough to push the hand through.

'See,' cried the fiddler, 'if you wish to learn to fiddle, just put your two fore-feet in there,' and he pointed to the rent in the tree. The wolf obeyed, and the fiddler, with a large stone, quickly wedged the feet of the wolf in the tree so fast that he could not move, and found himself a prisoner. 'Stay there till I come back,' said the musician, and went his way.

After wandering on for some distance, he again began to murmur to himself, 'I am still all alone in the wood, suppose I try for another partner;' so he took down his violin, and played with such spirit that the tones resounded on every side, and presently a fox made his appearance. 'Ah! here comes a fox,' said the fiddler, 'but I have no wish for his society.'

'What beautiful music!' exclaimed the fox. 'I should like to be able to play like you.'

'There is no difficulty in your learning to play as I do,' answered the fiddler, 'if you will only do as I tell you.'

'Indeed I will,' he replied; 'I will obey you as a scholar obeys his master.'

'Follow me then,' said the fiddler; so they walked on together till they came out upon a pathway on each side of which grew high shrubs.

The fiddler stopped, and bending down a branch of one of these shrubs to the ground, placed his foot on it. Then he bent a branch on the other side of the path, and also stood on it, and said:

'Come, little foxey, if you want to learn music, give me your left fore-foot.' The fox obeyed, and the fiddler tied it to a branch on the left hand. 'Now give me the right foot also.' The fox, remembering that he had promised to obey, did as he was told, and the fiddler tied this foot also to the branch on the right. Then, after seeing that the knots were tight, the fiddler lifted his feet and set the branches free. Up they sprang, carrying the fox with them suspended across the pathway from the boughs, and kicking as he hung.

'Wait till I return,' said the fiddler, and away he went.

After a while he began again to feel lonely, and taking down his violin, began to play with as much energy as ever, yet muttering all the while, 'Oh, if I only had a companion!'

In a few minutes a hare appeared in his path. 'Here comes a hare,' cried the fiddler; 'I don't want him as a companion.'

But the hare was so attracted by the music, that he came to the fiddler and exclaimed, 'Dear fiddler, how sweetly you play! I wish I could learn.'

'There is nothing so very difficult to learn,' cried the musician, 'if you will only do as I tell you.'

'Oh! fiddler,' answered the hare, 'only teach me to play as you do, I will obey you as a scholar does his master.'

So they walked on together for some distance, till they came to a clear place in the wood where an aspen-tree grew.

The fiddler then took a long string from his pocket, and tying one end loosely round the hare's neck, fastened the other end to the tree, and said to him:

'Brisk little hare, now do as I tell you; run twenty times round that tree.'

The hare obeyed, but by the time she had made twenty runs, the string was so firmly wound round the stem that she could not move without cutting her soft neck with the string.

And so the fiddler left his third prisoner, saying, 'Stay there till I come,' and went his way.

In the meantime the wolf had struggled hard to release his feet from the stone, and was hurting himself very much.

He succeeded at last, however, and then, full of anger and rage, hastened after the fiddler, determined to tear him in pieces. On his way he passed near to where the fox hung suspended between the trees in misery and pain.

'Dear, clever brother wolf,' he cried, 'do come to my help; the fiddler has betrayed me.'

At this appeal the wolf stopped—drew the branches down, untied the string with his teeth, and set the fox free. Then they both started off together, determined on revenge. On their way they discovered the imprisoned hare, whom they quickly set free, and then the three started together to find their enemy.

But while all this was going on, the fiddler had attracted another by his music; the tones of the violin reached the ears of a poor wood-cutter, who was obliged against his will to leave off work, and taking his axe under his arm, he went to meet the fiddler.

'At last, here comes the right companion for me,' he cried. 'It was men I wanted, not wild beasts.'

But while he played his sweetest notes to please the poor wood-cutter, who listened as if bewitched to the sounds, up came the wolf, the fox, and the hare, with their wicked intentions visible in their eyes.

At this the new friend placed himself before the musician, and raising his glittering axe, exclaimed, 'If you attempt to harm him, take care of yourselves, that's all; you have me to deal with now.'

At this the animals in alarm ran back into the wood, and the wood-man took the fiddler home to his cottage and remained his friend ever after.

THE TWELVE BROTHERS.

MANY years ago lived a king and queen who had twelve sons, all bright, intelligent lads; but they were not quite happy, although they loved each other very much. For one day the king had told his wife that as he had now twelve sons, if a daughter should be born, all the sons would die and their sister alone inherit his kingdom and riches.

So the king had twelve coffins made in readiness for his sons, in case his next child should be a daughter. These coffins, which contained their grave-clothes, were filled with shavings, and locked up in a private room, the key of which the king gave to the queen, praying her not to speak of it to the boys. But this dreadful preparation made the poor mother so unhappy that she wept for a whole day, and looked so sad that her youngest son noticed it.

He had the Bible name of Benjamin, and was more often with his mother than the rest.

'Dear mother,' he said to her, 'why are you so sorrowful?'

'My child, I cannot tell you,' she replied; but the boy was not satisfied, and he allowed her no rest till she unlocked the door of the private room and showed him the twelve coffins.

'Dearest Benjamin,' she said, 'these coffins are for you and your brothers; for if you should ever have a little sister you will all die, and be buried in them.'

She wept bitterly as she told him, but her son comforted her, and said, 'Do not weep, dear mother, we will take care of ourselves, and be far away from here before that time arrives.'

Then she took courage, and said, 'Yes, it will be better for you all to go away and remain for a time in a forest near to a hill, from whence you will be able to see the tower of the castle. If I should have a little son, a white flag shall be hoisted, and then you may venture to return home; but if you see a red flag, you will know it is a girl, and then hasten away as fast as you can, and may heaven protect you. Every night I will rise and pray for you, that you may not suffer from hunger or thirst, or the cold in winter, and the heat in summer.'

Then she blessed all her sons, and they went away into the forest, while each in turn mounted a high tree daily, to watch for the flag on the tower.

Eleven days passed, and it was Benjamin's turn to watch. He saw the flag hoisted, and it was red—the signal that they must die. The elder brothers were so angry at finding that, to save their lives, they were to be banished from home in consequence of a maiden's birth, that they vowed in revenge to destroy the first maiden whom they met in the forest.

However, as they must still hide themselves, they went still farther into the forest to find shelter. Strange to say, they had not travelled far before they came upon a most pleasant little cottage, neatly furnished, but uninhabited.

'We will make this our home,' they said, 'and Benjamin, as you are the youngest and weakest, you shall stay at home and keep house while we go out and procure food.'

So they wandered about the forest shooting hares, wild rabbits, pigeons, and other birds, and Benjamin gathered acorns, nuts, and berries, or whatever could be found for food. In this cottage they lived for ten years happily together, so that the time passed quickly, but they heard nothing from home.

During this time their little sister was growing a great girl. She had a sweet disposition, and was very beautiful to look upon. She wore rich clothes, and a golden star on her forehead.

One day, when she was about ten years old, she discovered in her mother's wardrobe twelve shirts.

'Mother,' she exclaimed, 'whose shirts are these? they are much too small for my father.'

The queen sighed deeply as she replied, 'Dear child, these shirts belong to your twelve brothers.'

'Twelve brothers!' cried the little maiden; 'where are they? I have not even heard of them.'

'Heaven knows where they are,' was the reply; 'but they are wandering about the world somewhere.'

Then the queen took her little daughter to the private room in the castle, and showed her the twelve coffins which had been prepared for her brothers, and related to her, with many tears, why they had left home.

'Dear mother,' said the child, 'do not weep. I will go and seek my brothers.'

So she took the twelve shirts with her, and wandered away into the forest.

She walked for a whole day, and by evening began to feel very tired, till at last she saw a light in a cottage, and stepped up to the door and knocked. It was opened by a young boy, who stared with astonishment at seeing a beautiful little girl dressed in rich clothing, and wearing a golden star on her forehead.

At last he said, 'Who are you, and what do you want?'

'I am a king's daughter,' she said, 'and I seek my twelve brothers, and I intend to search for them in every place under the sun till I find them; and these are their shirts,' she added, opening her parcel.

Then Benjamin knew that she was his sister, and said, 'I am your youngest brother, Benjamin.'

On hearing this the little maiden burst into tears, but they were tears of joy, for they kissed each other with deep affection, and they were for a time very happy. He made her rest by the fire, and gave her something to eat and drink, for she was very tired.

At last Benjamin remembered the vow made by his brothers, that the first young maiden they met should die, because through a maiden they had lost their kingly rights; and he told his little sister about it. 'I would willingly die,' she said, 'if by so doing I could restore my brothers to their rightful possessions.'

'But I do not fear anything so sad will happen,' he replied, 'if I explain to them before they see you; and I hear them coming,' he continued. 'Just hide yourself in this room till after supper, and I will see what can be done.' So the maiden hid herself where she could hear all that was said.

Presently the brothers returned from hunting; but the youngest would not speak about his sister till he had prepared the supper. While they sat at table, one of them said, 'Well, Benjamin, have you any news to tell us?'

'Perhaps I have,' he said; 'although it seems strange that I who stay at home and keep house should know more than you who have been out in the world.'

'Well, tell us your news,' said one, and they all looked very eager. So he said:

'I will tell you if you make one promise.'

'Yes, yes,' they all cried; 'what is it?'

'Well, then, promise me that the first maiden you meet with in the forest shall *not* die.'

To this they all readily agreed, and the eldest said, 'I will take care that mercy shall be shown to her.'

'Then,' said the youngest brother, 'our sister is here;' and, rising, he opened the door of the inner room, and the king's daughter came forth in her royal robes, and with a golden star on her forehead, and looking so fair and delicate and beautiful that the brothers were full of joy, and kissed and embraced her with the fondest affection.

She stayed with them some time, and was a great help to the youngest brother in keeping the house clean, and cooking the game which the others brought home. Everything was so nicely managed now, and with so much order; the curtains and the quilts were beautifully white, and the dinners cooked so well, that the brothers were always contented, and lived in great unity with their little sister.

There was a pretty garden around the house in which they lived, and one day when they were all at home to dinner together, and enjoying themselves, the maiden went out into the garden to gather them some flowers.

She had tended twelve lilies with great care, and they were now in such splendid bloom that she determined to pluck them for her brothers, and place one on each of their plates as a present.

But the moment she brought the lilies in from the garden, her twelve brothers were changed into twelve ravens, and flew away over the trees of the forest, while the charming house and garden vanished from her sight. Now was the poor little maiden left all alone in the wild wood, and knew not what to do; but on turning to go she saw a curious old woman standing near, who said to her, 'My child, what hast thou done? Why didst thou not leave those white flowers to grow on their stems? They were thy twelve brothers, and now they will always remain ravens.'

'Is there no way to set them free?' asked the maiden, weeping.

'No way in the world,' she replied, 'but one, and that is far too difficult for thee to perform; yet it would break the spell, and set them free.'

'Tell me, tell me!' she cried. 'I know I can do it, only tell me what it is.'

On hearing this the old woman replied: 'Hast thou firmness enough to remain dumb seven years, and not speak to anyone, or even laugh? for if ever you utter a single word, or fail only once in the seven years, all you have done before will be vain, and at this one word your brothers will die.'

'Yes,' said the maiden, and she spoke from her heart; 'I can do this to set my brothers free.'

The old woman left her, after hearing her determination, and the maiden climbed into a tree, for she had no home now, and, seating herself in the branches, began to knit.

For three days she remained here, living on the fruit that grew on the tree, and without laughing or uttering a word.

At the end of three days, as she sat in her tree, she saw the hunters pass near: and the king, who was hunting with them, had a favourite hound, who very soon discovered her, ran to the tree on which the maiden sat, sprang up to it, and bayed and barked at her violently.

The king, on this, came nearer, and saw with surprise the beautiful king's daughter with the golden star on her forehead sitting among the branches. He was so struck with her beauty that he begged her to come down, and asked her to be his bride. She did not speak a word, but merely nodded her head. Then the king himself climbed up into the tree, and, bringing her down, seated her on his own horse and galloped away with her to his home.

The marriage was soon after celebrated with great pomp, but the bride neither spoke nor laughed.

When they had lived happily together for some years, the king's mother, a wicked witch, came to visit them, and she soon began to raise wicked reports about the queen, and to set her husband against her. ‘ I dare say it is some beggar girl you have picked up,’ she said one day. ‘ Who can tell in what wretched home she may have been trained? Of course she can't help being dumb; but why does she never laugh, unless she has a guilty conscience?’ The king at first would listen to none of these suspicions; but she led him on by degrees, and accused the queen of such wicked conduct, that at last he gave up his beautiful wife to be burnt to death. If she could have spoken to defend herself, the king might have saved her; but she remained silent to save her brothers, and so he concluded she was guilty.

On the day of the execution the king stood weeping at a window overlooking the court of the palace, where the stake had been erected, for he still loved her dearly. He saw her brought forth and tied to the stake, the fire kindled, and the flames with their forked tongues creeping towards her, when suddenly a rustling noise of wings was heard in the air—twelve black ravens alighted on the earth, and instantly assumed their own forms; they were the brothers of the queen.

The last moment of the seven years had expired; the enchantment was broken, and they arrived in time to save her. The fire was quickly extinguished; the queen, when led by her brothers to the king, was able to speak to him, and to smile in joy at being allowed to explain the cause of her silence.

The delight of the king was only equalled by his anger against the wicked witch, who was brought to justice, and ordered to be thrown into a vat of oil full of poisonous snakes, where she died a dreadful death.

THE ROGUES' HOLIDAY.

'LITTLE hen,' said a young cock to his wife one day in autumn, 'this is the time for nuts and acorns ; let us go to the mountains and feast ourselves before they are all gone.'

'That will be a happy time,' said the hen. 'Yes, I am quite ready.'

So they started off together very early in the morning, and stayed all day feasting.

Now I cannot say whether they had eaten too much, or if they really were tired ; at all events, they could not walk home, so the cock made a little carriage of nut-shells. No sooner was it finished than the hen seated herself in it, and said to the cock, 'Come, you may as well harness yourself to the carriage and draw me home ; you are stronger than I am.'

'Very likely,' he replied, 'that I should allow myself to be harnessed like a horse and draw you ; it would be better to walk home than to do that. No ; if we have the carriage at all, I mean to be coachman, and sit on the box ; but I am not going to draw you, indeed, so don't expect it !'

While they were contending, a duck came by. 'You thieves,' she quacked, 'what are you doing in my nut mountains ? Be off quickly, or you will get the worst of it,' and she gave the cock a tremendous peck with her beak.

THE NUT-SHELL CARRIAGE.

But the cock was not going to stand that ; he flew at the duck, and beat her so with his spurs that she was obliged to beg for mercy, and at last allowed herself to be harnessed to the little carriage as a punishment for her interference.

The cock sat on the box and drove at a furious rate, crying out, ' Get on, duck! get on!'

After travelling some distance they overtook two foot passengers—a pin and a needle. ' Halt, halt!' they cried; ' do help us. We are so tired that we cannot go a step farther; night is coming on, the roads are so dusty, and we cannot sit down. We stopped at the door of a tailor's shop and asked for shelter, but he said he had too many like us already.'

The cock, seeing that they were slight, thin people who would not require much room, allowed them to enter the carriage, only making them promise not to step on the hen's feet.

Late at night they reached a roadside inn, and by this time the duck was getting so tired that her legs were unsteady, and she waddled terribly; so they stopped at the inn, and asked for supper and a night's lodging. The landlord made many objections at first—his house was already full, and he thought these new-comers did not look quite respectable.

However, the cock flattered the old landlord, and promised that whatever eggs the hen and the duck might lay while they stayed should be his. So the landlord gave them shelter, and glad enough they were of a night's rest.

Early in the morning, however, just as it began to dawn, and while everyone else was asleep, the cock and hen awoke, and seeing the egg which she had laid, they made a good breakfast on it, and threw the shell into the kitchen fire. Then they went to the pin-cushion, where the needle and pin still lay asleep, and, carrying them away, stuck the needle in the cushion of the landlord's armchair and the pin in his towel.

After performing these tricks, they flew away with the greatest indifference through the open window, and across the heath.

The duck, who preferred the open air, had roosted in the outer court, and was awoke by the rustle of wings. Rousing herself quickly, she plumed her feathers, and espying a stream near, partly flew and partly waddled down to it; for to swim home would be far better than drawing that heavy carriage.

A few hours after this the landlord arose, and prepared to wash himself; but on taking up his towel to wipe his face, the point of the pin made a long red scratch right across from one ear to the other.

It was rather painful; but he dressed himself quickly, and went into the kitchen to light his pipe. As he stooped to put in a match, out popped a piece of burnt egg-shell into his eye.

The pain made him start back and sink down into his grandfather's armchair, which stood near; but he started up again more quickly than he had sat down, for the needle in the cushion pricked him terribly.

Then was the landlord very angry, and began to suspect his guests, who had arrived so late the night before. He went out to look for them, and found they were gone.   Then he took an oath that he would never again admit such knaves into his house—ragamuffins who ate a great deal, paid nothing, and, above all, instead of thanks, performed knavish tricks.

THE ENCHANTED STAG.

THERE were once a brother and sister who loved each other dearly; their mother was dead, and their father had married again a woman who was most unkind and cruel to them.   One day the boy took his sister's hand and said to her, ' Dear little sister, since our mother died we have not had one happy hour.   Our stepmother gives us dry hard crusts for dinner and supper ; she often knocks us about, and threatens to kick us out of the house.   Even the little dogs under the table fare better than we do, for she often throws them nice pieces to eat.   Heaven pity us !   Oh, if our dear mother knew !   Come, let us go out into the wide world !'

So they went out, and wandered over fields and meadows the whole day till evening.   At last they found themselves in a large forest ; it began to rain, and the little sister said, ' See, brother, heaven and our hearts weep together.'   At last, tired out with hunger and sorrow, and the long journey, they crept into a hollow tree, laid themselves down, and slept till morning.

When they awoke the sun was high in the heavens, and shone brightly into the hollow tree, so they left their place of shelter and wandered away in search of water.

' Oh, I am so thirsty !' said the boy.   ' If we could only find a brook or a stream.'   He stopped to listen, and said, ' Stay, I think I hear a running stream.'   So he took his sister by the hand, and they ran together to find it.

Now, the stepmother of these poor children was a wicked witch.   She had seen the children go away, and, following them cautiously like a snake, had bewitched all the springs and streams in the forest.   The pleasant trickling of a brook over the pebbles was heard by the children as they reached it, and the boy was just stooping to drink, when the sister heard in the babbling of the brook :

> ' Whoever drinks of me, a tiger soon will be.'

Then she cried quickly, ' Stay, brother, stay ! do not drink, or you will become a wild beast, and tear me to pieces.'

Thirsty as he was, the brother conquered his desire to drink, at her words, and said, ' Dear sister, I will wait till we come to a spring.'   So they wandered farther, but as they approached, she heard in the bubbling spring the words—

> ' Who drinks of me, a wolf will be.'

'Brother, I pray you, do not drink of this brook; you will be changed into a wolf, and devour me.'

Again the brother denied himself and promised to wait; but he said, 'At the next stream I must drink, say what you will, my thirst is so great.'

Not far off ran a pretty streamlet, looking clear and bright; but here also, in its murmuring waters, the sister heard the words—

> 'Who dares to drink of me,
> Turned to a stag will be.'

'Dear brother, do not drink,' she began; but she was too late, for her brother had already knelt by the stream to drink, and as the first drop of water touched his lips he became a fawn. How the little sister wept over her enchanted brother, and the fawn wept also.

He did not run away, but stayed close to her; and at last she said, 'Stand still, dear fawn; don't fear, I must take care of you, but I will never leave you.' So she untied her little golden garter and fastened it round the neck of the fawn; then she gathered some soft green rushes, and braided them into a soft string, which she fastened to the fawn's golden collar, and then led him away into the depths of the forest.

After wandering about for some time, they at last found a little deserted hut, and the sister was overjoyed, for she thought it would form a nice shelter for them both. So she led the fawn in, and then went out alone, to gather moss and dried leaves, to make him a soft bed.

Every morning she went out to gather dried roots, nuts, and berries, for her own food, and sweet fresh grass for the fawn, which he ate out of her hand, and the poor little animal went out with her, and played about as happy as the day was long.

When evening came, and the poor sister felt tired, she would kneel down and say her prayers, and then lay her delicate head on the fawn's back, which was a soft warm pillow, on which she could sleep peacefully. Had this dear brother only kept his own proper form, how happy they would have been together! After they had been alone in the forest for some time, and the little sister had grown a lovely maiden, and the fawn a large stag, a numerous hunting party came to the forest, and amongst them the king of the country.

The sounding horn, the barking of the dogs, the holloa of the huntsmen, resounded through the forest, and were heard by the stag, who became eager to join his companions.

'Oh dear,' he said, 'do let me go and see the hunt; I cannot restrain myself.' And he begged so hard that at last she reluctantly consented.

'But remember,' she said, 'I must lock the cottage door against those huntsmen, so when you come back in the evening, and knock, I shall not admit you, unless you say, "Dear little sister let me in."'

He bounded off as she spoke, scarcely stopping to listen, for it was so delightful for him again to breathe the fresh air and be free.

He had not run far when the king's chief hunter caught sight of the beautiful animal, and started off in chase of him; but it was no easy matter to overtake such rapid footsteps.   Once, when he thought he had him safe, the fawn sprang over the bushes and disappeared.

As it was now nearly dark, he ran up to the little cottage, knocked at the door, and cried, ' Dear little sister, let me in.'   The door was instantly opened, and oh, how glad his sister was to see him safely resting on his soft pleasant bed !

A few days after this, the huntsmen were again in the forest ; and when the fawn heard the holloa, he could not rest in peace, but begged his sister again to let him go.

She opened the door, and said, ' I will let you go this time ; but pray do not forget to say what I told you, when you return this evening.'

The chief hunter very soon espied the beautiful fawn with the golden collar, pointed it out to the king, and they determined to hunt it.

They chased him with all their skill till the evening ; but he was too light and nimble for them to catch, till a shot wounded him slightly in the foot, so that he was obliged to hide himself in the bushes, and, after the huntsmen were gone, limp slowly home.

One of them, however, determined to follow him at a distance, and discover where he went.   What was his surprise at seeing him go up to a door and knock, and to hear him say, ' Dear little sister, let me in.' The door was only opened a little way, and quickly shut; but the huntsman had seen enough to make him full of wonder, when he returned and described to the king what he had seen.

' We will have one more chase to-morrow,' said the king, ' and discover this mystery.'

In the meantime the loving sister was terribly alarmed at finding the stag's foot wounded and bleeding.   She quickly washed off the blood, and, after bathing the wound, placed healing herbs on it, and said, ' Lie down on your bed, dear fawn, and the wound will soon heal, if you rest your foot.'

In the morning the wound was so much better that the fawn felt the foot almost as strong as ever, and so, when he again heard the holloa of the hunters, he could not rest.   ' Oh, dear sister, I must go once more ; it will be easy for me to avoid the hunters now, and my foot feels quite well ; they will not hunt me unless they see me running, and I don't mean to do that.'

But his sister wept, and begged him not to go : ' If they kill you, dear fawn, I shall be here alone in the forest, forsaken by the whole world.'

' And I shall die of grief,' he said, ' if I remain here listening to the hunter's horn.'

So at length his sister, with a heavy heart, set him free, and he bounded away joyfully into the forest.

As soon as the king caught sight of him, he said to the huntsmen, ' Follow that stag about, but don't hurt him.'   So they hunted him all day, but at the approach of sunset the king said to the hunter who had followed the fawn the day before, ' Come and show me the little cottage.

So they went together, and when the king saw it he sent his companion home, and went on alone so quickly that he arrived there before

THE KING AND THE MAIDEN.

the fawn; and, going up to the little door, knocked and said softly, 'Dear little sister, let me in.'

As the door opened, the king stepped in, and in great astonishment saw a maiden more beautiful than he had ever seen in his life standing before him. But how frightened she felt to see instead of her dear little fawn a noble gentleman walk in with a gold crown on his head.

However, he appeared very friendly, and after a little talk he held out his hand to her, and said, ' Wilt thou go with me to my castle and be my dear wife ?'

' Ah yes,' replied the maiden, ' I would willingly ; but I cannot leave my dear fawn : he must go with me wherever I am.'

' He shall remain with you as long as you live,' replied the king, ' and I will never ask you to forsake him.'

While they were talking, the fawn came bounding in, looking quite well and happy. Then his sister fastened the string of rushes to his collar, took it in her hand, and led him away from the cottage in the wood to where the king's beautiful horse waited for him.

The king placed the maiden before him on his horse and rode away to his castle, the fawn following by their side. Soon after, their marriage was celebrated with great splendour, and the fawn was taken the greatest care of, and played where he pleased, or roamed about the castle grounds in happiness and safety.

In the meantime the wicked stepmother, who had caused these two young people such misery, supposed that the sister had been devoured by wild beasts, and that the fawn had been hunted to death. Therefore when she heard of their happiness, such envy and malice arose in her heart that she could find no rest till she had tried to destroy it.

She and her ugly daughter came to the castle when the queen had a little baby, and one of them pretended to be a nurse, and at last got the mother and child into their power.

They shut the queen up in the bath, and tried to suffocate her, and the old woman put her own ugly daughter in the queen's bed that the king might not know she was away.

She would not, however, let him speak to her, but pretended that she must be kept quite quiet.

The queen escaped from the bath-room, where the wicked old woman had locked her up, but she did not go far, as she wanted to watch over her child and the little fawn.

For two nights the baby's nurse saw a figure of the queen come into the room and take up her baby and nurse it. Then she told the king, and he determined to watch himself. The old stepmother, who acted as nurse to her ugly daughter, whom she tried to make the king believe was his wife, had said that the queen was too weak to see him, and never left her room. ' There cannot be two queens,' said the king to himself, ' so to-night I will watch in the nursery.' As soon as the figure came in and took up her baby, he saw it was his real wife, and caught her in his arms, saying, ' You are my own beloved wife, as beautiful as ever.'

The wicked witch had thrown her into a trance, hoping she would die, and that the king would then marry her daughter ; but on the king speaking to her, the spell was broken. The queen told the king how cruelly she had been treated by her stepmother, and on hearing this he became very angry, and had the witch and her daughter brought to justice. They were both sentenced to die—the daughter to be devoured by wild beasts, and the mother to be burnt alive.

No sooner, however, was she reduced to ashes than the charm which held the queen's brother in the form of a stag was broken ; he recovered his own natural shape, and appeared before them a tall, handsome young man.

After this, the brother and sister lived happily and peacefully for the rest of their lives.

HANSEL AND GRETHEL.

NEAR the borders of a large forest dwelt in olden times a poor wood-cutter, who had two children—a boy named Hansel, and his sister, Grethel. They had very little to live upon, and once when there was a dreadful season of scarcity in the land, the poor woodcutter could not earn sufficient to supply their daily food.

One evening, after the children were gone to bed, the parents sat talking together over their sorrow, and the poor husband sighed, and said to his wife, who was not the mother of his children, but their stepmother, 'What will become of us, for I cannot earn enough to support myself and you, much less the children? what shall we do with them, for they must not starve?'

'I know what to do, husband,' she replied ; 'early to-morrow morning we will take the children for a walk across the forest and leave them in the thickest part ; they will never find the way home again, you may depend, and then we shall only have to work for ourselves.'

'No wife,' said the man, 'that I will never do ; how could I have the heart to leave my children all alone in the wood, where the wild beasts would come quickly and devour them?'

'Oh, you fool,' replied the stepmother, 'if you refuse to do this, you know we must all four perish with hunger ; you may as well go and cut the wood for our coffins.' And after this she let him have no peace till he became quite worn out, and could not sleep for hours, but lay thinking in sorrow about his children.

The two children, who also were too hungry to sleep, heard all that their stepmother had said to their father. Poor little Grethel wept bitter tears as she listened, and said to her brother, 'What is going to happen to us, Hansel?'

'Hush, Grethel,' he whispered ; 'don't be so unhappy ; I know what to do.'

Then they lay quite still till their parents were asleep.

As soon as it was quiet, Hansel got up, put on his little coat, unfastened the door, and slipped out. The moon shone brightly, and the white pebble stones which lay before the cottage door glistened like new silver money. Hansel stooped and picked up as many of the pebbles as he could stuff in his little coat pockets. He then went back to Grethel and said, 'Be comforted, dear little sister, and sleep in peace; heaven will take care of us.' Then he laid himself down again in bed, and slept till the day broke.

As soon as the sun was risen, the stepmother came and woke the two

HANSEL DROPPING THE PEBBLES ON THE GROUND.

children, and said, 'Get up, you lazy bones, and come into the wood with me to gather wood for the fire.' Then she gave each of them a piece of bread, and said, 'You must keep that to eat for your dinner, and don't quarrel over it, for you will get nothing more.'

Grethel took the bread under her charge, for Hansel's pockets were full of pebbles. Then the stepmother led them a long way into the forest. They had gone but a very short distance when Hansel looked back at the house, and this he did again and again.

At last his stepmother said, ' Why do you keep staying behind and looking back so ?'

' Oh, mother,' said the boy, ' I can see my little white cat sitting on the roof of the house, and I am sure she is crying for me.'

' Nonsense,' she replied ; ' that is not your cat ; it is the morning sun shining on the chimney-pot.'

Hansel had seen no cat, but he stayed behind every time to drop a white pebble from his pocket on the ground as they walked.

As soon as they reached a thick part of the wood, their stepmother said :

' Come, children, gather some wood, and I will make a fire, for it is very cold here.'

Then Hansel and Grethel raised quite a high heap of brushwood and faggots, which soon blazed up into a bright fire, and the woman said to them :

' Sit down here, children, and rest, while I go and find your father, who is cutting wood in the forest; when we have finished our work, we will come again and fetch you.'

Hansel and Grethel seated themselves by the fire, and when noon arrived they each ate the piece of bread which their stepmother had given them for their dinner ; and as long as they heard the strokes of the axe they felt safe, for they believed that their father was working near them. But it was not an axe they heard—only a branch which still hung on a withered tree, and was moved up and down by the wind. At last, when they had been sitting there a long time, the children's eyes became heavy with fatigue, and they fell fast asleep. When they awoke it was dark night, and poor Grethel began to cry, and said, ' Oh, how shall we get out of the wood ?'

But Hansel comforted her. ' Don't fear,' he said ; ' let us wait a little while till the moon rises, and then we shall easily find our way home.'

Very soon the full moon rose, and then Hansel took his little sister by the hand, and the white pebble stones, which glittered like newly-coined money in the moonlight, and which Hansel had dropped as he walked, pointed out the way. They walked all the night through, and did not reach their father's house till break of day.

They knocked at the door, and when their stepmother opened it, she exclaimed : ' You naughty children, why have you been staying so long in the forest? we thought you were never coming back.' But their father was overjoyed to see them, for it grieved him to the heart to think that they had been left alone in the wood.

Not long after this there came another time of scarcity and want in every house, and the children heard their stepmother talking after they were in bed. ' The times are as bad as ever,' she said ; ' we have just half a loaf left, and when that is gone all love will be at an end. The children must go away; we will take them deeper into the forest this time, and they will not be able to find their way home as they did before; it is the only plan to save ourselves from starvation. But the husband felt heavy at heart, for he thought it was better to share the last morsel with his children.

His wife would listen to nothing he said, but continued to reproach him, and as he had given way to her the first time, he could not refuse to do so now. The children were awake, and heard all the conversation; so, as soon as their parents slept, Hansel got up, intending to go

HANSEL AND GRETHEL RETURN HOME.

out and gather some more of the bright pebbles to let fall as he walked, that they might point out the way home; but his stepmother had locked the door, and he could not open it. When he went back to his bed he told his little sister not to fret, but to go to sleep in peace, for he was sure they would be taken care of.

Early the next morning the stepmother came and pulled the children out of bed, and, when they were dressed, gave them each a piece of bread for their dinners, smaller than they had had before, and then they started on their way to the wood.

As they walked, Hansel, who had the bread in his pocket, broke off little crumbs, and stopped every now and then to drop one, turning round as if he was looking back at his home.

'Hansel,' said the woman, 'what are you stopping for in that way?' come along directly.'

'I saw my pigeon sitting on the roof, and he wants to say good-bye to me,' replied the boy.

'Nonsense,' she said; 'that is not your pigeon; it is only the morning sun shining on the chimney-top.'

But Hansel did not look back any more; he only dropped pieces of bread behind him, as they walked through the wood. This time they went on till they reached the thickest and densest part of the forest, where they had never been before in all their lives. Again they gathered faggots and brushwood, of which the stepmother made up a large fire. Then she said, 'Remain here, children, and rest, while I go to help your father, who is cutting wood in the forest; when you feel tired, you can lie down and sleep for a little while, and we will come and fetch you in the evening, when your father has finished his work.'

So the children remained alone till mid-day, and then Grethel shared her piece of bread with Hansel, for he had scattered his own all along the road as they walked. After this they slept for awhile, and the evening drew on; but no one came to fetch the poor children. When they awoke it was quite dark, and poor little Grethel was afraid; but Hansel comforted her, as he had done before, by telling her they need only wait till the moon rose. 'You know, little sister,' he said, 'that I have thrown breadcrumbs all along the road we came, and they will easily point out the way home.'

But when they went out of the thicket into the moonlight they found no breadcrumbs, for the numerous birds which inhabited the trees of the forest had picked them all up.

Hansel tried to hide his fear when he made this sad discovery, and said to his sister, 'Cheer up, Grethel; I dare say we shall find our way home without the crumbs. Let us try;' but this they found impossible. They wandered about the whole night, and the next day from morning till evening; but they could not get out of the wood, and were so hungry that had it not been for a few berries which they picked they must have starved.

At last they were so tired that their poor little legs could carry them no farther; so they laid themselves down under a tree and went to sleep. When they awoke it was the third morning since they had left their father's house, and they determined to try once more to find their way home; but it was no use, they only went still deeper into the wood, and knew that if no help came they must starve.

About noon, they saw a beautiful snow-white bird sitting on the branch of a tree, and singing so beautifully that they stood still to listen. When he had finished his song, he spread out his wings and flew on before them. The children followed him, till at last they saw at a distance a small house; and the bird flew and perched on the roof.

But how surprised were the boy and girl, when they came nearer, to find that the house was built of gingerbread, and ornamented with sweet cakes and tarts, while the window was formed of barley-sugar. 'Oh!' exclaimed Hansel, 'let us stop here and have a splendid feast. I will have a piece from the roof first, Grethel; and you can eat some of the barley-sugar window, it tastes so nice.' Hansel reached up on tiptoe, and breaking off a piece of the gingerbread, he began to eat with all his might, for he was very hungry. Grethel seated herself on the doorstep, and began munching away at the cakes of which it was made. Presently a voice came out of the cottage:

'Munching, crunching, munching,
Who's eating up my house?'

Then answered the children:

'The wind, the wind,
Only the wind,'

and went on eating as if they never meant to leave off, without a suspicion of wrong. Hansel, who found the cake on the roof taste very good, broke off another large piece, and Grethel had just taken out a whole pane of barley-sugar from the window, and seated herself to eat it, when the door opened, and a strange-looking old woman came out leaning on a stick.

Hansel and Grethel were so frightened that they let fall what they held in their hands. The old woman shook her head at them, and said, 'Ah, you dear children, who has brought you here? Come in, and stay with me for a little while, and there shall no harm happen to you.' She seized them both by the hands as she spoke, and led them into the house. She gave them for supper plenty to eat and drink—milk and pancakes and sugar, apples and nuts; and when evening came, Hansel and Grethel were shown two beautiful little beds with white curtains, and they lay down in them and thought they were in heaven.

But although the old woman pretended to be friendly, she was a wicked witch, who had her house built of gingerbread on purpose to entrap children. When once they were in her power, she would feed them well till they got fat, and then kill them and cook them for her dinner; and this she called her feast-day. Fortunately the witch had weak eyes, and could not see very well; but she had a very keen scent, as wild animals have, and could easily discover when human beings were near. As Hansel and Grethel had approached her cottage, she laughed to herself maliciously, and said, with a sneer: 'I have them now; they shall not escape from me again!'

Early in the morning, before the children were awake, she was up, standing by their beds; and when she saw how beautiful they looked in their sleep, with their round rosy cheeks, she muttered to herself,

'What nice tit-bits they will be!' Then she laid hold of Hansel with her rough hand, dragged him out of bed, and led him to a little cage which had a lattice-door, and shut him in; he might scream as much as he would, but it was all useless.

After this she went back to Grethel, and, shaking her roughly till she woke, cried: 'Get up, you lazy hussy, and draw some water, that I may boil something good for your brother, who is shut up in a cage outside till he gets fat; and then I shall cook him and eat him!' When Grethel heard this she began to cry bitterly; but it was all useless, she was obliged to do as the wicked witch told her.

For poor Hansel's breakfast the best of everything was cooked; but Grethel had nothing for herself but a crab's claw. Every morning the old woman would go out to the little cage, and say: 'Hansel, stick out your finger, that I may feel if you are fat enough for eating.' But Hansel, who knew how dim her old eyes were, always stuck a bone through the bars of his cage, which she thought was his finger, for she could not see; and when she felt how thin it was, she wondered very much why he did not get fat.

However, as the weeks went on, and Hansel seemed not to get any fatter, she became impatient, and said she could not wait any longer. 'Go, Grethel,' she cried to the maiden, 'be quick and draw water; Hansel may be fat or lean, I don't care, to-morrow morning I mean to kill him, and cook him!'

Oh! how the poor little sister grieved when she was forced to draw the water; and, as the tears rolled down her cheeks, she exclaimed: 'It would have been better to be eaten by wild beasts, or to have been starved to death in the woods; then we should have died together!'

'Stop your crying!' cried the old woman; 'it is not of the least use, no one will come to help you.'

Early in the morning Grethel was obliged to go out and fill the great pot with water, and hang it over the fire to boil. As soon as this was done, the old woman said, 'We will bake some bread first; I have made the oven hot, and the dough is already kneaded.' Then she dragged poor little Grethel up to the oven door, under which the flames were burning fiercely, and said: 'Creep in there, and see if it is hot enough yet to bake the bread.' But if Grethel had obeyed her, she would have shut the poor child in and baked her for dinner, instead of boiling Hansel.

Grethel, however, guessed what she wanted to do, and said, 'I don't know how to get in through that narrow door.'

'Stupid goose,' said the old woman, 'why, the oven door is quite large enough for me; just look, I could get in myself.' As she spoke she stepped forward and pretended to put her head in the oven.

A sudden thought gave Grethel unusual strength; she started forward, gave the old woman a push which sent her right into the oven, then she shut the iron door and fastened the bolt.

Oh! how the old witch did howl, it was quite horrible to hear her.

HANSEL AND GRETHEL

HANSEL AND GRETHEL

But Grethel ran away, and therefore she was left to burn, just as she had left many poor little children to burn. And how quickly Grethel ran to Hansel, opened the door of his cage, and cried, 'Hansel, Hansel, we are free; the old witch is dead.' He flew like a bird out of his cage at these words as soon as the door was opened, and the children were so overjoyed that they ran into each other's arm, and kissed each other with the greatest love.

GRETHEL PUSHING THE WITCH INTO THE OVEN.

And now that there was nothing to be afraid of, they went back into the house, and while looking round the old witch's room, they saw an old oak chest, which they opened, and found it full of pearls and precious stones. 'These are better than pebbles,' said Hansel; and he filled his pockets as full as they would hold.

'I will carry some home too,' said Grethel, and she held out her apron, which held quite as much as Hansel's pockets.

'We will go now,' he said, 'and get away as soon as we can from this enchanted forest.'

They had been walking for nearly two hours when they came to a large piece of water.

'What shall we do now?' said the boy.   'We cannot get across, and there is no bridge of any sort.'

'Oh! here comes a boat,' cried Grethel, but she was mistaken; it was only a white duck which came swimming towards the children. 'Perhaps she will help us across if we ask her,' said the child; and she sung, 'Little duck, do help poor Hansel and Grethel; there is not a bridge, nor a boat—will you let us sail across on your white back?'

The good-natured duck came near the bank as Grethel spoke, so close indeed that Hansel could seat himself and wanted to take his little sister on his lap, but she said, 'No, we shall be too heavy for the kind duck; let her take us over one at a time.'

The good creature did as the children wished; she carried Grethel over first, and then came back for Hansel. And then how happy the children were to find themselves in a part of the wood which they remembered quite well, and as they walked on, the more familiar it became, till at last they caught sight of their father's house. Then they began to run, and, bursting into the room, threw themselves into their father's arms.

Poor man, he had not had a moment's peace since the children had been left alone in the forest; he was full of joy at finding them safe and well again, and now they had nothing to fear, for their wicked stepmother was dead.

But how surprised the poor wood-cutter was when Grethel opened and shook her little apron to see the glittering pearls and precious stones scattered about the room, while Hansel drew handful after handful from his pockets. From this moment all his care and sorrow was at an end, and the father lived in happiness with his children till his death.

RAPUNZEL.

THERE were once a man and a woman who wished very much to have a little child. Now, these people had a small window in their cottage which looked out into a beautiful garden full of the most lovely flowers and vegetables. There was a high wall round it, but even had there not been, no one would have ventured to enter the garden, because it belonged to a sorceress, whose power was so great that everyone feared her.

One day the woman stood at the window looking into the garden, and she saw a bed which was planted full of most beautiful lettuces. As she looked at them, she began to wish she had some to eat, but she could not ask for them.

Day after day her wish for these lettuces grew stronger, and the knowledge that she could not get them so worried her, that at last she became so pale and thin that her husband was quite alarmed.

'What is the matter with you, dear wife?' he said one day.

'Ah!' she said, 'if I do not have some of that nice lettuce which grows in the garden behind our house, I feel that I shall die.'

The husband, who loved his wife dearly, said to himself, 'Rather than my wife should die, I will get some of this lettuce for her, cost what it may.'

So in the evening twilight he climbed over the wall into the garden of the witch, hastily gathered a handful of the lettuces, and brought them to his wife. She made it into a salad, and ate it with great eagerness.

It pleased her so much and tasted so good that after two or three days had passed, she gave her husband no rest till he promised to get her some more. So again in the evening twilight he climbed the wall, but as he slid down into the garden on the other side he was terribly alarmed at seeing the witch standing near him.

'How came you here?' she said with a fierce look. 'You have climbed over the wall into my garden like a thief, and stolen my lettuces; you shall pay dearly for this.'

'Ah!' replied the poor man, 'let me entreat for mercy; I have only taken it in a case of extreme need. My wife has seen your lettuces from her window, and she wished for them so much that she said she should die if she could not have some of them to eat.'

Then the witch's anger cooled a little, and she replied; 'If what you tell me is true, then I will give you full permission to take as many lettuces as you like, on one condition. You must give up to me the child which your wife may bring into the world. I will be very kind to it, and be as careful of it as a mother could be.'

The husband in his alarm promised everything the witch asked, and took away with him as many lettuces as his wife wanted.

Not many weeks after this the wife became the mother of a beautiful little girl, and in a short time the witch appeared and claimed her, according to the husband's promise. Thus they were obliged to give up the child, which she took away with her directly, and gave her the name of Rapunzel,* after the name of the vegetable which grew in the garden.

Rapunzel was the most beautiful child under the sun, and as soon as she reached the age of twelve years, the witch locked her up in a tower that stood in a forest, and this tower had no steps, nor any entrance, excepting a little window. When the witch wished to visit Rapunzel, she would place herself under this little window and sing:

> "Rapunzel, Rapunzel, let down your hair
> That I may climb without a stair."

Rapunzel had most long and beautiful hair like spun gold, and when

---

*"Rapunzel" is a German word for lettuce.

she heard the voice of the witch, she would unbind her golden locks, and let them fall loose over the window-sill, from which they hung down to such a length that the witch could draw herself up by them into the tower.

Two years passed in this manner, when it happened one day that the king's son rode through the forest. While passing near the tower, he heard such a lovely song, and could not help stopping to listen. It was Rapunzel, who tried to lighten her solitude by the sound of her own sweet voice.

The king's son was very eager to obtain a glimpse of the singer, but he sought in vain for a door to the tower; there was not one to be found.

So he rode home, but the song had made such an impression on his heart that he went daily into the forest to listen. Once, while he stood behind a tree, he saw the witch approach the tower, and heard her say:

> "Rapunzel, Rapunzel, let down your hair,
> That I may climb instead of a stair."

Presently he saw a quantity of long golden hair hanging down low over the window-sill, and the witch climbing up by it.

'Oh!' said the young prince, 'if that is the ladder on which persons can mount and enter, I will take the first opportunity of trying my luck that way.'

So on the following day, as it began to grow dark, he placed himself under the window, and cried:

> "Rapunzel, Rapunzel, let down your hair,
> That I may climb instead of a stair."

Immediately the hair fell over the window, and the young prince quickly climbed up and entered the room where the young maiden lived.

Rapunzel was dreadfully frightened at seeing a strange man come into the room through the window; but the king's son looked at her with such friendly eyes, and began to converse with her so kindly, that she soon lost all fear.

He told her that he had heard her singing, and that her song had excited such deep emotion in his heart that he could not rest till he had seen her. On hearing this, Rapunzel ceased to fear him, and they talked together for some time, till at length the prince asked her if she would take him for a husband. For a time she hesitated, although she saw that he was young and handsome, and he had told her he was a prince. At last she said to herself, 'He will certainly love me better than old Mother Grethel does.' So she placed her hand in his, and said, 'I would willingly go with you, and be your wife; but I do not know in the least how to get away from this place.

Unless,' she said, after a pause, 'you will bring me every day some strong silk cord, then I will weave a ladder of it, and when it is finished I will descend upon it, and you shall take me away on your horse.'

The prince readily agreed to this, and promised to come and see her every evening till the ladder was finished, for the old witch always came in the daytime.

The witch had never seen the prince; she knew nothing of his visits; till one day Rapunzel said innocently, 'I shall not have such a heavy weight as you to draw up much longer, Mother Grethel, for the king's son is coming very soon to fetch me away.'

'You wicked child,' cried the witch, 'what do I hear you say? I thought I had hidden you from all the world, and now you have betrayed me.' In her wrath she caught hold of Rapunzel's beautiful hair, and struck her several times with her left hand. Then she seized a pair of scissors and cut Rapunzel's hair, while the beautiful locks, glistening like gold, fell on the ground. And she was so hard-hearted after this that she dragged poor Rapunzel out into the forest, to a wild and desert place, and left her there in sorrow and woe.

On the same day on which the poor maiden had been exiled, the witch tied the locks of hair which she had cut off poor Rapunzel's golden head into a kind of tail, and hung it over the window-sill.

> "Rapunzel, Rapunzel, let down your hair,
> That I may climb without a stair."

Then the witch let the hair down, and the king's son climbed up; but at the open window he found not his dear Rapunzel, but a wicked witch, who looked at him with cruel and malicious eyes.

'Ah!' she cried, with a sneer, 'you are come to fetch your loving bride, I suppose; but the beautiful bird has flown from the nest, and will never sing any more. The cat has fetched it away, and she intends also to scratch your eyes out. To thee is Rapunzel lost; thou wilt never behold her again.'

The prince felt almost out of his mind with grief as he heard this, and in his despair he sprang out of the tower window and fell among the thorns and brambles beneath. He certainly escaped with his life, but the thorns struck into his eyes and blinded them. After this he wandered about the woods for days, eating only wild roots and berries, and did nothing but lament and weep for the loss of his beloved bride.

So he wandered for a whole year in misery, till at last he came upon the desert place where Rapunzel had been banished and lived in her sorrow. As he drew near he heard a voice which he seemed to recognize, and advancing towards the sound came within sight of Rapunzel, who recognised him at once with tears. Two of her tears fell on his eyes, and so healed and cleared them of the injury done by the thorns that he could soon see as well as ever. Then he travelled with her to his kingdom, and she became his wife, and the remainder of their days were spent in happiness and content.

THE THREE LITTLE MEN IN THE WOOD

ONCE upon a time, there was a man who had lost his wife and had one daughter, and a widow, who also had a daughter. The maidens were brought up together, and played together as if they had been sisters.

One day the widow said to the man's daughter, 'Go and tell your father that I will marry him as soon as thou canst wash in milk and drink wine; but my child shall wash in water and drink water.'

Then the maiden went home and told her father what the woman had said.

Then said the man, 'What shall we do? This marriage would be a very happy thing, but it is also a great trouble.'

He thought for a while, and at last finding that he could make no excuse, he pulled off his boot, and said, 'Take this boot—there is a hole in the sole—and go with it to the loft; then hang it on a large nail, and pour water into it. If it holds the water, then I will again take a wife; but if it runs through the hole, I will not marry.'

Then the maiden did as her father had told her, and the water drew the hole together, so that the boot became full even to the brim, and she went to inform her father what had occurred.

As soon as he heard what had happened, he rose and went himself to see the boot; and, finding she had spoken the truth, he went at once to the widow, and after a short courtship they were married.

On the first morning the husband's daughter had milk placed for her to wash in and wine to drink, but the wife's daughter had water only. On the second morning there was nothing but water for both of them; but on the third day, the wine and milk were for the wife's daughter, while her stepchild had nothing but water, and so from this time it continued.

In the heart of the wife a bitter hatred soon arose against her stepdaughter, because she was beautiful and amiable and her own child was ugly and disagreeable. Not a day passed without some unkindness on the stepmother's part, which made the poor girl quite sad, but she bore it all patiently.

One day in the winter, when the ground was frozen hard and mountain and valley lay white with snow, the stepmother made a dress of paper. Then she called the maiden and said to her, 'Just put on this dress and go out into the woods and bring me that basket full of blackberries. I have a longing for them.'

'Oh, dear,' replied the girl, 'blackberries do not grow in winter, when the ground is frozen and the hedges are covered with snow. Besides, how can I go in this paper dress? It is so cold out of doors that even one's breath freezes, and the wind will cut through this thin dress, and the thorns tear my skin.'

'Hold your tongue, and don't answer me,' said the stepmother. 'Get off as fast as you can, and let me not see you again till you get the basket full of blackberries.' Then she gave her stepdaughter a small piece of dry bread, and said, 'That will be enough for you to-day: now go.'

'Ah,' thought the wicked woman, 'she will be frozen, or starved with hunger, and will never come before my eyes again.'

Now, as the maiden was always obedient, she put on the paper dress and went out. Far and wide there could be seen nothing but snow, not even a little blade of green grass; but she walked on, and at last came to a small cottage in the wood, from which peeped out three strange little men.

She wished to know what o'clock it was, so she knocked timidly at the door. 'Come in,' they cried, and she stepped in and seated herself on a stool near the stove, for she wanted to get warm and eat her breakfast. Presently one of the little men said to her, 'Give us some of your bread, maiden.'

'Willingly,' she replied. So she divided her piece of bread, and gave them half.

Presently they asked again, 'What brought you into the forest on such a wintry day as this with only a thin dress?'

'Ah,' she answered, 'I was sent into the wood to fill this basket with blackberries, and I dare not go home again till I have filled it.'

The tiny mannikins said no more till she had eaten her bread, and then one of them gave her a broom and said, 'Go and sweep the snow away from the back door.'

Without a word, the maiden took the broom and went out.

As soon as she was gone the little men began to talk together about her. 'She is a pretty, well-behaved girl,' said one; 'what good fortune shall we send her?' 'I will promise,' said the first, 'that she shall grow every day more beautiful.' 'And I will endow her with a wonderful gift,' said the second; 'every time she opens her mouth to speak, a piece of gold shall fall out.' Then the third foretold that a king's son should make her his wife.

All this while the maiden was busily employed sweeping away the snow from the pathway behind the cottage, and at last what do you think she found?—rich ripe strawberries of a deep red lying before her on the snow.

How quickly and joyfully she gathered them up and filled her basket we can easily guess, and, after shaking hands with the little men, she thanked them for their kindness and ran home; for she was longing to show her stepmother what she had brought for her. As she entered the house and said 'Good-evening,' a piece of gold immediately fell from her mouth on the floor.

Her stepmother was astonished; and then the maiden related what had happened to her in the wood, while at every word she uttered a piece of gold fell from her mouth, so that in a very short time the whole room glittered with the gold.

'I expect you will be proud and haughty,' said the stepsister, 'now that you can scatter gold in this way;' but she was deceitful and jealous about it, and asked her stepmother privately to let her go into the wood to find strawberries.

'No, my dear little daughter,' replied the mother; 'it is too cold for you; it is freezing hard.'

But the girl gave her mother no peace, till at last she allowed her to go. Not, however, till she had made her dress herself in a warm fur jacket, and given her bread and butter and cake to eat on the way.

The maiden went to the wood, and walked on till she reached the cottage. The three little men saw her coming, although she knew it not; and, without guessing or seeing anything wrong, walked right into the room, seated herself by the stove, and began eating her bread and butter and cake.

'Give us a little of your nice breakfast,' said one of the little men.

'I have not enough for myself,' she replied; 'how can I give you any?' So she went on eating, and they waited till she had finished.

Then they said, 'There is a broom in the corner; take it and sweep the pathway at the back door.'

'Go and do it yourself,' she cried; 'I am not your servant.'

However, when she saw that they did not move, she was half afraid, and, taking the broom, went out.

After she was gone the little men began to talk one to the other about her. 'What shall we send her?' asked one; 'for she has such a naughty, wicked, and envious heart, we cannot grant her a favour.' 'Then,' said the first, 'I ordain that she shall grow more ugly every day.' 'I will send her such a gift,' said the second, 'that at every word she speaks a toad shall spring out of her mouth;' while the third prophesied that she should meet with an unlucky death.

After sweeping away the snow, the maiden searched in vain for strawberries, but none could she find; so she went home quite sullen, and out of temper. But how terrified she was when, on opening her mouth to relate all that had happened to her in the wood, at each word a toad sprang out on the floor, so that she became disgusting to everyone.

After this, the stepmother became more spiteful against her husband's daughter than ever, and thought only of the means to make her suffer pain and annoyance, for her beauty grew more and more daily.

At last, one morning, she took a kettle, and set it on the fire to boil yarn. As soon as it was ready, she called the poor girl, and, hanging the thread on her shoulder, gave her an axe, and told her to go to the frozen river, break a hole in the ice, and wash the thread.

Always obedient, she took the axe and went to break a hole in the ice. But as she struck the first blow, a beautiful little carriage passed by in which sat a young king. He stopped the carriage when he saw the maiden, and said, ' My child, why are you out here in the cold, and what are you doing ?'

' I am a poor maiden,' she replied ; ' and I am cleaning yarn.'

Then the king was full of pity, and seeing such a beautiful maiden so cruelly served in such cold weather, he said, ' Will you ride with me ?'

' Oh yes,' she replied, ' with all my heart ;' for she was overjoyed at the thought of escaping out of sight of her stepmother and sister.

Then she entered the carriage, and the king drove her a long way from home, to his castle. And in a very short time after the king asked her to be his wife, and the marriage was celebrated with great splendour, as the little men in the wood had foretold.

In about a year the young queen had a little son, of whom she was very fond. And the stepmother, who had heard of her good fortune, went with her daughter to the castle, and they both made themselves so agreeable that they were invited to make a long visit.

But one day, while the king was from home and no one in the castle near, the wicked woman laid hold of the queen by the head, and her daughter held her by the feet; then they lifted her out of bed, and threw her from the window into a stream that flowed on one side of the castle.

After this wicked deed, the stepmother placed her own daughter in the bed, and covered her over with the clothes till only the top of her head could be seen. When the king came back, and wished to speak to his wife, the mother exclaimed, ' Hush, hush ! you must not disturb her ; she is in a sweet sleep.' However, the next morning the king would see his wife, although he never suspected such wickedness ; but when he spoke to her, and she answered him, there sprung out of her mouth at each word a toad, instead of the pieces of gold as before. Then the king inquired what could be the cause of this dreadful change, and the old woman said that if she could have another sound sleep, she would soon be all right again. So the king left her. That night the king's page saw something like a duck swimming across the moat under the king's window, and heard a voice saying :

> ' King, dost thou watchful keep ?
> Or dost thou close thine eyes in sleep ?'

There was no answer, and the spectre said again, ' What does my visitor ?'

Then the page replied, ' She is fast asleep.'

Again it spoke—' Where is my little child ?'

'He sleeps in his cradle, now,' answered the page.

Then the apparition took the form of the young queen, went into the infant's room, took him up and fed him, shook up his little bed, laid him to sleep, covered him warmly with the clothes, and then swam back again through the moat in the form of a duck. All this occurred again the next night; but when she appeared the third time she spoke to the page, and said, 'Go and call the king, and tell him to take his sword and swing it three times over me from the window-sill.' Then ran the page quickly and told the king. He came immediately with his sword and swung it three times over the apparition, and after the third time there stood before him his own beautiful wife, healthy, and charming as ever. Oh, how happy the king was now! He kept the queen concealed in the room where his baby lived till Sunday, when he was to be baptized. As soon as the ceremony was over, he said to the old stepmother, 'What does that man deserve who takes another out of his bed and throws him into the water?'

'He deserves nothing better,' she replied, 'than to be stuck in a barrel full of the points of nails and rolled down a mountain into the water.'

'Then,' said the king, 'you have pronounced your own sentence. Let such a barrel as this wicked woman has described be brought, and place her and her daughter in it, that they may be rolled into the water as a punishment for their cruel conduct.'

But the young queen begged the king to pardon them for her sake; and he consented to do so, on condition that they should be banished from his kingdom.

THE THREE WHITE SNAKES.

THERE lived once a father who was so poor that he could hardly earn enough to keep himself and his son from starving. One day the boy said to him, 'Dear father, I see you going about every day looking so sorrowful and tired, that I am determined to go out into the world and try to earn my own living.'

Then his father gave him his blessing and took leave of him with many tears. Just at this time a great king was going to war with the king of another country, and the youth took service under him and marched to the battlefield as a soldier. In the first conflict with the enemy he was in great danger and had a wonderful escape, for his comrades fell on each side of him. Their commander also was wounded, and several were inclined to take flight and run from the field. But the youth stepped forth to raise their courage, and cried, 'No, no, we will never allow our fatherland to sink to the ground!' Then they took courage and followed their young leader, who led them forward, attacked, and quickly vanquished the enemy. When the king heard to whom he owed this great victory, he sent for the youth, raised him to a position of great honour, gave him large treasures, and made him first in the kingdom next to himself.

Now, the king had a daughter who was very beautiful, but she was also very whimsical. She had made a vow that she would take no man for a husband who did not promise that if she should die, he would allow himself to be buried alive with her in the grave. 'If he loves me,' she said, ' he will not wish to outlive me,' and in return for this she would also promise to be buried in the grave with her spouse, should he die first.

This vow had hitherto frightened away all wooers, but the young soldier was so struck with the beauty of the princess that he disregarded the vow, although her father warned him, and said, ' Do you know what a terrible promise you will have to make ?'

' Yes,' replied the young man, ' I must be buried with her in the grave if I outlive her ; but my love for her is so strong that I disregard that danger.'

Then the king gave his consent, and the marriage was celebrated with great pomp.

After they had lived together for some time in great happiness and contentment, the young queen was seized with a terrible illness from which her physicians were unable to restore her. As she lay dead, the young husband remembered what he had promised, and the thought of lying in the grave alive filled him with horror, but there was no escape. The king placed a watch at every outlet from the castle, so that it was not possible to avoid his fate. When the day of the funeral arrived and the body had been carried down and placed in the royal vault, he was taken there also, and the door firmly fastened with locks and bolts. Near to the coffin stood a table upon which were four lights, four loaves of bread, and four bottles of wine, and he knew that when these provisions came to an end he must starve. So he seated himself, feeling full of grief and sorrow, but with a determination to take only a small piece of bread, and the least drop of wine, to make them last.

One day, when death seemed nearer than ever, he saw from a corner of the vault, just opposite to where he sat, a white snake creep out and approach the body. He rose in horror, thinking it was about to gnaw it, and drawing his sword, exclaimed, as with two blows he cut the snake into three pieces, ' As long as I live you shall not touch that.'

After a while a second snake crept out of the corner, but as soon as he saw the other lying dead in three pieces, he went back and quickly returned with three green leaves in his mouth. Then he took the three separate portions of the snake, placed them together and laid a leaf on each wound, and no sooner were they joined, than the snake raised himself as lively as ever, and went away hastily with his companion.

The leaves remained lying on the ground, and as he looked at them, the thoughts of the poor unfortunate man were full of the wonderful properties they possessed, and it suddenly occurred to him that a leaf which could restore a dead snake to life might be useful to human beings. He stooped and picked up the leaves, then advancing softly towards the body, he laid one on the mouth of the dead, and the others on both the eyes. In a moment he saw the effect of what he had done. The blood began to circulate in the veins, and flushed softly in the pale face and lips of his dead wife. She drew a deep breath, opened her closed eyes, and exclaimed faintly, ' Where am I ?'

' Thou art with me, dear wife,' answered her husband ; and then he told her all that had happened, and how he had wakened her to life.

THE YOUNG SOLDIER AND THE SNAKE.

After taking a little of the wine and bread she became stronger, and was able to rise from the bier and walk to the door of the vault with her husband. Here they knocked and called loudly for a long time, till at last the watchman heard them, and word was sent to the king. He came himself very quickly, and ordered the door of the vault to be opened, and, oh ! how astonished and joyful he was to find them both alive and uninjured, and to know that his anxiety was over, for the whole matter had been a great trouble to him.

The three leaves the young prince took with him, and gave them in charge to a servant to take care of, saying, ' Preserve them carefully for me, and see that they are safe every day ; who knows what help they may be to us in any future trouble ?'

In the wife of the young prince after this event a great change appeared—it was as if with her return to life all her love for her husband had vanished from her heart.

Not long after he wished to take a voyage across the sea to see his old father, and she accompanied him. While they were on board ship, she forgot all the true and great love he had shown for her in trying to restore her to life when she was dead, and made friends with the captain, who was as wicked as herself.

One day, when the young prince lay asleep on deck, she called the skipper to her and told him to take her husband by the feet, while she raised his head, and before he was awake enough to save himself, these two wicked people threw him overboard into the sea. As soon as this shameful deed was accomplished, she said to the skipper, 'Now let us sail home again, and say that the prince has died on the voyage. I will praise and extol you so greatly to my father, that I know he will readily give his consent to our marriage, and leave the crown to you after his death.'

But the faithful servant to whom the prince had given the wonderful leaves to take care of saw all that his master's wife had done. Unnoticed, he lowered one of the boats from the ship's side, got on board, and very soon discovered the body of the prince. Dragging it hastily into the boat, he rowed away and soon left the traitors far behind. As soon as he felt safely out of sight, he produced the precious leaves, which he always carried about with him, and laid one on each eye and one on the mouth of the dead man, who very quickly showed signs of life, and was at last sufficiently restored to help in rowing the boat. They both rowed with all their strength day and night, and their little bark flew so swiftly over the waves that they arrived at the king's palace long before his daughter and the captain.

The king wondered greatly when he saw his son-in-law and the servant enter, and asked them what had happened. But when he heard of his daughter's wickedness, he said, 'I can scarcely believe she would act so basely. However, the truth will soon be brought to light. For the present, I advise you both to hide yourselves in a private chamber, and make yourselves quite at home till the ship returns.'

The master and servant took the king's advice, and a few days afterwards the large ship made its appearance, and the king's guilty daughter appeared before her father with a sorrowful countenance.

'Why have you come back alone?' he asked. 'Where is your husband?'

'Ah! dear father,' she replied, 'I am come home to you in great sorrow, for, during the voyage, my husband was taken suddenly ill and died; and if the good captain had not stood by me, and conducted me home, I cannot tell what evil might have happened to me. He stood by my husband's deathbed, and he can tell you all that occurred.'

'Oh!' said the king, 'I can restore your dead husband to life again, so do not grieve any longer.' He threw open the door of the private room as he spoke, and told his son and the servant to come out.

When the wife saw her husband, she was thunderstruck, and sank on her knees imploring mercy.

'I can show you no mercy,' said the king. 'Your husband was not only ready to be buried and die with you, but he used the means which restored you to life, and you have murdered him while he slept, and shall receive the reward you so truly merit.'

Then was she with her accomplice placed in a boat full of holes, and driven out to sea, where they were soon overwhelmed in the waves and perished.

THE LANGUAGE OF ANIMALS.

IN times of old there once lived a king whose wisdom was so great that the whole land depended upon his judgments. Nothing remained long unknown to him; it appeared as if intelligence of the most carefully concealed event was carried to him through the air. It was the custom of this king each day at noon, when the dinner had been removed, and no one else present, for a trustworthy servant to bring in a large bowl, which was always covered up. Neither the servant nor anyone else knew what it contained, for the king never took off the cover to eat of the contents till he was quite alone. This had continued for a long time, but there came a day when the curiosity of the servant was too strong to be overcome, and after removing the dish from the king's table he took it to his own room. After carefully locking the door he lifted up the cover, and saw to his surprise a white snake lying at full length in the dish. He no sooner caught sight of it than he became unable to resist a desire to taste, so he cut a little piece off and put it in his mouth. Scarcely had it touched his tongue, than he heard outside his window strange whisperings and soft voices. He went and listened; and then noticed two sparrows who were talking together and relating to each other all that they had seen in the woods and fields. The little piece of snake which he had so enjoyed had given him the power to understand the language of animals.

Now it happened that on this very day the queen had lost one of her beautiful rings, and she suspected that this trustworthy servant had stolen it, because he, above all others, had most access to the room in which she had left it. The king sent for him, and with harsh, angry words told him he should be brought to justice and punished for a deed which till that moment he had never heard of. It was of no use for him to protest his innocence; the king was inexorable. In his sorrow and distress of mind he went out into the court behind the castle, and tried to think of some means by which he might get himself out of this trouble.

On the smooth surface water of the lake two ducks were swimming peacefully together, side by side. They plumed their shining feathers with their smooth bills, while they held a very confidential conversation. The servant stood still to listen, and heard them talking of where they had been waddling, and of the good food they had found.

'Ah, yes,' said one, 'but some of it lies very heavy on my stomach; I think it must be that ring which lay under the queen's window. In my hurry, I dare say I swallowed it.'

The servant no sooner heard this, than he seized the duck by the neck, and, carrying her into the kitchen, said to the cook, 'Kill this duck for dinner, will you? it is quite fat.'

'Yes, I see it is,' replied the cook, taking it in his hand. 'I shall not have the trouble of fattening this one, at all events, or waiting till it is ready.' Then he put an end to the poor duck's life; and, on opening it to prepare for roasting, he found the queen's ring in her stomach.

The servant was overjoyed when he saw the ring, for now he could easily prove his innocence to the king, who was very anxious to make amends for having so unjustly accused him. He not only gave him his friendship, but also promised him whatever high position in the court he wished. The servant readily accepted an office in which he could have a horse, and money to travel, for he had a great desire to see the world, and visit the different towns of which he had heard.

All his requests were granted, and he very speedily set out on his travels.

At the end of a few days he came to a pond, in which he saw three fish, which had been caught by the rushes on the bank, and were gasping for want of water. Although people say that fish are dumb, yet he understood the complaining tones well enough to know that without help they would quickly perish. He sympathized from his heart with their suffering. So he alighted from his horse, and, rescuing the little fish from the rushes, placed them again in the water. They wriggled about with joy, and one of them stretched out his head and cried:

'We will always think of thee; and thou wilt be rewarded for having saved us.'

He rode away, however, and presently beneath his feet a voice spoke, and he understood that the words were those of an ant-king mourning over the danger to his community. 'These human beings,' he said, 'ride by on awkward animals without the least thought. Here's a stupid horse coming along; no doubt, with his heavy hoofs he will tread down our people unmercifully.

But the rider turned his horse aside; and the ant-king cried out:

'I will often think of thee; and thou shalt be rewarded.'

Then the king's messenger travelled on till he reached a wood, and there he saw two ravens — a father and mother — and heard them say, as they stood by their nest: 'Go along with you, we cannot feed you any more; you are fat enough, and must now provide for yourselves ;' and the old birds threw the young ones out of the nest as they spoke.

The poor little birds lay on the ground, fluttering and beating their little wings, and crying, ' Oh! we poor, helpless children, we have to provide for ourselves, and we cannot even fly; there is nothing left for us but to die of hunger.'

Then the good young man dismounted, killed his horse with his dagger, and left it there for the young ravens to feed on. They hopped upon it, and began to feast themselves, crying out :

' We will always think of thee ; and thou shalt be rewarded.'

He was now obliged to use his own legs instead of riding ; so he walked on for a long distance, till at last he came to a large town. There was a great noise in the streets, and crowds of people, and presently a man on horseback rode up and made a proclamation that the king's daughter was seeking a spouse; but that he who was a candidate for her hand must first perform completely a very difficult task, and if he undertook it and did not succeed he would forfeit his life. The young man had at first no wish to be a suitor to such a great lady ; but he had no sooner seen the young princess than he became quite dazzled with her beauty, and promised to do everything she wished.

Then he was admitted by the king as her suitor, and sailed very soon after on a voyage to enable him to accomplish the undertaking she required. One day as he was seated on deck, he saw a gold ring fall before him, as if thrown by a hand. He took great care of it, and on his return gave it to the king, who at once ordered him to throw the ring back into the sea, and dive after it, adding, 'Every time you come up without it, you shall be thrust back into the waves till they overwhelm you.'

Everyone pitied the handsome youth who was required to perform such a difficult task. He went back to the sea, and while standing mournfully on the shore, he saw three fish swimming about, and they proved to be none other than those whose lives he had saved. One of them held a mussel in its mouth, and swimming to the shore laid it on the strand at the young man's feet. He took up the mussel and opened it, and there lay the gold ring. Full of joy he carried it to the king, and expected that the promised reward would be granted him.

But the king's proud daughter said, disdainfully, that she understood her suitor was not so well born as herself, and therefore he must have another difficult task to perform before she could consent to marry him. So she went out herself into the garden and scattered ten sacks full of grain over the grass. Then she called her lover and showed him what she had done, saying, ' These grains must all be separated from the grass before the sun rises to-morrow morning ; not the smallest grain must be overlooked.'

She left him after these words, and the poor young man seated himself in the garden and thought that for him to perform such a task as this would be impossible. So he sat still in sorrowful expectation that the break of day would be the hour of his death. But when the first sunbeam fell in the garden, he saw with surprise the ten sacks of grain standing quite full near each other, and not the smallest grain left behind in the grass.

The ant-king had arrived during the night with thousands from his ant kingdom, and the grateful creatures had with great industry picked up every tiny grain, and filled the sacks.

At sunrise, the king's daughter came herself into the garden and saw with wonder that the young man had in every way performed the allotted task. But she could not even now conquer the pride of her heart, and therefore she said, 'It is true he has accomplished two difficult tasks, but I require one more : he shall be my husband when he brings me an apple from the tree of life.'

The young man knew not even where this wonderful tree grew, but he was determined to make an effort to find it, so he set out to walk as far as his legs could carry him, but he had very little hope of success. He had travelled day after day through three kingdoms without success, when one evening he wandered into a wood, and, feeling very tired, laid himself down under a tree to rest. Presently, in the branches, he heard a chattering of birds in a nest, and a golden apple fell down into his hand. Immediately three young ravens flew down to him, perched themselves on his knee, and said, 'We are the three young ravens which you saved from being starved to death with hunger. As soon as we were grown large and strong enough to fly, we took our flight to distant countries, and heard that you were in search of a golden apple, so we have travelled over the sea, even to the end of the world, where the tree of life grows, and have brought away an apple for you.'

Full of joy, the young man forgot his fatigue, and, returning quickly, placed before the beautiful princess the golden apple. She had not now another word to say in opposition to their marriage. They divided the golden apple between them, and ate it together. Then was the heart of the princess softened and filled with love for the brave youth, and they lived in uninterrupted happiness to a good old age.

THE STRAW, THE COAL, AND THE BEAN.

IN a village there lived an old woman, who one day gathered some beans from her garden to cook for her dinner. She had a good fire on the hearth ; but to make it burn more quickly she threw on a handful of straw. As she threw the beans into the pot to boil, one of them fell on the floor unobserved by the old woman, and not far from a wisp of straw which was lying near. Suddenly a glowing coal bounced out of the fire, and fell close to them. They both started away and exclaimed,

'Dear friend, don't come near me till you are cooler. Whatever brings you out here?'

'Oh,' replied the coal, 'the heat luckily made me so strong, that I was able to bounce from the fire. Had I not done so, my death would have been certain, and I should have been burnt to ashes by this time.'

'Then,' said the bean, 'I have also escaped with a whole skin; for had the old woman put me in the pot with my comrades, I should, without mercy, have been boiled to broth.'

'I might have shared the same fate,' said the straw, 'for all my brothers were pushed into the fire and smoke by the old woman. She packed sixty of us in a bundle, and brought us in here to take away our lives, but luckily I contrived to slip through her fingers.'

'Well, now what shall we do with ourselves?' said the coal.

'I think,' answered the bean, 'as we have been so fortunate as to escape death, we may as well be companions, and travel away together to some more friendly country, for here we may expect nothing but new misfortunes.'

This proposal was gladly accepted by the two others; so they started immediately on their journey together. After travelling a little distance, they came to a stream, over which there was no bridge of any sort— not even one of wood—so they were puzzled to know how to get over to the other side.

Then the straw took courage, and said, 'I will lay myself across the stream, so that you can step over me, as if I were a bridge.'

So the straw stretched himself from one shore to the other, and the coal, who from his nature is rather hot-headed, tripped out quite boldly on the newly-built bridge. But when he reached the middle of the stream, and heard the water rushing under him, he was so alarmed that he stood still, and dared not move a step farther. Sad were the consequences; for the straw, being slightly scorched in the middle by the heat still in the coal, broke in pieces from its weight, and fell into the brook. The coal, with a hiss, slid after him into the water, and gave up the ghost.

The bean, who had cautiously remained behind on the shore, could not contain herself when she saw what had happened, and laughed so heartily that she burst. Now would she have been in a worse plight than her comrades; but, as good luck would have it, a tailor who was out on his travels came to rest by the brook, and noticed the bean. He was a kind-hearted man, so he took a needle and thread out of his pocket, and taking up the bean, sewed her together. She thanked him very much, but unfortunately he had only black thread to sew with, and, in consequence, since that time all beans have a black mark down them.

THE BRAVE LITTLE TAILOR.

ONE fine summer morning, a little tailor sat at his open window on a table at work; and many good things could he buy with the money he earned, for he was a clever little tailor.

A farmer's wife came down the street, crying, 'Good jam for sale—good jam for sale.' The voice had a lively sound to the ears of the

'SEVEN AT ONE STROKE.'

little tailor; so he put his soft head out of the window, and cried, 'Come here, my good woman; this is the place to sell your goods.'

The woman ascended the three steps with her heavy basket, and stood before the tailor, who asked her to uncover it, and show him how much she had. As soon as he saw the contents, he rose from his table, and putting down his nose to smell, he exclaimed, 'This jam smells so good that I must have four ounces—that is a quarter of a pound; I cannot afford more.' The woman, who had hoped to sell a large quantity, gave him what he wished for, but went away quite angry and discontented.

' Oh, how I shall enjoy this !' cried the tailor, who cared nothing for the woman's grumbling; ' it will give me strength and energy for my work.' Then he fetched the bread from his cupboard, cut off a piece the whole size of the loaf, and spread the jam upon it. ' That will not taste bitter,' he said; ' but before I take even a bite, I must finish this waistcoat.' Then he placed the bread on a chair near, and, seating himself, sewed and stitched away with a spirit full of joy.

THE TAILOR AND THE FLIES.

In the meantime, the smell of the jam rose to the wall, where numbers of flies were clustered together; so tempting was it, that they flew down in swarms just to taste.

' Hallo ! who invited you ?' cried the tailor, as he drove away the unbidden guests.

But it was of no use. The flies did not understand German. They would not be sent away, but returned again in larger companies than ever. Then ran the little tailor ' head over heels,' as people say, and pulling from the chimney-corner a piece of cloth, he said, ' Wait and see what I will give you ;' then he dashed the cloth unmercifully amongst them.

Presently he stopped to see the havoc he had made, and counted no fewer than seven lying with their legs stretched out, quite dead.

' Am I such a churl,' he exclaimed, ' that I must admire my own bravery alone? No, no; the whole town shall hear about it.' And the little tailor, in great haste, cut out a waist-belt, on which he sewed and stitched large letters forming these words, ' Seven at one stroke.' ' This town,' said he again, ' indeed, the whole world, shall hear of it !' And his heart waggled with pride like a lamb's tail.

The little tailor bound the girdle round his waist, and determined to go out into the world, for he considered his workshop too small for a display of such bravery. Before starting, he searched in every corner of the house to discover if there was anything he could take with him, but found nothing but an old cheese, which he stuck in his pocket.

As he passed out, he saw before the door a bird caught in the bushes: this he also placed in his pocket with the cheese. Then he set out on his journey, tripping lightly along on his legs, for he was so light and pliant that he could walk a long way without feeling fatigue.

The road he took led him up a high mountain. When he reached the summit, there, quite at his ease, sat an enormous giant, who looked at him in a friendly manner.

The brave little tailor went straight up to him, and said, 'Good-morning, comrade. Upon my word, you have a grand prospect of the world stretched out before you. As for me, I am travelling in search of adventures—will you go with me?'

The giant looked quite disdainfully at the little tailor, and exclaimed, 'You conceited little imp! What! go with a contemptible little morsel of a man like you?'

'Stop!' cried the tailor; 'not so fast;' and unbuttoning his coat, he pointed to the words on his girdle. 'If you can read, that will show you whether I am a man or not.'

The giant read, 'Seven at one stroke!' and thinking it must be seven men whom the tailor had killed, he began to feel more respect for him.

'Well, now, I will prove you,' said the giant. 'Look here, can you do this?' and he took up a large stone and squeezed it till the water came from it.

'Oh, that is nothing,' exclaimed the tailor; 'it is but play to me;' and, taking out the soft cheese from his pocket, he squeezed it till the whey ran from it, crying out at the same time, 'Beat that, if you can!'

The giant knew not what to say; the strength of the little tailor quite astonished him. However, he took up another stone, and threw it to such a height in the air that it was impossible to see where it went.

'Certainly, that is clever,' said the tailor; 'but the stone will fall somewhere. I will throw one up that shall not come down again.' He put his hand in his pocket, and drawing out the bird, threw it up into the air.

Overjoyed at regaining its freedom, the bird rose immediately, and, spreading its wings, was soon far out of sight.

'What do you think of that performance, comrade?' he asked.

'You can throw very well, certainly,' replied the giant; 'but I should like to see if you can draw a heavy weight as easily as you can throw.'

He led the little tailor to a forest, in which lay an enormous oak which had fallen to the ground. 'Now, then,' he said, 'if you are as strong as you say, just help me to carry this tree out of the forest.'

'Most willingly,' replied the little man. 'You take the trunk on your shoulders, and leave me the leaves and the boughs; they are the heaviest.'

The giant lifted the trunk on his shoulders, but the cunning little tailor seated himself among the branches, unseen by the giant, who had therefore to carry the whole tree and the tailor into the bargain, without knowing it.

Our little friend was so merry as he went along, that he could not help whistling and singing, 'Three tailors rode from the door away,' as if carrying trees was mere child's play.

The giant, however, had not gone far when he began to stagger under his heavy load. 'I cannot move a step further,' he cried. 'Don't you hear? I shall let the tree fall.'

At this, the tailor sprung lightly down, seized the tree with both hands, and exclaimed, 'Well, you can't be so very strong, not to be able to carry such a tree as this.'

They left the tree, and walked on together till they came to a cherry-tree loaded with ripe fruit. The giant seized the topmost branch, and, bending it down, placed it in the tailor's hand, and told him to eat as many as he liked. But the little man had not strength enough to hold the branch, so up it sprang again, carrying the little tailor high into the air and letting him fall on the other side, but without hurting him at all. 'What,' said the giant, 'had you not strength enough to hold such a twig as this?'

'My strength did not fail me,' he replied. 'Do you suppose a man who could kill seven at one stroke would find this a difficult task? I sprung over the tree because I saw a number of hunters shooting in a wood close by. Now, you do the same; I should so like to see you spring over.'

The giant made an attempt, but he could not clear the tree; he only entangled himself in the branches; so that in this, also, the tailor gained the upper hand.

Then the giant said to him, 'As you are such a clever little fellow, you had better come home with me to my cave and stay the night.'

The tailor was quite ready to accompany him, and when they reached the cavern, there sat two other giants before a blazing fire, each with a large roast sheep in his hands, eating his supper.

The little tailor seated himself, and thought, 'Well, this is a sight worth coming out into the world to see.'

The giant then showed him a bed in which he could sleep, but when he laid himself down, it was so large that he got up again, and, creeping into a corner, curled himself round and went to sleep.

At midnight, the giant, thinking his visitor was fast asleep, rose up, and taking a heavy iron bar, struck a blow at the bed, which broke it right through. 'Ah,' thought he, 'I must have killed the little grass-hopper, and got rid of his cunning tricks now.' But the next morning, when the giants went out into the wood, and were not thinking of the tailor, he walked up to them as brave as ever, and looking as fresh and merry as a bird.

The giants were so alarmed at the sight of him come to life again, as they thought, and remembering that he could kill seven at one stroke, they quite expected he would be the death of them all. So, taking to their heels, they ran away quickly, and were soon out of sight.

Then the little man journeyed on, always following his nose, as the saying is; till, after wandering a long time, he arrived at the entrance court of a king's palace. Feeling very tired, he lay down on the grass, and soon fell fast asleep.

While he lay there, the people passing read on his girdle, ' Seven at one stroke.' ' Ah,' exclaimed one, ' what can a great warrior like this want here in time of peace? He must be a great hero.'

So they went and told the king, and suggested to him that in case a war should break out, it would be a great advantage to secure the services of such a wonderful and clever man at any price.

The king listened to this counsel, and sent one of the gentlemen of the court to tell the little man, as soon as he awoke, that he wished to enlist him in his service.

The messenger remained by him, and waited till he at last opened his eyes and stretched his limbs ; then he delivered his message.

' Ah, yes,' exclaimed the little man, ' that is exactly what I came for; I wish to be enlisted in the king's service.'

Then was he received at the palace with high honours, and handsome apartments prepared for his use.

But the military men at the court were jealous of the little tailor, and wished him thousands of miles away. ' What will become of us,' they said one to another, ' if we should quarrel with him, or attempt to fight him? If he can kill seven at one blow, there will soon be an end of us all.' So they formed a resolution, and went together to the king, and resigned their commissions, saying they could not associate with a man who could kill seven men at one blow.

The king was very much vexed when he heard this determination, for he did not like the idea of losing all his old and tried servants on account of this stranger, and began to wish he had never seen the tailor.

But how to get rid of him he knew not, for he might kill them all and place himself on the throne. The king reflected long and deeply on the subject, till at last a plan suggested itself. So he sent for the tailor, and told him that, as he was such a great hero, he wished to make a proposal to him.

' In a forest, not far from here,' he said, ' two giants dwell, who have committed so many dreadful deeds of robbery, murder, and violence, that no one will venture near where they live, for fear of losing their lives. Now, to whosoever shall vanquish and destroy these dreadful giants, I will give my only daughter in marriage, and the half of my kingdom as her dowry ; and if you will undertake to do this, I will send an escort of one hundred knights with you, to assist you in any way you wish.'

' Well,' thought the tailor, ' that is a reward worth trying for, especially for such a man as I am; it is an offer not met with every day.'

So he replied to the king, ' Yes, sire, I will overcome the giants ; but the hundred knights will be of no use to me. I, who have slain seven at one blow, am not likely to be afraid of two.'

Then the tailor boldly set out on his enterprise, the hundred knights following him; but when they reached the borders of the wood, he told them to remain there till he returned, as he would rather go alone to attack the giants.

They stayed behind gladly, while the bold little tailor rushed into the forest and looked cautiously around.

After a while, he saw the two giants lying fast asleep under a tree, and snoring so loudly that the leaves above them were shaken from the branches and fell to the ground.

The little tailor was not idle; he ran quickly and filled both his pockets full of large stones. Then he climbed up into the tree, and sliding out to the end of a branch under which the sleepers lay, let fall upon the chest of one of the giants one stone after another.

It was a long time before even this could disturb him, but at last he woke, and pushing his companion roughly, exclaimed, 'What do you mean by knocking me about like this?'

'You are dreaming,' said the other; 'I never touched you.' And presently they were both asleep again.

Then the little tailor threw a heavy stone on the other giant, who woke up in a rage, and cried, 'You are striking me, now; what do you mean by it?'

'I never struck you,' he growled.

They were both so ill-tempered at being disturbed, that they quarrelled till they were tired, and then lay down to sleep again.

As soon as their eyes were closed, the tailor began again at his game, and choosing the largest stone he could find, threw it with all his strength on the chest of the first giant.

'This is really too bad,' cried he, springing up in a fury and striking his comrade against the tree so violently that it trembled.

The other returned him as good as he gave, and a regular combat followed. So furiously did they fight, that they uprooted the large trees near them to use as weapons, the earth shook under their feet, and the conflict only ended when they both lay dead on the ground.

Down sprang the little tailor, exclaiming, 'It is a lucky thing for me that they did not uproot the tree in which I sat, or I should have had to spring like a squirrel from one tree to another. However, it is all right now.'

Then he drew his sword, and after cutting the throats of the giants, went out of the forest and returned to the knights who were waiting for him.

'The deed is done,' he said. 'I have made an end of them both. It was no easy task, I can tell you, for in their struggles for life they rooted up trees for weapons; but all this was useless against one who has killed "seven at a stroke." '

'And are you not hurt or wounded?' asked one of the soldiers.

'Not a very likely thing,' he replied. 'No, not a hair of my head has been even ruffled.'

The soldiers would not believe him, till he led them into the wood, where they found the giants weltering in their blood, and the trees they had rooted up lying near them.

The little tailor returned to the court, and presented himself before the king to claim the promised reward; but the king regretted having promised, and all his anxiety now was to get rid of the little hero.

'Ere I can give you my daughter, and half my kingdom,' said the king, 'you must perform one more heroic deed. There is another dangerous creature in my forests, a fierce unicorn, who spreads destruction wherever he is found. You must kill him also.'

'One unicorn will be nothing, after two giants,' he replied. 'Seven at one blow, that is my business.'

So he started off again to the forest, taking with him a rope and an axe, and again asked those who accompanied him to remain outside.

He had not long to wait. The unicorn very quickly made his appearance, and as soon as he saw the tailor sprang forward to pin him to the ground with his horn.

'Softly, softly,' he cried; 'you cannot manage me so easily as that.'

Then he stood quite still, and waited for the animal to come nearer, and on seeing him prepared to make a final spring, the tailor jumped lightly behind the trunk of a large tree, at which the unicorn ran with all his force, and stuck his horn so fast in the trunk that he had not strength enough to pull it out, and therefore remained a prisoner.

'I have just caught my bird,' said the bold little man; and coming forth from behind the tree, he first fastened the rope round the neck of the unicorn, and with the axe cut the horn out of the tree, and then led the animal into the presence of the king.

But the king, even now, would not grant the promised reward, without requiring the little hero to perform another feat of valour. He made a bargain that before the marriage with his daughter took place, he should kill a wild boar, who did great mischief in the forest, and that the king's hunters should assist him.

'Oh, certainly,' replied the tailor; 'that will be child's play for me.' So he set out immediately for the forest, but left the hunters outside, to their great delight, for the wild boar had often hunted them, and they had no wish to join in the tailor's enterprise.

As soon as the wild boar caught sight of the tailor, he flew at him, with glaring tusks and a foaming mouth, and would have thrown him on the ground. But our clever little friend was too quick for him; he sprang through the open window of a little chapel that stood near, and out through another on the other side. The boar was soon after him; but the moment he entered the chapel through the door, the tailor ran round quickly to close it, and the wild animal found himself a prisoner, for he was much too heavy and excited to jump through the window.

The little hero called the hunters, and showed them the prisoner with their own eyes. After this, he presented the wild boar to the king, who this time, whether he would or no, was obliged to keep his promise to give to the hero his daughter and half his kingdom.

Had he known that a little tailor stood before him instead of the great hero he imagined him to be, it would have grieved the king to the heart.

So the wedding was performed with great pomp, but very little rejoicing, and thus was a tailor made into a king.

Some little time after, the young queen heard her husband talking in his sleep, and saying, 'Work away, youngster; I expect you to finish that waistcoat very quickly, for you have the seams of the trousers to sew. If you sit there idling, I will lay the yard measure about your ears.'

This sort of talk occurred several times, and the young queen discovered by it that her husband was of low birth, and only a tailor.

When she told her father of her trouble, and asked him to send away a husband who was only a tailor, the king tried to comfort her by saying, 'This evening, when night comes, leave your chamber-door unlocked, and as soon as your husband is fast asleep, my servants shall enter and bind him hand and foot, and carry him away to a ship, in which he shall sail to distant lands.

The young wife was overjoyed at hearing of this scheme, and readily consented to the arrangement. But the king's equerry had overheard the conversation, and as he had a regard for this young man, he discovered to him the whole of the plot.

'I'll soon settle that,' was the little tailor's reply; 'there shall be a bolt to the door they don't expect.'

'When night came, everyone retired to rest at the usual hour; and as soon as the queen thought her husband slept, she rose quietly and opened the door. But the tailor, who had only pretended to sleep, exclaimed in a loud voice, 'Be quick, youngster, and finish that waistcoat, and stitch the seams of these trousers, or you will soon have the yard measure about your ears. I have killed seven at a blow; I have destroyed two giants; I have hunted a unicorn, and taken a wild boar captive, and shall I be afraid of those who stand outside my chamber door?'

As soon as the conspirators heard this, they were in a great fright, and fled as if a wild host were at their heels; and from that time no one in the kingdom could be prevailed upon to take part against him, and so the tailor remained a king for the rest of his life.

THE FISHERMAN AND HIS WIFE.

A FISHERMAN once lived contentedly with his wife in a little hut near a lake, and he went every day to throw his line into the water.

One day, after angling for a long time without even a bite, the line suddenly sunk to the bottom, and when he pulled it up again there was a large flounder hanging to the end of it.

'Oh, dear!' exclaimed the fish; 'good fisherman, let me go, I pray you; I am not a real fish, but a prince in disguise. I shall be of no use to you, for I am not good to eat. Put me back again into the water, and let me swim away.'

'Ah,' said the man, 'you need not make such a disturbance. I would rather let a flounder who can speak swim away than keep it.'

With these words, he placed the fish back again in the water, and it sunk to the bottom, leaving a long streak of blood behind it. Then the fisherman rose up, and went home to his wife in the hut.

'Husband,' said the wife, 'have you caught anything to-day?'

'I caught a flounder,' he replied, 'who said he was an enchanted prince; so I threw him back into the water, and let him swim away.'

'Did you not wish?' she asked.

'No,' he said; 'what should I wish for?'

'Why, at least for a better hut than this dirty place. How unlucky you did not think of it! He would have promised you whatever you asked for. However, go and call him now; perhaps he will answer you.'

The husband did not like this task at all; he thought it was nonsense. However, to please his wife, he went and stood by the sea. When he saw how green and dark it looked, he felt much discouraged, but made up a rhyme and said:

> 'Flounder, flounder, in the sea,
> Come, I pray, and talk to me;
> For my wife, Dame Isabel,
> Sent me here a tale to tell.'

Then the fish came swimming up to the surface, and said, 'What do you want with me?'

'Ah,' said the man, 'I caught you and let you go again to-day, without wishing; and my wife says I ought to have wished, for she cannot live any longer in such a miserable hut as ours, and she wants a better one.'

'Go home, man,' said the fish; 'your wife has all she wants.'

So the husband went home, and there was his wife, no longer in her dirty hovel, but sitting at the door of a neat little cottage, looking very happy.

'FLOUNDER, FLOUNDER, IN THE SEA, COME, I PRAY, AND TALK TO ME.'

She took her husband by the hand, and said, 'Come in, and see how much better it is than the other old hut.'

So he followed her in, and found a beautiful parlour, and a bright stove in it, a soft bed in the bedroom, and a kitchen full of earthenware, and tin and copper vessels for cooking, looking so bright and clean, and all of the very best. Outside was a little farmyard, with hens and chickens running about, and, beyond, a garden containing plenty of fruit and vegetables.

'See,' said the wife; 'is it not delightful?'

'Ah, yes,' replied her husband, 'as long as it is new you will be quite contented; but after that, we shall see.'

'Yes, we shall see,' said the wife.

A fortnight passed, and the husband felt quite happy, till one day his wife startled him by saying, 'Husband, after all, this is only a cottage, much too small for us, and the yard and the garden cover very little ground. If the fish is really a prince in disguise, he could very well give us a larger house. I should like, above all things, to live in a large castle built of stone. Go to thy fish, and ask him to build us a castle.'

'Ah, wife,' he said, 'this cottage is good enough for us; what do we want of a castle?'

'Go along,' she replied; 'the flounder will be sure to give us what you ask.'

'Nay, wife,' said he; 'the fish gave us the cottage at first, but if I go again he may be angry.'

'Never mind,' she replied; 'he can do what I wish easily, and I have no doubt he will; so go and try.'

The husband rose to go with a heavy heart; he said to himself, 'This is not right,' and when he reached the sea he noticed that the water was now a dark blue, yet very calm; so he began his old song:

'Flounder, flounder, in the sea,
Come, I pray, and talk to me;
For my wife, Dame Isabel,
Wishes what I fear to tell.'

'Now then, what do you want?' said the fish, lifting his head above the water.

'Oh dear!' said the fisherman, in a frightened tone, 'my wife wants to live in a great stone castle.'

'Go home, man, and you will find her there,' was the reply.

The husband hastened home, and where the cottage had been there stood a great stone castle, and his wife tripped down the steps, saying, 'Come with me, and I will show you what a beautiful dwelling we have now.'

So she took him by the hand, and led him into the castle, through halls of marble, while numbers of servants stood ready to usher them through folding-doors into rooms where the walls were hung with tapestry, and the furniture was of silk and gold. From these they went into other rooms equally elegant, where crystal looking-glasses hung on the walls, and the chairs and tables were of rosewood and marble. The soft carpets sunk beneath the footstep, and rich ornaments were arranged about the rooms.

Outside the castle was a large courtyard, in which were stables and cow-sheds, horses and carriages, all of the most expensive kind. Beyond this was a beautiful garden, full of rare flowers and delicious fruit, besides several acres of field and park-land, in which deer, oxen, and sheep were grazing—all, indeed, that the heart could wish was here.

'Well,' said the wife, 'is not this beautiful?'

'Yes,' replied her husband, 'and you will think so as long as the humour lasts, and then, I suppose, you will want something more.'

'We must think about that,' she replied, and then they went to bed.

Not many mornings after this the fisherman's wife rose early. It was just daybreak, and she stood looking out, with her arms akimbo, over the beautiful country that lay before her. Her husband did not stir, and presently she exclaimed, 'Get up, husband, and come to the window! Look here, ought you not to be king of all this land? Then I should be queen. Go and tell the fish I want you to be king.'

'Ah, wife,' he replied, 'I don't want to be king. I can't go and ask that.'

'Well,' she replied, 'if you don't care about being king, I wish to be queen, so go and tell the fish what I say.'

'It's no use, wife; I cannot.'

'Why not? Come, there's a good man, go at once; I must be queen.'

The husband turned away in a sorrowful mood. 'It is not right,' he said; 'it is not right.' However, he went, and as he stood on the sea-shore, he noticed that the water looked quite dark and rough, while the waves foamed and dashed against the shore, as if they were angry. But still he said :

> 'Flounder, flounder, in the sea,
> Come, I pray, and talk to me ;
> For my wife, Dame Isabel,
> Wishes what I fear to tell.'

'What!' cried the fish, rising to the surface, "she is not content, and she wants to be queen? Very well, then ; go home, and you will find her so.'

When he got near home, he found the castle had disappeared, and he saw at a distance a palace, which seemed to grow larger as he approached it. At one end was a large tower, and a noble terrace in front. A sentinel stood at the gates, and a band of soldiers, with drums and trumpets, were performing martial music. On arriving at the palace, he found it was built of precious marble. Within no expense had been spared. The furniture was of the most precious materials, and the curtains and carpets fringed with gold. The husband passed through the doors into a state apartment of immense size, and there sat his wife upon a lofty throne of gold and precious stones. She had a crown of gold upon her head, and a golden sceptre in her hand adorned with jewels. On each side of her stood six pages in a row, each one a head taller than the one next him. He went up to his wife, and said, 'Ah, wife, so you are queen now!'

'Yes,' she said, 'I am queen.'

He stood looking at her for a long time, till at last he spoke again. 'Well, wife, now that you are queen, we have nothing left to wish for ; we must give up wishing.'

THE SEA WAS BLACK, AND THE WAVES RUSHED FURIOUSLY OVER THE ROCKS.

'No, indeed,' she replied, 'I am not yet satisfied. Time and tide wait for no man, nor will they wait for me. I am as impatient as ever. Go to your enchanted prince again, and tell him I want to be empress.'

'Empress!' cried the husband. 'It is beyond his power, I am certain ; the empress has the highest place in the kingdom.'

'What!' she replied, 'don't you know that I am queen, and that you must obey me, although you are my husband? Go at once ; if the prince in disguise can make a queen, he can also make an empress.'

So the husband went away muttering to himself, ' To keep on wishing in this way is not good; I am certain the fish will put an end to it this time.'

When he reached the shore the sea was quite black, and the waves rushed so furiously over the rocks that he was terrified, but he contrived to repeat his wild verses again, saying:

> 'Flounder, flounder, in the sea,
> Come, I pray, and talk to me;
> For my wife, Dame Isabel,
> Wishes what I fear to tell.'

Up came the fish.

' Well,' he said, ' what does she want now ?'

' Ah!' said the husband timidly, ' she wants to be empress.'

' Go home, man,' he replied. ' She has her wish.'

And on his return he found his wife acting as empress in a palace of marble, with alabaster statues, and gold, and pearls, and soldiers, and lords, and barons bowing to her; but she was not satisfied even now, and at last told her husband that she wished to be the Pope, and that he must go to the fish and tell him so.

' No,' he said, ' that is impossible. The Pope is the head of the Church. You cannot have that wish.'

' But I will be Pope,' she exclaimed.

So he was obliged to go, and when he reached the shore the sea was running mountains high, and roaring and beating against the shores, and it was such terrible weather that the sky looked quite black.

However, he ventured to call up the fish with the old song, and told him of his wife's wish.

' Go home,' he said. ' Your wife is Pope.'

He turned to go back, but what a change he found: the palace had vanished, and in its place stood a large cathedral surrounded by marble pillars.

On a high throne sat his wife, with thousands of lights around her, dressed in robes embroidered with gold, and wearing a large golden crown on her head. Candles of all kinds stood near her, some as thick as a tower, others as small as a rushlight, while emperors, kings, and nobles kneeled at her footstool, and kissed her slippers.

' Well, wife,' said her husband, ' so you are Pope?'

' Yes,' she said. ' I am.'

He stood still for a time watching her, and at length he remarked, ' You cannot be higher than the Pope, so I suppose now you are content?'

' I am not quite sure,' she said. But when evening came, and they retired to rest, she could not sleep for thinking of what she should next wish for. Her husband slept soundly, for he had tired himself the day before; but she rose even before the day broke, and stood at the window to watch the sun rise. It was a beautiful sight, and she exclaimed, as she watched it, 'Oh, if I only had the power to make the sun rise. Husband, wake up,' she added, pushing him in the ribs with her elbows; 'wake up, and go and tell the enchanted prince that I wish to be equal to the Creator, and make the sun rise.'

The husband was so frightened at this that he tumbled out of bed, and exclaimed, 'Ah, wife, what didst thou say?'

CINDERELLA WEEPING AT HER MOTHER'S GRAVE.

She repeated the words.

Her husband fell on his knees before her. 'Don't ask me to do this; I cannot,' he cried, but she flew into a rage, and drove him from the house.

The poor fisherman went down to the shore in terror, for a dreadful storm had arisen, and he could scarcely stand on his feet. Ships were wrecked, boats tossed to and fro, and rocks rolled into the sea.

In his terror and confusion he heard a voice from amidst the storm:
'Your wife wishes to be equal to the Creator. Go home, man, and find her again in her dirty hovel by the sea.'

He went home, to find the glories, the riches, and the palaces vanished, and his wife sitting in the old hut, an example of the consequences of impious ambition.

CINDERELLA.

ONCE upon a time the wife of a rich man fell sick, and as she knew her end was approaching, she called her only daughter to her bedside, and said, 'Dear child, when I am gone continue good and pious, and Heaven will help you in every trouble, and I will be your guardian angel.'

Soon after this the mother closed her eyes in death, and day after day the maiden went to her mother's grave to weep. But she never forgot her last words, and continued pious and gentle to all around her. Winter came and covered the grave with its dazzling drapery of snow; but when the bright sun of spring again warmed the earth, the husband had taken to himself another wife. This wife had been already married, and she brought with her two daughters who were fair and beautiful in appearance, while at heart they were evil-minded and malicious. It soon became a very sad time for their poor stepsister, of whom they were very envious, and at last persuaded their mother to send her to the kitchen.

'Is the stupid goose to sit in the parlour with us?' they said. 'Those who eat ought to work. Send her into the kitchen with the kitchen-maid.'

CINDERELLA IN THE KITCHEN

Then they took away all her nice clothes, and gave her an ugly old frock and wooden shoes, which she was obliged to put on.

'Look at our fine princess now! See how she has dressed herself!' they said, laughing, and driving her into the kitchen.

And there she was obliged to remain doing hard work from morning till night; and she had to rise early to draw water, to light the fire, to cook, and to wash. Besides all this, her stepsisters invented all sorts of ways to make her more unhappy. They would either treat her with scorn or else push her out of their way so roughly that she sometimes fell among the pea shells and cabbage leaves that lay in the yard.

At night, when she was tired with her work, she had no bed to lie on, and when the weather was cold she would creep into the ashes on the warm hearth, and get so black and smutty that they gave her the name of Cinderella.

It happened one day that the father was going to a fair, and he asked his two stepdaughters what he should bring back for them as a present.

'A beautiful dress,' said the eldest; 'a pearl necklace,' said her sister.

'And, Cinderella,' asked her father, 'what will you have?'

'Father,' she replied, 'please bring me the first twig that strikes your hat on your way home.'

So the father bought for his stepdaughters a beautiful dress and a pearl necklace, and, as he was returning home, he rode through a shrubbery, where the green bushes clustered thickly around him, and a hazel twig stretching across his path struck his hat. Then he stopped, broke off the twig, and carried it home with him.

As soon as he reached the house he gave his stepdaughters the presents they had wished for, and to Cinderella the hazel twig from the hazel bush. She thanked him for it even more than her sisters had done for their beautiful presents, and went out immediately to her mother's grave, where she planted the hazel twig, and wept over it so much that her tears fell and softened the earth.

The twig grew and became a beautiful tree, and Cinderella went three times every day to pray and weep at the grave; and on each visit a little white bird would perch on the tree, and when she expressed a wish, the bird would throw down whatever she wished for.

After a time the king of the country gave a grand ball, which was to continue for three days. All the beautiful young ladies in the land were invited to this ball, so that the king's son might make choice of a bride from amongst them.

The two stepsisters, when they heard that they were invited, knew not how to contain themselves for joy. They called Cinderella in haste, and said, 'Come and dress our hair and trim our shoes with gold buckles, for we are going to the ball at the king's palace.'

When Cinderella heard this she began to cry, for she was fond of dancing, and she wanted to go with her stepsisters, so she went to her stepmother and begged to be allowed to accompany them.

'You, Cinderella!' cried her stepmother, 'so covered with dirt and smut as you are; you go to a ball! Besides, you have no dress nor dancing shoes.'

Cinderella, however, continued to beg for permission to go, till her stepmother said at last:

'There, go away into the kitchen; I have just thrown a shovelful of linseed into the ashes; if you can pick these seeds all out and bring them to me in two hours you shall go.'

Away went the maiden through the back door into the garden, and called out:

> 'Little tame pigeons,
> Turtle-doves, too,
> If you don't help me
> What shall I do?
> Come, pick up the seeds,
> All the birds in the sky,
> For I cannot do it
> In time, if I try.'

Then came flying in at the kitchen window two pretty white doves, and they were followed by all the birds of the air, twittering in a swarm. Nodding their heads at Cinderella, they began to pick, pick, and very quickly picked every seed from the ashes, till the shovel was full. It was all finished in one hour, and then the birds spread their wings and flew away.

Full of joy, the maiden carried the shovelful of seed to her stepmother, believing that now she was sure to go to the ball. But her stepmother said:

'No, Cinderella, you have no dress, and you have not learnt to dance; you would only be laughed at.'

Still she cried and begged so hard to be allowed to go that her stepmother, to keep her quiet, threw *two* shovelfuls of linseed in the ashes this time, and told her she should go if she picked all these out in two hours.

'She can never do that in the time,' thought the cruel woman, as Cinderella ran away to the kitchen; but the maiden went again into the garden and called the birds:

> 'Little tame pigeons,
> Turtle-doves, too,
> If you don't help me
> What shall I do?
> Come, pick up the seeds,
> All the birds in the sky,
> For I cannot do it
> In time, if I try.'

Then the birds all came as before, and in less than an hour every seed was picked out and laid in the shovels. As soon as they had flown away Cinderella carried the shovelfuls of seed to her stepmother,

quite expecting now to go to the ball with her stepsisters. But she
said again :

'It is of no use to fret, Cinderella ; you have no dress, you cannot
dance, and were you to go it would be a disgrace to us all.'

Then she turned her back on the poor girl and hastened away with
her two proud daughters to the ball. There was no one at home now
but Cinderella, so she went out to her mother's grave and stood under
the hazel-tree and cried :

> 'Shake and shiver, little tree,
> With gold and silver cover me.'

Then the bird in the tree threw down a beautiful silk dress embroidered with gold and silver, and a new pair of glittering golden
slippers. In great haste she dressed herself in these beautiful clothes
and went to the ball. When she entered the ballroom, looking so
beautiful in her rich dress and slippers, her stepmother and sisters did
not know her; indeed, they took her for a foreign princess. The idea
that it could be Cinderella never entered their heads ; they supposed
she was safe at home picking linseed from the ashes.

The king's son took a great deal of notice of this unknown lady, and
danced with her several times, till at last he would dance with no
other, always saying, 'This is my partner.' So she danced all the
evening till it was time to go home, and the prince said he would
accompany her, for he wanted to discover where she lived. But she
avoided him, and with one bound sprang into the pigeon-house. The
prince was quite astonished, but waited till nearly all the company had
left, and then told his father that the strange lady was in the pigeon-
house.

'Could it be Cinderella?' thought the stepmother, who would not
leave till the last; 'I must find out.' So she advised the prince to send
for workmen to pull down the pigeon-house. This was soon done, but
they found no one there. When the stepmother and her daughters
reached home, they found Cinderella in her smutty dress, lying in
the ashes, and a dingy little lamp burning on the chimney-piece. The
truth was, Cinderella had slipped out from the back of the pigeon-house
even more quickly than she had jumped in, and had run to the hazel
tree. Here she hastened to take off her beautiful clothes, and lay them
on the grave while she put on her kitchen clothes, and the bird came
down and carried the ball-dress away, while Cinderella went home to
lie in the ashes.

A short time after this the king gave another ball, to which her
parents and stepsisters were invited. As soon as they were gone,
Cinderella went to the hazel-tree and said—

> 'Shake and shiver, little tree,
> Throw gold and silver over me.'

Then the bird threw down a far more elegant dress than the first, and when she entered the ballroom in her rich apparel, everyone was astonished at her great beauty. The king's son, who refused to dance till she came, took her hand and led her to her seat, and during the whole evening he would dance with no one else, always saying, 'This is my partner.'

Again, when it was time to go, the prince wanted to accompany her and find out her home, but she managed to avoid him and rushed out into the garden behind the palace, in which grew a beautiful tree loaded with pears. She climbed like a squirrel between the branches, and the prince could not find her anywhere.

When his father came home they even ordered the tree to be cut down, but no one could be found among the branches. The stepmother still had a fear that it might be Cinderella, but when they returned home, there she was in her kitchen dress lying among the ashes as usual. When they were looking for her, she had sprung down at the other side of the tree, and the bird in the hazel tree had brought her kitchen clothes and taken away the ball-dress.

A third fête took place, to which the stepmother and her daughters were invited, and Cinderella again went to her mother's grave and said to the tree—

> 'Shake and rustle, little tree,
> Throw gold and silver over me.'

Then the bird threw down a most magnificent dress, more glittering and elegant than ever, and the brightest pair of gilded slippers.

When she appeared at the fête in this dress, everyone was astonished at her beauty. The prince danced only with her, and to every other proposal replied, 'This is my partner.' When the time came to leave, Cinderella wanted to go, and the prince wished to accompany her, but she darted away from him and vanished so quickly that he could not follow her.

Now, the king's son had had recourse to stratagem in the hope of discovering the home of the lovely princess. He had ordered the steps of the castle to be strewed with pitch, so that as Cinderella hurried away her left slipper stuck to the steps, and she was obliged to leave it behind. The prince himself picked it up; it was very small and elegant, and covered with gold.

The next morning he sent for one of his servants and said to him, 'None other shall be my bride but the lady to whom that slipper belongs, and whose foot it shall fit.'

When the stepsisters heard of this proclamation from the prince they were delighted, for they both had small feet. The messenger went with the slipper from house to house, and the young ladies who had been present at the ball tried to put it on, but it would fit none of them, and at last he came to the two sisters. The eldest tried it on first in another room, and her mother stood by. She could have worn it if her great toe had not been so large, so her mother offered her a knife, and told

her to cut it off. ' When you are a queen,' she said, ' you will not want
to use your feet much.'

The maiden cut the toe off and forced on the slipper in spite of the
pain, and the messenger led her to the prince. But on their road they
had to pass the grave of Cinderella's mother, and on the hazel-tree sat
two doves, who cried—

> ' That is not the right bride,
> The slipper is much too small,
> Blood is flowing inside,
> The shoe does not fit her at all.'

Then the messenger examined the slipper and found it full of blood.
So he led her back and told the next sister to try. She also went
into another room with her mother, and found that she could not get
the slipper over her heel.

' Cut a piece off,' said her mother, offering her a knife ; ' when you
are queen you will not have to use your feet much.'

The maiden cut a piece off her heel, and fitted on the slipper in spite
of the pain, and then went to the prince. They also had to pass the
grave of Cinderella's mother, in which the two doves still sat and
cried :

> ' Go back, go back,
> There is blood in the shoe,
> The shoe is too small,
> That bride will not do.'

So the messenger examined the shoe, and found the white stocking
quite red with blood. He took the false bride back to the house, and
this time the king's son went with him.

' Hast thou not another daughter ?' asked the prince of Cinderella's
father.

' None,' he said, ' excepting the child of my first wife, a little Cinderella ; she could not possibly be your bride.'

' Send for her,' said the prince.

But the stepmother answered, ' Oh no ! I dare not let you see her,
she is much too dirty.'

But the prince insisted that Cinderella should be sent for, so at last
they called her in.

After washing her hands and face, she made her appearance, and
bowed to the prince, who offered her the golden shoe. She seated herself on a footstool, took off the heavy wooden shoe from her left foot,
and slipped on the golden slipper, which fitted her exactly. Then, as
she lifted up her head and looked at the king, he recognised the beautiful
maiden who had danced with him at the ball, and exclaimed, ' That is
the right bride !'

The stepmother and her two daughters were in a dreadful rage when
they heard this, and turned white with anger.

But the prince disregarded their anger, and taking Cinderella on his horse, rode away with her. As they passed the hazel-tree on the grass, the two white doves cried:

'Fair maid and true,
No blood in her shoe;
She is the bride,
With the prince by her side.'

As they rode by, the doves came and perched on Cinderella's shoulders, one on the right, and the other on the left.

When the marriage-day came, the two stepsisters, wishing to share Cinderella's fortune, contrived to be present. As the bridal party

WEDDING OF CINDERELLA.

walked to church, they placed themselves one on the right, and the other on the left of the bride. On the way, the doves picked out one eye from each of them. When returning, they changed places, and the doves picked out the other eye of each, so they were for their wickedness and falsehood both punished with blindness during the rest of their lives.

THE RIDDLE.

THERE was a king's son who had no greater pleasure than to travel, and with no other companion than his faithful servant.

During one of their journeys, they one day found themselves in a great forest, and knew not where to get shelter for the night. At last they espied a little maiden, and as they drew near to her they saw she was young and fair; so they followed her to a little cottage.

The king's son spoke to her, and said, 'Dear child, can I and my servant find accommodation for the night in your little cottage?'

'Ah, yes,' said the maiden, in a sorrowful tone, 'you can very easily; but I advise you not to stay, nor even to go in.'

'Why should I not?' he asked.

The maiden sighed, and said, 'My stepmother carries on a wicked trade. She is not good to strangers.'

It was evident to the travellers that this was the house of a witch; but as it grew darker every minute, they could not go farther, and they had no fear, so they stepped in.

As they entered, an old woman, who sat in an armchair near the fire, turned and looked at the strangers with her red eyes.

'Good-evening,' she said, in a tone that seemed quite friendly. 'Lie down there, and rest as long as you like.'

Then she blew up the fire to make the coals burn under a saucepan in which something was boiling; but the daughter cautioned them not to eat or drink anything in the house, for that her stepmother was brewing wicked drinks.

So they went to sleep without any supper, and slept quite peaceably all night till the next morning. Just as they were about to start——indeed, the king's son was already on his horse—the old woman came up to them and said:

'Wait a moment, till I give you some drink for a farewell cup.'

While she went to fetch it, the prince rode away, and his servant, who sprung hastily into the saddle, was just about to follow him, when the wicked witch returned with the drink.

'Carry this to your master,' she exclaimed, and at the same moment the bottle burst, and the poison spurted all over the horse. So virulent was the venom that the animal instantly fell dead.

The servant ran after his master, and related what had happened; but as he did not wish to lose the saddle, he went back to fetch it.

When he came to the place where he saw the dead horse lay, he found a raven already feeding upon the carcase.

'I will take this bird,' he said; 'it will do very well for our dinner to-day, unless we find something better.' So he killed the raven, and took it away with him.

After this the king's son and his servant travelled the whole day through the forest, but could find no resting-place till evening advanced, and then they came to a kind of inn, and entered. They were shown into a small parlour, and the servant gave the bird he had killed to the landlord, telling him to have it roasted for their supper.

But the young prince and his servant were in more danger now than while in the witch's hut; they had lighted on a den of murderers and thieves.

When it was quite dark, twelve evil-looking men surrounded the house, whose intention it was to get at the foreigners and rob them.

However, before commencing their evil operations, they seated themselves at the supper-table, prepared for the king's son and his servant, and presently they were joined, not only by the landlord, but also by the witch herself, for the travellers had wandered back through the wood nearly to the old woman's house. A dish full of soup was first placed on the table, in which the bird had been cooked, and they began to eat quite greedily; but scarce had they taken two mouthfuls when they all fell to the ground dead. The raven, in feeding on the poisoned flesh of the horse, was itself poisoned, and shared this poison with the robbers.

The prince and his servant were thus saved, and very glad to have lost their supper.

There was now no one left in the house but the daughter of the landlord, who was a truly honest girl, and would take no part in the terrible deeds done in the house. She opened all the doors for the strangers, and pointed out to them an accumulation of treasures; but the king's son said she might keep them, he would have none of them, and so he rode away with his servant. They had been travelling for many days, when they came to a large city in which lived a very proud and beautiful princess.

She had made known her determination that she would take for her husband any man who should propose to her a riddle which she could not find out. But if she did find out the answer, then his head would be cut off.

Three days was the time allowed for her to try, and she was so clever that she always discovered the meaning of the riddle before the appointed time had expired.

Already had nine of these *wise* men risked their lives for the beautiful princess, and the king's son, who had just arrived in the town, was so struck with her great beauty that he determined to follow their example.

So he presented himself before her and propounded his riddle. 'What is that which never slew anything, and yet slew twelve?'

The princess was puzzled now. She thought, and thought, but she could make nothing of it. Then she studied her riddle book, but all to no purpose. Her wisdom had come to an end.

So the princess determined to try some other means, and, calling her maid, she told her to hide herself in the stranger's room, for that very likely he might dream, and tell the answer of the riddle in his sleep.

But the prince's clever servant found out what was going on, and laid himself in bed in the room of his master, and when the maid came in, he pulled off the cloak in which she had tried to conceal herself, and drove her from the room.

The next night the princess sent her chambermaid to try her fortune as a listener, but she was just as unsuccessful; for the servant also pulled off her cloak, and drove her out.

On the third night, the princess, believing that the master himself was in the bed, came herself to the room. She wore a large dark-gray mantle, and thought, as she softly placed herself near him, that she should not be seen.

As soon as he closed his eyes, the princess began to question him in the hope that he would talk in his sleep as many do. Whereas, the prince's servant was wide awake, and knew very well what he was about.

Then asked the princess, 'What is it that never killed anyone?'

'A raven,' he answered, 'who ate the flesh of a dead and poisoned horse, and died in consequence.'

Again she inquired, 'What was it that killed twelve?'

'Twelve murderers ate the raven, and were poisoned also, and died.'

As soon as the princess knew the riddle, she wanted to run away; but the servant caught hold of her cloak, and held it so tight that she was obliged to leave it behind.

On the following morning the princess made known that she had found out the riddle, and sent for the twelve judges to hear her reply to it.

But the servant, who was present with his master, requested to be heard first.

'The princess,' he said, 'would never have found out the riddle, if she had not concealed herself in my master's room where she thought he slept, but I was there instead of him, and when she questioned me about the riddle, I told her all she knows about it, and she supposed I was talking in my sleep.'

'Can you,' the judges said, 'give us some proofs of what you have affirmed?'

The young man went immediately and fetched the three cloaks, and explained to the judges how he had obtained them.

As soon as they saw the dark-gray mantle which the princess had worn and tried to keep, they said, 'Let this mantle be stuck full of gold and silver, so that it can be worn as a wedding cloak when the princess is married.' But the prince would not marry her after all, and no wonder.

THE MOUSE, THE BIRD, AND THE SAUSAGE.

HERE was once a little mouse, a little bird, and a sausage, who formed a partnership. They had set up housekeeping, and had lived for a long time in great harmony together. The duty of the little bird was to fly every day into the forests, and bring home wood; the mouse had to draw water, to light the fire, and lay the table-cloth; and the sausage was cook.

How often when we are comfortable we begin to long for something new. So it happened one day that the little bird had met in his road another bird, to which he had boasted of their happiness and friendship at home.

The other bird replied scornfully, 'What a poor little simpleton you are to work in the way you do, while the other two are enjoying themselves at home! When the mouse has lighted the fire and drawn the water, she can go and rest in her little room till she is called to lay the cloth. The sausage can sit by the stove while he watches that the dinner is well cooked, and when the dinner-time arrives he devours four times as much as the others of broth or vegetables till he quite shines with salt and fat.'

The bird, after listening to this, came home quite disconcerted, and, laying down his load, seated himself at the table, and ate so much and filled his crop so full that he slept till the next morning without waking, and thought this was a happy life.

The next day the little bird objected to go and fetch wood, saying that he had been their servant long enough, and that he had been a fool to work for them in this way. He intended at once to make a change, and seek his living in another way.

After this, although the mouse and the sausage were both in a rage, the bird was master, and would have his own way. So he proposed that they should draw lots, and the lots fell so that the sausage was to fetch the wood, the mouse to be cook, and the bird to draw the water. Now, what was the consequence of all this? The sausage went out to get wood, the bird lighted the fire, and the mouse put on the saucepan, and sat down to watch it till the sausage returned home with the wood for the next day. But he stayed away so long that the bird, who wanted a breath of fresh air, went out to look for him. On his way he met a dog, who told him that, having met with the sausage, and considering him as his lawful prey, he had devoured him.

The bird complained greatly against the dog for his conduct, and called him a cruel robber, but it did no good.

'For,' said the dog, 'the sausage had false papers with him, and, therefore, his life was forfeited to society.'

The little bird, full of sorrow, flew home, carrying the wood with him, and related to the mouse what he had seen and heard. They were both very grieved, but quickly agreed that the best thing for them to do was to remain together.

From that time the bird undertook to prepare the table, and the mouse to roast something for supper, and to put the vegetables into the saucepan, as she had seen the sausage do; but before she had half finished her task, the fire burnt her so terribly that she fell down and died.

When the little bird came home, expecting to find something to eat, there was no cook to be seen, and the fire was nearly out. The bird, in alarm, threw the wood here and there, cried out, and searched everywhere, but no cook could be found.

Meanwhile, a spark from the fire fell on the wood, and set it in a blaze, so that there was danger of the house being burnt. The bird ran in haste to the well for water. Unfortunately he let the pail fall into the well, and being dragged after it, he sank into the water and was drowned.

And all this happened because one little bird listened to another who was jealous of the happy little family at home, and from being discontented and changing their arrangements they all met with their death.

CINDERELLA

THE WIDOW'S TWO DAUGHTERS

THE WIDOW'S TWO DAUGHTERS.

A WIDOW, who lived in a cottage at some little distance from the village, had two daughters, one of whom was beautiful and industrious, the other idle and ugly. But this ugly one the mother loved best, because she was her own child; and she cared so little for the other, that she made her do all the work, and be quite a Cinderella in the house.

Poor maiden, she was obliged to go every day and seat herself by the side of a well which stood in the broad highroad, and here she had to sit and spin till her fingers bled.

One day when the spindle was so covered with blood that she could not use it, she rose and dipped it in the water of the well to wash it. While she was doing so, it slipped from her hand and fell to the bottom. In terror and tears, she ran and told her step-mother what had happened.

The woman scolded her in a most violent manner, and was so merciless that she said, 'As you have let the spindle fall into the water, you may go in and fetch it out, for I will not buy another.'

Then the maiden went back to the well, and hardly knowing what she was about in her distress of mind, threw herself into the water to fetch the spindle.

At first she lost all consciousness, but presently, as her senses returned, she found herself in a beautiful meadow, on which the sun was brightly shining and thousands of flowers grew.

She walked a long way across this meadow, till she came to a baker's oven, which was full of new bread, and the loaves cried, 'Ah, pull us out! pull us out, or we shall burn, we have been so long baking!'

Then she stepped near to the oven, and with the bread-shovel took the loaves all out.

She walked on after this, and presently came to a tree full of apples, and the tree cried, 'Shake me, shake me; my apples are all quite ripe.'

Then she shook the tree till the fruit fell around her like rain, and at last there was not one more left upon it. After this she gathered the apples into one large heap, and went on farther.

At last she came to a small house, and, looking earnestly at it, she saw an old woman peeping out, who had such large teeth that the girl was quite frightened, and turned to run away.

But the old woman cried after her, ' What dost thou fear, dear child? Come and live here with me, and do all the work in the house, and I will make you so happy. You must, however, take care to make my bed well, and to shake it with energy, for then the feathers fly about, and in the world they will say it snows, for I am Mother Holle.'

SHAKE WITH ENERGY, FOR THEN THE FEATHERS
FLY ABOUT.

As the old woman talked in this kind manner, she won the maiden's heart, so that she readily agreed to enter her service.

She was very anxious to keep friendly with her, and took care to shake up the bed well, so that the feathers might fly down like snowflakes. Therefore she had a very happy life with Mother Holle. She had plenty to eat and drink, and never heard an angry word.

But after she had stayed a long time with the kind old woman, she began to feel sad, and could not explain to herself why, till at last she discovered that she was home-sick. And it seemed to her a thousand times better to go home than to stay with Mother Holle, although she made her so happy.

And the longing to go home grew so strong that at last she was obliged to speak.

' Dear Mother Holle,' she said, ' you have been very kind to me, but I have such sorrow in my heart that I cannot stay here any longer; I must return to my own people.'

' Then,' said Mother Holle, ' I am pleased to hear that you are longing to go home, and as you have served me so well and truly, I will show you the way myself.'

So she took her by the hand, and led her to a broad gateway. The gate was open, and as the young girl passed through, there fell upon her a shower of gold, which clung to her dress, and remained hanging to it, so that she was bedecked with gold from head to foot.

' That is your reward for having been so industrious;' and as the old woman spoke she placed in her hand the spindle which had fallen into the well.

Then the great gate was closed, and the maiden found herself once more in the world, and not far from her step-mother's house. As she entered the farmyard, a cock perched on the wall crowed loudly, and cried, ' Kikeriki! our golden lady is come home, I see.'

Then she went in to her mother; and because she was so bedecked with gold, both the mother and sister welcomed her kindly. The maiden related all that had happened to her; and when the mother heard how much wealth had been gained by her step-daughter, she was anxious that her own ugly and idle daughter should try her fortune in the same way.

So she made her go and sit on the well and spin; and the girl, who wanted all the riches without working for them, did not spin fast enough to make her fingers bleed.

BEDECKED WITH GOLD FROM HEAD TO FOOT.

So she pricked her finger, and pushed her hand in the thorn-bushes, till at last a few spots of blood dropped on the spindle.

Directly she saw these spots, she let it drop into the water, and sprung in after it herself. Just as her sister had done, she found herself in a beautiful meadow, and walked for some distance along the same path, till she came to the baker's oven.

She heard the loaves cry, ' Pull us out, pull us out, or we shall burn; we have been here so long baking !'

But the idle girl answered, ' No, indeed, I have no wish to soil my hands with your dirty oven;' and so she walked on till she came to the apple-tree.

'Shake me, shake me!' it cried; 'for my apples are all quite ripe.'

'I don't agree to that at all,' she replied, 'for some of the apples might fall on my head;' and as she spoke she walked lazily on farther.

When she at last stood before the door of Mother Holle's house, she had no fear of her great teeth, for she had heard all about them from her sister; so she walked right up to her and offered to be her servant. Mother Holle accepted the offer of her services, and for a whole day the young girl was very industrious, and did everything that was told her; for she thought of the gold that was to be poured upon her.

But on the second day she gave way to her laziness, and on the third it was worse. Several days passed, and she would not get up in the mornings at a proper hour. The bed was never made or shaken, so that feathers could fly about, till at last Mother Holle was quite tired of her, and said she must go away; that her services were not wanted any more.

The lazy girl was quite overjoyed at going, and thought the golden rain was sure to come when Mother Holle led her to the gate. But as she passed under it a large kettle full of pitch was upset over her.

'That is the reward of your service,' said the old woman as she shut the gate.

So the idle girl walked home with the pitch sticking all over her, and as she entered the court the cock on the wall cried out:

'Kikeriki! our smutty young lady is come home, I see.'

The pitch stuck closely, and hung all about her hair and her clothes, and do what she would as long as she lived it never would come off.

THE SEVEN RAVENS.

A MAN had seven sons, but not one little daughter, which made both him and his wife very unhappy. At last a daughter was born, to their great joy; but the child was very small and slight, and so weak that they feared it would die. So the father sent his sons to the spring to fetch water, that he might baptize her.

Each of the boys ran in great haste to be the first to draw the water for their little sister's baptism, but in the struggle to be first they let the pitcher fall into the well.

Then they stood still and knew not what to do; not one of them dared to venture home without the water. As the time went on, and they did not return, the father became very impatient, and said, 'I suppose in the midst of their play they have forgotten what I sent them for, the careless children.'

He was in such an agony lest the child should die unbaptized, that he exclaimed in his anger, 'I wish that the youngsters were all turned into ravens.'

The words were scarcely uttered, when there was heard a rushing of wings in the air over his head, and presently seven coal-black ravens flew over the house.

The father could not recall the dreadful words, and both parents grieved terribly over the loss of their seven sons; their only consolation now was the little daughter, who every day grew stronger and more beautiful.

For a long time the maiden was not told that she had brothers; her parents were most careful to avoid all mention of them. But one day she overheard some persons talking, and they said that no doubt the young girl was very beautiful, but that there must have been some strange cause for the misfortune which had happened to her seven brothers.

Oh, how surprised and sad she felt when she heard this! She went at once to her father and mother, and asked them if she really had had any brothers, and what had become of them. Then her parents dared not any longer keep the secret from her. They told her, however, that it was the decree of Heaven, and that her birth was the innocent cause of all. As soon as she was alone, she made a firm determination that she would try and break the enchantment in which her brothers were held.

She had neither rest nor peace till she had made up her mind to leave home and seek her brothers, and set them free, cost what it might.

When at last she left home, she took nothing with her but a little ring, in memory of her parents, a loaf of bread, a jug of water, and a little stool, in case she felt tired.

So she went from her home, and travelled farther and farther, till she came to the end of the world, and there was the sun; but it was so hot and fierce that it scorched the little child, and she ran away in such a hurry that she ran into the moon. Here it was quite cold and dismal, and she heard a voice say, 'I smell man's flesh,' which made her escape from the moon as quickly as she could, and at last she reached the stars.

They were very kind and friendly to her. Each of the stars was seated on a wonderful chair, and the Morning Star stood up and said, 'If you have not a key you will not be able to unlock the iceberg in which your brothers are shut up.'

So the Morning Star gave the maiden the key, and told her to wrap it up carefully in her little handkerchief, and showed her the way to the iceberg. When she arrived the gate was closed; she opened her handkerchief to take out the key, but found it empty; she had forgotten the advice of the kind stars. What was she to do now? She wished to rescue her brothers, and had no key to the iceberg.

At last the good little sister thought she would put her finger into the lock instead of a key.　After twisting and turning it about, which hurt her very much, she happily succeeded in opening it, and immediately entered.

Presently a little dwarf came forward to meet her, and said, ' My child, what are you seeking?'

' I seek my brothers, the seven ravens,' she said.

' The seven ravens are not at home,' replied the dwarf; ' but if you like to wait here till they return, pray step in.'

HERE COME THE SEVEN RAVENS.

Then the little dwarf took the maiden to the room where supper was prepared for the seven ravens, on seven little plates, by which stood seven little cups of water.

So the sister ate a few crumbs from each plate, and drank a little draught from each cup, and into the last cup she let fall the ring that she brought from home.

Before she could get it out again she heard the rushing of wings in the air, and the little dwarf said, ' Here come the seven Mr. Ravens flying home.'

Then she hid herself behind the door, to see and hear what they would do. They came in, and were about to eat their supper; but, as they caught sight of their little cups and plates, they said one to another, 'Who has been eating from my little plate?' 'Who has been drinking from my little cup?' 'It has been touched by the mouth of a human being,' cried one; 'and, look here, what is this?' He took up his cup and turned it over, and out rolled the little ring, which they knew had once belonged to their father and mother.

Then said the eldest, 'Oh, I remember that ring! Oh, if our sister would only come here, we should be free!'

The maiden, who heard the wish from behind the door, came forth smiling, and stood before them.

In that same moment the seven ravens were freed from the enchantment, and became seven handsome young men. Oh, how joyfully they all kissed each other, and their little sister, and started off at once in great happiness to their parents and their home!

LITTLE RED RIDING-HOOD.

THERE was once a sweet little girl, who had gained the love of every-one, even those who had only seen her once. She had an old grand-mother, who knew not how to do enough for her, she loved her so much. Once she sent her a little cloak with a red velvet hood, which became her so well that she obtained the name of Little Red Riding-hood.

One day her mother said to her, 'Come, Red Riding-hood, I want you to go and see your grandmother, and take her a piece of cake and a bottle of wine; for she is ill and weak, and this will do her good. Make haste and get ready before the weather gets too hot, and go straight on your road while you are out, and behave prettily and modestly; and do not run, for fear you should fall and break the bottle, and then grandmother would have no wine. And when you pass through the village, do not forget to curtsy and say "good-morning" to everyone who knows you.'

'I will do everything you tell me, mother,' said the child, as she wished her good-bye, and started for her long walk.

It was quite half an hour's walk through the wood from the village to the grandmother's house, and no sooner had Red Riding-hood entered the wood than she met a wolf.

Red Riding-hood did not know what a wicked animal he was, and felt not the least afraid of him.

'Good-day, Red Riding-hood,' he said.

'Good-morning, sir,' replied the little girl, with a curtsy.

'Where are you going so early, Red Riding-hood?' he asked.

'To my grandmother, sir,' she replied. 'Mother baked yesterday, and she has sent me with a piece of cake and a bottle of wine to her because she is sick, and it will make her stronger and do her good.'

'Where does your grandmother live, Red Riding-hood?'

'About half a mile from here through the woods; her house stands under three large oak-trees, near to the nut hedges; you would easily know it,' said Red Riding-hood.

RED RIDING-HOOD STARTING FOR HER WALK.

The wolf, when he heard this, thought to himself, 'This little delicate thing would be a sweet morsel for me at last, and taste nicer than her old grandmother, but she would not satisfy my hunger; I must make a meal of them both.'

Then he walked quietly on by the side of Red Riding-hood till they came to a part of the wood where a number of flowers grew.

'See, Red Riding-hood,' he said, 'what pretty flowers are growing here; would you not like to rest and gather some? And don't you hear how sweetly the birds are singing? You are walking on as steadily as if you were going to school, and it is much more pleasant here in the wood.'

Then Red Riding-hood looked up and saw the dancing sunbeams shining between the trees and lighting up the beautiful flowers that grew all around her, and she thought, 'If I were to take my grandmother a fresh nosegay, it would make her so pleased; it is early yet, and I have plenty of time.'

So she went out of her way into the wood to gather flowers. And when she had picked a few, she saw some more beautiful still at a little distance; so she walked on farther and farther, till she was quite deep in the wood.

SHE MET A WOLF.

Meanwhile the wolf went straight on to the grandmother's house, and knocked at the door.

'Who is there?'

'Little Red Riding-hood,' replied the wolf, imitating the voice of the child. 'Mother has sent me with a piece of cake and a bottle of wine for you. Open the door.'

'Lift up the latch and come in,' she replied; 'I am too weak to get up.'

So the wolf lifted the latch, and the door flew open; then he rushed in, sprang upon the poor old grandmother, and ate her up. Then he shut the door, dressed himself in the old woman's nightgown and night-cap, and laid down in the bed to wait for Red Riding-hood.

After Red Riding-hood had gathered as many flowers as she could carry, she found her way back quickly to the right path, and walked on very fast till she came to her grandmother's house, and knocked at the door.

'Who is there?' said the wolf, trying to imitate the grandmother. His voice was so gruff, however, that Little Red Riding-hood would have been frightened, only she thought her grandmother had a cold.

So she replied, 'It's Little Red Riding-hood. Mother's sent you a piece of cake and a bottle of wine.'

'Lift up the latch and come in,' said the wolf.

So Red Riding-hood lifted the latch and went in.

When she saw her grandmother, as she thought, lying in bed, she went up to her and drew back the curtains; but she could only see the head, for the wolf had pulled the nightcap as far over his face as he could.

'Good-morning,' she said; but there was no answer. Then she got on the bed, and cried out, 'Oh, grandmother, what great ears you have got!'

'The better to hear with, my dear,' he said.

'And what great eyes you have got!'

'The better to see with, my dear.'

'And, grandmother, what large hands you have got!'

'The better to hold you, my dear.'

'But, grandmother, what great teeth you have got!' cried Red Riding-hood, who began to be frightened.

'The better to eat you!' cried the wolf, jumping from the bed; and, seizing poor Red Riding-hood, he swallowed her up at one mouthful.

Now, as soon as the wolf had satisfied his hunger, he laid himself in the bed, and snored so loudly that he could be heard outside.

A hunter, who was out with his gun, was passing by, and thought to himself, 'How the old woman snores; I must go in and see what is the matter.'

Then he stepped into the room, and when he came to the bed he saw the wolf lying on it.

'Oh, you old sinner,' said the hunter, 'have I found you at last? I have been seeking you a long time, Mr. Wolf.'

He was just going to raise his gun when he missed the old grand-mother, and thinking that the wolf might have swallowed her, he remembered she might yet be saved. So he would not shoot, but, taking a pair of scissors, cut open the stomach of the sleeping wolf.

How surprised he was to see the smiling face of Red Riding-hood peep out at the first snip; and as he cut further, she sprang out, exclaiming: 'Oh, I have been so frightened; it was dreadfully dark in the wolf's stomach!'

Then they helped out the old grandmother, who was also unhurt and living, but she could scarcely breathe. The wolf awoke too late to save his own life; he sank back on the bed and died, and the hunter had his skin. After this they all sat down very contentedly, and drank the wine and ate the cake which Red Riding-hood had brought; and then the hunter took the little girl safely home.

'Ah,' she thought, 'I will never go out of my way to run in the wood again, when my mother has forbidden me.'

*   *   *   *   *   *

It is related that once after this, when Little Red Riding-hood was going again to her old grandmother with some of the nice things her mother had made, another wolf spoke to her, and wanted to entice her out of the way.

But Red Riding-hood was on her guard, and went straight forward without stopping till she came to her grandmother's house.

'Oh, grandmother,' she said, 'I met a wolf, who wished me " good-day;" but he looked at me with such wicked eyes, that if I had not been in the street I am sure he would have eaten me up.'

'Perhaps he will come here,' said the grandmother; 'so we will lock the door and keep him out.'

Sure enough, soon after the wolf came to the door and knocked, crying: 'Open the door, grandmother; I am Red Riding-hood, and I have brought you some cake and wine.' But all remained silent, and the door was not opened.

Then the sly old thief prowled round the house, and at last sprang on the roof to wait till Red Riding-hood went home in the evening, that he might seize her in the dark and devour her.

But the grandmother knew what was in his mind. Now there stood near the house a large stone trough, and she said to the child: 'Red Riding-hood, I cooked a large sausage yesterday; you can empty the water in which it was cooked into the stone trough.'

Red Riding-hood drew off the water from the copper, and emptied it into the trough until it was quite full, and the smell of the sausage reached the wolf's nose. He sniffed, and sniffed, and looked down, till at last he stretched his neck out to such a distance that he lost his balance, and fell from the roof into the great trough full of water, and was drowned. Red Riding-hood went home that evening in happiness and safety, and no one attempted to hurt her on the road.

THE TOWN MUSICIANS.

THE TOWN MUSICIANS.

An ass who had carried sacks to the mill for his master during many long years felt his strength fail at last, so that he could no longer work for his living. His master thought of getting rid of his old servant, that he might save the expense of his food. But the ass discovered his intentions, and determined to run away.

So he took the road to Bremen, where he had often heard the street band playing, and he thought he could be as musical as they were.

He had not travelled far when he saw a hound lying on the ground and gasping for breath, as if he were tired of running.

'Why are you panting so, friend?' asked the ass.

'Ah,' he replied, 'now that I am old, and get each day weaker and weaker, I can no more go to the hunt, and my master has ordered me to be killed, so I have run away, but how I am to earn my living I don't know.'

'Will you go with me?' said the ass. 'Do you know I am going to try my fortune as a street musician in Bremen; I think you and I could easily earn a living by music; I can play the lute, and you can beat the kettledrum.'

The dog was quite contented, and so they both walked on together.

Not long after, they saw a cat sitting in the road with a face as dismal as three days of rainy weather.

'Now, whatever has come across you, old whiskers?' asked the ass.

'How can one be merry when one has a collar on?' said the cat;
'now I am getting old, and my teeth are become stumps, I cannot

'WHY ARE YOU PANTING SO, FRIEND?' ASKED THE ASS.

'WITH ALL MY HEART,' SAID THE CAT.

catch mice, and I like to lie behind the stove and purr; but when I
found they were going to drown me and my wife, I ran away as fast as

I could; my experience has cost me dear, and now what am I to do?'

'Go with us to Bremen,' said the ass; 'you are accustomed to perform night music, I know, so you can easily become a street musician in the town.'

'With all my heart,' said the cat. So he walked on with them.

After travelling some little distance, the three fugitives came to a farm yard, and on the gate stood a domestic cock screaming with all his might.

'Why are you standing there on your marrow-bones and screaming so?' said the ass.

'I will tell you,' replied the cock. 'I prophesied fine weather at Lady-day, when the family went to perform some of their religious work, and there was fine weather; but the housekeeper has no pity, for I heard the cook say that there is company coming on Sunday, and she shall want me to put in the soup. So this evening my head will be cut off; therefore I shall scream at the top of my voice as long as I can.'

'WHY ARE YOU SCREAMING SO?' SAID THE ASS.

'Listen, Red Comb,' said the ass; 'would you like to run away with us? We are going to Bremen, and you will find something better there than to be made into soup; you have a fine voice, and we are all musical by nature.'

The cock readily fell in with this proposal, and they all four went away together.

They could not, however, reach Bremen in one day, and evening came on just as they entered a wood, so they decided to stay all night.

The ass and the dog laid themselves under a large tree, but the cat made himself comfortable on the branches. The cock flew to the summit of the tree, where he felt himself quite safe.

Before they slept, the cock, who from his high position could see to all points of the compass, discovered in the distance a tiny spark burning, and calling to his comrades, told them he was convinced that they were not far from a house in which a light was shining.

LITTLE RED RIDING-HOOD

THE TOWN MUSICIANS

'Then,' said the ass, 'we must rouse up and go on to this light, for there is plainly a harbour of refuge for us.' And the hound said he should be glad of a little piece of meat, or a couple of bones if he could get nothing else.

So they were very soon on their way to the place where the light shone, and it grew larger and brighter as they approached, till they saw that it came from the window of a robber's cave. The ass, who was the tallest, went near and looked in.

'What is to be seen, old gray horse?' said the cock.

'What do I see?' answered the ass; 'why, a table laid out with plenty to eat and drink, and robbers sitting at it and enjoying themselves.'

'WHAT DO I SEE?' ANSWERED THE ASS.

'That ought to be our supper,' said the cock.

'Yes, yes,' the ass replied; 'if we were only inside.

Then the animals consulted together as to what they had better do to drive the robbers away; at last they fixed upon a plan.

The ass was to stand on his hind legs and place his forefeet on the window-sill, and the dog to stand on his back. The cat was then to climb on the dog, and above them all, the cock promised to fly and perch on the cat's head.

As soon as this was accomplished, at a signal given, they all began to perform their music together. The donkey brayed, the hound barked, the cat mewed, and the cock crowed with such a tremendous force through the window into the room that the window rattled.

The robbers, hearing such a horrible outcry above them, thought it could only be caused by supernatural beings, and fled in great terror to the wood behind the house. Then our four comrades rushed in, placed themselves near or upon the table and took whatever was before them, which the robbers had left, and ate as if they had been hungry for a month.

When the four musicians had finished, they put out the light, and each sought a sleeping-place most easy and suitable to his nature and habits. The ass laid himself down at full length in the yard, the dog crouched behind the door, the cat rolled herself up on the hearth among the warm ashes, while the cock perched on the beam in the roof, and they were all so tired with their long journey that they were soon fast asleep.

About midnight, one of the robbers from a distance, seeing that the light was out and all quiet, told their chief, who said :

'I do not think there has been any cause for fear after all.'

Then he called one of their number and sent him to the house to see if it was all right.

The messenger, finding everything still, went into the kitchen to strike a light, and, seeing the glaring, fiery eyes of the cat looking like a live coal, held a match towards them that he might set fire to it. But puss, not understanding such sport, flew up, spit at him, and scratched his face. This frightened him so terribly that he rushed to the door ; but the dog, who lay there, sprang out upon him and bit him in the leg as he went by.

In the court he ran against the donkey, who gave him a kick with his hind-foot, while the cock on the beam. aroused by the noise, became alive and brisk in a moment, and cried out as loudly as he could, ' Cock-a-doodle-doo.'

Then ran the robber as fast as he could back to his chief.

THE ROBBERS.

' Ah me !' he said, ' in that house is a horrible witch, who flew at me, and scratched me down the face with her long fingers. Then by the door stood a man with a knife, who stabbed me in the leg ; and out in the court lay a black monster, who struck me a violent blow with his wooden leg ; and up in the roof sat the judge, who cried, "Bring me the scoundrels here." On that I made off as fast as possible.'

From the moment that they heard this, the robbers never again entered the house, but escaped as quickly from the place as they could ; and the four musicians found themselves in such good quarters that they would not leave, and the last heard of them was, that they intended to remain there.

THE SINGING BONE.

THERE was once in a country great trouble about a wild boar, who attacked the peasants in the fields, and had killed and torn to pieces several men with his tusks. The king of the country promised a large reward to anyone who would free the land from this plague. But the animal was so large and strong that no man would even venture near the forest where he lived.

At last, the king made a proclamation that he would give his only daughter in marriage to any man who would bring the wild boar to him dead or alive.

There lived two brothers in that country, the sons of a poor man, who gave notice of their readiness to enter on this perilous undertaking. The eldest, who was clever and crafty, was influenced by pride; the youngest, who was innocent and simple, offered himself from kindness of heart.

Thereupon the king advised that, as the best and safest way would be to take opposite directions in the wood, the eldest was to go in the evening, and the youngest in the morning.

The youngest had not gone far when a little fairy stepped up to him. He held in his hand a black spear, and said, 'I will give you this spear because your heart is innocent and good. With this you can go out and discover the wild boar, and he shall not be able to harm you.'

He thanked the little man, took the spear, placed it on his shoulder, and, without delay, went farther into the forest. It was not long before he espied the animal coming towards him, and fiercely making ready to spring. But the youth stood still, and held the spear firmly in front of him. In wild rage the fierce beast ran violently towards him, and was met by the spear, on the point of which he threw himself, and, as it pierced him to the heart, he fell dead.

Then the youngster took the dead monster on his shoulder, and went to find his brother. As he approached the other side of the wood, where stood a large hall, he heard music, and found a number of people dancing, drinking wine, and making merry. His eldest brother was amongst them, for he thought the wild boar would not run far away, and he wished to get up his courage for the evening by cheerful company and wine.

When he caught sight of his youngest brother coming out of the forest laden with his booty, the most restless jealousy and malice rose in his heart. But he disguised his bitter feelings and spoke kindly to his brother, and said:

'Come in, and stay with us, dear brother, and rest awhile, and get up your strength by a cup of wine.'

So the youth, not suspecting anything wrong, carried the dead boar into his brother's house, and told him of the little man he had met in the wood, who had given him the spear, and how he had killed the wild animal.

The elder brother persuaded him to stay and rest till the evening, and then they went out together in the twilight, and walked by the river till it became quite dark. A little bridge lay across the river, over which they had to pass, and the eldest brother let the young one go before him. When they arrived at the middle of the stream, the wicked man gave his youngest brother a blow from behind, and he fell down dead instantly.

But, fearing he might not be quite dead, he threw the body over the bridge into the river, and through the clear waters saw it sink into the sand. After this wicked deed he ran home quickly, took the dead wild boar on his shoulders, and carried it to the king, with the pretence that he had killed the animal, and that therefore he could claim the princess as his wife, according to the king's promise.

But these dark deeds are not often concealed, for something happens to bring them to light. Not many years after a herdsman, passing over the bridge with his flock, saw beneath him in the sand a little bone as white as snow, and thought that it would make a very nice mouthpiece for his horn.

As soon as they had passed over the bridge, he waded into the middle of the stream, for the water was very shallow, took up the bone, and carried it home to make a mouthpiece for his horn.

But the first time he blew the horn after the bone was in, it filled the herdsman with wonder and amazement; for it began to sing of itself. and these were the words it sang:

> 'Ah! dear shepherd, you are blowing your horn
> With one of my bones, which night and morn
> Lie still unburied, beneath the wave
> Where I was thrown in a sandy grave.
> I killed the wild boar, and my brother slew me,
> And gained the princess by pretending 'twas he.'

'What a wonderful horn,' said the shepherd, 'that can sing of itself! I must take it to my lord the king.'

As soon as the horn was brought before the king and blown by the shepherd, it at once began to sing the same song and the same words.

The king was at first surprised, but his suspicion being aroused, he ordered that the sand under the bridge should be examined immediately, and then the entire skeleton of the murdered man was discovered, and the whole wicked deed came to light.

The wicked brother could not deny the deed; he was therefore ordered to be tied in a sack and drowned, while the remains of his murdered brother were carefully carried to the churchyard, and laid to rest in a beautiful grave.

THE THREE GOLDEN HAIRS.

THERE was once a poor woman who was very happy when her little son was born, for he had a caul, and it was prophesied, therefore, that in his fourteenth year he should marry the king's daughter. It happened very soon after that the king came to the village, but no one knew that it was the king. So when he asked for news they told him that a few days before a child had been born in the village with a caul, and it was prophesied in consequence that he would be very lucky. Indeed, it had been said that in his fourteenth year he would have the king's daughter for his wife.

The king, who had a wicked heart, was very angry when he heard this; but he went to the parents in a most friendly manner, and said to them kindly, ' Good people, give up your child to me, I will take the greatest care of him.'

At first they refused; but when the stranger offered them a large amount of gold, and they mentioned that if their child was born to be lucky, everything must turn out for the best with him, they willingly at last gave him up.

The king placed the child in a box, and rode away with it for a long distance, till he came to deep water, into which he threw the box containing the child, saying to himself as he rode away, ' From this unwelcome suitor have I saved my daughter.'

But the box did not sink; it swam like a boat on the water, and so high above it that not a drop got inside. It sailed on to a spot about two miles from the chief town of the king's dominions, where there was a mill and a weir, which stopped it, and on which it rested.

The miller's man, who happened to be standing near the bank, fortunately noticed it, and thinking it would most likely contain something valuable, drew it on shore with a hook; but when he opened it there lay a beautiful baby, who was quite awake and lively.

THE KING PLACED THE CHILD IN A BOX AND RODE AWAY.

He carried it in to the miller and his wife, and, as they had no children, they were quite delighted, and said Heaven had sent the little boy as a gift to them. They brought him up carefully, and he grew to manhood clever and virtuous.

It happened one day that the king was overtaken by a thunder-storm while passing near the mill, and stopped to ask for shelter. Noticing the youth, he asked the miller if that tall young man was his son.

'No,' he replied; 'he is a foundling. Nineteen years ago a box was seen sailing on the mill-stream by one of our men, and when it was caught in the weir he drew it out of the water, and found the child in it.'

Then the king knew that this must be the child of fortune, and therefore the one which he had thrown into the water. He hid his vexation, however, and presently said kindly, 'I want to send a letter to the queen, my wife; if that young man will take it to her, I will give him two gold pieces for his trouble.'

'We are at the king's service,' replied the miller, and called the young man to prepare for his errand. Then the king wrote a letter to the queen, containing these words:

'As soon as the boy who brings this letter arrives, let him be killed, and I shall expect to find him dead and buried when I come back.'

The youth was soon on his way with this letter. He lost himself, however, in a large forest. But when darkness came on, he saw in the distance a glimmering light, which he walked to, and found a small house. He entered, and saw an old woman sitting by the fire, quite alone. She appeared frightened when she saw him, and said:

'Where do you come from, and what do you want?'

'I am come from the mill,' he replied, 'and I am carrying a letter to the wife of the king, and, as I have lost my way, I should like very much to stay here during the night.'

'You poor young man,' she replied, 'you are in a den of robbers, and when they come home they may kill you.'

'They may come when they like,' said the youth; 'I am not afraid; but I am so tired that I cannot go a step farther to-night.' Then he stretched himself on a bench and fell fast asleep.

Soon after the robbers came home, and asked angrily what that youth was lying there for.

'Ah,' said the old woman, 'he is an innocent child, who has lost himself in the wood, and I took him in out of compassion. He is carrying a letter to the queen, which the king has sent.'

Then the robbers went softly to the sleeping youth, took the letter from his pocket, and read in it that as soon as the bearer arrived at the palace he was to lose his life. Then pity arose in the hard-hearted robbers, and their chief tore up the letter and wrote another, in which it was stated that as soon as the boy arrived he should be married to the king's daughter. Then they left him to lie and rest on the bench till the next morning, and when he awoke they gave him the letter and showed him the road he was to take.

As soon as he reached the palace and sent in the letter, the queen read it, and she acted in exact accordance to what was written—ordered a grand marriage feast, and had the princess married at once to the fortunate youth.

He was very handsome and amiable, so that the king's daughter soon learnt to love him very much, and was quite happy with him.

Not long after, when the king returned home to his castle, he found the prophecy respecting the child of fortune fulfilled, and that he was married to a king's daughter.

'How has this happened?' said he; 'I have in my letter given very different orders.'

Then the queen gave him the letter, and said, ' You may see for yourself what is stated there.'

The king read the letter, and saw very clearly that it was not the one he had written. He asked the youth what he had done with the letter he had entrusted to him, and where he had brought the other from.

'I know not,' he replied, 'unless it was changed during the night while I slept in the forest.'

Full of wrath, the king said, ' You shall not get off so easily, for whoever marries my daughter must first bring me three golden hairs from the head of the Demon of the Black Forest. If you bring them to me before long, then shall you keep my daughter as a wife, but not otherwise.'

Then said the child of fortune, 'I will fetch these golden hairs very quickly; I am not the least afraid of the Demon.' Thereupon he said farewell, and started on his travels. His way led him to a large city, and as he stood at the gate and asked admission, a watchman said to him :

'What trade do you follow, and how much do you know?'

'I know everything,' he replied.

'Then you can do us a favour,' answered the watchman, ' if you can tell why our master's fountain, from which wine used to flow, is dried up, and never gives us even water now?'

'I will tell you when I come back,' he said ; ' only wait till then.'

He travelled on still farther, and came by-and-by to another town, where the watchman also asked him what trade he followed, and what he knew.

'I know everything,' he answered.

'Then,' said the watchman, ' you can do us a favour, and tell us why a tree in our town, which once bore golden apples, now only produces leaves?'

'Wait till I return,' he replied, ' and I will tell you.'

On he went again, and came to a broad river, over which he must pass in a ferry-boat, and the ferryman asked him the same question about his trade and his knowledge. He gave the same reply, that he knew everything.

'Then,' said the man, ' you can do me a favour, and tell me how it is that I am obliged to go backwards and forwards in my ferry-boat every day, without a change of any kind?'

Wait till I come back,' he replied, ' then you shall know all about it.'

As soon as he reached the other side of the water, he found the entrance to the Black Forest, in which was the Demon's cave. It was very dark and gloomy, and the Demon was not at home; but his old mother was sitting on the stool of care, and she looked up and said, 'What do you want? You don't look wicked enough to be one of us.'

'I just want three golden hairs from the Demon's head,' he replied; 'otherwise, my wife will be taken away from me.'

'That is asking a great deal,' she replied; 'for if the Demon comes home and finds you here, he will have no mercy on you. However, if you will trust me, I will try to help you.'

Then she turned him into an ant, and said, 'Creep into the folds of my gown; there you will be safe.'

'Yes,' he replied, 'that is all very good; but I have three things besides that I want to know. First, why a well, from which formerly wine used to flow, should be dry now, so that not even water can be got from it? Secondly, why a tree that once bore golden apples should now produce nothing but leaves? And, thirdly, why a ferryman is obliged to row forward and back every day, without ever leaving off?'

'These are difficult questions,' said the old woman; 'but keep still and quiet, and when the Demon comes in, pay great attention to what he says, while I pull the golden hairs out of his head.'

Late in the evening the Demon came home, and as soon as he entered he declared that the air was not clear. 'I smell the flesh of man,' he said, 'and I am sure that there is some one here.' So he peeped into all the corners, and searched everywhere, but could find nothing.

Then his old mother scolded him well, and said, 'Just as I have been sweeping, and dusting, and putting everything in order, then you come home and give me all the work to do over again. You have always the smell of something in your nose. Do sit down and eat your supper.'

The Demon did as she told him, and when he had eaten and drank enough, he complained of being tired. So his mother made him lie down, so that she could place his head in her lap; and he was soon so comfortable that he fell fast asleep and snored.

Then the old woman lifted up a golden hair, twitched it out, and laid it by her side.

'Oh!' screamed the Demon, waking up; 'what was that for?'

'I have had a bad dream,' answered she, 'and it made me catch hold of your hair.'

'What did you dream about?' asked the Demon.

'Oh, I dreamt of a well in a market-place from which wine once used to flow, but now it is dried up, and they can't even get water from it. Whose fault is that?'

'Ah, they ought to know that there sits a toad under a stone in the well, and if he were dead wine would again flow.'

Then the old woman combed his hair again, till he slept and snored so loud that the windows rattled, and she pulled out the second hair.

'What are you about now?' asked the Demon, in a rage.

'Oh, don't be angry,' said the woman; 'I have had another dream.'

'What was this dream about?' he asked.

'Why, I dreamt that in a certain country there grows a fruit-tree which used to bear golden apples, but now it produces nothing but leaves. What is the cause of this?'

'Why, don't they know,' answered the Demon, 'that there is a mouse gnawing at the root? Were it dead, the tree would again bear golden apples; and if it gnaws much longer the tree will wither and dry up. Bother your dreams; if you disturb me again, just as I am comfortably asleep, you will have a box on the ear.'

Then the old woman spoke kindly to him, and smoothed and combed his hair again, till he slept and snored. Then she seized the third golden hair, and pulled it out.

The Demon, on this, sprang to his feet, roared out in a greater rage than ever, and would have done some mischief in the house, but she managed to appease him this time also, and said, 'How can I help my bad dreams?'

'And whatever did you dream?' he asked, with some curiosity.

'Well, I dreamt about a ferryman, who complains that he is obliged to take people across the river, and is never free.'

'Oh, the stupid fellow!' replied the wizard, 'he can very easily ask any person who wants to be ferried over to take the oar in his hand, and he will be free at once.'

Then the Demon laid his head down once more; and as the old mother had pulled out the three golden hairs, and got answers to all the three questions, she let the old fellow rest and sleep in peace till the morning dawned.

As soon as he had gone out next day, the old woman took the ant from the folds of her dress, and restored the lucky youth to his former shape. 'Here are the three golden hairs for which you wished,' said she; 'and did you hear all the answers to your three questions?'

'Yes,' he replied, 'every word, and I will not forget them.'

'Well, then, I have helped you out of your difficulties, and now get home as fast as you can.'

After thanking the old woman for her kindness, he turned his steps homeward, full of joy that everything had succeeded so well.

When he arrived at the ferry the man asked for the promised answer.

'Ferry me over first,' he replied, 'and then I will tell you.'

So when they reached the opposite shore he gave the ferryman the Demon's advice, that the next person who came and wished to be ferried over should have the oar placed in his hand, and from that moment he would have to take the ferryman's place.

Then the youth journeyed on till he came to the town where the unfruitful tree grew, and where the watchman was waiting for his answer. To him the young man repeated what he had heard, and said, 'Kill the mouse that is gnawing at the root, then will your tree again bear golden apples.'

The watchman thanked him, and gave him in return for his information two asses laden with gold, which were led after him. He very soon arrived at the city which contained the dried-up fountain. The sentinel came forward to receive his answer. Said the youth, ' Under a stone in the fountain sits a toad ; it must be searched for and killed, then will wine again flow from it.' To show how thankful he was for this advice, the sentinel also ordered two asses laden with gold to be sent after him.

At length the child of fortune reached home with his riches, and his wife was overjoyed at seeing him again, and hearing how well he had succeeded in his undertaking. He placed before the king the three golden hairs he had brought from the head of the black Demon; and when the king saw these and the four asses laden with gold he was quite satisfied, and said, ' Now that you have performed all the required conditions, I am quite ready to sanction your marriage with my daughter ; but, my dear son-in-law, tell me how you obtained all this gold ? It is indeed a very valuable treasure ; where did you find it ?'

' I crossed the river in a ferry-boat, and on the opposite shore I found the gold lying in the sand.'

' Can I find some if I go ?' asked the king eagerly.

' Yes, as much as you please,' replied he. ' There is a ferryman there who will row you over, and you can fill a sack in no time.'

The greedy old king set out on his journey in all haste, and when he came near the river he beckoned to the ferryman to row him over the ferry.

The man told him to step in, and just as they reached the opposite shore he placed the rudder-oar in the king's hand, and sprang out of the boat ; and so the king became a ferryman as a punishment for his sins.

I wonder if he still goes on ferrying people over the river ! It is very likely, for no one has ever been persuaded to touch the oar since he took it.

THE LADY-BIRD AND THE FLY.

A LADY-BIRD and a fly once lived and kept house together, and they brewed their beer in an egg-shell. One day the lady-bird fell in and was burnt. Then the fly set up such a loud scream that the little door of the room asked, ' What are you screaming for, fly ?'

' Because lady-bird has burnt herself.'

Then began the door to creak. ' Why are you creaking?' asked a little broom in the corner.

' Shall I not creak ?—

> 'Lady-bird is burnt
> And little fly weeps.'

Then began the broom to sweep with all its might; and presently a stream passed the door, and said, 'Why are you sweeping so, broom?'
'Shall I not sweep?' replied the broom:

> 'Lady-bird is burnt,
> Little fly weeps,
> Little door jars,
> And little broom sweeps.'

Then said the stream, 'So I will run,' and it began to run rapidly.
'Why are you running so?' asked the fire.
'Shall I not run,' it replied,

> 'When lady-bird is burnt,
> And little fly weeps,
> Little door jars,
> And little broom sweeps,
> While little stream runs?'

Then said the fire, 'So will I burn,' and it burst into a dreadful flame.
A tree grew near the fire, and it said, 'Fire, why do you burn?'
'Shall I not burn,' it replied, 'when

> 'Lady-bird is burnt,
> And little fly weeps,
> The little door jars,
> And little broom sweeps,
> And little stream runs?'

Then said the little tree, 'So will I rustle,' and it began to shake so violently that the leaves fell off.
A maiden came by carrying her little pitcher to the well, and she said, 'Tree, why do you rustle so?'
'Shall I not rustle?' the tree replied:

> 'Lady-bird is burnt,
> Little fly weeps,
> Little door jars,
> Little broom sweeps
> Little stream runs,
> And little fire burns.'

'Then I will break my little pitcher,' said the maiden. So she broke her pitcher.
Then said the well, as the water flowed out, 'Maiden, why dost thou break thy pitcher?'
'Shall I not break my pitcher,' she said, 'when

> 'Lady-bird is burnt,
> And little fly weeps,
> Little door jars,
> And little broom sweeps,

Little stream runs,
Little fire burns,
And little tree rustles ?'

' Ah !' said the well, ' then I will begin to flow,' and the water began
to flow so rapidly that the maiden, the tree, the fire, the stream, the
broom, the door, the fly, and the lady-bird were all drowned together.

THE MAIDEN WITHOUT HANDS.

A MILLER, who had by degrees become very poor, had nothing at last
left but his mill and a large apple-tree behind it. One day, when he
went into the forest to gather wood, an old man, whom he had never
seen before, came towards him, and said, ' Why do you take the trouble
to cut down wood? I will give you great riches if you will promise to
let me have what stands behind your mill.'

' That can be no other than my apple-tree,' thought the miller; ' I
possess nothing else.' So he said to the old man, ' Yes, I will let you
have it.'

Then the stranger smiled maliciously, and said, ' In three years I
will come again to claim what belongs to me,' and after saying this he
departed.

As soon as the miller returned home, his wife came towards him
and said, ' Miller, from whence have all these riches come so suddenly to our house? All at once every drawer and chest has become
full of gold. No one brought it here, and I know not where it came
from.'

' Oh,' replied her husband, ' I know all about it. A strange man,
whom I met in the wood, promised me great treasures if I would make
over to him what stood behind the mill. I knew I had nothing there
but the large apple-tree, so I gave him my promise.'

' Oh, husband !' said the wife in alarm, ' that must have been the
wizard; he did not mean the apple-tree, but our daughter, who was
behind the mill sweeping out the court.'

The miller's daughter was a modest and beautiful maiden, and lived
in innocence and obedience to her parents for three years, until the day
came on which the wicked wizard was to claim her. She knew he was
coming, and after washing till she was pure and clean as snow, she drew
a circle of white chalk, and stood within it.

The wizard made his appearance very early, but he did not dare to
venture over the white circle, therefore he could not get near her. In
great anger he said to the miller, ' Take away every drop of water, that
she may not wash, otherwise I shall have no power over her.'

The frightened miller did as he desired, but on the next morning, when the wizard came again, her hands were as pure and clean as ever, for she had wept over them. On this account the wizard was still unable to approach her; so he flew into a rage, and said, ' Chop her hands off, otherwise I cannot touch her.'

Then the miller was terrified, and exclaimed, ' How can I cut off the hands of my own child ?'

Then the wicked wizard threatened him, and said, ' If you will not do as I desire you, then I can claim you instead of your daughter, and carry you off.'

The father listened in agony, and in his fright promised to obey. He went to his daughter, and said to her, ' Oh, my child, unless I cut off your two hands the wizard will take me away with him, and in my anguish I have promised. Help me in my trouble, and forgive me for the wicked deed I have promised to do.'

' Dear father,' she replied, ' do with me what you will, I am your child.'

Thereupon, she placed her two hands on the table before him, and he cut them off. The wizard came next day for the third time, but the poor girl had wept so bitterly over the stumps of her arms, that they were as clean and white as ever. Then he was obliged to give way, for he had lost all right to the maiden.

As soon as the wizard had departed, the miller said, ' My child, I have obtained so much good through thy conduct, that for thy whole lifetime I shall hold thee most precious and dear.'

' But I cannot stay here, father,' she replied; ' I am not safe; let me go away with people who will give me the sympathy I need so much.'

' I fear such people are very seldom to be found in the world,' said her father.

However, he let her go. So she tied up her maimed arms and went forth on her way at sunrise.

For a whole day she travelled without food, and as night came on found herself near one of the royal gardens. By the light of the moon she could see many trees laden with beautiful fruit, but she could not reach them, because the place was surrounded by a moat full of water. She had been without a morsel to eat the whole day, and her hunger was so great that she could not help crying out, ' Oh, if I were only able to get some of that delicious fruit ! I shall die unless I can obtain something to eat very soon.'

Then she knelt down and prayed for help, and while she prayed a guardian fairy appeared and made a channel in the water so that she was able to pass through on dry ground.

When she entered the garden the fairy was with her, although she did not know it, so she walked to a tree full of beautiful pears, not knowing that they had been counted.

Being unable to pluck any without hands, she went quite close to the tree and ate one with her mouth as it hung. One, and no more, just to stay her hunger. The gardener, who saw her with the fairy stand-ing near her, thought it was a spirit, and was too frightened to move or speak.

After having satisfied her hunger, the maiden went and laid herself down among the shrubs and slept in peace. On the following morning, the king, to whom the garden belonged, came out to look at his fruit trees, and when he reached the pear-tree and counted the pears, he found one missing. At first he thought it had fallen, but it was not under the tree, so he went to the gardener and asked what had become of it.

'Then,' said the gardener, 'there was a ghost in the garden last night who had no hands, and ate a pear off the tree with its mouth.'

'How could the ghost get across the water?' asked the king; 'and what became of it after eating the pear?'

To this the gardener replied, 'Some one came first in snow-white robes from heaven, who made a channel and stopped the flow of the water, so that the ghost walked through on dry ground. It must have been an angel,' continued the gardener; 'and therefore I was afraid to ask questions or to call out. As soon as the spectre had eaten one pear it went away.'

Then said the king, 'Conceal from everyone what you have told me, and I will watch myself to-night.'

As soon as it was dark the king came into the garden and brought a priest with him to address the ghost, and they both seated themselves under a tree, with the gardener standing near them, and waited in silence. About midnight the maiden crept out from the bushes, and went to the pear-tree, and the three watchers saw her eat a pear from the tree without plucking it, while an angel stood near in white garments.

Then the priest went towards her, and said, 'Art thou come from heaven or from earth? art thou a spirit or a human being?'

Then the maiden answered, 'Ah me! I am no ghost, only a poor creature forsaken by everyone but God.'

Then said the king, 'You may be forsaken by all the world, but if you will let me be your friend, I will never forsake you.'

So the maiden was taken to the king's castle, and she was so beauti-ful and modest that the king learnt to love her with all his heart. He had silver hands made for her, and very soon after they were married with great pomp.

About a year after, the king had to go to battle, and he placed his young wife under the care of his mother, who promised to be very kind to her, and to write to him.

Not long after this, the queen had a little son born, and the king's mother wrote a letter to him immediately, so that he might have the earliest intelligence, and sent it by a messenger.

The messenger, however, after travelling a long way, became tired, and sat down to rest by a brook, where he soon fell fast asleep. Then came the wizard, who was always trying to injure the good queen, took away the letter from the sleeping messenger, and replaced it by another, in which it was stated that the little child was a changeling.

Knowing nothing of the change, the messenger carried this letter to the king, who, when he read it, was terribly distressed and troubled. However, he wrote in reply to say that the queen was to have every attention and care till his return.

The wicked wizard again watched for the messenger, and while he slept exchanged the king's kind letter for another, in which was written to the king's mother an order to kill both the queen and her child.

The old mother was quite terrified when she read this letter, for she could not believe the king meant her to do anything so dreadful. She wrote again to the king, but there was no answer, for the wicked wizard always interrupted the messengers, and sent false letters. The last was worse than all, for it stated that instead of killing the mother and her child, they were to cut out the tongue of the changeling and put out the mother's eyes.

But the king's mother was too good to attend to these dreadful orders, so she said to the queen, while her eyes streamed with tears, ' I cannot kill you both, as the king desires me to do ; but I must not let you remain here any longer. Go now out into the world with thy child, and do not come here again.' Then she bound the boy on his mother's back, and the poor woman departed, weeping as she went.

After walking some time, she reached a dense forest, and knew not which road to take. So she knelt down and prayed for help. As she rose from her knees she saw a light shining from the window of a little cottage, on which was hung a small sign-board, with these words : ' Everyone who dwells here is safe.' Out of the cottage stepped a maiden dressed in snowy garments, and said : ' Welcome, queen-wife,' and led her in. Then she unfastened the baby from his mother's back, and hushed him in her arms till he slept so peacefully that she laid him on a bed in another room, and came back to his mother.

The poor woman looked at her earnestly, and said :

' How did you know I was a queen?'

The white maiden replied :

' I am a good fairy sent to take care of thee and thy child.'

So she remained in that cottage many years, and was very happy, and so pious and good that her hands, which had been cut off, were allowed to grow again, and the little boy became her great comfort.

Not long after she had been sent away from the castle, the king returned, and immediately asked to see his wife and child.

Then his old mother began to weep, and said :

' You wicked man, how can you ask me for your wife and child when you wrote me such dreadful letters, and told me to kill two such innocent beings ?'

The king, in distress, asked her what she meant ; and she showed him the letters she had received, which were changed by the dreadful wizard. Then the king began to weep so bitterly for his wife and child, that the old woman pitied him, and said:

' Do not be so unhappy; they still live: I could not kill them; but your wife and child are gone into the wide world, never to come back for fear of your anger.'

Then said the king:

' I will go to the ends of the earth to find them, and I will neither eat nor drink till I find my dear wife, even if I should die of hunger.'

Thereupon the king started on his expedition, travelling over rocks and valleys, over mountains and highways, for seven long years; but he found her not, and he thought she was starved to death, and that he should never see her again.

He neither ate nor drank during the whole time of earthly food, but heaven sent him help. At last he arrived at a large forest, and found the little cottage with the sign-board, and the words upon it, ' Every-one who dwells here is safe.'

While he stood reading the words, the maiden in white raiment came out, took him by the hand, and led him into the cottage, saying:

' My lord the king is welcome; but why is he here?'

Then he replied:

' I have been for seven years travelling about the world hoping to find my wife and child, but I have not yet succeeded. Can you help me?'

' Sit down,' said the angel, ' and take something to eat and drink first.'

The king was so tired that he gladly obeyed, for he really wanted rest. Then he laid himself down and slept, and the maiden in the white raiment covered his face.

Then she went into an inner chamber where the queen sat with her little son, whom she had named ' Painbringer,' and said to her:

' Go out together into the other chamber; thy husband is come.'

The poor queen went out, but still sorrowfully, for she remembered the cruel letters his mother had received, and knew not that he still loved her.

Just as she entered the room, the covering fell off his face, and she told her little son to replace it.

The boy went forward and laid the cloth gently over the face of the strange man. But the king heard the voice in his slumber, and moved his head, so that the covering again fell off.

' My child,' said the queen, ' cover the face of thy father.'

He looked at her in surprise, and said:

' How can I cover my father's face, dear mother? I have no father in this world. You have taught me to pray to " Our Father, which art in heaven;" and I thought my father was God. This strange man is not my father; I don't know him.'

When the king heard this, he started up and asked who they were.

Then said the queen, ' I am thy wife, and this is thy son.'

The king looked at her with surprise. 'Your face and your voice are the same,' he said; 'but my wife had silver hands, and yours are natural.'

'My hands have mercifully been allowed to grow again,' she replied; and, as he still doubted, the maiden in white entered the room, carrying the silver hands, which she showed to the king.

Then he saw at once that this was, indeed, his dear lost wife and his own little son; and he embraced them, full of joy, exclaiming, 'Now has a heavy stone fallen from my heart!'

The maiden prepared a dinner for them, of which they all partook together; and, after a kind farewell, the king started with his wife and child to return home to the castle, where his mother and all the household received them with great joy.

A second marriage-feast was prepared, and the happiness of their latter days made amends for all they had suffered through the wicked demon, who had caused them so much pain and trouble.

THE THREE LANGUAGES.

IN Switzerland, some years ago, lived an old count. He had an only son, whose intellect was so inferior that he seemed unable to learn anything.

One day his father said to him, 'My son, I have done everything I can for you, but your head can retain nothing, do what I will. I must send you away to an excellent master, who shall try what he can do with you.'

So the youth departed to a distant city, where he remained with the master a whole year. At the end of that time he returned home, and his father said to him, 'Well, my son, what have you learnt?'

'Father, I have learnt to understand what the dog says when he barks,' answered he.

'Heaven pity you!' cried the father; 'is that all the knowledge you have gained? Then I must send you to another master.'

So the youth was again placed under the care of a first-rate master for a year.

On his return, his father asked him the same question.

'Father,' said the boy, 'I can now understand the language of birds.'

Then was his father in a rage, and exclaimed, 'Oh! you lost creature, has all this precious time been wasted in learning nothing, and are you not ashamed to appear in my presence? However, I will try you once more with a third master; and if you make no more progress than you have done during the last two years with him, I will give you up—you shall be no longer my son.'

So the youth went for a year to a third master, and on his return, when his father asked him what he had learned, he replied, 'Dear father, I have this time learnt to understand the croaking of the frogs.'

Then was the father in a greater rage than ever. He started up, called the household together, and said, 'This youth is my son no longer; he shall not stay here. I order you to chase him from the house, and you are any of you at liberty to take his life!'

The servants drove him out, but they pitied him too much to kill him. So they let him go away unhurt; but they killed a stag, and sent the eyes and the tongue to the old count, to make him believe that his son had been killed, as he commanded.

The youth wandered away far from home in a very sad mood, and came at last to a roadside inn, and asked the landlord if he could give him a night's lodging.

'Willingly,' replied the burgomaster, 'if you do not mind taking up your abode for the night in the old tower; but I warn you that your life will be in danger, for the place is full of wild dogs, who bark, and howl, and constantly seize and devour human beings. The whole neighbourhood is kept in fear and terror about these dogs, and no one can do anything to get rid of them.'

But the young man had no fear, and he said, 'Let me go to these barking and howling dogs; only give me something to throw to them, and I'll warrant they won't injure me.'

As he would not sleep in the tower unless they agreed to his wishes, they gave him some meat for the wild animals, and then led him to the tower and left him.

As he entered, not one of the dogs barked at him, but wagged their tails in the most friendly manner, ate what he had brought for them, and did not ruffle even a hair of his head.

On the following morning the youth made his appearance, and stood before everyone safe and sound, and said to the burgomaster, 'I understand the language of dogs, and they have explained to me clearly why they have caused so much trouble in the land. They are kept in the tower by enchantment, to watch and protect a great treasure which is hidden beneath it; and until that treasure is removed, there will be no rest for themselves or others, and the spell will remain unbroken. This I have discovered from their conversation.'

All who heard this news were overjoyed at the discovery; and the burgomaster said that if the young man should be successful in bringing away the treasure, he would adopt him as his son, for he had no children of his own.

Then the youth went up again to the tower, and having understood well from the conversation of the dogs where to find the treasure, he knew what to do, and very soon returned to the burgomaster's house, carrying a chest full of gold.

The spell was broken; the howling and barking of the wild dogs ceased from that hour, and the land was freed from the dreadful plague.

A short time after this, the young man thought he should like to take a journey to Rome. On the way he came to a marsh, in which a number of frogs were croaking loudly. He stopped to listen, and as he understood their language, what he heard them say made him quite

'THE TWO DOVES WHISPERED THE WORDS INTO HIS EARS.'

thoughtful and sad as he continued his journey. He arrived at Rome just in time to hear of the Pope's death, and the great doubts which had arisen as to which of the cardinals should be chosen as his successor.

At last it was decided that whoever received a sign from heaven should be at once elected as Pope.

Scarcely had this decision been arrived at, when the young count entered the church; and no sooner did he appear than two snow-white doves flew towards him, and placed themselves one on each shoulder, and there remained.

The clergy who were present acknowledged at once that this was a sign from heaven, and asked the young count if he would accept the position of Pope.

At first he hesitated to reply, for he could scarcely believe he was suitable for such a high station; but the doves, whose language he understood, whispered that it was right to do as the people wished, so at last he said 'Yes.'

Then was he anointed and consecrated, and so was fulfilled the prophecy which he had heard in the frogs' croak, and which had made him so unhappy—namely, that before a month had passed he would be a priest.

Of course after this he had to be present at high mass, and sing the parts, although he could not read a word of the Latin. However, the two doves, who again perched themselves on his shoulders, whispered the words into his ears; and so, after all, his acquaintance with the languages of dogs, frogs, and birds was of as much use to him as if he had been a man of great learning.

THE CLEVER ELFE.

THERE were once a man and woman who had an only daughter, and they thought her so wonderfully clever that they gave her the name of 'The Clever Elfe.' One day her father said to his wife, 'Our daughter is now grown up, and we must get her married soon.'

'Yes,' replied the mother, 'if we find anyone who will have her.'

Not long after this a young man named Hans came to ask these good people for their daughter, yet he made one decided condition, that if he did not find her as clever as they said, he could not marry her.

'Oh,' exclaimed the father, 'she has a good headpiece, you may be sure of that.'

'Yes,' said the mother, 'and she can even see the wind running through the streets and hear the footsteps of the flies on the ceiling.'

But they did not tell him how much she disliked trouble or work, and how often she was idle—however, they sat down to supper together, and seemed very happy. Presently her mother said, 'Elfe, go into the cellar and draw some beer.'

The clever Elfe took the jug from the nail and went into the cellar, taking off the lid as she walked to save time. When she reached the cellar she fetched a chair and placed it in front of the cask, that she might not have to stoop and hurt her back. Then she stood the jug upon it under the tap, from which the beer ran slowly, and waited impatiently for it to fill.

But her eyes were not idle, and, while looking round the cellar, she observed upon the wall above her a crossbar, which the mason had by an oversight forgotten to remove.

Then the clever Elfe begun to weep, and to say that she was quite sure if she married Hans that one of them would be killed by a crossbar; and there she sat, weeping and wailing over this superstitious fear, till her strength was almost gone. Those above at supper waited for the beer, but none came, and at last they sent for the maiden and said to her, 'Go and see why the Elfe is staying so long.'

Then went the maiden and found her sitting before the cask, weeping bitterly.

'Elfe,' she said, 'why do you weep?'

'Ah!' she replied, 'shall I not weep, when I can foresee that a crossbar will cause my death if I marry Hans?' and she pointed to the wall as she spoke.

'What a clever Elfe you must be to find this out!' said the maidservant, beginning to weep and mourn over this misfortune.

The maiden remained so long in the cellar that her master sent the boy after her. He also began to cry and mourn when he heard what the clever Elfe had found out. At last the father and mother came themselves, and, on hearing the clever Elfe's story, they both joined in the crying and howling, and the noise became so loud that Hans went himself to discover what was the matter.

When he reached the cellar and heard them all screaming and crying, one louder than the other, as if they were trying who could weep the loudest, he exclaimed, 'What dreadful misfortune has happened?'

'Oh, dear Hans,' said the Elfe, 'look at that crossbar! I have a presentiment that if we are married you will be killed by it; for if it remains here, it may fall on your head when you come to draw the beer. No wonder we all weep.'

'Now,' said Hans, whose self-love was gratified, 'I believe that you are a clever Elfe to weep, and make everybody else weep, on my account, and I want nothing else to make my household complete but a clever wife.'

So he took her by the hand and led her away from the cellar to the supper-table; the evening passed pleasantly, and very soon after the marriage took place.

But the clever Elfe did not like work. After they had spent a few weeks in idleness, Hans said one day, 'Dear wife, I must go to work and earn money for a living. Don't you think you could go into our little corn-field and cut down the corn, that we may have some flour to make bread?'

Yes, my dear Hans,' she replied; 'I will if you wish it.'

So the next morning Hans went off to his daily work. As soon as he was gone, his wife made some nice broth for herself, and took it with her into the field; but when she arrived there she sat down and

'ALL SCREAMING AND CRYING, ONE LOUDER THAN THE OTHER.'

said to herself, 'What shall I do; shall I nap first, or eat first? Ah! I will eat first.'

So she ate up the whole potful of broth, and then, feeling heavy and stuffed with what she had eaten, she asked herself, 'Now, shall I

cut the corn, or sleep first? Ah! I know, I will have a nap before I
begin my work.'

Then she laid herself down in the corn and was soon fast asleep.
Hans returned home expecting his dinner; but no one was there, nor
anything ready. He waited a long time, but the Elfe did not come.

'What a clever Elfe she is to be sure!' he said; 'so industrious that
she cannot even come home to her dinner.'

But as the evening came on, and she still remained away, Hans went
out to look for her, and to see how much corn she had cut. On reaching the field he found that none had been touched, and after searching
some time for his clever Elfe, he found her fast asleep amongst the
corn.

Hans went away in great haste and fetched a fowler's net, covered
with little bells, which he spread over her; but she continued to sleep
as soundly as before. Then he returned home, locked the cottage door,
and seated himself to work on a chair as coolly as if no clever Elfe had
ever been his wife.

At last, when the clever Elfe awoke out of her long sleep and found
it quite dark, she recollected where she was, and rose to go home,
while the bells which hung round her tinkled at every step she took.
This alarmed her so much that she began to feel puzzled, and could
scarcely tell whether she really was the clever Elfe or not.

'Oh dear!' she said, 'am I myself, or am I some one else?'

She was scarcely able to answer this question, and stood a long time
as if in doubt; at last a thought struck her: 'I will go home and
ask Hans whether I am really myself or some one else; he is sure
to know.'

She found her way home, although it was dark, very quickly, the
bells tinkling as she ran; but when she reached the front-door of the
house it was locked. She knocked at the window, and cried:

'Hans, is the Elfe at home?'

'Yes,' he answered; 'she is at home.'

Oh, how frightened she felt as she heard this!

'Oh, dear!' she exclaimed; 'then I am not the clever Elfe after all.'

Then she went from door to door of the neighbours' houses, but when
they heard the bells jingling no one would admit her, and even the
neighbours did not recognise her. At last she ran away from the village,
and has not been heard of since. So, after all, it is better to be industrious than clever.

THE TAILOR'S THREE SONS.

ONCE upon a time lived a tailor who had three sons, and only one goat to supply them with milk. Of course, such a valuable animal had to be well fed, and the boys used to take her by turns every day to browse in the lanes and to crop the green grass which grew by the road-side. One day the eldest son took her into the churchyard, in which she not only enjoyed the green fresh grass, but frisked about quite merrily. In the evening, when it was time to go home, the boy said to her 'Have you had enough?' and the goat replied :

> 'I am so full,
> I could not pull
> Even a blade of grass,
> Baa, baa !'

'Then come home,' said the youth ; and he took hold of the rope, led her to the stable, and tied her up.

'Well,' said the father, as his son appeared, 'have you taken care of the goat?'

'Yes, indeed, father; she has eaten till she can eat no more.'

But the father, wishing to make quite sure, went to the stable himself, and, stroking his favourite, said, 'Nanny, have you had enough to-day?'

But the goat replied playfully :

> 'In the churchyard all day,
> I could frisk and play,
> But there was not a leaf to eat,
> Baa, baa !'

'What do I hear?' cried the tailor, rushing out of the stable and calling to his eldest boy. 'You have told me a falsehood—you said the goat had eaten as much as she liked, and was well fed, and after all she has been starved.'

And in great anger he took up the yard measure, and drove him with blows from the house.

On the next day it was the turn of the second son to take the goat out, and he soon found a nice spot near a garden wall full of sweet fresh grass, which the goat ate till there was not a blade left.

In the evening, when it was time to go home, the boy asked the goat whether she had had enough.

> 'I have eaten so much,
> I can eat no more,
>   Baa, baa!'

was the goat's reply: so the boy led her home, and, taking her to the stable, tied her up.

'Well,' said the father, as his second son entered the house, 'how has the goat fared to-day?'

'Ah!' replied the youth, 'she has eaten so much she can eat no more.'

But the tailor, remembering the previous evening, went again into the stable, and asked the goat the same question.

> 'How could I eat,
> When there was no meat,
> Not even a tiny leaf?
>   Baa, baa!'

'You dreadful child,' cried the tailor, 'to leave such a useful animal to starve!'

He ran to the house in great anger, and, after beating the boy with his yard measure, he drove him also from the house.

The turn of the youngest son came the next day, and he was determined to give the goat a feast this time. So he took her to a bank, where delicious wild flowers and young leaves grew, and left her to enjoy herself.

When he came to fetch her in the evening, he asked, 'Have you had enough to-day, Nanny?' She replied:

> 'I am so full,
> That I could not pull
> Even a blade of grass,
>   Baa, baa!'

'Then come home,' he said; and, after leading her to the stable, he tied her up, and went in to his father, and told him how well he had fed the goat; but the tailor could not trust him, and upon going out into the stable, and asking the goat, the wicked animal replied:

> 'How can I be full?
> There was nothing to pull,
> Not even a blade of grass.'

'Oh, dear!' cried the tailor, 'what dreadful boys mine are—one quite as bad as the other; he shall not stay here to make a fool of me.'

He beat the boy with the yard measure in his rage so dreadfully that he rushed out of the house and ran away.

Now the tailor remained at home alone with his goat, and the next morning he went into the stable himself, and said to her, 'Come, my precious animal, I will take you out to-day myself.' So he took her a little distance to some green hedges, near which grew bright, tender grass, of which goats are very fond, and said, 'This time you can enjoy yourself to your heart's content.'

He left her there till the evening, and then he asked, 'Have you eaten as much as you like, Nanny?' She replied:

> 'I have had enough
> Of the nicest stuff;
> I could not eat any more,
> Baa, baa!'

So he led her home, and tied her fast in the stable. He had not, however, gone far from the door when he turned back, and again asked her if she was satisfied. To his surprise, she said:

> 'How can I be?
> For I did not see
> A single blade of grass,
> Baa, baa!'

When the tailor heard this, he was greatly startled, and saw at once that he had punished his three sons unjustly.

'You ungrateful animal!' he cried. 'It would be a slight punishment to you to send you away as I did my sons. But wait a bit. I will mark you in such a manner that you will never dare to show yourself again amongst honest tailors.'

So he seized a razor, soaped the head of the goat, and shaved it as smooth as the back of his hand, and then, as a blow from the yard measure would have been too great an honour, the tailor fetched a whip, and gave the goat two or three such cuts with it that the animal rushed out, and ran away with all her might.

The tailor, being now quite alone in the empty house, began to feel very miserable; he would have been glad to have his three sons home again, but he knew not where to find them. And so years passed away without any news of the wanderers.

We will leave the hasty tailor to himself, and see what his sons have been about all this while. The eldest had apprenticed himself to a joiner, and acquired the knowledge of the trade so quickly that his master was quite pleased with him. When the time came for him to travel about, as young tradesmen do abroad, to improve their knowledge of the different branches of their trade, his master gave him a table. It was very small, and not at all wonderful to look at, for the wood was of the most common sort; but it possessed one remarkable quality. If anyone addressed it, and said, 'Table, prepare for dinner,' immediately the table obeyed, and quickly covered itself with a snowy cloth, on which stood plates, knives, and forks, with dishes and tureens full of good things to eat, and the bright, sparkling red wine in glass goblets, which makes glad the heart.

The young apprentice thought that with such a table he could want nothing else in the world, and started on his journey without troubling himself to find an inn, either good or bad, or perhaps where he might be unable to get anything to eat at all. And so it happened to him, that travel where he might, whether through wood or meadow, he had only to take his table from his back, place it on the ground, and say, ' Table, prepare thyself,' and immediately it was ready, and covered with all that heart could wish.

After travelling for some time, it came into his mind that he would return to his father, whose anger must be appeased by this time, and with such a wonderful table as he possessed, he was sure to receive a kind welcome. He therefore turned his steps homewards, and towards evening came to an inn by the roadside, which seemed full of guests. The landlord asked him in, and invited him to sit and eat with him, as the house was so full.

The young joiner looked at the scanty fare which was placed before him, and said : ' Do you think I am going to be satisfied with such a supper as that ? Why, I could eat it all in two mouthfuls ! No, wait a bit ; you shall be *my* guest, landlord.'

The host laughed, and thought his visitor was making jokes with him ; but how great was his surprise when he saw him unfasten the little table from his back, place it on the floor of the room, and heard him say, ' Table, prepare thyself.' In a moment the table was covered with a most splendid supper, as good as, and even better than the landlord himself could have provided. The smell even reached the noses of the guests, and they came down to the landlord's room to see what feast he had there.

Then the joiner said : ' Dear friends, seat yourselves ; you are quite welcome.' And when they saw that he was really in earnest, they did not allow themselves to be asked twice, but took their places at the table and used their knives and forks bravely. Their surprise was increased when they observed that as soon as a dish was empty, it was instantly replaced by a full one.

The landlord stood in a corner watching the affair in silence, but he thought to himself, ' If I had such a cook as that, it would make the fortune of my house.'

The joiner and his guests spent great part of the night enjoying themselves, but at last they went to their rooms, and the young man carried his table with him, and placed it against the wall. But the envious, avaricious thoughts of the landlord gave him no rest all night, he did so long to possess this wonderful table. At last he remembered that he had in his lumber-room an old table just like it in appearance. So he rose and went very quietly to fetch it ; then, creeping into the young man's room, he changed the tables, and carried off his treasure, for the joiner slept soundly.

The next morning the youth, after paying for the night's expenses, packed up his table and went his way, quite unaware of the false conduct of the landlord.

About noon he reached home, and the old tailor welcomed him back with great joy. 'Well, my son,' he asked, 'and what have you been learning all this long time?'

'Father,' he replied, 'I am a cabinet-maker, and can work well at my trade.'

'It is a good business,' said the tailor; 'but how much have you gained by it?'

'The best thing I have gained,' he said, 'is that little table.'

The tailor examined it on all sides, and then said: 'That cannot certainly be of much value; why, it is old, and nearly worn out.'

'Ah,' said the son, 'its value is not in its looks. It has such a wonderful power, that when I stand it up, and say, "Table, cover thyself," it will instantly prepare a splendid dinner, with plates, knives, forks, glasses, and dishes of various kinds, and such rich wines as will rejoice your heart. You go and invite all our friends and relations to dinner, and you will soon discover what my table can do.'

The tailor hastened to follow his son's advice, and when the company were all assembled, expecting a splendid feast, the young man placed his table in the centre of the room, and said, 'Table, prepare thyself.' But the table did not move; it stood there as empty as any other table, for, of course, it had no magic power, and did not understand what was said to it.

When the poor young man discovered that he had been deceived, and his table changed for another, he stood before the company covered with shame, for he felt sure they would look upon him as a liar. His relations, however, only laughed at him, although they did grumble a little, for they had all to go home again to get something to eat and drink. After this disgrace and disappointment, the father went back to his needle and thimble, and the son was obliged to seek for work with a master joiner.

We will now return to the second son. He had apprenticed himself to a miller, and when his time was up his master said:

'You have worked so well while you have been with me, that I mean to make you a present of a wonderful donkey; but I must tell you that he can neither draw a cart nor carry a sack.'

'Then he will be of no use to me,' said the youth, 'if he is ever so wonderful.'

'Stay,' replied his master; 'I would not give him to you if he were not useful.'

'In what way can I make him of use, if I can neither ride nor drive him?' asked the youth.

'Why,' said his master, 'he can supply you with gold. You have only to lay a cloth on the ground and lead the donkey on it, and say "Bricklebrit," and immediately pieces of gold will drop from his mouth.'

'That is a wonderful power, indeed!' said the young man, and quickly expressed his readiness to accept such a present; and, thanking his master with his whole heart, he bade him farewell and started on his travels.

He soon discovered the value of his donkey; for if he wanted money he could lead him on the cloth, say 'Bricklebrit,' and a shower of gold would cover the ground, which he had only the trouble of picking up. So wherever he went he had the best of everything that money could buy, for his purse was always full.

After he had been for some time travelling in different countries, he began to think of home. 'For,' he said to himself, 'if I can return with plenty of money, my father will forget his anger, and receive me kindly.'

So he turned his steps towards his native village, and after a long journey came at last to the same inn at which his brother's table had been changed. He led his donkey by the bridle, and the landlord wished to take the animal to the stable; but the young man said, 'Don't trouble yourself, landlord. I always tie up old Grizzle myself, for I like to know where he is.'

The landlord wondered at first, and then he thought that a guest who tied up his donkey himself had not much to spend; but when the stranger put his hand in his pocket and, pulling out two gold pieces, said he should like a good supper prepared for him, the landlord opened his eyes wide, and ran to order the best he had in the house.

After dinner the young miller asked for his bill, and the avaricious host had charged such tremendously high prices that it amounted to an immense sum. The young man, after searching in his pockets, found he had not enough to pay. 'Wait a moment, landlord,' he said, 'I will soon fetch some more;' and he rose up hastily, carrying the tablecloth with him.

The landlord, who could not in the least understand these movements, was, however, very curious. So he slipped out and followed his guest, whom he saw enter the stable and fasten the door behind him. Creeping nearer, he found a hole formed by a knot in the wood of the door, through which he peeped. Then he saw the stranger stretch out the tablecloth on the ground, lead the donkey on it, and heard him cry 'Bricklebrit.' At the same moment the animal began to pour a shower of gold pieces from his mouth, which fell on the earth like rain. 'On my word!' cried the landlord, 'and all newly-coined ducats, too. Such a coiner is indeed a valuable purse of gold to possess.'

The young man paid his reckoning and went to bed; but the innkeeper slipped into the stable during the night, led away the gold coiner, and tied up another donkey in its place. Early the next morning the young man rose, led the donkey from the stable, and continued his journey, not in the least aware of the trick which had been played him. He reached home about noon, and received as kind a reception from his father as his brother had done.

'And what trade have you been learning, my son?' asked his father.

'I am a miller, dear father,' he replied.

' And what have you gained by your travels ?' was the next question. ' Only a donkey.'

' We have donkeys enough here already,' said his father. ' Now, if you had brought a goat, it might have been useful.'

' Yes,' said the youth, 'so it might, but not so valuable as the animal I have brought—it is not like a common animal. Why, father, it can coin money ! If I only say " Bricklebrit," quite a shower of gold will fall from its mouth on a cloth which I lay under it. Let me show you,' he continued. ' Send for all our relations to come here, and I will give them each money enough to make them rich people at once.'

' That is good news,' said the father ; ' and if this happens I shall be able to give up stitching, and lay my needle aside for ever.' And away he went to invite his relations.

As soon as they had assembled, the young miller cleared a place on the floor, and spread the cloth over it. Then he went out, brought the donkey into the room, and led it on the cloth. ' Now pay attention !' he exclaimed, at the same time saying 'Bricklebrit' more than once; but no gold pieces fell, and the animal stood quite still, evidently not under-standing what was said to him. The poor young miller's face fell. He knew now that his real donkey had been stolen, and this one placed in its stead. He could therefore only explain, and, with every apology, send his relations away as poor as they came. His father also was obliged to continue his sewing and cutting out, and the young man obtained work at a miller's close by.

The third brother had bound himself apprentice to a turner, and as this is a difficult trade to learn, he remained longer than his brothers had done. They wrote to him, however, and told him how unfortunate they had been, and how the innkeeper had stolen from them such valuable possessions.

At last the young brother was free to travel, and before he started on his journey, his master offered him as a farewell gift a bag, and said, ' I give you this as a reward for your industry and steady conduct, and there is a stick in the bag.'

' I can carry the bag on my shoulders,' replied the youth, ' and it will be of great service to me ; but what do I want with the stick ? It will only make it heavier.'

' I will tell you,' replied his master. ' If anyone attempts to ill-treat you, you have only to say, " Now, stick, jump out of the bag," and immediately it will spring upon the shoulders of your assailant and give him such a thrashing that he will not be able to move for days after-wards—unless you stop it—for the stick will go on till you say, " Now, into the bag again." '

The youth, on hearing this, thanked his master for his present, and started on his travels. He found it very useful ; for if anyone ventured to molest him, he had only to say, ' Out of the bag, stick,' and out it sprung upon the shoulders of the offender, beating him sharply and quickly, and, although he felt the pain, he could not see who struck him.

One evening the young turner arrived at the inn where the landlord had so cruelly robbed his brothers. He went in, and, laying his bag on the table, began to talk of the wonderful things he had seen and heard in the world during his travels. 'Indeed,' he said, 'some have found tables which could spread themselves with a great feast when ordered to do so, and others have possessed donkeys who could coin gold from their mouths, besides many other wonderful things which I need not describe; but they are nothing when compared with what I carry in my bag; even the wonderful things I have seen myself in the whole world are nothing to it.'

The landlord pricked up his ears. 'What! could nothing in the world be compared to the contents of that bag?' thought he. 'No doubt, then, it is full of precious stones, and I ought in fairness to have it with my other two prizes. All good things go in threes.'

When bed-time came, the young man stretched himself on a bench and placed the bag under his head for a pillow. The landlord waited in another room till he thought the visitor was fast asleep; then he approached softly, and tried in the most gentle manner to pull the bag from under the sleeper's head, intending to put another in its place. But the traveller was not asleep; he lay watching the innkeeper's movements, and, just as he had nearly succeeded in pulling away the bag, he cried out suddenly, 'Stick, stick, come out of your bag.' In a moment the stick was on the thief's shoulders, thumping away on his back, till the seams of his coat were ripped from top to bottom. In vain he cried for mercy; the louder he screamed, so much the stronger were the blows he received, till at last he fell to the ground quite exhausted.

Then the youth bade the stick desist for a time, and said to the innkeeper, 'It is useless for you to cry for mercy yet. Where are the table and the golden ass that you stole? You had better go and bring them here, for if they are not given up to me, we will begin the same performance over again.'

'Oh, no, no!' cried the landlord feebly; 'I will give everything up to you directly, if you will only make that little imp creep back into the bag.'

'I will do so,' said the young man, 'and I advise you to keep to your word, unless you wish for another thrashing. Into your bag, stick,' he continued, and the stick obeyed; so the innkeeper rested in peace till the next day, when, still smarting with the chastisement he had received, he gave up the stolen goods to the owner of the bag.

The youth arrived at his father's house with the table and the donkey, and was received very joyfully. The tailor asked him about his trade, and whether he had brought home anything worth having.

'I have a bag, and a stick in it, dear father,' he replied.

'That was scarcely worth the trouble of bringing,' said his father, 'for you can cut as many as you like in any wood.'

'Ah! but not like mine, father. Why, I have only to say, "Out of the bag, stick," and it will jump out and thrash anyone who attempts to interfere with me, till they cry for mercy. Through this stick I have recovered the table and the donkey which the thievish innkeeper stole from my brothers. Let them both be sent for, and then invite our relations to visit us; I can not only give them a splendid feast, but fill their pockets with gold also.'

The tailor was half afraid to believe all these promises, after having been already so deceived, yet he went out and invited his relations to assemble at his house. Then the young turner laid a cloth on the floor of the room, led the ass upon it, and said, ' Now, dear brother, speak to him.'

'Bricklebrit!' exclaimed the young miller. At the word down fell the gold pieces on the floor as thick as rain, and continued to fall till everyone had gathered up as much as he could possibly carry. (Would not you have liked to be there, dear reader?) After this the donkey was led away, and the youngest brother placed the table in the middle of the room, and said to his eldest brother, ' Dear brother, it is your turn to speak now.'

No sooner had the young cabinet-maker exclaimed, ' Table, prepare the dinner!' than the most splendid dishes appeared upon it, with the richest wines, and every necessary for a feast; and you may fancy how they all enjoyed themselves. Never before had there been such an entertainment in the tailor's house, and the whole company remained together till nearly morning, feasting and making merry. After this the tailor locked up in a drawer his needle and thread, his yard measure, and his goose, and lived the remainder of his days with his three sons.

But where is the goat all this while, whose deceit caused the tailor to turn his sons out of doors? I am just going to tell you. She was so ashamed of her bald head, that she ran and hid herself in a fox's hole till the hair should grow again.

When the fox came home at night, he saw a pair of great eyes shining upon him out of the darkness like fire. In a great fright, he rushed back and ran away as fast as he could. On the way he met a bear, who, seeing the fox in such terror, exclaimed:

' Whatever is the matter, brother? Why, you look quite scared.'

' Oh!' he answered, ' there is a dreadful animal at the bottom of my den, who glared at me with such fiery eyes.'

' We'll soon drive him out,' said the bear quite boldly, as he walked to the hole and looked in; but no sooner did he catch a glimpse of those burning eyes than his terror caused him to take to his heels as the fox had done, rather than have any skirmish with such a fierce animal.

On his way home, a bee met him, and, observing that his hair stood on end, she said to him, ' Why, Grandpapa Bear, what is the matter? You have such a woeful face. And where is all your fun gone?'

' It is all very fine talking about fun,' replied the bear; ' but if you had seen the horrid monster with glaring eyes in the fox's den, you wouldn't have much fun left in you; and the worst is, we can't get him out.'

Then said the bee, 'I pity you, bear, very much, and I know I am only a poor, weak little creature, that you great animals scarcely notice when we meet. Yet I believe I can help you in this matter.'

And away she flew into the fox-hole, and, perching herself on the goat's head, stung her so fiercely that she rushed out quite frantic, crying, 'Baa, baa!' and has never been heard of since.

LITTLE THUMB.

A POOR peasant was one evening sitting by his hearth in a homely cottage, doing nothing but stirring the fire, while his wife sat spinning near him. At last he said, 'How sad and sorrowful it is to think that we have no children! The house is so lonely and still, while in our neighbours' homes the voices of children make everything cheerful.'

'Ah, yes,' replied the wife, 'if I had only a little child not bigger than my thumb, how happy I should be! We should have something to love then with all our hearts.'

Now it so happened that after a few months the wife's wish was accomplished; for a little baby was born, perfect in all its limbs, but not taller than a thumb. 'Ah!' said she, 'I have got what I asked for, and, small as he is, we will love him dearly.' And, because of his size, they named him Little Thumb.

The parents brought up the child very carefully. They fed him on the most nourishing food, and spared no care and attention. Yet he did not increase in size, but remained always as small as on the day of his birth. But intellect shone from his eyes, and he soon showed by his cleverness and ability that he would succeed in whatever he undertook, notwithstanding his small size.

One day when his father was getting ready to go to the forest, and cut down some trees, he said aloud to himself, 'I wish I had some one who could drive the cart, for I want to go on first by myself.' 'Oh, father!' cried Little Thumb, 'I can do that easily. Leave the cart with me. I will take care to be in good time.' 'Oh, yes,' replied the father, laughing; 'it is very likely I should trust you to drive. Why, you are much too little even to lead the horse by the bridle.' 'Never mind how small I am,' said the boy; 'only you go as soon as you like, and, if mother will harness the horse, I will seat myself on his ear, and tell him which way to go.' 'Well,' replied his father, 'I'll try for once what you can do.' So he went off to the forest, and when the hour to start arrived, the mother harnessed the horse in the cart, and seated Little Thumb on his ear.

'Gee up!' shouted the little one into the ear, and the horse went on immediately.

LITTLE THUMB

THE CLEVER ELFE

And so he kept on, using the right words when he wanted the horse to turn to the right or the left, and crying out, 'Gee, woa,' so cleverly that the cart reached the wood as safely as if his master had driven him. Just as the horse and cart were turning into a path through the forest, two strange men came by. They stood still in astonishment, for they heard the voice of the driver, and saw the horse take the right turning, but no one was visible.

'Hallo!' cried one; 'there is something queer about this. Let us follow, and see where the cart stops.'

So they turned, and went after the cart till it came to the place where several trees had been cut down, and there it stopped.

As soon as Little Thumb saw his father, he cried out: 'See, father, I have brought the horse and cart. Can't I drive well? And now, please, lift me down.' The father held the horse by the bridle with one hand, and, lifting his little son from the horse's ear with the other, placed him on the ground. In a few moments the merry little fellow seated himself on a shaving and felt quite comfortable.

When the strangers caught sight of Little Thumb they were much astonished, and scarcely knew what to think. Presently one took the other aside, and said: 'That little chap would make our fortune if we could exhibit him in great towns for money. Suppose we buy him.' So they went up to the father, and said: 'Will you sell this little man to us? We will take the greatest care of him.' 'No,' he replied; 'he is my dear child, and I would not sell him for all the gold in the world.'

But Little Thumb, who had crept into the folds of his father's coat, heard what was said, and, climbing to his shoulder, whispered into his ear: 'Father, let me go with these men. I am sure to come back again.'

So the father gave him up for a large sum in gold.

'Where shall we put you?' they asked. 'Oh!' replied Little Thumb, 'place me on the brim of your hat. I can walk about there, and see where I am going, and I'll take care not to fall off.'

They very willingly did as he wished, and as soon as Little Thumb had taken leave of his father, the men walked away with him.

They travelled all day, but, when evening came on, Little Thumb was tired of sitting up there so long, and cried out: 'Stop, lift me down, please.' 'No,' said the man, 'stay where you are, little one. I don't mind your being there in the least. The birds often perch on my hat without causing me the slightest inconvenience. Stay where you are, my little man.' 'No, no!' cried Little Thumb; 'I know best what to do. I want you to lift me down directly.' Then the man took his hat off, and placed it on the ground by the roadside.

In a moment the little fellow sprang from the hat, ran through the hedge into a field, in and out between the clods of earth, then suddenly slipped into the nest of a field-mouse, which he had seen from his seat on the man's hat. 'Good-evening, gentlemen, you must go home without me now,' he shouted, laughing merrily. They were terribly annoyed, and tried to catch him by poking their sticks into the hole; but it was useless trouble, for Little Thumb crept to the farthest corner of the nest; and so night came on, and the men were obliged to go home in a great rage without him and with empty purses.

As soon as Little Thumb knew they were gone, he crept through the underground passages, and got out of his hole; but at first he stood still, and said to himself, ' It will not be safe for me to cross the field in the dark; most likely I shall break my limbs or my neck if I do.'

All at once he saw an empty snail-shell. ' Oh, how lucky!' he exclaimed; ' I can spend the night here in comfort.'

So he crept in; but just as he was dropping off to sleep, he heard voices and the footsteps of two men, who were planning a robbery at the rector's house.

' There is gold and silver in abundance there,' said one; ' but how are we going to get at it?'

' I will tell you,' shouted Little Thumb.

' What was that?' cried one of the thieves, in a fright. ' I am certain I heard some one speak.'

They stood still to listen, and Little Thumb spoke again: ' Take me with you; I will help you,' he said.

' Where are you, then?' asked one.

' Look for me on the ground, where my voice comes from,' said he.

On this they began to search, and at last found him; and one of the thieves lifted him up, and said, ' You little mite, how can you help us?'

' Try me,' cried Little Thumb. ' Why, I can creep between the iron bars of the window into the rector's room, and pass out to you whatever you want.'

' Oh, well,' they replied, ' you are too small to do us any harm, so we will take you with us and see what you can do.'

The thieves did not remember what a loud, shrill voice the little fellow had, so they carried him to the rectory. It did not take him long to creep through the bars into the room; but no sooner was he inside than he cried out as loud as he could, ' Will you have everything from the room you can get?'

' Hush!' cried the thieves, in a fright. ' Speak lower; you will wake everybody in the house.'

But Little Thumb, as if he did not understand, kept crying out as loud as ever, ' What shall I give you first; do you want all?'

In the room adjoining slept one of the servants, and the noise woke her; she sat up in bed to listen, and heard what Little Thumb said.

The thieves, who had run away in terror when Little Thumb cried out, ventured back when all was quiet, and said, ' Come now, this is not a time for joking; get us what we want, and pass it through the window to us.'

Then cried the little man, ' Oh, you want everything, do you? Now then, hold out your hands.'

The maid-servant heard this plainly enough; she jumped out of bed, and, being in the dark, stumbled against the door. On hearing the noise the thieves took to their heels, and ran as if wild hunters were behind them. The girl, who had gone to fetch a light, quickly returned, and determined to examine every part of the room. As soon as Little Thumb saw her coming, he slipped out of window and hid himself in a barn, so that she did not even see him. After a good search in every corner, and finding no one there, she went back to bed, and fancied that she must have been dreaming.

Little Thumb found a snug bed in a truss of hay, and made up his mind to sleep comfortably there till morning, and then return home to his parents; but there were other troubles for him to endure first. This is a world of trouble.

At daybreak the next morning the maid-servant rose and went out to give the cattle their fodder. Her first visit was to the hayloft, and unluckily the truss of hay nearest the opening was the one in which Little Thumb lay sleeping, and in pulling out an armful she carried him away with it. So soundly did he sleep, that he knew nothing of what had happened till he awoke and found himself in the mouth of a cow, who had taken him up with the hay.

'Oh, dear! I might as well be in a crushing-machine,' he cried, as soon as he found out where he was. But he had little time for reflection, as he shifted from side to side to avoid the teeth of the cow, and presently he slided downwards into her stomach.

'This is a room without any windows, at all events,' he exclaimed; 'the sun cannot shine here, and to light a candle is out of the question.'

Most certainly he had fallen into unpleasant quarters; and, worse than all, fresh quantities of hay kept coming in at the door, till there was scarcely room to move. At last he could bear it no longer, and cried out, 'No more hay, please—no more hay!'

Now, the maid, who was milking the cow, no sooner heard some one speak, than she recognised the voice which had disturbed her in the night. In great alarm she screamed out, threw down her stool, upset the milk-pail, and ran to her master, exclaiming, 'Oh, sir, the cow has been talking!'

'Nonsense, girl,' replied the rector; however, he went himself to the stable to find out what was going on. No sooner had he set his foot within the door, than Little Thumb cried out, 'No more hay; I don't want any more hay.'

Then was the rector himself alarmed, and thought that the cow was possessed by an evil spirit, so he ordered it to be killed. The poor animal was slaughtered and cut up, and its stomach, in which Little Thumb lay hidden, thrown on the dung-hill. It gave him no little trouble to work his way out; but he had scarcely succeeded in popping up his head, when a new misfortune presented itself. A hungry wolf rushed up, and seizing the cow's stomach, swallowed it at one gulp.

Little Thumb did not lose his courage; he called out to him from his uncomfortable lodgings, 'Friend wolf, I know where you can get such a beautiful dinner.'

'And where am I to find it?' he asked.

'Oh, at a house not far from here. I will tell you the way to get in. You must creep through a large hole into the kitchen, and there you will find the best of everything in the way of eating and drinking, and take which you like.'

Then he described to the wolf his father's house.

The wolf did not need to be told twice, and in a very short time had found his way into the kitchen, through the hole; and a famous feast he made of the good things he found in the larder.

But after he had supped to his heart's content, he wanted to creep out by the same hole, but he had eaten so much that it was impossible to squeeze himself through. This was just what Little Thumb had expected, and he began to jump about inside the wolf and make such a disturbance and noise that the wolf said, 'Will you be quiet?—you will wake all the people in the house.'

'All very fine,' said the little one, 'you have been eating and enjoying yourself, and now it is my turn;' and then he began to scream and shout with all his might, and at last woke his father and mother.

In great alarm they ran to the room and peeped through the keyhole. As soon as they caught sight of the wolf, the husband fetched a hatchet and the wife a scythe.

'You keep behind me,' said the man to his wife as they opened the door: 'if I don't kill him with the first blow, you must rush in and cut at him with the scythe.'

Little Thumb, on hearing his father's voice, cried out, 'Dear father, here I am, in the wolf's body.'

'Thank Heaven,' he cried, 'here's our child again come back to us,' and called to his wife not to use the scythe for fear of hurting their son. Then he raised the axe, and with one blow struck the wolf dead at his feet. A knife and a pair of scissors were soon found, and with this they ripped open the wolf's body and set Little Thumb free. 'Ah,' said the father, 'what trouble we have suffered about you!'

'Yes, father, I dare say; but I have been out in the world, and shut up in strange places, and I am very thankful to find myself again in the fresh air.'

'Where have you been, then?' he asked.

'Oh, father, I have been in a mouse-hole, I have been swallowed by a cow, and just now I was shut up in the body of a wolf; but I don't care, for I am safe at home at last.'

'And we will never sell you again, for all the riches in the world,' said his parents, as they kissed him and pressed him to their hearts, and called him their dear Little Thumb.

They gave him something to eat and drink, and the next day he had new clothes, for those he had on were quite old and worn out on his travels. Perhaps we shall have some more to tell of this Little Thumb by-and-by.

THE WEDDING OF WIDOW FOX.

ONCE upon a time there lived an old fox who, strange to say, had nine tails, which did not, however, make him either wiser or better. He had a snug home near a wood, yet he was not happy, for he was jealous of his wife, and thought she was not true. At last he could bear it no longer, and he determined to find out by a cunning stratagem, and foxes, as we know, are very cunning.

So one day he lay down on a bench, stretched himself out at full length, held his breath, and kept as motionless as a dead mouse. When Mrs. Fox came into the room she thought he was dead, so she locked herself in a room with her maid, a young cat, and was for a little while very unhappy; but presently Mrs. Fox began to feel hungry, so she sent her young maid, pussy, downstairs to cook something nice for supper.

The news of poor old fox's death soon spread in the neighbourhood, and even before the funeral several lovers came to sue for the hand of Widow Fox.

The young cat was busy frying sausages when she heard a knock at the door, so she went out to see who it could be, and there stood a young fox. 'Oh, it is you, Miss Kitty,' he said; 'are you asleep or awake, and what are you doing?'

'Oh,' she replied, 'I'm wide awake, never fear; and do you want to know what I'm doing? Well, I'm getting supper ready, and warming some beer with a piece of butter in it for my mistress. Will you come in, sir, and have supper with me?'

'Thank you, my dear,' said the fox; 'but what is Widow Fox doing?'

'Oh,' replied the cat, 'she does nothing but sit in her room all day and cry her eyes out, because Mr. Fox is dead.'

'Then go and tell her, youngster, that a young fox is here who wishes to become her suitor.'

'Very good, young sir,' said the cat, as she turned away to go to her mistress.

She tripped upstairs, and, opening the room door, exclaimed, 'Are you there, dear Mother Fox?'

'Yes, little puss ; what is the matter ?'

'There is a suitor come already.'

'Nonsense, child ; what is he like ?'

'Oh, he is a handsome young fox, with a bushy tail and such whiskers !'

'Ah !' sighed the widow ; 'but has he nine beautiful tails, like my poor old husband had ?'

'No,' answered the cat ; 'he has only one.'

'Then I won't have him !' cried the widow.

The young cat went down and gave the message to the suitor, and sent him away.   But soon after there came another knock at the door, and when the cat opened it there stood a fox, who wished to court Widow Fox ; he had two tails, but had no better success than the first.

And so they kept coming one after the other, each with one tail more, till at last a fox made his appearance who had nine tails, like the widow's dead husband.   The cat ran upstairs to tell the widow, who asked, 'Has the gentleman red stockings and a pointed nose ?'

'No,' answered the cat.

'Ah ! then he won't do for me,' she said.

By-and-by came a wolf, a dog, a stag, a bear, and even a lion ; but she would have nothing to do with any of them.   By this time the old fox began to think that he had made a mistake about his wife ; and, indeed, he was getting so hungry, that he could hardly lie still and sham being dead any longer.   He opened his eyes, and was just going to spring up and say, 'Dear old wife, I'm not dead at all !' when in came the cat.

'Oh, Madam Fox !' she exclaimed, 'there's a young gentleman fox downstairs, and he's so handsome.   He has nine tails, a scarlet tongue, red stockings, and a pointed nose, and he wants to become a suitor.'

'That is just the husband for me, pussy,' said Widow Fox ; 'and we'll have a such a splendid wedding ; but first, open all the doors and windows, and throw the old fox out and bury him.'

At these words the old fox could stand it no longer.   Up he started from his place under the bench, gave the whole party a good thrashing, turned the young cat and all the other servants and suitors out of the house, and Widow Fox after them.   So he had the place all to himself, and made a firm resolve never to die again, if he could help it.

THE SHOEMAKER AND THE ELVES.

A SHOEMAKER once became so very poor—not by any fault of his own—
that at last he had only just enough leather left to make one pair of
shoes. So one evening he cut out the shoes from this piece of leather,
and laid them in readiness to begin work early the next morning. He
had a clear conscience, so he lay down on his bed and slept in peace.

In the morning he rose and went to his work, but how surprised he
was to find the shoes lying on the table beautifully made and quite
finished. In his wonderment, he knew not what to say or even think.
He took the shoes in his hand, and examined them inside and out, but
there was not a false stitch in either of them; they were beautifully
made—indeed, quite a masterpiece of workmanship.

The shoemaker placed them in his window, and very soon after a
customer came in who was so pleased with them that he offered to
purchase them at more than the usual price. The shoemaker could,
therefore, with this money buy leather enough to make two pairs of
shoes. He cut out and prepared the leather in the evening, that he
might begin to work next morning early with fresh energy. But he had
no need to begin, for on entering his workshop there stood two pairs of
shoes beautifully finished and ready for sale. He had no lack of
customers now, for two came in and paid such a good price for the two
pairs that he had money enough to buy leather for four pairs. This he
cut into four pairs of shoes, which he laid ready for work the next
morning; but, on coming down, as usual, there were the shoes quite
finished and ready for sale. And so it went on—what he cut out at
night was always completed by the morning, till he had nothing to do
but buy the leather and cut out shoes. In fact, so much money came
pouring in, that the poor shoemaker soon overcame all his difficulties,
and became, as he had formerly been, a wealthy tradesman.

Now it happened one evening, not long before Christmas, that after
the shoemaker had been cutting out several pairs of shoes, instead of
going to bed, he said : ' My dear, I should like to find out who these
good creatures are who help us every night in this way. Suppose we
sit up and watch ?'

The wife was overjoyed at the thought; and leaving the candle burning, they hid themselves in a corner of the room behind their clothes,

which hung there, and watched with great attention. As the clock struck twelve, there came into the room two pretty little elves, without a morsel of clothes to cover them; and seating themselves on the shoemaker's table, they took up the leather which he had cut out, and set to work so nimbly, stitching, sewing, and hammering with such swiftness, that the shoemaker became quite bewildered, although he could not take his eyes off them. They did not stop work for a moment till all the shoes were completed and placed on the table; then they skipped off the table and vanished.

The next morning the wife said to her husband: 'These little men have made us so rich that we ought to do something for them in return for their kindness. I will tell you what I have thought of. I am sure they must be almost frozen, running about naked, as they do. So I mean to make them little shirts, trousers, waistcoats and coats; and if you will get a pair of little shoes ready for each of them, I will knit some stockings, and then these good little men will be comfortably clothed from head to foot.'

'I shall only be too glad to help you,' said the husband.

So they set to work busily, and in a very few days the clothes were quite ready. In the evening, instead of cutting out any more shoes, the man and woman laid out their gifts on the table in the workshop, and hid themselves, as before, in a corner, to see what the little men would do. At midnight they came bounding in, and jumped on the table, expecting to see the leather cut out for them to begin work. But nothing was to be seen excepting these beautiful little clothes. At first they were much surprised, but as soon as they understood that the shirts, and stockings, and coats were for themselves, they began to dress themselves in eager haste, and were so delighted that they danced and jumped about the room, over stools and chairs, singing:

'Happy little men are we,
Smartly dressed, as you can see,
No more shoemakers to be.'

And at last danced out of the room through the door, and never came back to work any more.

But after this, the shoemaker, who had been kind to those who helped him, prospered in everything he did, and neither he nor his wife ever wanted money again as long as they lived.

THE MAIDEN'S VISIT.

THERE was once a poor servant-maid whose neatness and industry made her quite a favourite with her master and mistress. She swept and dusted and kept the house in such beautiful order that everybody said she must have help from the fairies.

One morning, while she was busy at her work, she found a letter on the doorstep, and, not being able to read the address, she placed her broom in a corner and carried the letter to her master. She was greatly surprised to find that it was addressed to herself, and that it contained an invitation for her to attend at the christening of one of the pixie's children. She knew that these pixies were good fairies, who are always kind to industrious human beings, yet she was half afraid to go.

At last, after much talk with her master and mistress, who said that they could not dare to allow her to refuse, she consented to go. No sooner had she done so than three of these good little people arrived and carried her away with them to a mountain, where the mother and the baby lived.

As soon as they arrived, the mountain opened to receive them and closed behind them after they had entered. What a beautiful place it was, all glittering with pearls and precious stones, very tiny, but so wonderfully neat and elegant that it cannot be described! The little lady was lying on a beautiful bed made of shining ebony with pearl ornaments ; the counterpane was of embroidered gold, the baby's cradle of carved ivory, and the font of burnished gold.

The maiden was at first too much astonished to speak, but they were kind and encouraging to her, and she stood godmother to the baby. After the ceremony was over she asked the fairies to take her home, but they begged her to remain for three days, and she consented, for they were all so kind and loving to her that she knew not how to refuse. These three days were passed in the most delightful manner, but they came to an end, and then she requested to be taken home, so they stuffed her pockets full of money, and sent her home through the mountain entrance back into the world. When she reached her old home, being willing to begin work at once, she took the broom which stood in the corner and began to sweep.

Then a strange servant came and asked her what she was doing there, and a strange mistress sent for her, and she found to her surprise that, instead of being only three days absent as she thought, she had been seven years with the good people in the mountain ; her former master had died during the time, and the house had been let to strangers.

THE CHANGELING.

A POOR woman had a pretty little child who was carried away by the fairies, and a changeling with a thick head and staring eyes left in its place, who did nothing but eat and drink all he could get. In her trouble the mother went to a neighbour and asked her advice.

'I will tell you what to do,' she said; 'take the changeling into the kitchen, seat him on the hearth, make up a good fire, and then fill two egg-shells with water, and place them on the fire to boil. That, perhaps, will make him laugh, and if he laughs you will get rid of him.'

So the woman went home and did as her neighbour advised, and when the changeling saw her fill the egg-shells with water and set them on the fire, he said :

> 'Now I am as old
> As a mine of gold,
> Yet I never saw
> In my life before,
> Water in egg-shells boiled.'

And after this he began to laugh.

The moment he laughed, one of the men from the fairy mountain came into the kitchen ; he brought the woman's own child with him, seated him on the hearth, and carried away the changeling.

THE THREE SPINNING FAIRIES.

THERE was once a young girl who was so idle that she hated work, and let her mother say what she would, nothing would induce her to spin. At last she became so angry that she was determined to try what effect a good flogging would have.

But at the first blow the girl set up such a loud screaming that the queen, who was passing near, stopped to inquire what was the matter ; she even alighted from her carriage, and stepped into the house and said :

'Why are you beating your daughter ? her screams are heard by people in the street.'

Then the mother was ashamed to expose the laziness of her daughter, and said :

'I cannot get her away from the spinning-wheel, and we are too poor to provide her with flax.'

'Oh,' answered the queen, 'there is nothing more pleasant to me than the sound of spinning ; the humming of the wheel delights me. Give me your daughter ; I will take her to the castle. I have plenty of flax, and she shall spin as much as she likes.'

The mother was in her heart quite overjoyed at this proposal, and glad to allow the queen to take the maiden away with her. As soon as they arrived at the castle, the queen took the idle girl into three rooms that were all quite full of beautiful flax.

'Spin me this flax,' she said, 'and as soon as it is finished come to me, and I will give you my eldest son for your husband. Although you may be poor, I do not care for that ; your unwearied industry is sufficient dowry.'

The maiden was in a terrible fright when she heard this, for she knew she could never spin all that flax if she worked every day from morning till night for a hundred years; and as soon as she was alone she began to cry. At the end of three days, when the queen came to see her, she had not raised her hand to begin her task. The queen was quite surprised, but the maiden excused herself by saying that she felt so unhappy at leaving her mother's home that she knew not how to begin.

The queen accepted the excuse, but as she left the room she said in a pointed manner, ' You had better begin to-morrow morning to work.'

When the young girl found herself alone, and knew that she was quite unable even to begin this task, she rose in her trouble and walked to the window. As she stood looking out mournfully, she saw three strange-looking women coming towards her. One had a broad flat foot, the second such a large under-lip that it hung over the chin, and the third had an enormous thumb.

These three women placed themselves before the window, looked up at the maiden, and asked her what was the matter. She was in such trouble that she could not help telling them all about it, and they immediately offered to assist her.

' You must first promise,' said one, ' that we shall be invited to your wedding, and allowed to sit at your table, and you must agree to call us your cousins, without being ashamed of us. If you will do this, we will come in and spin your flax in a very short time.'

' I promise, with all my heart,' said the girl. ' So come and set to work at once.'

She opened the window as she spoke, and let the three strange-looking women into the first flax-chamber, where they seated themselves and quickly commenced spinning.

The first turned the wheel and drew out the thread, another moistened it, while the third twisted it with her finger on the table, and, as she twisted, there fell on the ground skein after skein of the finest spun flax.

The queen came every day, as usual, to see how the work was getting on; but the maiden took care to hide the three spinners, and showed her each time so many skeins of the finest thread that she went away quite astonished.

When the first room was empty they went to the second, and at last to the third, till all the flax was spun into beautiful thread, and the maiden's task was finished.

Then the three women bade her farewell, saying, ' Don't forget what you have promised, for it will bring you good fortune.'

When the queen came and saw the empty rooms, and the quantity of skeins of thread, she was delighted, and fixed the day on which the marriage was to take place.

The prince, who had seen the maiden, and heard how clever and industrious she was, felt overjoyed at the prospect of such a wife, and soon learned to love her dearly. Just before the wedding-day he asked his bride if she wished for any favour to be granted her.

'Yes,' she replied. 'I have three cousins who have been very kind

'FROM TURNING THE SPINNING-WHEEL,' SHE REPLIED.

to me, and I should not like to forget them in the midst of my good fortune. Will you permit me to invite them to the wedding, and to give them seats at our table?'

The queen and the prince both replied that they could have no reason to object. So the three strange women were invited. On the wedding-day they came in great pomp and beautifully dressed; but this could not conceal their defects.

The bride give them a most kind reception, saying, 'Welcome, dear cousins.'

But the bridegroom was surprised, and he exclaimed, 'Ah! however came you to have such ugly acquaintances? Then he went up to them, and addressing the first, he asked, 'How did it happen that you have such a broad foot?'

'From turning the spinning-wheel,' she replied.

He turned away, and inquired of the second the cause of her over-hanging lip.

'From moistening the thread with my lips,' was the reply.

'And your thumb,' he asked the third; 'what makes it such a size?'

'From drawing and twisting the thread,' she answered.

'Then,' said the bridegroom, 'if these are the consequences of turning the spinning-wheel, my beautiful bride shall never touch it again with her hands or feet, or the thread with her lips, as long as she lives.'

So the young maiden was set free from the work she disliked, because she remembered her promise, and was not ashamed to own those who had helped her in her trouble.

THE ROBBER BRIDEGROOM.

A MILLER once had a beautiful daughter, and as soon as she was grown up, his great wish was to see her well married and happy. So he decided that if a suitable wooer came whom his daughter could love, he would give his consent.

Not long after a suitor came for his daughter's hand. He appeared to be very rich, and the miller could find nothing to say against him; so he promised him his daughter. But the maiden did not love this suitor as a bride should love her bridegroom. She had no confidence in him, and not only the sight, but the very thought of him filled her heart with horror.

One day he said to her, 'You are my affianced bride, but you have never once paid me a visit.'

Then said the maiden, 'I don't know where your house is.'

But when he told her he lived far down in the depths of the forest, she made many excuses, and said she should never find the way.

'Yes you will,' he said; 'and you must come next Sunday. I expect company on that day; and to enable you to find your way through the wood to my house, I will strew ashes along the pathway.'

So on Sunday the young bride-elect, who had a little curiosity about

her future husband's home, determined to try and find the road through
the wood; but so fearful was she of not being able to retrace her steps,
that she filled her pockets full of peas and linseed to drop on the path.
And as she walked along the road which was strewed with ashes, she
dropped peas right and left on the ground at every step. And thus she
walked for hours in the shade of the trees, till she came to the darkest
part of the forest, and there she found a solitary house, which did not
please her at all—it looked gloomy, and not at all home-like. The
door was open, so she walked in; but there was no one to be seen, and
the deepest silence reigned. Suddenly a voice cried out:

> 'Return, return, thou youthful bride!
> A murderers' house it is inside.'

The maiden glanced up and saw that the voice came from a bird,
whose cage hung on the wall. Again it cried:

> 'Return, thou youthful bride, return!
> This is a murderers' house—return!'

Yet still her curiosity led her on from room to room till she had been
all over the house, which was quite empty—not a single human being
could be seen. At last she found, in a cellar or cave behind the house,
a very old woman seated, who nodded at her.

'Can you tell me,' asked the maiden, 'if my bridegroom resides
here?'

'Alas, poor child,' answered the old woman, 'how did you find your
way here? This is a robbers' den. You imagine that you are a bride,
and that your wedding will soon take place, but there will be no marriage
for you but with death. Do you see that large kettle? Well, when
once the robber gets you in his power, he will cut you in pieces without
mercy, and I shall have to fill it with water and boil you in it, for he is
a man and woman eater. Unless I take pity on you and save you now,
you will be lost.'

So the old woman hid the young girl behind a large cask, where no
one could see her.

'Keep as still as a mouse,' she said to her; 'if you move or stir in
the slightest, I know not what will happen to you, but in the night,
while the robbers sleep, we will make our escape; I have long waited
for an opportunity of doing so.'

Scarcely had she finished speaking when the whole gang of robbers
returned home. They brought in another young girl whom they had
decoyed in their toils, and they were deaf to her cries and lamentations.
They gave her wine to drink, three glasses full, one of white, one of red,
and one golden, which caused her to swoon away. Then they tore off
her clothes, laid her on a table, cut up her beautiful form into pieces,
and strewed salt over them. The poor bride behind the cask trembled
with horror at what she saw, for she knew now to what a fate she had
been destined by her pretended bridegroom. Presently one of the robbers

noticed on the finger of the dead maiden a gold ring, and as he could not get the ring off, he took a hatchet and chopped off the finger. But as he did so the finger sprung up in the air, over the cask behind which the bride was hidden and fell into her lap! The robber took a light and searched for it everywhere, but could not find it. Then said one of them, ' Have you looked behind the cask?'

' Nonsense,' cried the old woman, ' come to supper, you can look for it in the morning; the finger cannot run away.'

' The old woman is right,' said their chief; ' leave off searching, and come to supper.'

As the old woman waited upon them, she was able to pour a sleeping draught into the wine, and they were soon lying fast asleep on the ground and snoring loudly.

As soon as the maiden heard this she came out from behind the cask, but when she saw that she had to step over the sleepers, who lay stretched on the ground, she was in dreadful terror lest she should awaken them. But God helped her, so that she happily escaped without arousing one of them. The old woman stepped over with her, opened the doors, and they both hastened away as quickly as they could from the murderers' den. The strewed ashes had been scattered away by the wind, but the peas and the linseed had germinated, and little plants were springing up all over the pathway, so that in the moonlight they could easily find their way.

They walked all night, and arrived next morning at the mill. And the maiden immediately described to her father all the horrors she had seen in the bridegroom's dreadful home. The miller made no movement in the matter until the day which had been fixed for the wedding arrived. He, however, invited all his relations and acquaintances to be present, so that when the bridegroom appeared, he found a large company assembled to meet him.

After dinner, as they sat at the table, the miller requested one or two of the guests to relate any wonderful circumstance which had occurred to them on their travels. After one or two interesting incidents had been told, the bridegroom said to the bride, who sat in silence, ' Now, my love, have you nothing to relate? Do tell us something.'

' I will tell you a strange dream, if you like,' she replied.

' Oh, yes,' they all cried; ' let us have it.'

' It was a horrible dream,' she said. ' But still I will describe it. I dreamt that I went through a forest for a long way, till at last I came to a lonely house in the densest and darkest part; there was not a single human being in sight, but on the wall outside hung a cage with a bird in, and the bird cried:

> "Return, return, thou youthful bride!
> This is a murderers' den."

And the bird kept repeating these words; yet I would not believe it, but went on through all the rooms, which were empty and gloomy. At last I came to a cellar, where sat a very old woman, who shook her head mournfully when she saw me. I asked her if my bridegroom dwelt in that house, and she answered, "Alas, poor child! he does dwell here, but this is a murderers' den."'

And then she went on to relate how the old woman had hidden her behind a cask, and the horrors she had seen. At last, after describing the manner in which one of the robbers had chopped off the poor girl's finger because he could not get at the ring, she said: 'The finger with the ring flew up as he chopped, and fell behind the cask right into my lap. And there is the finger and the ring.'

At these words she placed it on the table, rose up, and pointed it out to everyone present. The robber bridegroom, who during this description had been gradually becoming pale as death, sprung up and would have fled, but the guests held him fast and took him at once before the justices. And very soon the whole gang were arrested, and sentence of death passed upon them for their shameful deeds.

THE TROUBLESOME VISITORS.

A COCK and hen determined one day to go for a little trip into the country, to visit their old master, Dr. Korbes; so they built a very pretty carriage, which had four red wheels, and harnessed to it four mice. Then they seated themselves in it and drove away together.

They had not travelled far when they met a cat, who said to them, 'Where are you going?'

The hen replied, 'We are going to see Dr. Korbes, our old master.'

'Take me with you,' said the cat.

'With all my heart,' she replied; 'but you must get up behind, for if you sit in front you will fall:

> 'Eight of us can ride
> Outside and inside.
> Little red wheels roll,
> Little white mice pull,
> Till we reach Dr. Korbes' house.'

Then there came by a millstone, then an egg, after that a duck, and a darning-needle, and at last a pin, who were allowed seats in the carriage, and they all drove away together. When they arrived at Dr. Korbes' house he was not at home, but they made themselves quite comfortable. The mice drew the little carriage into the barn, the cock and hen flew to a perch, the cat seated herself in the fireplace, the duck waddled to the spring, while the egg rolled itself up in the towel. The darning-needle stuck point upwards in the chair cushion, and the pin, jumping on the bed, fixed itself in the pillow, while the millstone placed itself over the entrance door.

Dr. Korbes came home in a short time after this, and, as his servant was out, he went into the kitchen to light the fire; but while attempting to do this, the cat threw a quantity of ashes into his face. He ran quickly to the spring to wash them, and the duck, who was swimming about, splashed so much water over him that he was obliged to run into the house for his towel; but as he took it up the egg rolled over his face, broke, and, filling his eyes, stuck them together like glue. After this he wished to rest, but as he seated himself in his armchair the darning-needle ran into him. Up he jumped in a rage and threw himself on his bed, but this was quite as bad; for no sooner did he lay his head on the pillow than the pin scratched his face. At this last attack he cried out in great trouble, and declared that the things must all have been bewitched, and that he would run away; but as he opened the front door to go out, down fell the millstone on his head and killed him. This Dr. Korbes must really have been a very wicked, or a very injured man.

THE WONDERFUL GLASS.

A MAN once had so many children that all his friends had been asked to become sponsors, so when another child was born he had no one to ask, and knew not what to do.

One night, when he had lain himself down to sleep in great trouble, he had a wonderful dream. He dreamed that a voice said to him, ' Go out early to-morrow morning, and the first person you meet ask him to be godfather.' On awaking he determined to follow the advice given in his dream, and, dressing himself quickly, he went out. Near his door he met a man, and immediately asked him to be sponsor for his child.

The stranger, before giving his consent, presented the man with a glass, and said, ' This is a most wonderful glass. The water with which you fill it has the power of curing sick persons; you have only to observe where death stands. If he stands by the head of the sick person, then give him the water, and he will be soon well; but if he stands by the feet all your trouble will be useless—the sick person must die.'

So the stranger became sponsor for his child, and gave to the father the wonderful goblet, which endowed the water he put into it with such healing qualities. Besides this, he could always tell whether the sick person would recover or not, and could therefore speak confidently about curing him; by this he made a great deal of money, and his fame spread far and wide. Even the king sent for him when one of his children was ill; but as the wonderful doctor entered, he saw death standing at the head of the bed, and knew that the child would recover after drinking the water in the magic glass : and so he did. The second time he was sent for the same occurred ; but on his third visit the doctor saw death seated at the foot of the bed, and he told the parents that the child must die. After a while this doctor became curious, and thought he should like to see where his child's godfather, who had given him such a valuable present, lived, and tell him how he was getting on. But when he reached the house the domestic arrangements quite startled him. On the first step a mop and a broom were quarrelling together and fighting furiously.

'Where shall I find the master of this house?' he asked.

'A step higher,' answered the broom.

But when he arrived on the second step, he saw a number of dead fingers lying together, and he inquired again, ' Where is the master?'

'A step higher,' replied one of the fingers.

On the third step lay a heap of human heads, who directed him to go a step higher. On the fourth step he saw a fish frizzling in the pan, and cooking himself. He spoke to the man and told him to go a step higher. On he went, and at last, on the fifth step, he came upon the door of a room, and peeping through the key-hole, saw the godfather, and, to his surprise, he had large horns ; but as soon as he opened the door and went in, the strange man with the horns rushed away suddenly, laid himself on the bed, and drew the clothes over him. Then said the man, ' What is the meaning of this strange management in your house, good sir ? On the steps I met with all sorts of strange things, and was told to go up higher ; and when I came to the door of this room, I peeped through the key-hole and saw you with a pair of horns on your head.'

' That is not true,' cried the pretended godfather, in such a terrible voice that the man, in a fright, turned to run away; but no one knows what has become of him, for he has never been heard of since.

OLD SULTAN AND HIS FRIENDS.

A COUNTRYMAN once had a faithful hound, who was called Sultan, and who had grown old in his service. He had lost all his teeth, and could no longer follow with the pack.

One day the countryman stood before the door with his wife, and said to her, ' Old Sultan is no longer of any use. I shall shoot him to-morrow.'

But Sultan's mistress, who had great pity for the faithful animal, exclaimed :

' How can you destroy him, after he has served us so many years,

OLD SULTAN AND HIS FRIENDS

THE SLEEPING BEAUTY IN THE WOOD

and lived with us so long? I am sure we could spare him some allowance for his old age.'

'No, no,' replied her husband. 'That is not just reasoning. He has not a tooth in his head, and is of no further use in keeping away the thieves; for they are not afraid of him, so he may as well go. If he has served us well, so has he also been well fed, and could eat as much as he wanted.'

The poor dog, who was lying stretched out in the sun, not very far off, heard all that was said, and it made him very sad to know that the morrow would be the last day of his life.

Now, Sultan had a very good friend, a wolf, who lived near; so in the evening he slipped out into the forest to visit him, and complained to him of the fate which awaited him.

'Listen, grandfather,' said the wolf; 'take courage. I will help you out of your trouble. I have thought of something. To-morrow morning early your master and his wife are going out into the fields haymaking, and they will take their little child with them. While they are at work they will lay the child under the hedge in the shadow. You lay yourself by him as if you meant to watch him. I will wait till all is quiet, and then I will run out of the wood, seize the child, and carry it away. Then you must spring after me with the greatest zeal, as you used to do in your hunting days. I will let the child fall, and you shall bring it back to its parents again, and they will believe that you have saved it from me, and will be the more thankful because they intended to kill you. Instead of that you will be in full favour, and nothing will ever cause them to give you up.'

The dog followed this advice, and as it had been planned, so it was accomplished. The father screamed as he saw the wolf run away with his child through the wood; but when poor old Sultan brought it back, his joy and gratitude knew no bounds. He stroked and patted the old dog, saying, 'Nothing shall ever hurt you now, you dear old dog, and you shall never want for food and shelter as long as you live.'

To his wife he said, 'Go home at once, wife, and cook some bread and milk for poor old Sultan. It is soft, and will not require strong teeth to bite it. And bring the pillow from my armchair; he shall have it for a bed.'

And so from this time old Sultan had every comfort and contentment that his heart could wish. By-and-by Sultan went to pay the wolf a visit, and told him joyfully of his good-fortune.

'Grandfather,' he said slily, 'I suppose now you will shut your eyes and not see if I carry away a fat sheep from your master's flock? It is very hard to get food nowadays.'

'I can't help that,' said the dog. 'My master trusts in me, and I dare not allow you to touch his property.'

The wolf, however, did not believe the dog spoke in earnest; so he came in the night, slipped into the fold, and would have carried off a sheep, if Sultan had not forewarned his master of the wolf's intention.

He watched for him, and gave him a good combing with the flail, till he was almost bare of hair.

So he was obliged to rush away, crying out, however, to the dog, ' Only wait a little, you false friend ; you shall pay for this !'

The next morning the wolf sent a challenge to the dog by his friend the wild boar, who had promised to stand second. They appointed to meet in the wood ; and poor old Sultan had no one to stand by him but a cat who had only three legs. Puss had, however, plenty of spirit ; although she hobbled along on her three legs with great pain, yet her tail stood erect as if she cared for no one in the world. The wolf and the wild boar were already on the appointed spot ; but when they saw their adversaries approaching, they thought that the cat's tail was a sabre ; and that each time puss humped her back as she hopped it must be a large stone, which Sultan intended to throw at them. They were both so frightened that the wild boar crept in among the dried leaves, and the wolf sprang up a tree.

The dog and the cat were very much surprised when they reached the place to find no one there ; but the cat espied something on the ground which she took for a mouse.

Now the wild boar, when he crept among the dried leaves to hide himself, left his gray ears sticking out ; and when the cat began to smell about, she saw the ears move, and, taking one of them for a mouse, sprang forward, caught the ear in her teeth, and bit it in half. The wild boar started up with a terrible scream, exclaiming, 'There is the real offender, up in the tree,' and ran away as fast as he could. The dog and the cat looked up, and saw the wolf, who was so ashamed of his cowardice, and so angry with his pretended friend who had betrayed him, that he came down from the tree, and made friends with the cat and the dog from that moment.

THE SLEEPING BEAUTY IN THE WOOD.

ONCE upon a time there lived a king and queen who lamented every day because they had no children. One day, however, when the queen was in her bath, a frog crept out of the water, and, standing before her, croaked, and said, ' Thy wish will be accomplished before the end of the year. Thou shalt have a little daughter !'

And so it happened as the frog had prophesied. The queen had a little child, who was so beautiful that the king could hardly contain himself for joy, and determined to give a great entertainment in honour of the event. He not only invited his relations, friends and acquaintance, but also the wise women, who could endow his daughter with fairy gifts. There were thirteen of these wise women ; but only twelve were invited, and twelve golden plates were placed for them.

The feast was conducted with great pomp, and towards the end of it the wise women declared their readiness to endow the king's little daughter with their wonderful gifts. The first gave her virtue, the second beauty, the third riches, and so to the eleventh, with all that can be wished for in the world.

Before the twelfth could speak, in walked the thirteenth. She was in a terrible rage at not having been invited; and, without saluting or noticing anyone, cried with a loud voice, ' In her fifteenth year the king's daughter shall prick her finger with a spindle, and fall down dead !' and, without another word, she turned round and left the hall.

Everyone felt alarmed at this prophecy; but the twelfth, who had not yet spoken, stepped forward. She could not alter the wicked decree, but she could soften and alleviate it. So she said, ' The king's daughter shall not die, but a deep sleep shall fall upon her, in which she shall remain for a hundred years.'

The little child, who was endowed with such wonderful gifts, grew up to be the delight of her parents. But, as she approached her fifteenth year, the king became very unhappy, and issued a decree that all the spindles in his kingdom should be burnt.

In every other respect, the prophecies of the good fairies were fulfilled; for the young princess was so beautiful, so amiable, and so clever, that those who saw her could not help loving her; but this only made her parents more anxious, especially when they were absent from the castle.

However, as the king felt certain that his commands about spindles had been obeyed, her parents would sometimes, but not often, leave her in the castle with the servants.

One day, when she had been left in this way, the young princess took a fancy into her head that she would explore the castle. So she walked from room to room, through galleries and passages, till she came at last to an old tower.

She ascended the narrow, winding staircase, till at length she came to a little door. In the lock was stuck a rusty key, and as she turned it the door sprang open, and there, in a small room, sat an old woman spinning flax.

' Good-morning, old lady,' said the princess ; ' what are you doing?'

' I am spinning,' she replied, nodding her head.

' And what is this funny thing that jumps about so ?' the princess asked, at the same time taking the spindle in her hand and trying to spin. Scarcely had she given the wheel one turn, when the bad fairy's prophecy was fulfilled—the point of the spindle stuck into her finger. At the same moment the king's daughter fell back on a bed which stood near, while a deep sleep came upon her, and not only on the princess, but on the whole of the inhabitants of the castle, the king and queen, who had returned and were in the state chamber, and all their house-hold with them.

This deep sleep fell also on the horses in the stable, the dogs in the outer court, the pigeons on the roof, the flies on the wall—yes, and even the fire that flickered on the hearth became still and slept; the meat roasting before the fire stayed its frizzing; the cook in the kitchen, who was just going to box the ears of the scullion, let his hand drop and sank to sleep.

Outside the wind lay calmly at rest, and upon the trees which surrounded the castle not a leaf stirred. In a few hours there sprung up around the castle a hedge of thorns, which year after year grew higher and higher, till at last nothing could be seen of the castle above it, not even the roof, nor the flag on the tower.

And so the years went by, and a report spread over the country of the 'sleeping beauty,' as the king's daughter was called. And from time to time the sons of kings came to the spot, and tried to penetrate through the protecting hedge of thorns. But many found it impossible, and gave up the attempt; added to this, the thorns had hands, with which they seized the young men who persisted, and held them so fast that they could not free themselves, and died a miserable death.

Many more years passed away, and at length another prince came to that part of the country and heard an old man relate the story of the thorn-surrounded castle, in which the wonderful sleeping beauty, the king's daughter, lay, and who had already slept for nearly a hundred years, and with her the king and queen and the whole household.

The prince, when he heard his grandfather talk of the fate of former princes who had tried to force their way through the hedge of thorns, and how they were caught by the bushes, and died a miserable death, would say, 'It matters not to me, I have no fear; I am determined to discover this beautiful Briar Rose.' The good old man gave up attempting to dissuade the wilful prince, and said no more.

Just at this time the hundred years had nearly come to a close, and the day at last arrived for Briar Rose to be awaked from her long sleep. On this very day the prince started on his enterprise, and on reaching the hedge of thorns, what was his surprise to find it covered with large, delicately-beautiful flowers, which separated from each other to allow him to pass, and closed again behind him like a wall. And so without difficulty he reached the court of the castle.

Here he saw a dappled gray horse and a stag-hound, sleeping together. On the roof sat the pigeons, with their heads tucked under their wings.

He found the same silence in the castle; the cook, the kitchen-maid, and even the flies on the wall, still slept; and in the saloon he found the king and queen sleeping on their thrones, surrounded by the courtiers and the household, all slumbering peacefully. So deep was the stillness, that he could hear his own breathing; however, he wandered on from room to room, till he reached the tower where the beautiful princess lay asleep. He stood for awhile transfixed with surprise at the beauty of the sleeping maiden, which the hundred years had not

THE SLEEPING BEAUTY IN THE WOOD

injured or even changed. So strong was the fascination which held him, that he could not resist stooping to kiss her. At the touch Briar Rose opened her eyes and awoke, and with her the whole household.

At first they all stared at each other with wide open eyes, but not for long; very soon they resumed the employment in which they had been engaged when the enchantment fell upon them. The horse rose and shook himself; the dog sprung up and barked; the pigeons drew out their heads from behind their wings, plumed their feathers, and flew to the field; even the fire aroused itself, and its flickering flame soon burned into a steady blaze, to roast the dinner; and more than all this, the thorn hedge round the castle sunk down and disappeared.

The king and queen, who now remembered the wicked fairy's prophecy, and how it had been limited to a sleep of a hundred years instead of death, were overjoyed, and so thankful to the prince for disenchanting them, that they readily consented when he asked that the beautiful Briar Rose should be his wife. But when those around came to visit the restored and awakened household, they were much amused and surprised at the strange dresses worn by the awakened sleepers. They were equally astonished at the dress of the visitors, and no wonder, for in this hundred years the fashions had changed. The prince, however, did not care for this; he loved the princess for herself and not for her dress, and the marriage was celebrated in a very short time, with great splendour.

BIRDIE AND HER FRIEND.

A FORESTER went out one day shooting; he had not gone far into the wood when he heard, as he thought, the cry of a child. He turned his steps instantly towards the sound, and at length came to a high tree, on one of the branches of which sat a little child. A mother, some short time before, had seated herself under the tree with the child in her lap, and fallen asleep.

A bird of prey, seeing the child, seized it in its beak and carried it away; but hearing the sound of the sportsman's gun, the bird let the child fall, its clothes caught in the branches of a high tree, and there it hung, crying till the forester came by.

The mother, on awaking and missing her child, rushed away in great agony to find it, so that the poor little thing would have been left alone in the world to die had not the sportsman made his appearance.

'Poor little creature!' he said to himself, as he climbed up the tree and brought the child down, 'I will take it home with me, and it shall be brought up with my own little Lena.'

He kept his word, and the little foundling grew up with the forester's little daughter, till they loved each other so dearly that they were always unhappy when separated, even for a short time. The forester had named the child 'Birdie,' because she had been carried away by the bird; and Lena and Birdie were for several years happy little children together.

But the forester had an old cook, who was not fond of children, and she wanted to get rid of Birdie, who she thought was an intruder.

One evening Lena saw the woman take two buckets to the well, and carry them backwards and forwards more than twenty times.

'What are you going to do with all that water?' asked the child.

'If you will promise not to say a word, I will tell you,' replied the woman.

'I will never tell anyone,' she said.

'Oh, very well, then, look here. To-morrow morning, early, I mean to put all this water into a kettle on the fire, and when it boils I shall throw Birdie in and cook her for dinner.'

Away went poor Lena, in great distress, to find Birdie.

'If you will never forsake me, I will never forsake you,' said Lena.

'Then,' said Birdie, 'I will never, never leave you, Lena.'

'Well, then,' she replied, 'I am going away, and you must go with me, for old cook says she will get up early to-morrow morning, and boil a lot of water to cook you in, while my father is out hunting. If you stay with me, I can save you. So you must never leave me.'

'No, never, never!' said Birdie.

So the children lay awake till dawn, and then they got up and ran away so quickly that by the time the wicked old witch got up to prepare the water, they were far out of her reach.

She lit her fire, and as soon as the water boiled went into the sleeping-room to fetch poor little Birdie and throw her in. But when she came to the bed and found it empty, she was very much frightened to find both the children gone, and said to herself, 'What will the forester say when he comes home if the children are not here? I must go downstairs as fast as I can and send some one to catch them.' Down she went, and sent three of the farm servants to run after the children and bring them back.

The children, who were sitting among the trees in the wood, saw them coming from a distance.

'I will never forsake you, Birdie,' said Lena quickly. 'Will you forsake me?'

'Never, never!' was the reply.

'Then,' cried Lena, 'you shall be turned into a rose-bush, and I will be one of the roses.'

The three servants came up to the place where the old witch had told them to look; but nothing was to be seen but a rose-tree and a rose.

'There are no children here,' they said.

So they went back and told the cook that they had found only roses and bushes, but not a sign of the children.

The old woman scolded them well when they told her this, and said, ' You stupid fools! you should have cut off the stem of the rose-bush, and plucked one of the roses and brought them home with you as quick as possible. You must just go again a second time.'

Lena saw them coming, and she changed herself and Birdie so quickly that when the three servants arrived at the spot to which the old woman had sent them, they found only a little church with a steeple—Birdie was the church and Lena the steeple.

Then the men said one to another, ' What was the use of our coming here? We may as well go home.'

But how the old woman did scold.

' You fools!' she said, ' you should have brought the church and the steeple here. However, I will go myself this time.'

So the wicked old woman started off to find the children, taking the three servants with her.

When they saw the three servants coming in the distance, and the old woman waddling behind, Lena said, ' Birdie, we will never forsake each other.'

' No, no! never, never!' replied the little foundling.

' Then you shall be changed into a pond, and I will be a duck swimming upon it.'

The old woman drew near, and as soon as she saw the pond she laid herself down by it, and, leaning over, intended to drink it all up. But the duck was too quick for her. She seized the head of the old woman with her beak, and drew it under the water, and held it there till the old witch was drowned.

Then the two children resumed their proper shape, and went home with the three servants, all of them happy and delighted to think that they had got rid of such a wicked old woman. The forester was full of joy in his home with the children near the wood; and if they are not dead they all live there still.

KING ROUGHBEARD.

A KING once had a daughter who was beautiful beyond measure, but so haughty and proud that she considered no man good enough to marry her. She pretended to accept one after another the suitors who approached her, and then treated them with mockery and scorn. At last her father, the king, made a great feast, and invited all the most illustrious men for miles round to be present. All of them were introduced to the proud young princess by their rank. First, the king of a neighbouring country, then a duke, then a prince, and, after these, nobles of high position.

But the princess, when asked to choose for herself, had some fault to find with each. One was too fat, another too thin, a third was short and thick, and a fourth had a face as pale as a ghost; and so on, till they all went away quite offended, except one son of the king of a neighbouring country—the highest of them all. Now, the princess in her heart liked this one of her suitors best, but she made no difference in her manner to him. The young prince had a very good-looking face, but his chin was a little crooked, and he had a rough beard.

'Oh!' said the young princess, when she saw he still waited after the others were gone, 'what a chin he has, to be sure; just like a bird's beak! I shall call him King Roughbeard;' and she laughed heartily as she spoke.

The young prince turned away without a word, to show he was offended; but a report of what the princess had said soon got about, and people called him King Roughbeard from that day.

After the feast was over, and the king found that not only had his daughter dismissed all her lovers, but that she had mocked and insulted his guests, he was very angry, and took an oath that his daughter should take as a husband the first poor wayfarer who came to the castle. A day or two after the princess heard the sound of music under her window. The king also heard it, and said, 'Go at once and fetch the musician in.'

The servants obeyed, and presently returned with a wandering minstrel, who played and sang before the castle in hopes of receiving an alms. He was dressed in soiled and ragged clothes, but the king made him stay and sing to them, and when he had finished he asked for a little gift.

'Yes,' replied the king, 'you shall be rewarded. Your song has pleased me so well that I will give you my daughter to be your wife!'

The princess was terrified at her father's words, and would have rushed from the room, but the king prevented her. 'No,' he said, 'you shall not escape; I took an oath that you should marry the first wayfarer who came to the door, and I will keep my word.'

All objections on the princess's part were useless. The priest was sent for, and she was obliged to plight her troth to a poor minstrel.

As soon as this was accomplished the king said to his daughter, 'Now that you are the wife of a poor man you will see how unfit you are to remain in my castle. You must therefore depart at once with your husband.'

The musician took her by the hand as the king spoke, and led her away to travel on foot for a long distance. At length they came to the borders of an extensive forest, which the young wife knew belonged to King Roughbeard.

'Ah me!' she cried; 'this wood belongs to the prince that I mocked and insulted. Ah! poor delicate creature that I am! if I had only married him when he wanted me!'

By-and-by they entered a meadow, and she made the same lament, for it belonged to King Roughbeard. But when at last they came to

a large city, near which was his palace, the repeated lamentation at
length annoyed her husband.

'It is not pleasant to me to hear you constantly wishing that you had
married some one else; am I not good enough for you?'

She made no reply, and they continued to walk on till she was quite
tired, and at last her husband stopped before a mean little house.

'What are we stopping here for?' she asked; 'whose wretched house
is this?'

'It is my house and yours,' he replied, 'where we must live together,'
and he led her in; but the door was so low that they had to stoop
as they entered.

'Where are the servants?' asked the king's daughter.

'What servants?' replied her husband. 'You must wait upon yourself now; and you will have to do all the work—to light the fire, to
fetch the water, and cook my dinner, for I am too tired to help you.'

The princess was being punished now for her pride. Her husband,
although he could sing, looked so repulsive in his ragged clothes, and
with his face tied up as if he had the toothache, that she did not care
to do anything for him. Besides, she knew nothing of cooking or
lighting fires, so he had to get up and do it himself. After she had
taken a little—for she was too sad to eat much—she laid herself down
on a miserable bed quite tired out. In the morning, however, her
husband woke her very early, that she might clean up the house and
get breakfast; and she tried to do it to please him, for he was kind and
patient with her. Thus they continued for a few days till their stock
of provisions was all gone. Then said the husband, 'Wife, we cannot
go on in this way, staying here and earning nothing; you shall learn to
plait willow and make baskets—it is not difficult—while I go and earn
money some other way.'

So he went out, cut some willow twigs, and brought them home.
She soon learnt to plait; but the hard willow twigs wounded her soft
hands and made them quite sore.

'I see that will not do,' said her husband; 'you must try to spin,
dearest; perhaps you may manage that better.'

The king's daughter tried spinning also, but it was of no use; the hard
thread soon cut through her soft white fingers till the blood ran down.

'See, now,' said her husband, 'you are good for nothing at work. I
am badly off indeed with such a helpless wife; so I must find a trade
for you. If I purchase a basketful of different wares, you can sit in
the market and sell them.'

'Ah!' thought she, 'when the market-people from my father's kingdom come out and see me sitting there with things to sell, how they
will mock me.'

But she could not help herself; she was obliged to go, for she did
not want to die of hunger. The first time, however, everything turned
out well. People bought goods willingly of such a beautiful woman;
all she had was sold, even the basket, and they paid her whatever she

asked, so that she went home with plenty of money. They lived on this for some time—as long as it lasted—and then her husband bought another basketful of wares and gave it to his wife, who went again to the market, seated herself in a corner, and spread out her goods for sale.

SHE HAD TO WASH THE SAUCEPANS AND KETTLES.

Suddenly a drunken hussar came by on horseback, and not seeing the basket, rode right into it, breaking the delicate ware into a thousand pieces. Then she began to weep, and knew not in her distress what to do, crying out, ' Oh! what will become of me? what will my husband say?'
She ran home and related to him her misfortune.

'Why did you seat yourself at such a dangerous corner of the market?' he said. 'There, stop your weeping; I see that you are quite unfit to perform the simplest work. I have just been to our king's castle, and they told me they wanted a kitchen-maid. I have promised to send you over every day, and they are ready to take you; so come and have your supper, and don't weep any more.'

And so the proud king's daughter became a kitchen-maid in the castle of King Roughbeard. It was dreadfully hard work; she had to wait upon the cook, wash the plates and dishes, and the saucepans and kettles.

They brought her whatever pieces were left for her to take home for dinner and supper; and she was often very tired. But she could hear what went on in King Roughbeard's castle, and at last the servants told her that a great festival was about to take place in honour of the young king's marriage.

The poor wife, who remembered that she could once have been his wife but for her pride, felt very sad; yet she could not help going to the door of the grand saloon that she might see the company arrive.

The room was full of light, and each one who stepped in seemed more elegant and beautiful than the last; and as the glory and splendour surrounded her she thought with a sorrowful heart of her fate, and lamented over the pride and haughtiness which had brought her into such terrible poverty and disgrace.

From the costly supper which was laid out for the guests came the most delicious odours; and the servants who waited threw her pieces that were left on the plates as they passed her, which she gathered up and put into her basket to carry home.

After supper, the company adjourned to the dancing-room, and as the king's daughter was looking earnestly at the beautifully dressed ladies and gentlemen who passed, she saw all at once a noble-looking prince approaching her. He was richly dressed in velvet and silver, and wore a golden order across his shoulders. He saw the beautiful princess who had lost her position through her own pride standing at the door. He knew her at once, although she was so meanly dressed; but when he advanced and took her by the hand, to lead her into the ball-room, saying that she must dance with him, she was in a terrible fright, and struggled to get free, for she knew it was King Roughbeard, her lover, whom she had treated with contempt. But it was useless to refuse, he held her hand so tightly, and led her in.

In the struggle the band that fastened her basket round her waist broke, and all the broken pieces which the servants had given her were scattered on the floor, and rolled in all directions, while the company looked on and laughed, in tones of mockery. Her shame was now complete, and she wished she could at that moment hide herself a thousand fathoms deep in the earth. She rushed to the door to run away, but on the steps, in the dark, she met, as she supposed, her husband, for it was his voice.

He seized her firmly, and brought her back into the castle, and as

soon as he appeared in the light, she saw to her astonishment that it
was King Roughbeard.

'Do not fear,' said he in a gentle tone; 'I and the wandering minstrel
with whom you have lived in the wretched house in the wood are the
same. My love for you made me disguise myself that I might win you

HE ADVANCED, AND TOOK HER BY THE HAND.

through your father's oath. I was the hussar who upset your basket.
I have done it to try if, after all, you really loved King Roughbeard,
whom you refused and mocked; and I hoped that your proud thoughts
would be humbled, and your haughty spirit bend, and that it would be
a punishment for having mocked and spurned me.'

Then she wept bitterly, and said, ' I know I have done wrong, and I am not worthy to be your wife.'

But he said, ' Be comforted; all is past now. You are my wife, and we have a splendid festival to celebrate the event after all.'

Then he took her to a beautiful chamber, where the maidens of the court dressed her in royal robes, and when her husband came and conducted her to the great hall, there was her father and his whole court ready to receive her, and wish her joy on her marriage with King Roughbeard, and so was there a joyful end to all her troubles. I wish, dear reader, you and I had been there to see.

SNOW-WHITE AND THE SEVEN DWARFS.

ONE day in the middle of winter, when the snowflakes fell from the sky like feathers, a queen sat at a window netting. Her netting needle was of black ebony, and as she worked, and the snow glittered, she pricked her finger, and three drops of blood fell into the snow. The red spots looked so beautiful in the white snow that the queen thought to herself :

' Oh, if I only had a little child, I should like it to be as fair as snow, as rosy as the red blood, and with hair and eyes as black as ebony.

Very soon after this the queen had a little daughter who was very fair, had rosy cheeks, and hair as black as ebony; and they gave her the name of Snow-white. But at the birth of the little child the queen died.

When Snow-white was a year old, the king took another wife. She was very handsome, but so proud and vain that she could not endure that anyone should surpass her in beauty. She possessed a wonderful mirror, and when she stood before it to look at herself she would say :

> ' Mirror, mirror on the wall,
> Am I most beautiful of all ?'

Then the mirror would reply :

> ' Young queen, thou art so wondrous fair,
> None can with thee at all compare.'

Then she would go away quite contented, for she knew that the magic mirror could only speak the truth.

Years went by, and as Snow-white grew up, she became day after day more beautiful, till she reached the age of seven years, and then people began to talk about her, and say that she would be more lovely even than the queen herself. So the proud woman went to her magic looking-glass, and asked :

> ' Mirror, mirror on the wall,
> Am I most beautiful of all ?'

But the mirror answered :

> ' Queen, thou art lovely still to see,
> But Snow-white will be
> A thousand times more beautiful than thee.'

Then the queen was terrified, and turned green and yellow with jealousy. If she had caught sight of Snow-white at that moment, she would have been ready to tear her heart out of her body, she hated the maiden so fiercely.

And this jealousy and envy grew every day in her heart stronger and stronger, like a disease, till she had no rest day or night.

At last she sent for a hunter, who lived near a forest, and said to him, ' Hunter, I want to get rid of that child. Take her out into the wood, and if you bring me some proofs that she is dead, I will reward you handsomely. Never let her appear before my eyes again.'

So the hunter enticed the child into the wood; but when he took out his hunting-knife to thrust into Snow-white's innocent heart, she fell on her knees and wept, and said, ' Ah, dear hunter, leave me my life; I will run away into the wild wood, and never, never come home any more.'

She looked so innocent and beautiful as she knelt, that the hunter's heart was moved with compassion : ' Run away, then, thou poor child,' he cried ; ' I cannot harm thee.'

Snow-white thanked him so sweetly, and was out of sight in a few moments.

' She will be devoured by wild beasts,' he said to himself. But the thought that he had not killed her was as if a stone-weight had been lifted from his heart.

To satisfy the queen, he took part of the inside of a young fawn, which the wicked woman thought was poor little Snow-white, and was over-joyed to think she was dead.

But the poor little motherless child, when she found herself alone in the wood, and saw nothing but trees and leaves, was dreadfully frightened, and knew not what to do. At last she began to run over the sharp stones and through the thorns, and though the wild beasts sprang out before her, they did her no harm. She ran on as long as she could, till her little feet became quite sore ; and towards evening she saw, to her great joy, a pretty little house. So she went up to it, and found the door open, and no one at home.

It was a tiny little house, but everything in it was so clean and neat and elegant that it is beyond description. In the middle of the room stood a small table, covered with a snow-white table-cloth, ready for supper. On it were arranged seven little plates, seven little spoons, seven little knives and forks, and seven mugs. By the wall stood seven little beds, near each other, covered with white quilts.

Poor Snow-white, who was hungry and thirsty, ate a few vegetables and a little bread from each plate, and drank a little drop of wine from each cup, for she did not like to take all she wanted from one alone. After this, feeling very tired, she thought she would lie down and rest on one of the beds, but she found it difficult to choose one to suit her. One was too long, another too short; so she tried them all till she came to the seventh, and that was so comfortable that she laid herself down, and was soon fast asleep.

When it was quite dark the masters of the house came home. They were seven little dwarfs, who dug and searched in the mountains for minerals. First they lighted seven little lamps, and as soon as the room was full of light they saw that some one had been there, for everything did not stand in the order in which they had left it.

Then said the first, 'Who has been sitting in my little chair?'

The second exclaimed, 'Who has been eating from my little plate?'

The third cried, 'Some one has taken part of my bread.'

'Who has been eating my vegetables?' said the fourth.

Then said the fifth, 'Some one has used my fork.'

The sixth cried, 'And who has been cutting with my knife?'

'And some one has been drinking out of my cup,' said the seventh.

Then the eldest looked at his bed, and, seeing that it looked tumbled, cried out that some one had been upon it. The others came running forward, and found all their beds in the same condition. But when the seventh approached his bed, and saw Snow-white lying there fast asleep, he called the others, who came quickly, and holding

'OH, WHAT A BEAUTIFUL LITTLE CHILD!'

their lights over their heads, cried out in wonder as they beheld the sleeping child. 'Oh, what a beautiful little child!' they said to each other, and were so delighted that they would not awaken her, but left her to sleep as long as she liked in the little bed, while its owner slept with one of his companions, and so the night passed away.

In the morning, when Snow-white awoke, and saw all the dwarfs, she was terribly frightened. But they spoke kindly to her, till she lost all fear, and they asked her name.

' I am called Snow-white,' she replied.

' But how came you to our house?' asked one.

Then she related to them all that had happened ; how her stepmother had sent her into the wood with the hunter, who had spared her life, and that, after wandering about for a whole day, she had found their house.

The dwarfs talked a little while together, and then one said. ' Do you think you could be our little housekeeper, to make the beds, cook the dinner, and wash and sew and knit for us, and keep everything neat and clean and orderly? If you can, then you shall stay here with us, and nobody shall hurt you.'

' Oh yes, I will try,' said Snow-white. So they let her stay, and she was a clever little thing. She managed very well, and kept the house quite clean and in order. And while they were gone to the mountains to find gold, she got their supper ready, and they were very happy together.

But every morning when they left her, the kind little dwarfs warned Snow-white to be careful. While the maiden was alone they knew she was in danger, and told her not to show herself, for her stepmother would soon find out where she was, and said, ' Whatever you do, let nobody into the house while we are gone.'

After the wicked queen had proved, as she thought, that Snow-white was dead, she felt quite satisfied there was no one in the world now likely to become so beautiful as herself, so she stepped up to her mirror and asked :

> ' Mirror, mirror on the wall,
> Who is most beautiful of all ?'

To her vexation the mirror replied :

> ' Fair queen, at home there is none like thee,
> But over the mountains is Snow-white free,
> With seven little dwarfs, who are strange to see ;
> She is a thousand times fairer than thee.'

The queen was furious when she heard this, for she knew the mirror was truthful, and that the hunter must have deceived her, and that Snow-white still lived. So she sat and pondered over these facts, thinking what would be best to do, for as long as she was not the most beautiful woman in the land, her jealousy gave her no peace. After a time, she decided what to do. First, she painted her face, and whitened her hair ; then she dressed herself in old woman's clothes, and was so disguised that no one could have recognised her.

Watching an opportunity, she left the castle, and took her way to the wood near the mountains, where the seven little dwarfs lived. When she reached the door, she knocked, and cried, 'Beautiful goods to sell; beautiful goods to sell.'

Snow-white, when she heard it, peeped through the window, and said, 'Good-day, old lady. What have you in your basket for me to buy?'

'Everything that is pretty,' she replied; 'laces, and pearls, and ear-rings, and bracelets of every colour;' and she held up her basket, which was lined with glittering silk.

'I can let in this respectable old woman,' thought Snow-white; 'she will not harm me.' So she unbolted the door, and told her to come in. Oh, how delighted Snow-white was with the pretty things; she bought several trinkets, and a beautiful silk lace for her stays, but she did not see the evil eye of the old woman who was watching her. Presently she said, 'Child, come here; I will show you how to lace your stays properly.' Snow-white had no suspicion, so she placed herself before the old woman that she might lace her stays. But no sooner was the lace in the holes than she began to lace so fast and pull so tight that Snow-white could not breathe, and presently fell down at her feet as if dead.

'Now you are beautiful indeed,' said the woman, and, fancying she heard footsteps, she rushed away as quickly as she could.

Not long after, the seven dwarfs came home, and they were terribly frightened to see dear little Snow-white lying on the ground without motion, as if she were dead. They lifted her up, and saw in a moment that her stays had been laced too tight. Quickly they cut the stay-lace in two, till Snow-white began to breathe a little, and after a time was restored to life. But when the dwarfs heard what had happened, they said: 'That old market-woman was no other than your wicked stepmother. Snow-white, you must never again let anyone in while we are not with you.'

The wicked queen when she returned home, after, as she thought, killing Snow-white, went to her looking-glass and asked:

'Mirror, mirror on the wall,
Am I most beautiful of all?'

Then answered the mirror:

'Queen, thou art not the fairest now;
Snow-white over the mountain's brow
A thousand times fairer is than thou.'

When she heard this she was so terrified that the blood rushed to her heart, for she knew that after all she had done Snow-white was still alive. 'I must think of something else,' she said to herself, 'to get rid of that odious child.'

Now this wicked queen had some knowledge of witchcraft, and she knew how to poison a comb, so that whoever used it would fall dead. This the wicked stepmother soon got ready, and dressing herself again like an old woman, but quite different to the last, she started off to travel over the mountains to the dwarfs' cottage.

When Snow-white heard the old cry, 'Goods to sell, fine goods to sell,' she looked out of window and said:

'Go away, go away; I must not let you in.'

'Look at this, then,' said the woman; 'you shall have it for your

THE DWARFS FINDING SNOW-WHITE.

own if you like,' and she held up before the child's eyes the bright tortoiseshell comb which she had poisoned.

Poor Snow-white could not refuse such a present, so she opened the door and let the woman in, quite forgetting the advice of the dwarfs. After she had bought a few things, the old woman said, 'Let me try this comb in your hair; it is so fine it will make it beautifully smooth and glossy.'

So Snow-white, thinking no wrong, stood before the woman to have her hair dressed; but no sooner had the comb touched the roots of her hair than the poison took effect, and the maiden fell to the ground lifeless.

'You paragon of beauty,' said the wicked woman, 'all has just happened as I expected,' and then she went away quickly.

Fortunately evening soon arrived, and the seven dwarfs returned home. When they saw Snow-white lying dead on the ground, they knew at once that the stepmother had been there again; but on seeing the poisoned comb in her hair they pulled it out quickly, and Snow-white very soon came to herself, and related all that had passed.

Again they warned her not to let anyone enter the house during their absence, and on no account to open the door; but Snow-white was not clever enough to resist her clever wicked stepmother, and she forgot to obey.

The wicked queen felt sure now that she had really killed Snow-white, so as soon as she returned home she went to her looking-glass, and inquired:

> 'Mirror, mirror on the wall,
> Who is most beautiful of all?'

But the mirror replied:

> 'Queen, thou art the fairest here,
> But not when Snow-white is near;
> Over the mountains still is she,
> Fairer a thousand times than thee.'

As the looking-glass thus replied, the queen trembled and quaked with rage. 'Snow-white shall die,' cried she, 'if it costs me my own life!'

Then she went into a lonely forbidden chamber where no one was allowed to come, and poisoned a beautiful apple. Outwardly it looked ripe and tempting, of a pale green with rosy cheeks, so that it made everyone's mouth water to look at it, but whoever ate even a small piece must die.

As soon as this apple was ready, the wicked queen painted her face, disguised her hair, dressed herself as a farmer's wife, and went again over the mountains to the dwarfs' cottage.

When she knocked at the door, Snow-white stretched her head out of the window, and said, 'I dare not let you in; the seven dwarfs have forbidden me.'

'But I am all right,' said the farmer's wife. 'Stay, I will show you my apples. Are they not beautiful? let me make you a present of one.'

'No, thank you,' cried Snow-white; 'I dare not take it.'

'What!' cried the woman, 'are you afraid it is poisoned? Look here now, I will cut the apple in halves; you shall have the rosy-cheek side, and I will eat the other.'

The apple was so cleverly made that the red side alone was poisonous. Snow-white longed so much for the beautiful fruit as she saw the farmer's wife eat one half that she could not any longer resist, but stretched out her hand from the window and took the poisoned half. But no sooner had she taken one mouthful than she fell on the ground dead.

Then the wicked queen glanced in at the window with a horrible look in her eye, and laughed aloud as she exclaimed :

'White as snow, red as blood, and black as ebony; this time the dwarfs will not be able to awake thee.'

And as soon as she arrived at home, and asked her mirror who was the most beautiful in the land, it replied :

'Fair queen, there is none in all the land
So beautiful as thee.'

Then had her envious heart rest, at least such rest as a heart full of envy and malice ever can have.

The little dwarfs, when they came home in the evening, found poor Snow-white on the ground ; but though they lifted her up, there were no signs of breath from her mouth, and they found she was really dead. Yet they tried in every way to restore her ; they tried to extract the poison from her lips, they combed her hair, and washed it with wine and water, but all to no purpose : the dear child gave no signs of life, and at last they knew she was dead. Then they laid her on a bier, and the seven dwarfs seated themselves round her, and wept and mourned for three days. They would have buried her then, but there was no change in her appearance ; her face was as fresh, and her cheeks and lips had their usual colour. Then said one, 'We cannot lay this beautiful child in the dark, cold earth.'

So they agreed to have a coffin made entirely of glass, transparent all over, that they might watch for any signs of decay, and they wrote in letters of gold her name on the lid, and that she was the daughter of a king. The coffin was placed on the side of the mountain, and each of them watched it by turns, so that it was never left alone. And the birds of the air came near and mourned for Snow-white ; first the owl, then the raven, and at last the dove. Snow-white lay for a long, long time in the glass coffin, but showed not the least signs of decay. It seemed as if she slept ; for her skin was snow white, her cheeks rosy red, and her hair black as ebony.

It happened one day that the son of a king, while riding in the forest, came by chance upon the dwarfs' house and asked for a night's lodging. As he left the next morning he saw the coffin on the mountain-side, with beautiful Snow-white lying in it, and read what was written upon the lid in letters of gold.

Then he said to the dwarfs, 'Let me have this coffin, and I will give you for it whatever you ask '

But the elder dwarf answered, 'We would not give it thee for all the gold in the world.'

But the prince answered, 'Let me have it as a gift, then. I know not why, but my heart is drawn towards this beautiful child, and I feel

THE COFFIN WAS PLACED ON THE SIDE OF THE MOUNTAIN.

I cannot live without her. If you will let me have her, she shall be treated with the greatest honour and respect as one dearly beloved.'

As he thus spoke the good little dwarfs were full of sympathy for him, and gave him the coffin. Then the prince called his servants, and the coffin was placed on their shoulders, and they carried it away, followed by the king's son, who watched it carefully. Now it happened that one of them made a false step and stumbled. This shook the coffin, and caused the poisoned piece of apple which Snow-white had bitten to roll out of her mouth. A little while after she suddenly opened her eyes, lifted up the coffin-lid, raised herself and was again alive.

'Oh! where am I?' she cried.

Full of joy, the king's son approached her, and said, 'Dear Snow-white, you are safe; you are with me.'

'DEAR SNOW-WHITE, YOU ARE SAFE; YOU ARE WITH ME.'

Then he related to her all that had happened, and what the little dwarfs had told him about her, and said at last, 'I love you better than all in the world besides, dear little Snow-white, and you must come with me to my father's castle and be my wife.'

Then was Snow-white taken out of the coffin and placed in a carriage to travel with the prince, and the king was so pleased with his son's choice that the marriage was soon after celebrated with great pomp and magnificence.

Now it happened that the stepmother of Snow-white was invited, among other guests, to the wedding-feast. Before she left her house she stood in all her rich dress before the magic mirror to admire her own appearance, but she could not help saying :

> 'Mirror, mirror on the wall,
>   Am I most beautiful of all ?'

Then to her surprise the mirror replied:

> 'Fair queen, thou art the fairest here,
>   But at the palace, now,'
> The bride will prove a thousand times
>   More beautiful than thou.'

Then the wicked woman uttered a curse, and was so dreadfully alarmed that she knew not what to do.   At first she declared she would not go to this wedding at all, but she felt it impossible to rest until she had seen the bride, so she determined to go.   But what was her astonishment and vexation when she recognised in the young bride Snow-white herself, now grown a charming young woman, and richly dressed in royal robes !   Her rage and terror were so great that she stood still and could not move for some minutes.   At last she went into the ball-room, but the slippers she wore were to her as iron bands full of coals of fire, in which she was obliged to dance.   And so in the red, glowing shoes she continued to dance till she fell dead on the floor, a sad example of envy and jealousy.

THE FORTUNE SEEKERS.

ONCE upon a time, in a village, lived three brothers, who became so sunk in poverty and want that at last they had not even a morsel of bread to eat.   Then they said to each other, ' We cannot remain here to starve ; let us go out into the world and seek our fortunes.'

So they begged a few pence of their neighbours and started on their way.   They travelled for some distance over fields and meadows, but met with no good fortune till they came at length to a large forest and saw a mountain in the distance.   As they approached nearer they saw that the mountain was composed entirely of silver, and the eldest brother exclaimed, ' Now have I found the good fortune I hoped for; I can wish for nothing better than this.'

So he gathered up as much silver as he could carry, turned round, and went home.   The two younger brothers, however, were not yet satisfied, and one said to the other, ' We want something better for our fortunes than uncoined silver.'

So they continued on their way without attempting to take any.   In the course of a day or two the two brothers came to another mountain, which was composed entirely of gold. Then the second brother stood still and seemed for a time quite undecided.

'What shall I do?' he said; 'shall I take gold enough from here to last my life, or shall I go farther?'

After considering for a long time, he suddenly formed a resolution, and filling his pockets with as much as they would hold, wished his brother farewell, and returned home. After he was gone, the youngest said to himself, 'Silver and gold do not tempt me. I will not give up trying for a fortune yet. Who knows? Very likely mine will be the best after all.'

So he travelled on, and at the end of three days came to another forest, so much larger than the former that it seemed to have no end, and while there he found nothing to eat or drink, so that he was almost starved. At last he climbed to the top of a high tree, hoping to discover a way out of the forest; but as far as the eye could reach nothing could be seen but the tree-tops. So he began to descend the tree very slowly; for his hunger was becoming painful.

'Oh,' he exclaimed, 'if I could only find something to satisfy this dreadful hunger!'

But when he reached the foot of the tree, what was his surprise and astonishment to see a table laid out with a delicious supper, the odour from which was most tempting.

'This time,' cried he, 'my wish has been fulfilled at the right moment;' and, without asking any questions as to who had brought the supper or who had cooked it, he placed himself at the table and ate till his hunger was appeased. As soon as he had finished he thought, 'What a pity it would be to leave this nice little table here in a wood to spoil.'

So he packed it up very carefully, and carried it away with him. He now continued his journey through the wood in comfort, but towards evening, feeling again hungry and tired, he stopped to rest, and thought he would try his little table again in the hopes of another supper, so he unfolded it and said, 'I wish there could be a good supper for me again this evening.'

The wish had scarcely passed his lips when the table was covered with so many dishes, containing such good things, that there was no room for any more.

'I see now,' he said, 'who is to be my cook for the future; this table is as precious as the mountains of gold and silver;' and he saw at once that it possessed the magic power of preparing itself. But this good fortune was not enough to satisfy him; he could not rest without seeking farther; for he loved to wander about the world: he had a more restless spirit than his brothers. He travelled on for many days, till one evening he found himself in a lonely part of the wood, and came suddenly upon a black, dusty charcoal-burner, who had made a fire of charcoal on the ground, and was roasting potatoes for his supper.

'Good-evening, Blackbird,' said he; 'how do you get on here in your loneliness?'

'Pretty well, one day with another,' answered the charcoal-burner; 'and potatoes every evening. Do you wish to join me in my supper?'

'Many thanks,' replied the traveller; 'but I will not take your supper from you. There is not more than enough for yourself; but if you would like to take supper with me, I shall be glad to invite you.'

'How will you prepare a supper?' asked the stranger. 'No one could go to the town and get it under two hours, and I see that you have nothing with you.'

'Yet you shall have a supper,' said the younger brother, 'and a good one too, though it will cost nothing.'

Thereupon he unfastened the little table from his back, unfolded it, and placed it on the ground. Then he said, 'Table, prepare thyself!'

In a moment it was covered with the best of every good thing in the way of eatables and drinkables, all hot and nice, as if they had just been cooked. The charcoal-burner stared with wide open eyes, but he did not wait for a second invitation; placing himself before the table, he fell to with a great appetite, stuffing large pieces into his black mouth till he had eaten as much as he could. Then, with a grin of satisfaction, he said, 'Listen, friend: thy table has my approval, and it would be the very thing for me here alone in this wood, with no one to cook for me. I will make an exchange with you. Yonder in the corner hangs a soldier's knapsack; it is old and unsightly, but it possesses a wonderful power, and, as it is of no more use to me, I will give it to you in return for your table.'

'First, I must know what this wonderful power is,' said the young fortune-seeker.

'I will tell you,' replied the charcoal-burner. 'If you knock upon it with your hand there will instantly appear before you a corporal with six men, all in full uniform, and whatever you order them to do, they will perform it.'

'It's all the same to me,' replied the youth; 'I don't mind which I have, so we will make the exchange.'

He gave him the table as he spoke, slung the knapsack on his back, wished the charcoal-burner farewell, and went on his journey. He had not gone far, however, before he had a strong desire to try what this wonderful knapsack could do, so he put his hand over his shoulder and knocked.

In a moment there stood before him seven great warriors, and the corporal, with a military salute, said, 'What is my lord and master's pleasure?'

'Quick step, march! to the charcoal-burner in the forest,' he replied, 'and demand my wish-table back.'

They put their best foot foremost, and in a very short time returned with what he required, which they had obtained from the charcoal-burner without much difficulty. Then he told them to march off, as he wanted nothing more at present, and continued his way, hoping that such good fortune would still continue to shine upon him.

At sunset, next day, he came up to another charcoal-burner, who sat by his charcoal fire preparing his evening meal.

'Will you eat with me?' said the sooty fellow; 'potatoes and salt are wholesome food; so seat yourself by me.'

'No,' answered the other; 'for this once you must be my guest.' And, without waiting for a reply, he arranged his table, gave it the word of command, and very soon they were both seated at a splendid feast. They ate and drank together, and were very soon good friends.

After supper, the charcoal-burner said, 'Over there, on that bank, lies an old worn-out hat, which has a very peculiar quality—if the wearer lifts it up and turns it round above his head, instantly a number of shots are fired, like a discharge of artillery, so that no one could dare to approach. It is useless to me, so you may have it for your table, if you will make the exchange.'

'I have no objection,' said the young man; so he took the hat, placed it on his head, and left the table behind him.

He did not go far, however, before knocking on his knapsack, and when his soldiers appeared he sent them again to fetch the table.

'It passes from one to another,' he thought; 'but it is mine. It seems as if my luck would never end;' and his thoughts did not deceive him.

After regaining his table he travelled on through fields and woods, and one day he met with a third charcoal-burner, who, as the former two had done, invited him to share his supper of potatoes and salt. But the traveller, after ordering the table to prepare itself, gave the charcoal-burner such a feast that he also begged for the table, and offered to give him in exchange a wonderful horn, which had quite a different power to that of the table or the hat.

'If ever a man were to blow this horn near a town, or a city, or village, the walls, the fortresses, the houses, and all they contained, would be thrown down in one heap of confusion and ruin.'

For this wonderful horn, therefore, he was quite ready, not only to give up his table to the charcoal-burner, but to let him keep it. To have possession of the knapsack, the hat, and the horn, and to keep them as his own, was all he cared for.

'Now,' said he, 'I am a mighty man, and it is time for me to turn my steps homeward and see how my brothers are going on.'

By the time he reached his home, he found that his brothers had, with their gold and silver, built two beautiful houses, and were living in grand style.

Without thinking of his ragged coat, shabby hat, and the knapsack on his shoulder, he stepped in and presented himself to his brothers.

They would not, however, acknowledge him at all; they mocked and insulted him, and said, 'You pretend to be our brother, who despised gold and silver, and left us to seek a higher and a better fortune. Why, we shall expect him to arrive in pomp and splendour like a mighty

king, not in the dress of a poor beggarman,' and so they drove him
from their doors.

Then he fell into a passion, and knocked on his knapsack so many
times that a hundred and fifty warriors in rank and file stood before
him. He ordered them to surround his brothers' houses, and sent two
of their company with hazel-switches, to flog them till they acknowledged that he was their brother.

All this caused a great noise and disturbance in the town. The
people ran together, and wanted to render some assistance to the two
brothers; but they could not, because of the soldiers. At last information was sent to the king; he was very indignant, and sent a captain
and his troop to drive the peace-disturber from the town.

But the man with the wonderful knapsack had very soon a larger
number of soldiers at his command, who drove back the king's captain
and his company in no time, so that they were obliged to retreat in
disgrace.

Then said the king, 'This vagabond fellow must be put down;' and
the next day he sent a larger troop than before, but all in vain. A
great many people and soldiers now came forward, ready to oppose the
peace-destroyer, and to drive him from the town; but he quickly put an
end to the disturbance himself—he took off his hat, and whirled it twice
round his head. In an instant the shots fell among the people like
hail; many were slain, and the soldiers fled in alarm.

'Tell your king,' said the young fortune-seeker to the captain of the
soldiers, 'that there shall be no peace till he gives me his daughter as a
wife, or power to rule the whole kingdom in his name.'

Away ran the captain to the king with this announcement; and
seeing what the consequences would be if he did not agree to these
requests, he went to his daughter, and told her what the troublesome
man required to keep him quiet.

'There remains no other way for me,' he said, 'and if you will do
this, then I shall keep my kingdom, and peace will be restored.'

The king's daughter had no objection to a husband, so the marriage
took place very quickly, and, for a time, everything was peaceable.

But the princess, who could not endure that the people should think
of her husband as a common man, was much annoyed at his persisting
to wear such a shabby hat, and to carry an old knapsack about with
him. All her anxiety now was to get rid of these odious things, and
she thought day and night of the best way to manage it. At last it
occurred to her that perhaps his wonderful power was contained in the
old knapsack, and she determined to find out.

So she pretended to be very fond of him, and coaxed him till his heart
was softened towards her, and then she said, 'I wish you would not
wear that ugly old knapsack; it disfigures you so much, and makes me
quite ashamed of you.'

'Dearest child,' he replied, 'that knapsack is my greatest treasure;
as long as I have it, I fear no power in the world.'

Then she threw her arms round his neck, as if she were going to kiss him, and with great cleverness unfastened the knapsack from his shoulder and ran away with it.

As soon as she was alone, she knocked on it, and when the soldiers appeared, she ordered them to arrest their former master, and carry him out of the king's palace.

They obeyed, and the false wife called to a number of people to follow her, that her husband might be carried away out of the country.

Then would he have been lost if he had not had the wonderful hat. No sooner were his hands free, than he raised it and waved it twice over his head. In a moment the shots fell so thick and fast, that the soldiers and the people were glad to escape, and even the king's daughter herself was obliged to ask for pardon before the shooting was allowed to cease.

After this she was so gentle and affectionate, and spoke so kindly to him, that he allowed himself to be talked over, and willingly forgave them all. She behaved to him for a long time very kindly, and as if she loved him dearly, for she knew she could at any time deceive him. And as he had trusted her about the power he possessed in the knapsack, she hoped he would do the same about the hat; and she knew she could not get rid of him as long as he kept it. She soon knew that secret also, and only waited till he was asleep to take the hat away and throw it into the street.

But he still had his horn, and when he woke and missed the hat, in a great rage, he seized it and blew it with all his strength; and had he not ceased blowing, the whole town, walls, palace, fortress, and neighbouring villages would have fallen together with a loud crash. As it was, the king and his daughter were crushed beneath the ruins. And when he ceased blowing and looked around, there lay the palace all in a heap—not one stone remained upon another. Now there was no one to oppose him any more, and he proclaimed himself king, and reigned over the whole kingdom.

RUMPELSTILTSKIN.

THERE was once a miller who was very poor, but he had a beautiful daughter; and a thought struck him that he would speak about her to the king, and get some situation for her. So he obtained an audience, and told the king that he had a daughter who could spin straw into gold.

'Then,' said the king, 'that is a quality which pleases me well. If your daughter is, as you say, so very skilful, bring her to the castle to-morrow morning, and I will try what she can do.'

The miller next day took his daughter to the castle, and as soon as she arrived the king led her into a chamber which was quite full of straw, and placing a spinning-wheel before her, said :

' Now set to work at once, for if all this straw is not spun into gold before sunrise, you shall die.'

Then he locked the door himself, and left her alone.

The poor maiden sat for some time looking at the straw in despair. She had never in her life been taught to spin, and she had not the least idea how to turn straw into gold. Every moment her fear became greater, and at last she began to weep bitterly.

As evening came on, the door opened, and a little man entered, who said :

' Good-evening, young daughter of the miller. Why do you weep so sadly ?'

' Oh !' she replied, ' I have all this straw to spin into gold, and I know not how to do it.'

' What will you give me,' said the little man, ' if I spin it for you ?'

' My neck ribbon,' she said.

The man took the ribbon, seated himself before the spinning-wheel, and as the wheel went whirr, whirr, whirr, three times, the spool was full of gold. Then he fastened on more straw, and after three turns of the wheel the spool was a second time full ; and so he went on all night, and before the morning dawned the straw was all spun and the spools full of gold. Then he left her.

At sunrise the king came to the chamber, but when he caught sight of the glittering gold, he was first astonished and then full of joy. But his heart was greedy for gold, so he led the miller's daughter into another chamber full of straw, and much larger than the former, and ordered her, as she valued her life, to spin that into gold before sunrise next morning.

The maiden, when left alone, could only weep, for she knew it was an impossible task. But in the evening the same little man again appeared, and said, ' What will you give me if I spin all this straw into gold ?'

' My ring from my finger,' answered the maiden.

The little man took the ring, set to work at the spinning-wheel, and before morning the whole of the straw was spun into gold.

The king gloated with delight over the glittering heap, but he was not yet satiated with gold. So he led the maiden into a still larger room full of straw, and said, ' You must spin for me during one more night, and if all this straw is spun into gold by the morning, then you shall be my wife.'

' Although she is a miller's daughter,' thought the king, ' I could not find a richer wife in the whole world.'

No sooner was the maiden alone, than the mannikin again appeared for the third time, and said, ' What will you give me if I spin the straw for you this time ?'

' I have nothing more that I can give,' answered the maiden.

'Then promise when you are queen to give me your first child,' said the little man.

'Who knows if I shall ever be queen,' thought the maiden; and she knew also that in her trouble there was no other help for her. So she promised what he wished.

Immediately he set to work, and very soon spun all the straw into gold.

In the morning when the king came and found that what he required was done, he ordered preparations to be made for a splendid wedding, and in a few days the miller's beautiful daughter became a queen.

About a year after this a beautiful little child was born to the queen, who never thought of her promise to the little man, till one night he stepped suddenly into her chamber, and said, 'Now give me what you have promised.'

In great terror the queen offered him all the treasures in the kingdom if he would leave her the child.

But the little man said, 'No; something living I like better than all the treasures in the world.' Then the queen began to mourn and weep so bitterly, that the little man had compassion on her, and said, 'I will give you three days, and if in that time you can find out my name, then you shall keep your child.'

After he was gone, the queen lay awake till morning, thinking over all the names she had ever heard of, and determined to send a messenger all over the country to inquire far and wide what names had been given to people formerly.

The next night the little man came again, and she repeated all the names she could think of, Casper, Melchior, Balzar, and many others that she knew, in every rank of society. But the little man said, 'No, I have not one of these names.'

The next day she made every inquiry among the neighbours, and when the little man came at night for the second time, she mentioned most unearthly names, such as Brown-ribs, Dicky-calf, and Spindle-leg. But he answered always, 'No, it is none of these.'

On the third day the messenger returned and related his adventures. He had not been able to find a single new name, but on his way home he crossed a high mountain, and came to the borders of a wood, in which the foxes and the hares wished him 'good night.' After this he came to a tiny little house, and saw before it a fire burning, and hopping round it, on one leg, was a ridiculous-looking little man, who cried:

> 'To-day I brew, to-morrow I bake,
> Next morning I shall the queen's child take;
> How glad I am that she does not dream
> That Rumpelstiltskin is my name!'

The messenger could not think what made the queen so overjoyed when she heard this name, but she rewarded him handsomely and dismissed him.

On the third and last night, the little man appeared for the last time, and said, ' Now then, queen-mother, what is my name?'

' Well,' she replied, ' are you called **Conrad**?'

' No.'

' Henry ?'

' No.'

' Then your name is **Rumpelstiltskin**!'

' The fairies must have told you that! the fairies must have told you that!' screamed the little man, and in his rage struck the ground so fiercely with his right foot that it sunk in deeply into the earth, dragging his body after it. Then, in his fury, he laid hold of his left foot with both hands, and tore himself completely in halves.

THE SHEPHERD'S FLOWER.

A WOMAN, who was in reality a witch, had two daughters living with her. Her own daughter, who was ugly and wicked, she loved best; but her stepdaughter, who was beautiful and good, she hated

It happened once that the stepdaughter had a pretty apron, which pleased the other very much, and made her jealous. So she said to her mother, ' I must and will have that apron, mother.'

' Keep quiet, my child,' said her mother; ' you shall have it. Your stepsister ought to have been dead long ago. To-night, while she is asleep, I will go into her room and cut off her head. Be careful, when you go to bed, to get in first, and push her right in front of you.'

Now all this would have happened to the poor girl, if she had not fortunately stood in a corner of the room, unseen, while they were talking, and heard it all. She dared not go out of the house for the whole day, for she knew that when bedtime came she must get into bed before her stepsister. However, she kept awake till the other slept, and then she got behind her, next the wall, and pushed her stepsister in front. There she lay, trembling and in fear, till, in the middle of the night, her stepmother entered the room, in the dark, with an axe in her right hand. The poor girl lay quite still, as if asleep; indeed, she hardly dared to breathe, for she knew the wicked woman was feeling about the bed for the one outside. And presently she took the axe in both hands, lifted it up, and cut off the head of her own child. Then she went out of the room to her own bed.

In great fear, the poor girl lay still till all was quiet. Then she got up, dressed herself, and went softly out of the house to her lover, who was named Roland, and knocked at the door. As soon as he opened it,

she exclaimed, ' Oh, dearest Roland, we must take flight very quickly. My stepmother intended to kill me, and she has killed her own daughter by mistake. When daylight comes, and she sees what she has done, we are lost if we stay here.'

' But I would advise you,' said Roland, ' first to take away her witch's staff. Otherwise she will pursue and overtake us.'

In fear and trembling, the maiden returned home, and, after securing the magic wand, she went upstairs and carried away the dead head to bury it, and in doing so three drops of blood fell from it : one on the bed, another on the stairs, and one in the kitchen. Then she hastened back to her lover.

In the morning, when the old witch rose, she called to her daughter to get up, as she had got the apron for her. But she did not come.

' Where are you ?' she cried.

' Out here on the step, turning round,' answered one blood-drop.

The woman went out, but there was no one on the step, so she asked again, ' Where are you ?'

' Here in the kitchen, warming myself,' cried the second drop of blood.

She went into the kitchen, but on seeing nobody there, she called out angrily a third time, ' Where are you ?'

' In bed, asleep,' answered the third drop of blood.

Then she went to the sleeping-chamber, and approached the bed, and what did she see there !—Her own child, weltering in her blood, whose head she herself had cut off. In a terrible fury, the old witch sprang to the window, from which she could see to a very great distance, and soon espied her stepdaughter going hastily away with her lover Roland.

' It is useless for them to try to escape from me,' she cried; 'however far they may be on their way, I can overtake them.'

So she put on her one-mile shoes, in which she could travel an hour's walk in one step, and it was not very long before she had overtaken them both.

But as soon as the maiden saw her coming, she touched her dear Roland with the magic wand, and he was immediately turned into a lake; then she transformed herself into a duck, and swam upon its surface.

The witch stood on the shore, and threw breadcrumbs to the duck, and took a great deal of trouble to decoy her; but the duck would not allow herself to be enticed. So the old woman was obliged to return home that evening without having gained her object.

When she was gone, the maiden and her lover resumed their natural forms, and travelled during the whole night, till the day dawned. Then she transformed herself into a beautiful flower, growing in a hedge of thorns, and her lover into a fiddler.

Not long after, the witch stepped up, and said, ' Dear fiddler, may I pick the beautiful flower for myself ?'

'Oh yes,' answered he, ' and I will play you a tune.'

Now, the fiddle being produced by a witch's staff, was a magic fiddle; therefore, just as she had crept into the hedge of thorns to break off the flower, for she knew well who it was, the fiddler played a magic tune, to which she was obliged to dance. The faster he played, the higher she had to spring and dance in the thorn-hedge, while the thorns tore her clothes from her back, scratched her skin till the blood came, and, as he would not stop playing, she was obliged to dance till she fell down dead.

As they were now free from the power of the witch, they resumed their natural shape, and Roland said, 'Now I will go home to my father, and arrange about our marriage.'

'And I will stay here and wait for you, and, that no one may recognise me, I will turn myself into a red landmark.'

Then Roland went away, and the maiden placed herself as a red stone in the field, and waited for her lover.

But when Roland returned home, he met with another maiden, who so ensnared him that at last he quite forgot the maiden whom he had promised to marry.

The poor forsaken one waited a long time; but when she found that he did not come again, she was so sorrowful that she turned herself into a flower, and said to herself sadly, 'Perhaps he may come this way by-and-by, and crush me with his foot.'

Now it happened after a time that a shepherd, who was watching his sheep in the field, saw the flower, and as it was very pretty, he plucked it, carried it home, and laid it in his drawers. From that moment everything that was wonderful occurred in the shepherd's house. When he got up in the morning, all the work was already done: the fire on the hearth was lighted, the room swept, table and chairs dusted and placed in order, and water fetched from the well. At noon, when he came home to dinner, the cloth was laid and a nice dinner placed ready for him. He could not imagine how it all came to pass, for he never saw any human creature in his house, and no one could have concealed himself in the shepherd's little hut.

The careful housekeeping and care pleased him very much, but at last he began to feel uneasy; so he went to a wise woman and asked her advice.

'There is witchcraft concealed behind all this,' said the wise woman. 'I will tell you what to do. On some morning when you wake early, lie quite still and pay great attention; if you hear any movement, look out cautiously, and whatever you see, let it be what it may, as quick as lightning throw a white cloth over it; then will the enchantment be broken.'

The shepherd went home, determining to follow the advice of the wise woman. The next morning he woke early, and, just at daybreak, he saw his drawer open, and the flower he had plucked come out. Quickly he sprang up and threw a white cloth over it. In a moment the transformation took place, and a beautiful maiden stood before him, who confessed that she had been the flower he had plucked, and that she had taken care of his household ever since.

She related to him all that had happened to her, and the shepherd was so pleased with her that he asked her to marry him. But she said 'No.' For although her dear Roland had forsaken her, she would still be true to him. She promised the shepherd, however, that she would not go away, but continue to keep house for him.

The time came for Roland's marriage to take place; and it was a custom in that country that all the maidens that could be found should be present, and sing in honour of the bridal pair. The true maiden, when she heard of it, was so overcome with sorrow that she thought her heart would break when they came and asked her to go, and at first she refused, but at length several came and persuaded her to join them. The wedding-day arrived, and when the young maidens placed themselves in a row to sing, she stepped back and stood alone, unknown to the others. But as soon as the song began and the voice reached the ears of Roland, he started up, crying, 'I know that voice; that is the right bride; I desire no other.' All the old memories which had been forgotten and banished from his thoughts now came home to his heart again. Then was the marriage held with the true maiden, and all her sorrow was turned into joy.

THE GOLDEN BIRD.

ONCE upon a time there lived a king who had a beautiful pleasure-garden behind his castle, in which grew a tree which bore golden apples; as the apples ripened they were counted, but every morning one would be missing. The king noticed this, and ordered that every night watch should be kept under the tree.

The king had three sons, and he sent the eldest to watch for the first night in the garden, but when midnight came he could not keep himself awake, and the next morning another apple was missing. On the following night the second son tried to watch, but he succeeded no better; after struggling to keep awake for twelve hours he slept one, and in the morning, as usual, an apple was missed.

Now came the turn of the third son to watch, but at first the king did not trust him; he thought he would be as unsuccessful as his brothers. At length he gave him permission. The youth laid himself down under the tree and watched, but he did not allow sleep to gain the mastery over him, and as the clock struck twelve, he heard a sound of rushing wings through the air, and presently a bird flew by with plumage that glittered like gold. The bird alighted on the tree and was plucking an apple, when the young man raised his gun and fired. The bird escaped, but the shot had touched its plumage, and one of its golden feathers fell to the earth.

The youth picked it up, and the next morning carried it to the king, and related to him what he had seen during the night. The king assembled his counsellors and laid the whole case before them, and they all declared that such a feather as the bird had dropped was of more value than the whole kingdom. 'If one feather is so costly,' cried the king, 'whether I have help or not, I must and will have the whole bird.'

Then the eldest son, relying on his own cleverness, set out on a journey to find the bird, and felt sure he should do so very quickly. He had not gone far when he came to the borders of a wood, where he saw a fox, and immediately presented his gun at him. 'Do not shoot me,' cried the fox; 'I can give you good advice. I know you are searching for the golden bird, and if you keep straight on you will arrive towards evening at a little village in which there are two inns on exactly opposite sides of the road. You will find one lighted up brightly and with all sorts of amusement and gaiety going on, but do not enter there; go to the other inn, however dark and dismal it may appear to you.'

'Why should I listen to the advice of an ignorant animal, however cunning he may be?' thought the young man; yet he followed the fox, who stretched out his bushy tail and darted off quickly through the wood.

After walking a long time he came towards evening to a village, and there stood both the inns as the fox had said. In one, which was brilliantly lighted up, he heard music and dancing, but the other had a dark, gloomy, sorrowful appearance.

'I should be a fool indeed,' said the young man, 'if I went to such a dismal old lumber place as that, instead of to this, which looks so bright and cheerful.

So he walked into the attractive house, and lived there in such sumptuous luxury and dissipation that he soon forgot, not only the golden bird, but his father, and the lessons he had been taught at home.

As time went on and the eldest son did not return, the second son offered to do what he could; so he set out on his way to find the golden bird. As the eldest had done, he also met a fox, who gave him the same advice, to which he paid no attention.

When he arrived at the two hotels, his brother, who was standing at one of the windows from which sounds of merriment issued, saw him pass, and called to him to come in.

He could not withstand this invitation, so he entered, and was very soon, like his brother, living only a life of pleasure and luxury. Again the time passed on, and the youngest brother, finding the others did not return, offered to go and seek for them; but his father would not give him permission.

SNOW-WHITE

THE GOLDEN BIRD

'You are less likely to find the golden bird than your brothers,' he said; 'for if any misfortune should happen to them they know how to take care of themselves, and will not fail to act for the best.'

But at last, as the brothers did not return, and the king became anxious, he allowed the youngest to go. At the entrance to the wood the fox again appeared, begged to have his life spared, and offered the third brother the same advice. The youth had plenty of courage, and he said, 'Make yourself quite easy, dear fox; I will do thee no harm.'

'Neither shall you repent of your kindness,' answered the fox; 'and to enable you to go very fast on your journey, just climb up behind on my tail.'

No sooner was the youth seated than the fox began to run, and they went so fast over sticks and stones that the wind whistled through his hair. As soon as they arrived near the village the young man slipped from the fox's back, and, following his good advice, turned without being seen into the humble-looking inn, and remained there the night.

The next morning he rose and went out into the fields, and there was the fox waiting for him. 'I will tell you what to do next,' he said, when the youth appeared; 'you must go straight on from here till you come to a castle, before which you will find a whole band of soldiers lying down; but do not trouble yourself about that, for they will all be asleep and snoring. So pass in between them and enter the castle, and go through all the rooms. At last you will reach a chamber in which hangs a golden bird in a wooden cage. Near it stands an empty cage, made of gold for show; but be careful while you are taking the golden bird out of his common cage to put him in the handsome one, or he may do you some harm.'

At these words the fox again stretched out his tail, the king's son seated himself on it, and away they went like the wind.

As soon as they arrived at the castle, the young prince found all as the fox had told him. He passed the sleeping soldiers safely, entered the castle, and walked from room to room till he reached the chamber in which hung the golden bird in its wicker cage. The gilded cage also hung close by; and on the floor lay the three golden apples which had been plucked from the king's garden while his three sons watched.

The young man felt inclined to laugh at his wonderful success when he opened the mean-looking wicker cage; but he seized the bird rather carelessly while removing it to the gilded cage, and it uttered such a heart-rending scream that the soldiers awoke. Rushing suddenly into the room, they took the king's son off to prison without allowing him to speak.

The next morning he was carried before the judge, who, when he had heard the accusation, passed sentence of death upon him. The matter, however, was laid before the king in whose castle he had found the bird, and he consented to spare the young man's life, on condition that he discovered the golden horse which could run faster than the wind; and he promised, when he brought it to him, he should, in addition, have the golden bird as a reward. The king's son agreed that he would do this; but when they set him free he felt very sorrowful, and sighed deeply as he went on his way.

'Where and how shall I ever be able to find this golden horse?' he said to himself. At this moment who should he see sitting by the roadside but his old friend the fox.

'Cheer up, friend,' he said; 'remember you have not heard yet what I can do. Keep up your courage; I will myself tell you how you may find the golden horse, and lead you to it. You must travel for a long way without turning right or left, till you come to a castle, in one of the stables of which the horse stands. Near the stable many grooms and stable-boys will be lying about; but they will be asleep and snoring, and you can quietly lead the golden horse out. But you must be careful to place on the horse the common saddle, made of wool and leather, not the gilded one which hangs near it, or some harm will happen to you.' Then the fox stretched out his tail, and the king's son seated himself upon it, and away they went again like the wind.

Everything occurred as the fox had said, and he soon reached the stable where the golden horse stood; but as he was going to put on the common leather saddle, he thought to himself, 'Such a beautiful horse as this ought not to have a common saddle on his back; it is not suitable for him.' But no sooner had he touched the golden saddle than the horse began to neigh as loud as he could.

The grooms and stable-boys awoke, seized the young man, and carried him off to prison. The next morning he was again brought before the justice, and condemned to die. This time, when he appealed to the king, he promised to grant him his life, and to give him the golden horse, if he could bring the beautiful princess from the golden castle.

With a heavy heart the young man started on what appeared to him a hopeless journey, when, to his good fortune, he again met the faithful fox waiting for him.

'I should now leave you to your fate,' said he, 'for not following my directions; but I feel compassion for you, and once more I will help you out of your trouble. To find the golden castle you must keep straight on, without turning right or left, and you will arrive there about sunset. Late in the evening the princess, when all is still, will go alone through the garden to the bath. You must conceal yourself, and as she passes spring out upon her, and give her a kiss. Then she will follow you, and you can easily carry her away; but on no account allow her to stay to say farewell to her parents. If you do so, evil will befall you.' Then the fox stretched out his tail, the king's son seated himself upon it, and away they went like the wind.

When he came near the castle he found everything as the fox had described. He waited till midnight, when everyone slept, and then, as he heard the footsteps of the beautiful young princess coming towards the bath, he hid himself till she came near, when he sprung out and gave her a kiss. She was terribly frightened, but he talked gently to her, and after a while she promised to go away with him, if he would only allow her to take leave of her parents. He refused at first, but she prayed and wept piteously, and fell at his feet, begging him to grant her request, so that at last he could not withstand her tears, and gave his consent.

No sooner, however, had the young maiden entered her parents' chamber than every inhabitant of the golden castle awoke; the servants went out, found the young man, and took him prisoner.

The next morning the king of the golden castle sent for him, and said, 'Your life is forfeited, and you can only obtain pardon by removing that mountain which lies before my window, and over which I cannot see the distant country; and this task must be finished in eight days. If you succeed, then you shall have my daughter as a reward.'

The king's son went out directly and began digging and shovelling with all his might. Night and day he worked without any success; all he did seemed lost, and when the seventh day arrived he gave up hope, and was overcome with sorrow.

On the evening of the seventh day the fox presented himself to the mourner: 'You do not deserve that I should take any notice of you,' he said; 'but go away now and get a little sleep. I will finish your task for you.'

The next morning, when they all rose and looked out of window, the mountain had vanished.

The young man hastened, full of joy, to the king, and informed him that he had completed the conditions imposed upon him. The king, therefore, whether he would or not, was obliged to keep his word, and give him his daughter.

Then the two went out together to find the fox, and they did not wait long before the faithful animal made his appearance.

'This is, indeed, the best of your performances,' said the fox; 'but remember that the golden horse belongs to the young lady of the golden castle.'

'How am I to get it?' asked the prince.

'I will tell you this also,' he replied. 'First, take the beautiful princess to the king who sent you to the golden castle; he will be so overjoyed that he will at once give you the golden horse as he promised. When the horse is brought to the door, hold out your hand to everyone present to say farewell, and leave the princess till the last. Then, as soon as you take her hand to wish her good-bye, hold it fast, and, with a spring, lift her on your horse, and ride away with her. None of those who stand by you will attempt to overtake you, for the golden horse runs swifter than the wind.'

All this happily came to pass, and the young prince galloped off with the beautiful maiden far away from all pursuers.

But the fox was not far behind when they stopped, so he came up to them and said, 'Now I will help you to get the golden bird. When you approach the castle where it is concealed, you must leave the young lady under my protection, and ride into the castle court with your golden horse. They will all be so delighted at seeing the beautiful animal that they will bring out the golden bird to you; and as soon as you have the cage in your hand, then ride back to us, and fetch the beautiful princess.'

Everything happened as they expected, and the king's son, lifting the young maiden on the horse, was quite ready to ride home with his treasures.

' And now,' said the fox, ' what reward am I to have for my assistance to you?'

' What do you wish for?' asked the young man.

' I wish,' he replied, ' that when you reach the wood where you first saw me, you will shoot me dead, and cut off my head and feet.'

' That would indeed be a pleasant way of showing my gratitude,' said the king's son; ' but it is an impossibility for me to do.'

' Then,' replied the fox, ' if you will not do it, I must leave you here; but, before I go, I will give you once more good advice. For two miles be very careful of yourselves; on no account sit on the edge of a well, and do not buy gallows meat.' After saying these words, the fox ran away into the wood.

' What a wonderful animal that is!' said the young man to himself, ' and what curious, strange whims he has ! Who ever would think of buying gallows flesh? and the wish to sit on the edge of a well would never occur to me.'

So he rode away with the beautiful princess. The road led him through the village in which his two brothers were staying, and on arriving there they heard a great noise, and saw the people running about. Upon inquiring what was the matter, they were told that two people were going to be hung; and as they drew nearer, he saw that they were his two brothers, who had committed all sorts of wicked actions, and wasted and spent all their property.

Eagerly he asked if he could not set them free and save them.

' If you will pay a ransom for them, you can,' answered the crowd; ' but why should you give your gold for two wicked men who deserve to be hung?'

But the younger brother did not listen to this; he paid the ransom for them, set them free, and told them to travel home with him.

When they reached the wood where each of them had first met the fox, it was so cool and pleasant, and so sheltered from the burning sun, that the elder brother said, ' Let us stay here and rest for a time, while we take something to eat and drink.' The younger brother was quite willing; he alighted from his horse, and when one of them asked him to sit on the brink of the well with him he readily consented, quite forgetting the warning, and his promise to the fox. He had scarcely seated himself, when his two brothers suddenly turned upon him, and pushed him backwards into the well.

Then they started up, took possession of the young princess, the golden horse, and the golden bird, and travelled quickly home to their father.

'We have brought home not only the golden bird,' they said, 'but the golden horse and the young princess from the golden castle, as booty.'

There was great rejoicing on their arrival at first; but it caused much anxiety when it was found that the horse would not eat, the bird would not sing, and the young maiden only sat and wept.

The younger brother, however, was not dead. Fortunately the well was dry, and he fell on soft moss without receiving the least injury. He could not, however, get out without help, and help was at hand, for in his trouble the faithful fox did not forsake him. He came to the well, and, after looking over, he jumped down to him, and began to scold him well for having forgotten his advice.

'I cannot, however, leave you here,' he said; 'I will help you again into the daylight.'

So he told the young man to lay hold tightly by his tail, and then the fox climbed up, and dragged the young man after him. 'You are still in danger,' he said; 'for your brothers, not being sure of your death, have placed watchers about the wood to kill you if they see you.'

Presently the king's son saw a poor man sitting under a tree, begging. 'Change clothes with him,' whispered the fox, and then ran away.

The man was very ready to make the exchange, and then the younger brother took his way, as a poor beggar, across the fields, till he came to the courtyard of his father's castle. No one recognised him, so he went on still closer to the windows, and asked for alms. In a moment the bird in the cage began to sing, the horse in the stable ate his corn, and the beautiful young maiden ceased to weep.

'What is the meaning of this?' asked the king in wonder.

Then said the maiden, 'I cannot tell why, but I have been so sad, and now I feel quite happy. It is as if my real bridegroom had returned.'

At length she determined to tell the king all that had occurred, although the other brothers had threatened to kill her if she betrayed them.

The king, upon this, ordered everyone in the castle to appear before him, and among them came the poor man in ragged clothes. The princess recognised him immediately, and fell on his neck, and wept for joy to find him alive. The king also recognised his youngest son, after he had thrown off his disguise. Then the brothers were brought to justice and punished, while the youngest married the beautiful princess, and was named as the king's successor.

We must now hear what became of the poor fox. Not long after, the king's son met him, and the fox said, 'You have everything that you can wish for in the world, but to my misfortunes there appears no end, although you have the power of setting me free;' and once more he begged so earnestly to be shot dead, and to have his head and feet cut off, that the king's son at last, with sorrow, consented. What was his surprise, as soon as he had finished the painful task, to see a fine, tall young man stand up in the place of the fox, who was no other than the brother of the beautiful princess, whom the king's son had at last set free from the enchantment that lay upon him.

After this, nothing ever happened to interfere with their happiness and good fortune for the rest of their lives.

THE TWIN BROTHERS.

THERE were once two brothers, one of them rich, the other poor. The rich brother was a goldsmith, and had a wicked heart. The poor brother supported himself by making brooms, and was good and honest. He had two children, twin-brothers, who resembled each other as closely as one drop of water resembles another. The two boys went sometimes to the house of their rich uncle to get the pieces that were left from the table, for they were often very hungry.

It happened one day that while their father was in the wood, gathering rushes for his brooms, he saw a bird whose plumage shone like gold—he had never in his life seen any bird like it. He picked up a stone and threw it at the bird, hoping to be lucky enough to secure it; but the stone only knocked off a golden feather, and the bird flew away.

The man took the feather and brought it to his brother, who, when he saw it, exclaimed, 'That is real gold!' and gave him a great deal of money for it. Another day, as the man climbed up a beech-tree, hoping to find the golden bird's nest, the same bird flew over his head, and on searching farther he found a nest, and in it lay two golden eggs. He took the eggs home and showed them to his brother, who said again, 'They are real gold,' and gave him what they were worth. At last the goldsmith said, 'You may as well get me the bird, if you can.'

So the poor brother went again to the wood, and, after a time, seeing the bird perched on a tree, he knocked it down with a stone, and brought it to his brother, who gave him a large heap of money for it. 'Now,' thought he, 'I can support myself for the future,' and went home to his house full of joy.'

The goldsmith, however, who was clever and cunning, knew well the real value of the bird. So he called his wife, and said, 'Roast the gold brid for me, and be careful that no one comes in, as I wish to eat it quite alone.'

The bird was, indeed, not a common bird ; it had a wonderful power even when dead.   For any person who ate the heart and liver would every morning find under his pillow a piece of gold.   The goldsmith's wife prepared the bird, stuck it on the spit, and left it to roast.

Now it happened that while it was roasting, and the mistress absent from the kitchen about other household work, the two children of the broom-binder came in, and stood for a few moments watching the spit as it turned round.   Presently two little pieces fell from the bird into the dripping-pan underneath.   One of them said, ' I think we may have those two little pieces ; no one will ever miss them, and I am so hungry.'   So the children each took a piece and ate it up.

In a few moments the goldsmith's wife came in, and saw that they had been eating something, and said, ' What have you been eating ?'

' Only two little pieces that fell from the bird,' they replied.

' Oh !' exclaimed the wife, in a great fright, ' they must have been the heart and liver of the bird ;' and then, that her husband might not miss them, for she was afraid of his anger, she quickly killed a chicken, took out the heart and liver, and laid them on the golden bird.

As soon as it was ready, she carried it in to the goldsmith, who ate it all up, without leaving her a morsel.   The next morning, however, when he felt under his pillow, expecting to find the gold pieces, nothing was there.

The two children, however, who knew nothing of the good fortune which had befallen them, never thought of searching under their pillow. But the next morning, as they got out of bed, something fell on the ground and tinkled, and when they stooped to pick it up, there were two pieces of gold.   They carried them at once to their father, who won-dered very much, and said, ' What can this mean ?'

As, however, there were two more pieces the next morning, and again each day, the father went to his brother and told him of the wonderful circumstance.   The goldsmith, as he listened, knew well that these gold pieces must be the result of the children having eaten the heart and liver of the golden bird, and therefore that he had been deceived. He determined to be revenged, and, though hard-hearted and jealous, he managed to conceal the real truth from his brother, and said to him, ' Your children are in league with the evil one : do not touch the gold, and on no account allow your children to remain in your house any longer, for the evil one has power over them, and could bring ruin upon you through them.'

The father feared this power, and therefore, sad as is was to him, he led the twins out into the forest and left them there with a heavy heart.

When they found themselves alone, the two children ran here and there in the wood to try and discover the way home, but they wandered back always to the same place.   At last they met a hunter, who said to them, ' Whose children are you ?'

' We are a poor broom-binder's children,' they replied, ' and our father will not keep us any longer in the house because every morning there is a piece of gold found under our pillows.'

'Ah,' exclaimed the hunter, 'that is not bad! Well, if you are honest, and have told me the truth, I will take you home and be a father to you.'

In fact, the children pleased the good man, and, as he had no children of his own, he gladly took them home with him.

While they were with him, he taught them to hunt in the forest,

THE TWO CHILDREN RAN HERE AND THERE.

and the gold pieces which they found every morning under their pillows they gave to him; so for the future he had nothing to fear about poverty.

As soon as the twins were grown up, their foster-father took them one day into the wood, and said : 'To-day you are going to make your first trial at shooting, for I want you to be free if you like, and to be hunters for yourselves.'

Then they went with him to a suitable point, and waited a long time, but no game appeared. Presently the hunter saw flying over his head a flock of wild geese, in the form of a triangle, so he said, 'Aim quickly at each corner and fire.' They did so, and their first proof-shot was successful.

Soon after, another flock appeared in the form of the figure 2. 'Now,' he exclaimed, 'shoot again at each corner and bring them down!' This proof-shot was also successful, and the hunter directly said, 'Now I pronounce you free ; you are quite accomplished sportsmen.'

Then the two brothers went away into the wood together, to hold counsel with each other, and at last came to an agreement about what they wished to do.

In the evening, when they sat down to supper, one of them said to their foster-father, 'We will not remain to supper, or eat one bit, till you have granted us our request.'

'And what is your request?' he asked.

'You have taught us to hunt, and to earn our living,' they replied, 'and we want to go out in the world and seek our fortune. Will you give us permission to do so?'

The good old man replied joyfully, 'You speak like brave hunters ; what you desire is my own wish. Go when you will, you will be sure to succeed.'

Then they ate and drank together joyfully.

When the appointed day came, the hunter presented each of them with a new rifle and a dog, and allowed them to take as much as they would from his store of the gold pieces. He accompanied them for some distance on the way, and before saying farewell, he gave them each a white penknife, and said :

'If at any time you should get separated from each other, the knife must be placed cross-ways in a tree, one side of the blade turning east, the other west, pointing out the road which each should take. If one should die, the blade will rust on one side ; but as long as he lives, it will remain bright.'

After saying this, he wished the brothers farewell, and they started on their way.

After travelling for some time they came to an immense forest, so large that it was impossible to cross it in one day. They stayed there all night, and ate what they had in their game-bags ; but for two days they walked on through the forest without finding themselves any nearer the end.

By this time they had nothing left to eat, so one said to the other, 'We must shoot something, for this hunger is not to be endured.' So he loaded his gun, and looked about him. Presently an old hare came running by ; but as he raised his rifle, the hare cried :

'Dearest hunters, let me live ;
I will to you my young ones give.'

Then she sprang up nto the bushes, and brought out two young ones, and laid them before the hunters. The little animals were so full of tricks, and played about so prettily, that the hunters had not the heart to kill them; they kept them, therefore, alive, and the little animals soon learned to follow them about like dogs.

By-and-by a fox appeared, and they were about to shoot him, but he cried also:

> 'Dearest hunters, let me live,
> And I will you my young ones give.'

Then he brought out two little foxes, but the hunters could not kill them, so they gave them to the hares as companions, and the little creatures followed the hunters wherever they went.

Not long after a wolf stepped before them out of the thicket, and one of the brothers instantly levelled his gun at him, but the wolf cried out:

> 'Dear, kind hunters, let me live;
> I will to you my young ones give.'

The hunters took the young wolves, and treated them as they had done the other animals, and they followed them also.

Presently a bear came by, and they quite intended to kill him, but he also cried out:

> 'Dear, kind hunters, let me live,
> And I will you my young ones give.'

The two young bears were placed with the others, of whom there were already eight.

At last, who should come by but a lion, shaking his mane. The hunters were not at all alarmed; they only pointed their guns at him. But the lion cried out in the same manner:

> 'Dear, kind hunters, let me live,
> And I will you two young ones give.'

So he fetched two of his cubs, and the hunters placed them with the rest. They had now two lions, two bears, two wolves, two foxes, and two hares, who travelled with them and served them. Yet, after all, their hunger was not appeased.

So one of them said to the fox, 'Here, you little sneak, who are so clever and sly, go and find us something to eat.'

Then the fox answered, 'Not far from here lies a town where we have many times fetched away chickens. I will show you the way.'

So the fox showed them the way to the village, where they bought some provisions for themselves and food for the animals, and went on farther.

The fox, however, knew quite well the best spots in that part of the country, and where to find the hen-houses; and he could, above all, direct the hunters which road to take.

After travelling for a time in this way, they could find no suitable place for them all to remain together, so one said to the other, 'The only thing for us to do is to separate;' and to this the other agreed.

THEY HAD NOW TWO LIONS, TWO BEARS, TWO WOLVES, TWO FOXES, AND TWO HARES.

Then they divided the animals so that each had one lion, one bear, one wolf, one fox, and one hare. When the time came to say farewell, they promised to live in brotherly love till death, stuck the knife that their foster-father had given them in a tree, and then one turned to the east, and the other to the west.

The youngest, whose steps we will follow first, soon arrived at a large town, in which the houses were all covered with black crape. He went to an inn, and asked the landlord if he could give shelter to his animals. The landlord pointed out a stable for them, and their master led them in and shut the door.

But in the wall of the stable was a hole, and the hare slipped through easily and fetched a cabbage for herself. The fox followed, and came back with a hen; and as soon as he had eaten it, he went for the cock also. The wolf, the bear, and the lion, however, were too large to get through the hole. Then the landlord had a cow killed and brought in for them, or they would have starved.

The hunter was just going out to see if his animals were being cared for, when he asked the landlord why the houses were so hung with mourning crape.

'Because,' he replied, 'to-morrow morning our king's daughter will die.'

'Is she seriously ill, then?' asked the hunter.

'No,' he answered; 'she is in excellent health; still, she must die.'

'What is the cause of this?' said the young man.

Then the landlord explained.

'Outside the town,' he said, 'is a high mountain, in which dwells a dragon, who every year demands a young maiden to be given up to him, otherwise he will destroy the whole country. He has already devoured all the young maidens in the town, and there are none remaining but the king's daughter. Not even for her is any favour shown, and to-morrow she must be delivered up to him.'

'Why do you not kill the dragon?' exclaimed the young hunter.

'Ah!' replied the landlord, 'many young knights have sought to do so, and lost their lives in the attempt. The king has even promised his daughter in marriage to whoever will destroy the dragon, and also that he shall be heir to his throne.'

The hunter made no reply to this; but the next morning he rose early, and taking his animals with him, climbed up the dragon's mountain.

There stood near the top a little church, and on the altar inside were three full goblets, bearing this inscription : 'Whoever drinks of these goblets will be the strongest man upon earth, and will discover the sword which lies buried before the threshold of this door.'

The hunter did not drink; he first went out and sought for the sword in the ground, but he could not find the place. Then he returned, and drank up the contents of the goblets. How strong it made him feel; and how quickly he found the sword, which, heavy as it was, he could wield easily !

Meanwhile, the hour came when the young maiden was to be given up to the dragon, and she came out, accompanied by the king, the marshal, and the courtiers.

They saw from the distance the hunter on the mountain, and the princess, thinking it was the dragon waiting for her, would not go on. At last she remembered that, to save the town from being lost, she must make this painful sacrifice, and therefore wished her father farewell. The king and the court returned home full of great sorrow. The king's marshal, however, was to remain, and see from a distance all that took place.

When the king's daughter reached the top of the mountain, she found, instead of the dragon, a handsome young hunter, who spoke to her comforting words, and, telling her he had come to rescue her, led her into the church, and locked her in.

Before long, with a rushing noise and a roar, the seven-headed dragon made his appearance. As soon as he caught sight of the hunter, he wondered to himself, and said at last, ' What business have you here on this mountain ?'

' My business is a combat with you,' replied the hunter.

' Many knights and nobles have tried that, and lost their lives,' replied the dragon; ' with you I shall make short work.'

And he breathed out fire as he spoke from his seven throats.

The flames set fire to the dry grass, and the hunter would have been stifled with heat and smoke had not his faithful animals ran forward and stamped out the fire. Then in a rage the dragon drew near, but the hunter was too quick for him; swinging his sword on high, it whizzed through the air, and falling on the dragon, cut off three of his heads.

Then was the monster furious; he raised himself on his hind legs, spat fiery flames on the hunter, and tried to overthrow him. But the young man again swung his sword, and, as the dragon approached, he, with one blow, cut off three more of his heads. The monster, mad with rage, sank on the ground, still trying to get at the hunter; but the young man, exerting all his remaining strength, had no difficulty in cutting off his seventh head, and his tail; and then, finding he could resist no more, he called to his animals to come and tear the dragon in pieces.

As soon as the combat was ended, the hunter unlocked the church-door, and found the king's daughter lying on the ground; for during the combat all sense and life had left her, from fear and terror.

He raised her up, and as she came to herself and opened her eyes, he showed her the dragon torn in pieces, and told her that she was released from all danger.

Oh, how joyful she felt, when she saw and heard what he had done, and said, ' Now you will be my dear husband, for my father has himself promised me in marriage to whoever should kill the dragon.'

Then she took off her coral necklace of five strings, and divided it between the animals as a reward; the lion's share being in addition the gold clasp. Her pocket-handkerchief, which bore her name, she presented to the hunter, who went out, and cut the seven tongues out of the dragon's heads, which he wrapped up carefully in the handkerchief.

After all the fighting, and the fire and smoke, the hunter felt so faint and tired, that he said to the maiden, 'I think a little rest would do us both good, after all the fight and the struggles with the dragon that I have had, and your terror and alarm. Shall we sleep for a little while before I take you home safely to your father's house?'

'Yes,' she replied, 'I can sleep peacefully now.'

So she laid herself down, and, as soon as she slept, he said to the lion, 'You must lie near, and watch that no one comes to harm us.' Then he threw himself on the ground, quite worn out, and was soon fast asleep.

The lion laid himself down at a little distance to watch; but he was also tired and overcome with the combat, so he called to the bear, and said, 'Lie down near me; I must have a little rest, and, if anyone comes, wake me up.'

Then the bear lay down; but he was also very tired, so he cried to the wolf, 'Just lie down by me; I must have a little sleep, and, if anything happens, wake me up.'

The wolf complied; but, as he was also tired, he called to the fox, and said, 'Lie down near me; I must have a little sleep, and, if anything comes, wake me up.'

Then the fox came and laid himself down by the wolf; but he too was tired, and called out to the hare, 'Lie down near me; I must sleep a little, and, whatever comes, wake me up.'

The hare seated herself near the fox; but the poor little hare was very tired, and, although she had no one to ask to watch and call her, she also went fast asleep. And now the king's daughter, the hunter, the bear, the lion, the wolf, the fox, and the hare were all in a deep sleep, while danger was at hand.

The marshal, from the distance, had tried to see what was going on, and being surprised that the dragon had not yet flown away with the king's daughter, and that all was quiet on the mountain, took courage, and ventured to climb up to the top. There he saw the mangled and headless body of the dragon, and, at a little distance, the king's daughter, the hunter, and all the animals sunk in a deep sleep. He knew in a moment that the stranger hunter had killed the dragon, and, being wicked and envious, he drew his sword, and cut off the hunter's head. Then he seized the sleeping maiden by the arm, and carried her away from the mountain.

She woke, and screamed; but the marshal said, 'You are in my power, and therefore you shall say that I have killed the dragon!'

'I cannot say so,' she replied, 'for I saw the hunter kill him, and the animals tear him in pieces.'

Then he drew his sword, and threatened to kill her if she did not obey him; so that, to save her life, she was forced to promise to say all he wished.

Thereupon he took her to the king, who knew not how to contain himself for joy at finding his dear child still alive, and that she had been saved from the monster's power.

Then the marshal said, 'I have killed the dragon, and freed the king's daughter, therefore I demand her for my wife, according to the king's promise.'

'Is this all true?' asked the king of his daughter.

'Ah, yes,' she replied, 'I suppose it is true; but I shall refuse to allow the marriage to take place for one year and a day. For,' thought she, 'in that time I may hear something of my dear hunter.'

All this while on the dragon's mountain the animals lay sleeping near their dead master. At last a large humble-bee settled on the hare's nose, but she only whisked it off with her paw, and slept again. The bee came a second time, but the hare again shook him off, and slept as soundly as before. Then came the humble-bee a third time, and stung the hare in the nose, thereupon she woke. As soon as she was quite aroused, she woke the fox; the fox, the wolf; the wolf, the bear; and the bear, the lion.

But when the lion roused himself, and saw that the maiden was gone, and his master dead, he gave a terrible roar, and cried, 'Whose doing is this? Bear, why did you not wake me?'

Then said the bear to the wolf, 'Wolf, why did you not wake me?'

'Fox,' cried the wolf, 'why did you not wake me?'

'Hare,' said the fox, 'and why did you not wake me?'

The poor hare had no one to ask why they did not wake her, and she knew she must bear all the blame. Indeed, they were all ready to tear her to pieces, but she cried, 'Don't destroy my life; I will restore our master. I know a mountain on which grows a root that will cure every wound and every disease, if it is placed in the person's mouth; but the mountain on which it grows lies two hundred miles from here.'

'Then,' said the lion, 'we will give you twenty-four hours, but not longer, to find this root and bring it to us.'

Away sprang the hare very fast, and in four-and-twenty hours she returned with the root. As soon as they saw her, the lion quickly placed the head of the hunter on the neck; and the hare, when she had joined the wounded parts together, put the root into the mouth, and in a few moments the heart began to beat, and life came back to the hunter.

On awaking, he was terribly alarmed to find that the maiden had disappeared. 'She must have gone away while I slept,' he said, 'and is lost to me for ever!'

These sad thoughts so occupied him that he did not notice anything wrong about his head, but in truth the lion had placed it on in such a hurry that the face was turned the wrong way. He first noticed it when they brought him something to eat, and then he found that his

face looked backwards.   He was so astonished that he could not
imagine what had happened, and asked his animals the cause.   Then
the lion confessed that they had all slept in consequence of being so
tired, and that when they at last awoke, they found the princess gone,
and himself lying dead, with his head cut off.   The lion told him also
that the hare had fetched the healing root, but in their haste they had
placed the head on the wrong way.   This mistake, they said, could be
easily rectified.   So they took the hunter's head off again, turned it
round, placed it on properly, and the hare stuck the parts together with
the wonderful root.   After this, the hunter went away again to travel
about the world, feeling very sorrowful, and he left his animals to
be taken care of by the people of the town.

It so happened that at the end of a year he came back again to the
same town where he had freed the king's daughter and killed the dragon.
This time, instead of black crape, the houses were hung with scarlet
cloth.   ' What does it mean ?' he said to the landlord ; ' last year when
I came, your houses were all hung with black crape, and now it is
scarlet cloth.'

' Oh,' replied the landlord, ' last year we were expecting our king's
daughter to be given up to the dragon, but the marshal fought with him
and killed him, and to-morrow his marriage with the king's daughter
will take place : that is the cause of our town being so gay and bright—
it is joy now instead of sorrow.'

The next day, when the marriage was to be celebrated, the hunter
said, ' Landlord, do you believe that I shall eat bread from the king's table
here with anyone who will join me ?'

' I will lay a hundred gold pieces,' replied the landlord, ' that you will
do nothing of the kind.'

The hunter took the bet, and, taking out his purse, placed the gold
pieces aside for payment if he should lose.

Then he called the hare, and said to her, ' Go quickly to the castle,
dear Springer, and bring me some of the bread which the king eats.'

Now, the hare was such an insignificant little thing that no one ever
thought of ordering a conveyance for her, so she was obliged to go on
foot.   ' Oh,' thought she, ' when I am running through the streets,
suppose the cruel hound should see me.'   Just as she got near the
castle, she looked behind her, and there truly was a hound ready to
seize her.   But she gave a start forward, and before the sentinel was
aware, rushed into the sentry-box.   The dog followed, and wanted to
bring her out, but the soldier stood in the doorway and would not let
him pass, and when the dog tried to get in he struck him with his staff,
and sent him away howling.

As soon as the hare saw that the coast was clear, she rushed out of
the sentry-box and ran to the castle, and, finding the door of the room
where the princess was sitting open, she darted in and hid under her
chair.   Presently the princess felt something scratching her foot, and
thinking it was the dog, she said, ' Be quiet, Sultan ; go away.'   The

hare scratched again at her foot, but she still thought it was the dog, and cried, ' Will you go away, Sultan?' But the hare did not allow herself to be sent away, so she scratched the foot a third time. Then the princess looked down and recognised the hare by her necklace. She took the creature at once in her arms, carried her to her own room, and said, ' Dear little hare, what do you want?'

The hare replied instantly, ' My master, who killed the dragon, is here, and he has sent me to ask for some of the bread that the king eats.'

Then was the king's daughter full of joy; she sent for the cook, and ordered him to bring her some of the bread which was made for the king. When he brought it, the hare cried, ' The cook must go with me, or that cruel hound may do me some harm.' So the cook carried the bread, and went with the hare to the door of the inn.

As soon as he was gone she stood on her hind-legs, took the bread in her fore-paws, and brought it to her master.

' There!' cried the hunter, ' here is the bread, landlord, and the hundred gold pieces are mine.'

The landlord was much surprised, but when the hunter declared he would also have some of the roast meat from the king's table, he said: ' The bread may be here, but I'll warrant you will get nothing more.'

The hunter called the fox, and said to him, ' My foxy, go and fetch me some of the roast meat such as the king eats.'

The red fox knew a better trick than the hare: he went across the fields, and slipped in without being seen by the hound. Then he placed himself under the chair of the king's daughter, and touched her foot. She looked down immediately, and recognising him by his necklace, took him into her room. ' What do you want, dear fox?' she asked.

' My master, who killed the dragon, is here,' he replied, ' and has sent me to ask for some of the roast meat that is cooked for the king.'

The cook was sent for again, and the princess desired him to carry some meat for the fox to the door of the inn. On arriving, the fox took the dish from the cook, and, after whisking away the flies that had settled on it with his tail, brought it to his master.

' See, landlord,' cried the hunter, ' here are bread and meat such as the king eats, and now I will have vegetables.' So he called the wolf, and said, ' Dear wolf, go and fetch me vegetables such as the king eats.'

Away went the wolf straight to the castle, for he had no fear of any-thing, and as soon as he entered the room he went behind the princess and pulled her dress, so that she was obliged to look round. She recognised the wolf immediately by the necklace, took him into her chamber, and said, ' Dear wolf, what do you want?' He replied, ' My master, who killed the dragon, is here, and has sent me to ask for some vegetables such as the king eats.'

The cook was sent for again, and told to take some vegetables also to the inn door; and as soon as they arrived the wolf took the dish from him, and carried it to his master.

'Look here, landlord,' cried the hunter, 'I have now bread, meat, and vegetables; but I will also have some sweetmeats from the king's table.' He called the bear, and said: 'Dear bear, I know you are fond of sweets. Now go and fetch me some sweetmeats such as the king eats.'

The bear trotted off to the castle, and everyone ran away when they saw him coming. But when he reached the castle gates, the sentinel held his gun before him, and would not let him pass in. But the bear rose on his hind legs, boxed his ears right and left with his fore paws, and, leaving him tumbled all of a heap in his sentry-box, went into the castle. Seeing the king's daughter entering, he followed her and gave a slight growl. She looked behind her, and, recognising the bear, called him into her chamber, and said: 'Dear bear, what do you want?'

'My master, who killed the dragon, is here,' he replied, 'and he has sent me to ask for some sweetmeats like those which the king eats.'

The princess sent for the confectioner, and desired him to bake some sweetmeats, and take them with the bear to the door of the inn. As soon as they arrived, the bear first licked up the sugar drips which had dropped on his fur, then stood upright, took the dish, and carried it to his master.

'See now, landlord,' cried the hunter, 'I have bread, and meat, and vegetables, and sweetmeats, and I mean to have wine also, such as the king drinks!' So he called the lion to him, and said: 'Dear lion, you drink till you are quite tipsy sometimes. Now go and fetch me some wine, such as the king drinks.'

As the lion trotted through the streets all the people ran away from him. The sentinel, when he saw him coming, tried to stop the way; but the lion gave a little roar, and made him run for his life. Then the lion entered the castle, passed through the king's apartment, and knocked at the door of the princess's room with his tail. The princess, when she opened it and saw the lion, was at first rather frightened; but presently she observed on his neck the gold necklace clasp, and knew it was the hunter's lion. She called him into her chamber, and said: 'Dear lion, what do you want?'

'My master, who killed the dragon,' he replied, 'is here, and he has sent me to ask for some wine, such as the king drinks.'

Then she sent for the king's cupbearer, and told him to give the lion some of the king's wine.

'I will go with him,' said the lion, 'and see that he draws the right sort.' So the lion went with the cupbearer to the wine-cellar, and when he saw him about to draw some of the ordinary wine which the king's vassals drank, the lion cried, 'Stop! I will taste the wine first.' So he drew himself a pint, and swallowed it down at a gulp. 'No,' he said, 'that is not the right sort.'

The cupbearer saw he was found out; however, he went over to another cask that was kept for the king's marshal.

'Stop!' cried the lion again, 'I will taste the wine first.' So he drew

THE CUPBEARER CARRYING THE WINE TO THE DOOR OF THE INN.

another pint and drank it off. 'Ah!' he said, 'that is better, but still not the right wine.'

Then the cupbearer was angry, and said:

'What can a stupid beast like you understand about wine?'

But the lion, with a lash of his tail, knocked him down, and before the man could move himself, found his way stealthily into a little private cellar, in which were casks of wine never tasted by any but the king.   The lion drew half a pint, and when he had tasted it, he said to himself, 'That is wine of the right sort.'   So he called the cupbearer, and made him draw six flagons full.

As they came up from the cellar into the open air, the lion's head swam a little, and he was almost tipsy; but as the cup-bearer was obliged to carry the wine for him to the door of the inn, it did not much matter.   When they arrived, the lion took the handle of the basket in his mouth, and carried the wine to his master.

'Now, master landlord,' said the hunter, 'I have bread, meat, vegetables, sweetmeats, and wines, such as the king has, so I will sit down, and, with my faithful animals, enjoy a good meal;' and, indeed, he felt very happy, for he knew now that the king's daughter still loved him.

After they had finished, the hunter said to the landlord:

'Now that I have eaten and drank of the same provisions as the king, I will go to the king's castle and marry his daughter.'

'Well,' said the landlord, 'how that is to be managed I cannot tell, when she has already a bridegroom to whom she will to-day be married.'

The hunter, without a word, took out the pocket-handkerchief which the king's daughter had given him on the dragon's mountain, and, opening it, showed the landlord the seven tongues of the monster, which he had cut out and wrapped in the handkerchief.

'That which I have so carefully preserved will help me,' said the hunter.

The landlord looked at the handkerchief, and said:

'I may believe all the rest, but I would bet my house and farmyard that you will never marry the king's daughter.'

'Very well,' said the hunter, 'I accept your bet, and, if I lose, there are my hundred gold pieces;' and he laid them on the table.

That same day, when the king and his daughter were seated at table, the king said: 'What did all those wild animals want who came to you to-day, going in and out of my castle?'

'I cannot tell you yet,' she replied; 'but if you will send into the town for the master of these animals, then I will do so.'

The king sent, on hearing this, a servant at once to the inn with an invitation to the stranger who owned the animals, and the servant arrived just as the hunter had finished his bet with the landlord.

'See, landlord!' he cried, 'the king has sent me an invitation by his servant; but I cannot accept it yet.' He turned to the man who waited, and said: 'Tell my lord the king that I cannot obey his commands to visit him unless he sends me suitable clothes for a royal palace, and a carriage with six horses, and servants to wait upon me.'

The servant returned with the message, and when the king heard it, he said to his daughter : ' What shall I do ?'

' I would send for him, as he requests,' she replied.

So they sent royal robes, and a carriage and six horses with servants, and, when the hunter saw them coming, he said to the landlord : ' See ! they have sent for me as I wished.'

He dressed himself in the kingly clothes, took the handkerchief containing the dragon's tongues, and drove away to the castle.

As soon as he arrived, the king said to his daughter : ' How shall I receive him ?'

' I should go and meet him,' she replied.

So the king went to meet him, and led him into the royal apartment, and all his animals followed. The king pointed him to a seat by his daughter. The marshal sat on her other side as bridegroom, but the visitor knew it not.

Just at this moment the dragon's seven heads were brought into the room to show to the company, and the king said : ' These heads belonged to the dragon who was for so many years the terror of this town. The marshal slew the dragon, and saved my daughter's life ; therefore, I have given her to him in marriage, according to my promise.'

At this the hunter rose, and, advancing, opened the seven throats of the dragon, and said : ' Where are the tongues ?'

The marshal turned white with fear, and knew not what to do. At last he said, in his terror : ' Dragons have no tongues.'

' Liars get nothing for their pains,' said the hunter ; ' the dragon's tongues shall prove who was his conqueror !'

He unfolded the handkerchief as he spoke. There lay the seven tongues. He took them up, and placed each in the mouth of the dragon's head to which it belonged, and it fitted exactly. Then he took up the pocket-handkerchief which was marked with the name of the king's daughter, showed it to the maiden, and asked her if she had not given it to him.

' Yes,' she replied ; ' I gave it you on the day you killed the dragon.'

He called his animals to him, took from each the necklace, and from the lion the one with the golden clasp, and asked to whom they belonged.

' They are mine,' she replied ; ' they are a part of my coral necklace which had five strings of beads, which I divided among the animals because they aided you in killing the dragon, and afterwards tore him in pieces. I cannot tell how the marshal could have carried me away from you,' she continued, ' for you told me to lie down and sleep after the fatigue and fright I had endured.'

' I slept myself,' he replied, ' for I was quite worn out with my combat, and as I lay sleeping the marshal came and cut off my head.'

' I begin to understand now,' said the king ; ' the marshal carried away my daughter, supposing you were dead, and made us believe that he had killed the dragon, till you arrived with the tongues, the handkerchief, and the necklace. But what restored you to life?' asked the king.

Then the hunter related how one of his animals had healed him and restored him to life through the application of a wonderful root, and how he had been wandering about for a whole year, and had only returned to the town that very day, and heard from the landlord of the marshal's deceit.

Then said the king to his daughter, 'Is it true that this man killed the dragon?'

'Yes,' she answered, ' quite true, and I can venture now to expose the wickedness of the marshal; for he carried me away that day against my wish, and forced me with threats to keep silent. I did not know he had tried to kill the real slayer of the dragon, but I hoped he would come back, and on that account I begged to have the marriage put off for a year and a day.'

The king, after this, ordered twelve judges to be summoned to try the marshal, and the sentence passed upon him was, that he should be torn to pieces by wild oxen. As soon as the marshal was punished, the king gave his daughter to the hunter, and appointed him to the high position of stadtholder over the whole kingdom.

The marriage caused great joy, and the hunter, who was now a prince, sent for his father and foster-father, and overloaded them with treasures.

Neither did he forget the landlord, but sent for him to come to the castle, and said : ' See, landlord, I have married the king's daughter, and your house and farmyard belong to me.'

' That is quite true,' replied the landlord.

' Ah,' said the prince, ' but I do not mean to keep them : they are still yours, and I make you a present of the hundred gold pieces also.'

For a time the young prince and his wife lived most happily together —he still, however, went out hunting, which was his great delight, and his faithful animals remained with him. They lived, however, in a wood close by, from which he could call them at any time ; yet the wood was not safe, for he once went in and did not get out again very easily.

Whenever the prince had a wish to go hunting, he gave the king no rest till he allowed him to do so. On one occasion, while riding with a large number of attendants in the wood, he saw at a distance a snow-white deer, and he said to his people, ' Stay here till I come back ; I must have that beautiful creature, and so many will frighten her.'

Then he rode away through the wood, and only his animals followed him. The attendants drew rein, and waited till evening, but as he did not come they rode home and told the young princess that her husband had gone into an enchanted forest to hunt a white deer, and had not returned.

This made her very anxious, more especially when the morrow came and he did not return; indeed, he could not, for he kept riding after the beautiful wild animal, but without being able to overtake it. At times, when he fancied she was within reach of his gun, the next moment she was leaping away at a great distance, and at last she vanished altogether.

Not till then did he notice how far he had penetrated into the forest. He raised his horn and blew, but there was no answer, for his attendants could not hear; and then as night came on he saw plainly that he should not be able to find his way home till the next day, so he alighted from his horse, lit a fire by a tree, and determined to make himself as comfortable as he could for the night.

As he sat under the tree by the fire, with his animals lying near him, he heard, as he thought, a human voice. He looked round, but could see nothing. Presently there was a groan over his head; he looked up and saw an old woman sitting on a branch, who kept grumbling, 'Oh, oh, how cold I am! I am freezing.'

'If you are cold, come down and warm yourself,' he said.

'No, no,' she replied; 'your animals will bite me.'

'Indeed they will do no such thing. Come down, old mother,' he said kindly; 'none of them shall hurt you.'

He did not know that she was a wicked witch, so when she said, 'I will throw you down a little switch from the tree, and if you just touch them on the back with it they cannot hurt me,' he did as she told him, and as soon as they were touched by the wand the animals were all turned to stone. Then she jumped down, and touching the prince on the back with the switch, he also was instantly turned into stone. Thereupon she laughed maliciously, and dragged him and his animals into a grave where several similar stones lay.

When the princess found that her husband did not return, her anxiety and care increased painfully, and she became at last very unhappy.

Now it so happened that just at this time the twin brother of the prince, who since their separation had been wandering in the East, arrived in the king's country, of which his father-in-law was king. He had tried to obtain a situation, but could not succeed, and only his animals were left to him.

One day, as he was wandering from one place to another, it occurred to his mind that he might as well go and look at the knife which they had stuck in the trunk of a tree at the time of their separation. When he came to it there was his brother's side of the knife half rusted, and the other half still bright.

In great alarm he thought, 'My brother must have fallen into some terrible trouble. I will go and find him; I may be able to rescue him, as the half of the knife is still bright.'

He set out with his animals on a journey, and, while travelling West, came to the town in which his brother's wife, the king's daughter,

lived.   As soon as he reached the gate of the town, the watchman
advanced towards him, and asked if he should go and announce
his arrival to the princess, who had for two days been in great
trouble about him, fearing that he had been detained in the forest
by enchantment.

The watchman had not the least idea that the young man was
any other than the prince himself, especially as he had the wild
animals running behind him.   The twin brother saw this, and he said
to himself, 'Perhaps it will be best for me to allow myself to be taken
for my brother; I shall be able more easily to save him.' So he followed
the sentinel to the castle, where he was received with great joy.

The young princess had no idea that this was not her husband, and
asked him why he had remained away so long.

He replied, 'I rode a long distance into the wood, and could not
find my way out again.'   But she thought he was very cold and distant
to her.

In a few days he discovered all about his brother that he wished to
know, and was determined to go and seek for him in the enchanted
wood.   So he said, 'I must go to the hunt just once more.'

The king and the young princess said all they could to dissuade him,
but to no purpose, and at length he left the castle with a large company
of attendants.

When he reached the wood, all happened as it had done with his
brother.   He saw the beautiful white deer, and told his attendants to
wait while he went after it, followed only by his animals; but neither
could he overtake it; and the white deer led him far down into the
forest, where he found he must remain all night.

After he had lighted a fire, he heard, as his brother had done,
the old woman in the tree, crying out that she was freezing with cold,
and he said to her, 'If you are cold, old mother, come down and warm
yourself.'

'No,' she cried; 'your animals will bite me.'

'No, indeed they will not,' he said.

'I can't trust them,' she cried; 'here, I will throw you a little switch,
and if you gently strike them across the back, then they will not be able
to hurt me.'

When the hunter heard that, he began to mistrust the old woman,
and said, 'No; I will not strike my animals; you come down, or I
will fetch you.'

'Do as you like,' she said; 'you can't hurt me.'

'If you don't come down,' he replied, 'I will shoot you.'

'Shoot away,' she said; 'your bullet can do me no harm.'

He pointed his gun, and shot at her; but the witch was proof against
a leaden bullet.   She gave a shrill laugh, and cried, 'It 's no use trying
to hit me.'

The hunter knew, however, what to do; he cut off three silver
buttons from his coat, and loaded his gun with them.   Against

these she knew all her arts were vain; so, as he drew the trigger, she fell suddenly to the ground with a scream. Then he placed his foot upon her, and said, 'Old witch, if thou dost not at once confess where my brother is, I will take thee up and throw thee into the fire.'

She was in a great fright, begged for pardon, and said, 'He is lying with his animals, turned to stone, in a grave.'

Then he forced her to go with him, and said, 'You old cat, if you don't instantly restore my brother to life, and all the creatures that are with him, over you go into the fire.'

She was obliged to take a switch and strike the stones, and immediately the brother, his animals, and many others—traders, mechanics, and shepherds—stood before him, alive and in their own forms.

Thankful for having gained their freedom and their lives, they all hastened home; but the twin brothers, when they saw each other again, were full of joy, and embraced and kissed each other with great affection. They seized the old witch, bound her, and placed her on the fire, and, as soon as she was burnt, the forest became suddenly clear and light, and the king's castle appeared at a very little distance.

After this, the twin brothers walked away together towards the castle, and, on the road, related to each other the events that had happened to them since they parted. At last the youngest told his brother of his marriage to the king's daughter, and that the king had made him lord over the whole land.

'I know all about it,' replied the other; 'for when I came to the town, they all took me for you, and treated me with kingly state; even the young princess mistook me for her husband, and made me sit by her side.'

But, as he spoke, his brother became so fierce with jealousy and anger that he drew his sword and cut off his brother's head. Then, as he saw him lie dead at his feet, his anger was quelled in a moment, and he repented bitterly, crying, 'Oh, my brother is dead, and it is I who have killed him!' and, kneeling by his side, he mourned with loud cries and tears.

In a moment the hare appeared, and begged to be allowed to fetch the life-giving root, which she knew would cure him. She was not away long, and, when she returned, the head was replaced, and fastened with the healing power of the plant, and the brother restored to life, while not even a sign of the wound remained to be noticed.

The brothers now walked on most lovingly together, and the one who had married the king's daughter said, 'I see that you have kingly clothes, as I have; your animals are the same as mine. Let us enter the castle at two opposite doors, and approach the old king from two sides together.

So they separated; and, as the king sat with his daughter in the royal apartment, a sentinel approached him from two distant entrances at the same time, and informed him that the prince, with his animals, had arrived.

'That is impossible,' cried the king; 'one of you must be wrong; for the gates at which you watch are quite a quarter of a mile apart.'

But while the king spoke the two young men entered at opposite ends of the room, and both came forward and stood before the king.

With a bewildered look the king turned to his daughter, and said, 'Which is your husband? for they are both so exactly alike I cannot tell.'

She was herself very much frightened, and could not speak; at last she thought of the necklace that she had given to the animals, and, looking earnestly among them, she saw the glitter of the golden clasp on the lion's neck. 'See,' she cried, in a happy voice, 'he whom that lion follows is my husband.'

The prince laughed, and said, 'Yes; you are right; and this is my twin brother.'

So they sat down happily together, and told the king and the young princess all their adventures.

When the king's daughter and her husband were alone, she said to him, 'I thought you did not love me the other day, when you came home from the wood, for you never even kissed me.'

Then the prince knew how true and honourable his twin brother had been.

THE QUEEN BEE.

A KING once had two sons, who were considered clever; yet they wasted their time and money in folly and dissipation, and were scarcely ever at home. They had a younger brother, whom they called stupid because he was quiet and simple, and they used to make sport, and mock him, and say that such a simpleton as he would never fight his way through the world, for they, with all their cleverness, found it a very difficult matter.

One evening, however, they took him for a walk with them, and on their way they met with an ant-hill, and the two elder brothers wanted to overturn the hill, that they might see the little ants running and creeping about in their fright, and carrying their eggs away to a place of safety. But the simpleton said: 'No, no; leave the little creatures in peace. I do not like to see them disturbed.'

Then the brothers gave way to him, and they went on quietly till they came to a lake on which a large number of ducks were swimming, and the brothers wished to catch one or two of them for roasting; but the simpleton said: 'Leave the poor birds in peace; I cannot endure that you should kill any of them.'

So the ducks were left to live, and the three brothers walked on again till at length they came to a bees' nest in a tree, with so much

honey that it ran over on the trunk. The two brothers wanted to light a fire under the tree to smother the bees, that they might take away the honey ; but the younger brother held them back. ' Leave the poor insects in peace,' he said ; ' I cannot bear to think of their being burnt.'

Again they listened to him, stupid as they thought him, and the three brothers walked on till they came to a castle where in the stable stood horses of pure stone. They went all over the rooms and through the castle till they reached a door to which were three locks. The centre of this door was glass, through which one could see into the room. They looked, and saw a very old man sitting at a table. They called to him more than once, but he did not hear till they called a third time. Then he rose up, opened the three locks, and came out. Even then he uttered not a word, but led them to a richly prepared table, and, after they had eaten and drank as much as they wished, he allowed them to remain all night, and sleep in his own chamber.

The next morning the gray old man came to the eldest brother, made signs to him to follow, and led him to a stone table, on which were engraved three sentences, the first in the following words :

' In the wood under the moss are scattered the pearls of the king's daughter. They are a thousand in number, and whoever can find them all in one day before the sun goes down will release the castle from its enchantment ; but if he should search and not succeed before sunset, he will be turned into stone.'

The eldest brother read these words, and determined to try. He searched for the whole day, but when the hour of sunset arrived he had only found a hundred pearls, and, according to the writing on the table, he was turned into stone.

Notwithstanding this, the second brother made an attempt, and began his task in the evening, so that he searched all night, but with very little more success than his brother. By sunset next day he had found only two hundred pearls ; he was therefore turned into stone.

At last came the turn of the simpleton to seek amongst the moss ; but he had no confidence in himself, and he was so miserable at having to find the pearls that he went quite reluctantly, and when he reached the place sat down on a stone and wept. As he sat there weeping, he saw coming towards him the ant king, whose kingdom and life he had saved, with five thousand of his ants, and it was not long before they had found all the pearls, and piled them up in a large heap. Then they went home, scarcely waiting for his thanks ; they had only intended to show their gratitude. The poor simpleton was quite over-joyed ; but on returning to the castle he found the second task await-ing him. It was to fetch the key of the princess's sleeping-chamber from the bottom of the lake, into which it had been thrown ; so the simpleton went to the shore of the lake, wondering what he should do. But the ducks knew him in a moment, and were ready to help him, because he had saved their lives, and asked what he wanted. No sooner had he told them than they dived to the bottom, and in a few moments brought up the key and gave it to him.

There was still another task to perform, and the most difficult of all. He had to go into the room where the king's three daughters were sleeping, find out which was the youngest and the most beloved, and wake her. The sisters exactly resembled each other; the only thing by which they could be distinguished was that, before they went to sleep, the eldest had eaten barley-sugar, the second a little syrup, and the youngest a spoonful of honey. But in the midst of the youth's trouble and wonder how he should find out which was the youngest daughter, in came the queen bee, whose community he had saved from the fire, and she went to the mouths of the three sleepers, and quickly discovered by the breath of the youngest that she had eaten honey. She remained sitting on her mouth, and the youth knew by this which of the king's daughters to awaken. No sooner had he done so than the castle was disenchanted, and all who had been turned to stone resumed their proper forms.

The simple brother married the youngest daughter of the king, and became king after her father's death. His brothers married her two sisters. After all, it was better to be simple and kind-hearted than clever and cruel.

THE PRINCESS IN DISGUISE.

A KING once had a wife with golden hair, who was so beautiful that none on earth could be found equal to her. It happened that she fell ill, and; as soon as she knew she must die, she sent for the king, and said to him, 'After my death, I know you will marry another wife; but you must promise me that, however beautiful she may be, if she is not as beautiful as I am, and has not golden hair like mine, you will not marry her.'

The king had no sooner given his promise than she closed her eyes and died.

For a long time he refused to be comforted, and thought it was impossible he could ever take another wife. At length his counsellors came to him, and said, 'A king should not remain unmarried; we ought to have a queen.'

So he at last consented, and then messengers were sent far and wide to find a bride whose beauty should equal that of the dead queen. But none was to be found in the whole world; for even when equally beautiful they had not golden hair.

So the messengers returned without obtaining what they sought.

Now the king had a daughter who was quite as beautiful as her dead mother, and had also golden hair. She had all this while been growing up, and very soon the king noticed how exactly she resembled her dead mother. So he sent for his counsellors, and said to them, 'I will marry my daughter; she is the image of my dead wife, and no other bride can be found to enable me to keep my promise to her.'

When the counsellors heard this, they were dreadfully shocked, and said, 'It is forbidden for a father to marry his daughter; nothing but evil could spring from such a sin, and the kingdom will be ruined.'

When the king's daughter heard of her father's proposition she was greatly alarmed, the more so as she saw how resolved he was to carry out his intention. She hoped, however, to be able to save him and herself from such ruin and disgrace, so she said to him, 'Before I consent to your wish I shall require three things—a dress as golden as the sun, another as silvery as the moon, and a third as glittering as the stars; and, besides this, I shall require a mantle made of a thousand skins of rough fur sewn together, and every animal in the kingdom must give a piece of his skin towards it.'

'Ah!' she thought, 'I have asked for impossibilities, and I hope I shall be able to make my father give up his wicked intentions.'

The king, however, was not to be diverted from his purpose. All the most skilful young women in the kingdom were employed to weave the three dresses, one to be as golden as the sun, another as silvery as the moon, and the third as glittering as the stars. He sent hunters into the forest to kill the wild animals and bring home their skins, of which the mantle was to be made; and at last, when all was finished, he brought them and laid them before her, and then said, 'To-morrow our marriage shall take place.'

Then the king's daughter saw that there was no hope of changing her father's heart, so she determined to run away from the castle.

In the night, when everyone slept, she rose and took from her jewel-case a gold ring, a gold spinning-wheel, and a golden hook. The three dresses of the sun, moon, and stars she folded in so small a parcel that they were placed in a walnut-shell; then she put on the fur mantle, stained her face and hands black with walnut juice, and, committing herself to the care of Heaven, she left her home.

After travelling the whole night she came at last to a large forest, and, feeling very tired, she crept into a hollow tree and went to sleep. The sun rose, but she still slept on, and did not awake till nearly noon.

It happened on this very day that the king to whom the wood belonged was hunting in the forest, and when his hounds came to the tree, they sniffed about, and ran round and round the tree, barking loudly. The king called to his hunters, and said, 'Just go and see what wild animal the dogs are barking at.'

They obeyed, and, quickly returning, told the king that in the hollow tree was a most wonderful creature, such as they had never seen before —that the skin was covered with a thousand different sorts of fur, and that it was fast asleep.

'Then,' said the king, ' go and see if you can capture it alive. Then bind it on the waggon and bring it home.'

While the hunters were binding the maiden she awoke, and, full of terror, cried out to them, 'I am only a poor child, forsaken by my father and mother ; take pity on me, and take me with you!'

'Well,' they replied, 'you may be useful to the cook, little Roughskin. Come with us ; you can at least sweep up the ashes.'

So they seated her on the waggon and took her home to the king's castle. They showed her a little stable under the steps, where no daylight ever came, and said, 'Roughskin, here you can live and sleep.' So the king's daughter was sent into the kitchen to fetch the wood, draw the water, stir the fire, pluck the fowls, look after the vegetables, sweep the ashes, and do all the hard work.

Poor Roughskin, as they called her, lived for a long time most miserably, and the beautiful king's daughter knew not when it would end or how. It happened, however, after a time that a festival was to take place in the castle, so she said to the cook, 'May I go out for a little while to see the company arrive? I will stand outside the door.'

'Yes, you may go,' he replied; ' but in half an hour I shall want you to sweep up the ashes, and put the kitchen in order.'

Then she took her little oil lamp, went into the stable, threw off the fur coat, washed the nut-stains from her face and hands, so that her full beauty appeared before the day. After this, she opened the nut-shell, and took out the dress that was golden as the sun, and put it on. As soon as she was quite dressed, she went out and presented herself at the entrance of the castle as a visitor. No one recognised her as Roughskin; they thought she was a king's daughter, and sent and told the king of her arrival. He went to receive her, offered her his hand, and while they danced together, he thought in his heart, ' My eyes have never seen any maiden before so beautiful as this.'

As soon as the dance was over she bowed to the king, and before he could look round she had vanished, no one knew where. The sentinel at the castle gate was called and questioned, but he had not seen any-one pass.

But she had run to her stable, quickly removed her dress, stained her face and hands, put on her fur coat, and was again ' Roughskin.' When she entered the kitchen and began to do her work and sweep up the ashes, the cook said : ' Leave that alone till to-morrow; I want you to cook some soup for the king. I will also taste a little when it is ready, but do not let one of your hairs fall in, or you will get nothing to eat in future from me.'

Then the cook went out, and Roughskin made the king's soup as nicely as she could, and cut bread for it, and when it was ready, she fetched from her little stable her gold ring, and laid it in the dish in which the soup was prepared.

After the king had left the ball-room, he called for the soup, and, while eating it, thought he had never tasted better soup in his life.

But when the dish was nearly empty, he saw to his surprise a gold ring lying at the bottom, and could not imagine how it came there. Then he ordered the cook to come to him, and he was in a terrible fright when he heard the order.

' You must certainly have let a hair fall into the soup; if you have, I shall thrash you,' he said.

As soon as he appeared, the king said : ' Who cooked this soup ?'

' I cooked it,' he replied.

' That is not true,' said the king; ' this soup is made quite differently and much better than you ever made it.'

Then the cook was obliged to confess that Roughskin had made the soup.

' Go and send her to me,' said the king.

As soon as she appeared, the king said to her, ' Who art thou, maiden ?'

She replied, ' I am a poor child without father or mother.'

He asked again, ' Why are you in my castle ?'

' Because I am trying to earn my bread by helping the cook,' she replied.

' How came this ring in the soup ?' he said again.

' I know nothing about the ring,' she replied.

When the king found he could learn nothing from Roughskin, he sent her away. A little time after this there was another festival, and Roughskin had again permission from the cook to go and see the visitors; ' But,' he added, ' come back in half an hour and cook for the king the soup that he is so fond of.'

She promised to return, and ran quickly into her little stable, washed off the stains, and took out of the nut-shell her dress, silvery as the moon, and put it on. Then she appeared at the castle like a king's daughter, and the king came to receive her with great pleasure; he was so glad to see her again, and while the dancing continued, the king kept her as his partner. When the ball ended, she disappeared so quickly that the king could not imagine what had become of her. But she had rushed down to her stable, made herself again the rough little creature that was called Roughskin, and went into the kitchen to cook the soup.

While the cook was upstairs she fetched the golden spinning-wheel, and dropped it into the soup as soon as it was ready. The king again ate it with great relish; it was as good as before, and when he sent for the cook and asked who made it, he was obliged to own that it was Roughskin. She was also ordered to appear before the king, but he could get nothing out of her, excepting that she was a poor child, and knew nothing of the golden spinning-wheel.

At the king's third festival, everything happened as before. But the cook said: ' I will let you go and see the dancing-room this time, Roughskin; but I believe you are a witch, for although the soup is good, and the king says it is better than I can make it, there is always something dropped into it which I cannot understand.' Roughskin did not stop to listen; she ran quickly to her little stable, washed off the nut-stains, and this time dressed herself in the dress that glittered like the stars. When the king came as before to receive her in the hall, he thought he had never seen such a beautiful woman in his life. While they were dancing, he contrived, without being noticed by the maiden, to slip a gold ring on her finger, and he had given orders that the dancing should continue longer than usual. When it ended, he wanted to hold her hand still, but she pulled it away, and sprang so quickly among the people that she vanished from his eyes.

She ran out of breath to her stable under the steps, for she knew that she had remained longer away than half an hour, and there was not time to take off her dress, so she threw on her fur cloak over it, and in her haste she did not make her face black enough, nor hide her golden hair properly; her hands also remained white. However, when she entered the kitchen the cook was still away, so she prepared the king's soup, and dropped into it the golden hook.

The king, when he found another trinket in his soup, sent immediately for Roughskin, and as she entered the room he saw the ring on her white finger which he had placed there. Instantly he seized her hand and held her fast, but in her struggles to get free the fur mantle opened and the star-glittering dress was plainly seen. The king caught the mantle and tore it off, and as he did so her golden hair fell over her shoulders, and she stood before him in her full splendour, and felt that she could no longer conceal who she was. Then she wiped the soot and stains from her face, and was beautiful to the eyes of the king as any woman upon earth.

'You shall be my dear bride,' said the king, 'and we will never be parted again, although I know not who you are.'

Then she told him her past history, and all that had happened to her, and he found that she was, as he thought, a king's daughter. Soon after the marriage was celebrated, and they lived happily till their death.

THE BRIDE'S VENTURE.

THERE was once a king's son who was betrothed to a maiden, and he loved his bride very much. One day, as they were sitting very happily together, there came information that his father lay ill and dying, and wished to see him for the last time before his death. 'I must go and leave you, darling,' said the king's son, 'and directly too, for I have a long journey to take; but I will give you this ring as a memory token, and when I am king I will come and fetch you home.'

Then he rode away, and when he reached the castle, he found his father dying and his end very near. But he was able to speak, and said: 'Dearest son, I have sent for you because I want you to promise to do as I wish about your marriage.'

And then he named to him a king's daughter who was well known, and asked him to take her as his wife. The son was so sad at these words that he hardly knew at first what to say; still, he could not refuse his dying father, so he replied: 'Dear father, whatever your will is shall be done.'

Then the king closed his eyes and died. As soon as the son became king, and the mourning was over, he remembered that he must keep the promise which he had given to his father. He sent, therefore, to the king's daughter, and as she was willing to be his bride, they were betrothed to each other.

The first bride very soon heard of what he had done, and she grieved so bitterly over her lover's unfaithfulness that her life seemed passing away. At last her father, who was also a king, said to her: 'Dearest child, why are you so sad? If anything you wish can be done, I will do it for you.'

She roused herself in a moment, and said: 'Dear father, I should so like to have as companions eleven maidens exactly like myself in countenance, shape, and size.'

Her father replied: 'As soon as possible your wish shall be fulfilled.'

He sent messengers all over the kingdom, who were ordered to find eleven maidens who should resemble his daughter in face, figure, and size; and after a long time they succeeded, and brought them to the king's daughter.

As soon as they arrived, she ordered twelve hunting-dresses to be made exactly alike, and, when they were finished, each of the eleven maidens put one on, and she did the same. Then she bid her father farewell, and rode away to the castle of her former bridegroom, whom she still loved. On arriving, she sent a message to the king, saying she was the chief of twelve young huntsmen who wished to be taken into the king's service.

He came out to see them; but, in the huntsman's dress he did not recognise his former bride; but he was so pleased with their appearance that he said he should like them to serve him very much, and so they all became the king's huntsmen.

But the king had a lion who was a wonderful animal, for he found out every concealment or secret.

So it happened one evening that he said to the king, 'You think that you have engaged twelve young huntsmen to serve you.'

'Yes,' said the king, 'I have engaged twelve huntsmen.'

'You are mistaken,' replied the lion; 'they are maidens, not huntsmen.'

'Well,' said the king, 'that cannot be true; or, if it is, how can you prove it?'

'Oh, easily,' said the lion; 'strew peas in the ante-chamber, and you will soon see. A man has a firm step; he will either crush the peas or pass over without moving them; but maidens will come tripping or shuffling along, and set the peas rolling.'

The king was very much pleased with this advice, and ordered the room to be strewed with peas.

But one of the king's own servants was kind-hearted, and, as he had overheard the lion's advice, he went at once and told the young huntsmen how they were to be put to the proof, and said also, 'The lion wants the king to believe that you are women.'

The king's daughter thanked him, and when she spoke afterwards to the maidens about it, she said, ' Remember to step strongly, and with a firm foot, on the peas.'

The next morning the king sent for the twelve huntsmen, and met them in the ante-chamber; but as they passed through where the peas lay, they stepped upon them so heavily, and had such a firm strong walk, that not a single pea rolled or even moved.

After they were gone, the king said to the lion, ' You have spoken falsely to me; they walk like men.'

' Yes,' answered the lion; ' they knew that the peas were put there to prove them, so they exerted all their strength; but now give them another trial: have twelve spinning-wheels placed in the ante-room, and when they see them, they will look quite delighted, whereas no man would notice them.'

The king was pleased with this advice also, and gave orders for twelve spinning-wheels to be placed in the ante-room.

The servant, however, who really believed in the truthfulness of the young huntsmen, disclosed the plan to them. When they were alone, the king's daughter cautioned them not even to glance at the spinning-wheels, and to walk firmly.

The next morning the king sent for his twelve huntsmen; but as they passed through the ante-room with a firm step, not one of them took the slightest notice of the spinning-wheels.

' Wrong again, lion,' said the king; ' they must be men, for they did not even see the spinning-wheels.'

' Because,' answered the lion, ' they knew that you were trying them with another test.'

But after this the king would not believe the lion.

The twelve huntsmen generally followed or accompanied the king when he went hunting, and the more he knew of them the more he liked them.

It happened one day, while they were out hunting, that information was brought of the approach of the king's bride. As soon as the chief huntsman—who really was the king's first bride, and rode near him— heard the news, such a pang of grief came upon her that her heart seemed to stop, and she fell off her horse to the ground insensible. The king, who supposed that his favourite huntsman had met with an accident, ran to help him; and, in raising him up, his glove fell off.

Then the king saw with surprise that he wore on his finger a ring which he had given to his first bride, and looking earnestly in the face, he recognised her. Then was his heart so completely at rest that he kissed her, and, as she opened her eyes, he exclaimed, ' Thou art mine, and I am thine, and no one in the world shall separate us again.'

To his other bride he sent a messenger to say that he had a wife already whom he had chosen before he knew her, and that he prayed her to return to her own country.

Soon after, the marriage was celebrated, and the lion taken into favour; for, after all, he had spoken the truth.

FLORINDA AND YORINGAL.

IN olden times there stood, far down in the forest, an old castle, in which dwelt an aged woman, quite alone, who was a great sorceress. By day she took the form of a cat, during the night she was an owl, and for a few hours every evening she assumed the form of a human being.

If anyone came within a hundred steps of her castle, there he was obliged to remain, standing in the same place, and quite unable to move, till she spoke and set him free. If a young maiden came within the enchanted circle, the old witch changed her into a bird, fastened her up in a basket, and carried her to a chamber in the castle, where she had more than seven thousand of these rare birds shut up.

Not far from this wood lived a young maiden, named Florinda, who was more beautiful than all the other maidens in the village. She was betrothed to a very handsome young man, whose name was Yoringal. They were in their bridal days, and had great delight in the society of each other.

It happened sometimes that when they wanted to talk together they would go into the wood to walk.

' We must be careful not to go too near the castle,' Yoringal had often said.

One beautiful evening, however, they went to take their usual walk. The sun shone between the trunks of the trees, and brightened the dark leaves of the forest, while the cooing of the turtle-dove sounded so sweetly and mournfully from the beeches, that Florinda felt inclined to weep; indeed, they both felt as if something dreadful was about to happen to them, or as if they were going to die.

Meanwhile, the sun was setting behind the trees, and in their desponding mood they scarcely noticed it, but wandered on, forgetting that they must not go near the castle. Presently, Florinda looked up, and saw the walls of the castle close by, and was almost dead with terror. The next moment Yoringal missed Florinda; she had been turned into a nightingale, and began to sing ' Jug, jug, jug,' with the sweetest music. Just then a night owl with glowing eyes flew over them three times, each time screeching loudly. Then Yoringal found he could not move; there he stood like a stone; he could neither speak nor cry, nor move hand or foot.

The sun went down, and the owl flew into a bush, and from thence presently came forward a crooked old woman, thin and sallow, with great red eyes, and a hooked nose that almost touched her chin. Muttering to herself, she took hold of the nightingale, and carried it away in her hand. In a little while she returned, and said in a hollow voice, ' I greet thee, Zachiel; when the moon in a basket shines, bind; loose, Zachiel, till the good hour comes.'

Then was Yoringal free, and he threw himself upon his knees before the woman, and prayed her to give him back his Florinda; but she told him he would never have her back again, and went away. Yoringal cried and wept and wailed by turns. ' What, oh! what shall I do?' he exclaimed, but all to no purpose.

At last he went away to a distant town, and hired himself to tend the sheep. Here he remained for a long time. He could not go home without Florinda, though he sometimes went round by the castle—not too near—but there were no signs of her.

At length he dreamed one night that he had found a blood-red flower, in the middle of which was a large and beautiful pearl. He had plucked the flower, and while carrying it to the castle, he knew he was safe from all witchcraft or sorcery. He dreamed also that through this flower he had got back his dear Florinda.

In the morning when he awoke he rose hastily, and hurried away over mountain and valley to seek for such a flower as he had dreamed of. He had begun to give up all hope, when on the ninth day of his search, early in the morning, he found the blood-red flower, and in the centre was a dew-drop, as large and as beautiful as a pearl.

With this flower he travelled day and night till he came to the castle, and, when he arrived within a hundred paces, he found to his great joy that he was free to walk on even to the castle-gate. He went in through the court, and stood still to listen, hoping that he might find out where the birds were kept by their twittering. At last he heard, and went on till he reached the hall in which the wicked old woman had shut up the birds in the seven thousand wicker-basket cages. As soon as they saw Yoringal they were very spiteful; they scolded, and hissed, and spit poison and venom at him; but they could not reach to hurt him.

He did not turn back, however, but went on still farther, till he had found the nightingales. There were several hundred, and how among so many was he to find Florinda?

As he stood looking and considering, he saw all at once the old woman moving stealthily away towards the door with a basket containing a bird in her hands. Swiftly he sprung upon her, and, on touching the basket and the old woman with the flower, her power over Florinda was over; she could do them no more harm. In a moment the young girl stood before him in her own proper form, as beautiful as ever, and clasped him round the neck with her arms.

Then he touched all the other birds with his flower, and set the young women free from the spell. After this he went home with Florinda, and it was not very long before they were married, and lived in great happiness for the rest of their lives.

THE FATHER'S LEGACIES.

A FATHER once sent for his three sons to advise them how they should act after his death.

'I am old,' he said, 'my death is near, and I must prepare for the end. I have no money to leave you; but what I can leave, although it is very little, depends upon yourselves to be turned to some good account, if you understand how to employ it rightly.'

Then he gave to the eldest a cock; to the second a scythe; and to the third a cat, and said:

'Take these, seek a country where such things are unknown, and so will you each make a fortune.'

After the father's death, the eldest son started on his enterprise, and went through many towns where the cock was a well-known bird. Sometimes he saw at a distance one even sitting on the top of a tower and turning round with the wind.

In the villages it was the same. He heard the cocks crowing, and no one thought his bird at all wonderful. There seemed, therefore, no prospect of a fortune being made through the cock.

At last, after much consideration, he determined to visit an island where the bird was unknown and they had no division of time. They knew when it was morning and evening; but at night, if they did not sleep, they had no way of finding out the hour.

'See,' said he, 'what a proud creature this is! It has a ruby-red crown on its head, and wears spurs like a knight; it also calls out three times in the night to tell the hour, and the third time is just before sunrise. If it should call out during the day-time, we may be sure of a change in the weather.'

The people of the island were so pleased that none of them slept all night, and as they lay awake, they heard the cock call out the time quite loudly and clearly at two, four, and six o'clock. Next morning they asked the owner if the creature was to be sold, and how much he wanted for it.

'About as much gold as an ass could carry,' he replied.

'A very low price for such a valuable creature,' they said, as they collected the money, and gave him willingly what he asked.

When he returned home with all this wealth, his brothers wondered, and the second said:

'I think I may as well go and try if I can make as good a bargain for my scythe.'

At first, however, on starting, he did not meet with much encouragement. The farmers and labourers whom he met had on their shoulders scythes as good as his own.

At last he succeeded in reaching an island where the people had never heard of a scythe. When they wanted to reap their corn, they brought out cannons and shot it down. It certainly was a very singular proceeding, for many ears of corn fell outside, and others were struck off and shot away, so that few fell on the ground to be gathered up; and, above all, the cannons made a dreadful noise.

On seeing all this, the young man placed himself in a cornfield, and cut it down so quietly and swiftly with his scythe that the people were struck dumb with wonder, and were willing to give him whatever he asked for his scythe. Then he said he would be satisfied with as much gold as a horse could carry, and this they readily gave him.

After seeing the success of his brother, the youngest thought he would try his fortune with puss, if he could find the right way. So he went away as the others had done; but as long as he remained inland it was all useless. There were cats in every town, and in some places so numerous that the kittens were always drowned as soon as they were born.

At last he took ship and crossed over to an island, and came luckily to a place where they had never even seen a cat, and the mice had so gained the upper hand that they did as they pleased. They invaded the larder, and scampered over the tables and chairs in the rooms, whether the master was present or not.

The people complained terribly all over the place. The king, even in his castle, could do nothing to remove them; for in every corner, whether of cottage or castle, the mice picked and gnawed everything which their teeth could lay hold of. Then the young man sent his cat amongst them, and she soon cleared several houses of the mice by killing them or driving them away.

The people upon this hastened to the king and begged him to buy the wonderful animal for the sake of his kingdom. The king was quite willing to give what the owner asked, and the young man returned home with the largest treasure of them all—he had as much gold as a mule could carry. The cat made herself quite at home in the king's castle; she had mice to her heart's desire, and killed more than they were able to count. At last such hard work made her thirsty, so she stood still, lifted up her head, and cried, ' Mew, mew !'

The king immediately sent for his attendants, and, as puss again uttered the same cry, they were quite frightened, and rushed away from the castle.

Then the king held a council as to what was best to be done. At last it was resolved to send a herald to the cat, to request her to leave the castle, or, if she would not go, to expel her by force.

'For,' said the judge, 'it would have been better to dwell as we did before—plagued by mice, and endure the evil—than have our lives sacrificed to such a monster.'

A page was therefore told to go to the cat, and ask her if she would leave the castle of her own free will; but the cat, whose thirst had become still greater, merely answered, 'Mew, mew.'

The page, who did not in the least understand, carried the answer to the king.

'Now,' said the council, 'we must use force.' So the cannon were brought out, and the first shot fired into the room where the cat was sitting. In a great fright, she flew through the window and made her escape. The besiegers, however, did not know she was gone, and continued to fire upon the castle till it was completely razed to the ground.

THE BOASTING WOLF.

A FOX was one day speaking to a wolf of the great strength of human beings, especially men. 'No animal can stand against them,' he said, 'unless he employs craft and cunning.'

'Then,' said the wolf, 'I only wish I could see a man. I know he should not escape me; I would never let him go free.'

'I can help you to obtain your wish,' said the fox. 'If you come to me early to-morrow morning I will show you a man.'

The wolf took care to be early enough, and the fox led him to a hedge through which he could see the road, and where the fox knew huntsmen would pass during the day.

First came by an old pensioner.

'Is that a man?' asked the wolf.

'No,' answered the fox; 'not now—he was once.'

Then a little child passed who was going to school.

'Is that a man?' he asked again.

'No, not yet,' said the fox; 'but he will be one by-and-by.'

At last a hunter appeared, with his double-barrelled gun on his shoulder, and his hunting-knife by his side.

'There!' cried the fox; 'see, there comes a man at last! I will leave him to you to manage; but I shall run back to my hole.'

The wolf rushed out upon the man at once; but the hunter was ready for him, although when he saw him he said to himself, 'What a pity my gun is not loaded with ball!'

However, he fired the small shot in the animal's face as he sprung at him; but neither the pain nor the noise seemed to frighten the wolf in the least. The hunter fired again; still the wolf, struggling against the pain, made another spring—this time furiously; but the hunter, hastily drawing his bowie-knife, gave him two or three such powerful stabs that he ran back to the fox all covered with blood.

'Well, brother wolf, and have you succeeded in conquering a man?'

'Oh!' he cried, 'I had not the least idea of a man's strength; first, he took a stick from his shoulder, and blew something in my face, which tingled dreadfully; and before I could get closer to him, he puffed again through his stick, and there came a flash of lightning, and something struck my nose like hailstones. I would not give in, but rushed again upon him. In a moment he pulled a white rib out of his body, and gave me such dreadful cuts with it that I believe I must lie here and die.'

'See now,' said the fox, 'how foolish it is to boast. You have thrown your axe so far that you cannot fetch it back.'

THE FOX AND THE CAT.

ONE day a cat met a fox in the wood. 'Ah,' she thought, 'he is clever, and sensible, and talked of in the world a good deal; I will speak to him.' So she said, quite in a friendly manner, 'Good-morning, dear Mr. Fox; how are you? and how do affairs go with you in these expensive times?'

The fox, full of pride, looked at the cat from head to foot, and knew hardly what to say to her for a long time. At last he said, 'Oh, you poor little whisker-cleaner, you old, gray tabby, you hungry mouse-hunter, what are you thinking about to come to me, and to stand there and ask me how I am going on? What have you learnt, and how many tricks do you know?'

'I only know one trick,' answered the cat meekly.

'And pray what is that?' he asked.

'Well,' she said, 'if the hounds are behind me I can spring up into a tree out of their way, and save myself.'

'Is that all?' cried the fox; 'why, I am master of a hundred tricks, and have, over and above all, a sackful of cunning; but I pity you, puss, so come with me, and I will teach you how to baffle both men and hounds.'

At this moment a hunter with four hounds was seen approaching. The cat sprang nimbly up a tree, and seated herself on the highest branch, where, by the spreading foliage, she was quite concealed.

' Turn out the sack, Mr. Fox ; turn out the sack !' cried the cat ; but the hounds had already seized him, and held him fast.

' Ah, Mr. Fox,' cried the cat, ' your hundred tricks are not of much use to you ; now, if you had only known one like mine, you would not have so quickly lost your life.'

THE LOST SON.

THERE lived a queen once who had no children, and she prayed every day that she might have either a son or a daughter.

One day when she was walking in the garden an angel came to her, and said, ' Be happy ; thou shalt have a son with a wonderful power ; whatever he wishes for in the world he will have.'

Then she went to the king, and told him the joyful news ; and after a time a little son was born, to the great happiness of his parents.

Every morning the queen took her child into a park, in which was a menagerie, as she wished to wash him in the clear fountain which flowed there.

One day, when he was a few months old, the queen, after washing him, seated herself on a garden seat, with the child in her lap till he was asleep ; and, the weather being warm, she also slept. In the castle was a covetous cook, who knew what a wonderful power the child possessed ; and he came to the park where the queen was sleeping, and stole the child from her lap. Then he killed a chicken, cut off the head, and sprinkled the blood about on the grass, and on the queen's apron and dress. He carried the child away to a place of concealment, where he had a wet nurse ready for him, and then ran to the king, and complained to him that the queen had been asleep, and allowed the wild beasts to destroy the child.

The king, when he saw the blood on the apron, believed the cook's story, and, in his wrath against the queen, ordered a high tower to be built, in which the sun and moon could never shine. In this tower the poor queen was to be shut up for seven years, without food or water, and where he supposed she would soon die of starvation. But he was mistaken ; two good fairies were sent to her, in the form of white doves, who brought her meat and drink twice a day for the whole time.

After a while, the cook, who knew nothing about the doves, left the castle and the service of the king, for he thought, ' If the child should wish anything while I am here, it would be unlucky for me.' So he went to the place where the child was concealed, and found him much grown, and able to speak. After a time, he said to him, ' Why don't you wish that we may have here a beautiful castle, and garden, and furniture, and all that is necessary to make it complete ?'

The boy uttered the wish, and the words were no sooner out of his mouth than his wish was accomplished.

Time passed on, and again the cook said to the boy, ' Why don't you wish to have a pretty little girl as a companion ?'

No sooner was the wish expressed, than a little girl made her appearance, who was so beautiful that no painter could have truly represented her in a picture.

The children played together, and were very happy, and the cook went out hunting as if he had been a nobleman. At last, a fear arose in his mind that if the boy should one day wish for his father to come it would bring great trouble upon him; and, as he had a fine castle and plenty of money, he did not want the boy any longer.

So one day he called the little maiden to go out with him, and said, ' To-night, while the boy is asleep, you must take a knife and thrust it into his heart; for I have discovered that if he lives he can do us great harm.'

The poor child begged him not to ask her to do such a dreadful thing; but he said, ' If you disobey me it will cost you your life.'

So she went away; but in the morning she had not done the wicked deed. ' I could not do it,' she said, with tears. ' Why should I take away his innocent life, for he has never injured anyone ?'

' Very well,' he said; ' if you don't kill him to-night you shall die yourself.'

Then the poor child went out in the dark, and was obliged to kill a little fawn, and take out its heart and tongue to show to the wicked man, that he might think the boy was dead.

But he was in the room when the man came in, and still alive, concealed under the bed, and when he heard what the wicked man said, he thought to himself, ' You old sinner ! Now, as you wanted to kill me after all the good things I have obtained for you, I will pronounce your fate.'

Instantly he wished that the cook should be turned into a large black dog, which should be fastened up with a golden chain, and have only ashes to eat; and, as he uttered the wish in a low tone, it was immediately accomplished, and the wicked cook became a fierce black dog, who could, however, hurt no one, because he was always chained up.

The children, after this, remained for some time at the castle alone; but at last the boy began to think of his mother, and to wonder whether she was alive. So he said to the maiden, ' I should like to return to my fatherland. Will you go with me ? I will provide for all you want.'

' Ah !' she replied, ' it is such a long way; and what will become of me in a strange land where I am unknown ?'

So as he saw she could not bear to be separated from him, he wished that she might be changed into a beautiful carnation; and then he placed the flower in his coat, and took it with him.

The boy had a long distance to travel; and the black dog was obliged to follow, and go also into his own country. They went first to the tower where the queen was shut up, and, as it was so high, the boy wished for a ladder which should reach to the top. Then he climbed up and looked in, and cried, ' Dearest mother, queen wife, art thou living or dead ?'

She thought the fairies spoke to her, and said, ' I have enough to eat ; I am quite satisfied.'

But he spoke again, and said, ' I am thy dear son, whom they say was stolen from thy lap by wild animals; but I am still alive, and I will rescue thee very soon.'

He descended the ladder, and went to the king and informed him that he was a hunter from a foreign country, and wished to be taken into his service. The king replied that he would readily employ him, if he would tell him where the game could be found, for that he had hunted the whole country round for years, without once obtaining any.

The young huntsman immediately promised that he would very quickly bring him as much game as would cover the royal table. He went out after this, and called all the king's hunters together, and asked them to join him in the chase. As soon as they reached the entrance to the wood, he requested them to form a great circle, with an opening at one end. Then he placed himself in the centre, and wished. In a moment about two hundred head of game rushed into the circle, and these the hunters were not long in bagging. The dead game was then placed upon sixty farm waggons, and carried home to the king, who could now ornament his table with game, after being for many years without it.

The king was much pleased at the result of the young hunter's promise, and gave orders that the next day there should be an assembly of the whole court to dine with him, and to hold a great festival.

As soon as they were assembled, the king said to the hunter :

' You have been so skilful and clever in this affair that you shall sit by me.'

But he answered : ' My lord king, your majesty is doing me too much honour ; I am only a plain hunter.'

The king, however, stood up and said, ' I desire you to sit by me till the feast is ended.'

The youth obeyed, but, as he sat there in the place of honour, he could not help thinking of his lady mother, and wished that even now one of the king's chief courtiers would get up and ask about the queen in the tower, and whether she was still living or not.

No sooner had he wished, than the king's marshal rose and said : ' Your majesty the king, while we are here enjoying ourselves, may I ask what has become of our lady queen in the tower—is she still alive, or has she been starved to death ?'

But the king replied haughtily : ' She allowed the wild animals to tear my little son to pieces, therefore I will not hear a word about her.'

Then the young hunter stood up and said : ' My honoured lord and father, the queen is still alive, and I am your son. The wild beasts did not touch me. A wicked wretch—your old cook—carried me away from her lap while she slept, and sprinkled the blood of a chicken over her apron to deceive you.'

As he spoke he led the black dog forward by his chain, and said : ' This is the wicked creature, who has been turned into a fierce dog as a punishment. Shall I wish that he may be restored to his proper shape ?'

The king, in surprise, consented ; and no sooner was the wish expressed than the old cook appeared before them, with his white apron on and his knife by his side. The king recognised him at once, and was so exceedingly wroth that he ordered him to be thrown into the deepest dungeon of the castle.

Then the hunter related to the king all that had occurred since he had been stolen from his mother, and said : ' Will you, dear father, see the beautiful maiden who saved my life at the risk of her own ?'

' Yes,' he replied ; ' I am quite anxious to see her.'

' Honoured king and father,' said the youth, ' I will first show her to you in the form of a flower.'

He searched in his pocket as he spoke, brought out the beautiful carnation, and laid it on the table, and they all acknowledged that it was indeed a rare flower. But no sooner had he wished that she should resume her own form, than a beautiful maiden stood before them, whose beauty was beyond the painter's art to portray.

After this the king sent two waiting-maids and two attendants to the tower to fetch the queen, and bring her to the royal table ; but as soon as she appeared, and was seated at the table, she could not eat. From that hour she ate nothing, and in three days died quite happily.

After she was buried, the two fairies, in the form of white doves, who had fed her daily while she was in the tower, placed themselves on her grave. The old cook was kept in the dungeon, where he soon died. In due time the son married the beautiful maiden, whom as a flower he had brought home in his pocket, and after his father's death became king of the country.

THE FALSE BRIDE.

THERE was once an old queen whose husband had been dead many years, and she had a beautiful daughter. This daughter had been for some time betrothed to the son of a king, who lived many miles away.

THE QUEEN TOOK A SORROWFUL LEAVE OF HER DAUGHTER.

She was now grown up, and the queen knew that very soon her child must leave her, and travel into distant lands, to be the wife of the king's son; so she began to collect many costly things which were to be sent with her as marriage presents—dresses and trinkets, gold and silver, goblets and jewels ; indeed, everything suitable for the treasures of a royal bride, for she loved her child dearly.

She gave her also a waiting-maid to ride with her, and to place her hand in that of the bridegroom. The queen also provided each a horse for the journey; and the bride's horse, which was named 'Falada,' could speak.

When the farewell hour arrived, the queen repaired to her sleeping-room, took a small knife, and cut her finger till it bled. Then she laid a piece of rag on the table, and let fall three drops of blood on it, and, after folding it up, gave it to her daughter, and said, 'Dear child, take care not to lose this, and no harm will happen to you on the way.' The queen took a sorrowful leave of her daughter, who had placed the piece of rag in her bosom before she seated herself on her horse to ride away to her bridegroom.

After journeying about an hour the heat made the princess very thirsty, and, stopping her horse, she said to her waiting-maiden, 'Please alight, and draw me some water in one of my little cups which the queen, my mother, gave me. I must have something to drink, I am so thirsty.'

'If you are thirsty,' replied the waiting-maid, 'get down from your horse yourself, and lie down by the brook and drink; I am not going to be your servant !'

The princess got off her horse, for her thirst was very great, and, lying down, she drank from the stream; for she knew she durst not ask for the cup. But she could not help sighing, and then she heard a voice from the piece of rag in her bosom say, 'If the queen-mother knew this she would break her heart.' But the young bride was courageous; she said nothing, and again mounted her horse and rode away for several miles. The heat still continued, and the princess again suffered from thirst, and presently they came to a running stream. Forgetting all the unkind words of her companion, she once more asked her to alight and fetch her a little water in her cup. Again she replied haughtily that she might get it herself; she was not going to be her maid.

She was therefore obliged to get down and drink from the flowing stream as she had done before. This time, as she got off her horse, she wept, and heard the voice in her bosom say, 'Ah! if your mother knew this she would break her heart.' But as she stooped over the edge of the stream to drink, the piece of cloth, on which were the blood-drops, fell from her bosom into the water, and floated away without her noticing it in her sorrow and trouble.

Her companion, however, saw it, and congratulated herself that now she could do as she liked with the bride ; the piece of linen being lost, she had become weak and powerless to oppose her.

As she turned round to mount her horse again, her companion said to her, 'Falada belongs to me, and I mean to ride him, and you must ride on my horse.' Then, with harsh and cruel words, the woman

obliged her to take off her royal dress, and put on her own common one, and at last made her swear that when they reached the king's court she would not reveal to a single person that she was a princess; and she told her that if she had not taken this oath she would have killed her on the spot. But Falada saw and heard all that passed, and took care to remember it.

The lady's-maid rode after this on Falada, and the true bride on the inferior horse; and so they travelled farther, till at last they arrived at the royal castle. Their arrival was announced with great joy. The king's son hastened forward to receive them, and assisted the lady's-

LYING DOWN, SHE DRANK FROM THE STREAM.

maid to alight from her horse, thinking that she was his bride. He led her up the steps into the castle, while the real bride remained behind.

Presently the old king looked out of a window and saw her standing in the court, and he could not help noticing that she looked refined and delicate, and was very beautiful. He went out, and, with kingly gentleness, asked her why she was staying there, and what she wanted, and who she was.

She replied, 'I came all this way as a companion; but I cannot stay, because there is a maid to wait upon the bride, and I have no other employment.'

'I am sorry there is no situation suitable for you in the castle,' replied the king; 'but I know a little maiden who has a number of geese. She is called Kürdchen; she may help you.'

The real bride, being anxious to remain near the castle, was glad to do as the king proposed; and so the king's daughter went to help in the care of the geese.

Soon after this, the false bride said to the king's son, 'Dearest prince, will you do me a favour?'

'Certainly I will do it,' he replied.

'Well, then, I want you to have the horse that I rode on in my journey here destroyed; for it was very restive more than once, and made me quite fearful.'

The truth was, she knew that the horse could speak, and feared he would some day tell the prince she was not the king's daughter nor the real bride.

The order to kill the true Falada came to the ears of the true bride, and she found out the man, and promised him a piece of gold if he would do her a service.

In the town was a large gloomy-looking door, through which the geese had to be driven morning and evening, and she told the man who was going to kill Falada to fasten the head on this gloomy door, that she might see it every day as she passed through.

The man thought it a strange request, but he promised to comply; so poor Falada's head was cut off and nailed to the door.'

Early the next morning, when she and Kürdchen passed through, she spoke to the head, and said, 'Falada, dost thou know me?'

'Ah, yes!' replied the head; 'you are the young princess, and if your mother knew she would break her heart.

Then she joined Kürdchen, and they drove the geese into the field. As soon as they could sit down, the young princess unfastened her hair that she might comb it and make it neat.

Kürdchen was quite delighted when she saw the hair, for it was bright and golden, and the princess had always hitherto worn it hidden under a cap; so she came over to cut off a lock for herself. But the princess did not wish to lose her hair, so she cried out:

> 'Blow, blow, wind; take Kürdchen's hat in the air,
>   And do not let her catch it till I have done my hair.'

Then there came such a strong wind that Kürdchen's little hat was carried away to a long distance, and before she could get back from fetching it her companion had finished combing her hair, so she could not cut any off. Kürdchen was so cross that she would not speak to her all day till they went home.

Next day the princess again stayed behind when they drove the geese out from the gloomy door, and spoke to the horse's head; and Falada again replied that she was the queen's daughter, and that her mother, if she knew, would break her heart. Also, when they reached

FLORINDA AND YORINGAL

THE FALSE BRIDE

the field, and Kürdchen wanted a lock of her hair while the princess was combing it, she again said :

> 'Blow, blow, wind ; take Kürdchen's hat in the air,
> And do not let her catch it till I have done my hair.'

This happened several times, and at last Kürdchen went to the old king, and said, 'I cannot have this maiden to help me to watch the geese any longer.'

'Why, what has she done ?' asked the king.

'BLOW, BLOW, WIND ; TAKE KÜRDCHEN'S HAT IN THE AIR.'

'Oh, she worries me the whole day, and every morning when we drive the herd out through the dark gates, she stops to talk to a horse's head which is nailed there, and says, "Falada, dost thou know me ?" and the head answers, "You are a king's daughter, and if your mother knew she would break her heart.'"

And then Kürdchen told the king of her beautiful golden hair, which she combed in the field ; and how often the strange maiden had made the wind blow her hat away that she might not cut off a lock.

The king advised Kürdchen to bear it all for a few days longer; for he determined after this to find out for himself what it all meant.

The next morning he went out early and placed himself near the dark gate, where no one could see him, and as the two maidens passed through driving the geese, he saw the stranger stop and speak to the head, and heard the reply. After seeing this he hastened to the field, hid himself in the bushes, and, as the maiden unfastened her hair, he saw with his own eyes that it was very beautiful, and glittered like gold. He was not surprised at Kürdchen's anger when he heard the other maiden call upon the wind to blow away her hat, and saw what trouble she had to catch it.

The king went back to the castle unnoticed; but in the evening, when the girls returned home, he sent for the strange maiden, and asked her the meaning of all he had seen and heard.

' I dare not tell,' she replied, ' neither can I venture even to complain of my trouble to anyone; for I have sworn in the sight of Heaven that I will divulge nothing, and were I to do so my life will be forfeited !'

The king pressed her very much to tell him, but all to no purpose; he could get nothing out of her. Then he said : ' Go and complain of your trouble in that iron closet. Till you tell me all, there you shall stay.'

Then she crept into the iron closet with a trembling heart, and began to lament and weep, and said aloud : ' I am now forsaken by the whole world, and yet I am a king's daughter. A false lady's-maid has done this she got me into her power, made me take off my royal dresses and give them to her, and has taken my place with my bridegroom, while I must go out and serve as a tender of herds of geese, and if I tell she will kill me. Oh! if my mother knew, she would break her heart !'

The king, who had been standing near the closed door listening, heard all she said. So he opened the door, and called her to come out. Without a word he sent for some of her royal clothes, and desired her to put them on, and made her uncover her golden hair. As soon as she had done so, he was astonished to find her so beautiful.

The old king now sent for his son, and disclosed to him that he had a false bride, who was merely the lady's-maid to the princess, whom she had frightened into silence, and that the maiden who had been obliged to keep the secret was the real bride.

The prince, notwithstanding his astonishment, could not help seeing how beautiful the true bride was, and how much more gentle and refined than the woman who had been so cruel to her, and whom he could not love. He listened to the story of her sorrow, and was full of joy when he told her it was at an end, and a day was fixed for his friends and acquaintances to be invited to meet the true bride; but not a word was said to the deceiver.

When the day arrived, the bridegroom placed the king's daughter on one side of himself, and the lady's-maid on the other. But the lady's-maid never expected to see the goose-tender at the king's table, and did not recognise her in her rich and glittering dress. When the feast ended, and they were all in good spirits and merry, the old king asked the lady's-maid: 'What does he deserve who betrays his master?' and then he related the circumstances he had learnt from the princess; but as the betrayer in the king's story was a man, not a woman, the lady's-maid never supposed that she had been found out. 'Pronounce his sentence,' cried the king as he finished.

'He deserves nothing better,' said the false bride, 'than to be torn to pieces by wild horses, and rolled down a hill in a cask full of spikes till he is dead.'

'You have pronounced your own doom,' said the king; 'you are the guilty person.'

So the false bride was led away to punishment, and very soon after the young king married the right bride, and they both ruled the kingdom in peace and happiness all their lives.

THE YOUNG GIANT.

A COUNTRYMAN once had a son who was not taller than his father's thumb, and year after year grew not a hair's breadth bigger. One day, when the father was going into the fields to plough, the little dwarf said: 'Father, I want to go with you; do take me.'

'No, no,' replied his father, 'you stay here; you would be useless yonder, and you would soon be lost.'

Then the little creature began to cry, and for the sake of peace the father put him in his pocket and carried him away. As soon as they reached the field, the father took him out of his pocket, and seated him in a fresh furrow.

While he sat there, who should be seen coming over the mountain but a great giant.

'See, there comes a big man,' cried the boy's father, who wanted to frighten the child, and prevent him from being troublesome; 'he is coming to fetch you away.'

The giant, however, with his long legs, had only two steps to take before he reached the furrow. He lifted the little dwarf with two fingers, looked at him earnestly, and then without a word carried the little creature away. The father, who stood by, could not utter a sound for fright, and thought that he had lost his child, and should never see him again as long as he lived.

The giant took the little dwarf to his home and gave him such wonderful food that he grew big and strong after the manner of giants. When two years had passed, the giant took the boy into the wood, and said to him, ' Cut a switch for yourself ;' but the boy was so strong that he took a young tree and tore it up by the roots. The giant was not, however, yet satisfied ; he took the boy home for another two years, and at the end of that time his strength was so great that he was able to pull up an old oak-tree in the forest with ease.

But the giant considered he could make the boy still stronger, so he continued to feed him with giants' food, and at the end of another two years he led him to the forest and told him to break off a large bough for a switch. The young giant, however, pulled up the thickest trunk of a tree that he could find, and it was to him a mere trifle.

' That will do,' said the giant ; ' your education is finished ;' and sent him back to the ploughed field from which he had taken him. His father was behind the plough, and the young giant, going up to him, said :

' See, father, what a man your son has become.'

' No !' cried the father, in terror ; ' you are not my son. I don't want you ; go away from me.'

' Indeed, I am your son,' he replied. ' Let me do your work ; I can plough as well as you, and better.'

' No, no !' he cried ; ' you are not my son ; you cannot plough. Go away.'

He was, however, in such terror of the big creature that he removed his hands from the plough and stepped out of his way. Then the youngster took hold of the handles of the plough, and pressed them so heavily that the shares sank quite deeply in the ground. The father, seeing this, cried out, ' If you will plough, you need not use so much force ; that will make the work bad.'

The young man, without listening to his father, unyoked the horses and drew the plough himself, saying, ' Go home, father, and tell my mother to get a plentiful dinner ready for me while I plough this piece of ground for you.'

The countryman went home and carried the message to his wife, while the youngster ploughed the whole field of quite two acres. Then he harnessed himself to the harrow and harrowed it, drawing two harrows at a time. When it was finished, he went to the wood and pulled up two oak-trees, laid one on each shoulder, and suspended from one the harrows, and from the other the horses, and carried them home just as easily as if they had been a truss of straw.

As he entered the yard, his mother saw him, and cried : ' Who is this frightful giant coming in ?'

' That is our son,' said the peasant.

' No, it cannot be,' she cried ; ' our son is no more. We never had such a son as that ; ours was a very little creature. Go away,' she cried, as he approached ; ' we don't want you here.'

The young man did not reply ; he took the horses into the stable, gave them plenty of oats and hay, and made them quite comfortable. When this was done, he went in, seated himself on a bench, and said :

'Mother, is dinner nearly ready? I am very hungry.'

'Yes,' she replied, as she brought two immense dishes containing enough to have lasted his parents for a week, and placed them before him. The youngster ate it all up, and asked if she had any more.

'No,' she said; 'that is all I have.'

'That was only a taste,' he answered; 'I must have something more.'

She was afraid to refuse him, so she placed a large kettleful of soup on the fire, and when it was ready brought it in.

'Ah, this is better than nothing,' he said, as he broke some bread into it and quickly ate it all. Yet still his hunger was not appeased. By-and-by he said: 'Father, I can see very well that there is not enough at home to supply me with food; but if you will get me a bar of iron too strong for me to break over my knee, I will go away and travel about the world on my own account.'

The peasant was rejoiced at the thought of getting rid of him; so he harnessed two horses to a waggon, and fetched from the smith a bar of iron so large and thick that his two horses could scarcely draw it. The young giant took hold of it, laid it across his knee, and crash —it broke like a bean-prop in the middle, and he threw the pieces away.

Then the father harnessed four horses to the waggon and fetched another bar of iron stronger and thicker than before, and so heavy that it was as much as his four horses could do to draw it. But his son snapped it across his knee with very little trouble, and said: 'Father, this is of no use at all; you must harness your horses again and fetch me something better and stronger than this.'

So the father harnessed eight horses to his waggon this time, and even they could scarcely draw the immense bar of iron he brought. When the son took it in his hand he broke a piece off it, and said: 'Father, I see you cannot procure a bar of iron such as I want, so I will not stay here any longer.'

He went away, and after travelling some distance came to a town in which lived a blacksmith. He was a covetous man who gave nothing away, but kept all he earned to himself. The young man walked into the smithy and asked the smith if he wanted an assistant.

'Ah,' thought the smith, 'this is a strong, clever fellow, no doubt; he has an arm for the forge, and will earn his bread well.' So he asked, 'What wages do you require?'

'None,' replied the youngster; 'only every fortnight, when you pay the others, you must agree to let me strike you twice.'

The avaricious smith was quite overjoyed at the thought of saving his money, and as to the blows, why, he could easily return them if that was all; his arm was very strong, and though the youngster was such a giant, he was not afraid of him.

On the following morning the new workman had to take his place at the forge, and when the master brought out the red-hot iron bar and placed it on the anvil, the young giant's first blow shivered the iron into a thousand pieces, and drove the anvil so deep into the ground that it could not be got out again.

The smith was terribly angry, and exclaimed, 'This won't suit me, young man; such blows as that do more harm than good, so take yourself off; and what am I to pay you?'

'I don't ask for payment; all I want is to give you one tap, that's all;' and lifting his foot, he gave him a kick that sent him flying over three haystacks. Then he picked out the strongest iron bar he could find for a walking-stick, and went on his way.

After travelling some distance he came to a farm, and asked the bailiff if he wanted a head man amongst his labourers.

'Well, yes, I do,' he replied; 'and as you seem likely to suit me, I may as well engage you; but what do you ask a year?'

He replied that he did not care for wages, but only to be able by right to give his master three hard knocks at the end of the year; and he must promise him this. The bailiff readily agreed to this proposal, for he also was avaricious.

The following morning the men had to rise early to fetch timber from the forest, but the stranger lay still in bed. One of the men called to him, 'It is time to get up; we are going to the forest, and you must come with us.'

'Be off!' he cried quite roughly; 'I shall be there as soon as you.'

Then one of them went to the master and told him that the new man was in bed, and would not get up to go with them to the forest.

'Go and tell him I say he is to get up directly and harness the horses to the waggons.'

But it was all useless, the great fellow wouldn't move, and told them to go by themselves. He remained in bed after they were gone for two hours, and then got up, went into the garden, picked two dishfuls of peas and boiled them into soup, and ate them for his breakfast quite contentedly.

When he had finished, he harnessed the horses and drove them to the forest. Not far from the spot where the forest lay was a narrow lane. Through this lane he led his horses, and when they reached the other end, he made them stand still, while he went back, broke down great boughs and stems of trees, and laid them across the lane, forming barriers, over which neither horses nor waggons could pass.

When he reached the forest, the other labourers were just going home with their loaded waggons. He said to them, 'Go home, all of you, as fast as you please; I shall be there as soon as you are.'

Then, without going farther, he tore up two full-grown trees from the ground, threw them on his waggon, and turned to go home.

On arriving at the end of the lane, he found the others standing there with their waggons, not knowing how to get over the barriers thrown across the road.

'See,' cried he, 'you might as well have stayed and had another hour's sleep, for I shall be at home after all as quickly as you.'

Then, as his own horses could not get over the barriers, he unharnessed them, placed them on the top of the trees which lay on the waggon, and, taking hold of the shafts himself, drew the whole as if it had been laden with feathers. Then he called out to the men, ' You see I shall be home first after all,' and he was right, for they had to set to work to clear the lane of the obstruction before they could lead their horses through it. On reaching the farmyard, he took one of the trees in his hand, and showing it to the bailiff, said, ' Is not that a beautiful flag-staff?'

The bailiff said afterwards to his wife, ' That is a clever fellow; after all, if he does sleep longer than the others, he gets back before them.'

The young giant served at the farmyard for a year, and when the other labourers went up for their wages he said it was also time for him to take his. The bailiff, by this time, had found out the young man's strength, and he was rather afraid of a blow from such a hand, and he knew he dared not quarrel with him. So he tried to get off his bargain, and even offered to make the young man bailiff instead of himself, or to give him anything he asked for, but all to no purpose. Then the bailiff begged for a fortnight's respite, that he might think the matter over, and the young giant promised that the fortnight he should have.

Then the bailiff assembled all his farm people and neighbours, and asked for their advice. The clerks considered for a long time, and then they said that with a labourer on the estate who with one blow could crush them as easily as a man would crush a gnat, no man's life was in safety. So they decided at last that he should be sent to clean out a dry well, and while he was down they were to throw millstones upon his head, that he might never again see daylight. This counsel pleased the bailiff, and he sent the young man down into the well to clean it.

While he was down, they rolled great stones upon him, and thought that he must be crushed to death; but he cried out, ' Drive those hens away; they are scratching in the sand by the well and throwing it into my eyes, so that I cannot see what I am doing.'

' Hish, hish!' cried the bailiff, as if he were driving away the hens, and presently, having finished his work, the young giant climbed up, and said, ' See what a handsome necklace I have got,' and there was one of the millstones hanging on his neck.

After this he again asked if he might take his wages, but the bailiff begged for another fortnight to consider, and assembled once more his clerks and people for their advice. So they proposed that he should send the young man to the enchanted mill, to grind corn in the night, for that no man who went there ever lived to come out again. The advice pleased the bailiff; he sent for the young giant, and told him to carry eight sacks of corn to the mill to be ground during that day, as the flour was wanted greatly.

Away went the young man to the barn, put two sacks in his right pocket, two in his left, and four he placed in his wallet, half in front and half behind, and, thus laden, walked off to the enchanted mill.

'You must grind them all before dark,' said the miller; 'for the mill is enchanted, and no man ever comes out alive who stays there all night.'

'Oh, that doesn't matter,' said the youngster; 'you make yourself quite comfortable and go to sleep.'

'Ah,' thought the bailiff, 'he will never be able to grind all that corn before dark, so there is an end of him.'

Away went the giant to the mill, shook out the corn into the mill troughs, and when the clock struck eleven he went into one of the rooms of the mill, and seated himself on a bench. After he had been seated a little while, the door opened, and he saw a large table come in all by itself, and on it were placed bread, wine, and many dishes of good things, but no one could be seen carrying them. He drew his stool back a little, and watched till at last he saw fingers, and then hands holding knives and forks, and laying pieces on the plates, but still he saw no one.

At last, as he felt hungry, and the supper looked very tempting, he seated himself at the table, and ate, and enjoyed himself very much. As soon as he had finished, and the other plates and dishes were also empty, all at once the lights were blown out with a puff which he heard quite plainly, and in the darkness he suddenly felt something like a blow on the face.

'Oh!' cried he, 'if they do that again I shall give it them back.'

And when a second blow came, he returned it quickly, and then a third, and so they kept on the whole night; for every blow from the unseen hands he struck out right and left, and was not idle till the day broke, and then all became suddenly still.

When the miller rose in the morning he went into the mill, and was quite surprised to see the young man still living.

'Oh!' he said, 'I have had a good supper, and some terribly hard blows, but I have given them back without mercy.'

On hearing this, the miller was overjoyed, for the mill was now freed from enchantment, and he offered him a large amount of money as a reward.

But he refused, saying, 'I do not want money. I have enough.'

Then the young giant took the sacks of flour on his back, and returned to the farm, and told the bailiff that now the matter was all settled he would have the stipulated wages. When the bailiff heard this he was in a terrible fright, and knew not what to do. He walked up and down the room for some time, while the drops of perspiration stood on his forehead from terror. Presently he opened the window, that the fresh air might blow upon him, and, before he was aware, the young giant was behind him, and with one kick sent him through the window, flying in the air still higher and higher, till at last he was out of sight.

The young man then turned to the bailiff's wife, and said, ' The second blow must be for you, as your husband does not return.'

' No, no!' she cried. ' It is impossible. I could not bear it.' And she ran to the open window; for the perspiration also stood on her forehead in great drops from fear.

He was not, however, to be deterred from his purpose. With one kick, though more gentle, he sent her flying through the air after her husband, and, as she was lighter, she rose higher. Her husband saw her, and called to her to come to him; but, as she could not, she kept begging him to come to her. All to no purpose. They remained floating in the air unable to reach each other, and, for aught I know, they may be floating there still. As for the young giant, he took up his iron walking-stick, and went on his way.

THUMBLING'S TRAVELS.

A TAILOR once had a son who was so very small that he gave him the name of Thumbling. The little mite was, however, very courageous, and one day said to his father : ' Father, I must go out in the world and get my living.'

' Very well, my son,' he replied. Then he took a darning-needle, polished it till it was very bright, and made a top to it with sealing-wax. This he gave to his son, and said : ' There is a sword to hang by your side, and help you on your way.'

Before he started, the little fellow thought he should like to have something to eat, so he hopped into the kitchen to see what the good old cook could give him for his last meal. He was just in time, for a dish stood on the hearth.

' Good mother, what can you give me to eat to-day?' he said.

' See for yourself,' she replied.

Away sprung Thumbling to the hearth, and peeped into the dish, but as he was stretching his neck over, the steam caught him and carried him up the chimney.

For a time he floated on the steam in the air, but at last he sunk down again to the earth, and found himself, as he wished, out in the wide world alone. His father had taught him to work at his own trade, so he went and engaged himself to a master tailor, but the food did not please him, and one day he went to his master's wife, and said : ' Mistress, if you don't give me something better to eat, I shall go away early to-morrow morning, and write with chalk on your house door, " Too many potatoes, too little meat. Adieu, Sir Potato King." '

' You little grasshopper!' cried the mistress angrily, ' I'll teach you to talk like that.' Then she seized a duster, and was going to beat him with it, but he crept nimbly under her thimble, which stood on the table, and put out his tongue at her. She lifted up the thimble, and tried to catch hold of him, but the little dwarf hopped into the duster, and as his mistress unrolled it to seek for him, he jumped on the table, and called out: 'He, he! Madame Mistress, here I am!' And when she tried to strike him, he slipped into the table-drawer. At last, however, she caught him, and drove him from the house.

The little tailor wandered on till he came to a large forest, and here he met a robber chief on his way to steal the king's treasures. As soon as he saw the little man, he said to himself: 'A little fellow like that would make a capital picklock; he could creep through the key-holes.'

'Hi!' he cried, 'come here, you Giant Goliath. Will you go with us to the king's treasure-chamber? you can easily slip in and throw the gold out to us.'

Thumbling thought for awhile, and then said: 'Yes, I will go with you to the treasure-chamber.'

When they reached the door, they examined it well, but there appeared not a hole or a crevice under or above it. At last they discovered one just wide enough for Thumbling to creep through, and left him to himself. He was standing close to the hole, when one of the sentinels who stood before the door noticed him, and said to the other: 'Look at that ugly little spider creeping there, I shall just crush it to death with my foot.'

'Let the poor animal go,' said the other; 'it has done you no harm.'

Thumbling, on hearing this, crept through out of their way as quickly as he could, got into the treasure-chamber, opened the window under which the robbers stood, and threw out dollars to them one after the other.

In the midst of this work he heard the king coming to visit his treasures, and ran away quickly to hide himself. The king very soon missed a number of dollars, but he could not imagine how they had been stolen, for the locks and bolts were in perfect order, and all appeared carefully guarded. Thereupon he went out and said to the sentinels: 'Watch carefully, there is some one after the money.'

When the king was gone, Thumbling set to work again, and the sentinels could hear some one moving, as well as the clink of money. They rushed into the room quickly to seize the thief, but Thumbling was as quick as they were; he ran into a corner, and covered himself with one of the dollars, so that he could not be seen.

Then he began to tease the sentinels, and cried: 'Here I am.' But by the time they had reached the place from whence the sound came, he had jumped into another corner, under another dollar, and cried: 'Hi! here I am.' And so he kept them rushing about from one corner of the room to another, making fools of them till they were quite tired out, and went away. After they were gone, he again threw dollars out of the window one after another as swiftly as possible, and then with a spring jumped after them, and was caught by the robbers.

They were so pleased that one of them said : ' You are quite a mighty hero. Will you serve with us under our chief ?'

Thumbling reflected for awhile, and then said he should like to see a little more of the world first. On this they divided the spoil into shares, but Thumbling only had a kreutzer, for he could not carry any more. Thumbling again took his sword by his side, wished the robbers good-bye, and walked away on foot.

After awhile he engaged himself as workman to other masters ; but they did not fancy him, or like his appearance, so at last he became foot-boy at an hotel. The maids did not like him at all ; for, without being seen himself, he found out all their secrets, and told the master of what they took from the plates or fetched from the cellar. Then they said : ' Only wait, we'll catch you some day, and drown you.' And they made an agreement among themselves that they really would serve him out.

One morning the cook went into the garden to cut some cabbages, and she saw the dwarf jumping and creeping about. Then she cut the grass quickly round him, wrapped it up in a cloth, and threw it to the cows, and one of them gobbled him up with the grass. Here he found himself in great darkness, but in swallowing him the cow had fortunately not hurt him with her teeth. However, he did not like his position at all, so when anyone came near he cried out with all his might : ' Let me out ! let me out !' The herdsman, who heard the voice, was much alarmed, and sent for his master, who also distinctly heard the words : ' Let me out ! let me out !'

' Where are you ?' he asked.

' In the dark,' replied the dwarf.

' The cow is bewitched,' said the master, and after ordering it to be slaughtered, he went away.

The next morning the cow was killed, and fortunately while it was being cut up, Thumbling was not hurt, but to his terror he found himself with that part of the cow that was to be made into sausages. When the butcher began to chop, Thumbling screamed out with all his strength : ' Don't cut too deep ! don't cut too deep ! I am just under.'

But the man did not hear, because of the noise made by the chopping-knife. Now was poor little Thumbling in great trouble and danger, but the danger made him sprightly. He jumped aside and between the chopping-knives so quickly and nimbly that he got no hurt, and came off with a whole skin.

But jump about as he might, he could not save himself from being mixed with the sausage-meat and forced into the skin, where he was obliged to remain for a long time ; for the sausages were hung in the chimney to be smoked, as they were not required till winter.

At last a day came on which sausages were wanted for some guests at the hotel, and when the landlord's wife took them down to divide them, Thumbling kept himself carefully out of the way of her knife ; for if he had stretched out his neck his head most certainly would have been cut off. But he managed to escape when the opening was made at the end of the sausage without being hurt, and no sooner did he breathe the fresh air than he sprung out again to freedom.

It was not likely he would wish to remain at a house where he had been so badly served, and soon, therefore, he started again on his travels, and returned home to his father.

'I have brought you a beautiful piece of gold,' he said ; ' as much as I could carry,' and he offered him the kreutzer.

'If that is all you have gained by your travels you might as well have remained at home,' replied his father.

THE GOLDEN GOOSE.

A MAN once had three sons, the youngest of whom was considered very silly, and everybody used to mock him and make fun of him. The eldest son, who was a woodcutter, was often sent by his father to cut wood in the forest ; and, before he left home, his mother would prepare beautiful pancakes and a bottle of wine for him to take with him to eat and drink while he was at work.

One day, just as he entered the forest, he met a gray old man, who bade him good-morning, and said, ' Give me a little piece of cake out of your basket, and a drop of wine out of your bottle, for I am very hungry and thirsty.'

But the youth, who was considered clever, replied, ' What ! give you my cake and my wine ? Why, if I did I should have none for myself. Not I, indeed ; so take yourself off.'

The old man went away, and the young man began cutting down a tree, till presently he made a false stroke ; the axe slipped and cut his arm so badly that he was obliged to go home and have it bound up. Now this false stroke was caused by the little gray old man.

Next day the second son went into the forest to cut wood, and his mother gave him also a cake and a bottle of wine. As he entered the wood the same little old man met him, and begged for a piece of cake and a drop of wine. But the second son answered rudely, ' What I might give to you I shall want myself ; so be off.'

Then he left the little old man standing in the road, and walked on. His punishment soon came ; he had scarcely given two strokes on a tree with his axe, when he hit his leg such a terrible blow that he was obliged to limp home in great pain.

Then the stupid son, whom nobody cared for, went to his father, and said, ' Let me go for once and cut wood in the forest.'

But his father said, ' No ; your brothers have been hurt already, and it would be worse for you, who don't understand woodcutting.'

The boy, however, begged so hard to be allowed to go, that his father said, 'There, get along with you; you will buy your experience very dearly, I expect.'

His mother, however, gave him a cake which had been made with water and baked in the ashes, and a bottle of sour beer.

When he reached the wood the very same little old man met him, and, after greeting him kindly, said, 'Give me a little of your cake, and a drop from your bottle, for I am very hungry and thirsty.'

'Oh,' replied the simple youth, 'I have only a cake which has been baked in the ashes, and some sour beer; but you are welcome to a share of it. Let us sit down and eat and drink together.'

So they seated themselves, and, lo and behold! when the youth opened his basket the cake had been turned into a beautiful pancake, and the sour beer into wine. After they had eaten and drank enough, the little old man said, 'Because you have been kind-hearted, and shared your dinner with me, I will make you in future lucky in all you undertake. There stands an old tree; cut it down, and you will find something good at the root.'

Then the old man said farewell, and left him.

The youth set to work, and very soon succeeded in felling the tree— what was his surprise to find sitting at the roots a goose, whose feathers were of pure gold! He took it up, and, instead of going home, carried it with him to an inn at a little distance, where he intended to pass the night.

The landlord had three daughters, who looked at the goose with envious eyes; they had never seen such a wonderful bird, and longed to have at least one of its feathers. 'Ah!' thought the eldest, 'I shall soon have an opportunity to pluck one of them;' and so it happened, for not long after the young man left the room. She instantly went up to the bird and took hold of its wing; but as she did so the finger and thumb remained and stuck fast. In a short time after the second sister came in, with the full expectation of gaining a golden feather; but, as she touched her sister to move her from the bird, her hand stuck fast to her sister's dress, and they neither of them could free themselves. At last, in came the third sister with the same intention. 'Keep away, keep away!' screamed the other two; 'in Heaven's name keep away!'

But she could not imagine why she should keep away. If they were near the golden bird, why should not she be there? So she made a spring forward and touched her second sister, and immediately she also was made a prisoner, and in this position they were obliged to remain by the goose all night.

In the morning the young man came in, took the goose on his arm, and went away without noticing that the three girls were following close behind him. And, as he walked quickly, they were obliged to run one behind the other, left or right of him, just as he happened to change the goose from one arm to the other.

In the middle of a field they were met by the parson of the parish, who looked with wonder at the procession as it came near him. 'Shame on you!' he cried out. 'What are you about, you bold-faced hussies, running after a young man in that way through the fields? Go home, all of you!'

He placed his hand on the youngest to pull her back; but the moment he touched her he also became fixed, and was obliged to follow and run like the rest. In a few minutes the clerk met them, and when he saw the parson running after the girls he wondered greatly, and cried out, 'Halloa, master parson, where are you running in such haste? Have you forgotten that there is a christening to-day?' And, as the procession did not stop, he ran after it and seized the parson's gown.

In a moment he found that his hand was fixed, and he also had to run like the rest; and now there were five trotting along, one behind the other. Presently two peasants came by with their sickles from the field. The parson called out to them, and begged them to come and release him and the clerk. The men hastened over and made the attempt, but with the same result. They were stuck fast as the others, and the simpleton with his golden goose travelled on quite unconcerned about the seven who were obliged to trot along after him.

After a while they came to a city in which reigned a king who had a daughter of such a melancholy disposition that no one could ever make her laugh. Therefore he issued a decree that whoever would make the princess laugh should have her in marriage.

Now, when the simple youth heard this, he was determined to try what effect the appearance of himself and his train would have on the princess. So he ran before her, and the whole seven trotted after him. The sight was so ridiculous that the moment the princess saw it she burst into a violent fit of laughter, and they thought she would never leave off.

After this the youth went to the king and demanded his daughter in marriage, according to the king's decree; but his majesty did not quite like to have the young man for a son-in-law, so he said that before he could consent to the marriage the youth must bring him a man who could drink all the wine in the king's cellar.

So the simpleton released his prisoners from the golden goose, locked it away carefully, and went into the forest, for he thought, 'If anyone can help me it is the little gray man.' When he arrived at the spot where he had cut down the tree, there stood a man with a very miserable face.

The youth asked him why he looked so sorrowful.

'Oh,' he exclaimed, 'I suffer such dreadful thirst that nothing seems able to quench it, and cold water I cannot endure. I have emptied two casks of wine already, but they were just like a drop of water on a hot stone.'

'I can help you,' cried the young man; 'come with me, and you shall have your fill, I promise you.'

Upon this he led the man into the king's cellar, where he opened the casks one after another, and drank and drank till his back ached, and before the day closed he had quite emptied the king's cellar.

Again the young man asked for his bride, but the king was annoyed at the thought of giving his daughter to such a common fellow, and to get rid of him he made another condition. He said that no man should have his daughter who could not find some one able to eat up a whole mountain of bread.

Away went the simpleton to the forest as before, and there in the same place sat a man binding himself round tightly with a belt, and making the most horrible faces. As the youth approached, he cried, 'I have eaten a whole ovenful of rolls, but it has not satisfied me a bit; I am as hungry as ever, and my stomach feels so empty that I am obliged to bind it round tightly, or I should die of hunger.'

The simpleton could hardly contain himself for joy when he heard this.

'Get up,' he exclaimed, 'and come with me, and I will give you plenty to eat, I'll warrant.'

So he led him to the king's court, where his majesty had ordered all the flour in the kingdom to be made into bread, and piled up in a huge mountain. The hungry man placed himself before the bread, and began to eat, and before evening the whole pile had disappeared.

Then the simpleton went a third time to the king and asked for his bride, but the king made several excuses, and at last said that if he could bring him a ship that would travel as well by land as by water, then he should, without any further conditions, marry his daughter.

The youth went at once straight to the forest, and saw the same old gray man to whom he had given his cake.

'Ah,' he said, as the youth approached, 'it was I who sent the men to eat and drink, and I will also give you a ship that can travel by land or by sea, because, when you thought I was poor, you were kind-hearted, and gave me food and drink.'

The youth took the ship, and when the king saw it, he was quite surprised, but he could not any longer refuse to give him his daughter in marriage. The wedding was celebrated with great pomp, and after the king's death the simple woodcutter became king over the whole kingdom.

THE WONDERFUL TRAVELLERS.

THERE once lived a man who was clever in all kinds of trades. He had been a soldier, but when the war was over they discharged him, with the paltry pittance of threepence to help him on his way.

'Wait a bit,' said he to himself; 'this treatment does not please me, and if I can only get the proper people to help me, I will make the king give me all the treasures in his kingdom.'

So he went first in his vexation into a forest, and there saw a man pull up six trees as if they were blades of grass. He spoke to the man, and said :

'Will you enter my service and travel with me ?'

'Yes,' was the reply; 'but I must first carry home to my mother these few faggots of wood.'

Then he took one of the trees, twisted it like a twig round the other five, lifted them as if they had been a bundle of real faggots on his shoulder, and carried them away. Very soon he returned to his new master, and as they walked on together, he said :

'We two shall get on in the world splendidly, I fancy.'

After a while they came upon a sportsman, who was kneeling on one knee and pointing his loaded gun at some object.

'What are you aiming at ?' asked the soldier.

'Oh,' he replied, 'there sits a fly on the branches of an oak two miles off, and I wish to shoot him in the left eye.'

'Ah,' exclaimed the soldier, 'you had better come with me; three such as we are will soon make a noise in the world.'

The sportsman was quite ready to join the party, so the three went on together till they came to seven windmills. The sails were turning round with wonderful rapidity, although there was not wind enough even to stir a leaf.

'I cannot think what turns the windmills,' said the soldier, 'for there is not a breath of air stirring.' So he and his two servants continued their journey.

About two miles further on they saw a man perched on a tree, who closed one nostril with his finger, and blew out of the other.

'My friend,' asked the soldier, 'what are you about up there ?'

'Can't you see ?' he replied. 'Two miles off there stand seven windmills, and I am blowing to make their sails turn round.'

'Oh, come along with us,' he replied; 'when four such fellows as we go together in the world, we may do wonders.'

So the blower came down from the tree, and went with them.

After a time they passed a man standing on one leg, and the other, which had been cut off, lay on the ground near him.

'Well!' exclaimed the master, 'you have a queer way of resting yourself, certainly.'

'I am a courier,' he replied, 'and as I do not wish to run too fast, I have taken off one of my legs. When they are both on, I can run as swiftly as a bird flies.'

'Oh, then you must come with us,' was the reply; 'five such as we can carry the world before us.'

So they set off again, and before long met another curious being who wore a hat, but it hung quite on one side, over his ear. Then the chief said to him: 'Pardon me, sir, but you should not hang your hat on your ear; it makes you look like a fool.'

'I dare not alter it,' he replied, 'for if I place it on my head, there is such a dreadful frost that the birds in the air freeze, and fall dead on the ground.'

'Oh!' cried the master, 'come with us; you are the very man, and we six will do wonders in the world.'

After a time the six travellers arrived at a city in which the king had made a proclamation that if any man would run a race with his daughter and win, he should have her for a wife, but if he was beaten he would lose his head. Then the soldier came forward and informed the king that he should like to win the race, if one of his servants might be allowed to run for him.

'Certainly,' replied the king, 'but you must pledge your own life as well as his, and if he fails, you will both lose your heads.'

As soon as matters were arranged, the runner quickly screwed on his other leg, while his master said to him: 'Do your best, friend, and help us to win.'

It had been decided that whichever of the runners brought back water in a cup from a distant well first should be declared the winner. The courier and the king's daughter each received a cup for this purpose, and then started at the same moment. But the princess had scarcely run any distance before the courier was out of sight as completely as if the wind had carried him away.

On reaching the fountain, he filled his cup full of water, and turned to go back, but when he arrived about half way he began to feel overcome with fatigue, so he placed his cup of water on the ground, laid himself down, and was soon asleep. He had placed, however, a horse's skull, which he had found near, under his head for a pillow. Being hard, it would not let him sleep long. In the meantime the princess, who could really run very fast, arrived at the well. Hastily filling her cup, she turned back and very soon came to the place where her rival lay sleeping. She was overjoyed, and said: 'Ah, my enemy is in my power now.' So she emptied the water from his cup, and continued her rapid footsteps homeward with greater speed than ever.

Now all would have been lost but that the sportsman who stood on the castle wall saw with his keen eyes what had occurred.

'The princess must not be allowed to win,' he said, and, raising his gun, he took such a correct aim that the skull was shot away from under the courier's head without injuring him in the least. The noise awoke him, and starting up, he saw that his cup was empty, and the princess far ahead of him. But he did not lose courage ; running back to the spring, he refilled his cup with water, and then with a few rapid strides overtook the princess, passed her, and arrived home ten minutes before her.

The king and the princess were dreadfully mortified when they found that she was beaten, for he could not endure to think of his daughter marrying a discharged common soldier. So they held a council together as to the best means of freeing themselves from him and his companions. At last the king said : 'Don't be uneasy, my child ; I have thought of a plan ; they shall not come near to you again.'

Then he sent for the six travellers to a feast, and when they arrived, led them to a room in which stood a table covered with every delicacy, and left them to enjoy themselves.

But this room had an iron floor, iron doors, and iron-bound windows, and as soon as they were inside, he had all the doors bolted and locked. When this was done the king sent for the cook, and ordered him to light a fire under the room, and keep it blazing until the iron became red hot. This the cook did, and it was not long before the six travellers seated at the table began to feel very warm. At first they thought it arose from the steam of their dinner, but the heat increased so much that they determined to open the doors and windows, and then found them all barred and locked. At once they knew that it had been the wicked king's intention to shut them in and suffocate them.

'Don't fear, he shall not succeed,' cried the man with the little hat to his companions ; 'I will make it so cold and freezing that the fire shall creep away and hide itself for shame.'

He placed the little hat on his head as he spoke, and it became immediately so bitterly cold and freezing that the heat vanished, and the provisions left on the dishes were actually frozen.

After two hours had passed, the king, supposing that by this time they must all be dead, opened the door and looked in himself. But what was his surprise when the six men came forward, safe and sound, and said they should be glad to get out to warm themselves, for the room was so very cold that the dishes were even frozen to the table.

Away went the king, full of anger, to the cook, whom he scolded well, and asked him why he had not obeyed his orders. But the cook, pointing to the fire under the room, said, 'It is hot enough there.'

The king was much surprised, for he saw an immense fire burning under the iron room, and knew at once that he should not be able very easily to get rid of the six visitors. However, he thought he would try another plan, so he sent for the soldier, and said, ' If you will resign your claim to my daughter, I will give you as much gold as you like.'

' Oh, yes, my lord king, I am quite ready to do so,' he replied, ' if you will give me as much gold as one of my servants can carry.'

The king was delighted, especially when the soldier said he would go away at once and come again for the money in fourteen days. Thereupon the soldier sent for all the tailors in the kingdom, and desired them to make him such an immense sack that it took them fourteen days to finish it. As soon as it was ready, he called the strong man, who was one of the six, and who could pull up trees by the roots, and telling him to take the sack on his shoulders, they went together to the king. As soon as they appeared, the king asked, ' Who is this powerful fellow that I see with a woollen sack on his shoulders as large as a house?' and when they told him it was the servant of the soldier, and that the sack was to be filled with gold, he was greatly alarmed. ' My money will all be swallowed up,' he thought. However, he ordered a ton of gold to be brought, and it took sixteen strong men to carry it. But the soldier's servant took it up with one hand easily and threw it into the sack.

' Fetch some more,' he said ; ' that only just covers the bottom.' So the king ordered more to be brought, which the strong man threw into the sack also, yet still it was not half full. ' Bring me more,' he cried ; ' these crumbs are nothing at all.' So at last they brought seven hundred cartloads of gold from all parts of the kingdom, and these the strong man stuffed into his sack, gold and waggons, with even the oxen that drew them. ' I can't stay much longer,' he said at last, ' so bring me all you can to fill my sack.' But when he had got everything in that they could find, he said, ' The sack is not near full, but I must make an end of the matter, so it does not signify.' Then he hoisted the sack on his shoulders, and went away with his companions.

When the king saw plainly that all the riches of the country had been taken away by one man, he was in a terrible rage, and ordered all his cavalry to mount their horses and pursue the travellers, and, above all things, to bring back the man with the sack.

Two regiments, therefore, rode after the six travellers, and soon overtook them, and cried, ' You are our prisoners ; lay down the sack of gold immediately, or we will cut you in pieces.'

' What did you say?' asked the blower ; ' that we are prisoners ? I think before you take us prisoners I can treat you to a dance in the air.'

Then he closed up one nostril, and with the other blew the two regiments up into the air, right over a mountain, sending one to the right and the other to the left. One old sergeant-major begged for mercy ;

he had received nine wounds, and was a brave fellow, who did not deserve to be so disgraced. The blower therefore sent him only a little way, so that he came back quite safely to the ground. Then he said to him, ' Now go home to the king, and tell him that if he sends any more cavalry regiments here, they will be blown away into the air in the same manner.'

When the king received the message, he said, ' Let the rascals go; they will meet their reward.'

So the six travellers carried the treasure home, divided it among themselves, and lived upon it contentedly ever after.

CLEVER GRETHEL.

THERE was once a cook named Grethel who had shoes with red heels, and when she wore them out of doors she would draw herself up and walk proudly, and say to herself, ' I really am a handsome maiden.' At home she would sometimes, in a frolic, drink a glass of wine, or if she took it in her head, she would eat up all the best things in the house till she was satisfied, and say to herself, ' The cook ought to know the taste of everything.'

One day her master said to her, ' Grethel, I have invited some friends to dinner to-day; cook me some of your best chickens.'

' That will I do, master,' she replied.

So she went out and killed two of the best fowls, and prepared them for roasting.

In the afternoon she placed them on the spit before the fire, and they were all ready, and beautifully hot and brown by the proper time, but the visitors had not arrived. So she went to her master, and said, ' The fowls will be quite spoilt if I keep them at the fire any longer. It will be a pity and a shame if they are not eaten soon.'

Then said her master, ' I will go and fetch the visitors myself,' and away he went.

As soon as his back was turned, Grethel put the spit with the birds on one side, and thought, ' I have been standing by the fire so long that it has made me quite thirsty. Who knows when they will come? While I am waiting I may as well run into the cellar, and have a little drop.' So she seized a jug, and said, ' All right, Grethel, thou shalt have a good draught. Wine is so tempting,' she said again, ' and it does not do to spoil your draught,' and then she drank without stopping till the jug was empty.

After this she went into the kitchen, and placed the fowls again before the fire, basted them with butter, and rattled the spit round so furiously that they browned and frizzled with the heat. 'They would never miss a little piece, if they searched for it ever so carefully,' she said to herself. Then she dipped her finger in the dripping-pan to taste, and cried, ' Oh, how nice these fowls are ! It is a sin and a shame that there is no one here to eat them.'

She ran to the window to see if her master and the guests were coming; but she could see no one. So she went and stood again by the fowls, and thought, ' The wing of that fowl is a little burnt. I had better eat it out of the way.' She cut it off as she thought this and ate it up, and it tasted so nice that when she had finished it, she thought, ' I must have the other. Master will never notice that anything is missing.'

After the two wings were eaten, Grethel again went to look for her master, but there were no signs of his appearance.

' Who knows,' she said to herself, ' perhaps the visitors are not coming at all, and they have kept my master to dinner, so he won't be back. Hi ! Grethel, there are lots of good things left for you; and that piece of fowl has made me thirsty. I must have another drink before I come back, and eat up all these good things.'

So she went into the cellar, took a large draught of wine, and, returning to the kitchen, sat down, and ate the remainder of the fowl with great relish.

There was now only one fowl left, and, as her master did not return, Grethel began to look at the other with longing eyes. At last she said, ' Where one is, there must the other be ; for the fowls belong to each other, and what is right for one is also fair and right for the other. I believe, too, I want some more to drink. It won't hurt me.'

The last draught gave her courage. She came back to the kitchen, and let the second fowl go after the first.

As she was enjoying the last morsel, home came her master.

' Make haste, Grethel,' he cried. ' The guests will be here in a few minutes.'

' Yes, master,' she replied. ' It will soon be all ready.'

Meanwhile, the master saw that the cloth was laid, and everything in order. So he took up the carving-knife, with which he intended to carve the fowl, and went out to sharpen it on the stones in the passage.

While he was doing so, the guests arrived, and knocked gently and courteously at the house-door. Grethel ran out to see who it was, and when she caught sight of the visitors, she placed her finger on her lips, and whispered, ' Hush, hush ! go back again as quickly as you came. If my master should catch you, it would be unfortunate. He did invite you to dinner this evening; but with no other intention than to cut off both the ears of each of you. Listen ; you can hear him sharpening his knife.'

The guests heard the sound, and hastened as fast as they could down the steps, and were soon out of sight.

Grethel was not idle. She ran screaming to her master, and cried, 'You have invited fine visitors, certainly !'

'Hi ! Why, Grethel, what do you mean ?'

'Oh !' she exclaimed, 'they came here just now, and have taken my two beautiful fowls from the dish that I was going to bring up for dinner, and run away with them.'

'What strange conduct !' said her master, who was so sorry to lose his nice dinner that he rushed out to follow the thieves. 'If they had only left me one, or at least enough for my own dinner,' he cried, running after them. But the more he cried to them to stop, the faster they ran; and when they saw him with the knife in his hand, and heard him say, 'Only one ! only one !'—he meant, if they had left him 'only one fowl'; but they thought he spoke of 'only one ear,' which he intended to cut off—they ran as if fire were burning around them, and were not satisfied till they found themselves safe at home with both ears untouched.

THE OLD GRANDFATHER'S CORNER.

ONCE upon a time there was a very old man who lived with his son and daughter-in-law. His eyes were dim, his knees tottered under him when he walked, and he was very deaf. As he sat at table, his hand shook so that he would often spill the soup over the table-cloth, or on his clothes, and sometimes even he could not keep it in his mouth when it got there. His son and daughter were so annoyed to see his conduct at the table that at last they placed a chair for him in a corner behind the screen, and gave him his meals in an earthenware basin quite away from the rest. He would often look sorrowfully at the table with tears in his eyes, but he did not complain.

One day, thinking sadly of the past, the earthenware basin, which he could scarcely hold in his trembling hands, fell to the ground and was broken. The young wife scolded him well for being so careless, but he did not reply, only sighed deeply. Then she bought him a wooden bowl for a penny, and gave him his meals in it.

Some days afterwards his son and daughter saw their little boy, who was about four years old, sitting on the ground and trying to fasten together some pieces of wood.

'What are you making, my boy ?' asked his father.

'I am making a little bowl for papa and mamma to eat their food in when I grow up,' he replied.

The husband and wife looked at each other without speaking for some minutes. At last they began to shed tears, and went and brought their old father back to the table, and from that day he always took his meals with them, and was never again treated unkindly.

THE GOLDEN GOOSE

THE OLD GRANDFATHER'S CORNER

THE WATER SPRITE.

A LITTLE brother and sister were one day playing together by the side of a well, and not being careful they both fell in. Under the water they found a fairy, who said to them: 'Now I have caught you, and I intend you to work for me.'

So she carried them both away. When they arrived at her home, she set the maiden to spin hard, tangled flax, and gave her a cask full of holes to fill with water; and she sent the boy to the wood with a blunt axe, and told him to cut wood for her fire.

The children became at last so impatient with this treatment that they waited till one Sunday, when the fairy was at church, and ran away. But the church was close by, and as they were flying away like two birds she espied them, and went after them with great strides. The children saw her coming in the distance, and the maiden threw behind her a great brush, which instantly became a mountain covered with prickly points, over which the fairy had the greatest trouble to climb. But the children saw that she had managed to get over, and was coming near.

The boy then threw a comb behind him, which became a mountain of combs, with hundreds of teeth sticking up; but the fairy knew how to hold fast on this, and soon clambered over it.

The maiden next threw a looking-glass behind, which became a mountain also, and was so slippery that is was impossible to get over it.

Then thought the fairy, 'I will go home and fetch my axe and break the looking-glass.'

But when she came back and had broken the looking-glass, the children had been for a long time too far away for her to overtake them, so she was obliged to sink back into the well.

THE COCK'S FUNERAL.

ONCE upon a time a cock and a hen went to a nut mountain to gather nuts, and they promised each other that whoever found the first nut, it should be divided between them.

One day the cock found a very large kernel, which he thought he should like to eat all by himself. But the kernel was so large that when he tried to swallow it it stuck in his throat, and, fearing that he should be choked, he screamed out so loudly that the hen came running up to see what was the matter.

'Water, water, water! quick, or I shall be choked!' he cried.

Away ran the hen as fast as she could to the spring. 'Spring!' she cried, 'pray give me some water; my husband has swallowed a kernel, and he is choking.'

'Go first to the bride,' answered the spring, 'and ask her for a piece of red silk.'

The poor hen ran to the bride, and said, 'Dear bride, pray give me a piece of red silk for the spring, that I may get some water for my husband, who has swallowed a large nut-kernel, and will be choked.'

The bride answered, 'Run first and fetch me my wreath which hangs on the willow yonder.'

Then ran the hen to the willow and fetched the wreath. The bride gave her the red silk, which she took to the spring, and got some water at last. But it was too late; when she brought the water to the cock, she found him lying dead on the ground, for the nut had choked him.

The hen was in such distress that she gave a loud scream, which brought all the animals running in a great fright to see what was the matter. Then they all mourned for the cock, and six mice offered to build a little carriage for the funeral, and when it was finished they harnessed themselves to it, and drew it to the grave, while the hen followed. On the way they met a fox, who asked where they were going.

'I am going to bury my husband,' replied the hen.

'May I go with you?' asked the fox.

'Yes, if you follow behind; for my little horses could not draw the carriage with you on it.'

So the fox placed himself behind; and then came up a wolf, a bear, a stag, and a lion, and many other beasts of the forest, and joined the procession. They had not gone far when they came to a brook.

'How are we to get over here?' asked the hen.

There was a stalk of straw lying on the brook, and it said, 'I will place myself across from one side to the other, and you can easily get over me.'

But when the six mice stepped on the bridge it broke under them, and they all fell in and were drowned. This was a new trouble; but presently a coal came by and said, 'I think I am big and strong enough to carry you over safely.'

So the coal placed himself in the water; but he had nothing to rest upon, and, being too heavy to swim, he sank to the bottom and was drowned.

At last a large stone took compassion on them, and laid itself across the stream from one side to the other. Over this the hen drew the waggon with her dead husband upon it, and landed it quite safely on the opposite shore.

The rest of the procession wished to follow, so the empty carriage was sent back for them; but it was very small, and as they all crowded upon it at once, it upset, and they all fell into the water and were drowned. The hen was therefore left alone with her dead husband; so she dug a grave and laid him in it, and raised a mound over him. On this she seated herself, and grieved so much and so long that at length she died of grief.

BROTHER FROLICK'S ADVENTURES.

THE king of a certain country had been for some time at war, which at last came to an end, and several soldiers were discharged. Amongst them was a man called Brother Frolick, because he was such a light-hearted, jolly fellow; and although he only received a small loaf and four kreutzers in gold, he started on a journey through the world with a merry heart.

He had not gone far, when he saw a poor beggar sitting by the road-side begging, but he did not know that it was a fairy in disguise. The beggar asked for alms, and Brother Frolick said: 'What shall I give you? I am only a poor discharged soldier, and all they have given me is a loaf of bread and four kreutzers, and when it is all gone I must beg as well as you. However, I will give you something.'

Then he divided the loaf into four pieces, and gave one to the beggar, as well as one of his gold pieces.

The beggar thanked him, and went away, but only to a little distance; for, changing his appearance and face, he seated himself by the highway, waited for Brother Frolick to pass, and again begged for alms. The good-natured soldier gave this beggar also a fourth of his bread and a gold piece.

The fairy thanked him, and, after walking some distance, a third time seated himself in another form to beg of Brother Frolick. This time, also, he gave him a third piece of the divided loaf and another kreutzer. The beggar thanked him and went away.

The kind-hearted fellow had now only a fourth part of the loaf and one gold piece left, so he went to an inn, ate the bread, and paid his kreutzer for a jug of beer. As soon as he had finished, he went out, and travelled on for some distance, and there again was the fairy in the form of a discharged soldier like himself.

'Good-evening, comrade,' he said; 'could you give me a piece of bread, and a kreutzer to buy something to drink?'

'Where am I to get it?' answered Brother Frolick. 'I had my dis-charge to-day, and they gave me a loaf of bread and four gold kreutzers. But I met three beggars on the high road, and I gave them each a fourth part of my bread and a kreutzer, and the last kreutzer I have just paid for something to drink with my last piece of bread. Now I am empty, and, if you also have nothing, we can go and beg together.'

'No,' answered the fairy; 'we need not do that. I understand a little of medicine and surgery, and can soon earn as much as I shall want.

'Well,' replied Brother Frolick, 'I don't understand doctoring at all, so I must go and beg alone.'

'No; come with me,' cried the other; 'whatever I earn, you shall have half.'

'That is good news for me,' said Brother Frolick; so they went away together.

After a time, as they passed a peasant's house, they heard great cries and lamentations; so they went in, and found the husband very ill and at the point of death, and the wife weeping and howling with all her might.

'Leave off that noise,' said the fairy; 'I will soon cure your husband.'

Then he took some salve out of his pocket, and healed the man so quickly that he could stand up and was quite well.

The husband and wife joyfully thanked the stranger, and said, 'What can we give you in return for this kindness?'

But the fairy would name nothing, and, worse still, refused all they brought to him; and although Brother Frolick nudged him more than once, he still said, 'No; I will take nothing—we do not want it.'

At last the grateful people brought a lamb, and said that he must take it whether he would or not. Then Brother Frolick nudged him in the side, and said: 'Take it, you stupid; you know we do want it.'

Then the fairy said at last, 'Well, I will take the lamb, but I cannot carry it; you must do that, if you want it so much.'

'Oh, that will be no trouble to me,' cried the other, and taking it on his shoulder they went away together. After a while, they came to a wood, and Brother Frolick, who began to feel tired and hungry, for the lamb was heavy, proposed that they should stop and rest. 'See,' he said, 'this is a beautiful place for us to cook the lamb and eat it.'

'It's all the same to me,' replied the fairy, 'but I can have nothing to do with the cooking; you must do that, if you have a kettle, and I will go away for a little while till it is ready. You must not, however, eat any till I come back; I will be here quite in time.'

'Go along,' said Brother Frolick, 'I understand how to cook, and I will soon have dinner ready.'

Then the fairy went away, and Brother Frolick slaughtered the lamb, lighted a fire, and threw some of the flesh into the kettle to boil. The meat was quite ready, however, before the fairy returned, and Brother Frolick became so impatient, that he took out of the kettle a part of the flesh, in which was the heart. 'The heart is the best of all,' he said, tasting it; and finding it very good, he ate it all.

At last his comrade returned and said : ' You may eat all the lamb yourself ; I only want the heart, so just give it me.'

Then Brother Frolick took a knife and fork and began searching amongst the pieces of meat for the heart, which, of course, he could not find. Then he said pertly, ' It is not there.'

' Then where can it be ?' said the fairy.

' I do not know,' said Brother Frolick ; ' but see,' he added, ' why, what a couple of fools we are, searching for a lamb's heart ; of course there is not one to be found, for a lamb has no heart.'

' Ah,' said the other, ' that is news ! Every animal has a heart ; why should not a lamb ?'

' No, certainly, brother,' he said, ' a lamb has no heart ; reflect a little, and you will be convinced that it really has none.'

' Well, certainly, it is quite clear that there is no heart to be found in this one, and as I do not want any other part, you may eat it all yourself.'

' I cannot eat it all,' replied Brother Frolick, ' so what is left I will put into my knapsack.'

When this was done, the two started to continue their journey, and Brother Peter, as the fairy called himself, caused a large quantity of water to rise on the road just across where they had to pass. Said Brother Peter, ' You go first.'

' No,' answered the other, ' I would rather see you across ;' for he thought, ' if the water is very deep, I won't go at all.'

So Brother Peter stepped over, and the water only came up to his knees. His comrade prepared to follow, but he had not gone far when the water came up to his neck. ' Brother, help me,' he cried.

' Will you confess, then, that you ate the lamb's heart ?' he replied.

' No,' he said, ' I did not eat it.'

Immediately the water became deeper, and flowed to his mouth. ' Help ! help me, brother,' he cried.

' Will you confess now that you have eaten the lamb's heart ?' cried Brother Peter.

' No,' he replied, ' I did not eat it.'

Now the fairy did not intend to drown him, so he allowed the water to subside, and Brother Frolick crossed over safely. They travelled after this till they reached a foreign land, and in the chief city heard that the king's daughter was very ill, and not expected to live.

' Holloa ! brother,' said the soldier, ' that is a good chance for us if you cure her, we shall never know want again.'

But Brother Peter did not hurry himself, and when his comrade begged him to put his best foot foremost, he went slower than ever. Brother Frolick pushed him and dragged him on, but all to no purpose, and at last they heard that the king's daughter was dead. ' There now,' cried Brother Frolick, ' we have lost our chance, all through your sleepy walking.'

' Be quiet, now,' said Brother Peter ; ' I can not only cure the sick, but I can restore the dead to life.'

' If that is the case,' replied his comrade, ' you may be sure that the king will be ready to give us the half of his kingdom for joy.'

They therefore went to the king's castle, and found them all in great grief. But Brother Peter said to the king: ' Do not mourn; I can restore the princess to life.'

He and his comrade were at once led to her room, and telling every-one to go out, they were left alone with the dead princess. Brother Peter immediately stripped the body of the grave-clothes, and laid it in a bath of very hot water, which he had ordered to be brought. Then he uttered a few strange words, which his comrade tried to remember, and turning to the princess, said: ' I command thee to come out of the bath, and stand on thy feet.'

Immediately the princess rose, and was again alive and well. The chamber-women were sent for, and the princess in her royal clothes was taken to her father, who received her with great joy, and said to the two strangers: ' Name your reward; it shall be yours, even to the half of my kingdom.'

But Brother Peter replied: ' No, I will take no reward for what I have done.'

' Oh, you foolish fellow,' thought Brother Frolick to himself. Then he nudged him again in the side: ' How can you be so stupid? If you don't want anything, I do.'

Brother Peter, however, still refused; but the king, seeing that his comrade was quite willing to accept something, told his treasurer to fill the soldier's knapsack with gold.

They left the city after this, and travelled on till they came to a wood. Then said Brother Peter: ' We may as well divide that gold.'

' With all my heart,' replied the good-natured fellow.

Peter took the gold, and divided it into three portions.

' What is that for?' asked Brother Frolick. ' What have you got in your head now? There are only two of us.'

' Oh!' he replied, ' it's all right. One-third is for myself, one-third for you, and one-third for him who ate the lamb's heart.

' Oh, I ate that!' cried Brother Frolick, gathering the money up quickly. ' I did indeed; can't you believe me?'

' How can it be true?' replied Peter; ' a lamb has no heart.'

' Nonsense, brother,' he said, ' what are you thinking of? A lamb has a heart as well as other animals. Why should he not have one?'

' Now, really this is too good,' replied Brother Peter. ' However, you may keep all the gold to yourself; but I will go on my way alone in future.'

' As you please, brother,' answered the soldier. ' Farewell.'

Then Peter started on another road, and left Brother Frolick to pursue his way by himself. ' It is just as well,' thought he; ' but still he is a most wonderful man.' The soldier had now quite as much money as he wanted, but he knew not how to spend it properly; he wasted it or gave it away, till as time went on he was again almost penniless. At last he arrived at a city where he heard that the king's daughter had just died. 'Holloa!' thought he, 'here is an opportunity; I know how to restore her to life, and they will pay me something worth having this time.' So he went to the king and told him that he could restore his daughter to life.

Now the king had heard of the discharged soldier who had lately given new life to a princess, and he thought Brother Frolick was the man; still, as he was not quite sure, he asked him first for his opinion, and whether he would venture if the princess was really dead.

The soldier had no fear, so he ordered the bath to be filled with hot water, and went into the room with the dead princess alone. Then he stripped her of her clothes, placed her in the bath, and said, as he supposed, the words which Brother Peter had said, but the dead body did not move, although he repeated the words three times. He now began to feel alarmed, and cried out in angry tones: 'Stand up, will you, or you will get what you don't expect.'

At this moment the fairy appeared in his former shape as a discharged soldier, and entered the room through the window.

'You foolish man!' he cried, 'how can you raise the dead to life? I will help you this time; but don't attempt it again.'

Thereupon he pronounced the magic words, and immediately the princess rose and stood on her feet, and was as well and strong as ever. Then the fairy went away through the window, the maids were sent for to dress the princess in her royal robes, and then the soldier led her to her father. He knew, however, that he was not free to ask for a reward, for Peter had forbidden him to take anything; and therefore when the king asked him what he would have, he said he would take nothing, although he wanted it so much through extravagance and folly. Yet the king ordered his knapsack to be filled with gold, and with many thanks he took his departure.

Outside, near the castle gate, he met the fairy, who said to him: 'See now, I forbade you to take anything, and yet you have received a knapsack full of gold.'

'What could I do,' he replied, 'when they would put it in for me?'

'Then I can only tell you,' was the reply, 'that if you get into trouble a second time by undertaking what you cannot perform it will be worse for you.'

'All right, brother; I don't care now I have the gold, and I shall not care about putting dead people into a bath again after this.'

'Ah!' said the fairy, 'your gold will not last long. However, if you do not after this go into unlawful paths, I will give to your knapsack the power of containing in itself whatever you may wish for. And now farewell; you will see me no more.'

'Good-bye,' said the soldier, as he turned away. 'Well,' he thought, 'I am glad that he is gone. He is a wonderful fellow, no doubt; but I am better without him for a companion.'

Of the wonderful power with which he had endowed his knapsack Brother Frolick never thought then.

He went on his way with his gold from place to place, and spent and wasted it as he did before, and at last he had nothing left but four kreutzers. With this sum he entered an inn by the roadside, and felt that the money must go; so he spent three kreutzers in wine, and one in bread.

As he sat eating his bread and drinking his wine, the fragrant smell of roast goose reached his nose. Brother Frolick looked round and peeped about, and at last saw that the landlady had two geese roasting in the oven.

Then he suddenly remembered what his old comrade had said, that whatever he wished for he would find in his knapsack. 'Holloa,' he said to himself, 'then I must wish for the geese to be there.' Then he went out, and before the door he said, 'I wish that the two geese roasting in the oven were in my knapsack.' When he had said this he took it off, peeped in, and there they both lay. 'Ah!' he exclaimed, 'this is all right; I am a mighty chap after all,' and going farther into a meadow, sat down to enjoy his good fare.

Just as he had finished eating one goose, two farm-labourers came by, and when they saw the remaining goose, they stood still and looked at it with hungry eyes. 'Well,' thought Brother Frolick, 'one is enough for me.' So he beckoned the labourers nearer, and said, 'Here, take this goose, and drink my health as you eat it.'

They thanked him, and went away quickly to the inn, bought some wine and bread, and then unpacked the goose which had been given them, and began to eat it.

The landlady, when she saw it, went to her husband, and said, 'Those two are eating goose; just see if one of ours is gone from the oven.'

The landlord ran to look, and found the oven empty. 'You thieves!' he exclaimed, running out to them, 'where did you get roast goose to eat? Tell me instantly, or I will give you a taste of green hazel-juice!'

'We are not thieves!' they cried; 'a discharged soldier gave us this goose yonder in the meadow.'

'You are not going to make me believe that!' cried the landlord. 'That soldier has been here, and a most respectable fellow he is. I watched him when he left the house, and he had nothing with him then. No; you are the thieves, and shall pay for the goose.' But as they could not pay for it, he took a stick and thrashed them out of the house.

Quite ignorant of all this, Brother Frolick went on his way, till he came to a place where stood a beautiful castle, and not far from it a large but mean-looking inn. The soldier went up to the inn and asked for a night's lodging. But the landlord said, 'There is no room here; the house is full of noble guests.'

'I wonder at that,' said Brother Frolick. 'Why should they come here instead of going to that beautiful castle yonder?'

' Ah, yes !' said the landlord, ' many have thought as you do. They
have gone to spend a night at the castle, but they have never returned
alive. None are allowed to remain,' said the landlord, ' who do not go
in on their heads.'

' I am not likely to walk in on my head,' said the soldier. ' But now,
landlord, let me take something with me to eat and drink, and I'll go.'

So the landlord brought him a good supper to take with him, and
then Brother Frolick set out to go to the castle. On arriving, he first sat
down and ate with great relish, and when he began to feel sleepy laid
himself on the ground, for there was no bed, and was soon asleep.

In the night, however, he was awoke by a terrible noise, and when
he roused himself he saw nine hideous imps in the room, dancing round
a pole, which they held in their hands.

' Dance away,' he cried, ' as long as you will, but don't come near
me.' The imps, however, disregarded his orders; nearer and nearer
they approached as they danced, till one of them trod on his face
with his heavy foot. ' Keep away, you wretches,' he cried, but still
they came nearer. Then was Brother Frolick in a rage ; he started up,
seized a chair, and struck with the legs right and left. But nine imps
against one soldier were rather too much, and if he struck one before him,
another behind would pull his hair most unmercifully. ' You demons,'
he cried all at once, ' I will serve you out ; wait a bit—now then, all
nine of you into my knapsack.' Whisk ! and they were all in ; quick as
lightning he fastened the bag and threw it into a corner.

Then all was quiet, and Brother Frolick laid himself down again and
slept till broad daylight, when the arrival of the landlord of the inn and
the nobleman to whom the castle belonged woke him. They were
astonished to find him alive and full of spirits, and said to him, ' Have
you not seen any ghosts during the night, and did they not try to hurt
you ?'

' Well, not very much,' answered Brother Frolick ; ' I have them all
nine quite safe in my knapsack there,' and he pointed to the corner.
' You can dwell in your castle in peace now,' he said to the nobleman ;
' they will never trouble you again.'

The nobleman thanked the soldier, and loaded him with presents ;
he also begged him to remain in his service, and promised to take care
of him for the remainder of his life.

But the soldier said, ' No; I have a roving disposition ; I could never
rest in one place, I will go and travel farther.'

Then Brother Frolick went to a smith's, and laying the knapsack
containing the imps on the anvil, asked the smith and his man to strike
it with their great hammers with all their strength. The imps set up a
loud screech, and when at last all was quiet, the knapsack was opened.
Eight of them were found quite dead, but the ninth, who had laid himself in a fold, was still living. He slipped out when the knapsack was
opened, and escaped.

THE GOLD CHILDREN.

A LONG time ago there lived in a little cottage a poor fisherman and his wife, who had very little to live upon but the fish the husband caught. One day as he sat by the water throwing his net, he saw a fish drawn out which was quite golden. He examined it with wonder; but what was his surprise to hear it say, 'Listen, fisherman; if you will throw me again in the water I will change your little hut into a splendid castle.'

The fisherman replied, 'What would be the use of a castle to me when I have nothing to eat?'

'On that account,' said the gold fish, 'I will take care that there shall be a cupboard in the castle, in which, when you unlock it, you will find dishes containing everything to eat that heart can wish.'

'If it is so,' said the man, 'then I am quite willing to do as you please.'

'There is, however, one condition,' continued the fish; 'you must not mention to a living creature in the world, be it who it may, the source of your good fortune; if you utter a single word, it will at once be at an end.'

The man, upon this, threw the fish back into the water, and went home. But where his little hut had once stood now rose the walls of a large castle.

He stared with astonishment, and then stepped in, and saw his wife dressed in costly clothes, and sitting in a handsomely-furnished room. She seemed quite contented, and yet she said: 'Husband, how has all this happened? I am so pleased.'

'Yes,' said the man, 'it pleases me also; but I am so hungry, give me something to eat in our fine house.'

'Oh, dear,' she replied, 'I have nothing, and I don't know where any is to be found here.'

'There will be no trouble on that account,' he replied. 'Do you see that great cupboard? just unlock it.'

When the cupboard was opened, they saw with surprise that it contained every requisite for a beautiful feast. Bread, meat, vegetables, cake, wine, and fruit.

'Dear husband,' cried the wife, full of joy, 'what more can we desire than this?'

Then they sat down, and ate and drank together in great comfort.

After they had finished, the wife said : 'Husband, where do all these good things and riches come from ?'

'Ah !' he replied, 'do not ask me ; I dare not tell you. If I disclose anything, all our good fortune will come to an end.'

'Very well,' she replied, 'if I am not to be told, I shall not desire to know ;' but this was merely pretence, for she gave her husband no peace night or day, and she tormented and worried the poor man so terribly that she exhausted his patience, and he told her at last.

'This good fortune,' he said, 'all comes from a wonderful gold fish which I caught, and afterwards gave it freedom by throwing it back into the water.'

No sooner had he uttered these words than the castle with its wonderful cupboard disappeared, and they were again sitting in the fisherman's hut.

The husband was now again obliged to follow his trade and go fishing, and, as luck would have it, he again caught the golden fish.

'Listen !' cried the fish, 'if you will again throw me into the water, I will once more give you a castle and a cupboard full of good things ; but be firm this time, and reveal to no one from whom it comes, or all will be again lost.'

'I will keep it to myself,' answered the fisherman, and threw the fish into the water.

Everything at home now was in its former splendour, and the fisherman's wife joyful over their good fortune ; but her curiosity gave her no peace, and two days had scarcely passed before she began to ask how it all happened, and what was the cause.

Her husband kept silence for a long time, but at last she made him so angry that he incautiously revealed the secret. In a moment the castle and all that it contained vanished, and they were again sitting in their little old hut.

'See what you have done !' he said, 'we shall have again to starve with hunger.'

'Oh, well,' she replied, 'I would rather not have such riches if I am not to know where they come from ; it destroys my peace.'

The husband again went fishing, and, after a time, what should he again pull up in his net but the gold fish for the third time.

'Listen !' cried the fish ; 'I see I am always to fall into your hands ; therefore, you must take me to your house, and cut me in two pieces. These you must place in the ground, and you will have gold enough to last your life.'

The man took the fish home, and did exactly as he had been told.

It happened, after a while, that from the pieces of the fish placed in the earth two golden lilies sprung up, which were taken great care of.

Not long after the fisherman's wife had two little children, but they were both golden, as well as the two little foals in the stable. The children grew tall and beautiful, and the lilies and the foals grew also.

One day the children came to their father: 'We should like to ride out and see the world on our golden steeds. Will you let us?'

But the parents answered sorrowfully: 'How shall we be able to endure the thought that you are far away from us, and perhaps ill, or in danger?'

'Oh,' they replied, 'the two golden lilies will remain, and by them you can always tell how we are going on. If they are fresh, we are in health; if they fade, we are sick; and when they fall, we shall die!'

So the parents let them go, and they rode away for some time till they came to an inn where a number of people were staying. But when they saw the two gold children, they began to laugh and make a mockery of them.

As soon as one of them heard the laughter and mocking words, he would not go any farther, but turned back and went home to his father. The other, however, rode on till he came to a large forest. As he was about to enter the forest, some people came by and said: 'You had better not ride there, for the wood is full of robbers, who will overcome you and rob you, especially when they see that you and your horse are golden, and you will both be killed.'

He would not, however, allow himself to be frightened, but said: 'I must and will ride through!'

He took bearskins and threw them over himself and his horse, that the gold might not be seen, and rode confidently into the wood. He had not ridden far when he heard a rustling in the bushes, and voices speaking audibly to each other.

'That is one!' said a voice; but the other said: 'No; let him alone —he has nothing on but a bearskin, and is, I dare say, as poor and cold as a church mouse. What do we want with him?'

So the gold child rode through the wood, and no harm happened to him.

One day he came to a town in which he saw a maiden who appeared to him so beautiful that he did not think there could be another so beautiful in the world.

And as his love became stronger for her, he went to her and said: 'I love you with my whole heart. Will you be my wife?'

The maiden was so pleased, that she answered willingly: 'Yes; I will be your wife, and be true to you as long as I live.'

Very soon after they were married, and, just as they were enjoying themselves with the guests on the wedding-day, the bride's father returned home. When he found his daughter already married, he was much astonished, and said: 'Where is the bridegroom?' He was pointed out to him, and he still wore the bearskin dress. On seeing him, he exclaimed in great anger, 'My daughter shall never have a bearskin-wearer for a husband,' and wanted to murder him.

But the bride interceded for him as much as she could, and said, 'He is already my husband, and I shall always love him with my whole heart.' And at last her father was appeased. However, he could not help thinking about it all night, and in the morning, when the bride-groom was dressing, he peeped into his room, and saw a noble-looking golden man, and the bearskin lying on the ground. Then he went back to his own room, and said to himself, 'How fortunate it is that I restrained my anger last night, or I should have committed a great crime.'

The same morning the gold child told his wife that he had dreamed of being in the hunt, and catching a beautiful stag, so that he must on that day go out hunting.

She was very uneasy at the thought, and said: 'Pray, don't go; a misfortune might so easily happen to you.'

But he replied, 'I will and must go.'

As soon as he was ready he rode out into the wood, and had not been there long before he saw just such a stag as the one in his dream. He raised his gun to shoot it, but the stag sprang away, and he followed it over hedges and ditches the whole day without feeling tired. At last, as night came on, it vanished from his eyes.

Then the gold child looked round him, and saw close by a small house, in which sat an old woman, who was a witch; but he did not know it. He knocked at the door, and she came out and asked him what he wanted so late as that in the middle of the wood.

He said, 'Have you seen a stag pass this way?'

'Yes,' she replied; 'I know the stag well.'

And while she spoke, a little dog, that had come out of the house with the old woman, began to bark furiously.

'Be quiet, will you,' he cried, 'you spiteful cur, or I will shoot you?'

'What! you will kill my dog?' cried the old witch, in a rage. 'Ah, I'll soon stop that.'

And in a moment he lay on the ground turned into stone.

His bride waited for his return in vain, and thought, 'Something has certainly happened to him, or else why am I so anxious and troubled in my heart?'

On the same evening, the brother, who was at home, was standing by the golden lily, when it suddenly fell drooping on its stem.

'Ah me!' he exclaimed, 'there has some misfortune happened to my brother; I must go to him. Very likely I shall be able to save him.'

Then said his father: 'No, no; stay here. If I were to lose both of you, what should I do?'

But the youth answered, 'I must and will go and find my brother.'

Then he mounted his golden horse, and rode away quickly to the wood where his brother lay turned to stone.

The old witch saw him in the distance, and came out of her house, and tried to mislead him about his brother, and called to him to come in. But he would not go near her, and, raising his gun, he cried, 'If you do not this moment restore my brother to life, I will shoot you dead.'

She saw he was in earnest, yet she moved unwillingly towards a stone that lay near the door, touched it with her finger, and immediately the gold child stood before his brother in his own form. They were both overjoyed to meet again, and kissed and embraced each other. Then they rode together out of the wood, and there they parted—the one to hasten back to his bride, the other home to his parents.

'Ah,' said his father, 'we knew that your brother had been released from his trouble, for the golden lily is again erect and in full bloom.'

And after this they lived in happiness and contentment for the rest of their days.

THE FOX AND THE GEESE.

A FOX came once to a meadow, where a herd of fine fat geese were enjoying themselves. 'Ah,' he said, laughing, 'I am just in time. They are so close together that I can come and fetch them one after another easily.'

The geese, when they saw him, began to cackle with fear, sprung up, and, with much complaining and murmuring, begged for their lives.

The fox, however, would not listen, and said, 'There is no hope of mercy—you must die.'

At last one of them took heart, and said: 'It would be very hard for us poor geese to lose our young, fresh lives so suddenly as this; but if you will grant us only one favour, afterwards we will place ourselves in a row, so that you may choose the fattest and best.'

'And what is this favour?' asked the fox.

'Why, that we may have one hour to pray in before we die.'

'Well, that is only fair,' replied the fox; 'it is a harmless request. Pray away, then, and I will wait for you.'

Immediately they placed themselves in a row, and began to pray after their own fashion, which, however, was a most deafening and alarming cackle. In fact, they were praying for their lives, and so efficaciously that they were heard at the farm, and, long before the hour had ended, the master and his servants appeared in the field to discover what was the matter, and the fox, in a terrible fright, quickly made his escape, not, however, without being seen.

'We must hunt that fox to-morrow,' said the master, as they drove the geese home to safe quarters. And so the cunning fox was outwitted by a goose.

THE FAIRY'S TWO GIFTS.

In olden times, when the fairies lived on earth in the forms of human beings, a good fairy, once wandering for some distance, became tired, and night came on before she could find shelter. At last she saw before her two houses just opposite to each other—one large and beautiful, which belonged to a rich man; the other, small and mean in appearance, was owned by a poor peasant.

The fairy thought, 'I shall not be much trouble to the rich man, if he gives me shelter.' So she went up to the door of the beautiful house, and knocked. At the sound, the rich man opened a window, and asked the stranger what she wanted.

'I beg you to give me a night's lodging,' she replied.

Then the owner of the beautiful house looked at the wanderer from head to foot, and he saw that she was dressed in mean and ragged clothes, but he could not see how much gold she had in her pocket. So he shook his head, and said, 'I cannot take you in; my rooms are full of valuable things, and if I were to admit into my house every one who knocks at my door, I should soon have to take the beggar's staff myself. You must seek for what you want elsewhere.'

Then he shut down the window, and left the good fairy standing outside.

She turned her back upon the grand house and went across to the other. Scarcely had she knocked, when the poor man came and opened the door, and begged the wanderer to enter.

'You must remain all night with us,' he said: 'it is already quite dark, and you cannot attempt to go farther.'

The fairy was so pleased with this reception that she stepped in, and the wife of the poor man came forward to welcome her, and led her in and told her to make herself quite comfortable.

'We have not much,' she said, 'but what there is, we will give you with all our hearts.'

She placed the potatoes on the fire, and, while they were cooking, milked the goat, that the visitor might have a little milk. As soon as the cloth was laid the fairy seated herself at the table and ate with them, and the poor fare tasted good, because it was partaken amid contentment and peace.

After they had finished, and bed-time came, the wife called her husband away privately and said : 'Dear husband, let us for to-night make up a straw bed for ourselves, that the traveller may lie in our bed and rest ; after walking the whole day she must be tired.'

'With all my heart,' he replied ; 'I will go and ask her to do so.'

The good fairy, however, would not at first consent to accept this kind offer, but they were so earnest in their request that at length she could not refuse. The poor man and his wife, therefore, slept on their bed of straw, and the fairy rested comfortably in the bed.

In the morning when she rose she found the wife cooking an early breakfast for her of the best they had. The fairy again took her place at the table, the sun shone brightly into the room, and the faces of the poor people wore such a happy, contented expression that she was sorry to leave them.

As she rose to go she wished them farewell, and thanked them for their hospitality. But at the door she turned and said : 'As you have been so kind and compassionate to me when you thought I was poor and in need, therefore I will show you that I have power to reward you. Three times shall your wish be granted you.'

'What greater blessings can I wish for,' said the husband, 'but that we two, as long as we live, may be healthy and strong, and that we may always have our simple daily wants provided for ? I cannot think of a third wish.'

'Would you not like a new house instead of this old one?' she asked.

'Oh yes,' they both cried ; 'if we have these three wishes granted we shall want nothing more.'

Then the fairy changed the old house into a new one, and promising them the fulfilment of their other wishes, went her way. About noon the owner of the fine house happened to look out of his window, and saw with surprise opposite to him a pretty new cottage with red tiles, on the spot where the old house once stood. He stared at it for some time, and at last called his wife, and said to her : 'Tell me how this can have happened : yesterday there stood an old, wretched-looking hut ; to-day, this beautiful new cottage. Run over, and ask how it has all come about.'

The wife went over to ask the poor man to explain this wonderful change. 'Yesterday evening,' he said, 'came a poor traveller to our door and begged for a night's lodging. She was very poorly clad, but we gave her all we had, and our bed. This morning when she left us she offered to grant us the fulfilment of three wishes. We wished for continued health and our daily food as the greatest blessings, and at last she changed our old hut into this new and beautiful cottage.'

On hearing this, the rich man's wife ran hastily back, and related to her husband what she had heard. 'I could tear and beat myself to pieces,' he exclaimed. 'Oh, if I had only known ! That stranger came here first, such a shabby-looking woman she was, and begged me to give her a night's lodging, but I refused her.'

'Never mind,' said his wife; 'now make haste, get on your horse and ride after this woman; if you can but overtake her you can ask her to grant you three wishes also.'

The rich man followed this good advice, saddled his horse, rode after the traveller, and at last overtook her. He spoke to her then most gently and kindly, and hoped that she would not take it amiss that he had not admitted her the evening before. 'I assure you,' he said, 'I was only looking for the key of the house door, and in the meantime you went away; if you should pass our way again you must stay with us.'

'Yes,' she replied, 'I will do so, if I ever pass your house again.'

Then the rich man asked the poor woman if she would not grant him three wishes as well as his neighbour. 'I would grant you this willingly,' replied the fairy, 'but I do not think it would be good for you; you have nothing to wish for.'

The rich man replied that he could easily find something to wish for that would bring him good fortune, if he only knew that his wishes would be accomplished.

'Very well then,' replied the fairy; 'ride home, and whatever your three wishes are shall be granted.'

The rich man had obtained his desire, and he rode homewards, thinking deeply of what the wishes should be. As he thus thought, he allowed the bridle to hang so loosely that his horse began to caper and dance about till his thoughts were all so scattered that he could not collect them again. He struck the horse and said, 'Be quiet, Bess'; but the animal pranced and reared till he was nearly thrown off. At last he became angry, and cried out, 'What do you mean by it? I wish your neck was broken.'

No sooner had he spoken the words than his horse fell under him, and lay dead and motionless, and so was his first wish fulfilled. As he was by nature avaricious, he would not leave the saddle and bridle behind him, so he cut the straps, hung them on his back, and prepared to walk home, as he was now obliged to do on foot. 'We have still two wishes remaining,' he said, and comforted himself with the thought.

As he now walked along through the hot sand, with the burning noonday sun shining brightly upon him, he became fretful with the heat and fatigue. The saddle dragged him back, and seemed ready to fall, and he could not decide what to wish for. 'If I were to wish for all the riches and treasures in the world,' he said to himself, 'what would be the use? I should not know which to choose. I will contrive, however, that when I have gained my two wishes, I shall have nothing else left to wish for.' Then he sighed, and said, 'If I were only like the Bavarian peasant, who had three wishes offered him. First he wished for a draught of beer; the second time for as much beer as he could drink; and the third time for a whole cask. Each time he thought he had gained what he wanted, but afterwards it seemed to him as nothing.'

Presently, there came to him a thought of how happy his wife must be, sitting in their cool room at home, and enjoying something very nice. It vexed him so much not to be there with her, that, without a thought of the consequences, he exclaimed, 'Ah! I wish this heavy saddle would slip from my back, and that she was sitting upon it, not able to move.'

As the last word fell from his lips, the saddle and bridle vanished, and he became aware that his second wish was fulfilled.

Heated as he became at this thought, he yet ran home, for he wanted to sit alone in his chamber, and think of something great for his last wish. But when he opened the room door, there sat his wife on the saddle, screaming and lamenting that she was fixed, and could not get down.

'Make yourself quite happy,' he said. 'I can wish for all the riches in the world to be ours; and my wish will be accomplished if you will only remain sitting there.'

'But,' she replied angrily, 'you stupid head, what would be the use of all the riches in the world to me if I am obliged to sit always on this saddle? No, no; you wished me here, and now you must wish me off again.'

He was obliged, therefore, much against his will, to utter as his third wish that his wife might be set free, and able to alight from the saddle, and the wish was immediately granted.

The rich and selfish man had, therefore, no other result from his three wishes than anger, vexation, trouble, hard words from his wife, and the loss of his horse. The poor man, who was charitable and kind to others, had gained happiness and contentment for the rest of his days.

THE LION'S CASTLE.

A MERCHANT once, who had three daughters, was obliged to leave them to go on a long journey. Before he started he asked each of them what he should bring them as presents. The eldest asked for diamonds, the second for pearls, but the youngest said:

'Dear father, if you would bring me a little skylark, I should like it better than anything else.'

'If I can catch one you shall have it,' he replied. Then he wished them good-bye, kissed them all three, and left them.

A long time passed, and the father of the maidens was on his way home. He had the pearls and the diamonds for his two elder daughters, but he had not yet found a lark for the youngest, although he had searched and inquired everywhere on the way. This made him very unhappy, for she was his favourite child.

On his way home, however, he had to pass through a wood, in which stood a magnificent castle, and near it, above his head, hovered a lark, fluttering and singing to the morning sun. Presently the lark fluttered downwards, and, gradually sinking to the ground, was hidden in the long grass.

'Just the very thing I want,' he said in a satisfied tone; and, calling to his servant, he desired him to go cautiously to the spot he pointed out, and catch the lark.

But before he could catch it, a lion sprung out from the thicket, shook his mane, and roared so loudly that the leaves on the trees trembled.

'Whoever dares to steal my singing, fluttering lark,' he said, 'never leaves this place alive!'

The traveller replied : 'I did not know that the bird belonged to you ; but I will rectify the mistake, and pay you with a large amount of gold if you will spare my life.'

The lion replied : 'I do not want gold. You can only save yourself by at once promising to give up to me whatever shall first meet you on your return home. If you do this, I will grant your life, and give you the bird for your daughter.'

But the request grieved the merchant sadly ; for his youngest daughter, who loved him dearly, generally ran out to meet him on his return home, and he said so to his servant.

But the man, who was terribly frightened, begged his master to promise, and said : 'It might be a cat or a dog who came to meet you first, and not your daughter.'

So he allowed himself to be persuaded, took the lark, and promised to send the lion whatever first met him on his return home. The journey soon came to an end, and, as he approached his home, who should come running out to meet him but his youngest daughter, laughing and happy. She kissed him, and welcomed him home with all her heart ; and when she saw the lark, she was beside herself with joy.

But her father could not join in her pleasure. He began to weep, and said : 'Ah, my child, that bird has cost you dear. I have promised to send you to a fierce lion, who will, I fear, tear you in pieces the moment he sees you.' And then he related all that had happened, and what he had promised, and ended by begging her not to go, let the consequences be what they might.

She consoled him, however, and said : 'Dearest father, what you have promised must be performed. I will go to this lion, and soften and appease him so completely that I shall soon come back to you safe and sound.'

The next morning she got ready to leave home, and, after a sorrowful farewell, took her way to the wood with great confidence.

The lion was really a king's son under the spell of enchantment. By day he and all his servants were changed to the form of lions ; but at sunset and until sunrise they were allowed to assume their proper shapes.

On her arrival at the castle, the maiden was received very kindly by the lion and the servants, and led into the castle. But what was her surprise as the evening came on to see the lion changed to a handsome young prince, and the other lions to nobles and servants, who treated her with the greatest respect.

'You must be my wife,' said the prince, 'for the enchantment will only be broken if the maiden who obtains a lark from my estate should consent to marry me.'

There were still, however, some difficulties to overcome before the enchantment could be entirely dispelled. Yet the maiden consented to be married at once, and a splendid wedding took place at night, for during the day the lions all slept.

They lived happily together for a long time, till one day the prince told her that her eldest sister was going to be married, and that if she liked to go and join the festival with the rest, one of the lions should accompany her. So she said she should be delighted to see her father again; and then the lion was ordered to lead her to her home in safety.

When they arrived there was great joy, for they all supposed she had been torn to pieces long ago. But when she told them of the handsome prince whom she had married, and who was so kind to her even when in the form of a lion, they were all very happy, and she stayed with them till the marriage festivities were over, and then travelled back to the wood.

After a time, the marriage of her second sister was to take place, and she was invited to the wedding; but she told the lion she would not go unless he went with her.

'Ah,' he replied, 'that would be a great risk for me, for if while there one ray of a burning light should fall upon me, I shall be changed into a dove, and join the flock, and for seven long years I should have to fly with them.'

'Oh!' she cried, 'only go with me, and I will take care to hide you from all lights.'

So they set out together, took their little child with them, and arrived at night, when the young prince could appear in his own shape. He placed himself in a room near the great hall, of which the walls were so thick that no ray of light could penetrate, and here he promised to remain till the marriage ceremony was over. The door, however, owing to the wood of which it had been made not being properly seasoned, had a small crack which no one noticed. The prince sat alone in this room in total darkness while the wedding party went to church.

On their return, however, many candles and lamps were carried into the hall, and so it happened that through the crevice in the door a ray of only a hair's breadth fell upon the prince, and, as it rested upon him, he was changed in a moment.

After the festival was over his young wife came to seek for him, but there was nothing in the room excepting a white dove.

'Ah, me!' said the dove, 'I must now fly about the world for seven

THE FAIRY'S TWO GIFTS

THE LION'S CASTLE

years; but you must follow me, and at every seventh step you will see on your path a white feather and a drop of blood, which I will let fall to show you the way, and, if you keep on that track, you will at last be able to set me free.'

Then the dove flew out at the door, and the poor young wife sadly followed, observing where the white feathers and the blood-drops fell, and following the track carefully.

Steadily she kept on her way through the world as the dove flew, not looking to the right hand or the left. At last the seven years drew towards a close, and she was full of joy, for she thought the time was near when she should be able to break the enchanter's spell.

But in the midst of this hope she was one day alarmed at finding that the feathers and the blood-drops had ceased to fall, and, when she raised her eyes to look, the dove had vanished.

'Oh,' she said to herself, 'man cannot help me now!' So she climbed up to the Sun, and said to him, 'Oh, Sun! thou shinest everywhere, and thy rays penetrate the smallest crevice and gild the highest pinnacle! Hast thou seen a white dove flying near?'

'No,' replied the Sun, 'I have seen no dove; but I will give you this little casket, which you may open when you are in great trouble.'

She thanked the Sun, and went away, wandering about till evening came on. She saw the Moon shining at last.

So she said to her, 'Moon, thou shinest the whole night over field and meadow! Hast thou seen a white dove flying near?'

'No,' said the Moon, 'I have seen no dove; but here is an egg for you, which you may break when you are in any great trouble.'

She thanked the Moon and went on farther; and presently the Night-wind arose and blew upon her, so she spoke to him, and said, 'Night-wind, thou wavest with thy breath the summits of the forest trees, and the boughs bend and toss beneath thy power! Hast thou seen a white dove flying near?'

'No,' said the Night-wind, 'I have not seen it; but I will ask the other three winds, probably they may have seen the white dove.'

The East-wind and the West-wind were both questioned, but they had seen nothing. The South-wind, however, said, 'Yes, I have seen the white dove. It has flown to the Red Sea, and has again become a lion, for the seven years are over. The lion is at this moment in combat with a dragon, who is a bewitched king's daughter.'

'Then,' said the Night-wind, 'if this is the case, I can give you some good advice. Go to the Red Sea, and on the right shore you will see several large reeds. Count them till you come to the eleventh, cut the eleventh off, and strike the dragon with it; then the lion will conquer, and they will both return to their human shape. After this look round quickly, and you will see a griffin near you with wings like a bird, sitting on the waters of the Red Sea; leap on his back with the greatest swiftness, and the bird will carry you over the ocean to your home. I will also give you this nut,' continued the North-wind, 'and, while you are crossing the ocean, you must drop it into the sea. As soon as it reaches the bottom a great nut-tree will grow out of the water, on which the griffin can rest; for without rest he would not be strong enough to carry you over. Should you forget to drop the nut, he will let you fall into the sea.'

On hearing this, the young wife took the nut, the egg, and the casket, and went on her way to the Red Sea. Here she found it all as the Night-wind had told her. She counted the reeds by the sea, cut off the eleventh, took it with her, and struck the dragon. Immediately the lion became the conqueror, and they both appeared in their own proper forms. But no sooner was the enchanted princess released from the sorcerer's spell, than she seized the king's son, who had been a lion, by the arm, sprung with him on the griffin's back, and was soon carried away far out of sight.

There stood the poor wife, who had wandered so far in search of her husband, again left alone. She could at first only sit and weep, but presently her courage returned, and, rousing herself, she said : 'I will again travel as the wind blows, and as long as the cock crows, till I find him.'

She started again according to her resolution, and after travelling a long long time, came at last to the castle where they both were living together. She heard of the preparations for a great feast, and knew that he was going to marry another.

' Heaven help me now,' she said.

Then she opened the casket that the Sun had given her, and in it lay a dress which glittered like the Sun itself. She took it out, arrayed herself in the shining robe, and entered the castle. All the guests and the bride herself looked astonished, and the dress pleased the bride so much that she thought she should like it for her wedding-dress, and asked the stranger if she would sell it.

' No,' she said, ' not for gold or silver.'

The bride asked her what she would sell it for.

' Well,' she said, ' you shall have the dress if you will let me speak to the bridegroom alone in his sleeping-chamber.'

The bride at first refused, but as she wanted the dress so much, she was obliged to consent. She told his servant, however, to give him a sleeping-draught, so that when the poor wife entered the room he was fast asleep, and she did not like to disturb him. She sat still for some time, only murmuring: 'I have followed you for all these seven years; I went to the sun and the moon, and the four winds to find you. It was I who struck the dragon, and helped you to conquer it and resume your natural shape, and will you quite forget me now?'

But the prince slept so heavily that he heard only a sound like the rushing of the wind through the fir-trees.

When the hour was up which the bride had allowed her, she was obliged to leave the room, although he still slept, and the bride at once claimed the beautiful dress according to the agreement. The poor wife seemed now to have no hope left, and going out into the meadows, she sat down and wept. Presently she remembered the egg which the Moon had given her; taking it out of her pocket, she broke it, and out came a hen, with twelve beautiful little chicks, looking like balls of gold. They ran here and there, chirped and pecked, and then crept under their mother's wings in the prettiest manner possible. It was a most beautiful sight. At last she stood up, and drove the hen and her chickens gently out of the meadow, till they came in front of a window where the bride sat. As soon as she saw them she wanted to buy them, as she did the dress, but she was told, as before, they were not to be sold for silver or gold.

'Then what will you let me have them for?' asked the bride.

'For permission to stay another hour in the bridegroom's chamber,' she replied.

The bride agreed, but she intended to deceive her as before; she had cause to fear what this stranger might say to the bridegroom, and determined to prevent them from speaking to each other. But the prince had been slightly disturbed the evening before by the complaining tones of his true wife, and he asked his servant what caused it. Then the servant told him all, and said that his evening slumber had been caused by a sleeping-draught, which he had been told to give him, and that while he was asleep a poor maiden had come secretly to his room.

'I believe she is coming in again this evening,' added the servant.

'If you have another sleeping-draught for me,' said the prince, 'throw it away; I shall not take it.'

On that evening, when the prince heard the stranger coming, he laid himself on a couch, and closed his eyes as if he slept. His poor wife crept softly into the room, and, thinking he was sleeping heavily as before, she began to talk of her trouble, as she had then done, in a mournful tone.

But not for long; the prince recognised the voice, and, starting up, exclaimed, 'That is the voice of my own dear wife whom I had lost.' He sprung from the couch as he spoke, and exclaimed, 'I am awake, but not lost. I appear as if I had been in a dream. I must have been bewitched by the strange king's daughter to make me forget thee, my dearest; but the infatuation has been taken from me just in time.'

Then they both left the castle secretly in the night, for the prince was afraid of the new bride's father, who was a wizard.

Fortunately they found the griffin, who had wings like a bird, and seating themselves on his back, he carried them over the Red Sea. When they reached half-way, she threw the nut into the water, and immediately a great nut-tree grew up, on which the griffin rested, and afterwards carried them safely home to her father's house. Here she found her little child, who had grown tall and beautiful, and from this time they were free from all unhappiness to the end of their lives.

THE MAN IN THE BEAR'S SKIN.

THERE was once a young fellow who enlisted as a soldier; he was brave and courageous, and always foremost in the thick of the battle. As long as the war continued he got on very well; but when peace was proclaimed, he received his discharge, and the captain told him he might go as soon as he pleased.

He had, however, no home to go to, for his parents were dead; so at last he thought he would try his brothers, and ask them to give him a home till war broke out again.

But his brothers were hard-hearted, and said, ' What could we do with you here? You are not fit to help us, so you had better try to provide for yourself.'

The soldier had nothing of his own but his gun, so he placed it on his shoulder, and went out into the world to seek for a living.

After walking some distance he came to a heath, on which only a few trees were to be seen, and these grew in a circle. So, feeling very sorrowful, he sat down under the trees, and began to reflect upon his fate.

' I have no money,' he said to himself; ' I have never learnt anything but soldiering, and now peace is proclaimed I am not wanted. I can see that there is nothing before me but starvation.'

At that moment he heard a rustling sound, and looking round he saw a strange man standing before him; he wore a green coat, and looked rather stately, but had a very ugly cloven foot.

' I know very well what you want,' said he to the soldier, ' and money and possessions you shall have, as much as you can spend, however extravagant you may be. But I must discover first whether you are a coward, that my money may not be thrown away.'

' A soldier and afraid! who can put those two words together?' he replied. ' You can try me if you like.'

' Willingly,' answered the man; ' now just look behind you.'

The soldier turned and saw an immense bear, who was growling and trotting towards him.

' Oho,' cried the soldier; ' I will tickle your nose for you presently, my friend, and stop your growling;' and, raising his gun, he shot the bear in the head so surely that he fell all of a heap on the ground, and moved no more.

'I see clearly,' said the stranger, 'that you are not wanting in courage; but there is one more condition you must agree to.'

'If it does not harm me in the future,' replied the soldier, who knew well who he was talking to, 'I don't care what I promise to do.'

'You can tell for yourself whether the conditions are likely to injure you in the future,' was the reply; 'they are these : you must neither wash yourself, nor comb your hair, nor cut your nails or beard, nor say your prayers, for the next seven years, and I will give you this coat and cloak, which you must wear the whole time. Should you die during the seven years, you are mine ; but if you live beyond that time, you will be rich and independent for the rest of your life.'

The soldier sat for some minutes thinking of the great poverty in which he then was, and how often he had faced death without fear, and at last decided to accept the stranger's conditions.

The wicked old demon immediately took off the green coat, and, offering it to the soldier, said, 'Whenever you have that coat on your back, you will find plenty of money in the pocket, if you put your hand in it.' Then he pulled off the skin of the dead bear, and, giving it to him, said, 'This is to be used by you as a cloak and a bed ; you must not, for the whole seven years, dare to sleep in any other bed, nor to wear any other cloak, and on this account you shall be called "Bear-skin."'

Having said this, the stranger vanished.

The soldier immediately put on the coat, and, putting his hands in the pockets, found that the money was a reality. Then he hung the bearskin on his shoulders, and went out into the world rejoicing in his good fortune, and buying all he wished for with his money.

For the first year his unwashed face, his uncombed and uncut hair and beard, did not disfigure him so very much ; but during the second year he began to look like a monster. The hair covered the whole of his face, his beard looked like a piece of coarse blanket, his fingers had claws instead of nails, and his face was so covered with dirt that if mustard and cress had been sown there it must have grown on it.

Those who saw him for the first time always ran away ; but wherever he went he gave money to the poor, and therefore they all prayed that he might live for the seven years, and as he paid well for a night's lodging, on all occasions he was always sure of a shelter.

In the fourth year he came to an inn, but the landlord on seeing him would not take him in, nor even let him sleep in the stables, for he thought such a monster would frighten the horses.

However, when Bearskin put his hand in his pocket and pulled out a handful of gold pieces, the landlord began to soften, and gave him a room in one of the out-buildings, but he made him promise that he would not allow himself to be seen, for fear of getting the house into bad repute.

In the evening, when Bearskin was sitting by himself, and wishing that the seven years were over, he heard in an adjoining room loud lamentations. The soldier had a pitying heart, so he opened the door, and saw an old man with his hands clasped over his head and weeping bitterly.

BEARSKIN AND THE INNKEEPER.

Bearskin advanced towards him, but the old man sprang up to run away. When, however, he heard a kind, human voice speaking to him in friendly tones, he was inclined to remain; and the soldier's soothing words at last encouraged him to disclose the cause of his grief. His property, he said, had dwindled away by degrees, and now his daughters must starve. He had not, he said, even money enough to pay the landlord, and supposed he should be sent to prison.

'If you have no other trouble,' replied Bearskin, 'I can help you, for I have plenty of money.' Then he sent for the landlord, paid the old man's bill, and gave him a purse full of gold to put in his pocket.

When the old man found himself so quickly relieved from his present anxieties, he knew not how sufficiently to express his thanks. But at length he thought of his daughters. 'Come home with me,' he said. 'I will introduce you to my three daughters; they are wonders of beauty, and you shall have one of them, if you like, for a wife. When they hear all you have done for me, they will not refuse you. You are certainly a strange-looking man, but that is easily got over.'

Bearskin was very much pleased with this invitation, and went home with the old man quite readily. No sooner, however, did the eldest daughter catch sight of him than with a scream of terror she rushed away. The second stood still and looked at him from head to foot.

'How could I accept such a man for a husband?' she said; 'why, he has not the slightest resemblance to a human being. Why, the grizzly bear who came to see us once, and called himself a man, pleased me much better; for he did wear a Hussar's cap and white gloves. If he were only ugly I might get used to him, but not as he is.'

The youngest, however, spoke gently, and said, 'Dear father, that must be a good man, if he has helped you so generously out of your trouble; and if you have promised him a bride, you must keep your word.'

It was a pity that Bearskin's face was so covered with dirt and hair, or she would have seen how happy he looked at these words. However, he took a ring from his finger, broke it in half, gave her one half, and kept the other for himself. On one half he wrote her name, and on the other his own, and begging her to take care of it, he said, 'For three years longer I must travel about, but at the end of that time I will return; if I do not you will be free, for I shall be dead. But pray to God every day that my life may be preserved.' Then he said farewell, and left her.

After he was gone the bride dressed herself in black, and when she thought of her bridegroom the tears would come into her eyes. To her sisters it was a great amusement, and they did nothing but mock and jeer her about her lover. 'You must pay attention to the manner in which he takes your hand,' said the eldest, 'for his claws may be sharp.'

'And take care,' said the other, 'that he does not eat you up if you please him, for bears are fond of sweet things.'

'Ah, yes,' continued the eldest; 'and you must always do as he pleases, or he will growl at you.'

'Well,' said her sister, 'we shall have a merry wedding at all events, for bears are noted for their dancing.' The bride kept silence, and her sisters soon found that they could not make her angry with anything they said to her.

Meanwhile Bearskin was travelling about from one place to another, doing good on every opportunity, and relieving the poor and afflicted with the greatest sympathy, so that he had many to pray for him, that he might live long.

The last day of the seventh year dawned, and Bearskin went out to the heath and seated himself under the trees which grew in a circle. He did not wait long, for with a rush of wind came the demon who had appeared to him just seven years before, and looked at him with a most ill-tempered and disappointed face. He threw down the soldier's own coat, and asked him for his green coat and bearskin cloak.

'Stop a bit,' said the soldier, 'you are going too fast; you must wash me first.'

So the demon was obliged, whether he liked it or not, to fetch water and wash and shave the soldier, and afterwards to comb his hair and cut his nails. When this was done the brave soldier looked himself again, and, indeed, much handsomer than before.

As soon as his unpleasant companion had happily left him, he rose with a light heart, and went to the town, bought a magnificent velvet suit, and seated himself in a carriage drawn by four splendid white horses, and drove to the house of his bride. No one recognised him. The merchant took him for a nobleman or a field-officer, and led him into the room where his three daughters sat. He was obliged to yield to the request of the two eldest that he would sit between them at dinner. They helped him to wine, and placed all the choicest dishes before him, while they thought they had never seen such a handsome man before.

The bride, who sat opposite to him in her black dress, with downcast eyes, did not utter a word. At last, when they were alone, the father asked the soldier if he would like to marry either of his daughters. On hearing of this the two eldest ran away to their rooms to change their dresses; and both arrayed themselves in the gayest attire they possessed, for each fancied she would be the chosen one in preference to her sister.

Meanwhile the soldier found himself alone with his bride, and taking out the half of the ring which he had kept from his pocket, he threw it into a glass of wine which stood on the table, and presented it to her. As she took it she saw at the bottom of the glass the half of the ring. With a beating heart she lifted a ribbon which hung round her neck, to which the other half was suspended. She placed the two halves together, and found that they exactly joined.

Then the soldier, looking fondly at her, exclaimed, 'I am your bride-groom, whom you once knew as Bearskin. Through the mercy of Heaven I have recovered my natural shape, and am made free from the evil power which caused me to be so disfigured.' Then he went over to her, took her in his arms, and embraced her fondly.

Just at this moment the sisters entered the room in full dress; but when they discovered that this handsome young soldier belonged to their sister, and heard that he was the man they had laughed at who was called 'Bearskin,' they were so overcome with rage and vexation that one went and drowned herself in the well, and the other hung herself on a tree in the garden.

In the evening there was a knock at the door, and when the bride-elect opened it there was a strange man in a green coat, and he said to her, 'See, now, I have lost one, but I have gained two instead.'

THE KING OF THE BIRDS.

ONE summer's day a bear and a wolf were taking a walk together in the wood. The bear presently heard a very beautiful song, and he said, 'Brother wolf, what bird is that singing so splendidly?'

'That is the king of the birds,'* replied the wolf; 'and we must treat him with great respect.' But the wolf was in fun, for it was only a little wren.

'If it is the king of the birds,' said the bear, 'he certainly ought to have a palace. Come and show it to me.'

'That is not a very easy task,' replied the wolf. 'At all events, we must wait till the queen comes home.'

At this moment Jenny Wren appeared with her husband, and they both carried food in their beaks for their little ones. The bear wanted to follow them, but the wolf held him back, and said, 'No! we must wait till the king and his wife go out again.'

They took particular note of the place where the nest was, and went farther. But the bear could not rest till he had seen the kingly palace of the little wren. So he persuaded the wolf, and they went back together to the wren's nest.

The parent birds were absent, and the bear, climbing up to peep in, saw five or six little creatures lying in the nest.

'Is that a palace?' cried the bear. 'Why, it is a wretched place; and if you are the king's children, you are miserable little creatures.'

When the wrens heard this they were terribly angry, and one of them cried out, 'We are not miserable little creatures. Our parents are noble people, and you shall pay dearly for insulting us.'

The bear and the wolf were much alarmed at this threat, and, turning round, ran back quickly to their holes. But the young wrens kept

* In German the word for wren is Zaun-könig—*Hedge King.* On the word König, King, this tale is founded.

on crying and lamenting till their parents returned with food for them. Then they said, 'We will not eat a morsel; not even a fly's leg, till you have taught the bear to know that we are noble children; for he has been here and insulted us dreadfully.'

'Make yourselves quite easy, children,' said the wren. 'We will do what you wish immediately.' Then the father-bird, with Jenny Wren, flew to the bear's hole, and cried, 'Old growler, why have you insulted my children? You shall suffer for it. War to the knife shall be declared between us.' And saying this they flew away.

Upon hearing this declaration of war the bear started off to summon to his aid all the four-footed animals—the ox, the cow, the ass, the stag, the roe, and all that he could find on the earth. The wren hastened also to assemble creatures that fly in the air—not only the birds, great and small, but also flies, gnats, bees, and hornets.

When the time arrived for this great battle, the wren was determined to send out spies to discover who was the general chosen to command the enemy's army. The gnat, being the most crafty of the insects, was chosen. So he cautiously wandered into the wood, and on reaching the place where the enemy was assembled, he hid himself under a leaf on a tree near which they were holding council together and heard all they said. The bear first stood up, and calling the fox, said to him: 'Fox, you are the most cunning of all the animals; so you shall be our general, and lead us to battle.'

'Good,' said the fox; 'but what signal shall we agree upon?' No one seemed to know. So he said: 'I have a beautiful, long, bushy tail, that looks at a distance almost like a red plume of feathers, and you must remember that as long as I hold it up everything is going on right, and you will advance to victory. But if I lower it, then run away as fast as you can.'

The gnat listened attentively without being seen; then flew back and told the wren everything that had passed, word for word. At daybreak, when the battle was to begin, the four-footed animals rushed to the field with such fury that the earth trembled. The wren also appeared in the air with his army, some buzzing and croaking, and others hovering about wildly enough to make anyone giddy and scared who saw them, till the two armies met for conflict.

The first act of the wren was to send for a hornet, and tell him to go at once and settle on the fox's tail, and the moment he raised it in the air to sting it with all his might. Away went the hornet, and presently in the midst of the battle, when the fox felt the first sting, he could not help leaping up, yet he still kept his tail erect. At the second stab he was forced to lower it for a moment. But when a third time the hornet stung him he could bear it no longer. He dropped his tail between his legs with a great scream, and rushed away.

As soon as the animals saw this, they made sure that all was lost. A panic ensued; and they began flying and running to their dens in the greatest confusion. And so the birds won the battle.

The wrens returned to their nest in great haste. 'Be joyful, children,' they cried, 'and eat and drink to your hearts' content; for we have won the victory.'

But the young wrens said, 'No, we will not eat or drink till the bear comes and makes an apology, and acknowledges that we are nobly born.'

Upon this the wren flew to the bear's den, and said, 'Old growler, unless you come to the nest, and apologize to my children, and tell them they are of noble descent, you will have every rib in your body broken.'

The bear in great alarm crawled to the nest, and made the most humble apology. After this the little wrens were quite satisfied. They ate, and drank, and made themselves merry till quite late in the evening.

THE MAGIC FIDDLE.

A RICH man once had a servant who always served him honestly and faithfully. He was the first to rise in the morning, and the last to go to bed at night, and if any difficult work arose, which no one else could manage, he was ready to undertake it. Added to this, he never complained, but was contented with everything, and always merry.

At the end of his first year of service, his master paid him no wages, for he said to himself, 'It is the most prudent way, and I shall save the money. He will remain in my service, I know, and work as pleasantly as ever.'

The servant made no complaint, and during the second year continued to work well and faithfully, yet at the end of the time he was in the same manner kept without any wages. Still he worked on till the third year came to an end, and then the master put his hand in his pocket, as if he were going to pay him, but drew it out again empty. At last the young man spoke.

'Master,' he said, 'I have served you well for three years, and now I want to go out and see the world for a time; will you, therefore, give me what is right and just for me to have?'

'Yes,' answered the greedy old man; 'you have served me with the greatest willingness, and I am ready to reward you liberally.' He put his hand into his pocket as he spoke, and drew out three pence, and, counting them into the servant's hand, he said, 'There are three pence —one for each year—and those are as liberal wages as you would get from any master.'

The young man, who knew very little of the value of money, took up his earnings, and said to himself: 'Now that my pocket is full, I need not trouble myself any longer with hard work.'

Away he went, over hill and dale, singing and dancing with joy at his freedom, till he came to a road with thick bushes on one side.

Out of these bushes stepped a little man, who said to him: 'Where are you going, you merry fellow? The cares of the world don't appear to trouble you much, from what I can see.'

'Why should I be sad?' answered the youth. 'Have I not three years' wages jingling in my pocket?'

' How much is your wonderful treasure?' asked the dwarf.

'How much? why, three bright pennies, good coin, rightly told.'

'Listen,' said the stranger, in reply: 'I am a poor destitute man, too old to work; but you are young, and can easily earn your living: will you give me those three pennies?'

The young man had a kind heart, and could not help pitying those who were old, so he offered him the money, and said, 'Take it, in Heaven's name; I shall never miss it.'

The little man took the money, and said, 'I see you have a kind and generous heart, therefore I will grant you three wishes—one for each penny—and each wish shall be fulfilled.'

'Aha!' cried the youth, ' you are a magician, I see. Well, if what you say is true, I will wish first for a gun which shall hit everything at which I aim; secondly, for a fiddle, which, when I play it, shall oblige everyone to dance who hears it; and, thirdly, that whoever I make a request to shall not be able to refuse me.'

'All these you shall have,' said the little man. Then he thrust his hand into the bush, separated the branches, and there lay a beautiful fiddle and gun, all in readiness, as if they had been ordered for him beforehand.

He gave them to the young man, and said, 'Whatever request you may make, no man on earth will be able to refuse.'

'What more do I want now?' said he, as the little man left him. And he continued his way, feeling more light-hearted and merry than ever. In a short time, he met a greedy man with a long beard like a goat's, who stood listening to the song of a bird perched on the branch of a tree.

'How wonderful,' he cried, 'that such a little creature should have such a powerful voice! I wish it was mine. Oh, if I could only sprinkle a little salt on its tail, and bring it down!'

'If that is all,' cried the youth, 'the bird shall soon come down.' And, raising his gun, he aimed so correctly that the bird fell into the hedge of thorns beneath the tree.

'Go and fetch out your bird, you knave!' said he to the man.

'Mine?' he replied. 'Oh, I'll run like a dog to find it, if I may have it myself.'

Then he laid himself on the ground, and began to work his way into the bushes till the thorns held him fast. The young man, seeing him in this position, felt a little mischievous, and inclined to tease the man, so he took up his fiddle and began to play.

In a moment the man was on his legs, dancing and springing in the bush, and the longer the violin continued to play, the faster the man danced; and as the thorns tore his shabby coat, pulled out his long beard, and at last scratched him all over terribly, he cried out, ' Master, master, stop playing! leave off playing! I don't want to dance any more.'

But the youth would not listen, or stop, for he thought : ' You have fleeced others often enough, my friend, and now you shall see how you like it yourself;' and as he played, the man danced higher and higher till his rags were torn off and hung on the bush.

' Ah, woe is me !' cried the man. ' Master, master, I will give you whatever you ask me—even a purse full of gold—if you will leave off playing.'

' If you are really going to be so generous,' said the young man, ' I will stop my music ; but indeed I must praise your dancing—your style is perfection.' So saying, he put up his fiddle, took the purse of money the man had promised him, and went on his way.

The man stood and watched him till he was out of sight; then he screamed after him as loud as he could : ' You miserable musician—you wretched fiddler ! wait till I can catch you alone; I will hunt you then till you lose the soles of your shoes, you ragamuffin! I dare say you were not worth sixpence till you got all that money out of me.' And so he went on calling him all the dreadful names he could think of. At last he stopped for want of breath, and, making his way quickly to the next town, he bought some clothes to make himself decent, and then went before the magistrate.

' My lord judge,' he said, in a woful voice, ' I have been robbed and cruelly treated on the king's highway, by a rascally fellow who met me on the road. The very stones on the ground might pity me for what he made me suffer ; my clothes torn to rags ; my body all scratched, and my little bit of savings taken with my purse. Bright golden ducats, each as beautiful as the other. For the love of heaven let the man be found and put in prison.'

' Was it a soldier,' asked the judge, ' who cut you about in this manner with his sword?'

' No, no,' replied the man, ' he had not even a dagger with him, but he had a gun on his shoulder and a violin which hung round his neck; the rascal can easily be recognised.'

So the judge sent his people out to find the offender, and it was not long before they met him walking along quite wearily, and upon searching they found upon him the purse of gold. When he was brought before the judge and heard the accusation against him, he said : ' I never touched the man, nor his gold, but he gave me the purse of his own free will because I stopped my fiddling when he asked me, and said he could not endure it.'

' Heaven defend us !' cried the man; ' his lies swarm like flies on a wall.'

But even the judge refused to believe the young man's assertion. 'It was not likely,' he said, 'that the man would act so foolishly.'

Therefore the good servant was condemned to be hung for having committed a robbery on the king's highway. As he was being led away to the scaffold the man screamed after him, 'You dog of a fiddler, you thief! you are justly paid now for your conduct to me.'

The young man paid not the least attention to the man's abuse; quite calmly he ascended the steps to the scaffold, but on the last step he turned round and said to the judge, 'Grant me but one request before I die.'

He replied, 'You must not ask for your life; any other request I will accede to.'

'I shall not ask for my life,' replied the prisoner; 'I only request to be allowed once more to play on my violin.'

Up sprang the man with a loud outcry. 'I beg, I entreat you not to allow it. Pray, pray don't!' he almost howled in his terror.

But the judge said: 'Why should we not grant him this short pleasure? It is the last he will have, therefore it is granted.'

Indeed, the judge could not have refused the young man because of the power which had been given him by the dwarf in the wood. No sooner was permission granted, however, than the man cried: 'Oh, oh! bind me tight, tie me fast!'

But it was too late; the young man had quickly turned his violin round, and at the first chord, the man who was going to bind the man let the rope fall, the judge, the clerk, and the officers of the court began to move and to tremble, and presently, as the full tones of the violin struck out, they all jumped up and began dancing with all their might; even the hangman dropped the rope and joined in the dance, and he, with the judge and the man, were the chief performers.

Soon the sounds of the fiddle reached the market-place, and many who came from curiosity to listen were soon among the dancers, fat and lean, young and old, capering madly away among the rest. Even the dogs who ran by stood upon their hind legs and began dancing about; and the longer he played, the faster they all danced and the higher they sprung in the air, till at last they knocked each other's heads together and began to scream and cry out. At length the judge, quite out of breath, cried: 'I will give you your life if you will stop your fiddling.'

The young man, on hearing this, was quite ready to stop his playing, and, hanging his violin again on his neck, he stepped down from the ladder, and approaching the man, who lay panting on the ground, he said: 'You rascal, now confess where you got that purse of money that you gave me, or I will begin fiddling again.'

'Oh me, oh me! I stole it, I stole it,' cried the man, 'and you earned it honestly.'

Then was the man taken before the magistrate and condemned to the gallows, from which the honest servant had been saved.

THE KING OF THE GOLDEN MOUNTAIN.

A MERCHANT had two children, a boy and a girl, who were both so very young that they could not run alone. About this time, the merchant sent two richly-laden ships to sea, which contained the whole of his possessions, and while he was expecting to receive a large amount of profit, news came that his ships had been both wrecked, and all they contained lost. His position was now changed from that of a rich man to a poor one, for he had nothing left but a field of about an acre in extent.

One day, when he wished to divert his thoughts from his misfortunes, he went out to walk in his field. As he wandered along, thinking sorrowfully over the future, he saw a dark little man standing near him, who asked him what made him so sad.

'If you could help me,' replied the merchant, 'I might be inclined to tell you.'

'Who knows? Perhaps I may be able to help you,' replied the little man. 'Now tell me your trouble.'

Then the merchant described the great loss he had sustained in the wreck of his two ships, adding, 'All my possessions are lying at the bottom of the sea.'

'Do not make yourself unhappy,' replied the dark man. 'If you will promise that whatever comes first out of your house to meet you on your return home, and clings to your knees, shall be brought to this spot in twelve years, I will give you as much gold as you like.'

'Well,' thought he, 'my dog is the only one who can do that; my children are too young to walk.'

So he promised, and gave the little strange man a written agreement, and sealed it with his own seal to ensure that he would honourably keep his promise, and after doing this he returned home. As he came near the house, his little son saw him coming, and he was so delighted that he let go the chair by which he was holding, and, toddling towards him, caught him by the knees. In a moment the father, with terror, remembered his promise, and knew now what his written agreement would cost him.

But on finding that his chests and coffers were still empty, he thought after all it might only be a joke on the part of the little man. A month,

however, passed, and one day, when he again went out to try and dissi-
pate the old sad thoughts about money, he saw lying on the barn-floor
a large heap of gold. Now he was again all right, and able to trade so
well with the money that he became after a time a richer merchant
than before.

In the meantime, the children grew tall as well as clever and good;
but when the end of the twelve years approached, the merchant became
so full of care that it showed itself on his countenance to everyone.

One day his little son asked him what was the cause of his being
so sad. At first his father would not tell him, but day after day
he so persisted in his questions, that at length he told him what he
had done.

'I wrote down my promise and sealed it,' he said, 'and, therefore,
when the twelve years are at an end, I shall lose you.'

'Oh, father,' said the boy, 'do not allow yourself to be uneasy; it
will be all right. The little black man will have no power over me.'

The boy, however, went to a clergyman, and asked him for his
blessing, and, when the hour came, the father and son went to the field,
and stood at the spot where the promise had been made. Then the
boy made a cross on the ground, placed his father and himself on it, and
waited.

Presently the little black man appeared, and said to the father:
'Have you brought me what you promised?' But he did not reply.

Then said the son: 'What do you want here?'

The dark man replied: 'I am here to speak to your father, not to
you.'

'You have betrayed and misled my father!' answered the boy fearlessly. 'Give up the bond!'

'No,' he replied; 'I will not give up my right to anyone!'

They talked together for a long time, and at last it was arranged that
the son, who by inheritance was an enemy to the dark man, and yet
did not any longer belong to his father, should place himself in a little
ship, and that his father should with his own foot upset it, that the boy
might be lost in the water.

Father and son took leave of each other, and then they went down to
a flowing stream that was not far distant, where the little ship lay.
Bravely the boy stepped in, and his father, touching it with his foot, it
turned over, and sank till every part was covered with water. Then the
father, believing that his son was lost, went home and mourned for him
deeply.

The little ship, however, did not sink, but righted itself again, and,
as the boy had clung to it closely, he was able to regain the boat, and,
seating himself once more, was carried away over the waters for a long
distance.

At length it reached an unknown shore, and immediately became
fast. The youth stepped out on the land, and, seeing before him a
beautiful castle, he walked up to it. But the moment he entered he

was under the sorcerer's power. He went, however, from room to room, and found them all empty, except the last, in which lay a snake coiled round in rings on the floor.

The snake, however, was a bewitched maiden, who was delighted when she saw him, and said: 'Are you come, my deliverer? I have waited for you for twelve years already, and it is you who are to set me free.'

'How can I do so?' he asked.

'I will tell you,' she replied. 'To-night there will come here twelve dark men bearing chains and fetters, who will ask you what you are doing here. Then must you be silent, and not answer a word in reply,

'ARE YOU COME, MY DELIVERER?'

let them do what they will to you. They will beat and torment you dreadfully; but, whatever happens, do not speak, and at twelve o'clock they will be obliged to go away. To-morrow night another twelve men will come, and on the third night twenty-four. These last will cut off your head; but at twelve o'clock, if you have not spoken a word during the three nights, their power is over, and I am free. Then I shall be able to restore you to life; for I have a bottle of water which can cure everything, and if I touch you with this you will soon be well, and as healthy as ever.'

Then said he: 'All that you have told me I will remember to do, for I am quite willing to release you from this enchantment.'

It all happened exactly as she had said. The dark men came, but they could not make him speak a word, and so, on the third night, the snake was changed to a beautiful princess. The moment she was free, she opened the bottle of wonderful water, and, after anointing the youth with it, he was restored to life, and as healthy and strong as before. There was great joy then over the whole castle, for the spell of enchantment was broken for them all, and the servants and officers were soon in attendance.

As for the princess, she was so grateful that she willingly consented to be the wife of her deliverer, and they were soon after married. By this marriage the husband of the princess became king of the golden mountain.

Eight years passed in great happiness, and the young queen had one little son; but at the end of that time her husband began to think of his father, and wished very much to go home and see him once more.

The queen wished him not to leave her, and said, 'I am sure that some misfortune will happen to me if you do;' but he allowed her no rest, till she at last consented.

When they parted she gave him a wishing-ring, and said, 'Take that ring, and put it on your finger, and whenever you desire to change your place, you have only to touch it and wish, and you are there; but promise me that you will not use it to desire me away from here to your father's house.'

He promised what she asked, placed the ring on his finger, and wished himself at the town where his father lived. Immediately he found himself there; but when he reached the gates the sentinels would not let him pass, for he still wore his splendid and kingly robes.

Then he went to a hill close by, where a shepherd was keeping his sheep, changed clothes with him, and, putting on the shepherd's coat, walked into the town unnoticed.

When he appeared before his father, he did not recognise him at all; he could not believe he could be his son, and said he had no son. He had one once, who had long been dead, But seeing that the poor shepherd looked tired and hungry, he ordered something to be brought for him to eat.

Then the shepherd said to his parents, 'I am in very truth your son. Is there not any mark on my body by which you might know me?'

'Yes,' cried his mother; 'our son had a curious raspberry mark under his right arm.'

Instantly he turned up the sleeve of his shirt, and there was the mark of the raspberry quite plainly to be seen; so they could no longer doubt that he was their son.

Thereupon he told them all that had happened to him, and how he had been saved when the boat was upset. He said also that he was now king of the golden mountain, and that the princess whom he had rescued was his wife, and that he had a little son, nearly seven years old. But his father still doubted, especially when he said this.

'What you say cannot be true,' he remarked; 'for grand kings, such as you describe, do not wear ragged clothes and a shepherd's coat.'

Upon this the son became very angry, and, quite forgetting his promise to his wife, turned the ring on his finger, and wished both the queen and her son to be present.

In a moment they were there; but the queen wept and complained, and said, as he had broken his word, that misfortune would be the consequence.

'I did it inadvertently,' he said, 'and not with any wrong intention,' and tried so much to persuade her to forgive him, that at last she made it appear that she did so; but she was still angry in her heart.

He led her out through the town to the field, and showed her where the little ship had been upset; and presently he said to her, 'I am tired now; sit down for a little while, and let me lay my head in your lap and sleep.' She seated herself, and, lying down, he placed his head in her lap, and was soon asleep.

While he slept, she first slipped the ring off his finger and placed it on her own, then she quietly and gently lifted his head from her lap and laid it on the ground. As soon as this was done, she took her child by the arm, and wished herself and her boy back in her kingdom.

When he awoke he found himself quite forsaken, his wife and child gone, and the ring taken from his finger. 'I cannot go home to my parents after this,' he said to himself; 'they will say truly that I am a sorcerer. No; I must try and get back to my kingdom.'

He travelled on after this for a long time till he came to a mountain, before which stood three giants, contending about the division of their father's property.

As soon as he appeared, they called to him, and said that little men were often very clever, and that they would leave it to him to divide their inheritance fairly.

It consisted of a sword, which one took in his hand, and said, 'When I wield this all the heads must lie on the ground except mine.' The second giant produced a cloak, which made everyone who wore it invisible; and the third put on a pair of boots, and said that those who wore these boots had only to wish themselves in any particular spot, and they would be there immediately.

Then the king of the golden mountain said to the giants, 'Before I decide upon the division of these wonderful possessions of which you boast so much, you must let me prove their value.'

They gave him the cloak first, and the instant he put it on he was invisible to them, and changed into a fly. He quickly resumed his own shape, and said, 'The cloak is good; now give me the sword.'

'No,' they replied, 'we cannot give you that; for if you said, "Heads down, all but mine," you would have power over us, for your head would be the only one erect.' They gave it to him at last, however, on condition that he would first try its strength on a tree.

He did so, and the sword cut the trunk of the tree in two, as if it had been a stalk of straw. Then he wanted the boots; but they again refused, 'Because,' they said, 'if you put them on, and should wish yourself over this mountain, we should be down here, and have nothing.'

'HE TOOK THE CAKE FROM HER PLATE, AND DRANK THE WINE FROM HER GLASS.'

But he told them it was not likely he should have such a wish as that. So they let him try the boots; but the moment he had them on his feet he forgot everything but his wife and child, and said to himself, 'Oh, if I were only on the golden mountain!' In a moment he had vanished from the eyes of the giants, and with him all their shares of the inheritance.

As soon as he arrived at the castle, he heard sounds of merry-making, the flute and violin playing joyous music, and he was told that his wife was celebrating her marriage with another. 'The false one!' he exclaimed angrily, 'she has betrayed and forsaken me while I slept, and now she is marrying another.' He threw on his cloak, and went into the castle invisible.

When he entered the dancing-saloon, he saw a table richly spread for the feast, and the guests eating, drinking, laughing, and joking. His wife sat among them, splendidly dressed, on a royal seat, and with a crown of gold on her head.

He placed himself behind her, but no one saw him; and presently, when a piece of cake or a glass of wine was placed before her, he took the cake from her plate, and drank the wine from her glass. The company were always giving her some of the rich things on the table; but it was useless—her plate and her glass always vanished immediately.

At last she became alarmed, rose up, and went to her own chamber, and thither her husband followed. She wept and said, 'What can it be? am I not yet delivered from the wizard's spell?'

He struck her in the face, invisible as he was, and said, in a deep tone of voice, 'Thou wilt never be free, thou betrayer; the spell is over thee still.' Then he assumed his own shape, went into the saloon, and cried, 'The marriage is at an end; the real king has returned!' The kings, princes, and councillors there assembled laughed and defied him; but he merely answered them shortly, in a few words, 'Will you leave this house or not?'

Instead of going, they crowded round him, and tried to seize him; but he drew his sword, and said, 'Every head on the ground but mine.' In a moment all the heads were rolling on the ground, and he was alone, master of the castle, and king of the golden mountain.

THE GOLDEN CASTLE OF STROMBERG.

THERE lived once a queen who had a little daughter still so young that she had to be carried in arms. One day the child was naughty, and do what the mother might, she could not make her quiet.

At last the mother became impatient, and just as a raven flew over the castle, she opened the window and cried, ' I wish you were a raven, and would fly away, then I should have peace.'

No sooner had she uttered the words, than her child became a raven, and flew away from its mother's arms through the window, to a dark wood, and remained there a long time, during which the parents heard nothing of her.

But one day, a man travelling through the wood heard a voice calling him, and on going to the place from whence it came, he saw a raven on a tree. 'I am a king's daughter by birth,' said the raven, as he came near, 'and have been changed by magic; but it is in your power to set me free.'

'What am I to do?' he asked.

'Go farther into the forest,' she replied, 'and there you will see a tiny house, in which lives an old woman, who will offer you something to eat and drink; but do not dare to take anything; if you do you will fall into a deep sleep and be unable to set me at liberty. In the garden behind the house is a large tanyard, and there you must stand and wait for me. I shall come to you at two o'clock each day, for three days, and each time in a carriage; on the first day drawn by four white horses, on the second by four red horses, and the third time four black horses. If, however, you should not be awake, but sleeping at any time when I come to you, then I shall not be free.' The man promised to do all she desired; but the raven said, 'Ah, I know already that you will not deliver me; you are sure to take something the old woman offers you.' The man promised again that he certainly would not touch anything, either to eat or to drink, and then he left her.

As he approached the house, the woman came out to him and said: 'Poor man, you seem tired out; but come in and refresh yourself, and have something to eat and drink.'

'No,' he replied, 'I do not want anything.' But she gave him no peace till he came in, and then she said:

'If you won't eat, perhaps you will just drink a little from this glass; once is nothing at all.'

At last he allowed himself to be persuaded, and drank from the glass. Next day at noon he went out to wait for the raven, till two o'clock, at the tanyard. But while he stood there, a feeling of fatigue came at once upon him so painfully that he could not overcome it. 'I must lie down,' he said; 'but I will not sleep.'

No sooner, however, had he stretched himself on the ground, than his eyes closed involuntarily, and presently he slept so soundly that nothing on earth could awake him.

At two o'clock came the raven in her carriage, drawn by four white horses; but she was already full of grief, and said, 'Ah, I know he will be asleep.'

When she entered the garden, there he lay in a deep sleep by the tanyard. She descended from the carriage, went to him, shook him, and tried all she could to wake him, but it was quite useless.

The next day, at noon, the old woman came again, and brought him meat and drink; he refused to take any, but she would not leave him alone; she did and said all she could to persuade him, and at last he drank a second time from her glass. At the hour of two he went out again to stand by the tanyard, for he wanted to keep awake for the raven. But he found himself again so overcome with fatigue that his limbs could not support him; he could not help himself, but was obliged to lie down, and soon fell fast asleep.

In the meantime the raven drove up in a carriage drawn by four red horses; but she was still sorrowful. 'I know he sleeps,' she said; and so she found him lying in a deep sleep, from which nothing could awake him.

The next day the old woman said to him, 'If you do not eat or drink you will die.'

He replied, 'I will not, and I dare not eat or drink.'

However, she brought a dish with something very nice on it, and a

THE RAVEN'S CARRIAGE AND WHITE HORSES.

glass of wine; and when the smell reached him he could withstand it no longer, and ate a good meal. When the time came for him to go out to the tanyard and wait, he was as tired as on the previous day, and, laying himself down, slept as soundly as if he had been a stone. At two o'clock came the raven again, this time with four black horses, and the carriage and all the harness were black also. She was, however, already sorrowful, and said, 'I know that he sleeps, and cannot set me free.' And she found her fears verified; there he lay fast asleep. She shook him and called to him, but he did not awake.

Then she placed a loaf of bread, a piece of meat, and a bottle of wine by his side, from which he could take what he liked. She also took a gold ring from her finger, on which her name was engraven, and placed it on his. And last of all she laid a letter on the ground close to him, in which she told him he might eat and drink what she had left for him; but that while he stayed in that place he would be unable to set her free. She then advised him to come to her at the golden castle of Stromberg; for she knew certainly that her freedom could only be obtained through him. After this, she seated herself in her carriage and drove away to the golden castle of Stromberg.

When the man awoke and found that he had been sleeping, he was deeply grieved, and said, 'Certainly now it is all over, and I have not set her free.' Then his eyes fell on the things that lay near him, and he took up and read the letter, which stated what she expected him to do.

He rose immediately and left the garden; but much as he wished to go to the golden castle, he could not do so, as the way was unknown to him. The first thing, however, was to get out of the wood; but this was not easy, for after wandering for fourteen days, he could find no outlet. One evening he felt so tired that he laid himself down in the copse and slept. Another day he went on farther and again lay down to rest, but he heard such crying and howling this time that he could not sleep.

After a while he saw the reflection of a light, and going towards the spot at which it appeared, he came in front of a house that appeared small, because before it stood a great giant. Then thought he to himself, 'If I go in and the giant gets a glimpse of me, my life may not be safe.' However, he did venture to show himself.

As soon as the giant saw him, he said: 'Is it wise for you to come here? I have eaten nothing for some time, and I shall most likely swallow you for my supper.'

'Leave my life alone,' said the man; 'I should not willingly allow myself to be swallowed, but if you are hungry I have quite enough with me to satisfy your appetite.'

'If that is true,' replied the giant, 'I will leave you in peace; I don't want to eat you if there is enough without it.'

So they went in and seated themselves at a table, and the man brought out bread, and meat, and wine, and placed them before the giant. 'This pleases me well,' he said, and ate away to his heart's content.

After he had finished, the man said to him, 'Could you tell me which road I am to take to find the golden castle of Stromberg?'

The giant replied; 'I will fetch my map, in which all the towns, villages and houses are easily found.' He brought the map from another room, and searched for the castle, but it was not there. 'This won't do,' said he. 'However, there is a larger map in that cupboard.' He brought out this map also, but it was as useless as the other—the castle was not mentioned.

After this the man wished to go, but the giant begged him to stay for a day or two longer till his brother came home, who, he said, was gone out to fetch provisions. As soon as the brother returned, the man asked if he could tell him what road to take for the golden castle of Stromberg.

'After I have eaten my supper,' he replied, 'then I will look in the map.'

As soon as he had finished, they went with him into his room, and searched on his map, but it could not be found even there. He then brought out another very old map, and would not give up the search, till at last they found the golden castle of Stromberg, but it was many thousand miles away.

'How shall I ever get there?' asked the man.

'Well,' said the giant, 'I have two hours to spare, and will carry you, if you like, to the neighbourhood of the castle; but after that, I must return and look after my child.'

The man was glad of the help, and the giant took him up, and carried him in the two hours to a spot that was not a hundred leagues from the castle, and said: 'The rest of the way you can easily find for yourself.'

He turned away without waiting for thanks, and the man went forward day and night till at last he came to the golden castle of Stromberg. It stood on a mountain of glass, and as he was looking at it, he saw the enchanted king's daughter riding in her carriage to the castle, which she entered. He was delighted when he saw her, and began eagerly to climb the mountain; but he only went a few steps and then slid backwards, for the glass was so slippery.

When he found that it was impossible for him to reach the castle, he felt quite unhappy, and at last said to himself: 'I will remain down here and wait for her.' He built himself a little hut in which he lived for a whole year, and every day saw the enchanted princess drive round the mountain, but could not get near her.

One day he saw outside his hut three robbers who were fighting with each other, and he cried out: 'Heaven defend us!' They stopped for a moment at the cry, but, seeing no one, they returned to the fight in the most terrible manner. Then cried he a second time: 'Heaven defend us!' They heard the sound again; but after looking about in every direction, and seeing no one, continued their furious battle. At last he thought: 'I must see what these three men are about.' So he went out and asked them why they were fighting with each other.

Then said one: 'I have found a stick which when you knock with it at any door it will instantly fly open.' Another said he had in his possession a cloak which would make anyone who wore it invisible. A third had a horse on which a man could ride over every sort of ground, even over the glass mountain. And now, as they could not agree, they scarcely knew what to do—whether to continue in partnership or to separate.

Then said the man: 'I will make an exchange with you for these three things. I have not money to buy them, but what I have is still more valuable. However, before I make the exchange I should like to try whether what you have said of them is true.'

They allowed him, as he wished, to mount the horse, gave him the stick in his hand, and threw the cloak over him.

Immediately he became invisible, and giving each of them a sharp cut with the stick, said: 'You dolts, you have just got what you deserve, and I hope you are contented.' Then he rode quickly up the glass mountain and arrived at the castle. The door was locked, but he struck it with the stick and it flew open instantly.

He entered, and went up the steps into the saloon, and there sat the princess with a golden cup of wine before her. She could not see him, for he still wore the invisible cloak. But he went near to her, and taking the ring which she had given him from his finger, he threw it into the cup, where it clinked against the side.

'That is my ring,' she cried; 'and the man to whom I gave it must be here, and will be able to break the enchanter's spell.'

She rose as she spoke, and went all over the castle, but could find no one. Meanwhile he had gone out and seated himself on the horse, and as she approached the open door he threw off the cloak; then she saw him, and screamed out for joy. He alighted from his horse, took the king's daughter in his arms, and she kissed him and said: 'Now you have broken the spell, and I am free, and to-morrow morning we will celebrate our marriage.'

THE PEASANT'S CLEVER DAUGHTER.

THERE was once a peasant who was very poor; he had a small house, but no land in which to grow corn or vegetables. The peasant had an only daughter, and she said one day to her father; 'I am sure if the king knew how poor we are he would give us a little piece of waste land. I shall ask somebody to tell him.'

When the king heard how poor they were he not only sent the peasant a piece of ground but also a small quantity of turf. The father and daughter dug up the ground carefully, for they wished to sow a little corn and make the place fruitful. But while they were digging and turning up the earth they found a piece of pure gold. On seeing it the father took it up eagerly, and said to his daughter: 'As the king has been so kind as to give us the field, we ought to send him this piece of gold.'

But the maiden was not willing for her father to do so. 'Father,' she said, 'if we speak of this we shall have to work for nothing, and give up all we find in future, therefore we had better keep silent.'

He would not listen, however, to her advice, but took up the piece of gold, carried it to the king, told him where he had found it, and asked if he would accept it as a token of his respect and gratitude. The king took the gold in his hand and asked him if he had not found more. The peasant replied truthfully, 'No.' But he was not believed. 'I

THE MAGIC FIDDLE

THE PEASANT'S CLEVER DAUGHTER

must have the whole of the gold,' said the king; 'it is not likely you would bring me all you have found, so go and fetch it.'

In vain the peasant assured the king that he had found no more; it was as if he spoke to the winds, and at last the poor honest fellow was placed in confinement and told that he must remain there till he gave up the rest of the treasure. The servants were told to take him bread and water every day, which were all the provisions allowed to prisoners, but he would neither eat nor drink, and was constantly crying out, 'Oh, that I had listened to my daughter! oh, that I had listened to my daughter!'

Then the servants went to the king and told him what the prisoner was always crying out, and that he would neither eat nor drink. So the king sent for him and asked him what his daughter had said which he wished he had listened to.

'She prophesied,' he replied, 'that if I took the small piece of gold to the king we should have to give up all we found afterwards.'

'Have you such a clever daughter?' said the king. 'Then send for her at once, that I may see her.'

So the peasant's daughter was obliged to come, and the king was so pleased with her that he talked to her quite pleasantly, and said: 'People tell me that you are very clever. I will therefore give you a riddle to guess, and if you solve it you shall be my wife.'

Then she said at once that she would try. So the king said: 'Come to me neither clothed nor naked, neither riding nor walking, neither on the road nor on the path; and if you can do all this I will marry you.'

The maiden immediately went home, quickly stripped herself, got a large hank of yarn, placed herself in it, and wound it round and round her body till she was quite covered. Then a neighbour, for a small payment, lent her an ass, and she tied the end of the yarn to the ass's tail, so that he dragged her along behind him, therefore she neither rode nor drove. The ass also walked, so that she was dragged along in a carriage-wheel rut, and only her great toe touched the ground, and thus she appeared before the king—neither clothed nor naked, neither riding, walking, nor driving, and neither on the road nor on the path.

When the king saw her he said she had guessed the riddle, and fulfilled the contract, and therefore he was ready to make her his wife. Her father was immediately released from confinement, and the king married the daughter and bestowed upon them all the necessary kingly honours.

A year passed, and one day the king went out on the parade in front of the castle. It happened just then that a number of peasants of whom he had bought wood stood with their waggons before the castle. To some of the waggons oxen were harnessed, and to others horses; among them was a peasant who had two horses and a young foal, and while they stood there the foal ran away and laid itself down between two oxen who were yoked in the waggon of another peasant. On this a dreadful quarrel arose among the peasants. The owner of the oxen said the foal belonged to one of his beasts, and the peasant declared it was the foal of one of his horses, and that it was his. The noise and the fighting became at last so great that the matter was brought before the king, and he gave as his decision that where the foal was found lying there it should remain, and, as that was with the oxen, therefore to the owner of the oxen the foal belonged, and might be taken by him. The other went home mourning and lamenting over the loss of his foal. Now he had heard that the queen was very kind and gracious, although she had been herself a peasant. So he went to her and begged her to help him to get back his foal. She readily agreed to do so, on condition that he would promise not to betray her. 'To-morrow morning early,' she said, ' when the king goes out with the officers to relieve guard, you place yourself in the road by which they must pass. Take with you a fishing-rod and act as if you were fishing in the ditch, which will be dry; but never mind, pull in your line, and jerk it up and down just as if you had a bite; and if the king or anyone asks you what you are doing, give them the answer that I will tell you.'

So the next day the peasant seated himself by the road and began to fish in a dry ditch. As soon as the king came by he saw him, and sent his attendants to ask the foolish man what he was about. The peasant, on being questioned by the attendant as to what he was doing, replied, ' I am fishing.'

' Fishing?' he replied; ' why you will get none if you fish for a year; there is no water.'

' Ah,' said the peasant, ' it is quite as easy for me to get fish without water as for an ox to be the parent of a horse's foal.'

The attendant went back with this answer to the king. The king desired the peasant to be brought before him, and told him he was quite sure that he could not have thought of such an answer himself, and desired him instantly to tell him from whom he had it.

But the peasant refused to admit that the answer was not his own, and he was therefore taken away from the king's presence and beaten, and ill-treated, and bound in fetters, till at last he was obliged to disclose that the queen had told him what to say and do.

As soon as the king returned home he went to his wife in great anger, and said: ' You have been false to me, and have been plotting with a peasant to insult me; now go home to where you came from, to your peasant's home; you shall not be my wife any longer.'

He told her, however, to take with her from the castle whatever she loved best in the world, and that should be her farewell gift from him.

' Dear husband,' she replied, ' if you wish it, I will do so.'

Then she threw her arms round his neck, kissed him, and said she was ready to wish him good-bye, if he would take one parting cup with her. Some wine, into which she had poured a sleeping-draught, was brought, and the king drank a large cupful off at once. In a few minutes he sank into a deep sleep, and then the queen, after covering him with a beautiful white linen cloth, called a servant, and desired him to carry the king out and place him in a carriage that stood at the door. The queen then got in and drove the king to her father's little cottage, and on arriving there he was laid on the bed. The king slept for many hours, but at last he awoke, and finding himself alone, exclaimed, 'Where am I?' and called his servants, but none were there. At last his wife came in and approached the bed, and said: 'Dear lord and king, you told me to take with me from the castle whatever was best and dearest; now I have nothing in the world better or dearer than you, therefore I have brought you with me.'

The tears, on hearing this, stood in the king's eyes.

'Dearest wife,' he said, 'from this hour we belong to each other; you shall never leave me more.'

So he took her back to the royal castle; she was again his dear wife, from whom nothing but death could divide him.

THE SILVER AXE.

THERE lived once a poor woodcutter, who worked hard from morning till night, and at last contrived to lay by a good sum of money. He had an only son; so he called the boy to him one day, and said: 'My son, you are my only child, and the money I have saved by the sweat of my brow will be yours; therefore, I wish you to learn how to lay it out to the best advantage, so that in my old age, when my limbs are stiff, and I am obliged to sit still at home, you may be able to support me.'

So the youth was sent to the high school, and studied so diligently that his teachers commended him, and begged for him to remain another year longer.

But this education was so expensive that at the end of the second year the father said all his hard earnings were dwindling away so fast that the boy must return home, and give up his school.

'I cannot give you any more education,' said his father sorrowfully, 'for I have now only just enough left to supply us with daily bread, and not even a penny to spare for anything else!'

'Dear father,' said the boy, 'make yourself quite happy about it. I am satisfied with what I have learnt, and I will do my best without any more instruction. I am already quite contented.'

One day—the boy had been at home some little time—his father talked of going to the forest to cut some wood for the wood market.

'I will go with you,' said the son, 'and help you.'

'No, no, my son,' said the father; 'the work would be too rough for you to attempt. You have not been accustomed to it, and could be no help to me.   Besides, I have only one axe, and no money to buy another.'

'Go to one of our neighbours,' said the boy; 'he will lend you an axe till I am able to buy one for myself.'

So the father borrowed an axe of a neighbour, and the next morning at daybreak they went off together to the wood.

The youth worked well, and was a great help to his father, and quite lively and cheerful.   As noon drew near, the wood-cutter said : ' Come, my son, let us sit down and eat our dinner, otherwise we shall not get on so well with our work by-and-by.'

But the boy took up his share of the dinner, and said : ' Rest yourself, father, it will do you good; I am not in the least tired.   I will go farther into the wood to look for bird's-nests, and eat my dinner as I go along.'

'Oh, you silly boy!' said his father; 'if you go running about the wood, you will be too tired by-and-by to lift your arm.   Stay here, and sit by me.'

The boy, however, would not be persuaded, so he went off to the wood, ate his dinner, and was soon running along full of spirits, for he saw in the green branches here and there the form of a nest.   He went on for some distance, however, till at last he came to an immense weird-looking oak, which was certainly many hundred years old, and its trunk so large that five men, with their hands joined together, could not have spanned it.

The boy stood still and looked at it, and thought : ' How many birds must have built their nests in that oak.'

Presently, as he stood admiring it, he thought he heard a voice. He listened, and it sounded again in smothered tones, and cried : 'Let me out; let me out!'   He looked about, but could discover nothing.   Still, it appeared to him as if the voice came from under the ground.

At last he cried : ' Where are you ?'

The voice answered : ' Here I am, just under the roots of the oak. Let me out ! let me out !'

The scholar at once commenced clearing away the underwood from the roots, and searching carefully, till at last he discovered in a corner a glass bottle.   He took it up, and held it against the light, and saw something in the shape of a frog springing up and down, and crying : 'Let me out; let me out !'   The scholar, suspecting no harm, took the cork out of the bottle, and instantly a spirit rose in the air; and, spreading as it rose, became in a very few moments a frightful looking creature half as high as the tree.

'Knowest thou,' he exclaimed to the youth, in a terrible voice, 'what will be thy reward for this ?'

'No,' answered the youth fearlessly, 'how should I ?'

'Well, then, I will tell you,' cried the ghost; 'I shall have to break your neck !'

'If you had told me that before,' said the scholar, 'I should certainly have let you stick fast in your bottle. As for my head, that shall remain on my shoulders for all your threats. There are more people to consult than myself in the matter.'

'More people coming! more people here!' cried the giant. 'Do you think that after being shut up so long I can have any inclination to mercy? No, indeed, I have had my punishment, and I will be revenged! I am the great and mighty Mercury, and you have set me free; therefore must I break your neck!'

'Gently,' replied the scholar, 'there need not be such haste as this. First, I must be sure that you are the same little spirit which was shut up. If you can make yourself small enough to go back into the bottle, then I will believe you, and you shall do as you like with me.'

The spirit replied, full of haughty courage: 'That is a mere trifle for me to do,' and immediately drew himself together, made himself as thin and small as he was before, so as to enter the opening of the bottle, and crept in.

No sooner had he done so than the scholar popped in the drawn cork, pushed it down tightly, and threw the bottle in its old place among the roots of the oak, and so the spirit was entrapped.

He was turning to go back to his father, when the ghost cried out again most pitifully: 'Oh, let me out again! let me out again!'

'No,' answered the scholar, 'it is not likely I shall let you out a second time after you have threatened my life. What should I expect if I did?'

'If you will set me free,' cried the ghost, 'I will give you more than enough money to last your life!'

'No,' said the scholar, 'you would deceive me as you did the first time.'

'You are throwing away your luck,' said the spirit; 'I will, indeed, do you no harm this time; but you shall be richly rewarded.'

The scholar thought to himself: 'I will venture it; most likely he may keep his word, and will not injure me.'

Then he took out the stopper, and, the spirit rising up as before, spread itself outwards, and was soon as large as a giant.

'Now you shall have your reward,' he said, 'as I promised;' and he handed him a small piece of rag like a plaster, and said: 'If you use one end to strap on a wound, it will heal it directly; ' and if you spread the other half on steel and iron, they will immediately be changed into gold and silver.'

'I must just prove it first,' said the youth. So he went to a tree, and with a stroke of the axe split the bark, and then spread the rag over it. Immediately it closed together again, and was healed. 'It is all right,' said he to the spirit, 'and now we may as well part.'

The spirit, on this, thanked him for setting him free, and the scholar, after thanking him for his gift, went back to his father.

'Where have you been running,' said his father, 'forgetting all about helping me? I said you would not work for an hour without getting tired.'

'Never mind, father,' said the boy. 'Do not be uneasy; I will soon make up for it.'

'Make it up, indeed,' said the father angrily; 'that is not the way to get on in the world.'

'Have patience,' said the youth. 'See, father, I will give this tree one stroke that shall crack it.'

As he spoke he took up the plaster, spread it over the axe, then, lifting it, struck a heavy blow on the tree; but, as the axe had been changed into silver, the blow turned the edge at once.

'Oh, look here, father!' said the boy, 'what a bad axe they have given you for me. See how it is turned on one side!'

'Ah! what have you done?' cried the father, in a great fright. 'Now I shall have to pay for the axe, and I know not how I am to do so; and this is all the use your work has been to me.'

'Don't be angry, father,' answered the boy; 'I can easily pay for the axe.'

'You idiot!' cried his father. 'How are you to pay for it, I wonder? You have nothing but what I give you. There are plenty of schoolboy tricks in your head, I can see; but you know nothing about wood-cutting.'

Presently the youth said to him, 'Father, I cannot work any more. Let us go home and keep holiday this evening together.'

'Eh, what?' he cried. 'Do you think I can go home to sit with my hands in my lap as you do? No, indeed, I must still work; but you may pack off home, if you like.'

'Father,' he replied, 'I have only been into the wood once, and I don't know my way home alone. Do go with me.'

As his anger became a little appeased, the father allowed himself to be talked over, and went home with the boy.

When they reached the house, he said, 'Now go and sell the defaced axe, and see what you can get for it; but remember that our neighbour must be paid, whatever you bring home.'

The boy took up the axe, and went into the town to a goldsmith, who proved it, and, laying it on the scales, said, 'This is worth four hundred dollars, but I have not so much cash in the house.'

The scholar said, 'Give me what you have, the overplus I will lend you.'

The goldsmith then gave him three hundred dollars, and there remained one hundred owing.

Thereupon the scholar went home to his father, and said, 'Father, I have money now! Go and ask our neighbour how much he wants for his axe.'

'I know that already,' he replied. 'One dollar and six groschens.'

'Ah, well! then you can give him two dollars and twelve groschens. That is just double, and I am sure it is enough. See here, I have money in abundance!'

And as he gave his father one hundred dollars, he said, 'We shall never miss the two dollars; for there is still quite enough for us to live at our ease.'

'Good heavens!' cried the father. 'Where have all these riches come from?'

Then the boy related what had happened to him in the wood, and how he had trusted the bottle spirit, and what a good fortune he had made. With all this money the scholar was again able to go to the High School, and continue his education; and, as he was not only clever, but had in his possession a plaster that could heal every wound, he became the most renowned doctor in the whole world.

CLEVER PEOPLE.

ONE day a countryman fetched his boxwood stick out of the field, and said to his wife, 'Irine, I am going away into the country, and shall return in three days. If the cattle-dealer should come to trade with us, and wish to buy our three cows, you can let him see them; but you must not allow them to go for less than two hundred dollars—not a farthing less, do you hear?'

'Be off with you, if you are going,' she replied. 'I will do as you say.'

'I hope you will,' he cried; 'but you are little better than a child who has fallen on its head. You'll forget all I have told you in an hour. But I can only promise you that if you make a stupid mess of this business I will stripe your back till it is black and blue, and that without any colour, but with this bare stick that I hold in my hand, and the marks shall last for a whole year; therefore you had better not forget.'

The next morning the cattle-dealer came, and the wife had no occasion to say much to him. When he had seen the cows, and had asked the price, he said, 'I am quite willing to take the animals; they are very cheap.' Then she unfastened the chain, and drove them out of the stable.

But when they reached the yard gate, and the driver wished to lead them out, the wife seized him by the sleeve, and said, 'You must first give me the two hundred dollars, or I cannot let them go with you.'

'All right,' answered the man; 'but I have forgotten to buckle on my money-pouch this morning. Do not be uneasy; you shall have security till I pay. I will take two cows with me, and leave the third behind with you, so that will be a good guarantee for my return.'

The woman was deceived. She allowed the man to march off with the two cows, and said to herself, 'How pleased Hans will be when he sees how cleverly I have managed.'

The farmer came home as he had said on the third day, and asked immediately whether the cows had been sold.

'Yes, most certainly, dear Hans,' answered the wife, 'and for two hundred dollars, as you told me. They are scarcely worth so much, but the man took them without the slightest objection to the price.'

'Where is the money?' asked the farmer.

'I have not got it yet,' she replied. 'He had forgotten his money-bag; but he will bring it soon, and he has left good security behind him.'

'What has he left?' asked the farmer.

'One of the three cows,' she said; 'he would not take that one till he had paid for the other two. I have managed very cleverly. I have kept back the smallest cow because it eats the least.'

In a rage and fury the man lifted his stick to inflict upon his wife the stripes with which he had threatened her. Suddenly he let it fall again without touching her, and said, 'You are the most stupid goose that ever waddled about on this earth; but I pity you. However, I am going again into the country for three days, and if I find anyone during that time as silly as you are, then you will escape; but if I do not, then you shall receive your well-deserved reward without mercy.'

Then he went out into the highroad, seated himself on a stone, and waited for something to help him in his search. Presently he saw a waggon coming along, in which sat a woman on a truss of straw, but near enough to guide the oxen who drew it. 'Ah!' thought the man, 'here is what I seek; I will try her.' He sprang up as he spoke, and ran before the waggon, here and there, as if he was undecided which way to go.

'What do you want, grandfather?' said the woman. 'I do not know you; where do you come from?'

'I have fallen from heaven,' he replied, 'and have no idea how to get back again. Can you take me there?'

'No,' said the woman, 'I do not know the way; but as you have come from heaven, can you tell me how my husband is going on? He has been there this three years; you must have seen him.'

'I have seen him, certainly,' replied the man; 'but it is not every man that is contented, even there. Your husband has to watch the sheep, and the dear animals give him plenty of work. They run from the mountains, and wander into the wilderness, and he has to run after them and bring them home. In consequence of this his clothes are torn to rags, and are falling off his back; and there are no tailors there. They are not admitted, as you know we are told in the story.'

'Now, who would have thought that?' cried the wife. 'But stay, I'll tell you what I'll do—I'll go and fetch my husband's Sunday coat which hangs in the wardrobe, then he will look respectable; that is, if you will be good enough to take it.'

'No use at all,' said the farmer. 'No one can venture to take clothes to heaven; they are always taken away at the door.'

'Well, then,' cried the woman, 'I sold yesterday my beautiful meadow, and a fine lot of money I got for it. I will send him that. If you stick a purse of money in your pocket, no one will notice it as you go in.'

'If nothing else can be done,' said the man evasively, 'then I will oblige you in this matter.'

'Stay here, and sit down for awhile, then,' said the woman; 'I will go and fetch the purse, and be back again very soon. I shall not sit on the truss of straw, but stand up, so that I can guide the oxen better.'

Away she drove as she spoke, and the man thought to himself: 'She has a good stock of folly at all events, and if she really brings the money, my wife will be lucky, and escape without a single stripe.' He had not waited long before he saw her running back to him with the purse of money in her hand, which she herself placed in his pocket. Then she thanked him a thousand times for his kindness, and went away.

But, on reaching home, she met her son coming from the field, and told him what an unexpected thing had happened to her. 'I am so delighted,' she continued, 'that I really met with some one who has seen my poor husband, and to be able to send him something, for the man told me he was suffering for want of clothes and money.'

The son was full of wonder at this account; but presently he exclaimed, 'Mother, men do not come from heaven every day. I will go out immediately and try to find this man, for I should like to see him; he will be able to tell me how it looks up there, and what work there is to do.' So he went out, saddled his horse, and rode away quickly.

He had not gone far before he saw the farmer sitting under a willow-tree, counting the money that was in the purse. 'Have you seen a man pass here who has just come from heaven?' asked the youth.

'Yes,' answered the farmer; 'but he has set out to return, and has taken the road over yonder mountain, which is rather a nearer way. You could overtake him, if you rode quickly.'

'Ah,' said the young man, 'I have been the whole day hard at work, and the ride here has tired me. You know the man, so will you be so good as to seat yourself on my horse, and overtake him, and bring him back here?'

'Ah,' thought the farmer, 'here is another with no wick in his lamp. Why should I not do you this favour?' said he aloud, as he mounted the horse, and rode away at a rapid trot.

The young man remained sitting where the farmer had left him till night came on, but he did not return. 'Ah, well,' he thought, 'the man was, no doubt, in a great hurry to get back to heaven, and the farmer has lent him the horse to take to my father.' He went home, and told his mother what had happened, and finished by saying, 'The man has, no doubt, sent the horse to my father, that he may not have to run about so much on foot after the sheep.'

'It is all right,' she replied, 'for your legs are still young, and you can easily go about on foot,' and so they submitted to their losses.

As soon as the farmer returned home, he placed the horse which the youth had lent him in the stable, near the remaining cow, and then went in to his wife. 'Irine,' he said, 'you are very lucky. I have found two who are still more silly fools than you are; this time, therefore, you will get off without one stripe. I will reserve them for another occasion.'

Then he took out his pipe, lighted it, seated himself in the old arm-chair, and said: 'This has been a good speculation—a sleek horse for two poor, lean cows, and a purse full of money into the bargain. If stupidity always brought me so much as this, I should be quite willing to keep you in grand style, wife. But,' thought the farmer, 'after all, she is a silly dear.'

THE MILLER'S BOY AND HIS CAT.

A MILLER once lived in an old mill; he had neither wife nor children, and three miller's apprentices worked for him in the house and in his business. When they had been with him some years, he said to them one day: 'I am getting old, and I shall soon want to sit in the chimney-corner without work. Whichever of you, therefore, brings me the best horse shall have the mill, and only have to support me till my death.'

The youngest of these apprentices was quite a boy, and the others considered him silly; they were also envious at the thought that he might have the mill, so they determined to prevent him from trying for it. They started, however, together on their expedition, but when they got outside the town, the two said to him: 'Silly Hans, you had better stay here; you will never find a horse, if you were to try for your whole life.'

Hans, however, would go with them, and as night came on they arrived at a cave, in which they laid themselves down to sleep. The two elder youths, who fancied themselves very clever, waited till Hans was asleep, and then rose up and ran away as fast as they could, leaving him behind alone, and thought they had managed most cleverly to get rid of him.

Hans awoke with the sun, and found himself lying in a deep hole, and after looking all about him, and seeing no one near, he exclaimed: 'Oh, dear! where am I?' Then he roused himself and scrambled out of the hole, and wandered into the wood. 'Ah,' he thought, 'here I am in the wood quite forsaken and alone. How am I ever to find a horse?'

As he walked on in deep thought, a little tabby cat met him, and said to him in a most friendly manner: 'Hans, what can I do for you?'

'Ah,' he replied, 'you can't help me, puss.'

'Well,' she said, 'I know exactly what you are longing for: you want a beautiful horse. Come with me, then, and be my true knight for seven years, and I will give you one more beautiful than you have ever seen in all your life.'

'This is a wonderful cat,' thought Hans: 'however, I will see if what she says is true.'

Then she took him with her to a little enchanted castle, in which there were nothing but cats as servants, who waited upon the tabby cat. They sprung nimbly up the steps before the visitor, and seemed good-natured, merry creatures.

In the evening, while the mistress and Hans sat at supper, three of them came in and performed music. One played the violin, another the bass-viol, and the third blew out his cheeks as much as possible in playing the bugle. When supper was ended, the other cats cleared the table and moved it away.

Then said the mistress cat: 'Come, Hans, we will have a dance: will you dance with me?'

'No,' he replied; 'I could not dance with a pussy-cat—I never did such a thing in my life.'

'Oh, well, never mind,' she said, and told the other cats to take him to bed. They lighted him to a little sleeping-room: and then one pulled off his shoes, another his stockings, and as soon as he was in bed, they blew out the light and left him.

The next morning they came again and helped him out of bed: one pulled on his stockings, another tied on his garters, and a third washed his face, while a fourth dried it with her tail.

'That is certainly a very soft towel,' he said to himself, and went to his breakfast.

During each day the cats had to cut up wood into little pieces, as well as wait upon their mistress, and for this purpose they had an axe and a wedge of silver, and a chopper of gold. But at first Hans did very little; he remained in the house, had plenty of good eating and drinking, and saw no one but the tabby cat and her domestics.

At last one day she said to him: 'Go out into my meadow, Hans, and mow the grass, and make it into hay.' And for this purpose she gave him a silver scythe, and a gold whetstone and rake, and told him to be sure to bring them back again safely.

Away went Hans, and soon accomplished his task, bringing home the hay and the tools to the house as he had been told.

'Am I to have my reward now?' he asked.

'No,' she replied; 'you must do something else for me first. You will find timber outside, and carpenter's tools all of silver, and everything necessary for building, so I want you to build me a house.'

Hans set to work and soon built the house, and when it was finished, he said: 'I have done all you told me, but still there is no horse for me.'

By this time the seven years had really gone by, so the cat asked him if he would like to see his horse.

'Yes, indeed,' he replied.

So she led him out to the door, and when it was opened he saw standing before it twelve horses. Ah, how proud and spirited they looked! and their skins shone and glittered so brightly that his heart was in his mouth for joy.

After he had admired them, the cat took him into the castle, gave him a good dinner, and said: 'I shall not give you the horse yet; but you must go home, and in three days I will come myself and bring it to you.'

So she started him off, and herself showed him the way back to the mill.

During the time he had stayed with her, however, she had given him no new clothes; so that he was obliged to wear those he had brought with him, and a smock frock, which was not only too short and small for him, but all in rags. When he reached home he found the two other lads had returned and brought their horses with them; but although they looked sleek and fine, one was lame and the other blind.

'Well, Hans,' they said, when they saw him, ' where is your horse?'

'It will be here in three days,' he replied.

They laughed at him, and said, 'Ah, that is very likely; just catch any fine horses coming here for you.'

Hans said nothing, but went into the room; and when the miller saw him, he cried, 'You shall not sit at the table with us in such a torn and ragged condition; if anyone should come in, I should be ashamed to see you here.'

So they gave him something to eat outside.

When evening came, the other apprentices would not let him sleep in the same room with them, so he was obliged to go out and creep into the hen-house and lie down on the straw.

The third morning came, and very early, not long after they were all up, a splendid carriage, drawn by six horses, drove to the door. The horses were as beautiful and as sleek as those Hans had seen, and their harness glittered in the light. But with the carriage were several servants, and one of them led a most beautiful horse, which was for the poor miller's boy.

The carriage stopped, and a beautiful princess alighted, who was no other than the tabby cat whom Hans had released from enchantment, by serving her willingly for seven years. She entered the mill and asked the miller where his youngest apprentice was.

'We cannot have him in the mill now,' he replied; ' he is so torn and ragged; ' he is outside in the hen-house.'

'I will fetch him myself then,' said the princess.

So she called her servants, and they followed her with new and elegant clothes, and told them to lead him to the house, and desire him to throw off the rags and the old smock frock, and wash and dress himself in the new attire; and when he had done so, no prince could look more elegant.

Meanwhile, the princess returned to the mill and asked to see the horses which the other apprentices had brought, and she found that one was blind and the other lame. Then she desired her servants to bring the horse which was intended for Hans; and when it was brought into the court, and the miller had looked at it, the princess said, 'That horse is for your youngest apprentice.'

'A SPLENDID CARRIAGE, DRAWN BY SIX HORSES, DROVE TO THE DOOR'

'Then,' said the miller, 'he must have the mill.'

'No,' said the princess, 'he will not need it; you may keep the mill and the horse also.'

And then Hans appeared splendidly dressed, and she desired him to take a seat in her carriage, and they drove away together.

They went first to the small house which Hans had built with the silver tools ; it was now a beautiful castle all shining with gold and silver. They were soon after married, and Hans became so rich that

'THEY WERE SOON AFTER MARRIED.

he never wanted anything again as long as he lived. No one, therefore, can ever say that because a man is silly he will never be rich.

THE GOOD-TEMPERED TAILOR.

It is as easy for mountain and valley to meet as for mankind to be good and wicked at the same time. It happened once that a shoemaker and a tailor went on a friendly journey together : it came about in this way. The tailor was a good-looking little fellow, always good-tempered and merry ; and one day he met the shoemaker in the village, and saw that he carried his box of tools with him, so he cried out jocosely, in the words of a merry song :

> 'Sew well your seams,
> Draw out your thread,
> Rub it right and left with wax,
> Work till 'tis time to go to bed."

The shoemaker, however, would not stop, but he made a wry face as if he had been drinking vinegar, and looked as if he were going to collar the tailor. The merry little fellow, however, only laughed, and holding up a bottle to him, said, 'I did not mean any harm ; friend, just have a drink ; it will help you to swallow down the bile.'

The shoemaker did not refuse, and took such a large draught that the thunder-clouds on his face began to disperse. He gave back the bottle to the tailor, and said, 'I have often heard it said, that men speak better after drinking than when they are thirsty. Shall we travel together ?'

'With all my heart,' said the tailor, 'if your inclination is to go to a large town, where we may most likely find plenty of work.'

'That is just what I should wish to do,' replied the shoemaker ; 'in a little nest like our village there is no work to be had, and in the country people like to go bare-footed.'

So they agreed to travel together, and went away on their journey, always placing one foot before the other like a weasel in the snow. They had plenty of time for walking, but very little to eat and drink ; so when they arrived at a town they each tried for work in his different trade, and the tailor looked so fresh and lively, and had such bright, rosy cheeks, that he readily obtained work ; and when he had the luck, he would contrive to give the master's daughter a kiss behind the door as he went away. Generally, when he again joined the shoemaker, he had the most money in his purse.

The peevish shoemaker would make a long face, and say : 'The greater the rogue, the greater the luck.' But the little tailor only laughed and sang, and shared all that he earned with his comrade. If he had only a couple of pence jingling in his pocket, he would take them out and throw them on the table so joyfully, that the glasses would dance again, and it might be said of him : 'Easily earnt, easily spent.'

They had been travelling for some time, when they arrived near a large forest, through which lay the road to the chief town of the kingdom, and in which the king dwelt. Two footpaths led to this town, one of which would occupy seven days to traverse, and the other only two ; but neither of them knew which was the shorter way.

The two wanderers seated themselves under an oak-tree, and began to consult respecting what quantity of food they should take with them.

The shoemaker said : 'A man ought always to prepare for the future. I shall take bread enough to last seven days.'

'What!' cried the tailor, 'drag bread enough for seven days on your back, like a beast of burden, and not be able to look about you? I shall trust to Providence, and drive away care. The money in my pocket will keep as good in summer as in winter, but bread will become dry in the heat, and mouldy in the damp weather. My coat also is a little out at elbows; besides, after all, why should we not find the right way? Two days' provisions is all I shall carry.'

So they each bought what he chose, and started with the hope that by good fortune they might find the shortest path.

The forest was as still as a church when they entered it; not a breath of air stirred, the brook flowed silently, the song of the birds was hushed, and through the thick foliage not a sunbeam could penetrate. The shoemaker said not a word, but the pressure of the weight of bread on his shoulders obliged him every now and then to wipe off the drops of perspiration from his morose and sullen countenance. The tailor, however, was quite lively, sprang here and there, picked off a leaf or sang a song, and thought that heaven itself must be pleased to see him so happy.

Two days passed, but on the third day the end of the forest seemed as far off as ever, and the tailor had eaten all his bread. By this time his spirits had sunk an ell lower; he did not lose his courage, however, but still trusted to Providence and his own good luck. On the evening of the third day he laid himself down hungry and tired under a tree, and rose again next morning still hungry; and so he went on till the fourth day, and when the shoemaker sat down on the stump of a fallen tree to eat his supper, the tailor could not help seeing him. But when he begged for a piece of bread, the other laughed scornfully, and said: 'You that have always been so merry, can now know what it is to feel miserable. The birds sing in the morning early, but in the evening they become the prey of the hawk.' In short, he was quite without pity or sympathy.

But on the fifth morning the poor tailor could not hold out any longer, and from exhaustion could scarcely utter a word; his cheeks were white, and his eyes quite red.

Then said the wicked shoemaker: 'I will give you a piece of bread to-day, if you will let me put out your right eye.'

The unhappy tailor, whose only thought then was how to save his life, felt that he had no other means of doing so, and that he could not help himself. He wept once more with his two eyes, and then submitted to the cruel shoemaker, who must have had a heart of stone.

There came into the mind of the poor tailor at this moment something that his mother had once said when he had stolen something nice out of the store-room: 'Eat as much as you may, and suffer what you must.'

As soon as he had eaten his dearly-bought bread, he was able again to get on his legs, forget his misfortune, and comforted himself with the reflection that he could still see well enough with the eye that was left.

But on the sixth day the hunger was fiercer than ever, and seemed as if it were consuming his very vitals. In the evening he fell under a tree, and on the morning of the seventh day was unable to rise from exhaustion, while death stared him in the face.

Then the wretched shoemaker spoke again : 'I will have compassion on you, and give you another piece of bread if you will consent to lose your left eye also ; but you can do as you like.'

Then the tailor recalled his light-hearted, thoughtless life, and, praying for pardon, said to his comrade : 'Do what you will, I will endure what I must, but remember that every moment of your life is judged, and an hour will come when your wicked acts to me will be requited. Neither have I deserved this cruelty. In my best days I have always shared with you what I had earned. My trade is an art that requires to be carried on stitch by stitch, and if I lose both eyes, I shall be unable to work any more, and shall be obliged to beg; but if I am to be blind, do not leave me here alone in the forest, or I must die of starvation.'

The shoemaker, who had driven all good thoughts out of his heart, would not listen; he made the poor tailor blind in both eyes, and then, after placing a piece of bread in his hand, waited till he had eaten it, gave him a stick to guide his footsteps, and led him away. About sunset they came out of the forest, and in a field near stood a gallows. To this the shoemaker led the blind tailor, laid him down under it, and went away and left him.

Overcome with fatigue, pain, and hunger, the unfortunate man sunk to sleep, and slept the whole night. At daybreak he awoke, but knew not that above where he lay hung two poor criminals, and that on each of their heads sat a crow.

Just as he awoke, one of the crows began to speak to the other : 'Brother,' he said, 'are you awake?'

'Yes, I am awake,' replied the other.

'Then I will tell you something,' said the first again. 'The dew which has fallen around us to-night will restore the eyesight to any blind person who washes with it. If the blind only knew how many have been restored to sight by this dew, even those who never believed in its wonderful power, they would all come here.'

When the tailor heard this, he took out his pocket-handkerchief, dragged it over the grass, and when it was well saturated with dew, he washed out the cavities of his eyes with it. Almost at the same moment was fulfilled what he had heard, and a pair of new, perfect eyes filled up the empty sockets. A little longer, and then the tailor looked up, and saw the sun rising behind the mountain-top, and on the plain before him lay the great city, with its noble gates and its towers, while the golden pinnacles and crosses that crowned their summits glittered in the sun's first morning rays. He could distinguish every leaf on the trees, he saw the birds fluttering among the branches above him, and the gnats dancing in the morning air. Then he took a sewing-needle out of his pocket, and when he found that he could thread it as well as ever, his heart bounded for joy. He threw himself on his knees, and thanked God for the unmerited mercy, and sung his morning song of praise. He did not forget to pray for the two poor criminals who hung there, like clock-weights, swinging to and fro as the wind moved them. Then he took his bundle on his back, and soon forgetting his past pain and sorrow, continued his journey, singing and whistling as he went.

The first living thing he met was a brown foal, running and frisking in freedom in the field. He caught him by the mane, for he wished to mount and ride to the city; but the foal begged for his freedom.

'I am still young,' said he, 'and even a lighter tailor than you would break my back. Leave me to run free till I become strong. Very likely a time may come when I shall be able to repay your kindness.'

'Run away, then,' said the tailor; 'I see you are a wild young colt.' He gave him one gentle stroke with a switch over his back, which sent him kicking up his hind-legs with joy at his freedom, and galloping over hedges and ditches, like a hunter in the hunting-field.

The tailor, however, had not eaten anything since the day before. 'The dew,' he said, 'has filled my eyes, but bread has not filled my mouth; the first that I meet of anything eatable, I must keep for food.'

At this moment a stork stepped quite gravely across the meadow. 'Stop, stop!' cried the tailor, and caught him by the leg. 'I do not know whether you are good to eat, but my hunger allows me no time to inquire. I must cut off your head and roast you.'

'Do not do that,' answered the stork. 'I am a sacred bird, whom no one ever thinks of injuring, and I am of very great use to man; leave me my life, and I may be able, at some time or other, to recompense you for it.'

'Take yourself off then, cousin long-legs,' said the tailor.

The stork rose, let his long legs hang down, and flew gently away.

'What shall I do now?' said the tailor to himself; 'my hunger is constantly increasing, and my stomach is getting more empty; whatever comes in my way next is lost.' Almost as he spoke, he came to a pond where two young ducks were swimming about. 'You have come at my call,' said he, seizing one of them; and he was just going to wring its neck, when an old duck, who stood among the rushes on the bank, began to quack loudly; and swimming towards him with stretched-out beak, begged him most earnestly to spare her dear children.

'Think, now,' she said, 'how your own mother would have grieved if you had been taken away from her to be killed.'

'Be still now,' said the good-natured tailor; 'you shall keep your children.' And he placed the captive again in the water.

As he turned away, he saw before him an old tree, partly hollow, and from the hole wild bees were flying in and out. 'Here I shall find a reward for my kind actions,' said the tailor; 'the honey will refresh me.'

But the queen-bee came out in great displeasure, and said, ' If you disturb my people, and destroy my nest, we will use our stings upon you, and they will be in your skin like ten thousand red-hot needles ; but if you leave us at peace, and go your way, at some time or another we may be able to do you a service.'

The tailor saw at once that there was nothing to be got from the hollow tree. ' Three empty dishes,' he said, ' and out of the fourth nothing ; this is a bad dinner-time.' So he dragged himself on with his hungry stomach to the town, at which he arrived about noon. At the inn he found a dinner already cooked for him, and he lost no time in seating himself at the table.

As soon as his hunger was appeased, he determined to go out and seek for work, and very soon found a master and a good situation. He had, however, learnt the groundwork of his trade so thoroughly that it was not long before he became quite a noted tailor. Everyone wanted to have his coat made by the clever little man. Each day gained him fresh employment, and although he would say, ' I cannot rise any higher now,' at last he was appointed by the king to be tailor to the court.

However, as it often happens in the world, on the very same day his former comrade was made court shoemaker. When he caught sight of the tailor, and saw that he had again two perfect eyes, his conscience so tormented him that he thought to himself : ' I must dig a pit for this man ere he takes revenge on me.'

But those who dig a pit for another generally fall into it themselves.

So in the evening, when he had finished the day's work, and twilight drew on, the shoemaker slipped quietly in and obtained an audience of the king, and said : ' My lord king, the tailor who is appointed to the court is, no doubt, a very clever man, but he has boasted that he can recover the golden crown belonging to the kingdom, which was lost in days gone by.'

' Indeed,' replied the king, ' that is very pleasant news. Let the tailor know that I expect him to set about finding this crown to-morrow morning, and, unless he succeeds, he is to leave this city for ever.'

' Oho !' cried the tailor, who had no idea that his enemy, the shoemaker, had influenced the king, ' if this surly king desires what it is not possible for anyone to perform, I shall not wait for to-morrow morning, but take myself out of the town at once.'

He corded his bundle ; but he did not put it on his back till he got outside the gates, for he had been so fortunate and done so well there that he did not wish to be seen going away as if in disgrace.

He had not travelled far when he came to the pond where he had once made a friendly acquaintance with the ducks. The old duck was on the shore ; she had left her young ones to enjoy the water, and as he passed she was pluming her feathers with her beak. She recognised him immediately, and asked him what made him hang down his head so sadly.

'You would not wonder if you knew what has happened to me,' he said; and then he told her of his fate.

'Which, after all, is nothing,' said the duck. 'We can advise you what to do, and help you also. The crown was thrown into the water of this pond, and there it now lies at the bottom. I and my children can soon fetch it for you. In the meantime, spread your pocket-handkerchief on the shore in readiness.'

Away she swam with her young ones as she spoke, and quickly diving down under the water, in less than five minutes appeared again on the surface carrying the crown on her wings, and the twelve young ones swam round her, each supporting it with its beak. Then they came to land, and laid the crown on the pocket-handkerchief.

You would have been surprised to see how beautiful it looked when the sun shone upon it, for it glittered with thousands of precious stones. The tailor tied the crown up in his handkerchief, and carried it to the king, who was so overjoyed at seeing it again that he hung a gold chain round the tailor's neck.

When the shoemaker found that he had made a false move, he had no rest till he thought of something else to ruin the tailor. So he went to the king, and said: 'My lord king, the tailor is still boasting of his great cleverness. He says that a royal castle, complete in every way, both inside and out, can be built of wax.'

On this the king sent for the tailor, and commanded him to build a castle such as the shoemaker had described, and said that if he did not bring it in a few hours, or if there should want even a nail in the wall, he would be confined underground for the remainder of his life.

'Oh,' thought the tailor, when he heard this, 'it gets worse and worse; that is more than mortal man can do.'

So he again took his bundle on his back, and wandered away from the town.

On his road he came again to the hollow tree, on which he seated himself with his head drooping, and feeling very sad. Presently the bees came out, and amongst them the queen-bee, who, when she saw him, asked him if he had a stiff neck, as he held his head so low.

'Ah, no,' said the tailor, 'something more painful depresses my head.' Then he told her what the king required him to do.

Immediately the bees began to buzz and to hum, and the queen-bee said to him: 'Go back to your house, and come again in the morning; bring a large cloth with you, and you will find it is all right.'

So he turned his steps homewards. But the bees flew to the king's castle; and, as they found the windows open, they crept in, and examined every corner, and saw exactly how everything was arranged.

Then they hastened back, and reproduced the castle in wax in the most perfect manner, so that it appeared to grow before the eye. By evening it was finished; and, when the tailor made his appearance in the morning, there stood the beautiful building quite ready for him—not a nail on the wall missing, nor even a tile on the roof. It was delicately white like snow, and yet sweet as honey. The tailor packed it up carefully in his handkerchief, and carried it to the king.

The king could not help wondering as he looked at this curious piece of workmanship. He placed it in a saloon, and in return he presented the tailor with a large stone-built residence. The shoemaker, however, was not yet satisfied.

A third time he appeared before the king, and said: 'My lord king, it has come to the ears of the tailor that in the court of the palace there is not a well or a fountain; and he boasts that he could cause water to flow there as clear as crystal, and to the height of a tall man.'

So the king sent for the tailor, and said to him: 'If by to-morrow morning you do not cause a stream of water to flow in my court as you have promised, then shall the executioner in the same court make you shorter by a head!'

The poor tailor, as he went from the king's presence, did not take long to decide what to do. He hastened away from the town with the tears rolling down his cheeks, for this time his life was at stake.

As he walked along full of grief the foal to which he had granted liberty came springing towards him. It had now grown to a beautiful bay horse.

'I am here just in time,' he said as he saw the tailor, 'to requite your kindness to me. I know already what you want, and I shall soon be able to help you. Jump up,' he continued; 'my back could carry two such as you now.'

The tailor, on hearing this, took heart, sprung with one leap on the horse, which started off at full speed, and did not stop till he reached the gate of the castle. Then he galloped round the court as quick as lightning three times. The third time he plunged violently; and as he did so a terrible crack appeared in the ground under his feet, and in the same moment a quantity of earth was shot into the air and over the castle, and after it rose a stream of water as high as the man and the horse. The water was as clear as crystal, and the sun's rays sparkled on it in various colours.

When the king saw it he stood still in wondering amazement, and then embraced the tailor in the presence of all his people.

But this happiness did not last long; the shoemaker made a fourth trial in hopes of getting rid of the man he had injured. Now the king had several daughters, each very beautiful, but no son; so the wicked shoemaker came to the king and said to him: 'My lord king, there is no end to the tailor's haughty boasting; he is declaring now that he can bring a little son to the king through the air.'

Upon this the king sent for the tailor, and said to him: 'If within nine days a little son is brought to me through your means, then you shall have my eldest daughter to wife.'

'That is really a tempting reward,' thought the tailor, 'but it is out of the power of any man to accomplish. The cherries hang too high for me; if I attempt to climb for them the branch will break under me, and I shall have a fall.' He went home, seated himself cross-legged on his work-table, and reflected on what would be the best way to act. 'It is no use,' he said at last; 'I will go away; they will not let me live here in peace.' He got down from the table once more, tied up his bundle, and passed out through the town as he supposed for the last time.

It was not long before he reached a meadow, and there he saw to his surprise his old friend the stork, standing like a philosopher contemplating a frog which croaked near him, and which he at last swallowed. Then he turned, saw the tailor, and advanced to greet him. 'I see,' he said, raising himself, 'that you have your knapsack on your back. Why are you leaving the town?'

Then the tailor told him that the king required of him what it was impossible for him to do, and then began to mourn over his unhappy fate.

'Don't let any gray hairs grow out of that trouble,' said the stork; 'I will help you in your difficulty. I have already brought many babies to your town, and I can just as well bring a little prince out of the well this time as any other child. Go home and make yourself quite comfortable; in nine days from to-day go up to the king's castle, and I will be there.'

The tailor went home, and was careful to be at the castle at the appointed time. He had not been long there when the stork appeared flying through the air, and quickly tapped at the window with his beak. The tailor opened it, and 'Cousin Long-legs' stepped cautiously in, and walked gravely across the smooth marble floor. He had a little child in his beak, who was as beautiful as an angel, and it stretched out its little hands to the queen. The stork advanced and laid the child on the queen's lap, and she kissed it, and pressed it to her heart, and was almost beside herself with joy.

Before he flew away, the stork took his travelling pouch from his shoulder and presented it to the queen. It contained a horn full of coloured sugar-plums to be divided among the young princesses. The eldest, however, would not take any. She said, as she was going to be married, she would give up her share to her sisters.

The tailor was again the merry tailor of past days, and he said: 'It seems to me as if I had been drawing lots and winning. My mother was right: she said that if we trusted to Providence and acted honestly we should never want.'

After this the shoemaker was ordered to leave the town; but before he went he was obliged to make the shoes in which the tailor was to dance at his wedding. He turned his steps towards the forest in which he had so cruelly served his comrade, and travelled on till he reached the gallows. Full of rage and fury, and tired with the heat of the day, he threw himself down under it, for he wished to sleep; and while he slept the two crows, who still sat on the heads of the hanging men, flew down and picked out his eyes. With a great scream, he rose and ran blindly into the wood, where it is supposed he died of starvation, for he has never been seen or heard of since.

THE CLEVER HUNTER.

THERE was once a young lad who had learnt the business of a lock-smith, and he told his father he should like to go out into the world and seek his own living. His father was quite pleased that he should do so, and gave him some money for his travelling expenses, and told him which was the best place to find employment. But after a time he got tired of his trade, and nothing else would do for him than to be a hunter, for he had already great skill with a gun. One day in his wanderings he met a hunter in a suit of green, who asked him where he came from, and where he was going. He replied that he was a locksmith's apprentice, but that he did not like the trade and had a great desire to be a hunter, and asked the man if he would take him as a pupil. 'Oh yes,' replied the hunter; 'if you will go with me I will teach you.'

So the youth hired himself to the hunter, and remained for some years with him, and in that time learnt all the ins and outs of hunting. After this he wished to travel, and the hunter gave him for wages only an old air-gun, which had, however, one good property—whoever shot with it never missed his aim. Then he left his companion, and went away farther till he came to a great wood, in which after wandering about for a whole day he could not find a way out. When evening came on, he climbed up a high tree and seated himself on the branches, to be out of reach of the wild beasts, and about midnight thought he saw the glimmer of a small light in the distance; he looked cautiously through the foliage of the trees and discovered where it was. But before moving he took off his hat and threw it in the direction of the light, so that when he came down from the tree it might show him which way to turn. Then he scrambled down, went to where his hat lay, picked it up, and placing it on his head, turned his steps towards the light.

The nearer he approached the larger the light appeared, till at length he saw an immense fire with an ox roasting on a spit, and three giants sitting round it. As he drew near he heard one of the giants say, 'I must just see if this meat is ready for eating.'

So he cut off a piece, and was just going to put it into his mouth when the hunter shot it out of his hand. 'Now then,' cried the giant, 'the wind has blown that piece away; I must have another.'

But before he could get even a bite this also was shot away. The giant in a rage turned to the one who sat next him, and boxing his ears, cried : ' What did you snatch that piece away for ?'

' I didn't snatch it away,' said the other ; ' it must have been some sharp-shooter on the road.'

The giant cut off a third piece, but it was scarcely in his hand before the hunter shot it out again. ' That must be a good shot, whoever he is,' said the giants one to another, ' to shoot pieces out of one's mouth in that way ; he might be useful to us.'

So they called aloud, ' Come here, you sharpshooter ; come and sit down by our fire with us and have some supper ; we will do you no harm. If you won't come we will fetch you by force, and then good-bye to you.'

The youth on this stepped forward and said : ' I am a trained hunter, and wherever I aim with my gun I am sure to hit.'

So they asked him to join them, and said he should have the best of everything they had. They told him also that not far from where they sat was a large piece of water, and beyond it stood a castle, in which lived a beautiful princess whom they wished to carry off. ' Oh, that is easily managed,' he replied. But they said again : ' It is not so very easy, for the princess has a sharp little dog, which begins to bark loudly when anyone approaches the tower in which she sleeps, and the moment he barks everyone in the royal household wakes, and we cannot therefore get in. Do you think you could undertake to shoot that dog ?'

' Oh, yes,' he replied, ' that would be to me a mere trifle.'

So they went down to the water and seated themselves in a little boat, and were very soon across. As they approached the shore, out ran the little dog, but before he could utter a single bark, the hunter with his air-gun shot him dead. When the giants saw this they were mightily pleased, and thought now they were certain to have the princess ; but the hunter wished to see first how the affair was to be managed, so he told them to remain outside till he called them.

Then he entered the castle alone, and found everything as still as a mouse, for they all slept. In the first room he entered there hung upon the wall a sword of pure silver, with a golden star upon it, in which was inscribed the king's name. On a table near lay a sealed letter ; the hunter took it up, broke open the seal, and read what was written—that whoever wielded that sword could take the life of anyone who came in his way.

He took the sword from the wall, fastened it on, and went farther. Presently he came to the chamber where the princess lay sleeping, and she was so beautiful that he stood still and held his breath as he looked at her.

' Ah,' thought he to himself, ' I dare not allow this innocent maiden to fall into the power of those wild giants who have wickedness in their thoughts.'

Then he looked round the room, and saw a pair of slippers; on the right slipper was embroidered a star with the king's name, and on the left another star with the princess's name. There was also a silk neckerchief, embroidered with gold, on which her father's and her own name were worked, and all in gold letters. The hunter took a pair of scissors, and cut a strip off the silk neckerchief, and put it in his knapsack; he also took the slipper with the king's name on it, and placed it with the strip of silk. And all this while the princess slept peacefully, and she did not even wake while he cut a piece from the sleeve of her nightdress, which he also placed in his bag, and went away without disturbing anyone.

Outside the door he found the three giants waiting impatiently, and wondering that he did not bring the princess. He called to them, however, to come in.

'One at a time,' he said, 'for I cannot open the door for you; but there is a hole through which you can creep.'

Then the first giant came near, and stooped with his head through the opening; in an instant the hunter seized him by the hair, dragged the head through, cut it off with the silver sword at one blow, and pulled the rest of the giant's body in after it. He then called up the second and the third, and served them exactly in the same manner, and then feeling very joyful at having freed the beautiful young maiden from such enemies, he left the castle.

'Ah,' thought he, 'I will now go home and tell my father what I have already done, and afterwards go out again into the world to see what other good fortune awaits me.'

On arising in the morning and going to the door of the castle; the king saw with surprise the three dead giants. He instantly went to his daughter's room, woke her, and asked her if she knew who had killed the giants.

'Dear father,' she replied, 'indeed I do not know; I have slept all night.'

However, when she got up and began to dress, she first missed her right slipper; then she noticed that a strip had been cut off her silk necktie, and at last that her nightdress sleeve was in pieces.

On hearing of this, the king called together the whole household, soldiers, servants, and all who were there, and inquired if they knew who had destroyed the giants, and delivered his daughter from their power. Now, the captain of the soldiers was a wicked and ugly man, with one eye, and he came forward and said he had done this noble deed.

'Then,' said the king, 'as you have accomplished this so completely, I will give you my daughter in marriage.'

But the maiden said: 'Dear father, why should I be married? I would rather go out into the world and travel about on foot till I could walk no farther, than marry that man.'

The king replied: 'If you will not be married as I wish, you shall take off all your royal robes, and put on peasant's clothes, and I shall send you to a potter to learn how to be useful in selling earthenware vessels.'

Then the princess took off her beautiful clothes, dressed herself as a peasant, and went to a potter, and hired of him a basket of earthenware goods, and promised him that if she had sold any by the evening, she would pay him for the hire. Her father, however, made her go and stand in a corner of the market-place to sell her goods, close to the road where waggons were constantly passing, for he wanted to make her position as unhappy as he could, and he knew that if they drove by quickly, her goods would be soon shaken to a thousand pieces.

The poor maiden took her basket to the corner, as the king had desired her to do, knowing nothing of the waggons. Consequently, one soon drove by, and smashed her goods to atoms. Then she began to weep and cry: ' Oh, how shall I pay the potter ?'

The king, however, who still wanted her to marry the captain, sent for the potter, and asked him not to lend her another basket of goods, and so when she went to him the next morning, he refused to let her have any more. Then she went to her father weeping and lamenting sadly, and declaring that she would go out into the world and wander about by herself, rather than be married to the captain. Her father then told her that he would have a small cottage built for her in the wood, where she could live all her life by herself, and cook for anyone who passed by, but receive no money for it.

As soon as the house was finished, a sign was hung up over the door, on which was written: ' For nothing to-day, to-morrow we pay.'

She lived in this cottage for a long time, and it was soon noised abroad in the world that a maiden lived there who cooked for nothing, and that over the door of her cottage hung a sign. The hunter who had killed the giants heard of this, and thought to himself: ' That is the very place for me to have my dinner cooked; I am hungry, and have not much money.'

So he took his air-gun and his knapsack wherein everything still remained which he had taken from the castle as proofs of what he had done, and going to the forest soon found the tiny house, and read the words upon the sign: ' For nothing to-day, to-morrow we pay.' He carried also the sword with which he had cut off the heads of the three giants. So he went in like a traveller, and asked for something to eat.

He was quite delighted to find such a beautiful maiden there; for indeed she was as beautiful as a picture. She asked him where he came from, and he replied that he was travelling about the world. After he had eaten and drank they began to talk again, and she told him about the three giants being killed at the castle, and that the sword with her father's name was missing; and, as he listened, he knew she must be the king's daughter whom he had saved from the giants.

He then asked her why she was in such a cottage as that, and working like a peasant's daughter; and, oh, how overjoyed he was to hear that she was being punished for refusing to marry the false captain! Then he drew the sword, and said: 'With this sword *I* cut off the giants' heads.'

'Yes,' she cried, 'that is my father's sword. It bears his name.'

'And here,' he continued, opening his knapsack, 'is the slipper, and the pieces of the silk neckerchief and the nightdress. I have also the tongues of the giants, which I cut out after they were dead; so that I have every proof.'

Then how happy she was; for she knew that he had been the one to set her free. After this they went together to the old king, and the princess led her father away to her chamber, and told him she had found the man who had really slain the giants. When they showed him all the proofs, the king could no longer doubt, and told the hunter it was a great pleasure to him to know how it all happened; and that as he had spoken the real truth, he would give him his daughter as a wife.

The princess heard this, and there was no fear of her refusing this time; for she was too happy in her heart. Thereupon the hunter was presented with a dress suitable for a royal castle; and the king gave orders for a grand evening entertainment. The hunter was invited as a stranger, and at table he was placed at the right hand of the princess. On her left sat the captain, who of course had no idea who the strange gentleman was, and supposed him to be only a visitor.

After dinner the king told the captain he wished to ask him a question. 'If anyone should assert that he had killed three giants,' said the king, 'and on examining the heads they were found to be without tongues, how could you account for it?'

'Perhaps they had no tongues,' replied the captain.

'That is an impossibility,' said the king; 'every creature has a tongue.' And he continued, 'What should be done to the man who claims an unmerited honour and reward?'

'He deserves to be torn in pieces,' was the reply.

'You have pronounced your own sentence,' replied the king. 'Here is the man who killed the giants, and cut out their tongues, which he has, with other proofs, in his possession.'

So the captain was made a prisoner, and led away to punishment; and the hunter married the young princess. He soon after sent for his father and mother, and they lived with their son in great happiness till the king's death, and then he became king of the country.

THE HATCHET AND THE FLAIL.

A PEASANT once went out with a pair of oxen to plough. As soon as they were in the fields the horns of the two animals began to grow, and kept on growing all day, till by the time they returned home they had grown too large to get in at the stable door. Luckily a butcher came by, to whom the oxen were soon made over, and the bargain settled in this matter. The peasant agreed to carry to the butcher a quart of rape-seed, and for every seed the butcher promised to pay a dollar, which was a first-rate bargain, although payment for the oxen was included in it.

The peasant went home, and very soon returned with the rape-seed for the butcher, but on the way he dropped one seed. The butcher counted the seeds, and paid for them justly; but if the peasant had not lost that one seed he would have had another dollar. However, he set out to return home quite satisfied; but on reaching the place where the seed had dropped, what was his surprise to find that it had taken root and grown into a tree, the top of which reached to heaven.

Then thought the peasant, 'I should like to have a peep at what they are about up there, and see what the angels are doing, and here is a splendid opportunity.' So he climbed up the tree, and, peeping in, saw the angels at work threshing oats, and stood watching them for some time.

Presently, as he stood there, he felt the tree on which he stood totter under him. He looked through the branches and saw that they were cutting it down. 'If I should fall from such a height as this it would be terrible,' he thought; and in his trouble he scarcely knew what to do.

There seemed, however, nothing better than to take a piece of cord which lay near the heaps of chaff, and let himself down by it; but before he did so he laid hold of a hatchet and a flail which the angels had left behind them, and, tying them both to a rope, slid gently down from the tree. When he reached the earth, however, he sunk into a hole so deep that it was fortunate he had a hatchet with him, for with it he was able to cut steps in the side of the hole, and climb once more into daylight.

He took care to carry the hatchet and the flail with him, that no one might doubt his story when he related it.

THE BLUE LIGHT.

THERE once lived a soldier who had served the king faithfully for many years; but when the war ceased, and the soldier, who had many wounds, was disabled, the king said to him, 'You can go home now; I do not want you any more. You have had all your pay, and only those can receive a pension who have served me longer than you have."

The soldier on hearing this went away, feeling very sad; he knew not how he should get his living, and he wandered about for a whole day, full of care.

As evening came on he entered a wood, and as soon as it grew quite dark he saw at a distance a blue light, and on going towards it, he found a house in which dwelt an old witch. 'Give me a night's lodging,' he said to her, 'and something to eat and drink; I am almost starved.'

'Ah!' she cried, 'whoever gives anything to a runaway soldier? But I will take pity on you, if you will do as I wish to-morrow.'

'What do you want me to do?' asked the soldier.

'First, I want you to dig my garden.'

To this the soldier readily agreed, and worked all the following day as hard as he could; but, though he exerted all his strength, it was not finished by the evening.

'Ah! I see plainly,' said the witch, 'that you cannot do any more to-day. Well, I will give you another night's lodging, and to-morrow you shall split up a cartload of wood into fire-wood.'

Next day the soldier worked hard at woodcutting till evening, and then the witch again proposed that he should remain the night. 'You shall do one more little task for me,' she said. 'Behind my house is an old empty well into which my light has fallen. It burns blue, and will not go out; and you shall go down and fetch it up for me.'

The next day the old woman took him to the well, and let him down in a basket. He soon found the blue light, and made signs to her to pull him up again. She drew him up till he was near the brink, and stretched out her hand to take the light from him.

'No,' said he, perceiving her wicked intentions; 'I do not give up the light till I am standing with both feet on the ground.'

On this the witch flew into a rage, let him fall back again into the well, and went away. The poor soldier flew, without taking any harm, on the moist ground of the well. The blue light was still burning; but how could that help him? He saw plainly that death must come to him at last, and he sat for a while feeling quite sorrowful. By chance he put his hand in his pocket, and found his tobacco pipe half full of tobacco. 'That shall be my last comfort,' thought he, and, taking it out, he lighted it at the blue light, and began to smoke.

The smoke had no sooner ascended in the air, than he saw standing before him a little dark man, who said, 'Master, what is your pleasure?'

'What have you to do with what pleases me?' answered the soldier, in wonder.

'I must do all that you bid me,' he replied.

'Good,' said the soldier; 'then first help me out of this well.'

The little man took him by the hand, and led him through an underground passage; but he did not forget to take the blue light with him. Then he showed him the hidden treasures which the witch had collected together and concealed underground, and the soldier took away as much gold as he could carry. As soon as they were above ground again, he said to the little man, 'Now go in and bind the witch, and carry her before the judge.'

Not long after out she came, riding swift as the wind, on a wild cat, and screaming frightfully. In a very short time, however, the little man returned, and said, 'It is all right, and the witch is already hanging on the gallows. Now, master, what is your pleasure?'

'At this moment, nothing,' replied the soldier. 'You can go home; but be at hand to answer when I call you.'

'It is not necessary to call me,' he said; 'you have only to light your pipe at the blue light and I shall immediately stand before you.' Then he vanished from his eyes.

The soldier went back into the town from which he had wandered. He took up his abode at the best inn, ordered new clothes, and desired the landlord to have a room furnished for him as elegantly as possible.'

When it was ready, and he had taken possession of it, he summoned the little man, and said to him, 'I have served the king faithfully for many years, but he sent me away and left me to starve; therefore now I will have my revenge.'

'What am I to do?' asked the mannikin.

'Late in the evening,' he replied, 'when the princess is in bed and asleep, fetch her from the castle and bring her here; she shall be my maid-servant.'

Then said the little man: 'For me this is a very trifling task, and I will do it; but for you it is a very dangerous thing to do, for if it should be found out, you will suffer for it.'

As the clock struck twelve the door sprung open, and the little man appeared carrying the king's daughter. 'Aha! there you are,' cried the soldier, 'fresh to your work; go and fetch the broom and sweep the floor.' When this was finished he called her to his chair, stretched out his foot towards her, and said, 'Pull off my boot.' When she had done so he threw it in her face, and told her to pick it up and clean and polish it. She did all that he told her without resistance, mutely, and with half-closed eyes. At the first cockcrow the little man carried her back to the castle, and placed her again in her bed.

The next morning, when she rose, she went to her father, and told him she had had such a wonderful dream. She said she had dreamed that she was carried through the streets as quick as lightning to a room in which was a soldier, who made her wait upon him, and do all kinds of menial work, such as sweeping the room and cleaning his boots. 'It was only a dream,' she said, 'and yet I feel as tired as if I had really done it all.'

'The dream could not possibly have been true,' said the king; 'however, to make sure, I will advise you what to do. Fill your pocket full of peas, and make a little hole in it, so that if you are really carried away in the night, they will fall out and leave a trace behind you in the street.'

While the king spoke the little man, who was invisible, stood by him, and heard all he said.

That night, when he carried the sleeping princess through the streets, the peas fell out of her pocket; but they left no trace, for the cunning little man had strewed peas beforehand in all the streets. And she was obliged, therefore, again to be servant to the soldier till the cock crowed.

The following morning the king sent his servants out to find the track; but it was quite impossible, for the streets were crowded with poor children gathering up canfuls of peas, and saying: 'It has been raining peas all night!'

'We must think of something else,' said the king. 'You had better keep on your shoes when you go to bed, and before you come back, if you are carried away, leave one of them behind wherever you are, then I am sure to find it.'

The little man heard of the king's plan, and in the evening, when the soldier desired him to fetch the princess, he advised him not to do so again.

'Against this contrivance there is no way to avoid discovery,' he said, 'and, if the shoe is found here, the king can do you great injury.'

'Do as I tell you!' cried the soldier, and so the princess was for the third night brought to work as a servant-maid. Before she was carried back, however, she took off her shoe, and placed it under the soldier's bed.

The next morning the king ordered search to be made all over the town for his daughter's shoe, and it was found in the soldier's room. The soldier, who had begged the little man not to let them open the door, was seized and carried off to prison. In his fright he forgot to take with him his best and most valuable possessions, the blue light and the gold, and he had, therefore, only a ducat in his pocket. As he stood loaded with chains at the window of his prison, he saw one of his old comrades pass by, and he tapped on the window-pane, and beckoned him over.'

When the man came nearer he said to him : 'Will you be so kind as to fetch for me a little parcel that I have left at the inn, and I will give you a ducat for your trouble ?'

Away ran his comrade, and fetched him what he wanted.

As soon as the soldier was again alone, he took out his pipe, lit it, and began to smoke, and immediately the little man stood before him.

'Do not be afraid,' said he to his master, 'go with them wherever they lead you ; let what will happen, only remember to take your blue light and your pipe with you.'

The next day the trial of the soldier took place, and, although he had really done nothing very wicked, he was sentenced to death.

As he was being led away, he begged the king to grant him one last favour.

'What is it ?' asked the king.

'That I may smoke one pipe on my road,' he replied.

'You may smoke three if you like;' said the king, 'but do not suppose I shall grant you your life.'

The soldier, on this, took out his pipe, lit it ; and began to smoke ; and, as a pair of rings of smoke ascended in the air, the little man appeared with a little cudgel in his hand, and said : 'What is my master's pleasure ?'

'Knock down the false judges and their abettors to the ground,' said the soldier ; 'and do not spare the king for treating me so shamefully !'

Away flew the little man like lightning, striking right and left, here and there, and so scaring them that, if the cudged merely touched them, they fell to the ground and remained there, not daring to move. The king was terribly alarmed, and at last obliged to beg for his life. His prayer was not granted till he had promised to give his kingdom to the soldier, and his daughter to be his wife.

THE SEVEN WISE MEN.

ONCE upon a time there lived seven wise men together, and they all had different names. After much consultation, they decided to travel together through the world to seek adventures and to perform great deeds. When they first started, each walked separately, but as they considered it best to keep all together, they procured a long spear, which was very strong. This spear kept them all seven together, as they each clasped it with one hand. The cleverest and manliest, who was of course the eldest, walked first, and the others followed in a row, the youngest last.

Now it happened that they began their travels in the haymaking

month, and one day, after walking a long distance, they found themselves still some leagues from the town in which they intended to pass
the night. Twilight was coming on as they crossed a meadow, and
sometimes a cockchafer or a hornet would fly from behind a shrub or a
bush and buzz or hum round their heads. The gentleman who walked
first was terribly afraid of these intruders, and when one of them
buzzed close to his face he let fall the end of the lance, while the perspiration broke out all over him from fear. 'Listen,' he cried to his
companions, 'listen; I hear a drum.'

The second, who held the spear behind him, and had a very keen
nose, exclaimed: 'Something is without doubt near us, for I smell
powder and matches.'

At these words, the foremost of the wise men prepared to fly, and,
springing forward, quickly jumped over a hedge, and unfortunately over
the prongs of a rake which the haymakers had left there, and the steel
prong struck him an ugly blow in his face. 'Oh dear, oh dear!' he
cried; 'take me prisoner; I give myself up! I give myself up!'

The other six, running after him in confusion, one over the other,
screamed out, 'If you give yourself up so do we! if you give yourself
up so do we!'

And, after all, no enemy was there to bind them or carry them away,
and at last they discovered that they had made a great mistake. In
their fear of being laughed at and called fools by the people of the
town, they swore among themselves not to open their mouths to anyone of what had happened, but to keep it quiet. Then they again
started on their journey, consoling themselves with the reflection that
the second danger which might threaten them could not certainly
compare with the first. For some days nothing occurred, but one
morning, on passing through an unploughed field, they saw a hare
lying asleep in the sun, with her large ears raised, and her glassy eyes
wide open. They were so terrified at the sight of the wild and horrible
creature that they held a council together as to the least dangerous
way of passing it. At first they wished to fly from it, but if they did,
most likely the monster would follow them, seize them, and swallow
them up. 'But,' said one, 'as we must go on, it is better to prepare
for a great combat. To venture is half to win.'

Then they all seven seized the spear, and walked on cautiously, the
eldest foremost and the youngest behind. Mr. Pride, as the eldest
called himself, was not always able to hold the spear, from fright, but
the youngest, who was behind, feeling very courageous, began to sing.
The rest followed his example, one after another, till it came to Mr.
Pride's turn, and he said very gravely:

> 'In the town from roof and steeple,
> Soon they'll see some clever people.'

They were now approaching the dreadful dragon, still keeping close
together, and Brother Stultz crossed himself. As, however, this was

not much help, and they were approaching nearer to their dreaded enemy, they all screamed out in alarm, 'Hie! hie! ho ho! ho hi!' The noise woke the hare, who started up in a fright and sprung away like wind. When Brother Stultz saw her flying through the field, he cried, full of joy:

> 'See, brothers, just see what is there!
> The frightful monster is a hare!'

The band of seven wise men then continued their journey in search of fresh adventures, and at length arrived at the Blue Moselle, with its calm and deep waters, over which are so few bridges. The usual way, however, is to travel from place to place in boats or ships. When the seven wise men had reached the shore they called to a man who was at work on the opposite side and asked him how they were to get over.

The man understood very little of the question, partly from the distance of the voices, and partly because of the strange phraseology used by these wise men. So he cried out very distinctly, 'What! what!'* Then Brother Stultz thought the man meant that they were to wade across through the water. So as he was foremost, he advanced to the edge of the bank and at once stepped into the water; the next moment he sank in the mud and was drawn down by the deep waves. His hat, however, was carried by the wind to the opposite shore, and a frog, seating himself upon it, croaked, 'What! what! what!'* The other six heard it, and said one to another, 'Our companion, Brother Stultz, is calling us; if he can wade across why should not we also?'

Then they all ran down to the water in great haste to follow him, and were soon drowned; so the frog was the cause of the death of six, at least it is supposed so, for not one of the seven wise men ever returned to their homes.

THE FEARLESS PRINCE.

THERE was once a king's son so courageous that the quiet of his father's house did not please him at all, and he thought if he could go out into the world, it would not be long before he met with some wonderful adventures. So he took leave of his parents and started on his journey, and kept wandering on farther and farther, for it mattered not to him which way the road led him.

He went on till at last he came to a house inhabited by giants, and feeling very tired, he seated himself before the door to rest; but he was not inclined to sleep, so he let his eyes wander about here and there, and at last they rested on an immense ball, and skittles as tall as a man, which lay in the outer court, and were the giant's playthings.

* German, 'Was, was, was.'

After looking at them for some minutes, a longing came over him to try and play a game. So he rose, placed the skittles up, and rolled the great ball at them with all his might. In his delight at finding that he could make the skittles fall, he cried aloud and made such a noise that the giants stretched out their necks from the window, to see what was the matter.

As soon as they saw a little fellow not bigger than other men playing with their skittles, they were astonished, and cried out: 'You little worm, do you suppose you have the strength to play with our skittles, or even to lift our ball?'

The prince looked up, and when he saw the giants, he exclaimed: 'Oh, you clodhoppers! you think that no one has any strength but yourselves. You look here, now; I can do anything I like.'

The giants on this came out, and were quite astonished when they saw how cleverly he played with their skittles. At last one of them said: 'You little child of a man, as you are so clever, I wish you would go and fetch me a golden apple from the top of an enchanted tree.'

'What do you want it for?' asked the youth.

'Oh, not for myself,' he replied; 'but I have a sweetheart who wishes for one very much; I have been all over the world, but I could never find the tree.'

'I will find it,' said the king's son, 'and I should like to see anyone try to prevent me from getting an apple and carrying it away, if I choose.'

'Ah,' said the giant, 'it is not so easy as you think. I have heard that the garden in which the tree grows has iron railings all round it, and outside these railings lie a number of wild beasts close together, who keep watch, and allow no one to enter.'

'They will let me pass,' he said.

'Even if they do,' replied the giant, 'your difficulties are not over, for you will have to find the right tree, and, when it is found, the thing is not done. On the tree hangs a ring, through which you must put your hand to reach the apple you wish to pluck, or else you will not succeed.'

'I mean to succeed,' said the prince.

He then took leave of the giants, and went away over hill and valley, through fields and woods, till at last he found the wonderful garden. Wild animals were crouching round it, but their heads were lowered, for they slept. He had to step over them, however, but he did it so cautiously that they did not wake; so he climbed over the railings, and found himself in the garden without having been molested.

In the middle of the garden stood the enchanted tree, and the rosy golden apples glittered on its boughs. He climbed up the stem, and just as he discovered the apple he wanted, he saw the ring hanging before him. He put his hand through it without trouble, and broke off the apple, but on drawing it back he found that the ring closed tightly over his arm, and he felt through every vein a rush of new strength. He climbed down from the tree, and now did not care to jump over the railings, but went to the great gate, and had only to give it one shake, and it opened wide immediately for him to pass through.

As he went out, a lion, who appeared to be lying there waiting for him, sprung up, not in anger or wildness, but to follow him meekly, as as dog follows his master. The prince travelled back with all speed to the giant, and gave him the promised apple, and said to him: 'See, I have fetched it for you without any trouble.'

The giant, who was very much pleased that his wish had been accomplished, hastened to his sweetheart, and gave her the apple which she so desired to have. But she was a clever as well as a beautiful maiden, and she saw that the ring was not on the giant's arm, as she knew it must be if he had plucked the apple. So she said: 'I will not believe that this is the apple I want unless you can show me the ring on your arm.'

'Oh,' said the giant, 'I need only go home and fetch it for you.'

He thought it was a very easy thing for him to take it away by force from the weak little man, whether he was willing or not. But the king's son refused to give it up.

'Where the apple is, there must the ring be,' said the giant; 'and if you do not give it up willingly, you must fight for it.'

On this a struggle commenced, and continued for a long time; but the giant could not overcome the prince, because of the strength given to him by the enchanted ring. So the giant tried stratagem.

'This fighting has made me very warm,' he said, 'and you appear heated also. Suppose we go down to the river and bathe; that will cool us.'

The king's son, who suspected nothing, was taken off his guard, and went down with the giant to the water, threw off his clothes, and with them the ring from his arm, and jumped into the water. In a moment the giant seized the ring and ran off with it; but the lion, who had followed them unseen, quickly observing the theft, sprang after him, tore the ring from his hand, and carried it back to his master.

The giant, on this, placed himself behind an oak, and, while the prince was engaged in putting on his clothes, he struck him from behind a violent blow, that blinded him in both eyes.

The poor prince now stood helpless; for he was blind, and knew not how to help himself. The giant, however, approached, and, seizing his hand as if he were going to lead him home, dragged him to the top of a high rock, and left him standing near the edge.

'Ah,' thought the giant, as he went away, 'two steps more, and he will fall headlong and kill himself, and then I shall get the ring.'

But the faithful lion had not left his master; he now held him fast by the clothes, and pulled him gradually back.

When the giant returned, expecting to find the prince dead, he saw that all his cunning had been fruitless.

'Is a little weak child of man to conquer me like this?' said the giant, in a rage with himself; so he seized the king's son, and dragged him again to another precipice. But the lion knew his wicked intentions, and also here saved his master from the danger. When they came near the edge of the precipice, the giant let fall the hand of the blind prince, and turned to go back alone; but at this very moment the lion gave the giant a push, and over he went, fell on the ground below, and was smashed to pieces.

The faithful lion now drew his master again back from the edge of the abyss, and led him to a tree by which flowed a clear brook. The prince seated himself under the tree, and the lion, lying down by his side, splashed the water in his master's face with his paws. A few drops fell on the injured eyes, and presently he could see, but indistinctly, a bird that flew near him, and struck himself against the tree, as if his eyes also were dim. Immediately the bird flew down to the brook, and bathed himself in it; after this, he again flew up to a branch of the tree, this time without striking himself, but like one whose sight has been restored.

Then the prince understood what to do; he stooped over the water, and washed and bathed his face and eyes with it, and when he rose up, his eyes were as clear and bright as they had ever been in his life.

With his heart full of thankfulness for this great mercy, he travelled on farther through the wood, his faithful lion following, and, after a time, they approached an enchanted castle.

At the gate of the castle stood a maiden with a beautiful face and form, but she was quite black. She spoke to him, and said, 'Ah! if you could only set me free from the sorcerer's spell which is over me!'

'How am I to do it?' asked the youth.

'It is difficult,' said the maiden; 'you will have to stay for three nights in the large hall of the enchanted castle; but you must have no fear in your heart. And if you can be firm enough to endure all that occurs, without a sound or an expression of pain or vexation, for no one can dare to take your life, then I am free.'

'I have no fear,' said the king's son, 'and I therefore am ready to make the attempt.'

He went into the castle full of spirits, and, as it grew dark, seated himself in the great hall, and waited. About midnight, he heard suddenly a great noise, and presently, from every nook and corner, rushed out little imps. They appeared for a time not to see him; but, after lighting a fire, they seated themselves in the middle of the room, and began to gamble with cards and dice.

After a while, one of the losers cried out, 'I am sure some one is here who does not belong to us, and it will be his own fault if he gets the worst of it.'

'Wait you there, behind the stove,' cried another; 'I am coming.'

On this, the noise became so tremendous that, without shrieking, no one could have made himself heard. The prince sat calm and still, and had no fear, till, at last, they all rushed upon him suddenly, and they were so many that he could not avoid them. They pulled him down on the ground, and then pinched, and pricked, and thumped, and tormented him; but he uttered not a sound of fear or complaint.

At the first dawn of morning, however, they all vanished, and he lay still, quite worn out, for he could scarcely move his limbs. At sunrise the black maiden came in. She carried in her hand a little flask, containing healing waters, and with this she washed and bathed his limbs, and as she did so, all his pain vanished, and he felt new strength coursing through his veins.

'You have luckily kept firm for one night,' she said; 'but there are still two nights more before you.'

As she left him, he noticed that her feet were already white.

On the following night the little imps came again, and began their game anew, and with fresh violence. They beat and tormented the king's son much more cruelly than on the former night, so that he was covered with wounds; but he bore it all in silence, till they were at last obliged to leave him, and, at the first blush of morning, the young maiden appeared with her healing water, which soon restored him.

As she turned to go away, he saw that her skin had already become white on her arms and neck; only her face still remained black, and he determined to hold out for one more night, and this proved the worst of all.

'So you are still here!' screamed the imps, when they saw him. 'Well, you shall be tormented this time till there is no breath left in your body.'

They beat and pinched him, threw him from one place to another, and dragged him about by the arms and legs, as if they meant to tear him to pieces; but he endured it all, and uttered no sound.

At last the imps vanished, leaving him on the ground quite exhausted, and not even able to open his eyes when the maiden came in. However, after bathing his limbs and pouring the healing water on his eyes, all the pain was relieved, and he felt quite well and strong, as one just awakened out of sleep; and when, at last, he opened his eyes, he saw the young maiden standing near, snow-white, and bright and beautiful as the day.

'Stand up,' she said, ' and swing your sword three times over the steps of the castle; then the spell of enchantment will be broken.'

He had no sooner done so than the witchcraft was at an end, and he found that a king's daughter, rich and beautiful, was its owner.

Servants came, and said that the table was already prepared for the morning meal, and the prince and princess seated themselves in the great hall, where he had suffered so much, and were very happy together; and in the evening their marriage took place.

THE WONDERFUL PLANT.

A YOUNG hunter went once into a forest, which he had heard was full of witchcraft, without hesitation, for he was brave and light-hearted, and went on his way whistling, and picking a leaf here and there with careless good-humour.

Presently an ugly little old woman met him, and said, 'Good-day, dear hunter; you are full of health and contentment, but I am suffering from hunger and thirst; pray give me something to buy food.'

The hunter did not delay to help the poor old woman; he put his hand in his pocket, and pulled out as much as he could afford and gave it to her.

He would have passed on, but the old woman held him by the coat. 'Stay, dear hunter,' said she; 'hear what I have to say to you; for your kind good-nature, I will give you some information as a reward. Go on for a little way, and you will come to a tree on which are perched nine birds, with a cloak in their claws, about which they are quarrelling. Take aim amongst them with your gun and shoot; the cloak will then fall, and one of the birds drop dead at your feet. Take up the cloak, for it possesses a wonderful power; and if you place it on your shoulders and wish yourself in any place, there you will be in that moment. You must also carry the dead bird with you, open it, and take out the heart, which you must carry in your pocket carefully; for while it is there you will find a piece of gold under your pillow every morning.'

The hunter thanked the wise woman, and went away full of joy at the good fortune she had promised him should happen. And he did not exult in vain, for he had not walked a hundred steps, when he heard in a tree above him a screaming and twittering. He looked up, and saw a whole host of birds tearing a cloth to pieces with their beaks and talons, and chirping, screaming, and pecking each other, as each wanted to have it.

'Well,' cried the hunter, 'this is wonderful! it has just happened as the old mother said.' So he levelled his gun and shot in amongst them. Oh, what a screaming and fluttering there was, and how the feathers flew about as the flock took flight! One, however, was dead, and the cloak fluttered down after them to the ground. The hunter did as the

old woman had told him; he took out the heart, wrapped it up carefully, and put it in his pocket; then he carried the cloak home.

The next morning, when he awoke, he at once wished to prove
whether the promise of the woman would be accomplished. So he
lifted his pillow, and there were the pieces of gold sparkling as they
lay. The next morning it was the same, and the next, and so it continued, as she had said it would. At last he gathered the gold into a
heap, and thought, 'What is the use of all this gold if I remain here?
I will go out and see the world.'

So he took leave of his parents, hung up his game-bag and his gun,
and set out on his travels. It so happened that one day he passed
through a dense wood, to which there seemed no end; but he saw in
the distance a noble-looking castle. At the window stood two women
looking out; one very old, the other a wonderfully beautiful maiden.

The old woman, however, was a witch, and she said to the maiden:
'Yonder comes one through the wood who has wonderful treasures
about him; we must therefore entrap him, my heart's life, and get it
from him. He has in his possession a bird's heart, and, therefore,
every morning finds a piece of gold under his pillow.'

Then she explained how she wished her daughter to act, and the sort
of game she had to play, and at last threatened her, and said, with
angry eyes, 'And if you do not obey me, misfortune will follow you all
your life.'

As the hunter drew near he espied the maiden, and said to her, 'I
have been wandering about for a long time, and if I might be allowed
to rest in this beautiful castle I have plenty of money to pay for it.'

The reason, however, of his wish to stay was in reality that he wished
to become acquainted with the beautiful maiden the moment he had
cast his eyes upon her. He was received into the house in a very
friendly manner, and entertained most courteously, and in a very short
time found himself so much in love with the bewitching maiden that he
could not bear her to be out of his sight, and whatsoever she wished
he was ready to agree to.

Then the old woman said, 'Now is the time to get the bird's heart
from him; he will not be able to discover who has taken it even when
he misses it.' So she prepared a sleeping draught, and when it was
ready she gave it to the maiden in a goblet, and told her she must coax
him to drink it.

So the maiden went to do the bidding of the old witch, who was not,
however, her real mother, and she said to the hunter, 'Dearest, drink
with me, will you?'

Instantly he took the glass and drank a large draught, and in a few
minutes fell into a deep sleep.

Then she searched in all his pockets, but it was not there; and, after
great trouble, she at last found it in a little bag hanging round his neck.
The maiden carried it to the old woman, who fastened it at once round
the maiden's neck. The next morning the hunter found no money

under his pillow; for the piece of gold lay under the pillow of the maiden, and from whence the old woman fetched it every morning. But the hunter was so completely in love, and so foolishly fond of the maiden, that he cared for nothing else so long as he had her by his side.

Then said the old woman, ' We have the bird's heart, and now we must have the wishing-cloak.'

' We must leave him that,' said the maiden ; ' for he has lost all his riches already.'

At this the old woman was angry, and said, 'The cloak is a wonderful thing, seldom found in this world, so I must and will have it !' She gave the maiden a slap as she spoke, and said, ' If you do not obey me it will be dreadful for you.'

She could not obey the commands of the old woman at first, but went and stood by the open window, and looked out on the wide prospect, feeling very sad.

There the hunter found her, and he asked, ' Why are you standing here, and looking so sad, my treasure ?'

' Ah !' she replied, ' I know that in yonder mountain of granite the most costly precious stones can be found. I have such a great longing to see them ; but it is too far to go, and it makes me very sad when I think of it. We could not fetch any ; for only birds who can fly can possibly rise so high as that mountain—human beings never.'

' You shall have no occasion to complain of this difficulty any longer,' said the hunter ; ' I will soon remove this sorrow from your heart.'

Immediately he threw on his cloak, seized her in his arms, and wished himself over on the granite mountain, and in a moment they were both there. The glittering and sparkling stones lay around them on very side, so that it was quite a joy to see them ; and the hunter and the maiden gathered the most beautiful and costly to carry away with them.

Now the witch, by her witchcraft, had still power over the hunter, even at that distance ; so she caused his eyes to become so heavy that he could not keep them open.

So he said to the maiden, ' We will sit down here and rest; for I am so tired that I can scarcely put one foot before the other.'

Then she seated herself, and he placed his head in her lap, and was very soon fast asleep.

While he slept she unfastened the cloak from his shoulder and hung it on her own, gathered up the precious stones from the granite mountain, and wished herself at home.

When the hunter had finished his nap and awoke, he found that his beloved had betrayed him, and left him alone on the wild mountain. ' Ah !' he exclaimed, ' was ever such deceit in the world as this !' and for a time sat quite still, his heart so overwhelmed with sorrow and care that he knew not what to do.

The mountain, however, belonged to wild and monstrous giants, who resided within it; and it was not long before he saw three of them striding towards him. He instantly laid himself down again, and appeared to be in a deep sleep. Up came the giants, and the first pushed him with his foot.

'Crush him with your foot,' said the second.

'Ah!' said the third scornfully, 'he is not worth the trouble; let him live! He cannot remain here and live; and if he attempts to climb higher, to the top of the mountain, the clouds will soon take him up and carry him away.'

On this the giants passed on, and as soon as they were out of sight, the hunter, who had heard every word, stood up, and climbed at once to the mountain summit.

After he had been seated there a little while, a cloud floating by caught him up, and carried him away through the air for a long time, till at last it sank down and left him on the ground in a large vegetable garden, surrounded by walls.

The hunter raised himself and looked round.

'I am very hungry,' he said, 'but what is there here to eat? No apples, or pears, or fruit of any kind; nothing but vegetables, and the best are only cabbages.'

At last he thought that in a time of need a salad was better than nothing, especially when it was fresh.

So he searched for what appeared to be a beautiful cabbage, cut it off, and began to eat. No sooner had he swallowed two mouthfuls than a strange sensation came over him, and he felt himself becoming quite changed. His arms were growing to legs, his head became thicker, and out of it grew two long ears, and he discovered with terror that he had been changed into an ass. Still his hunger urged him to go on eating the juicy vegetable, which to his new nature tasted so good, till it was all gone. Then he turned to another part of the garden and commenced eating another, but he had scarcely swallowed any of this one when he found himself changed anew, and presently he recovered his former shape as a man.

After this the hunter laid himself down and slept, from exhaustion and fatigue, till the morning. When he awoke he broke off one of the good and one of the bad vegetables, and carried them away with him; and thought, 'These shall be the means by which I shall be able to punish those who were so unfaithful to me.'

Then he concealed the two cabbage heads under his coat, climbed over the wall, and went away to seek the castle where his sweetheart lived.

After wandering about for a few days, he luckily found it again; but before entering he stained his face, neck, and hands with brown juice, that the old woman might not recognise him, went up to the door of the castle, and begged for a night's lodging.

'I am so tired,' he said, 'I cannot go any farther.'

The witch on this came out and said:

'Countryman, who are you, and what is your business?'

'I am a messenger of the king,' he replied, 'and have been sent to seek the costliest salad that grows under the sun. I have been also fortunate enough to find what I sought and to bring it with me; but the burning heat of the sun dries up the costly vegetable, and I know not how to carry it any farther without placing it in water.'

When the old woman heard of this delicate salad, she longed so much to taste it that she said:

'Dear friend, let me see this beautiful salad.'

'With all my heart,' he said; 'I have two heads, and you are quite welcome to one.' So he opened his bag, and gave her the bad one. The old witch never thought of anything wrong, and her mouth watered so much at the thought of such a dish, that she went at once to the kitchen to prepare it.

When it was ready, she could not wait till it was placed on the table, but took two or three leaves and put them in her mouth. No sooner had she swallowed them than her human form was lost, and she ran out, in the shape of an ass, into the yard of the castle.

Meanwhile, the maid-servant came into the kitchen, and seeing a beautiful salad standing on the table, she could not resist tasting it. The consequences were the same: after eating a few leaves, she also was changed into an ass, and ran out after her mistress, while the dish of salad fell to the ground.

In the meantime, the pretended messenger sat with the beautiful maiden, and as no one came with the salad, and she wished very much to taste it, she said:

'I wonder why they don't bring in the salad.'

'Oh,' thought the hunter, 'it must be ready by this time, and perhaps has already produced its wonderful changes.' So he said: 'I will go into the kitchen and inquire.' When he reached the kitchen, he saw the two asses running about the yard, and the salad lying on the ground.

'All right,' said he; 'those two have had their share.' Then he gathered up from the floor the scattered leaves, laid them on a dish, and brought them to the maiden. 'I have brought you some of this delicate dish,' said he, 'that you might not wait any longer.'

She ate some of the wonderful leaves, and in a moment her delicate form was changed, and she also was an ass, and ran out to the court of the castle with the other two.

After this, the hunter washed the dark stain from his face, and, that they might recognise the change, he went out into the court and said:

'This is now your reward for your treacherous conduct to me.'

Then he tied them all together with a rope, and led them away till they came to a mill. He knocked at the window, and the miller put his head out, and asked what was his pleasure.

'I have three troublesome animals here,' he replied, 'and I cannot keep them any longer. Will you take care of them for a time, and provide them with fodder and shelter, and I will pay you whatever you ask for your trouble?'

'Well,' said the miller, 'I am quite willing; but how am I to manage these unruly brutes?'

'Oh,' replied the hunter, 'that one'—pointing to the old witch— 'requires good flogging and little food; the dark one'—which was the maid—'you may feed pretty well, and perhaps she will require a little chastisement sometimes; but this delicate one requires good food and no beating.'

For, treacherous as the maiden had been to him, he could not find it in his heart to have her beaten. After this he went back to the castle, and whatever was necessary for his own comfort he found there.

In two days came the miller, and said that the old ass who required so much beating was dead.

'The other two,' he added, 'who have had as much to eat as they like, are not quite dead, but they are so unhappy that I do not think they will live long.'

Then the hunter allowed his anger to cool. He pitied the two young girls whom he had punished, and he told the miller to bring them back immediately. The moment they arrived he gave them some of the good salad to eat, and they at once recovered their human shape.

The maiden then fell on her knees before the hunter, and exclaimed: 'Forgive me, dearest, for all the wicked things I did to you; my old stepmother forced me to do it all against my will, for I have always loved you from my heart. Your wishing-cloak hangs in the cupboard, and I will find the bird's heart for you to-morrow. My old mother took it from me.'

After this confession all the hunter's thoughts of revenge were changed.

'Never mind what has passed!' he cried; 'I can keep you now, and you shall be my own dear wife.'

The marriage took place soon after, and they lived in great happiness with each other till their death.

THE ENCHANTED TREE.

A POOR servant-maid was once travelling through a wood with her master and mistress, when they were attacked by robbers, who came out of the thicket and murdered all that passed that way. None of the party escaped, excepting the maid-servant, who in the fight had sprung aside, and hidden herself behind a tree.

As soon as the robbers had made off with their booty, she ventured out of her hiding-place, and saw what dreadful trouble had happened.

Then she began to weep bitterly, and said: 'What shall I, a poor maiden, do now? I know not how to find my way out of the wood, for not a living creature dwells here, and I shall certainly be starved to death.'

She tried to find a way out of the wood, however, but without success. At length, tired out, she seated herself under a tree, and determined to remain there, whatever might happen, without attempting to go away, and trust in Heaven to help her.

After she had been sitting there a short time, a white dove flew down from the tree, and he carried in his beak a little golden key. This golden key he placed in the hand of the maiden, and said: 'Do you see yonder a large tree? On it is a little lock, which can be opened with that key. If you open it you will find plenty to eat and drink, and to relieve the pain of hunger from which you are suffering.'

She went to the tree, unlocked it, and found to her surprise a basin full of white bread and milk, so that she could eat and be satisfied. When she had finished she said to herself: 'This is the time for the chickens to go home to roost; I am so tired I wish I had a bed to lie on.'

Again the white dove flew down, and brought another key, and said: 'Unlock the tree with this, and you will find a bed!'

She did as she was told, and there she found a pretty little white bed, and, praying to Heaven to watch over her during the night, she laid herself down and slept.

In the morning came the dove the third time, and brought her another little key, and said: 'Unlock the tree again, and you will find clothes!'

And when she did so, there she saw beautiful dresses embroidered with gold and precious stones, such as none but a king's daughter could wear.

She remained after this for a long time in the wood, and the dove came every day and took care of her. She was poor, but it was a peaceable and happy life.

At last the dove came one day, and said to her, 'Will you do something for me, only for love?'

'With all my heart,' she replied.

Then said the dove, 'I will take you to a small cottage on the heath, in which lives an old woman. When you go in she will say, "Good-day" to you; for your life give her no reply; let her do what she may, but turn away to the right, and you will see a door, which you must open, and in the room on a table lies a heap of rings of all sorts and descriptions, some of them set with beautiful and glittering precious stones. But leave all these alone, and look only for a plain gold ring which must be among them, and bring it to me as quickly as you can.'

The maiden hastened to do the commands of the little dove. He led her to the house, and she stepped in.

There sat the old woman, and said, 'Good-day, my child.' But she gave no reply, and went on to the other door. As she was opening it

the old woman cried : ' Where are you going ?   This is my house—no
one can enter there without my permission,' and she seized her by the
dress, and tried to hold her fast.   But the maiden kept silent, freed
herself from the old woman's grasp, and went right into the room.

There on the table lay an immense number of rings that shone and
glittered before her eyes ; but she threw them on one side, and searched
for the plain one, which, however, she could not find.

While she was searching, she happened to look up, and saw the old
woman slipping away with a bird-cage in her hand.   The maiden
followed her out quickly, took the cage from her ; and, as she opened
it and looked inside, there was a bird with the plain ring in its beak.

She took the ring, and went away full of joy from the house, and
was soon back to the tree where she expected to see the white dove
waiting for her ; for she expected him to fetch the ring, but he did not
come.   While she waited, she leaned against the tree, and, as she so
stood, she felt that the tree became soft and flexible, and the branches
sunk down.

All at once two of the branches wound themselves round her, and
they were the arms of a human being ; and, as she looked up, she saw
that the tree had changed to a handsome man, who kissed her, and
pressed her to his heart, and said : ' You have broken the spell, and
delivered me from the power of the old woman, who is a wicked witch.
She changed me into a tree, and every day for two hours I was able to
take the form of a white dove ; but so long as she kept the ring I could
not recover my human form.'

At the same time the horses and servants were set free from the
witchcraft, for they also had been changed into trees, and stood near
their master.

Then they all travelled away to his kingdom, for he was a king's
son, and he took the maiden with him, and made her his wife.

THE FOUR CLEVER BROTHERS.

A POOR man had four sons, who were nearly grown up, and one day he
called them to him, and said, ' Dear children, you must now go out
into the world and earn your own living.   I have nothing to give you,
so you had better choose some trade at which you can work, and when
you have learnt it you can make a fortune.'

Then the four brothers took each a traveller's staff, said farewell to
their father, and went away from the door together.   When they had
travelled some little distance, they arrived at a point where four roads
met and crossed each other.   Then said the eldest, ' Here we had
better separate, and this day four years we will again meet together in
this spot, and in the meantime seek our fortune.'

So each went his way, and the eldest presently met a man who asked him where he was going, and what he wanted. 'I wish to learn a trade,' he replied.

'Oh,' said the man, 'go with me, and learn to be a thief.'

'No,' replied the youth; 'that would unfit me for any respectable trade afterwards, and the end is trouble, or to swing at last, like a clapper in a bell.'

'Oh,' replied the man, 'there is no fear of the gallows in my trade; I will only teach you to accomplish what other people cannot attain to, and so cleverly that no man can ever find it out.'

So he allowed himself to be persuaded, and was instructed by the man so well that he became quite skilful in sleight of hand, and at last in his presence no one knew if what he held belonged to him or not.

The second brother also met a man, who asked him, in a similar way, what he would like to learn in the world.

'I do not know,' he replied.

'Ah, well, then go with me, said he, 'and become a star-gazer. There is no trade better than that, for nothing can be hidden from you.'

So the second brother became an astronomer, and so very clever that his master, when he left him, made him a present of a beautiful tele- scope, and said to him, 'With this you can discover whatever is going on both in heaven and earth; nothing can be hidden from you.'

A hunter took the third brother under his tuition, and taught him everything that a clever hunter should know, and gave him such good instruction that very few hunters could equal him.

On parting, his master presented him with a gun, and said ,'What- ever you aim at with this you will not fail to hit.'

The youngest brother also met with a man who entered into conver- sation with him about his future, and asked him if he should like to be a tailor.

'I think not,' replied the youth; 'the cramped position from morn- ing to night, and the constant in-and-out sewing with the needle and thread, and the ironing with the tailor's goose, would not suit me at all.'

'Ah, indeed,' replied the man, 'you are talking of what you do not understand; with me you would learn something far more respectable and seemly; quite another description of tailor's work, in which you could take an honourable part.'

So he allowed himself to be talked over, and went with the man, who taught him to sew so neatly that he could make old articles look new, for not a stitch was visible.

When his master took leave of him he gave him a needle, and said: 'You can with that needle repair whatever comes in your way, were it as soft as an egg-shell, or as hard as steel, and it will join anything so beautifully that not even the seam will be visible.'

At the end of the appointed four years, the brothers met together at the cross roads, and embraced and kissed each other, and then turned towards home to visit their father.

He was quite pleased to see them, and said, 'It is a pleasant wind which has blown you all back to me again.'

Then they each related to him where they had travelled, and what each had learnt.

They were all seated in front of the house, under a great tree, and their father said, 'I should like to see very much what you can all do, and to prove whether you are as clever as you say. He looked up as he spoke, and said to his second son, 'Among the branches of this tree, near the top, sits a bullfinch on her nest ; tell me how many eggs are there ?'

The star-gazer took his glass, looked up, and said, 'There are five.'

Then the father said to the eldest, 'Go and fetch the eggs, without disturbing the bird who sits brooding upon them.'

The accomplished thief climbed up the tree, took the five eggs from under the bird so quietly that she never noticed it, but remained sitting in her nest quite peacefully, and brought them down to his father. The father took them, placed them on a table, one at each corner, and the fifth in the middle, and said to the hunter, 'Can you, with one shot, divide those five eggs in half ?'

The hunter pointed his gun, and shot the eggs as his father desired— all five completely, with one shot.

'Now,' said the father to the youngest, 'here is a trial of your skill. Can you join those eggs together so that the young birds that are half formed in them may still grow to perfection, and suffer no injury from the shot ?'

The tailor took out his needles, and sewed up the eggs as his father wished. When they were finished, the thief had again to climb up the tree and lay the eggs under the bird without disturbing her or attracting her notice. The little creature continued to brood over her eggs, and in a few days the young ones crept out of the shells uninjured, excepting that where the tailor had sewn the eggs together a red streak appeared on their necks.

Then the old man said to his sons : 'I must praise you for the cleverness of the trades you have learnt. You have employed your time most usefully, and I cannot tell which deserves the preference. If an opportunity would only arise to employ these talents, and prove them, it might be the making of you.'

And it was not long before such an opportunity did occur. A great outcry arose in the country—the king's daughter had been carried away by a dragon. Day and night the king mourned her loss, and made a proclamation that he would give his daughter in marriage to whoever would bring her back. The four brothers talked together about this, and said it really was an opportunity for them to prove their skill, and they determined to go together and try to release the princess from the dragon.

' I will first find out where she is,' said the star-gazer; so he raised his telescope, looked through it, and said: ' I can see her already; she is far away from here, sitting on a rock in the sea, and near her is the dragon, whom she is watching.' Then he went to the king, and begged him to let him and his brothers have a ship to seek the princess; and when it was ready, they sailed away over the sea till they came to the rock.

There sat the king's daughter, looking very sad, and the dragon, who was fast asleep, had his dreadful head in her lap.

The hunter said: ' I could aim at the dragon and kill him, but I dare not shoot lest I should kill the beautiful princess.'

' I will try my luck,' said the thief; so he climbed up the rock and stole the princess away from under the dragon's head so lightly and nimbly that the monster did not move, but went on snoring hideously. They hastened away full of joy with her, and steered for the open sea.

But the dragon soon after awoke, and, missing the princess, was in a terrible rage. He rose in the air and followed, snorting vengeance as he hovered over the ship, and seemed about to pounce down on them like a hawk on a brood of chickens. But at this moment the hunter levelled his gun and shot him through the heart.

Terrible consequences followed: the monster was at the moment hovering over the ship, and consequently he fell dead upon it, crushing it beneath his great weight, and making it a complete wreck. Happily they contrived to catch hold of a few planks, on which they were able to float on the waves, but they were still in great danger.

The tailor, however, took out his wonderful needle, and with a few great stitches sewed the planks quickly together so that they formed a raft; then they seated themselves upon it, and gathered up the fragments of the ship. These, also the masts and sails, he sewed cleverly together, so that in a very short time the ship was again ready for sea, and they were able to complete the voyage home safely and without further difficulty.

When the king again saw his daughter, his joy knew no bounds, and he said to the four brothers:

' One of you shall have my daughter, but which it is to be you must decide among yourselves.'

Then arose a violent contention amongst them, for each claimed his right to the princess.

The star-gazer said:

' If I had not discovered first where the king's daughter was, all your art would have been useless, so she must be mine.'

Then said the thief:

' And after you had seen her, what would have been the use of that if I had not taken her away from under the dragon's head? Therefore she is mine.'

' Ah !' exclaimed the hunter, ' even then the king's daughter would have been torn to pieces by the dragon, had I not killed him with my bullet. Therefore she is mine.'

' And,' exclaimed the tailor, 'if I had not been there with my skill to sew together the planks and sails of the ship, you and the princess would all have been drowned. Therefore I have the greatest claim to the princess.'

Upon this the king spoke:

' Each of you,' he said, ' has an equal claim; but as you cannot all have the maiden, I shall not give her to either of you; but you shall for a reward have the half of my kingdom to divide amongst yourselves.'

The brothers were much pleased with this decision, and they said ·

' It is better so, than that we should fall out and be at variance.'

So they shared the half of the kingdom between them, and lived with their father in great comfort and happiness for the rest of their lives.

ONE EYE, TWO EYES, THREE EYES.

THERE was once a woman who had three daughters, of whom the eldest was named ' One Eye,' because she had only one eye in the middle of her forehead. The second had two eyes, like other people, and she was called ' Two Eyes.' The youngest had three eyes, two like her second sister, and one in the middle of her forehead, like the eldest, and she bore the name of ' Three Eyes.'

Now because little Two Eyes looked just like other people, her mother and sisters could not endure her. They said to her, ' You are not better than common folks, with your two eyes; you don't belong to us.'

So they pushed her about, and threw all their old clothes to her for her to wear, and gave her only the pieces that were left to eat, and did everything that they could to make her miserable. It so happened that little Two Eyes was sent into the fields to take care of the goats, and she was often very hungry, although her sisters had as much as they liked to eat. So one day she seated herself on a mound in the field, and began to weep and cry so bitterly that two little rivulets flowed from her eyes. Once, in the midst of her sorrow she looked up, and saw a woman standing near her who said, ' What are you weeping for, little Two Eyes?'

' I cannot help weeping,' she replied; ' for because I have two eyes, like other people, my mother and sisters cannot bear me; they push me about from one corner to another and make me wear their old clothes, and give me nothing to eat but what is left, so that I am always hungry. To-day they gave me so little that I am nearly starved.'

' Dry up your tears, little Two Eyes,' said the wise woman; ' I will tell you something to do which will prevent you from ever being hungry again. You have only to say to your own goat:

'"Little goat, if you're able,
Pray deck out my table."

and immediately there will be a pretty little table before you full of all sorts of good things for you to eat, as much as you like. And when you have had enough, and you do not want the table any more, you need only say:

'"Little goat, when you're able,
Remove my nice table."

and it will vanish from your eyes.'

Then the wise woman went away. 'Now,' thought little Two Eyes, 'I will try if what she says is true, for I am very hungry,' so she said:

'Little goat, if you're able,
Pray deck out my table.'

The words were scarcely spoken, when a beautiful little table stood really before her; it had a white cloth and plates, and knives and forks, and silver spoons, and such a delicious dinner, smoking hot as if it had just come from the kitchen. Then little Two Eyes sat down and said the shortest grace she knew—'Pray God be our guest for all time. Amen'—before she allowed herself to taste anything. But oh, how she did enjoy her dinner! and when she had finished, she said, as the wise woman had taught her:

'Little goat, when you're able,
Remove my nice table.'

In a moment, the table and everything upon it had disappeared. 'That is a pleasant way to keep house,' said little Two Eyes, and felt quite contented and happy. In the evening, when she went home with the goat, she found an earthenware dish with some scraps which her sisters had left for her, but she did not touch them. The next morning she went away with the goat, leaving them behind where they had been placed for her. The first and second times that she did so, the sisters did not notice it; but when they found it happened every day, they said one to the other, 'There is something strange about little Two Eyes, she leaves her supper every day, and all that has been put for her has been wasted; she must get food somewhere else.'

So they determined to find out the truth, and they arranged that when Two Eyes took her goat to the field, One Eye should go with her to take particular notice of what she did, and discover if anything was brought for her to eat and drink.

So when Two Eyes started with her goat, One Eye said to her, 'I am going with you to-day to see if the goat gets her food properly while you are watching the rest.'

But Two Eyes knew what she had in her mind. So she drove the goat into the long grass, and said, 'Come, One Eye, let us sit down here and rest, and I will sing to you.'

One Eye seated herself, and, not being accustomed to walk so far, or to be out in the heat of the sun, she began to feel tired, and as little Two Eyes kept on singing, she closed her one eye and fell fast asleep.

When Two Eyes saw this, she knew that One Eye could not betray her, so she said :

> 'Little goat, if you are able,
> Come and deck my pretty table.'

She seated herself when it appeared, and ate and drank very quickly, and when she had finished she said :

> 'Little goat, when you are able,
> Come and clear away my table.'

It vanished in the twinkling of an eye; and then Two Eyes woke up One Eye, and said, 'Little One Eye, you are a clever one to watch goats; for, while you are asleep, they might be running all over the world. Come, let us go home !'

So they went to the house, and little Two Eyes again left the scraps on the dish untouched, and One Eye could not tell her mother whether little Two Eyes had eaten anything in the field; for she said to excuse herself, 'I was asleep.'

The next day the mother said to Three Eyes, 'You must go to the field this time, and find out whether there is anyone who brings food to little Two Eyes; for she must eat and drink secretly.'

So when little Two Eyes started with her goat, Three Eyes followed, and said, 'I am going with you to-day, to see if the goats are properly fed and watched.'

But Two Eyes knew her thoughts; so she led the goat through the long grass to tire Three Eyes, and at last she said, 'Let us sit down here and rest, and I will sing to you, Three Eyes.'

She was glad to sit down, for the walk and the heat of the sun had really tired her; and, as her sister continued her song, she was obliged to close two of her eyes, and they slept, but not the third. In fact, Three Eyes was wide awake with one eye, and heard and saw all that Two Eyes did; for poor little Two Eyes, thinking she was asleep, said her speech to the goat, and the table came with all the good things on it, and was carried away when Two Eyes had eaten enough; and the cunning Three Eyes saw it all with her one eye. But she pretended to be asleep when her sister came to wake her and told her she was going home.

That evening, when little Two Eyes again left the supper they placed aside for her, Three Eyes said to her mother, 'I know where the proud thing gets her good eating and drinking;' and then she described all she had seen in the field. 'I saw it all with one eye,' she said; 'for she had made my other two eyes close with her fine singing, but luckily the one in my forehead remained open.'

Then the envious mother cried out to poor little Two Eyes, 'You wish to have better food than we, do you? You shall lose your wish!' She took up a butcher's knife, went out, and stuck the good little goat in the heart, and it fell dead.

When little Two Eyes saw this, she went out into the field, seated herself on a mound, and wept most bitter tears.

Presently the wise woman stood again before her, and said, 'Little Two Eyes, why do you weep?'

'Ah!' she replied, 'I must weep. The goat, who every day spread my table so beautifully, has been killed by my mother, and I shall have again to suffer from hunger and sorrow.'

'Little Two Eyes,' said the wise woman, 'I will give you some good advice. Go home, and ask your sister to give you the inside of the slaughtered goat, and then go and bury it in the ground in front of the house-door.'

On saying this the wise woman vanished.

Little Two Eyes went home quickly, and said to her sister, 'Dear sister, give me some part of my poor goat. I don't want anything valuable; only give me the inside.'

Her sister laughed, and said, 'Of course you can have that, if you don't want anything else.'

So little Two Eyes took the inside; and in the evening, when all was quiet, buried it in the ground outside the house-door, as the wise woman had told her to do.

The next morning, when they all rose and looked out of the window, there stood a most wonderful tree, with leaves of silver, and apples of gold hanging between them. Nothing in the wide world could be more beautiful or more costly. They none of them knew how the tree could come there in one night, excepting little Two Eyes. She supposed it had grown up from the inside of the goat; for it stood over where she had buried it in the earth.

Then said the mother to little One Eye, 'Climb up, my child, and break off some of the fruit from the tree.'

One Eye climbed up, but when she tried to catch a branch and pluck one of the apples, it escaped from her hand, and so it happened every time she made the attempt, and, do what she would, she could not reach one.

'Three Eyes,' said the mother, 'climb up, and try what you can do; perhaps you will be able to see better with your three eyes than One Eye can.'

One Eye slid down from the tree, and Three Eyes climbed up. But Three Eyes was not more skilful; with all her efforts she could not draw the branches, nor the fruit, near enough to pluck even a leaf, for they sprang back as she put out her hand.

At last the mother was impatient, and climbed up herself, but with no more success, for, as she appeared to grasp a branch, or fruit, her hand closed upon thin air.

'May I try?' said little Two Eyes; 'perhaps I may succeed.'

'You, indeed!' cried her sisters; 'you, with your two eyes, what can you do?'

But Two Eyes climbed up, and the golden apples did not fly back from her when she touched them, but almost laid themselves on her hand, and she plucked them one after another, till she carried down her own little apron full.

The mother took them from her, and gave them to her sisters, as she said little Two Eyes did not handle them properly; but this was only from jealousy, because little Two Eyes was the only one who could reach the fruit, and she went into the house feeling more spiteful to her than ever.

It happened that while all three sisters were standing under the tree together a young knight rode by. 'Run away, quick, and hide yourself, little Two Eyes; hide yourself somewhere, for we shall be quite ashamed for you to be seen.' Then they pushed the poor girl, in great haste, under an empty cask, which stood near the tree, and several of the golden apples that she had plucked along with her.

As the knight came nearer they saw he was a handsome man; and presently he halted, and looked with wonder and pleasure at the beautiful tree with its silver leaves and golden fruit.

At last he spoke to the sisters, and asked: 'To whom does this beautiful tree belong? If a man possessed only one branch he might obtain all he wished for in the world.'

'This tree belongs to us,' said the two sisters, 'and we will break off a branch for you if you like.' They gave themselves a great deal of trouble in trying to do as they offered; but all to no purpose, for the branches and the fruit evaded their efforts, and sprung back at every touch.

'This is wonderful,' exclaimed the knight, 'that the tree should belong to you, and yet you are not able to gather even a branch.'

They persisted, however, in declaring that the tree was their own property. At this moment little Two Eyes, who was angry because her sisters had not told the truth, caused two of the golden apples to slip out from under the cask, and they rolled on till they reached the feet of the knight's horse. When he saw them, he asked in astonishment where they came from.

The two ugly maidens replied that they had another sister, but they dared not let him see her, for she had only two eyes, like common people, and was named little Two Eyes.

But the knight felt very anxious to see her, and called out, 'Little Two Eyes, come here.' Then came Two Eyes, quite comforted, from the empty cask, and the knight was astonished to find her so beautiful.

Then he said, 'Little Two Eyes, can you break off a branch of the tree for me?'

'Oh yes,' she replied, 'I can, very easily, for the tree belongs to me.' And she climbed up, and, without any trouble, broke off a branch with its silver leaves and golden fruit and gave it to the knight.

THE GOOD-TEMPERED TAILOR

ONE EYE, TWO EYES, THREE EYES

He looked down at her as she stood by his horse, and said: 'Little Two Eyes, what shall I give you for this?'

'Ah!' she answered, 'I suffer from hunger and thirst, and sorrow, and trouble, from early morning till late at night; if you would only take me with you, and release me, I should be so happy.'

Then the knight lifted the little maiden on his horse, and rode home with her to his father's castle. There she was given beautiful clothes to wear, and as much to eat and drink as she wished, and as she grew up the young knight loved her so dearly that they were married with great rejoicings.

Now, when the two sisters saw little Two Eyes carried away by the handsome young knight, they were overjoyed at their good fortune. 'The wonderful tree belongs to us now,' they said; 'even if we cannot break off a branch, yet everybody who passes will stop to admire it, and make acquaintance with us, and, who knows? we may get husbands after all.'

But when they rose the next morning, lo! the tree had vanished, and with it all their hopes. And on this very morning, when little Two Eyes looked out of her chamber window of the castle, she saw, to her great joy, that the tree had followed her.

Little Two Eyes lived for a long time in great happiness; but she heard nothing of her sisters, till one day two poor women came to the castle, to beg for alms. Little Two Eyes saw them, and, looking earnestly in their faces, she recognised her two sisters, who had become so poor that they were obliged to beg their bread from door to door.

But the good sister received them most kindly, and promised to take care of them and give them all they wanted. And then they did indeed repent and feel sorry for having treated her so badly in their youthful days.

THE FOX AND THE HORSE.

A PEASANT once had a faithful horse who had grown old and could not serve his master any longer, and therefore he did not care to provide him with food, so he said to him; 'I really do not want you any more, for you are of no use to me; but if you can prove your strength by bringing me a lion, I will keep you as long as you live; but now just walk out of my stable and go and make yourself a home in the fields.'

The horse, feeling very sad, wandered away till he came to a wood, so that he might shelter himself under the trees in bad weather. A fox met him, and said: 'Friend, why do you hang your head and look so lonely?'

'Ah,' replied the horse, 'avarice and fidelity cannot dwell together in one house. My master has forgotten for how many years I have served him and borne him safely from place to place, and now that I am unable to plough any longer he will not provide me with food, and has sent me away.'

'Without any consolation?' asked the fox.

'The consolation was worthless,' he replied. 'He told me that if I was strong enough to bring him a lion he would take me back and keep me, but he knows very well that I could not possibly do that.'

Then said the fox, 'Don't be downhearted, I can help you; so just lie down here, stretch yourself out as if you were dead, and do not move.'

The horse did as the fox desired him, while the fox went to a lion, whose den was not far off, and said to him, 'Yonder lies a dead horse; come with me, and I will show you where it is, and you can have a good feast.'

The lion went with him, but when they reached the spot the fox said, 'You cannot make a meal comfortably here; I'll tell you what I will do, I will tie the horse on to you by the tail, and then you can drag him to your den and consume him at your leisure.'

The lion was pleased with this advice; he placed himself near the horse, and stood quite still to enable the fox to tie the tail securely. But in doing so he contrived to twist it round the lion's legs so tightly that with all his strength he could not move them. When the fox had accomplished this feat, he struck the horse on the shoulder and cried, 'Gee up, old horse, gee up.'

Up sprang the horse, and started off at full speed, dragging the lion with him. As they dashed through the wood the lion began to roar, and roared so loud that all the birds flew away in a fright. But the horse let him roar, and dragged him along over field and meadow to his master's door. As soon as the master saw what his horse had done, he said to him, 'As you have accomplished what I required, you shall now stay with me and have food and shelter as long as you live.'

THE DANCING SHOES.

A KING once had twelve daughters, one quite as beautiful as another. They slept together in the large hall of the castle, where their beds stood side by side. Every evening, when they retired to rest, the door of the saloon in which they slept was locked and bolted and barred by the king himself. The princesses had dancing shoes, which they wore when the king had grand entertainments; but this was not often enough to wear out many pairs, and yet sometimes, when they each had a new pair, they were found the next morning, when the king unlocked the door, completely worn out and in holes.

No one could imagine how it happened, for they could not possibly get out of the bolted and barred doors and windows. It occurred so often, and so many shoes were worn out, that the king at last made known his determination, that whoever would discover where his daughters went in the night to dance, and how they got out of the room, should have one of them for a wife, whichever he liked best, and the kingdom after the king's death.

But he also announced that whoever did not succeed, after trying for three nights, should forfeit his life. Notwithstanding this, it was not long before a king's son presented himself, and begged to be allowed to take his chance. He was well received, and placed in a chamber adjoining the sleeping hall, to enable him to see all that took place, and whether they went out to dance, and if they did go, to follow them. The door leading into the sleeping hall was left open, and his bed was placed opposite to it.

But, when he laid down, it was as if lead had been placed on his eyelids; he could not keep awake, and in the morning the dancing shoes were found more worn than ever; they had even holes in the soles, proving that they had been to a dance somewhere. The second and the third night it was the same, and then the head of the poor prince was cut off without the least pity.

Even this did not prevent others from trying, and they all lost their lives.

Now it happened that a poor soldier, who had been wounded, and could not serve any more in the army, was passing on his way to the town in which this king dwelt, and an old woman met him.

'Why are you going to this town?' she asked.

'I hardly know myself,' he replied; and then added, in joke, 'unless I felt inclined to find out where the king's daughters go to wear out their dancing shoes, and then become the future king!'

'That is not so very difficult, after all,' said the old woman. 'All you have to do is to keep awake, and therefore on no account drink the wine that is brought to you in the evening, or you will sleep without waking.' She then gave him a little cloak, and said: 'When you wear that you will be invisible, and can slip after the twelve dancers easily.'

As she gave the soldier this good advice, she was so earnest with him that he took courage, and determined to go before the king and present himself as a suitor. He was as well received as the others had been, and royal robes were given to him to wear.

In the evening, when sleeping time arrived, he was led to the little antechamber, and, when the princesses came to bed, the eldest brought him a goblet of wine; but he had fastened a piece of sponge under his chin, so that, as he put the cup to his lips, he let it all run into the sponge, and drank not a drop. Then he laid himself down, and after a little while began to snore as if he were fast asleep.

When the twelve princesses heard this, they began to laugh, and the eldest said:

' There is another that does not care for his life !'

Thereupon they all got up, opened wardrobes and drawers and boxes, and took out the most elegant dresses, in which they arrayed themselves before the glass, and jumped and danced about for joy, except the youngest, who said :

' I don't know how it is, but I feel quite miserable, as if something were going to happen.'

' What a goose you are !' cried the eldest ; ' you always fear without a cause. Do you forget how I have always managed the kings' sons already ? The soldier has had his sleeping draught, and such a clown as he is not likely to wake !'

When they were all ready, they came in and looked at the soldier ; but he had his eyes fast closed, and neither moved nor stirred ; so they believed he was quite sound asleep.

The eldest, on this, went up to her own bed, and struck it gently. Immediately it sank down into the earth, and through the opening appeared a flight of steps, down which the princesses disappeared one after the other, the eldest leading the way.

On seeing this the soldier sprang out of bed, threw on his invisible cloak, and followed the youngest, who went last, unseen. About halfway down he trod lightly on her dress, which so frightened her that she screamed out : ' What was that? who is pulling my dress ?'

' Don't be so silly,' cried the eldest ; ' I dare say you have a hook hanging down, which has caught in something.'

When they all arrived at the lowest step, the soldier saw before him a most beautiful avenue of trees with silver leaves, which shone and glittered in the light of many lamps.

' Well,' thought the soldier, ' it will be a proof that I have really followed the king's daughters if I take a branch with me.'

So he broke one off, and put it in his pocket ; but the branch made such a crack that the youngest again cried out : ' I'm sure there is something wrong ; did you not hear that crack ?'

' It is the first salute gun from the princes for joy that we are coming,' said the eldest sister.

They went on till they came to another avenue, where all the leaves were golden, and at last to a third on which sparkled diamonds. From each of these trees the soldier broke off branches, and the youngest, when she heard them crack, seemed terribly afraid, although her eldest sister persisted in calling them salute guns.

After awhile they reached the borders of a large lake, on which lay twelve pretty little boats, and in the boats sat twelve handsome young princes, who were waiting for the king's daughters. Each of them took one in his boat, and the soldier seated himself unseen with the youngest.

As this prince rowed away, he said : ' I cannot tell how it is, but the boat seems heavier to-day than it has ever been before. I am obliged to use all my strength to keep up with the rest.'

'It cannot really be heavier,' she replied; it must be the heat which makes you weaker; it is most oppressive weather.'

On the opposite shore stood a noble castle brilliantly lighted up, and from the rooms came sounds of soul-stirring music from fife and drum. The boats were rowed towards it, and the princes, assisting their companions to land, led them to the ball-room of the castle, and they were all very soon joining in the dance with great spirit.

The soldier danced among them unseen, and often when a glass of wine was brought and placed on the table, he would empty it while they turned their heads, and by so doing greatly alarmed the youngest sister, whose fears, however, were always silenced by the eldest.

They danced till three o'clock in the morning, when all their shoes were completely worn out. The princes accompanied the king's daughters to the boats, and rowed them back again over the lake, and this time the invisible soldier seated himself in the boat with the eldest.

On reaching the shore they said farewell to each other, and promised to be there on the following night. As soon as they reached the steps, the soldier ran on before them and laid himself on his bed, so that when the twelve princesses, tired and sleepy, came slowly tripping back, he snored so loudly that they all heard him, and said: 'From him we are quite safe.' Then they took off their beautiful clothes, put them away, and, after placing their dancing-shoes under the bed, laid themselves down and slept till it was time to rise.

The soldier next morning, however, said not a word of what he had seen; he wished to go again to those wonderful places, and so on the second and third nights he was with them as before. The proceedings were the same as at the first, and they danced till their shoes were worn out. On the third night, however, he took away with him a goblet as another proof of his visit.

When the hour arrived in which he was expected to state whether he had made the expected discovery, he took the three branches which he had broken off, and the goblet, and appeared before the king. The twelve princesses placed themselves secretly behind the door to listen and hear what he would say.

The king asked the question: 'How have my twelve daughters worn out their dancing-shoes during each night?'

'By dancing with twelve princes,' replied the soldier, 'in a subterranean castle.'

And then he described all that he had seen, and pointed to the proofs he had brought with him.

On hearing this the king sent for his daughters, and asked them if what the soldier had said was true. They saw at once that all was discovered; they could deny nothing, and must therefore take the consequences of their conduct. Thereupon the king asked the soldier which of them he would have for a wife, so he replied: 'I am no longer young, so give me the eldest.'

On that very day the marriage was celebrated and the kingdom promised to the soldier after the king's death. The rest of the king's daughters were condemned to be placed under the spell of enchantment for as many days as they had danced nights with the princes in the enchanted castle.

THE DRUMMER.

A YOUNG drummer was one evening walking across the fields, and as he came to a lake, he saw lying on the shore three pieces of white linen. 'What fine linen!' he said; and taking up one piece, he put it in his pocket. He went home, thought no more of what he had found, and went to bed. Just as he was going to sleep, he thought he heard some one call out his name, and heard distinctly a gentle voice say: 'Drummer, drummer, wake up!'

At first in the dark he could distinguish nothing, but presently he saw hovering over his bed a light form.

'What is it?' he asked.

'Give me back my dress,' answered the voice, 'which you took away from the lake yesterday.'

'You shall have it,' said the drummer, 'if you will tell me who you are.'

'Ah,' cried the voice, 'I am the daughter of a mighty king, but I have fallen into the power of a witch, and am confined to a glass mountain. Each day I am obliged to bathe in the lake with my two sisters; but without my dress I cannot fly back to the iceberg, and my sisters have already gone away and left me alone. I pray you, therefore, to give me back my dress.'

'Be at peace, poor child,' said the drummer; 'you shall have your dress very soon.' Then he took the piece of linen out of his pocket, and offered it to her in the darkness. She seized it hastily and was going away. 'Wait one moment,' he said; 'can I not help you in any way?'

'You could only help me,' she replied, 'by climbing on the glass mountain and freeing me from the witch's power. But you could not reach the mountain; or even if you did, you would be unable to climb to the top.'

'What I wish to do I can do,' said the drummer. 'I feel great compassion for you, and I fear nothing; but I do not know where the mountain is, nor the way to it.'

'The road lies through a large forest,' she replied; 'and you must pass several inns on your way. More than this I dare not tell you.'

Then he heard the rush of wings and she was gone. By the break of day the drummer was up and ready. He hung his drum on his shoulder, and went without fear to cross the forest. After walking for some time, and not meeting any giants, he thought to himself, 'I must wake up the lazy sleepers.' So he turned his drum before him, and played such a tantara that the birds on the trees flew away screaming.

Not long after, a giant who had been sleeping in the grass rose up and stood before him. He was as tall as a fir-tree, and cried out to the drummer :

'You wretched little creature! what do you mean by waking people up out of their best sleep with your horrid drum ?'

'I drummed to wake you,' he replied, 'because, as many thousands have done before, I did not know the way.'

'What do you want here in my wood ?' asked the giant.

'Well, I wish to free the forest from such monsters as you are !'

'Oho !' cried the giant, 'why, I could crush you beneath my foot as I would crush an ant !'

'Don't suppose you are going to perform any such thing,' cried the drummer. 'If you were to stoop down to catch hold of one of us, he would jump away and hide himself, and when you were lying down to sleep, his people would come from every bush and thicket, each carrying a steel hammer in his girdle. They would creep cautiously upon you, and soon with their hammers beat out your brains !'

This assertion made the giant rather uneasy. 'If I meddle with these cunning little people,' he thought, 'they can, no doubt, do me some mischief. I can easily strangle wolves and bears, but I cannot defend myself against these earthworms.'

'Listen, little man,' he said. 'I pledge myself that you and your companions shall for the future be left in peace. And now tell me what you wish, for I am quite ready to do your pleasure.'

'You have long legs,' said the drummer, 'so that you can run more swiftly than I can. Carry me to the glass mountain, and I will take that as a proof of your kind feeling towards us, and my people shall leave you in peace.'

'Come here, worm,' said the giant; 'seat yourself on my shoulders, and I will carry you wherever you wish.'

The giant then lifted him up, and the drummer soon began to play away on his drum to his heart's content. The giant was quite satisfied; he thought this would be a sign to the rest of the little people that he was friendly with them.

After a while a second giant made his appearance, and he took the drummer from the first, and stuck him in the buttonhole of his coat. The drummer seized the button, which was as large as a dish, and, holding fast by it, looked about him quite contentedly. Presently came a third, who took him from the buttonhole, and placed him on the brim of his hat, from which elevation he could look over the tree-tops.

All at once, in the blue distance, he espied a mountain. 'Ah!' thought he, 'that is certainly the glass mountain ;' and so it was.

The giant, after a few more steps, reached the foot of the mountain, and then he lifted the drummer from his hat, and placed him on the ground. The little man wished to be carried to the top of the mountain; but the giant shook his head, murmured something in his beard, and went back to the wood.

There stood the poor little drummer at the foot of the mountain, which looked as high above him as if three mountains had been placed one upon another. The sides were as slippery as a mirror, and there seemed no possible means of reaching the top. He began to climb, but he slid backwards at every step. 'If I were a bird, now,' he said to himself; but it was only half a wish, and no wings grew.

While he thus stood, not knowing how to help himself, he saw at a little distance two men struggling together. He went up to them, and found that they were quarrelling about a saddle, which lay on the ground between them, and which they each wished to have.

'What fools you must be,' he cried, 'to want a saddle when you have not a horse to place it upon!'

'This saddle is worth a contest,' said one of the men; 'for whoever seats himself upon it, and wishes himself somewhere, even were it to the end of the world, he would have his wish accomplished the moment it was uttered.'

'The saddle is our joint property, and it is my turn to ride it; but my companion will not let me.'

'I will soon put an end to this contention,' said the drummer. 'Go to a little distance, and stick a white staff in the ground; then come back, and start from here to run to the mark, and whoever is there first is to ride first.'

They did as he advised, and then both started off at a full trot; but scarcely had they taken two steps when the drummer swung himself on the saddle, and wished to be on the top of the mountain, and, ere a man could turn his hand, there he was.

The top of the mountain formed an extensive plain, on which stood an old stone-built house; in front of it a large fish-pond, and behind it a dark dreary forest. Neither man nor animals could be seen; not a sound disturbed the peaceful stillness, excepting the wind rustling the leaves, while the clouds floated silently over his head.

He stepped up to the door of the house and knocked. No one answered, and he knocked a second time; but it was not till the third time that the door was opened by an old woman with a brown face and red eyes. She had a pair of spectacles on her long nose, and looked at him very sharply as she asked, 'What is your business here?'

'I want admission, food, and a night's lodging,' he replied.

'All these you shall have,' she replied, 'if you will perform three tasks for me.'

'Willingly,' he replied; 'I do not shrink from work, however difficult it may be.'

The old woman, on this, led him in, gave him a supper, and a good bed in the evening.

THE DRUMMER

THE DRUMMER

Next morning, when he got up, breakfast was ready for him, and after eating it he expressed his readiness to perform the tasks she had spoken of.

In reply, the old woman took a thimble from her lean finger, and, offering it to him, said, ' Now go, for your first task, and scoop out the water from the fish-pond outside with this thimble, and the work must be finished before night. All the fish, also, that are in the water must be laid together, according to their size and species !'

' That is a strange task !' said the drummer. However, he went out to the pond and commenced his work.

He scooped industriously for the whole morning; but how can a man empty a large quantity of water with only a thimble to dip with at a time? Why, it would occupy a thousand years.

When noontide came he thought to himself, ' All I am doing is quite useless ; it will be just the same, whether I work or not.' So he gave it up, and seated himself.

Presently he saw a young maiden coming towards him from the house. She had a basket in her hand containing some dinner for him, and she said, ' Why are you sitting here and looking so sad? What is the matter ?'

He looked up at her, and saw that she was very handsome. ' Ah !' he exclaimed, ' I cannot perform the first task which has been given me, and how shall I succeed with the other two? I have come to seek for a king's daughter who dwells here, but I have not found her, so I may as well go away.'

' No ; stay here,' she replied ; ' I will help you out of your trouble. You are tired now, so lay your head in my lap and go to sleep. When you awake again your work will be done.'

The drummer did not require to be told twice, and, as soon as his eyes were closed, the maiden turned a wish-ring on her finger, and said, ' Water, rise out; fish, come out.'

In a moment the water rose in the air like a white mist, and floated away to the clouds above the mountain, while the fish came springing and jumping on the bank, and laid themselves down near each other, each according to its size and species. When the drummer awoke, he saw with astonishment that all had been done for him.

' It is not quite right now,' said the maiden ; ' one of the fish is lying away from its own species, quite alone. When the old woman comes this evening to see if all is done as she desired, she will ask why that little fish is left out. Then throw it in her face, and say, " That is left for you, old witch !"'

In the evening she came, and, when she asked the question as the maiden said she would, he threw the fish in her face, and repeated the words he had been told to. The old woman stood still, and appeared not to notice what he had done, excepting that she looked at him with malicious eyes.

The next morning she said to him : ' The task I gave you yesterday was too easy ; you must have something more difficult to-day. I expect you, therefore, to cut down all the trees of the forest behind this house, to split them into logs and stack them, and when evening comes all must be finished !'

She gave him an axe, a chopper, and a wedge. But the axe was made of lead, and the chopper and wedge of tin ; so that when he began his work the axe stuck fast in the wood, and the chopper and wedge struck one against the other, and became useless.

He knew not what to do ; but at noon the maiden came again with his dinner and comforted him. 'Lay your head in my lap,' said she, 'and sleep, and when you awake the work will be done.'

While he slept, she turned the wish-ring on her finger, and in a moment the whole of the forest trees fell together with a crash. The wood divided itself into logs and stacked itself in piles ; it was as if an invisible giant had accomplished the task. When the dreamer awoke, the maiden said : ' You see how all the wood is cut down and stacked, except one little bough. When the old woman comes this evening, and asks what the bough is left there for, you must give her a blow with it and say, " It is for you, old witch." '

The old woman came, and when she saw the work all done, she said : 'Ah, it was an easy task I gave you, but what is that bough left there for?'

'For you, witch,' he replied, giving her a blow with it. But she appeared not to feel it, laughed scornfully, and said : ' To-morrow you shall place all this wood in a heap, set fire to it, and burn it.'

He was at the forest by daybreak, and began his work of gathering the wood into a heap ; but how was it possible for one man to carry the trees of a whole forest into one spot ? The work went backwards, not forwards. The maiden, however, did not forget him in his trouble ; she brought him his mid-day meal, and, when he had eaten, made him lay his head in her lap and sleep. When he awoke, the whole stack of wood was burning in one vast flame, the tongues of which reached to the clouds. ' Listen now,' said the maiden ; ' when the witch comes she will give you all sorts of orders. If you perform courageously whatever she desires, she cannot injure you or touch your life. But if you show any fear she will put you in the fire, and you will be consumed. At last, when you have done all she tells you, take her up with both hands and throw her into the flames.'

Then the maiden went away, and presently the witch came sneaking up.

' Ha !' she exclaimed, ' I am so cold, and here is a fire to warm my old bones and do me good ; but there lies a log that will not burn ; just fetch it out for me. If you can do that you are free to go where you will. Now be brisk and do as I tell you.'

The drummer did not hesitate long ; he sprang into the flames, but they did him no harm, and not even a hair of his head was singed as he drew out the log and placed it before her. Scarcely, however, had it touched the ground than it was transformed, and the beautiful maiden, who had helped him in his trouble, stood before him, the silk and gold-embroidered clothes she wore proving at once that she was a king's daughter. The old witch laughed spitefully, and said :

' You think you are going to have the princess, but you shan't; I will take care of that;' and she advanced to lay hold of the maiden and carry her away. But the drummer started forward, seized the old witch with both hands, and threw her into the very midst of the flames, which gathered over her as if in joy at being able to consume a witch.

The king's daughter looked earnestly at the drummer, and saw that he was really a handsome youth, and remembered that he had saved her life and set her free from the witch's spell. So she held out her hand to him, and said :

' You have risked everything for me, therefore I will now do something for you. Promise to be true to me, then shall you be my spouse. I have plenty of riches and possessions which the old witch has accumulated.'

She led him into the house and showed him chests and boxes which were full of treasures. They left the gold and silver, took only the precious stones, and prepared to leave the mountain of glass. Then the drummer said to her, ' Seat yourself with me on my saddle, and we can fly through the air like birds.'

' The old saddle is useless to me,' she said ; ' I only require to turn my wish-ring over, and we are at home.'

' All right !' he cried ; ' then let us wish ourselves at the gate of my native city.'

In a trice they were there, and then the drummer said :

' I will first go and see my parents and tell them all the news ; wait here for me in this field ; I will soon return.'

' Ah,' said the king's daughter, ' let me beg of you to be careful when you arrive ; remember to kiss your parents only on the left cheek, otherwise you will forget me and all that has happened, and I shall be left behind in the field alone.'

' How can I ever forget you ?' he said, and pledged her with his right hand to return to her very soon.

When he reached his father's house no one knew who he was, he had so changed; for the three days which he had, as he supposed, spent on the mountains, had been really three long years. At last they recognised him, and his parents were so overjoyed at his return that they fell on his neck and embraced him. He was also so moved in his heart that he kissed them on both cheeks, and thought not once of the maiden's words. As soon as he had kissed them on the right cheek, all gratitude to the king's daughter vanished from his heart. He turned out his pockets and threw great handfuls of precious stones on the table, his parents wondering how and where he had obtained all these riches. They were, however, very happy to accept them.

The father's first act was to build a beautiful castle, around which were gardens, and woods, and meadows, as if a prince had been going to reside in it.

And, when it was finished, the mother said to her son, ' I have chosen a maiden to be your wife, and in three days the wedding must take place.'

The drummer was quite contented to do as his parents wished.

The poor princess stood for a long time outside the town, waiting for the return of the young man. When evening came, she said to herself, ' No doubt he has kissed his parents on the right cheek, and I am quite forgotten.'

Her heart was so full of grief that she wished herself in a lonely house in the wood close by.

Every evening she went into the town, and wandered about the grounds of his father's castle. She saw him many times, but he never saw her; and one day she heard people talking of his marriage, and saying that it would take place the following day.

Then she said to herself, ' I will try to win him back again.'

So, on the first day of the betrothal, she wished for a beautiful dress that should shine as the sun. And, when it lay before her, it glittered like sunbeams. All the guests were assembled when she entered the room; every one present was surprised at her beauty and her rich dress; but the drummer did not recognise her among so many, and she had disguised herself. That night, however, when all was still, she placed herself outside his window, and sang:

> ' Drummer, should I forgotten be?
> Was it not I who tended thee,
> And to your tasks lent all my aid,
> When on the mountain top we strayed?
> You freed me from the witch's power,
> And swore to love me from that hour:
> These riches all were gifts from me,
> Then why should I forgotten be?'

But the song was all lost; the young man slept soundly, and heard it not. On the second evening she was again at the festival, and afterwards sung her mournful song outside the window.

But she had mistaken the sleeping-room of her lover, and again her complaints would have been useless, had not the servants of the castle told their young master that they had heard a beautiful voice singing during the night. His curiosity was excited, and he determined to listen at the window himself.

In the night, after the third day of the betrothal, when the festivities were over, the young man placed himself at the window to listen; but no sooner had he heard the sound of the voice singing,

> ' Drummer, should I forgotten be?
> Was it not I who tended thee,

And to your tasks lent all my aid,
When on the mountain top you strayed?
You freed me from the witch's power,
And swore to love me from that hour:
Your riches all were gifts from me;
Drummer, should I forgotten be?'

than to his memory everything returned.

'Ah,' he cried, 'how nearly have I lost my true and only love! In the joy of my heart I kissed my parents on the right cheek. There is the fault; but I will atone for my conduct.' He started up, as the song still continued in plaintive accents, rushed out, and exclaimed, 'Forgive me, dearest!' and, as he pressed her to his heart, she forgot her sorrow and forgave him all.

Then he led her to his parents, and said, 'This is the true bride,' and told them what she had done for him, and the cause of his forgetfulness. They were ready to receive her at once as their daughter-in-law, and the other intended bride was made quite contented by being presented with the beautiful dresses which the real bride had worn at the festival.

THE ROYAL TURNIP.

THERE were once two brothers, who had both served in the war as soldiers; one was rich, the other poor. The poor brother was determined to work for his living, so he took off his soldier's uniform, and became a farmer. In one of his fields, after he had dug and ploughed it well, he sowed turnip seed. After a time, when the grains sprung up, one of them grew to such an enormous size, and continued to increase, and became so thick and large, that it almost seemed as if it would never stop growing at all.

People called it the prince of turnips, for none had ever been seen like it before, nor ever would again. At last it grew so big that it would have quite filled a waggon, and would have required two oxen to draw it. The farmer hardly knew what to do with it, or whether it would bring him luck or misfortune.

At last he thought to himself, 'Suppose I sell it. I should not get much certainly for such a great thing, and why should I eat it myself when little turnips would do just as well? No. I think the best thing I can do is to carry it to the king, and make him a present of it.'

So he laid the turnip on his waggon, harnessed the oxen to it, carried it to the castle, and presented it to the king.

'What a strange looking thing!' said the king, when he saw it. 'Many most wonderful things have passed before my eyes, but never such a monster as this. From what kind of seed did you grow it? or has it come to you as a favourite of fortune?'

'Ah! no!' replied the farmer. 'I am no child of fortune, only a poor soldier; and, as I have no pension, and nothing to live upon, I hung up my soldier's coat on a nail, and took to tilling the land. I have a brother who is rich; but, my lord king, you yourself know that those who have nothing are forgotten by all the world.'

Then the king felt so much sympathy for the poor man that he promised to present him with enough, not only to overcome his poverty, but to make him as rich as his brother. So the king gave him money, and fields, and meadows, and made him so very rich that his brother's possessions could not be compared with his.

When the brother heard of these riches, and that they had all been acquired through a large turnip, he was envious, and thought over every possible way in which he might be able to obtain such luck. He decided at last to present to the king fine horses and gold, and thought that, of course, he would give him pure, really valuable presents in return. If the king had given so much to his brother for a turnip, what might he not expect for these beautiful things?

The king accepted the presents, and said he could think of nothing better or more uncommon to offer him in return than the large turnip. So the rich brother was obliged to hire a waggon and oxen, lay his brother's turnip on it, and drive the waggon home.

In his anger and rage at the king's treatment, he knew not what to do, till at last his wicked thoughts excited him to go and shoot his brother.

To effect this, he found it necessary to have recourse to stratagem; and so he went to him, and said, 'Dear brother, I have discovered a hidden treasure, not far from here. Shall we go together to dig it up, and divide it?'

Without the least suspicion of wrong, the brother agreed to go with him, and they went out together, and walked on till they approached a stream of water. At the most lonely part, the wicked man suddenly overpowered his brother, bound him hand and foot, and was about to hang him on a tree. He had almost accomplished his wicked intention when there sounded in the distance a voice singing merrily, and the clatter of horse's hoofs.

In great terror the intending murderer unfastened the string from the branch of the tree, pushed the bound body of his brother into a sack, and took to flight. The brother, however, struggled till he worked a hole in the sack, through which he could push his head. Just as he had done so, there came walking his horse along the road a travelling scholar, a young fellow full of life and joy, singing a song as he rode through the wood or on the highway. As he came near the sack where the poor farmer lay, a prisoner bound, the farmer called out, 'I wish you good-day, traveller.'

The scholar looked about in every direction to see where the sound came from. At last he said, 'Who calls me?'

'Raise your eyes,' cried the voice from above. 'Here sits Wisdom in a sack. I have in a very little while learnt great things, in comparison to which all scholars are vanity; and I have ascertained also that every-one who climbs up here may quickly become wiser than other men. I understand the stars and the heavenly bodies, the way the wind blows, the sand of the sea, the healing of sickness, and the strength of vegetables, birds, and stones. Were you once in my position, you would feel how gloriously wisdom flows out of a sack.'

The scholar, when he heard all this, was astonished, and cried, ' Blessed be the hour that we have met! Cannot I come into the sack for a little while now ?'

This was just what he up above wanted; so he said, ' I will let you stay here for a little while presently as a reward for your kind words; but you can remain only an hour. I have learnt all I know in less time than that.'

The scholar waited; but the time appeared so long to him that he begged to be allowed to go into the sack at once—his thirst for wisdom was so great.

The man in the sack hesitated a little longer, and at last said, ' Well, then, let me down, and unbind me, and you shall get in.'

The scholar lowered the sack, and set him free. ' Now, then,' he cried, ' draw me up quickly,' and prepared to step into the sack.

' Stop, stop!' cried the other; ' not so fast.' He seized him by the head as he spoke, stuck him into the sack head foremost, drew the string tight, and raised the searcher after wisdom to the bough of the tree till he swung in mid air. Then he said to him, ' Stay there, my dear fellow, for a while. Do you not already feel something of the wisdom that comes from experience? Sit there, and rest till you become clever.'

Thereupon he mounted the scholar's horse and rode away, with the determination, however, that he would send some one in an hour to let him down and release him.

WHITE AND BLACK.

A WOMAN one day was going to a field with her daughter and her step-daughter to cut clover for their cattle. A good fairy met them disguised as a poor woman, and said, ' Will you show me the way to the town?'

' If you want to know, find out for yourself,' said the mother.

' As you are very anxious to find the way,' said her daughter, ' you had better engage a guide.'

But the stepdaughter said, 'Poor woman, come with me; I will take you a little way and show you.'

Then the fairy in anger turned her back on the mother and daughter, leaving upon them the power of enchantment, by which they both became as black as night and as ugly as sin.

She then accompanied the stepdaughter, and as they drew near the town, she said, 'Choose for yourself three things, and I will grant them.'

Then said the maiden, 'I should like to become as pure and beautiful as the sun.' Immediately she became fair and beautiful as the daylight. 'Then I should like to have a purse of money which would never be empty.' This the fairy gave her, and said, 'Do not forget what is good.' And then, as her third request, the maiden asked that she might reach heaven when she died. This was also granted, and immediately the fairy vanished.

When the mother and daughter came home, and saw that they had both become coal-black and ugly, while the stepdaughter was fairer and more beautiful than ever, wicked thoughts rose in their hearts, and they thought only of how they could make her unhappy.

The stepdaughter, however, had a brother named Rudy, whom she loved very much, and she told him everything that happened to her. One day her brother said to her, 'Dear sister, I love you so much that I mean to have your likeness taken, and then I shall have your face always before my eyes.'

'Very well,' she replied; 'but pray do not let anyone else see the picture.'

So he had her picture painted, and hung up in his room at the king's castle where he lived, for he was coachman to the king.

Every day he felt thankful that his dear sister had gained these precious gifts from the fairy. Not long before this time the queen had died, and the king was full of grief; for she had been so beautiful that none like her could be found anywhere.

One day a servant of the castle peeped into the coachman's room, and saw him standing before a beautiful picture which hung on the wall. He watched him again and again, and saw that not a day passed without his standing before the picture and seeming to admire it; so he told the other servants, and they, being envious, informed the king.

Upon this the king desired the picture to be brought to him, and he saw with surprise that it was the picture of a maiden who exactly resembled his dead wife, only still more beautiful, and he at once fell desperately in love with the picture. He sent for his coachman, and when he appeared asked him whose likeness it was. The coachman replied that it was that of his sister. Upon hearing this, the king resolved that no other woman should be his wife.

So Rudy was ordered to take a royal carriage and horses, and beautiful clothes embroidered with gold, and go at once for his sister, and bring her back to the castle to be the king's bride. When Rudy arrived in all his grandeur to fetch his sister, and she heard the message and saw the clothes, she was full of joy.

But her black sister was overpowered with jealousy at this good fortune, and vexed herself beyond measure, and said to her mother, ' What is the use of all your cleverness if you can't get me such luck as this ?'

' Be quiet,' said the old woman ; ' I will manage it all for you !' And, through the power of her witchcraft, she dimmed the eyes of the coachman so that he could hardly see, and deadened the sound in the ears of his sister till she became almost deaf.

Then they all got into the carriage—the fair maiden in her beautiful dress, and the mother with her daughter—while Rudy sat on the box and drove. After they had travelled a little way, Rudy said to his sister, ' Take care, dear sister, that you do not crush your beautiful clothes ; I want you to look well and neat when you are taken to the king.'

But the maiden could not hear distinctly, so she said to her mother : ' What does my dear brother say ?'

' Oh,' she replied, ' he says you must take off your gold embroidered clothes and give them to your sister.'

She immediately did as her stepmother said, and the black maiden dressed herself in the royal clothes, and gave her dark gray frock to her beautiful stepsister.

Then they travelled on still farther, and Rudy again told his little sister to take care of her clothes and keep herself nice, that she might appear beautiful before the king, but she could not hear, and said : ' What does my brother say ?'

' He says now,' replied the stepmother, ' that you are to give your sister your golden cap.'

So the cap was taken off, and the beautiful maiden's hair fell around her face and shoulders without any other ornament. And so they travelled on till they came near to a brook, in which the water was very deep. Again her brother said something to her which she could not hear, and she asked her stepmother.

' He says,' replied the wicked woman, ' that we must all get down here while he rests his horse.'

The maiden stood up, thinking the carriage was going to stop, but as it still moved on she lost her balance, and the cruel woman gave her a push, which sent her backwards into the deep water. At the moment she sank a snow-white duck appeared on the surface of the water, and swam about. The brother, who had not noticed what happened, drove on till they came to the castle. They alighted, and the coachman, who really thought the black maiden was his sister, when he saw the sparkle and glitter of her dress, led her to the king. When the king caught sight of the dreadful ugliness of the maiden, he was so angry with the coachman that he ordered him to be thrown into a dungeon full of snakes and vipers. The old witch, however, knew how to bewitch the king and blind his eyes, and she managed him so completely that he allowed her and her daughter to remain at the castle, and at last the ugly maiden became less unpleasant to him, and he appeared inclined to make her his wife.

One evening, when the king was sitting with the ugly and wicked maiden, there came to the kitchen door a beautiful white duck, and said to the kitchen-maid, 'Please make a fire here that I may warm and dry my feathers.'

So the kitchen-maid lighted a fire on the hearth, and the duck came in, and seating herself by it, plumed and stroked her feathers with her beak. Presently she said, 'What is my brother Rudy doing now?'

'Nothing,' said the maid; 'Rudy is shut up in a dungeon with snakes and adders.'

'And what is the black witch doing, and where is her daughter?'

'They are both with the king, and he will marry the daughter.'

'Heaven forbid,' said the duck, and she went out and swam away. The next evening she came again and said the same words. But when this happened a third time, the kitchen-maid felt that she ought to tell the king, so she went to him and described what the duck had said and done.

'I will come and see for myself,' he said, and the next evening, when the duck pushed her head through the kitchen door, the king drew his sword and cut it off. The next moment there stood before him a beautiful maiden, exactly like the picture which his coachman had shown him of his sister, and he knew it must be his right bride. So he sent for beautiful clothes and told her to put them on, and led her into the castle quite joyfully. She then told him of the falsehood and cunning which had been used to betray her, till at last she had been pushed into the water of the brook, and the king deceived by the witch; she begged, however, as her first request, that her brother should be released from the dungeon into which he had been unjustly thrown.

When the king had granted this petition, which he did readily, he went to the old witch, told her that her wickedness had been discovered, and that if she and her daughter did not at once leave his dominions they should be dragged to death by horses in a cask full of spikes. After they were gone the king married the beautiful maiden, whose picture he had seen, and rewarded her brother so handsomely that he became quite a rich man.

IRON HANS.

NEAR the castle of a king stood once a large forest inhabited by wild beasts of every kind. One day the king sent a hunter into the forest to hunt a stag, and kill him and bring him to the castle, but the hunter was never seen or heard of again. 'He has met with some accident,' said the king, and sent two hunters to search for him, but they remained absent also. On this, the king summoned his staff of hunters, and said:

'Go and search through the wood in every direction, and do not give up till you find the three men who are missing.'

But of all this number none returned, and not one of the pack of hounds who went with them was ever seen again. After this no one would venture into the wood, or even near it. The still and lonely place seemed uninhabited by any living creature, for, excepting that sometimes an eagle or a hawk would fly over the tree tops, nothing could be seen.

Many years had passed, when a foreign hunter made himself known to the king, and stated his wish to go into the dangerous wood. He only asked to be provided with the necessary means to support him during the enterprise. The king, however, was very unwilling to grant him permission, and said: 'The wood is no doubt haunted, and I fear you will not fare better than those who have gone before—if you go you will never come back.'

'My lord king,' he replied, 'I will venture at all risks, and I know not what fear is.'

The hunter, true to his determination, started on his expedition, taking with him one hound. They had not gone far into the wood, when the hound became suddenly wild, and turned to run back. He had, however, scarcely taken two steps when a dark pool rose before him, a naked arm was stretched out of the water, and the dog was seized and quickly drawn under.

On seeing this the hunter went back quickly and fetched three men, whom he told to bring pails and buckets to empty the pool. They were not long in performing this task, and, when they reached the bottom, there lay a wild-looking man, whose body was brown like rusty iron, while his long, tangled hair hung over his face, and reached even to his knees.

They bound him with cords and led him away to the castle. Everyone was astonished at seeing such a wonderful creature, and the king had him locked up in an iron cage and placed in the outer court, and forbade any person to open the cage door under pain of death; he also kept the key himself. After this the forest was quite safe to walk in.

The king had a little son eight years old, who often played in the outer court of the castle, and one day, while tossing his gilded ball, it fell into the iron cage. The boy ran fearlessly to the wild man, and said: 'Give me my ball.'

'No,' he replied; 'not unless you open the door of my cage.'

'I must not do that,' said the boy; 'the king has forbidden it;' and he ran away.

The next day he came again, and asked for his ball; but the wild man replied: 'Open the door, and you shall have it.' The boy still refused, and went away.

On the third day, while the king was out hunting in the forest, the boy came again, and said: 'You may as well give me my ball, for I cannot open the door even if I wanted to, for I have not the key.'

'It is under your mother's sofa pillow; you can easily fetch it,' was the reply.

The boy, who wanted very much to have his ball, threw to the wind all thoughts of wrong or danger, went in, fetched the key, and unlocked the cage-door.

It opened so quickly that the boy pinched his finger, and in a moment the wild man was out of the cage, gave up the ball, and rushed away. The boy, in a terrible fright, ran after him, screaming: 'Wild man, wild man, don't go away. I shall be beaten if you do.' The wild creature turned round, lifted up the boy, seated him on his shoulder, and walked with hasty steps to the forest.

On the king's return he noticed the empty cage, and asked the queen how it happened.

'I do not know,' she replied; 'the key was under my pillow.' But when she looked the key was gone.

They then called the boy, but he did not answer; and at last, after a search all over the castle and the grounds, they found that he was gone also.

The king sent messengers in every direction, but all to no purpose, and then they rightly guessed that he had been taken away by the wild man; and the whole castle was thrown into deep sorrow.

When the wild man reached the dark wood, he lifted the boy from his shoulders, and, placing him on his feet, said, 'You will never see your father and mother again; but I will take care of you because you set me free, and I have some gratitude and pity. If you do all I tell you, I will make you very happy, and I have more gold and richer treasures than anyone in the whole world.' He then made the boy a nice bed in the moss, where he slept peacefully all night.

The next morning the man led him to a well, and said: 'See how bright and golden this water is, and yet it is as pure as crystal. Now you must sit here, and take particular care that nothing falls into it; otherwise it will be disturbed. In the evening I will come and see if you have followed my instructions.'

The boy seated himself on the brink of the well, and saw that many goldfish and golden snakes were swimming about in the water, and was very careful to let nothing fall in. While he thus sat, his finger began to ache so terribly that he could not help putting just the tip into the water to cool it. He pulled it out again very quickly, and oh, how surprised he was to find it covered with gold! In great trouble, he tried to wipe it off, but without success.

In the evening came Iron Hans, as he called himself, and, when he saw the boy, he said, 'What is the matter with the well?'

'Nothing, nothing,' he answered, holding his finger behind his back that Iron Hans might not see it.

But the man said, 'You have dipped your finger in the water. This time it does not matter, you may go; but be careful in future not to let anything fall in, or even touch the water.'

The boy went to the well early the next morning, to watch as before. The finger was again painful, and to avoid touching the water he raised his hands above his head, and in so doing, unluckily a hair fell into the water of the well. He took it quickly out, but it was already covered with gold.

When Iron Hans came in the evening, he knew at once what had happened. 'You have let a hair fall into the well,' he said. 'I will try you once more; but if it happens again the well is disgraced, and you will not be able to remain any longer with me.'

On the third day the boy again seated himself by the well, and would not even move his finger, although it was still painful. But the time seemed so long that he tried to amuse himself by watching the different objects reflected on the surface of the water. While stooping over it he saw the image of himself; and when bending lower, to examine it, his long hair drooped over his face, and fell around him into the water. He raised his head quickly, but it was too late; the hair had already become golden, and shone like the sun.

You cannot imagine how terrified the poor child was. He took his pocket-handkerchief and bound it round his head, hoping that the man would not see the gold.

But when Iron Hans came, he knew all that had happened, and said: 'Take off that handkerchief.' And, as the boy did so, the golden hair fell on the boy's shoulders, and, excuse himself as he might, it was all useless.

'You have not been able to stand the test,' said the man, 'therefore you cannot remain here. You must go out into the world and learn by experience what it is to be poor. But while you keep your heart free from wickedness, and have a kind feeling for me, I will allow you to call upon me to help you. If you fall into great trouble, come to the forest and cry, "Iron Hans," and I will render you assistance immediately. My power is great—greater than you think—and gold and silver I have in abundance.'

The king's son on hearing this left the wood, and travelled for a long time over beaten paths and unfrequented roads till he came to a large town. Here he sought for employment, but as he had not been taught any trade, he found it very difficult to obtain. At last he went to the castle, and asked the people of the court to take him in. They were rather puzzled to know what the boy was fit for, but they were very much pleased with his appearance, and told him he might stay.

At last the cook said he might make the boy useful in the kitchen, to cut wood, and draw water, and sweep up the ashes. Once, however, after he had been some time at the castle, the cook told him to go and lay the cloth for the king and wait upon him. He went to the king's chamber, but, wishing to hide the golden hair, he kept on his hat.

The king, noticing this, said to him:

'If you come to a royal table, you should take off your hat.'

'Ah, my lord king, I cannot,' he replied; 'I have a sore head.'

The king on hearing this sent for the cook, scolded him well, and asked him how he could take such a youth as that into his service, and ordered that he should be immediately dismissed. The cook, however, pitied the boy, and exchanged him with the gardener's helper. In the garden the boy had to dig and rake, and plant and sow, let the wind roar and rain and weather be as bad as they might.

One day in summer, while he was in the garden at work, the heat was so great that he was obliged to take off his hat to cool himself. As he did so, the sun shone upon his gold-covered hair, and it glittered and sparkled in its light so brightly that the reflection was thrown into the sleeping-chamber of the king's daughter, and she started up to see what caused it. She was surprised to find that the bright locks belonged to a youth at work in the garden. She, however, called him, and said:

'Bring me a bunch of flowers, will you?'

In all haste the youth put on his hat, and then commenced gathering the most lovely wild-flowers he could find to make a bouquet for the princess. As he was ascending the steps, he met the gardener, who said to him:

'How can you take such a nosegay as that to the princess, with nothing but common field flowers? Go away quickly and fetch others —the rarest and most beautiful in the garden.'

'Ah, no,' said the youth; 'wild flowers are stronger and will please her better.'

When he entered the room in which the princess sat, she said:

'Take your hat off; you don't appear to know how to behave yourself before me.'

'I dare not,' he replied; 'pray do not ask me.'

Without another word she rose, and, coming towards him, seized the hat and pulled it off. Down rolled the golden hair over his shoulders —the most beautiful that ever was seen. He wanted to run away, but she held him by the arm and gave him a handful of ducats. He thanked her, but did not care for the money, and as he left the castle he met the gardener, and said to him:

'See, here is all this money; I don't want it; give it to your children to play with.'

The next day the princess again desired him to bring her a nosegay of fresh flowers, and when he entered her room, she suddenly caught hold of his hat to pull it off, but he held it firmly with both hands, and she could not remove it. However, she gave him again a handful of ducats, which he would not keep, but sent them to the gardener's children.

The third day the same occurred. He took the princess a nosegay; she tried to pull off his hat, but without success, and he would not keep the money she gave him.

Not long after this, war was declared in the country in which he now lived, and the king assembled his troops to go to battle; but he knew

WHITE AND BLACK

IRON HANS

not the strength of the enemy's forces, or whether they had a more numerous host of warriors than his own.

On hearing of the war, the gardener's boy said:

'I am grown up now, and I should like to go to battle, if I could have a horse.'

The soldiers laughed at him, and said:

'When we are gone, then you go and look in the stable; we will leave a horse there for you.'

He went to the stable, as they had told him, and found a horse certainly; but it was lame in one foot, and halted as it walked. He mounted his sorry steed, however, and rode away to the borders of the forest, and, standing still, called out three times, 'Iron Hans,' so loud that the trees echoed the sound.

In a moment the wild man appeared, and said:

'What do you wish for?'

'I want a strong horse to carry me to the battle,' he replied.

'That you shall have, and still more if you want it.'

On saying this, the wild man went back into the forest; and presently appeared a groom coming towards the young man, and leading a beautiful horse, snorting and curvetting, which could scarcely be held in; and behind him followed a troop of warriors clothed in bright steel, their swords glittering in the sun.

The youth gave up to the groom his three-legged horse, mounted the spirited creature, and rode away at the head of his troop of warriors. When they reached the battle-field, they found that a large number of the king's troops had already fallen, and those who remained were too weak to attack the enemy.

Then the young knight rode into the field with his troop of steel-clad warriors, drove like a storm over the enemy, and overpowered all resistance. Those who remained took to flight; but he rode after them, and he and his soldiers put them to total rout. Instead, however, of going to the king to claim the honour of this victory, he turned and led his troop back to the wood, and called for Iron Hans.

'What do you wish for now?' said the wild man, when he appeared.

'Take back your horse and your warriors, and give me my three-legged nag again.' His wish was complied with, and he rode home on his three-legged horse.

Meanwhile, the king returned to the castle, and his daughter came to him and congratulated him on his good fortune.

'It is not my victory at all,' he said, 'but owing to a strange knight who came to our help with steel-clad warriors.'

The princess wanted to know who this strange knight was, but the king could not satisfy her. He told her that he and his soldiers had followed the flying enemy, and had not been seen since. The princess also inquired of the gardener where his garden-assistant was gone.

The gardener laughed, and said: 'He has been away, and returned again on his three-legged horse, and the other servants have been jeering and laughing at him, and crying out, ' Here comes our Hunkypuns back again!' And they asked which hedge he hid behind while the battle was going on; and his was a strange reply. He said he had done better than any of them, and that the victory would not have been won without him! And at this they laughed more than ever.'

The king told his daughter a few days after that he intended to celebrate the victory in a festival which should last three days. 'And you shall have a golden apple to throw among the visitors,' he said, ' and perhaps this unknown warrior may be there.'

As soon as the invitations were sent out, the young man went into the forest, and called Iron Hans.

' What do you wish for now?' he asked.

' I want to be the fortunate one at the feast, and to catch the golden apple when the princess throws it.'

' You may be as sure of it as if you had it now,' said Iron Hans. ' And you shall have a red suit of armour and a chestnut horse to ride on!'

The appointed day arrived, the young man presented himself at the castle, and mixed so quickly with the other knights that no one re-cognised him. During the entertainment, the princess stepped forward, and threw among the knights a golden apple. It was caught by the stranger, who immediately slipped out and disappeared.

On the second day Iron Hans provided him with a white suit of armour, and he rode a gray horse. Again he caught the apple, and after doing so did not stop a moment, but rode quickly away. At this the king became angry, and said he could not allow it, and that who-ever caught the apple ought to show himself and give up his name. He therefore gave orders that if this strange knight again caught the apple, and left in such haste, he was to be pursued and brought back, and if he would not return willingly they were to use force.

The third day of the festival arrived; and the young knight this time appeared in black armour, and riding a splendid black horse with which Iron Hans had supplied him. Again he caught the apple, and instantly rode away, followed by the king's people; but it was not possible to overtake that fleet horse, although one approached near enough to wound the young knight in the leg with the point of his sword. He kept his seat, however; but his horse started so violently that his helmet fell off, and they could see the golden hair that lay scattered on his shoulders. So they rode back, and told the king all that had happened.

The next day the princess asked the gardener where his young assistant was. ' He is at work in the garden to-day,' he replied. ' But the wonder to me is that he should have been absent during the three days of the festival, and only came back last night; and he has also shown to my children three golden apples, which he says he has won.'

On hearing of this the king ordered him to be sent for; and he made his appearance as usual with his hat on. But the princess went quickly towards him, and as she pulled it off, down fell the golden hair on his shoulders, making him look so beautiful that they were all astonished.

' Are you the knight,' asked the king, ' who has attended the feast each day in different coloured armour, and caught the three golden apples?'

' Yes,' he replied ; ' and there are the apples,' he continued, taking them out of his pocket and offering them to the king. ' If you wish for further proof, I can show you the wound which one of your people inflicted with his sword when they followed me. I am also the knight who helped you to conquer the enemy on the battle-field.'

' If you can perform such deeds as these,' said the king, ' you cannot be a common gardener. Who is your father ?'

' My father is a mighty king,' he replied ; ' and I have money quite as much as I want.'

' I see plainly,' said the king, ' that I owe you more than thanks. Can I do anything to show my gratitude ?'

' Yes, indeed,' replied the young knight. ' You can give me your daughter to be my wife.'

The young maiden laughed as she said, ' I shall raise no obstacle; for I knew long ago by his golden hair that he was no gardener's son.'

And then she went forward and kissed him.

To the marriage came his father and mother, who were overjoyed at finding him alive ; for they had given up all hopes of seeing their dear son again.

On the day of the marriage, while they sat at the wedding-feast, all at once the music ceased, the door opened, and a noble-looking king stepped into the room, followed by a magnificent retinue. He approached the bridegroom, embraced him, and said, ' I am Iron Hans. I was once a wild man while under the sorcerer's spell; but you have set me free. All the treasures that I possess shall now be yours.'

MOUNTAIN SESIMA.

THERE once lived two brothers—one was poor, the other rich ; but the rich brother gave the poor one nothing, and he had to work hard for his living. Times were sometimes so bad that his wife and children had not even bread to eat.

One day he was driving his cart through a wood, and noticed at the side of the path an opening through the trees, and behind them a large barren mountain which he had never observed before. So he stood still, and looked at it with surprise.

As he so stood he saw twelve fierce-looking men coming towards him. Thinking they were robbers, he drew his cart behind the bushes, and climbed up a tree to see what would happen. The twelve men went and stood before the mountain, and cried, ' Mountain Sesima, Mountain Sesima—open thyself !' Immediately the sides of the mountain parted asunder, and the twelve men walked in, and immediately it closed after them.

In a short time, however, it again opened, and the twelve men came out carrying heavy sacks on their backs, and as soon as they were all in the open air they turned to the mountain, and said, ' Mountain Sesima, Mountain Sesima, close thyself !'

The sides instantly came together, and there was no longer any entrance to be seen, and the twelve men went away.

As soon as they were out of sight, the poor man came down from the tree, and felt very curious to know what could be concealed in the mountain. So he placed himself before it, and said, 'Mountain Sesima, Mountain Sesima, open thyself !' and the mountain stood open before him. He stepped in, and found that the whole interior was a mine full of silver and gold, and behind the gold lay heaps of pearls and sparkling precious stones like hoarded grain.

The poor man hardly knew what to do, or whether he dare take anything from these treasures. At last he filled his pockets with gold, leaving the pearls and precious stones lying untouched. When he wished to go out of the mine, he remembered to say, Mountain Sesima, Mountain Sesima, close thyself !' And immediately the mountain closed, and the poor man took his cart from behind the bushes, and drove it home to his house.

He now wanted for nothing, care had fled, and he could buy bread and wine, and all he required for his wife and children. They lived for a long time in happiness and peace, but he did not forget to give to the poor, and was kind to everyone.

When he went a second time to the mountain, he borrowed of his brother a bushel measure to carry the gold and silver; but the rich treasure he did not touch. At his third visit he also borrowed the bushel of his brother, whose suspicions were now aroused. He had for a long time been jealous of his brother's fortune and his happy household, and he could not imagine where he obtained these riches, and what he wanted the bushel for. Then a cunning thought came into his head : he would spread pitch over the bottom of the bushel ; and when the measure came back, there, sure enough, was a piece of gold sticking to it.

Immediately he went to his brother, and asked him, ' What have you been measuring with my bushel ?'

' Wheat and barley,' said the other. Then he showed him the piece of gold, and threatened him that if he did not tell the truth he would complain of him to the justices. Then the poor man told his brother all that had occurred.

On this, the rich brother had the horses harnessed to a waggon, and drove away, quite determined to make good use of the opportunity, and bring away richer treasure than mere gold and silver. When he came to the mountain, he cried, 'Mountain Sesima, Mountain Sesima, open thyself!' The mountain obeyed; and, as he went in, the mountain closed upon him.

There lay the riches all before him, and he for a long time was in doubt what first to lay hold of. At last he selected as many precious stones as he could carry, and turned to go out of the mountain with his load.

But his heart and thoughts had been so full of riches and treasures that he had forgotten the words, and said, 'Mountain Simeli, Mountain Simeli, open thyself!' but that was not the right word, and the mountain did not move itself, but remained closed.

He became terribly frightened; but the longer he thought over the word the more puzzled he became, and all his treasures now were useless to help him. Evening came, and then the mountain opened, and the twelve robbers came in. They quickly saw him, and laughed as they said, 'Have we caged you at last, little bird? Did you think that your visits were not noticed? The first and second times we could not touch you; but this is the third time, and you shall not escape.'

Then he cried out piteously, 'It was not me, indeed it was not me until to-day; it was my brother!'

But he might beg for his life, and say what he would all was useless; they very quickly cut his head off.

THE THREE FEATHERS.

THERE was once a king who had three sons. Two of them were considered wise and prudent; but the youngest, who said very little, appeared to others so silly that they gave him the name of Simple. When the king became old and weak, and began to think that his end was near, he knew not to which of his sons to leave his kingdom.

So he sent for them, and said, 'I have made a determination that whichever of you brings me the finest carpet shall be king after my death.'

They immediately prepared to start on their expedition, and, that there might be no dispute between them, they took three feathers. As they left the castle, each blew a feather into the air, and said, 'We will travel in whatever direction these feathers take.' One flew to the east, and the other to the west; but the third soon fell on the earth, and remained there. Then the two eldest brothers turned one to the right, and the other to the left, and they laughed at Simple, because where his feather fell he was obliged to remain.

Simple sat down after his brothers were gone, feeling very sad; but presently, looking round, he noticed, near where his feather lay, a kind of trap-door. He rose quickly, went towards it, and lifted it up. To his surprise he saw a flight of steps, down which he descended, and reached another door; hearing voices within, he knocked hastily. The voices were singing:

> 'Little frogs, crooked legs,
> Where do you hide?
> Go and see quickly
> Who is outside.'

At this the door opened of itself, and the youth saw a large fat frog seated, with a number of little frogs round her.

On seeing him, the large frog asked what he wanted.

'I have a great wish for the finest and most beautiful carpet that can be got,' he replied. Then the old frog called again to her little ones:

> 'Little frogs, crooked legs,
> Run here and there;
> Bring me the large bag
> That hangs over there.'

The young frogs fetched the bag, and, when it was opened, the old frog took from it a carpet so fine and so beautifully worked that nothing on earth could equal it. This she gave to the young man, who thanked her and went away up the steps.

Meanwhile, his elder brothers, quite believing that their foolish brother would not be able to get any carpet at all, said one to another: 'We need not take the trouble to go farther, and seek for anything very wonderful; ours is sure to be the best.' And as the first person they met was a shepherd, wearing a shepherd's plaïd, they bought the large plaid cloth and carried it home to the king.

At the same time the younger brother returned with his beautiful carpet, and when the king saw it he was astonished, and said: 'If justice is done, then the kingdom belongs to my youngest son.'

But the two elder brothers gave the king no peace; they said it was impossible for Simple to become king, for his understanding failed in everything, and they begged their father to make another condition.

At last he said: 'Whoever finds the most beautiful ring, and brings it to me, shall have the kingdom.'

Away went the brothers a second time, and blew three feathers into the air to direct their way. The feathers of the two eldest flew east and west, but that of the youngest fell, as before, near the trap-door, and there rested. He at once descended the steps, and told the great frog that he wanted a most beautiful ring. She sent for her large bag, and drew from it a ring which sparkled with precious stones, and was so beautiful that no goldsmith on earth could make one like it.

The elder brothers had again laughed at Simple, when his feather fell so soon to the ground, and, forgetting his former success with the carpet, scorned the idea that he could ever find a gold ring. So they gave themselves no trouble, but merely took a plated ring from the harness of a carriage horse, and brought it to their father.

But when the king saw Simple's splendid ring he said at once : 'The kingdom belongs to my youngest son.'

His brothers, however, were not yet inclined to submit to the decision; they begged their father to make a third condition, and at last he promised to give the kingdom to the son who brought home the most beautiful woman to be his wife.

They all were again guided by blowing the feathers, and the two elder took the roads pointed out to them. But Simple, without hesitation, went at once to the frog, and said : 'This time I am to take home the most beautiful woman.'

'Hey-day !' said the frog, 'I have not one by me at present; but you shall have one soon.' So she gave him a carrot, which had been hollowed out, and to which six mice were harnessed.

Simple took it quite sorrowfully, and said : 'What am I to do with this?'

'Seat one of my little frogs in it,' she said.

The youth, on this, caught one up at a venture, and seated it in the carrot. No sooner had he done so, than it became a most beautiful young lady; the carrot was turned into a gilded coach; and the mice were changed to prancing horses.

He kissed the maiden, seated himself in the carriage with her, drove away to the castle, and led her to the king.

Meanwhile his brothers had proved more silly than he ; not forgetting the beautiful carpet and the ring, they still thought it was impossible for Simple to find a beautiful woman also. They therefore took no more trouble than before, and merely chose the handsomest peasant maidens they could find to bring to their father.

When the king saw the beautiful maiden his youngest son had brought, he said : 'The kingdom must now belong to my youngest son after my death.'

But the eldest brothers deafened the king's ears anew with their cries, 'We cannot consent to let our stupid brother be king; give us one more trial. Let a ring be hung in the hall, and let each woman spring through it.' For they thought the peasant maidens would easily manage to do this, because they were strong, and that the delicate lady would, no doubt, kill herself. To this trial the old king consented.

The peasant maidens jumped first; but they were so heavy and awkward that they fell, and one broke her arm and the other her leg. But the beautiful lady whom Simple had brought home sprung as lightly as a deer through the ring, and thus put an end to all opposition.

The youngest brother married the beautiful maiden, and, after his father's death, ruled the kingdom for many years with wisdom and equity.

THE WOLF AND THE FOX.

A WOLF once made friends with a fox, and kept him always by him, so that whatever the wolf wanted the fox was obliged to do, because he was the weakest, and could not, therefore, be master. It happened one day that they were both passing through a wood, and the wolf said: ' Red fox, find me something to eat, or I shall eat you.'

' Well,' replied the fox, ' I know a farmyard near in which there are two young lambs ; if you like, I will go and fetch one.'

The wolf was quite agreeable, so the fox went to the field, stole the lamb, and brought it to the wolf; he then returned to find something for himself.

The wolf soon ate up the lamb, but he was not satisfied, and began to long so much for the other lamb, that he went to fetch it himself. But he managed so awkwardly that the mother of the lamb saw him, and began to cry and bleat fearfully; and the farmer came running out to see what was the matter. The wolf got so terribly beaten that he ran limping and howling back to the fox.

' You have led me into a pretty mess,' he said. ' I wanted the other lamb, and because I went to fetch it, the farmer has nearly killed me.'

' Why are you such a glutton, then ?' replied the fox.

Another day, as they were in a field, the greedy wolf exclaimed, ' Red fox, if you don't find me something to eat, I shall eat you up.'

' Oh ! I can get you some pancakes if you like,' he said ; ' for I know a farmhouse where the wife is frying them now.'

So they went on together, and the fox sneaked into the house, sniffed, and smelt about for some time, till he at last found out where the dish stood. Then he dragged six pancakes from it, and brought them to the wolf.

' Now you have something to eat,' said the fox, and went away to find his own dinner.

The wolf, however, swallowed the pancakes in the twinkling of an eye, and said to himself, ' They taste so good I must have some more.'

So he went into the farm kitchen, and, while pulling down the pancakes, upset the dish, and broke it in pieces.

The farmer's wife heard the crash, and came rushing in; but when she saw the wolf she called loudly for the farm servants, who came rushing in, and beat him with whatever they could lay their hands on, so that he ran back to the fox in the wood with two lame legs, howling terribly.

'How could you serve me such a dirty trick?' he said. 'The farmer nearly caught me; and he has given me such a thrashing.'

'Well, then,' replied the fox, 'you should not be such a glutton.'

Another day, when the wolf and the fox were out together, and the wolf was limping with fatigue, he said, 'Red fox, find me something to eat, or I shall eat you.'

The fox replied, 'I know a man who has been slaughtering cattle to-day; and there is a quantity of salted meat lying in a tub in the cellar. I can fetch some of that.'

'No,' said the wolf; 'let me go with you this time. You can help me if I cannot run away fast enough.'

'You may come for aught I care,' replied Reynard, and showed him on the way many of his tricks; and at last they reached the cellar safely.

There was meat in abundance. The wolf made himself quite at home, and said, 'There will be time to stop when I hear any sound.'

The fox also enjoyed himself; but he kept looking round now and then, and ran often to the hole through which they had entered to try if it was still large enough for his body to slip through.

'Dear fox,' said the wolf, 'why are you running about and jumping here and there so constantly?'

'I must see if anyone is coming,' replied the cunning animal, 'and I advise you not to eat too much.'

The wolf replied, 'I am not going away from here till the tub is empty.'

At this moment in came the farmer, who had heard the fox jumping about in the cellar. The fox no sooner saw him than with a spring he was through the hole. The wolf made an attempt to follow him; but he had eaten so much and was so fat that he stuck fast. The farmer, on seeing this, fetched a cudgel and killed him on the spot. The fox ran home to his den, full of joy that he was at last set free from the old glutton's company.

THE THREE TRADES.

A MAN who had three sons was very anxious respecting their future career after his own death. He had nothing to leave them but the house in which they lived, and was rather puzzled which to make his heir. He thought, it is true, that he could sell the house and divide the money between them; but at last he determined to call them together, and talk over the matter. So he said to them, 'I think you had better each go out into the world, and learn some trade, and on your return whoever shall bring the greatest masterpiece shall have the house.'

The young men were very much pleased with this proposal. The eldest chose the trade of blacksmith, the second of a barber, and the third determined to become a fencing-master. So they appointed a time to meet together again at the house, and set out on their journey.

Fortunately they all fell in with first-rate masters, who taught them the higher branches of their trade. The eldest son was at last appointed to shoe the king's horses, and thought to himself, ' After this, I am sure to get the house.'

The second son, who was a barber, had first-rate appointments at the houses of nobleman, and thought of the house as already his.

The fencing-master had received many hard knocks, but he clenched his teeth, and did not complain; for he thought to himself, ' If I am afraid of being knocked about, I shall never be able to claim the house.'

At length the time came for them to meet again at home for their father to decide; but they could not at first find an opportunity to make their cleverness known. So they sat down together in the field to consider the matter. As they thus sat, they saw a hare running across the field towards them.

' Hi!' exclaimed the barber, ' here comes an opportunity for me.' So he hastily filled his basin with lather, and as the hare ran by he shaved off a piece of his beard without cutting him or shortening another hair besides.

' I like that,' said the father; ' and unless your brothers can do something more wonderful still, the house is yours.'

Before long another opportunity occurred to display the skill of the second son. A gentleman drove by at a rapid rate in a carriage drawn by four horses. ' Now you shall see what I can do, father,' said the farrier; so he sprang out, took off the shoes of the leader, and replaced them with new ones, without stopping the carriage.

' Well,' exclaimed his father, ' you are a clever fellow; you have performed your task as skilfully as your brother, and I am puzzled now to know which of you ought to have the house.'

' Father,' said the youngest son, ' let me try before you decide.' At this moment it began to rain, and the fencing-master, looking up, cried, ' Here is my opportunity !' As he spoke he raised his fencing-stick, and made such rapid passes with it over and across their heads that not a drop of rain fell upon them, although it poured faster and heavier, as if the sky was being emptied with buckets; but where the father and his sons sat the ground remained as dry as if they had been under their own roof.

When the father saw the effect of this fencing he was astonished, and said : ' Most certainly the youngest has performed the best masterpiece; the house must be his.'

The elder brothers were quite content; they had already received praise for their work, and they were all so attached to each other, that they readily agreed to live together in the house, and follow their different trades. These trades had been so well learnt, and were so skilfully performed, that they soon made a great deal of money, and lived for many years in great contentment till old age came upon them. At last one of them was taken ill and died, and the other two grieved so greatly that they did not long survive him; and, as they had lived together in love and harmony, so, after their death, they were buried in the same grave.

THE DRAGON'S GRANDMOTHER.

A KING, who was at war with a neighbouring country, had a large number of soldiers; but he paid them so badly that they could scarcely manage to live. At last, three of them determined to run away on the first opportunity. 'If we are caught, we shall be hung on the gallows without mercy,' said one, who was fearful.

'Nonsense,' replied another; 'do you see that great cornfield in the distance? We can hide ourselves safely there; the army will not dare pass through a field of standing corn; besides, they are to march to-morrow morning.'

The others agreed to follow this advice, so the three soldiers deserted that night, and hid themselves in the standing corn. They had made a mistake, however, about the movements of the army, for it still remained encamped near to the cornfield in which they had concealed themselves.

For two days and nights they were obliged to remain there, not daring to move, till they were nearly starved, and death appeared inevitable. Then said one of them, 'What is the use of our deserting, if we are to die of hunger? We may as well give ourselves up at once.'

At this moment a great dragon appeared in the air above them, and, gradually sinking down to the place where they lay, asked them why they were concealing themselves.

'We are three soldiers who have deserted,' was the reply, 'because our pay was so small; but now we must die of hunger, for if we return we shall be hanged on the gallows.'

'Will you serve me for seven years?' said the dragon. 'I will carry you safely through the army, and no one shall see you.'

'We have no choice,' they replied, 'and must therefore accept your proposal.'

The dragon, on this, seized them in his claws, and carried them through the air, over the heads of their comrades, and landed them safely on the ground, at a great distance. He then gave each of them a whip, and said:

'When you crack these whips smartly, money will flow around you in abundance, as much as you desire.   You can then live in style, like great lords, and have horses, and carriages, and every luxury ; but at the end of seven years you will belong to me.'

At these words he handed them a book, in which they were expected to sign their names.   After this was done, he said :

' I will, however, give you one chance to escape me.   If at the end of the time you are able to guess three riddles which I shall then propound to you, my power will be over, and you will be free.'

The dragon then flew away, and the three soldiers immediately began to crack their whips joyfully, and soon had money enough and to spare. They had horses and carriages, and could travel all over the world, and they ate and drank, lived and dressed like gentlemen—happy and contented—but did nothing wicked or wrong.

Time, however, passed on quickly, and as the end of the seven years approached, two of the soldiers became very sad and uneasy ; the third, however, who was naturally light-hearted, said to them :

' Brothers, do not fear, I have my wits about me still ; I will find out the dragon's riddles.'

They were walking in the fields a few days after this, and the two fearful ones seated themselves on a mound with most woeful faces while the other stood by.   Presently an old woman passed them, and said :

' Why are you two looking so miserable ?'

' What does it matter to you ?' they replied.   'You cannot help us.'

' How do you know that ?' she replied.   'Come now, trust me with your sorrow, and see if I cannot help you.'

Then they told her about the dragon, and how that he had given them the means of making gold like hay for seven years, but that they had signed their names to be his servants at the end of that time, which had nearly arrived, unless they could guess three riddles. Therefore it was no wonder they felt so sad.

' If I am to help you,' replied the old woman, ' one of you must go into the forest.   There he will find a steep, overturned rock, which is used as a house.   If he enters this house, he will obtain help.'

The two desponding soldiers could not see much to hope for in this advice, so they remained seated in the wood, but the third exclaimed in a merry voice : ' I shall go and try my luck.'

He went at once deeper into the forest till he came to the overturned rock, which formed a hut, and immediately went in.   In the hut sat a very old woman who was the dragon's grandmother, and when she saw the soldier she asked him what he wanted and where he came from.   He answered all her questions, and told her his business so pleasantly that she was quite pleased with him, and so full of pity that she promised to help him.

Then she lifted up a great stone in the floor, and showed him a cellar beneath it, and said : ' You can hide yourself there, and listen to all

THE DRAGON'S GRANDMOTHER

SNOW-WHITE AND RED-ROSE

that passes up here. When the dragon comes home, you must remain quite still, without moving. I will then ask him about the riddle, and if you pay great attention, you will find out the answers.'

The soldier readily agreed to her wishes, and creeping down into the cellar, the old woman replaced the stone over him in the floor.

At about twelve o'clock the dragon came flying home with rushing wings, and crying out for his supper. The grandmother quickly laid the cloth, and brought out plenty of good things to eat and drink, and they supped together.

The dragon enjoyed his supper so much that he was in quite a good humour, and the old woman began to question him.

'Well,' she said, 'what success have you had to-day? How many poor creatures have you caught?'

'I have not had much luck,' he replied; 'but there are three soldiers who cannot escape me; I have them fast enough.'

'Ah, indeed; three soldiers? I suppose you have given them some impossible task to perform?'

'Yes, I have,' he said, with a chuckle; 'the riddles I shall ask them they will never find out; they are mine safe enough.'

'What are the riddles?' she asked.

'Oh, I don't mind telling you,' he replied. 'In the great North Sea lies a dead sea-cat, this will serve them for roast meat; the ribs of a whale shall be their silver spoon; and an old, hollow horseshoe they shall use for a wine-glass.'

After telling the riddle, the dragon rose and went to bed, and then the old grandmother lifted up the stone and set the soldier free.

'Have you listened attentively?' she asked.

'Indeed I have,' he replied; 'I know quite enough now to help us out of all our difficulties.'

The old woman then opened the window cautiously, and let him out that way instead of through the door; she also went with him a short distance to show him a new and a shorter road to his comrades.

With many thanks he parted from her, and reached their home in all haste. The two soldiers listened with surprise as he told them of the dragon's cunning old grandmother; and when they heard the riddle and its solution, they were full of joy, and, taking up their whips, began to crack them so fast that the floor of the house was soon covered with gold.

A few days afterwards the seven years came to an end, and the dragon appeared with his book under his arm, and, pointing to the signatures of the soldiers, said: 'You will have to go with me to my kingdom, and a festival shall be held to celebrate the event unless you can solve my riddle. You will have to tell me what your roast meat will be on that occasion.'

'Oh, that is easy enough,' replied the first soldier quickly. 'In the great North Sea lies a dead sea-cat; that will be our roast meat.'

'Hem! hem!' said the dragon in a rage, and then asked the second what would be their spoon.

'One of the ribs of a whale shall be our silver spoon.'

The dragon made a wry face, and snarled again three times, 'Hem! hem! hem!' and then said to the third: 'And pray what will your wineglass be?'

'An old horse's hoof shall our wineglass be,' he cried joyfully.

With a cry of rage the dragon spread his wings and flew away, for his power over them was now quite gone; but they had kept their whips, and continued to whip money till they had as much as they wanted, and on this they lived happily together for the rest of their lives.

THE IRON CHEST.

In olden times, when people had no power against the wicked wishes of others, a king's son was placed under enchantment by an old witch, and shut up in an iron chest in the forest.

Years rolled by, but no one was able to set him free. At length one day a king's daughter, who had been wandering through the wood for some days and lost her way, came near the iron chest; and, while she stood wondering what it could be, a voice proceeded from it, and said, 'Where do you come from? and what are you doing here?'

'I have missed my way to my father's kingdom, and know not how to find my way home.'

Then the voice from the iron chest replied, 'I will help you to reach your home by a very short road, if you will give me your word of honour to do as I wish. I am the son of a great king, and in the same rank as yourself, and if I am set free from this enchantment you shall be my wife.'

She was quite frightened at this, and said to herself, 'What can I do with this iron chest?' However, as she wanted to be shown the way to her home, she promised to do all he asked.

'Very well,' he replied; 'come back here again to-morrow, and bring with you a knife to scrape a hole in this iron chest that I may escape.' He then gave her directions how to find a road which was very little known, and it led her to her home in a few minutes.

When the king's daughter arrived at the castle there was great joy, and the old king clasped her in his arms, and kissed her with happiness and love at finding her at home in safety. But the princess looked very mournful, and said, 'Dear father, such a strange thing has happened to me. I should never have returned home, or found my way out of the wood, if I had not stooped to look at a large iron chest; and while I stood there a voice came from the chest, and said I should be directed in the shortest way if I would give my word of honour to return and set the owner of the voice free and marry him.'

This account so alarmed the old king that he nearly fell into a swoon, for this was his only daughter. So, after some reflection, he decided to send for the miller's daughter, and take her to the place instead of his own. When she came to the castle, he led her out into the wood, gave her a knife, and told her to scrape a hole in the iron chest. She scraped away at one spot for a whole day and night, but not the slightest hole could she make.

At daybreak a voice came from within the chest, and said, 'Is not the day breaking?'

'Yes,' she replied, 'I believe it is; for I can hear the click of my father's mill.'

'What! are you a miller's daughter?' cried the voice. 'Then go back at once and send the king's daughter here.'

She went immediately to the castle, and told the old king that whoever was shut up in the iron chest would not have her there, but wanted the king's daughter.

The good king was still more alarmed at this, and his daughter wept. However, this time they thought of the swineherd's daughter, who was even still more beautiful than the miller's daughter. She was sent for, and the king promised her a piece of gold, if she would go into the forest and scrape the iron chest instead of the princess.

She readily agreed to go; but after working for many hours till daybreak without any result, the voice said, 'Is it not morning?'

'Yes,' she replied, 'it must be; for I hear my father blowing his horn.'

'What! are you a swineherd's daughter?' said the voice. 'Then go away directly and send the princess; and tell her that if she does not come back here as she promised, the whole of her father's kingdom will be destroyed, and the castle thrown down, till not one stone remains upon another.'

When the princess heard this she began to weep; but there was nothing else to be done. She knew she must keep to her promise. She therefore took leave of her father, and, with a knife in her hand, went away into the forest where the iron chest stood.

As soon as she arrived she began at once to scrape away with all her might, and in less than two hours she had succeeded in making a small hole. Through this hole she peeped in, and, to her great surprise, saw a handsome young man, whose dress glittered with gold and precious stones.

She was so pleased with her discovery that she went on scraping, and in a very short time the hole was large enough for him to creep out.

'Now you have set me free, and broken the spell,' cried the king's son; 'and you shall be my bride, for we belong to each other.' He wanted to take her to his father's kingdom at once; but she begged him to let her go and say farewell to her father. The king's son gave her permission ; but he cautioned her on no account to speak to her father more than three words.

She went home quickly ; but she spoke more than three words ; and in consequence the iron chest was lifted up, and carried away from the forest over rocky mountains and snow-clad peaks. The king's son, however, was still free, and could never again be locked up in the iron case. After taking leave of her father, the king's daughter took a little money in her pocket, and turned her steps to the wood, to seek for the iron case ; but it was gone. For nine days she searched the forest round, and at last became so faint with fatigue and hunger that she felt ready to die.

One evening she climbed up as usual into a tree to be safe during the night ; for she was afraid of the wild beasts. As she sat thinking with sorrow of her lost bridegroom, she saw a light at a little distance. ' Oh !' she exclaimed, ' perhaps I may find help now.'

She descended from the tree and turned her steps towards the light, and on coming nearer she found a small, old, wooden house surrounded by high grass.

It looked so lonely and dismal that she wished she had not come. However, she ventured to peep through the window, and saw no living creature inside, but frogs of all sizes, big and little. There was, however, a supper-table richly spread with bread and wine, and the plates and cups were of silver.

Then she took heart and knocked at the door. At this she heard an old frog say, ' Go quickly, and see who is outside.' A little frog came immediately and opened the door ; and as the king's daughter entered, they all bid her welcome, asked her to sit down, and inquired where she came from, and what she wanted.

In answer to their questions she related all that had happened, and acknowledged that in consequence of her having overstepped the order not to utter more than three words, the iron chest and the king's son had both disappeared. But she said, ' I mean to seek him over hill and valley till I find him.'

On hearing all this the old frog desired the little ones to bring her the large bag, and while they dragged it across the room she told the king's daughter to sit down to the table, and eat her supper.

After she had finished the little frogs led her to a beautiful bed, which was of velvet embroidered with gold, and on it she laid herself, and slept in great comfort.

In the morning when she rose the old frog told her that she would have to climb one high slippery mountain, to cross three snowy peaks, and a great lake. She then gave her some articles from the bag, namely, three large needles, one ploughshare and three nuts, of which she was to take the greatest care, and use them when necessary.

Promising to attend to the frog's advice, the king's daughter started on her journey, and very soon came to the glassy mountain. Here she stopped, took off her shoes, and stuck the needles into the soles. This enabled her to clamber without difficulty over the slippery mountain.

On reaching the other side she pulled out the needles, and stuck them carefully in a corner that they might not be lost. She came after this very quickly to the snow-clad peaks. Across these she passed easily with the help of the ploughshare, and at length reached the large lake, over which she crossed in a ferryboat and saw before her a noble castle.

She went up to the gate, and asked to be engaged as a servant in the kitchen; for she wanted to discover if the king's son still loved her. Here she quickly heard to her sorrow that he was going to marry another; for he thought as she did not return that she was either dead or had forgotten him.

The wedding-day was approaching, but she knew what to do; and, on the evening of the first festival, she took one of the nuts which the old frog had given her, broke it, and took out a most beautiful dress, and went to the ball.

The king's son, supposing her to be one of the guests, led her out to dance; and, as they danced together, she whispered, 'Have you forgotten the iron chest, and the king's daughter who set you free?' In a moment the enchantment was broken, the prince recognised his true bride, and they travelled back, full of joy, to his own kingdom.

The new bride was the daughter of a witch, who, when the young princess had forgotten the order not to speak more than three words, had carried away the iron chest and the prince to her castle, that he might marry her daughter.

But now he was set free, and, as he travelled homewards with his true bride, they came to the wood in which once stood the house with the frogs; but now they found on its site a noble castle. On entering, instead of the young frogs, a number of princes and princesses advanced to receive them. The spell over them had been broken, and they were full of joy.

At this castle the marriage festival was held, and they wished to reside there, as it was much larger than their father's castle. The old king, however, complained of being left alone, so they returned to him, united the two kingdoms, one to be ruled over by the old king, and another by his son-in-law, whose married life was very happy.

THE LAMB AND THE FISH.

THERE lived once a little brother and sister who were very fond of each other. Their own mother was dead, and they had a stepmother who did not love them at all, and tried secretly to injure them.

It happened one day that the two children were playing in a meadow near the house with several other children, very happily.   Through this meadow ran a stream of water, which passed one side of the house, and on its banks the children were singing :

> ' Encké Bencké, that's the word,
> Will you be my little bird ?
> Birdie a sugar-stick will give,
> That will I to the good cook give ;
> The cook will give to me some milk ;
> The milk I will to the baker take,
> And he will make me a sugar-cake ;
> The cake I shall then give to puss,
> And she will quickly catch a mouse !
> I shall hang it up in the house,
> And then it is mine.'

While singing this, the children held hands, and danced round in a circle.   One, who stood in the middle, pointing with her finger to each child at each word, and when the word *mine* occurred the child who was pointed at ran from the circle, and the others had to run after him to catch him.

As the children were thus amusing themselves, and chasing each other about merrily, the stepmother looked out of the window, and, when she saw them so happy, wicked envy rose in her heart, and in her spite she used her power of witchcraft, and changed them both; the boy into a fish, the girl into a lamb.

A sorrowful little fish might now be seen swimming about in the stream, while near its banks, in the meadow, stood a pretty little lamb, too sad to eat even a blade of grass.

It happened, not long after, that the stepmother had visitors at her house, and she thought it would be a nice opportunity to get rid of the children.   So she called the cook, and told her to fetch the lamb from the meadow, and the fish from the pond, and kill them, to be cooked and eaten at the feast, and the woman innocently promised to obey.

But when the lamb and the fish were brought into the kitchen, and she took up the knife to kill them, the lamb—who was really the little sister—cried out :

> ' Ah ! little brother in the sea,
> Sadly my fond heart weeps for thee ;
> The cook is whetting the cruel knife,
> To take away my life.'

Then the little fish answered :

> ' Ah ! little sister, my heart is sad,
> And oh, my fate will be quite as bad,
> Down in the deep, deep sea.'

When the cook heard the lamb speak these sorrowful words, and the fish answer them, she was frightened, and knew they were not natural animals, but some human beings which her wicked mistress had be-witched. So she said : 'Do not fear ; I will not hurt either of you.' So she fetched another lamb from the field and another fish from the brook, and prepared them for the visitors.

She then took the bewitched lamb to a peasant's wife, and told her all about it. This woman had been wet nurse to the little girl, and she seemed drawn towards the lamb so tenderly, that at last she took her to a wise woman and asked her advice.

Without hesitation, the wise woman pronounced some good words over the lamb and the fish, and at once the spell was broken, the children returned to their proper shapes, and went away together to a great forest, in which stood a small, but very pretty house. Here they lived, although lonely, yet contented and happy, for the rest of their lives.

THE ASS'S SKIN.

THERE lived once a king and queen who had riches and everything they wished for except a little child, and at last this wish also was granted to them, and a little prince was born into the world.

Now, the queen had once offended a wicked witch, and she by her witchcraft altered the baby's face till it looked like an ass's, and was so ugly that the mother, when she saw it, was quite frightened ; she even wanted to have it thrown into the water and drowned, for she said it was only fit to be food for fishes.

But the king said, 'No. Ugly as the child may be, he is my son, and after my death this kingdom and my crown will be his.'

So the ugly little child was taken care of, and grew up healthy and strong, and not so very frightful after all, although he had such large ears. He was a lively, good-tempered little fellow—jumping and running here and there like a squirrel. But the most remarkable of his tastes was a love of music, and when he grew old enough he went to a first-rate professor, and asked to be taught to play on the lute.

Now, unfortunately, one of the young prince's defects was the form of his fingers, and the professor of music said to him :

'My lord prince, I fear I could never teach you to play the lute, your fingers are too thick and clumsy.'

The boy, however, was not to be daunted, and he persevered with so much determination that he soon played as well as his master. As he grew older, he began to think of his personal appearance, and one day happening to notice his looks in the glass, he became very sad and miserable at finding himself so ugly. He determined, therefore, to leave home, and go out into the world with only one faithful com-panion.

After travelling about for some time, they came at last to a country the king of which was a powerful monarch who had an only daughter, a most beautiful maiden.

'We will stay here for a while,' said the ugly prince. So he knocked at the door of the king's castle, and cried : 'Here is a visitor outside ; open and let him in.'

But the gates were not opened ; and then the prince seated himself on the steps, took out his lute, and began to play in the most delightful manner.

On hearing the music, the guard looked out, and, seeing the player, whose face was so like an ass, he ran to the king and told him that there was a strange animal before the door playing music like a first-rate musician.

'Let him come in,' said the king.

But as soon as he appeared, everyone began to laugh, and some of them told him to sit with the servants.

'No, indeed,' he said ; 'I may be ugly, but I am nobly born.'

'Well, then, take your place among the soldiers.'

But to this he would not consent, and exclaimed : 'I mean to sit by the king.'

On hearing of this, the king laughed, and said good-naturedly, 'So you shall, if you wish it ; come here by me.' After awhile the king said to him : 'Well, how do you like my daughter ?'

The ugly prince turned and looked at her earnestly ; then he nodded his head, and said, 'Very much indeed ; she is the most beautiful maiden I ever saw in my life.'

'Well, then, you shall sit by her side if you will.'

'That will be my right place,' he replied, seating himself by the princess ; and he treated her so kindly and politely that she quite forgot how ugly he was, and began to like him very much.

They kept him at the castle for some time, till he said to himself at last : 'What is the use of staying here ? I may as well go home.' But the thought of leaving the princess made him look very sorrowful when he went to bid the king farewell.

He had by this time, however, won the love of the king, and he said to him : 'Why, my friend, you look as sour as a vinegar-cruet ! Why do you wish to go away ? Stay with me, and I will give you whatever you wish. Will you have money ?'

'No,' he replied, shaking his head.

'Do you want jewels or trinkets ?'

'Oh no !'

'Shall I give you half of my kingdom, then, to keep you here ?'

'No ; oh no !' he cried earnestly.

'I wish I knew what would really content you,' said the king, and then exclaimed, 'Ah, perhaps you want to marry my beautiful daughter ?'

What a change came over the ugly face as the young prince said : 'Ah, yes; that is all I crave, if I only thought she could love me.'

But there seemed no doubt of this, for the wonderful music and the gentle ways of the high-born prince had made the princess quite forget his ugliness. So the marriage was celebrated with great pomp and splendour; and at the wedding, instead of an ugly bridegroom, with the face and long ears of an ass, there stood before them a handsome young prince.

On the night before the bridal a good fairy—who had waited till now to destroy the cruel sorcery which had so disfigured the king's son—came and touched him with her wand; the ass's skin immediately fell off, and he was restored to his natural shape and form.

The young princess was overjoyed to think that she had loved him for his good qualities alone. The king, however, could scarcely believe him to be the same till he showed him the ass's skin which had fallen off at the touch of the fairy's wand.

The king immediately ordered a large fire to be lighted, into which he threw the skin, and watched it till it was burnt to ashes.

There was great joy in the whole household after this, and the king gave to his son-in-law the government over half his kingdom, and at his death he became king. In a short time his own father died, and so he was king of both countries, and he and his queen lived in great happiness and splendour. It is better, therefore, to be good than handsome.

SNOW-WHITE AND RED-ROSE.

Once upon a time there lived in a lonely cottage, surrounded by a garden, a poor widow. In the garden grew two rose-trees, one of which bore white roses, the other red.

Now, the widow had two daughters, who so much resembled the rose-bushes that she gave to one the name of Snow-white, and to the other Red-rose.

These two children were the best, the most obedient, and most industrious children in the world; yet they differed in some respects. Snow-white was quiet and gentle, Red-rose was fond of running about the fields and meadows in search of flowers and butterflies.

Snow-white would often stay at home with her mother, help her with the house-work, and then read to her after it was done. The two children were very fond of each other, and whenever they walked out together they would hold each other's hands, and when Snow-white would say, ' We will never leave each other,' her sister would reply, ' No, never, as long as we live.'

The mother encouraged this; she would often say, ' Whatever nice things are given to either of you must be shared with the other;' and the sisters always did so.

They frequently rambled together alone in the wood, to gather berries: but not a creature ever did them any harm, although wild animals often passed them; they seemed to have such confidence in the sisters that they were quite friendly with them.

The little hares would eat cabbage-leaves out of their hands, the deer would graze by their side, the stag bound merrily near, while the birds would remain sitting and singing on the branches.

No danger ever threatened them, even if they stayed in the forest till late, or after night-fall. They would lie down on the mossy bed and sleep safely till morning, and their mother knew there was no cause for fear.

Once, when they had remained in the wood all night, they did not awake till the rising sun had reddened the eastern sky, and, as they opened their eyes, they saw near them a beautiful little child, whose clothes were white and shining. When he saw they were awake he looked kindly at them, and, without a word, vanished from their sight.

On rising, they found that they had been sleeping on the edge of a steep rock, down which they must have fallen had they moved in the dark. When they told their mother, she said it must have been one of the guardian angels who watch over good children.

Snow-white and Red-rose kept their mother's cottage so neat and clean that it was quite a pleasure to look at it. Every morning, in summer, Red-rose took care always to place a bouquet of fresh flowers by her mother's bed, in which was a flower from each of the rose-trees. In winter, Snow-white lighted the fire, filled the kettle, and placed it over the bright blaze, where it shone and glittered like gold; for it was of burnished copper, and was always kept bright and polished.

In the evening, when the snow was falling, and the door closed and locked, they would seat themselves round the fire, in the bright, snug little room, and knit busily, while their mother would put on her spectacles, and read to them out of the Good Book.

One, evening they were sitting in this peaceful happiness, with a pet lamb sleeping on the hearth near them, and above them, on a perch, a white dove, with its head behind its wing.

Presently came a knock at the door, and the mother said, 'Red-rose, open it quickly; no doubt some poor traveller, lost in the snow, wants shelter.' Red-rose hastened to obey; but, on opening the door, instead of the poor man she expected to see, a great bear pushed his great black head in.

Red-rose screamed aloud, and started back; the lamb bleated; the dove flew wildly about the room; and Snow-white hid herself behind her mother's bed.

The bear, however, began to speak very gently: 'Do not fear,' he said; 'I will not hurt you. I only want to warm myself by your fire, for I am half frozen.'

'Poor bear,' said the mother. 'Come in and lie down by the fire if you want to; but take care not to burn your furry coat.'

Then she called out, 'Snow-white and Red-rose, come here. The bear is quite gentle; he will do you no harm.'

So they both came near to the fire; and, by degrees, the dove and the lamb got over their fright, and settled themselves to sleep. Presently the bear said, 'Dear children, will you sweep off the snow from my fur?'

So they got the broom, and cleaned the bear's skin, till it looked quite smooth, and then he stretched himself at full length before the fire, grunting now and then to show how contented and comfortable he felt. In a very short time they lost all fear of their unexpected guest, and even began to play with him. They jumped on his back, rolled him over on the floor, and tapped him with a hazel-twig, pulled his thick fur, and when he growled they only laughed.

The bear allowed them to do as they liked, only saying, when they were too rough with him, 'Leave me my life, dear children, and don't quite kill your old sweetheart.'

When bedtime came, the mother said to him, 'You can stay here by the fire all night if you like. I will not turn you out in this dreadful weather, and here you will at least be sheltered from the cold.'

In the morning, when they all rose, the two children let him out, and he trotted away over the snow into the wood.

After that, he came each evening at the same hour, laid himself on the hearth, and allowed the children to play with him just as they pleased. They became so used to his visits that no one thought of bolting the door till his black muzzle was pushed in. The winter passed, and spring was again covering the meadows and forest trees with her robe of green, and one morning the bear said to Snow-white, 'I am going away now, during the summer, and you will not see me again till the end of autumn.'

'Where are you going, dear bear?' asked Snow-white.

'I must go to the forest,' he replied, 'to hide my treasures from those wicked dwarfs. In winter these treasures are safe under the frozen earth, but now, when the sun has warmed and softened the ground, it is easy for them to break it and dig up what I have buried, and when once anything valuable is in their hands it is not easy to recover it. They will take care that it does not see daylight again.'

Snow-white felt quite sorrowful when the bear said good-bye, but as he passed out of the door the latch caught his fur and tore a little piece off. Snow-white thought she saw something glittering like gold under the skin, but she was not sure, for the bear trotted away very quickly and was soon lost to sight amongst the trees. Some time after this the mother sent the children into the forest to gather brushwood, and they found a large tree which had fallen to the ground. As they stood looking at it they saw something jumping up and down on the other side of the trunk, but they could not think what it was till they went nearer, and then they saw a little dwarf with a shrivelled face, whose long white beard had been caught in the cleft of the tree. The dwarf was jumping about like a puppy at the end of a string, but he could not get free. He glared at the children with his red fiery eyes, and cried :

'Why are you standing there, staring, instead of offering to assist me ?'

'Poor little man,' said Red-rose, 'how did you do this ?'

'You stupid goose,' he replied angrily, 'I wanted to split up the tree that I might get some shavings for our cooking. A great coal fire burns up our little dinners and suppers ; we don't cram ourselves with food as your greedy people do. I drove my wedge into the tree and it seemed all right, but the horrid thing was so slippery that it sprung out again suddenly, and the tree closed so quickly that it caught my long white beard, and now holds it so fast that I cannot extricate it. See how the white milk-faced creatures laugh,' he shouted. 'Oh, but you are ugly.'

Notwithstanding his spiteful words and looks, the children wished to help him, and they went up to him and tried to pull out the beard, but all to no purpose.

'I will run home and call somebody,' said Red-rose.

'What !' snarled the dwarf, 'send for more people ! why, there are two too many here already, you sheepheaded madcaps.'

'Don't be impatient,' said Snow-white ; 'I think we can manage to release you.'

She took her scissors out of her pocket as she spoke and cut the dwarf's beard off close to the trunk of the tree. No sooner was he at liberty than he caught hold of a bag full of gold which was lying among the roots, grumbling all the time about the dreadful children who had cut off his magnificent beard, a loss which nothing could repay him. He then swung the bag across his shoulders and went away without one word of thanks to the children for helping him.

Some time after this, Snow-white and Red-rose went out one day to catch fish. As they sat fishing on the banks of the stream they saw something like a large grasshopper jumping about as if it were going to jump into the water. They ran forward, and recognised the dwarf.

'What are you doing here ?' asked Red-rose ; 'why do you wish to jump into the water ?'

'Do you think I am such a fool as that ?' he cried ; 'don't you see how this dreadful fish is dragging me ?'

The little man had been angling, but unfortunately the wind caught his beard, and entangled it in the line, so that when a large fish came up and swallowed the bait he had not strength to extricate himself, and the fish, in its efforts to escape, was dragging the dwarf into the water.

He held tightly by the reeds and rushes that grew on the bank, but with very little use, and the children were only just in time to save him from being dragged in by the fish. They both pulled him back with all their might, but as long as the beard remained entangled in the line, their efforts were useless, and they could not disentangle it. There remained no other means of saving him than by cutting off his beard, and this time so much of it that only a short piece remained.

Although by so doing they saved his life, the dwarf was in a dreadful rage ; he screamed out, ' Is it your custom, you wretches ! to disfigure people's faces in this way ?—not satisfied with cutting off a large piece the other day, you must now deprive me of nearly all. I dare not show myself such a fright as this. I wish you were obliged to run till you had lost the soles off your shoes.'

He lifted a bag of pearls which he had hidden among the rushes, and, throwing it on his shoulder without another word, slunk away and disappeared behind a stone. It happened on another occasion that the mother of the two maidens sent them to the town to purchase needles, thread, and ribbon. Their way lay across a heath, on which here and there great rocks lay scattered. Presently they saw a large bird hovering over a certain spot on the heath, till at last he pounced down suddenly to the earth, and at the same moment they heard terrible cries and piteous lamentations close to them. The children ran to the place, and saw with great alarm that a large eagle had got their old acquaintance the dwarf in his talons, and was carrying him away. The good-natured children did all they could—they held the little man fast to pull him back, and struggled so fiercely with the eagle, that at last the bird relinquished his prey and set him free.

But he had no sooner recovered from his fright than the ungrateful little wretch exclaimed :

' What do you mean by catching hold of me so roughly ? You clawed at my new coat till it is nearly torn off my back—awkward little clowns that you are !'

Then he took up his sack of precious stones, and slipped away among the rocks. The maidens were accustomed to his ingratitude, and did not care for it. So they went on their way to the town, and made their purchases.

On their return, while crossing the heath, they came unexpectedly again upon the dwarf, who had emptied his sack of precious stones in a quiet corner, not supposing that anyone would pass at such a late hour. The evening sun shone brightly on the glittering jewels, which sparkled and flashed out such beautiful colours in his golden light that the children stood and gazed in silent admiration.

' What are you standing there gaping at ?' asked the dwarf, his usually gray face quite red with rage. He was going on with his spiteful words when suddenly a terrible growl was heard, and a large black bear rushed out of the thicket.

The dwarf sprang up in a great fright, but he could not escape to a place of concealment, for the bear stood just in his way. Then he cried out piteously in his agony :

'Dear Mr. Bear, do spare my life. I will give you up all my treasures, and those jewels that you can see lying there, if you will only grant me my life. Such a weak little creature as I am would scarcely be a mouthful for you. See, there are two nice little tender bits—those two wicked maidens. They are as fat as young quails. Just eat them instead of me.'

But the bear paid no attention to his complaints. Without a word he lifted up his left fore-paw, and with one stroke laid the ugly, wicked little wretch dead on the ground.

The maidens in a fright were running away; but the bear called to them :

'Snow-white, Red-rose, don't be afraid. Wait; and I will go home with you.'

They instantly recognised his voice, and stood still till he came up to them; but as he approached, what was their astonishment to see the bearskin suddenly fall off, and instead of a rough bear there stood before them a handsome young man, with beautiful, gold-embroidered clothes.'

'I am a king's son,' he said; 'and that wicked dwarf, after robbing me of all I possessed, changed me into a bear; and I have been obliged to wander about the woods, watching my treasures, but not able to catch the dwarf and kill him till to-day. His death has set me free, and he has met with a well-deserved fate.'

Not many years after this Snow-white was married to the prince, and Red-rose to his brother, with whom he had shared the riches and treasures which the dwarf had stolen, and had concealed in his den till the prince recovered them at his death.

There was great joy in the village when these weddings took place, and Snow-white and Red-rose sent for their mother, who lived for many years in great happiness with her children.

The two rose-trees were brought to the castle and planted in the garden near the windows of the two sisters; and every year they bore the same beautiful red and white roses as they had done in the cottage-garden at home.

THE WATER OF LIFE.

A KING was once taken seriously ill, and everyone expected he would die. On hearing this, his three sons were so full of sorrow that they went into the garden of the castle, and wept bitterly.

In the midst of their sorrow they saw an old man approaching, who asked them the cause of their grief. They replied that their father was ill and expected to die; and that they wished to help him, and knew not how.

The old man replied:

'There is a way in which your father can be cured, if you do not mind trouble. He must drink a draught of the water of life. He will soon be well; but to find it is a very difficult task.'

'I will try,' said the eldest son, and he went at once to the sick king and begged for permission to go and seek this wonderful water, which could alone heal him.

'No,' replied the father; 'the risk is too great. I would rather die than allow you to incur such danger.'

But the prince begged so hard that at last the king unwillingly consented. The prince thought, 'If I bring this water I shall be my father's favourite son, and inherit his kingdom.'

In a very short time he was able to start on his journey, and after riding for some distance he at last saw in the road a dwarf, who stopped him, and cried, 'Where are you riding in such haste?'

'Stupid little pigmy!' replied the prince proudly. 'Where I am going is not for you to know;' and away he rode.

He had, however, made the little man in a rage, and he uttered a bad wish against the king's proud son.

He continued his journey, and came at last to a pass between two mountains; but as he rode on it appeared as if the mountains were closing together; and at last the way became so narrow that his horse could not possibly proceed a step either backwards or forwards, neither could he dismount from the saddle; so that he found himself a prisoner enclosed in the mountains.

The sick king anxiously expected his son day after day, but he did not return. Then the second son begged to be allowed to seek this wonderful remedy; and he also thought selfishly, 'If my brother is dead, the kingdom will belong to me.'

The king was as unwilling as before to let his son go, but he gave way at last, and the prince started and travelled by the same road which his brother had taken.

After a while he, too, met the dwarf, who stopped him, and asked him where he was going in such haste.

' You want to know, I daresay,' said he ; ' but, my little mannikin, I shan't tell you.'   And he rode away as he spoke.

The dwarf again threw over the prince the sorcerer's spell, and he rode away, as his brother had, down to the mountain pass, where he quickly found himself enclosed on all sides and unable to move backwards or forwards ; and this is how it often happens to those who boast of their high courage.

As the second son also remained away, the youngest entreated his father to let him go and fetch the healing water, and the king was at last obliged to consent.   He also was met by the dwarf with the question : ' Where are you riding in such haste ?'

But at the words he halted, and said, ' I am seeking for the water of life to cure my father, who is near to death.'

' Do you know where to find it ?' asked the dwarf.

' No,' answered the prince.

' Well, then,' replied the little man, ' as you have behaved properly to me, and not proudly as your false brothers did, I will give you the information you require, and tell you where this wonderful water flows. It flows from a well in the court of an enchanted castle, into which you could never enter unless I gave you an iron wand and two loaves of never-failing bread.   With the iron wand you must strike three times on the gate of the castle, and it will immediately spring open.   Within the gate lie three lions, who will stand before you with open mouths.   If you can then, with one effort, throw a loaf into each open throat, they will be quite quiet for a time, and you must as quickly as possible rush to the fountain, draw off some of the water, and return to the gate ; and as soon as you are outside, with one blow of your wand the gate will close, and you will be safe and free from the danger of enchantment.'

The prince thanked the dwarf, took the iron rod and the bread, and started again on his journey full of hope.   And it all happened as the dwarf had said.   The gate sprang open at three strokes from the wand, and the bread stopped the lions' mouths, and the young prince walked into the castle till he came to a splendid hall, in which sat an enchanted princess ; he took a ring from her finger, and, seeing by her side a sword and a loaf, he carried them both away with him.

A little farther on he came to a room in which stood a beautiful maiden.   She was full of joy when she saw him, kissed him, and said he had set her free from the enchantment, and that now she should have her kingdom restored to her, and if he would come again in a year to fetch her, she would be his wife.

She then told him where to find the well from which flowed the wonderful water, and cautioned him not to delay, for the water must be obtained before the clock struck twelve at midnight. He continued to explore the castle, till he came to a chamber in which stood a beautiful bed; the hangings were new and elegant, and the bed looked so tempting that, tired as he was, he could not help lying down for a little while to rest.

So he laid himself down and slept till the clock struck three-quarters past eleven. He sprang up in terror at the sound, ran out to the well, and as quickly as he could dipped in the bucket which stood by, drew out the water, and hastened away.

When he reached the iron door the clock struck twelve, and it swung to so violently that it grazed a piece of skin off his heel. He was, however, full of joy to think that he had obtained the water of life for his father, and hastily turned his footsteps towards home.

On his way he met the dwarf; and when the little man saw the sword and the bread, he said: 'You have indeed gained a valuable possession: with that sword you will be able to slay great hosts.'

But the prince could not bear to continue his journey and return home to his father without his brothers, so he said: 'Dear dwarf, will you not tell me where I can find my two brothers? They set out on a journey to discover the water of life long before I did, but they have not returned.'

'They were proud and haughty in their behaviour to me,' said the dwarf, 'so I threw a spell over them, and they are now shut up between two mountains, and cannot get out.' On this the young prince begged so hard for them that the dwarf at last promised to set them free, but he said: 'Take care of yourself when they are at liberty, for they will be jealous of your success, and their hearts are wicked.'

When his brothers arrived, the youngest was delighted to see them, and related all that had happened to him, and how he had obtained a bucketful of the wonderful water from a well, and of the beautiful princess whom he had set free in the enchanted castle. He said also that she had promised to be his wife, and that he was to fetch her at the end of a year, when she succeeded to her kingdom. After this they travelled towards home, and on the road came to a kingdom in which the people were suffering from the effects of war and famine, and the king himself was on the point of starvation—indeed, there was great trouble.

The young prince, on hearing this, went to the king, gave him the bread which never failed, and with it the whole kingdom was fed and satisfied; he also lent him the sword, with which he soon slew the enemy's hosts, and the land was restored to peace and joy.

The young prince, after reclaiming the sword and the never-failing bread, rode away with his two brothers. On their way they heard of two other countries suffering from war, and these he also rescued from death and suffering with his sword and the wonderful bread. They travelled far out of their way to help these cities, therefore to reach home quickly they were obliged to take ship and cross the sea.

During the voyage the elder brothers held a secret consultation, and the eldest said: 'Now that our youngest brother has obtained the healing water which we could not find, our father will be sure to give him the kingdom when he dies, which belongs to us, and he will take away all our fortune from us.'

These jealous thoughts made them determined at last to destroy his hopes. They waited, however, till one day when he lay fast asleep on the deck of the vessel; then one of them fetched the goblet containing the water of life, and emptied it into a jar of their own. They then filled their brother's goblet with the salt sea water, and replaced it safely. On reaching home, the youngest son hastily produced his goblet and offered some of its contents to his sick father; but no sooner had he drunk a very little of the bitter sea water, than he became more sick than before. And while he was complaining over it, the brothers came forward, declaring that the youngest must have poisoned the water, and producing the true water which they had stolen from him, they offered it to their father.

He had no sooner drunk a small quantity than he felt his sickness vanish, and was as well and strong as he had ever been in his young days. On this the two brothers went to the youngest and said to him in a tone of mockery: 'You, no doubt, are the one who discovered the water of life; but you had all the trouble, and we have gained the reward. You have been very clever, but you should have kept your eyes open; we changed the water at sea while you were asleep, and now in a year's time one of us will be at liberty to go and claim the beautiful princess. But take care not to betray us. Our father does not believe in you now, and if you say the least word you shall lose your life into the bargain. Remain silent, and you are safe.'

The king was, in truth, very angry with his youngest son, for he believed he had had a design on his life. He even called a council together, and himself pronounced a sentence upon him that he should be secretly shot. It was arranged, therefore, that when the prince went out hunting, and suspected nothing wrong, the king's hunter should accompany him and take his life. On the appointed day the prince and the hunter were riding together, and the prince, noticing that the hunter looked sad, said:

'Dear hunter, what is the matter?'

The hunter replied: 'I cannot, I dare not tell you yet.'

'Yes,' said the prince, 'tell me at once; it will ease your mind.'

'Ah,' he exclaimed, 'I may well be sad; the king has ordered me to shoot you and kill you.'

On hearing this the prince was not alarmed, but he said: 'Dear hunter, spare my life, and I will give you my royal robes in exchange for your forester's dress.'

The hunter was glad to escape from his unkind task so easily, and said : ' I will do that willingly ; I could not bear to take away your life.'

Then they exchanged clothes ; the hunter went home, and the prince remained in the forest. After a while, there arrived at the old king's castle three waggon-loads of gold and precious stones as a present to his youngest son, from the three kings whose countries he had rescued with his sword and bread, as proofs of their gratitude. The account of all he had done which the messengers brought made the old king very unhappy. Perhaps, after all, his youngest son might be innocent ' Oh, that he were still alive !' he said to his people. ' Oh, that I had not allowed him to be killed.'

' He lives still,' said the hunter. ' I had not the heart to carry out your orders to kill him.'

And then he related to the king all that had passed. On hearing this, the king felt as if a stone had fallen from his heart, and he caused a proclamation to be made all over his kingdom that if his son would return home he should have a free pardon. Meanwhile, the beautiful princess began to prepare for the return of the prince, so she ordered a pathway to be made in front of the castle which glittered with gold, and told her people that whoever came to see her on horseback by that road was the prince whom she expected, and they should admit him ; but whoever approached the castle by another road was a stranger and unknown to her.

The year was drawing to a close, and the eldest brother thought he would be beforehand with the king's daughter, who had been freed from enchantment by his brother, and declare himself her deliverer ; and by this deceit obtain her for a wife, and her kingdom also.

So he rode away, but as he approached the castle and saw the glittering golden road he thought to himself : ' It would be a thousand pities to ride over such a beautiful road ;' so he turned aside, and rode to the castle another way.

When he appeared, however, before the door, the people of the court told him he would not be admitted, as he was not known to the princess, so he was obliged to ride home again. Thereupon the second brother thought he would try ; but when he came to the golden path, and the horse was about to place his foot upon it, he drew him quickly back, thinking, as his brother had done, that it was a pity to ride on such a beautiful road. So he approached the castle-gate another way ; but he was refused admittance, and obliged to ride away, for the people told him he was not the right person.

By this time a year had quite passed, and the third son determined to leave his forest home and proceed to the castle where his betrothed lived, and with her forget his trouble.

So he set out on horseback, and, on approaching the castle, his thoughts were so absorbed in thinking of the love of the princess, and wishing to be with her, that he never noticed the golden road, but rode his horse right over it up to the gate.

It was opened to him immediately, and the princess came out herself, and received him joyfully, and told him he was her deliverer, and the master of her whole kingdom, and soon after the marriage was performed amid great splendour and rejoicing. At length he told the young queen how his father had sent him away and discarded him.

She immediately rode over to the old king and told him all; and how his elder sons had deceived and betrayed him, and made him keep silence by threats. The king wished to punish his eldest sons, but they had already sailed across the sea, hoping to reach another country out of the way of justice; the ship was wrecked, and they were never heard of after.

THE TAILOR AND THE BEAR.

THERE once lived a princess so very haughty that, when a suitor came, she would have nothing to do with him unless he could solve one of her riddles; and if he tried, and did not succeed, he was dismissed with mockery and contempt. She allowed it to be generally known, however, that the man who could find out her riddle should be her husband.

Now, it happened that three tailors came to the town in which the princess lived. The two eldest, who had done so many fine stitches, and guessed all sorts of puzzling riddles, were sure of being able to guess what the princess propounded; it was not possible such clever people could fail.

The third tailor, however, was a useless little fellow, who knew scarcely anything of his trade; yet he fancied he might be lucky as well as any of them, and wished to try. But the other two said to him: 'You had better stay at home with your half-witted head; you will never guess anything.'

The little tailor, however, was not to be diverted from his purpose. He said he had set his heart upon it, and he would go as well as everybody else. They all three, therefore, informed the princess that they were ready to receive the riddle if she would lay it before them. They said that the right people had arrived at last—people who had fine understanding, and could thread a needle with anyone!

The princess immediately sent for them, and propounded the riddle. 'I have two different sorts of hair on my head,' she said; 'what colour are they?'

'If you were old, I should say the colours were black and white, like the clothes people call pepper and salt,' replied one.

'You are wrong,' said the princess, and she turned to the second.

'The hairs are neither black nor white,' he replied, 'but brown and red, like my father's holiday coat.'

'Wrong again,' said the princess, turning to the third; 'most certainly these are not the answers.'

Then the little tailor stepped boldly forward, and said : ' The princess has a silver and a golden hair on her head, and they, of course, are of different colours !'

When the princess heard this she turned quite pale, and almost fell down with fright. The little tailor had guessed her riddle, and she had firmly believed that not a man upon earth could do so.

When she at last recovered herself, she said : ' You have guessed my riddle, but I am not won yet ; you must do something more than this before I can be your wife. Down in the stable there lives a bear ; you must spend the night with him, and if in the morning you are still alive, I will be your wife.'

She thought as she said this that she should easily get rid of the little tailor ; for the bear had never yet allowed any to escape alive when once he had them in his power. The tailor, however, did not allow himself to be frightened ; he went away, feeling quite contented, and saying : ' Boldly ventured is half won.'

When evening arrived, the little tailor was taken down to the stables where the bear lived. The bear was quite ready to bid him welcome with a pat of his paw.

' Gently, gently, friend; I will soon make you quiet !' thought the tailor. So he sat down, made himself quite comfortable, as if he had no care, pulled some nuts out of his pocket, cracked them, and ate the kernels quite at his ease.

When the bear saw this, he began to wish for nuts also, and asked the tailor to give him some. The tailor put his hand in his pocket and brought out a handful of what appeared to be nuts, but were really pebbles. The bear stuck them in his muzzle, and rolled them about in his teeth, but he could not crack them, try as he would.

' What a stupid blockhead I certainly must be,' thought the bear, ' not to be able to crack a nut !' So he said to the tailor, ' Crack my nuts for me, will you?'

' Now, what a fellow you are,' said the tailor, ' with such a great muzzle as yours, and yet not to be able to crack a nut !'

He took the pebble from the bear, and, quickly changing it for a nut, put it in his mouth, and in a moment crack it went.

' I really must try to do that myself,' said the bear.

So the little tailor gave him again more pebbles, and the bear worked hard, and bit with all his strength, but, as you may be sure, without success ; the tailor, meanwhile, keeping him in a good humour by pretending to crack the stones for him, but always cleverly changing them for real nuts.

Presently the little tailor took a violin from under his coat, and began to play upon it. On this, the bear, who understood music, could not help standing up and beginning to dance, and, after he had danced for a little while, he was so pleased with the music that he said to the tailor: 'Is it very difficult to learn to play upon that fiddle?'

'Oh no; quite easy,' replied the tailor. 'Look here, I lay my left

'THE BEAR STUCK THEM IN HIS MUZZLE, AND ROLLED THEM ABOUT IN HIS TEETH.'

hand on the strings, and with my right I draw the bow across them, making all sorts of sounds.'

'I must learn to play it,' said the bear, 'for then I shall be able to dance whenever I like. What do you think about it? Will you undertake to teach me?'

'With all my heart!' replied the tailor, 'if you have the ability for it. But first show me your paws; the nails are tremendously long, and I must cut them a little before you begin to play.'

In a corner of the stable stood a vice, which the tailor brought out, and told the bear to place his foot upon it. As soon as he did so, the tailor screwed it so tight that he could not move. Then he left the bear grumbling, and said: 'Wait a little while till I bring the scissors.'

The bear might grumble as he liked now, the tailor did not care; he felt quite safe, so he laid himself down in the corner on a bundle of straw, and went fast asleep.

During the night the princess heard the growling, and she made sure that the bear was growling for joy over the little tailor, of whom he was making a meal. So she rose in the morning quite contented and careless; but when she went to the stable, and peeped in, she felt quite astonished. There stood the tailor, quite lively, and as safe and sound as a fish in the water!

She could not say a single word against him, for she had spoken openly about the arrangement, and the king even ordered a carriage to take her to the church to be married to the tailor. The princess was not really unwilling, for she admired the young man's courage; so they entered the king's open carriage, and drove off to church together. Meanwhile, the other tailors, who envied his good fortune, made one more effort to destroy it. They went to the stable, set the bear's feet free from the vice, and no sooner did he regain his liberty than he immediately set off in a rage to run after the carriage. The princess heard him growling and snorting behind it, and in her terror she cried out, 'Oh, the bear is behind, and if he overtakes us we shall be lost!'

The tailor was quite prepared and self-possessed; he stood on his head, and, sticking his legs through the window, cried out, 'Bear, do you see the vice? If you don't go away now, you shall be screwed down and never again set free.'

When the bear heard this, he turned round and ran back with all his might. Our young tailor travelled with his bride to church, where he was happily married, and on their return the princess took him by the hand and led him into the castle, where they continued to live in peace and were as happy as skylarks. Whoever will not believe this story must pay a forfeit of one dollar.

THE SPARROW AND HIS YOUNG ONES.

A SPARROW had brought up four little ones in a swallow's nest; just as they were all fledged, a dreadful wind knocked in the nest and destroyed it. They were all, however, fortunately able to fly and take care of themselves, but the old bird was very sad because her children had been driven into the world so young, and before she had warned them of the dangers to which they would be exposed, and taught them how to escape from them. In the autumn, a large number of sparrows met together in a ploughed field, and, among others, the old birds met their children, and, full of joy, led them home to the old tree where they had been brought up.

'Ah, my dear children,' said the mother-bird, 'you cannot think how anxious I have been about you all the summer, for you were carried away by the wind before I could teach you a single lesson. Now listen to my advice and follow the example of your father, for little birds have many great dangers to withstand.'

Then she asked them how they had fared during the summer, and if they had found plenty of food.

'Oh yes,' said one; 'we stayed in a garden and sought for worms and caterpillars till the cherries were ripe.'

'Ah, my son,' said the father-bird, 'it is not wrong to indulge in good things, but there is great danger, and it requires you to be very careful, especially when people are walking in these gardens. Sometimes you will find a long green twig like a perch placed ready for you, but inside it is hollow, and underneath is a little hole.'

'Yes, my father, and the little green leaves are stuck all over the hole with bird-lime,' said the son.

'Where have you seen this?' asked the old bird.

'In a merchant's garden,' replied the young one.

'Ah, my child,' cried the father, 'merchant people are fast people; if you had been brought up in the world you would have learned enough of their smooth deceitful ways; however, you must take care not to want more than is right, and do not be too confiding.'

Then the old bird questioned another of his children.

'Where have you been living?' he asked.

'At court,' was the reply; 'sparrows and other simple birds know nothing of the place where there is so much gold, velvet, silk, harness, hawks, and all sorts of good and wonderful things in the stables. There they measure oats and thresh wheat, so that we are always lucky enough to find a few grains of corn for breakfast, and every day, indeed, more than we can eat. Yes, father, and when the stable-boys measure out the corn, or make a mash for the horses, we have such a feast.'

' Where did you find all this?' asked the old bird.

' Oh, in the court of the castle and with the stable-boys.'

' Oh, my son, stable-boys are often unkind and wicked, but if you have been to court and associated with great people without even losing a feather, you may think yourself well off. You have also learnt a great deal no doubt of the ways of the world which will help you to defend yourself bravely; but take care, the wolf often eats the most sensible little dog.'

The father after this called the third son before him, and asked : ' Where have you been trying your fortune, little one?'

' On the streets and highways,' he replied ; ' for there they draw up large sackfuls of corn by ropes, and a few grains of wheat or barley are sure to be dropped for us.'

' I can quite understand,' said the father-bird, ' but still you must keep a sharp look-out, for otherwise, if a stone should be thrown, there would be an end of you.'

' I am aware of that,' said the young bird, ' especially if you are near a wall, or see anyone put his hand in his pocket or his bosom.'

' Where have you learnt your wisdom then?' asked the father.

' Among the mountaineers, dear father, who, when they travel, carry secretly stones with them.'

' Mountain people! working people! striking people! Have you been with the mountain lads? then indeed you have seen and learnt something.'

At last the father called over his youngest son, and said to him : ' My dear little nestling, you, who were always the simplest and weakest, stay here with me now. In the world are many rough and wicked birds with crooked beaks and long claws who lie in wait for little birds to gobble them up, so you had better stay here with your own relations, and pick up the spiders and caterpillars from the trees or houses, and you will be safe and contented.'

' My father,' replied the little bird, ' you have lived and been fed in safety all your life; people have never hurt you, nor has any hawk or kite, or other bird of prey been near you to do you injury, and this is because the great God has sent you food morning and evening. For He is the Creator and Preserver of all the birds of the forest, or the city, and He hears the young ravens when they cry, and not even a sparrow can fall to the ground without His permission.'

' My son,' said the old bird, ' where did you learn all this?'

' I will tell you,' he replied. ' When the great storm of wind separated us from you, I was driven into a church, and remained there all the summer, living upon the flies and spiders. Once I heard these words preached, and it was the Father of all the sparrows who gave me food during the summer, and preserved me from injury and from fierce birds.'

'Truly, my son,' replied his father, 'if you fly to a church, and help to clear it from spiders and summer flies, and chirp to God like the young ravens do, and will trust in Him, as your own Creator, then you will be safe, even if the whole world were full of ravenous and malicious creatures.'

THE COFFIN OF GLASS.

No one should ever say that a poor tailor cannot rise to honour: it is only necessary for him to hit the right nail on the head, and he is sure to be lucky. A polite, pleasant little apprentice-boy was once on his travels, and at length reached a large forest, and, as he knew nothing of the road, he wandered about till he lost himself.

Night came on, and there seemed nothing for him to do but to seek a lodging in this dreadful solitude. The soft moss might have made a most pleasant bed for him, but the fear of the wild beasts would have disturbed his rest, so he was obliged at last to climb to the top of a high tree and make a sleeping-room of the branches.

The wind, which was very high, however, waved the branches about so terribly that he could not sleep, and indeed felt thankful that he had brought his goose with him ; the weight of this in his pocket kept him firm on the branch, otherwise he would certainly have been blown away.

After having been in the tree about an hour in the darkness—not without great trembling and shaking—he spied at a little distance the glimmer of a light. The thought that he might be near the dwelling of a human being gave him courage; no doubt he should find some better night's lodging than the top of a tree; he therefore descended cautiously and went towards the light.

It led him to a little cottage that was covered with reeds and rushes. He knocked courageously ; the door opened of itself, and he could see by the light which had shone outside a hoary-headed old man, dressed in many-coloured, patchwork clothes which had been sewn together.

'Who are you, and what do you want here ?' asked the man, in a snarling voice.

'I am a poor tailor,' he replied, 'and night has overtaken me in this wilderness. I pray you earnestly to take me in till the morning.'

'Go your way,' answered the old man, in a surly tone ; 'I will have nothing to do with strolling vagabonds ; you must find a night's lodging elsewhere.'

At these words he was about to close the door, but the young man held him by the coat, and begged so touchingly not to be sent away that the old man, who was not so bad as he pretended to be, softened at last and took him in. He also gave him something to eat, and pointed him to a corner of the room in which was a comfortable bed.

The tired tailor required no rocking; he slept till morning, but would not have thought of getting up, had he not been frightened by a loud noise—a violent screaming and roaring which pierced through the thin walls of the house in which he found himself alone.

The tailor was seized with unusual courage; he sprang up quickly, threw on his clothes, and hastened out. There he saw, not far from the house, a great black ox fighting furiously with a stag. Their rage was so fierce, and the tramp of their feet so terrible, that the earth trembled under them.

For a long time it seemed doubtful which would conquer, but at last the stag thrust his horns into the body of his adversary, and with a terrible roar he sunk to the ground; then with another stab from the stag's horn, the ox lay dead at his feet.

The tailor had been too terrified to move, at the sight of the conflict; and when the ox fell dead, he stood looking on almost stunned.

In a moment the stag in full spring pounced upon him, and, before he could escape, picked him up with his horns. The youth had not time to reflect on his position, when he felt himself carried at a rapid rate through wood and meadow, over mountain and valley; he could only hold on with both hands to the end of the horns and give himself up to his fate, for it appeared to him as if he were flying.

At last the stag stood still near a wall of rock and let the tailor sink gently down on the ground. Feeling more dead than alive, he yet did not take long to consider; but as he made a slight attempt to move, the stag stuck his horns so violently into what appeared like a door in the rock, that it sprang open, and flames of fire rushed out, followed by smoke, in which the stag disappeared.

The tailor knew not what to do or which way to turn, or, indeed, whether he should ever find himself safely out of this dreadful wilderness and again amongst human beings.

While he stood thus irresolute, a voice sounded from the rock, and called him, saying, 'Enter in without fear. No harm shall happen to you.'

He hesitated, certainly; but a hidden power seemed to draw him forward. He therefore obeyed the voice; and, passing through the iron door, found himself in a lofty and spacious hall. The ceiling, the walls, and the floor of this hall were formed of square polished stones which glittered in the light, and, unknown to him, were symbols containing some particular meaning.

He gazed around him with wonder and fear, and was on the point of going away, when the voice spoke again, and said to him:

'Step on that stone which lies in the centre of the hall, and there wait for good fortune.'

His courage appeared to have grown so rapidly that he at once obeyed the command; but no sooner had he placed his feet on the stone than it sank slowly down into the depths beneath.

When it again became stationary, and the tailor was able to look about him, he found himself in a spacious hall, quite as large as the one he had just left, but still more wonderful.

In the walls were niches in which stood elegant glass vases full of brightly coloured spirits or blue vapour. On the floor of the hall he observed, one opposite the other, two large glass cases which at once excited his curiosity.

He walked across the hall to one of them, and saw within a beautiful building—an ancient castle in miniature—containing everything requisite for a nobleman's household—barns, stables, outhouses, and everything beautifully and artistically arranged, showing the work of a skilful hand, and the most correct eye for elegance and minuteness.

He would have been quite unable to take his eyes from this wonderful sight if he had not again heard the voice advising him to turn and examine the wonderful chest of glass which stood opposite the castle.

He stepped across the hall at these words, and saw with astonishment through the glass case in which she lay, as if in a coffin, a maiden of the greatest beauty.

She appeared to be asleep, and her long flaxen hair covered her like a veil of costly material. Her eyes were closed; but the blush tinge on her cheek, and the heaving bosom as she breathed, proved that she still lived.

The tailor stood looking at her with a beating heart; when suddenly her eyes opened, and she gazed at him with a mingled look of joy and terror. 'Righteous Heaven!' she cried at last, 'my deliverance is near. Quick, quick! help me to escape from my prison. Just push aside the bolt of this glass coffin, and I am free.'

The tailor obeyed without a moment's hesitation; and as soon as he raised the coffin lid the beautiful maiden stepped out, and, hastening to a corner of the hall, arrayed herself in a large mantle.

She then seated herself on a stone, called the tailor to her, and as she pressed a friendly kiss on his lips, she exclaimed:

'My long-expected deliverer, kind Heaven has sent you to me to put an end to my sorrow. On the day this happens your good fortune begins. You are chosen by Heaven to be my future husband, and you will receive from me not only my fondest love, but I can lavish upon you every earthly good, so that you may live in happiness to the end of your days. Sit down again, and listen to the story of my fate.

'I am the daughter of a rich count, and my father died while I was still very young. He left me in his last will to the care of my elder brother, who brought me up.

'We loved each other so tenderly, and were so entirely of the same mind in thought and inclination, that we both made a determination never to marry, but to live with each other to the end of our lives. In our home we had no lack of companions. We had neighbours and friends in abundance, with whom we often exchanged friendly visits.

' It happened one evening, however, that a stranger on horseback arrived at our castle, and, under the pretext that he could not reach his destination before midnight, begged for a night's lodging.

' We granted his request with ready courtesy, and invited him to join us at supper. During the repast he conversed so pleasantly, and related so many agreeable and amusing adventures, that my brother was quite delighted with him, and asked him to remain with us for a few days.

' The stranger willingly accepted the invitation, and we stayed up talking till quite late. At last, after showing him to his chamber, I hastened to my own room, feeling very tired and glad to rest my weary limbs on the soft feathers.

' I had just fallen asleep, when I was aroused by the tones of soft and lovely music. I started up at the sounds, but I could not understand where it came from. I was about to rise and call my lady's maid, who slept in the chamber next mine ; but, to my astonishment, I found myself unable to move. It was as if a mountain lay on my breast, and, by some unseen cause, the power of speech was taken from me, and I could not utter a sound.

' At the same time I saw by the light of the night-lamp that the stranger had entered my room through two doors which I knew had been locked. He approached, and presently told me that through his knowledge of witchcraft he had not only been able to produce the sweet music, but to pass easily through doors both closely locked, and also to prevent me from moving or arousing the house ; that he was there to offer me his hand and his heart. But I felt so repelled by this account of his evil power that I did not deign to answer him a word.

' He stood for a long time immovable, waiting for my answer, and I could see on his countenance a look that made me shrink from him.

' As I still remained silent, he flew into a rage, declaring that he would have revenge, and find means to punish my pride; and with these words he disappeared through the closed doors, and left me. I passed a restless night, and only slept a little towards morning. On awakening, I rose and hastened to my brother, to tell him the strange things that had happened to me, but he was not in his room, and the servants told me that he had started with the stranger to the hunt at break of day.

' I foreboded some evil from this, and dressing myself very quickly, ordered my palfrey to be saddled, and rode away at full gallop, attended by one servant, to the forest. The servant's horse stumbled and fell, and, in so doing, injured his foot, so that I was obliged to go on alone. After riding rapidly a short distance, I saw the stranger standing near a beautiful white stag ; and, as soon as I appeared, he came towards me, leading the stag by a string.

THE COFFIN OF GLASS

'I asked him where he had left my brother. And then, as I saw tears flowing from the large eyes of the poor animal, I exclaimed: 'Have you changed him to this stag?'' Instead of answering me, he burst into a loud laugh.

'On this I became angry, drew a pistol, and fired at the monster; but the ball rebounded from his breast, struck my horse in the head and killed him, while I fell to the ground, and the stranger, murmuring a few words, deprived me of my senses.

'When I recovered consciousness, I found myself here in this underground tomb, shut up in a glass coffin. The wretch appeared to me once more, and said that he had changed my brother into a stag. My castle, with all belonging to it, had shrunk to a small size, and was now locked up in another glass case, and my servants and people had been changed into vapour or smoke, and were confined in vessels of glass. If, however, even now, I would accept his offer, he said, it would be very easy for him to put everything back into its former position. It was only for him to open the vessels, and we should all return to our natural form. I made no reply, but remained as silent as before.

'He then vanished, and left me in my prison, and presently I fell into a deep sleep. Among the pictures which have passed before my imagination, whether dreaming or waking I know not, was one which consoled me. I dreamed that a young man would come and set me free; and, when I opened my eyes and saw you, I knew that my dream was accomplished. Help me now to complete the change by doing as I ask you. And first, to open the glass chest in which the castle is confined, we must place it on this stone, and stand by it ourselves.'

The moment the stone felt the weight, it raised itself with all upon it, and the young man and the lady were lifted through the opening in the ceiling to the upper hall, and out into the open air. Here they had space to set the castle free; and, as the young lady opened the cover of the glass chest, what followed was wonderful to see, for castle, houses, and courts expanded, and spread swiftly, till they resumed their proper shape and size.

They then returned to the underground hall, and placed on the stone the vessels containing spirits and smoke, and no sooner had the young lady opened them, than the vapour and smoke arose, and in a few moments were changed into living men, in whom the young lady recognised her servants, and the people of her household.

Her joy was complete when her brother, who, while a stag, had killed the sorcerer in the form of a bull, came out of the forest in his own manly form, and embraced his sister. And on the very same day the young lady, according to her promise, gave her hand and heart to the lucky tailor at the altar.

THE WATER-SPRITE OF THE LAKE.

In olden times once lived a miller and his wife in great happiness; they had money enough and to spare, for it went on increasing year after year. But misfortune often comes at night, or, as the proverb means, when we least expect it; and so it was with the miller. He gradually lost all he had gained, and at last became so poor that he could scarcely call his mill his own.

He was so full of sorrow that, although he worked hard all day, he would lie tossing on his bed all night unable to sleep.

One morning he rose at daybreak, and went out, thinking that the fresh air of the morning would lighten his heart. As he passed along by the mill-dam, the first ray of sunlight glittered upon it, and he heard behind him a strange ripple of the water.

He turned quickly, and saw a beautiful woman rising gently out of the stream. Her long hair hung over her shoulders, and she put it back from her face with her delicate hands, and allowed it to fall over her like a veil. The miller saw at once that it was the water-sprite of the lake, and knew not whether to stay or fly in his fright.

But the fair vision called him by name in her soft voice, and inquired why he looked so sad. The miller had at first been almost stunned; but on hearing her speak so kindly, he took courage, and told her that, after having lived in wealth and honour for many years, he was now so poor that he knew not how to help himself.

'Be at rest, then,' said the water-sprite; 'I will make you richer and happier than you have ever been before, if you will promise to give me the first young thing that is born in your house.'

'That will be, no doubt, a puppy or a kitten,' thought the miller, and at once promised what she asked.

The water-sprite immediately disappeared in the water, and the miller returned with renewed courage to his mill.

He had scarcely reached the house when a maid-servant came from the door, and told him in a joyful voice that his wife had a fine little boy. On hearing this, the miller stood as if thunderstruck. He saw at once that the malicious water-sprite had betrayed him into a fatal promise.

He went into his wife's room, with his head bowed down and looking so sad that she said:

THE TAILOR AND THE BEAR

THE WATER SPRITE OF THE LAKE

'Are you not pleased at having a little son?'

Then he was obliged to tell her all that had occurred, and what a terrible promise he had made to the water-sprite.

'What is the use of all the riches and honours in the world,' he said, 'if I am to lose my child?'

And now what could he do? None of his relations who came to wish him joy could give him any advice. However, from that day good fortune came back to the miller's house. Everything he did prospered. It seemed as if his chests and coffers filled themselves, and the money in his desk increased during the night, and in a short time the miller was richer than ever.

But his wealth could not bring him happiness, for the fatal promise to the water-sprite cruelly tormented his heart. Every time he passed by the lake, he expected to see her rise out of the water and claim her debt. He would not allow the child to go near it, and often said to him:

'Take care, my boy; if you ever touch that water, a hand will rise up and drag you under.'

But as days and years rolled by, and the water-sprite never again made her appearance, the miller began to feel more at ease.

When the boy grew up to a young man, he was placed with a game keeper, to learn the use of a gun. He was a clever lad, and soon became so expert in the business that a gentleman near the town took him into his service as gamekeeper.

In this town lived a beautiful and true maiden, with whom the young keeper fell in love. His master, on hearing this, gave them a small but pretty cottage when they were married, and they lived in peace and contentment, loving each other very fondly.

One day, when the keeper was hunting a deer in full chase, the animal ran out of the forest into a field, where he overtook it, and with one shot brought it to the ground. So earnest was he over his sport that he did not notice his nearness to the dangerous water in which lived the water-sprite.

After he had killed and cut up the deer, he went to wash his blood-stained hands in the water. No sooner, however, had he touched it than the water-sprite rose, and, with a smile, entwined her arms around him, and drew him down so quickly that the waves closed over him, and scarcely a ripple remained to show where he had gone.

When evening came on, and the keeper did not return, his wife was in great trouble, and at last went out to look for him. He had often told her of the danger to which he was exposed by his father's promise to the water-sprite, and how he was obliged to avoid carefully the water of the mill-stream, and to this she hastened at once in great fear.

On arriving at the bank of the stream, she saw the game that her husband had killed lying near the water, and knew directly the fate which had come upon him. Wringing her hands, and with loud lamentations, she called him by name, again and again running from side to side of the water. She reproached the water-sprite for her cruelty with hard words, but there was no reply.

The water remained as smooth as a mirror, in which the face of the half-moon was clearly reflected. The poor young wife would not leave the mill-stream; she kept walking up and down without ceasing, sometimes in silence, and at other times complaining in low murmurs, or uttering cries of despair.

At last she became so worn out that she sank to the ground, and fell into a deep sleep, in which she dreamed a wonderful dream. She dreamed that she was walking over rugged rocks, and, as she walked, thorns and nettles pricked and stung her feet. The rain beat in her face, and the wind blew her long hair in wild confusion. But on reaching the top a very different scene presented itself. The sky was blue, the air soft and warm, while the sides of the mountain sloped downwards to verdant meadows, enamelled with bright flowers, in which stood a charming cottage.

She approached and opened the door of the cottage, in which sat an old woman with white hair, who looked kindly at her; but just as she was about to speak the poor wife awoke from her dream.

Day was just breaking, and she knew she had slept a long time; but she felt refreshed, and she remembered that just such a mountain as she had seen in her dream was not far distant. She immediately turned her steps towards it, and, after climbing up with some difficulty, reached the top, and found all as it had appeared in her dream.

The old woman of the cottage received her very kindly, and, pointing to a chair, asked her to be seated. 'You must be suffering from some great misfortune,' she said, 'or you would not have sought my lonely hut. Tell me what it is.'

The poor wife then related with tears all that had happened.

'Be comforted, poor child,' said the old woman; 'I will help you. Take this golden comb, and, when the moon is full, go to the mill-pond, seat yourself on the bank, and comb out your long black hair. When you have done this, lay the comb on the shore, and wait and see what happens.'

The keeper's wife returned home, but the time till the moon became full seemed very long. At last, as the luminous disk appeared in the heavens, she went quickly out, seated herself by the mill-pond, and began combing her long black hair with the golden comb. When she had finished, she placed the comb on the brink of the mill-stream and waited.

In a very short time the water bubbled up from the deep, a wave rose, rolled towards the shore, and carried away the golden comb as it receded. The comb could scarcely have sunk to the bottom, when the water divided, and the head of the gamekeeper appeared just above it.

He did not speak, and had only time to look sorrowfully at his wife before a second wave rose with a rushing sound, and covered the man's head. In a few moments the water lay at rest, tranquil and calm as ever, while on its smooth surface nothing could be seen but the face of the full moon reflected on it.

The poor wife returned home with all her hope fled; but during the night she again dreamed of the little cottage in the meadow, and the old woman. So in the morning she hastened to visit the good fairy, and tell her tale of sorrow.

The wise woman comforted her as before, and, giving her this time a golden flute, she said, 'Wait for another full moon, and then take this flute, seat yourself on the shore, and play upon it one of your sweetest songs, and when it is finished lay the flute on the ground near the brink, and you will see what happens!'

The keeper's wife did exactly as the old woman had told her. Scarcely had she finished her music, and placed the flute on the shore, than the water began to bubble and foam as before, and a wave rose and carried the flute away with it.

Almost at the same moment the water divided, and not only the head and shoulders, but nearly half the body of her husband rose above the surface. He held out his arms towards her with loving eyes; but a second wave rose with a rushing sound, covered the poor man, and drew him under.

'Ah, me,' cried the unfortunate wife, 'what is the use of my only having a passing glance at my dear husband, and then to lose him again immediately?'

Sorrow again took possession of her heart, but on dreaming the same dream about the cottage and the old woman, her hopes revived, and she once more paid her a visit.

This time the good fairy gave her a golden spinning-wheel, comforted her, and said:

'You have not done all that is necessary yet; you must wait for another full moon, then take your golden spinning-wheel, seat yourself on the shore, and spin till the bobbins are full, then place the spinning-wheel near the water and wait.'

The wife followed out all these directions correctly, but when she placed the spinning-wheel on the shore, the water bubbled up more violently than ever; a mighty wave arose, and in a moment swept it away. No sooner had it disappeared, than with a sudden flash the head and then the whole body of the gamekeeper rose above the water, and quick as lightning he sprang ashore, seized his wife by the hand, and fled.

But scarcely had they gone a few steps, when the whole water raised itself with a rushing noise, and with irresistible force spread over field and meadow. Already the two fugitives saw nothing but death before them; and just as they gave themselves up for lost, they were in a moment changed—the wife into a frog, the husband into a toad.

The flood reached them, and although they escaped death, the waters separated them from each other and carried them in different directions.

As soon as the waters receded and left them on dry ground, they resumed their proper shapes, but neither of them knew what had become of the other.

They found themselves among strange people, in a foreign country, and separated from their own home by high mountains and deep valleys which lay between them. To support themselves they were both obliged to keep sheep, and for many years they tended their herds and flocks in field and meadow, weighed down with sorrow and regret at being separated from each other.

Time passed on, and the sweet flowers bloomed at the breath of spring, when one day the two sad ones were tending their flocks, and the husband, seeing a flock of sheep grazing on the hillside, in a pleasant green spot, led his own flock towards it, and very soon the two flocks were feeding together; but their keepers did not recognise each other; still, they were each pleased to find a companion in their loneliness. From that day they led their sheep to the pasture side by side, and although they did not talk much, there was consolation in each other's society.

One evening, when the full moon was shining in the sky, and the sheep at rest around them, the shepherd took a flute out of his pocket and played a charming though mournful air upon it. When he had finished, he looked at the shepherdess, and saw that she was weeping bitterly.

'Why do you weep so?' he asked.

'Ah,' she replied, 'the full moon was shining as brightly in the sky the last time I played that air on my flute, and my dearest one appeared to me above the water.'

He looked at her earnestly as she spoke; a veil seemed to fall from his eyes, and he recognised his dear and long-lost wife; and the moon, as he looked at her, shone brightly on his face, causing her to recognise him at the same moment. They instantly fell into each other's arms, and kissed each other with joy, and from that happy moment neither of them wanted nor asked any greater good fortune.

THE YOUNG COUNT'S REWARD.

THERE was once a very old woman who lived with her flock of geese in a lonely spot between the mountains, in which stood also her little cottage. The waste land was surrounded by a large forest, into which the old woman hobbled with her crutch every morning, for she was very active—more than anyone would have believed, considering her age. She gathered grass for her geese, plucked quantities of the wild fruit that she could reach, and carried it all home on her back.

One might have expected that such a heavy burden would weigh her to the ground, but she always brought it safely home. If she met any one on her road, she would greet him in a friendly manner, and say, 'Good-morning, farmer; it is beautiful weather to-day. You wonder how I can drag this load, but you know we must all bear our own burdens on our backs.'

The people, however, at last avoided meeting her, and went another way; and if a father saw her when he was walking with his children, he would say to them: 'Avoid that old woman, she has mischief behind her ears; she is a witch.'

One morning a very handsome young man was walking in the forest. The sun shone brightly, the birds sang in the branches, a cool breeze rustled the leaves, and everything seemed full of joy.

For a time he met no one, when suddenly he espied the old witch kneeling on the ground and cutting the grass with her sickle. Already she had a large bundle of it packed away into her sack, and by her side stood two baskets filled with wild pears and wild apples.

'Ah, good mother,' said the youth, 'how are you going to carry all that?'

'I must carry it, dear sir,' she replied. 'Rich people's children need not do such hard work, but with us peasants it is different. Will you help me?' she added, as he still stood near her. 'You have a straight back and young limbs: to you it would be a light burden.'

The youth could not help pitying the old woman, so he said: 'My father is certainly not a peasant but a rich count; but to prove to you that peasants are not the only people who can carry burdens, I will carry yours for you.'

'If you will do this for me,' she replied, 'I shall be very thankful. It is not more than an hour's walk, and there are those baskets to carry, but that will be nothing to you.'

The young man became very thoughtful when he heard of an hour's walk, but the old woman would not let him off; she loaded him with the sack of grass and hung the baskets on his two arms, and said, 'See now, isn't it very light?'

'No, it is not at all light,' said the young count, making a woful face; 'the bundle weighs as heavy as if it were full of large pebble stones, and the apples and pears seem like lead. I can scarcely breathe.'

He wished to place the burden on the ground again, but the old woman would not allow him. 'See now,' she said scornfully, 'the young gentleman cannot even support a load which an old woman like me has carried so often. You are very ready with your fine words, but when it comes to the real thing you are as ready with your excuses. Why do you stand there? Come, step out and lift up your legs; no one can take that bundle from your back now.'

So the young count started, and as long as he walked on level ground he got on very well, but when they reached a mountain and he found he had to climb up he began to lose strength, and the stones rolled under his feet as if they were alive. Drops of perspiration stood on his fore-head and ran down his back, making him feel hot and cold alternately. ' Good mother,' he said, ' I cannot go any farther ; I want to rest.'

' You must not rest yet,' replied the old woman ; ' by-and-by, when we reach the end of the journey, will be the time to rest ; now you must go forward, and it may bring you good fortune in the end.'

' You are a shameless old woman,' said the young count, trying to throw the sack from his shoulders ; but he tried in vain ; it stuck as fast as if it had grown there, and twist and turn as he might, he could not get free. The old woman only laughed and danced round him on her crutches. ' Don't excite yourself, my dear sir,' she said; ' you are getting as red in the face as a turkey-cock. Carry your burden with patience, and when we get home you shall have a good draught to refresh you.'

What could he do ? He was obliged to submit to his fate with patience, and follow the old woman, who appeared to grow stronger and more active as his burden grew heavier. All at once she made a spring, jumped on the sack and seated herself there, and though she was so thin and withered, she was heavier than the stoutest farm servant.

The weight was so much increased that the youth's knees trembled under him, and if he stopped for a moment the old woman struck him with a strap and with stinging nettles on the legs. Under this constant goading he at last ascended the hill, and reached the old woman's cottage just as he was ready to drop with fatigue. As soon as the geese saw the old woman they spread out their wings and ran to meet her, crying, ' Wulle, wulle.'

Behind the flock walked a middle-aged woman with a staff in her hand, strong and big, but as ugly as night. ' Mother,' she said, ' has anything happened ? What makes you so late ?'

' Don't be alarmed, my daughter,' replied the old woman ; ' nothing wrong has occurred; quite the reverse. This young count has not only carried my burden for me, but when I was tired he actually carried me on his back also. The way has not seemed long, for we have been quite merry together, joking and laughing as we came along.'

At last the old woman slipped the sack from the youth's shoulders and took the baskets from his arms; then, looking at him kindly, she said : ' Now go and sit on that bench before the door and rest yourself ; you have honestly earned your reward, and it shall not be kept from you.'

Then she turned to the goose-tender and said : ' Go into the house, my daughter ; it is not proper for you to be alone with this young count, or he may fall in love with you. We ought not to pour oil on fire.'

The young count hardly knew whether to laugh or to cry at the idea of falling in love with such a ' treasure.' ' Why, if she were thirty years younger,' he thought, ' she would fail to move my heart.'

Meanwhile, the old woman caressed and stroked her geese as if they had been children, and at last went into the house to her daughter. The youth stretched himself on the bench in great comfort, the breeze blew soft and warm through the apple-tree above his head, around spread a green meadow covered with primroses, wild thyme, and a thousand other flowers. Through the meadow flowed a clear stream which reflected the sun's rays, while the white geese swam gently on its surface, or dived beneath its tranquil waters.

'It is delightful here,' he said to himself, 'but I am so tired I cannot keep my eyes open; I think I will sleep for awhile. I hope, however, the wind will not rise and blow away my legs; they seem to have lost all their power.'

After he had been asleep some time the old woman came and shook him till he woke. 'Stand up,' she said; 'you must not stay here. I certainly did treat you rather badly, but it has not killed you after all, and now you shall have your reward; it is neither money nor property, but something better still.'

Thereupon she placed in his hands a small casket which had been cut out of one emerald. 'Take great care of it,' she said; 'it will bring you good fortune.'

On hearing this the count jumped up, and, feeling himself quite refreshed and strong, he thanked the old woman for her kindness, and started on his homeward journey without one look at her beautiful daughter. Although after walking for some distance he still heard the loud cackling of the geese, yet the poor young count lost his way in the wilderness. He had been wandering about for three days before he could discover the right road, which at length led him to a large town. Of course he was unknown, so they took him to the castle where the king and queen were seated on their thrones. The count knelt on one knee before the queen, and, taking out the emerald casket from his pocket, laid it at her feet.

She requested him to stand up and to let her examine it. But no sooner had he done so than she opened it, and the next moment fell to the ground as if dead.

The count was immediately seized by the king's servants, and would have been led off to prison had not the queen quickly recovered, and, opening her eyes, ordered him to be released.

'Let everyone leave the room,' she said. 'I must speak privately to this stranger.'

They were no sooner alone than the queen began to weep, but presently, drying her tears, she said: 'You may think it strange that I should be unhappy and weep, when I am surrounded by grandeur and pomp, and show; but what are the use of all these when I wake every morning to sorrow and care? Listen, and I will tell you the cause of my grief. I once had three daughters, the youngest of whom was so beautiful that all the world looked upon her as a wonder. She was fair as a snow-flake, with a tint on her cheeks like apple-blossom, and her hair was as bright as a sunbeam. When she wept pearls and precious stones fell from her eyes instead of tears. As soon as she reached the age of fifteen, the king sent for his daughters to be presented at court. But when the youngest appeared she attracted all eyes by her great beauty; and the people said it was as if the sun had just risen upon them.

'The king then spoke: "My daughters, I know not when my last hour may come, but to-day I will decide what each of you is to have after my death. But I should like to know which of you loves me best, for whichever it is shall have the best place in my will. You all three love me, I know."

'They each said they loved him best.

'"Well, then, give me some resemblance of your love for me, that I may judge."

'Then said the eldest, "I love my father better than the sweetest sugar."

'The second said, "I love him better than the most beautiful of my dresses."

'But the youngest remained silent.

'At last the king said, "And you, my dearest child, how much do you love me?"

'"I know not what to compare my love to," she replied. But her father pressed her to make some comparison, and at last she said, "The best food does not taste good without salt, therefore I love my father as I love salt."

'When the king heard this he fell into a rage, and said, "If you love me like salt, then with salt shall your love be rewarded."

'He then divided his kingdom between the two eldest, and after ordering a bag of salt to be bound on the back of his youngest daughter, she was led out in the wild forest by two servants, and left there. We all prayed and entreated for her,' continued the queen; 'but nothing would soften the wrath of the king. She wept so much when she found she must go, that the whole way she went was strewn with pearls which fell from her eyes. The king soon regretted his cruel harshness, and had the whole forest searched to find her, but she has never been heard of since. When I think she may have been devoured by wild animals, I am overwhelmed with grief, and I can only console myself by the hope that I am wrong, and that she is living concealed in some cavern, or that she has been protected under the care of some charitable person who took pity on her.

'When I opened the emerald casket which you presented to me, you may imagine my surprise at seeing within it one of the pearls which used to fall from my daughter's eyes when she wept; and you will understand how the sight moved my heart. You must now tell me how that pearl came into your possession.'

On this the young count related what had happened in the wood, and described the old woman who had met him, and who had given him the casket. He said this old woman appeared to be a witch, who held the forest under her enchantments; but of the king's daughter he had heard or seen nothing.

On hearing all this the king and queen decided to go and seek the old woman. They thought that where the pearl had been found they should be sure to hear news of their daughter, and find her.

The old woman sat by the door of the cottage, spinning at her wheel. It was growing dark, and a burning fagot on the hearth gave but a feeble light. All at once a noise was heard outside: the geese were coming home from the meadows, cackling as loudly as they could. The daughter took them to their roosting-place, and then stepped into the cottage; but her mother scarcely thanked her, only nodded her head. She seated herself, however, without a word, to her spinning-wheel, and spun away as fast as any young girl could have done.

They both sat like this for two hours, without speaking a word to each other. At length something rushed against the window, and the fiery eyes of a night-owl appeared, and presently screamed her weird note three times.

The old woman slightly raised her head at the sound, and said, ' Now is the time, my daughter, for you to go out and do your work.'

She rose immediately and went to the meadows, which lay far away in the valley, till she came to a fountain, near which stood three old oak-trees. The moon, round and full, shone so brilliantly over the mountain that it would have been easy to pick up a pin. The first thing she did was to take off a skin that covered her face, and then stoop down and bathe in the cool water. After this she dipped the skin into the water, and then laid it on the grass to dry and whiten in the moonlight.

But how the maiden was changed! You could scarcely imagine her to be the same. The gray wig fell off, and her golden hair, sparkling like sunbeams, flowed over her shoulders and enveloped her like a mantle. Her eyes glittered like the stars of heaven, while her cheeks glowed with the soft bloom of the apple-blossom.

But the beautiful maiden was sorrowful, for she seated herself on the ground and wept bitterly. Tear after tear fell from her eyes, and trickled through her long hair to the ground.

She sat mourning in this way for some time, and might have remained there longer had she not heard a strange cracking and rustling sound among the trees. She sprang up like a doe that hears the crack of the hunter's gun. A dark cloud at the same moment covered the face of the moon, and in the twinkling of an eye she had disguised herself again in the skin and the gray hair, and disappeared like a light blown out by the wind. Trembling like an aspen leaf, she ran back to the house, and told what had occurred to the old woman, who stood at the door; but she only smiled pleasantly, and said, ' I know all about it, my child.'

Then she led her in, and lighted a fresh fagot; but instead of again seating herself to spin, she took a broom, and began sweeping and dusting the room.

' We must have everything clean and neat,' she said to the maiden.

' But, mother,' she replied, ' why do you begin to work at such a late hour as this ? What is it for ?'

' Well, what o'clock is it ?' asked the old woman.

' Not yet midnight,' she replied, ' but the clock has struck eleven.'

' Do you not remember,' said the woman presently, ' that it is three years to-day since you came to me ? The time is up, and we cannot remain any longer together !'

' Oh ! dear mother,' cried the maiden, in alarm, ' are you going to drive me away ? What shall I do ? I have no friends and no home, and where can I go ? I have always done everything you wished, and you have been satisfied with me. Oh, do not send me away !'

But the old woman seemed unwilling to tell the maiden what was going to happen, so she said :

' I cannot stop here any longer, and, when I leave this house, every room must be in perfect order, so do not hinder me while I work. Don't fear; there will always be a roof to cover you, and the reward I shall give you will be sure to satisfy every wish.'

' But tell me what is going to happen,' said the maiden.

' You must not ask,' replied the woman ; ' and you will disturb me in my work if you say another word. All you have to do is to go into your own chamber, take the skin off your face, and the wig from your head; then put on the silk dress that you wore when I first saw you, and remain in your room till I call you.'

We must now return, and see what the king and queen have been doing at the castle. They sent the young count first into the forest alone ; but he wandered about for two days before he could find the right road, and it was then quite dark ; so he climbed a tree to rest till morning, for he feared losing his way again in the darkness.

When the moon arose and shone brightly over the forest, he saw the figure of a woman coming over the mountains. She did not carry the staff in her hand, but he knew her at once as the goose-tender whom he had met at the old woman's cottage.

' Oho !' he said to himself, ' here comes one of the witches, so the other cannot be very far off !'

How astonished he was, however, to see her come up to the fountain near the tree in which he sat, and take the skin off her face to bathe in the cool water. He saw, also, that when she removed the gray wig, and her own golden hair fell around her like a veil, she was the most beautiful maiden he had ever seen in the world.

He could scarcely draw his breath as he gazed at her with earnest, wondering eyes ; but he stretched his neck so far through the foliage that the branch cracked with his weight. At the same moment a dark cloud passed over the moon, and before he could recover himself the maiden had resumed her disguise and disappeared.

The count quickly descended from the tree, and followed her with hasty strides. He had not gone far when he saw in the dim light two figures crossing the meadow, and knew it was the king and queen. They had seen the light in the distance shining from the window of the old woman's cottage, and were hastening towards it. The count overtook them, and described the wonderful sight he had seen at the fountain, and they did not doubt for a moment that the beautiful maiden was their own lost daughter.

Full of joyful hope, they hastened their steps and soon arrived at the cottage. Outside they found the geese in a row, standing on one leg, and fast asleep, with their heads behind their wings, but none of them stirred.

They approached, and, looking through the window, saw the old woman seated quietly at her spinning, with her head bent over her work, so that she did not see them. The room, and everything in it, was as clean and neat as if the spirits of the mist had dwelt there, whose feet are never soiled by earth's dust. Their daughter, however, was not to be seen, so after looking for some time, they at last took courage and tapped at the window.

It seemed really as if the old woman expected them, for she rose up and cried in a friendly voice: 'You may come in; I know who you are!' As they entered the room, she said: 'You might have been spared this long journey if you had not sent away your dear and sweet-tempered child unjustly. However, she has met with no injury; for three long years she has tended the geese, but she has learnt nothing wicked—her heart is still pure. You have been punished by the anxiety about her in which you have lived ever since you sent her away.'

Then she stepped up to the chamber-door, and said: 'Come out, my daughter.'

The room-door opened, and the king's daughter came forth in her silken robe, with her long golden hair hanging round her like a veil, and her brilliant eyes cast down. It was as if an angel had descended from the skies.

On seeing her father and mother, she ran towards them, threw herself in their arms, and kissed them, while nothing could check their tears of joy. The young count stood by; but when the young princess raised her eyes and saw him, her delicate cheeks became red with blushes, like a moss rose, and she hardly knew why.

Presently the king said: 'Dear child, I have given away my kingdom, and what can I give to you?'

'She wants nothing,' said the old woman. 'I have saved up the tears she has wept, and they are all pearls—far more beautiful than those found in the sea, and worth more than the whole of your kingdom. And as a reward for her services in tending my geese, I give her this cottage.'

As the old woman said this, she vanished from their sight. At the same moment a cracking sound was heard in the walls, and, when they turned to look, the whole cottage was changed into a noble palace, a royal banquet was already spread for them, and numerous servants were in attendance.

The story does not end here, but the old grandmother who related it to us has forgotten the termination; and lately her memory has become weak.

It is very probable, however, that the beautiful daughter of the king was married to the count, and that they lived together ever after at the palace in great happiness.

Whether the snow-white geese, whose guardian the princess had been, were really young maidens (in saying this we do not wish to be rude to our lady readers) whom the old woman had brought around her, or whether after they regained their human shapes they became maids of honour to the princess, we cannot say, but it is very probable.

This we do know, that the old woman was not a witch, as people supposed, but a good fairy, who only wished to do good. Very likely it was she who had given the princess at her birth the power of weeping pearls instead of tears. This gift is unknown in the present day, or how very soon the poor would become rich!

THE AVARICIOUS BLACKSMITH.

A TAILOR and a blacksmith were returning together one evening from a town in which they had been working at their different trades. As evening came on, they saw the sun setting behind the hills, and presently, as the moon rose, came the sound of distant music, which grew more distinct as they proceeded on their way. The tones were rather unearthly, but so charming that they quite forgot their fatigue, and went forward with rapid steps.

After walking a little distance they reached the hillside, and presently caught sight of a crowd of little men and women, holding hands, and dancing merrily in a circle to the strange music they had heard.

In the centre of the ring round which the pixies danced stood a little old man, yet larger and stouter than the rest. He wore a coat of many colours, and his snow-white beard descended to his breast. The travellers stood still and gazed in wonder at the dancers, and presently the old man made signs to them, and the little people separated that they might come within the circle.

The blacksmith, who was a bold fellow, and had a slight hump on his back, stepped in without fear; but the tailor was at first rather timid, and held back. In a very short time, however, seeing how merry and good-natured they all looked, he took heart, and entered the circle. Immediately they closed the ring again, and the little folks danced and sprung about in the wildest manner.

Meanwhile, the old man in the centre took out a large knife which hung at his girdle, sharpened it on a stone, and feeling the edge with his finger, turned and looked at the strangers in a manner that caused them to tremble with fear.

They were not kept long in suspense, however, for the little man seized the smith, and with the greatest rapidity shaved off his hair and beard clean at one stroke! He then turned to the tailor, and did the same to him.

But their alarm vanished when the old man, after finishing his performance, slapped them on the shoulder in the most friendly manner, as if to tell them that they had done well in submitting to be shaved without resistance. He then pointed with his finger to a heap of coals that lay on one side, and made signs that they should fill their pockets.

They both obeyed, although they could not imagine what could be the use of coals to them. They soon left the little people after this, for it was getting late, and they wanted to find a night's lodging.

Just as they reached the valley, a clock from the neighbouring cloisters struck twelve. Immediately the music ended, the little people vanished, and the hillside lay calm and still in the moonlight.

The two travellers found after a time a roadside inn, but there was no accommodation for them excepting a bundle of straw, on which they laid themselves down, dressed as they were, too fatigued to think of removing the coals from their pockets. But towards morning the heavy weight awoke them earlier than usual, and on putting their hands into their pockets, they could scarcely believe their eyes when they saw that, instead of coals, their hands were full of pure gold!

Their surprise was as great at finding that their beards had grown again, and that their heads were covered with hair. They had suddenly become very rich; but the blacksmith, who had a greedy disposition, had filled both pockets with coals, so that he possessed twice as much gold as the tailor.

Yet he was not satisfied, and he proposed to his companion that they should stay till the next day, go again in the evening, and get more treasures out of the little old man.

The tailor, however, refused,

'I have enough,' he said, 'and I am quite contented. I only wish to be master of a business of my own, and to marry the charming maiden whom I love, and then I am a happy man.'

However, to oblige his friend, he stayed another day at the inn, and in the evening the blacksmith took two sacks on his shoulders, and went alone to the hillside. He found the little people dancing and singing as on the previous night.

They received him into the ring, and the old man again shaved him, and made a sign as before that he should take as much coal as he liked. He did not hesitate to fill not only his pockets, but the two sacks, and returned home, congratulating himself on his good fortune.

Although he had a bed for this night, he laid himself down in his clothes, saying:

'I shall know when the gold becomes heavy, for it will wake me;' and at last he fell asleep with the pleasant expectation of awaking in the morning a very rich man.

As soon as he opened his eyes he started up, and began to dive into his pockets; but what was his astonishment at finding they contained nothing but black coals! Handful after handful he pulled out, but no gold.

'Well, I have still the gold I got on the first night,' he said, 'that is safe;' but what was his surprise and alarm to find it all turned back again to coal, and that he was penniless!

He put up his black hands to his head and found that it was still bald and his chin smooth and without a beard. But he had not come to the end of his misfortunes, for the hump on his back had grown larger and made him more deformed than ever. When he discovered at last that he was being punished for his covetousness, he began to groan and lament so loudly as to wake up the good tailor. He kindly comforted him in his misfortune and said generously, 'Don't grieve any more, we have been companions and travellers together, and now you can stay with me and share what I have, it will be enough for us both.'

He kept his word, but the poor blacksmith never could get rid of the hump on his back, and was always obliged to wear a cap to cover his bald head.

IDLENESS AND INDUSTRY.

THERE lived once a young maiden who was very beautiful, but so idle and careless that she hated work. When she was required to spin a certain quantity of flax, she was too idle to untie the little knots in it, but would break the thread and throw down whole handfuls of flax on the floor to be wasted. This idle young lady had a little servant maid who was as industrious as her mistress was idle; she collected these little pieces of flax, disentangled them, spun them into fine thread, and had them made into a beautiful dress for herself.

Now it happened that a young gentleman in the village had asked the idle maiden to be his wife, and the marriage-day was fixed. But a few evenings before it took place, the bride and bridegroom were walking together near the village green, where several young people were dancing. 'Look,' exclaimed the bride, with a laugh, 'that is my little maid servant; how merrily she is dancing, and thinks herself so fine in **my** leavings.'

'What do you mean?' asked the bridegroom.

Then she told him that her little servant had made that dress out of the tangled pieces of flax which she had thrown away because it was so much trouble to unravel the knots. On hearing this the bridegroom began to reflect that an industrious young maiden, although she might be poor, would make a better wife than a careless idle young lady with all her beauty. So by degrees he broke off the engagement, and married the industrious servant maid.

THE SHOWER OF GOLD.

ONCE upon a time lived a poor little maiden whose father and mother were both dead, and the child was so very poor that she had no little room to live in nor even a bed to lie on. At last all her clothes were gone excepting those she wore, and she had nothing to eat but a piece of bread given to her by some one who had a kind pitying heart. Still, she was good and pious, and although forsaken by all the world she knew that God would take care of her, and she went out into the fields and prayed to Him to help her. On the day when the kind-hearted person had given her the piece of bread, she was walking along the road when she met a poor man who said to her, 'Pray give me something to eat, for I am so hungry.'

Immediately she offered him the whole of her bread and went away after he had taken it, saying: 'Heaven has sent it to you.'

Presently she saw a little child sitting by the roadside crying, and as she passed, the child exclaimed, 'Oh, my head is so cold; do give me something to cover it.'

Instantly the poor maiden took off her own cap and gave it to the child. A little farther, she met another child, who said she was freezing for want of a jacket, so she gave up her own. Another begged for her petticoat, and that she gave also. At last she entered a wood, where it was quite dark, and here she intended to sleep. But she had not gone far, before she found another little child with scarcely any clothes at all, and who appeared to be almost dying with cold. The good child thought to herself, 'It is quite dark night now, no one will see me.'

So she took off all the clothes she had on, covered the poor little shivering child with them, and went away. This pious child had now nothing left in the world at all, and she was turning to go into the wood and cover herself with the fallen leaves, when all at once a golden shower fell around her from heaven. At first she thought that the stars, which look like golden money in the heavens, were falling, but when the drops reached the ground they were real golden dollars, and as she stood still under the golden shower she found herself covered from head to foot with warm and beautifully fine clothes. She gathered up the golden dollars, carried them away, and was rich instead of poor all the rest of her life.

THE SPINDLE, THE NEEDLE, AND THE SHUTTLE.

A YOUNG girl who had lost both parents in her infancy lived in a little cottage at the end of the village with an old woman, who took care of her and brought her up to be industrious and pious. The maiden earned enough by spinning to support herself and the old woman. When she was in her fifteenth year the old woman fell sick, and one day called her to her bedside, and said to her, ' Dear daughter, I feel that my end is approaching, so I will leave you this cottage and all that is in it. Here you will have shelter from wind and weather ; and with the needle, the spindle, and the shuttle, you can easily earn your bread.'

Then, laying her hand on the maiden's head, she blessed her, and said, ' Keep God always in your heart, and you will never go wrong.'

Not many days after this the old woman closed her eyes and died, and the poor girl followed her to the grave behind the coffin weeping bitterly. After this the maiden lived in the little cottage quite alone, working diligently at her spinning and weaving, and the blessing of the old woman seemed to rest upon all she did.

It was as if the flax in the room would never be exhausted ; and no sooner had she finished weaving a piece of cloth or carpet, or had made a shirt, than a purchaser was quickly found who paid her well ; so she had as much as she needed for all her wants, and a little also to spare for the poor.

It happened about this time that the son of the king of the country started on his travels to find a bride. The prince could choose for himself, excepting that his wife must not be poor, and he did not care for riches. So he decided in his heart that he would try and find one who was at the same time both the richest and the poorest.

When he arrived at the village near which the maiden dwelt, he inquired first for the richest maiden in the place, and, on being told, he then asked, ' And which is the poorest ?'

' The poorest is a maiden who lives at the end of a village, in a little cottage alone,' was the ready reply. ' Her cottage is easily found, for a winding path through a field leads to it.'

The prince, in going to this cottage, rode through the village, and at the door of a stately house sat a maiden richly dressed, and as the king's son approached, she went out and bowed herself before him in a most courtly manner. The prince looked at her, but he said not a word, and rode on without stopping till he arrived at the house of the poor maiden.

She, however, was not seated at the door, but in her own little room busily at work. The prince drew rein, alighted from his horse, and peeped into the neat apartment. Just at that moment a ray of sunshine darted through the window, and lighted up everything within, so that he could see the maiden spinning at her wheel with the most earnest diligence.

Presently she glanced up, and, seeing a noble-looking gentleman looking at her through the window, she cast down her eyes and continued her spinning, while her cheeks were covered with a rosy blush.

Whether the threads were even and regular at that moment we cannot say; but she continued to spin without looking up again till the prince remounted his horse and rode away.

Then she rose and opened the window, saying to herself, 'How very warm the room is to-day!' But she looked out and watched the stranger till she could no longer distinguish the white plume in his hat, and not till after he was quite out of sight did she return to her spinning-wheel and work as busily as ever.

Her thoughts were now on the handsome prince, although she knew not who he was; still, it was such an unusual event for a gentleman to look in at the window of her lonely cottage that she could not forget it.

At last strange ideas came into her head, and she began to sing some curious words which the old woman had taught her:

'Spindle, spindle, run away;
Fetch my lover here to-day.'

To her astonishment, the spindle leaped from her hands that very moment, and rushed out of the house. She followed to the door, and stood looking after it with wondering eyes, for it was running and dancing quite merrily across the field, trailing behind it a bright golden thread, and presently it was lost to her eyes.

Having no longer a spindle, she took up her shuttle, seated herself, and commenced weaving. The spindle, meanwhile, kept on its way, and just as the thread came to an end, it overtook the prince.

'What do I see?' he cried. 'The thread behind this spindle will lead me to good fortune, no doubt.'

So he turned his horse and rode back in the trail of the golden thread.

The maiden, who still worked on, thought presently of another of the rhymes taught her by the old woman, so she sang:

'Shuttle, shuttle, thou art free;
Bring my lover home to me.'

Instantly the shuttle slipped from her hand, and ran to the door, but on the door-sill it stopped and began to weave the most beautiful carpet ever seen. In the centre, on a golden ground, appeared a green creeping plant, and around it blush roses and white lilies were scattered. Hares and rabbits appeared running upon it; stags and deer stood beneath the foliage, in which were birds of beautiful colours which seemed able to do everything but sing. The shuttle sprang here and there, and the carpet seemed to grow of itself.

As the maiden had now lost both spindle and shuttle, she was obliged to take out her needle, and while she sewed she sang:

> 'Needle, needle, while you shine,
> Make the house look neat and fine.'

On this the needle sprang from her fingers, and flew about the room as quick as lightning. It was just as if a number of invisible spirits were at work, for the table and benches were quickly covered with green cloth, the chairs with velvet, and curtains were hung to the windows and on the walls of silk damask.

Scarcely had the needle finished the last stitch than the maiden saw through the window the white plume on the prince's hat; for he had followed carefully the golden thread till it reached her cottage.

He alighted from his horse, and quickly stepped in upon the beautiful carpet; when he entered the room, he saw the maiden, who even in her homely dress looked blooming and lovely as a wild rose.

'You are exactly what I seek,' he said: 'at once the poorest and the richest maiden in the world. Will you come with me and be my bride?'

She did not speak, but she held out her hand to him. He kissed the hand she offered, led her out, lifted her on his horse, and rode away with her to his father's castle.

The marriage was shortly after celebrated with great splendour and rejoicings. The needle, the spindle, and the shuttle were preserved in the treasure-chamber ever after with great honour.

THE RICH MAN'S GRAVE.

A RICH farmer was one day standing in his farmyard, and looking with pride on his possessions. The cornfields were full of grain, and the trees laden with fruit. The corn of the previous years, carefully preserved in the granaries, lay in large heaps on the floors, the beams bending beneath its weight. His stables, also, were full of fat oxen, milch cows, and well-fed horses.

After looking over all these stores, he returned to the house, and, entering a room, cast his eyes on the iron chest in which his money lay. As he thus stood contemplating his riches, something knocked sharply—not, however, on the door of the room, but on the door of his heart.

He stood still for a moment, and heard a voice within say : ' Have you done well with all your gold and possessions? Have you taken care of the poor? Have you shared your bread with the hungry? Are you satisfied with what you possess, or do you long for more ?'

His heart and conscience did not hesitate to reply : ' I have been hard and unsympathizing ; I have never done anything good for my own relatives ; I have never thought of God, but only how I should increase my riches. Had all the world been in my possession, I should still have wanted more !'

As these thoughts arose in his mind, his knees trembled under him, and he was so overcome as to be obliged to sit down. At this moment he heard another knock, but now it was at the door of the room.

' Come in,' he cried ; and, as the door opened, he saw one of his neighbours, a poor man, who found it a hard matter to support his large family of children.

' I know,' thought the poor man as he entered, ' that my neighbour is as hard as he is rich ; I do not suppose that he will help me ; but my children are crying for food, and I must venture.'

So he said to the rich man as he entered : ' I know you do not like giving or lending, but I have come to you in my trouble as a drowning man catches at straws. My children are hungry : will you lend me four measures of wheat ?'

The rich man looked at his neighbour, and a beam of pity for the first time melted the ice of avarice which bound his heart.

' I will not lend you four measures,' he said, ' but I will give you eight, on one condition.'

' What am I to do ?' asked the poor man.

' You must promise to watch at my grave for three nights after my death !'

The peasant was secretly troubled by this proposal; but in his present need he would have agreed to anything, so he gave his promise, and carried the corn home with him.

It was as if the rich man had foreseen what would happen to him, for three days later he suddenly died, and no one mourned for him. After he was buried the peasant remembered his promise. Gladly would he have withdrawn from the task, but he thought, ' The man was kind to me ; he gave me corn to make bread for my hungry children ; besides, I made a promise, and I am bound to keep it.'

At nightfall he went to the churchyard, and seated himself near the grave. All was still, the moon threw her soft light over the tomb-stones, and only the hoot of the owl disturbed the peaceful silence. At sunrise he returned home unhurt, and went again the second night without anything happening even to alarm him.

When the third evening arrived, however, he felt a kind of foreboding that something would occur, and, on entering the churchyard, he saw a man standing by the wall whom he had never seen before. He was not young; he had a scarred face, and eyes that were sharp and piercing.

'What do you want here?' cried the peasant. 'Are you not afraid of the lonely churchyard?'

'I want nothing,' replied the man, 'and I fear nothing. I am like the young man who went out to learn how to fear, and had his trouble for nothing, excepting that he married a king's daughter, and obtained great riches. I am always poor. I am a discharged soldier, and I came to the churchyard to pass the night here, for I have no other shelter.'

'If you are not afraid,' said the peasant, 'then stay with me and help me to watch by this grave.'

'Willingly,' he replied; 'for to mount guard is my trade. Whatever we meet with here, good or bad, I will share the consequences with you.'

The peasant consented, and they seated themselves by the grave together. All remained quiet till midnight; at that moment a shrill whistle was heard in the air, and the two watchers saw all at once, standing before them, the Evil One himself in person.

'Be off, you scoundrels!' he cried; 'he who lies in this grave is mine; I have come to fetch him, and if you do not go away at once I will wring your necks.'

'My lord of the red feather,' replied the soldier, 'you are not my captain. I cannot, therefore, obey orders from you, and I have never yet learnt to fear. So take yourself off; we shall remain here as long as we please.'

On seeing the men so firm, the Evil One thought he might easily bribe two such poor scamps as these with gold; so, assuming a gentle tone, he asked them if they would resign their position for a purse of gold.

'Come, now, that is worth hearing,' said the soldier; 'but a purse of gold is not enough. If, however, you can fill my boot with as much gold as it will contain, then we will quit the field and leave the way clear for you.'

'I have not so much money with me,' he replied, 'but I can fetch it. In the neighbouring town lives a usurer; he is a great friend of mine, and he will no doubt advance me the money.'

When the Evil One had vanished, the soldier pulled off his left boot, and said: 'We will lead the black gentleman by the nose this time. Give me your knife, friend.' He then cut off the sole of his boot, and fastened the upper-leathers to a tomb close by, so that the foot hung down under the long grass. 'All right,' said the soldier; 'now let the black sweep come back again as soon as he likes.'

Then they both seated themselves and waited, but not for long; back came the old gentleman with a little bag of gold in his hand.

'Pour it in,' said the soldier, lifting the boot a little. 'I'm afraid there's not enough even now.' And as he emptied the bag, the money fell to the ground and the boot remained empty.

'You old stupid,' cried the soldier, 'you don't know what you are about! I told you it was not enough; go and fetch some more.'

The old deceiver shook his head as he went away, and returned in an hour with a much larger sackful of gold under his arm.

'That looks more like business,' said the soldier; 'but I doubt whether it will fill the boot after all.'

The gold clinked as it fell, but the boot remained empty. The black intruder looked in and discovered the fact for himself; then he fell into a rage: 'What abominably large calves you must have, to be sure!' he cried, with a sardonic grin.

'What!' exclaimed the soldier, 'do you suppose I have a cloven foot like yours? And what makes you so stingy all at once? Go and fetch some more money, or there will be no dealings between us.'

The Evil One turned away once more. This time he remained much longer, and at last appeared carrying such a heavy sack on his shoulder that he quite bent under the weight. He poured the contents into the boot, but it remained as empty as before. On seeing this he fell into a furious rage, and was just about to drag the boot from the soldier's hand; but at that moment the first beam from the rising sun appeared in the sky, and with a loud yell the wicked spirit fled; the poor soul was saved.

The peasant wished to divide the gold, but the soldier said: 'No; give my share to the poor. I will go home again with you, and we will live upon what is left in peace and happiness to the end of our days.'

THE TWELVE IDLERS.

TWELVE farm servants, who had been doing nothing the whole day, were still as unwilling to exert themselves when evening came, and therefore lay down in the grass to enjoy their time of rest in idleness.

Presently the first spoke and said, 'What is the use to me of leisure time? I have nothing to do for myself, and my chief anxiety is to take care of my body and to eat and drink as much as I can. I can have four meals a day, but I like best to fast for a while after eating, till I feel really hungry, and then I can enjoy my food better. I don't like early rising—getting up at noon would suit me best. So when I am up I find a resting-place and lie down, and if my master calls me I

will not hear, neither the first time nor the second. And if at last I
am obliged to rouse myself, I go as slowly as I can; and so I pass my
life away.'

' I manage quite as well as you do,' said the second. ' I have a horse
to take care of, but I can leave him with food in the manger, and go
and sleep in the hayloft for hours. Sometimes I forget to give him his
corn, but I always say he has had it. And when I wake up I put my
best foot foremost, and comb him down once or twice with the curry-
comb, to make him look a little clean and polished. Why should I
take much trouble over that? Oh, I can assure you my work is not
very hard.'

' Why should we plague ourselves with work?' said the third; 'no
good comes from it. I know I take mine easy enough. I often lie in
the sun and sleep; or if it rains, and the drops fall on me, don't suppose
I get up. No, I just lie and let it dry of itself. Once there came down
such a large splash of rain that it tore the hair from my head and made
a hole in my skull; but what mattered? I laid a plaister on the place,
and it was soon all right, and no harm done.'

' I think my plan is best,' said the fourth. ' Before I begin my work
I always dawdle about for an hour to spare my strength; and, even
after this, I move very slowly, and ask everyone who comes near me
to help me. In this way I manage to get through the chief of my work;
and so it is done properly at last. But it is not much that I do after
all.'

' Oh, that is nothing to my idleness,' cried the fifth. ' Only think, I
have to remove the manure from the stables, and load a waggon
with it. I take it very easy, I assure you, for when I toss the manure
on a pitchfork, I raise it only half-way in the air, and then rest for
a quarter of an hour before I throw it quite into the cart. It is as
much as I can do to load a cart in a day. I have no wish to kill myself with work.'

' You ought to be ashamed of yourself,' said the sixth. ' I am not
afraid of work, but I save time for idleness in other ways. I sometimes
do not take my clothes off for weeks. And suppose I have no strings
to my shoes, what does it matter if they fall off my feet? There is
no harm done. I can drag one foot after the other slowly, and get on
by degrees; and I manage my time so well that I know when I can
rest.'

' All this is nothing to what I do,' said the seventh. ' My master
examines my work, but he is away from home all day. I neglect
nothing, however, for I can do in a very short time what slow people
would take days to perform, and it is quite as well done as if I had four
strong men to help me.'

' Ah,' said the eighth, ' I see plainly that I am the only wideawake
chap amongst you. Why, if a stone lies before my path I never trouble
myself to lift my leg and step over it. If I lie down on the ground and
get wet or covered with mud and dirt, I do not stir, but remain there

till the sun has dried up the wet or the mud. This way appears to me the easiest and the simplest in the world.'

'I can beat you all,' said the ninth. 'This very day my bread and cheese lay before me, but, although I was starving with hunger, I was too lazy to reach my hand and take it. A jug stood by, and because it was heavy I endured thirst rather than attempt to lift it. Indeed, rather than take the trouble to move, I remained the whole day lying still like a log of wood.'

'Well,' said the tenth, 'my laziness has obtained for me a broken leg and a swelled calf. Three of us were lying on the roadway, and I had my legs stretched out. A waggon came along the road, and the wheels went over them both. I could easily have drawn them back, for I heard the waggon coming, but I was too lazy. Besides this, the flies buzzed in my ears, crept up my nose, and into my mouth; but who would give himself the trouble to drive away a fly?'

The eleventh then spoke.

'Yesterday,' he said, 'I gave my master warning. I was tired of waiting upon him, brushing his clothes, and carrying his heavy books backwards and forwards, and working from morning till night. I know I used to waste my time on the road, and, truth to tell, I expected he would discharge me, for I let his clothes lie in the drawer uncovered till they were all moth-eaten.'

At last the twelfth spoke, and said:

'To-day I was sent with a waggon to the field. The goods in it were covered with straw, in which I made a capital bed and slept soundly. The reins slipped out of my hand, and when I awoke I found the horse, the traces, the collar, the bit, and most of the harness gone. Some one had come by and taken them all away while I slept. The waggon had also fallen into a rut, and stuck fast. I left it standing as it was, stretched myself again on the straw, and went to sleep. My master came at last himself, and dragged the waggon out of the rut, turned me out of the straw, and sent me about my business. But for this you would not have seen me here, for I should have slept peacefully on my bed of straw till morning without moving.'

THE SHEPHERD BOY AND THE KING.

THERE was once a shepherd boy who was known far and wide for his clever answers to every question. The king of the country heard of his wisdom, but he could not believe it, so he sent him an order to appear at court.

When he arrived the king said to him, 'If you can answer wisely three questions which I will give you, then you shall be as my own child, and dwell with me in my royal castle.'

The shepherd boy replied: 'Will your majesty ask me the three questions?'

On this the king said: 'First I want to know how many drops of water there are in the ocean.'

'My lord king,' said the boy, 'if you could have all the rivers in the world stopped up, so that not a drop could run into the sea, and I could count them, then I might be able to tell you how many drops the ocean contains.'

Without a remark the king propounded the next question. 'How many stars are there in the heavens?'

The shepherd boy replied: 'Give me a large sheet of paper. If I make a number of points with a pen, close together, then whoever casts his eyes upon it will be dazzled if he attempts to count them. If, however, it were possible to count these points, even then it would not be easy to count the stars.'

No one, however, would attempt to count them, so the king asked his third question: 'How many seconds of time are there in eternity?'

The shepherd boy replied: 'In Pomerania there is a diamond mountain, one league high, one league broad, and one league deep. If a little bird could go once in every hundred years, and with his little beak peck away a morsel from the mountain until the whole mountain was removed, not even then would one second of eternity be passed!'

Then the king replied: 'You have answered all my questions wisely, and shall from this time dwell with me in my royal castle, and be to me as my own son.'

DOCTOR KNOW-ALL.

THERE lived once a poor peasant named Krebs, who drove with two oxen and a cart containing a load of wood through the town, and sold it to a doctor for two dollars. When he went in to receive his money the doctor was at dinner, and the peasant looked at all the good things on the table till he began to long for some of them, and to wish he had been a doctor.

He remained standing for a while after he had received his money, and at last asked if he could not also become a doctor.

'Oh yes,' was the reply; 'that can easily be managed, if you wish it.'

'What must I do?' asked the peasant.

'You must first buy an A B C book, one in which there is a picture of a farmyard cock. Secondly, you must turn your waggon and oxen into money, and buy a suit of clothes such as a doctor should wear.

Thirdly, have a sign painted and placed over your door with these words, "I am Doctor Know-all!"'

The peasant followed the doctor's advice, and after a while obtained patients, but not many.

About this time a large robbery was committed at the house of a rich nobleman living near the town, who made it known that he would give a handsome reward to anyone who would discover the thief, or restore the money.

It was told to this nobleman that a clever doctor, named Doctor Know-all, lived in the town, who would most likely tell him where to find the lost treasure, and who had stolen it. So the nobleman ordered his carriage, and drove into the town. On seeing him he asked him if he were Dr. Know-all, and, on finding that he really was that great person, he invited him to his house, saying that he required his assistance in discovering the thief and the stolen property.

'I am willing to accompany you, my lord,' he replied, 'if my wife, Grethel, may go also.'

The nobleman was quite agreeable to this request, and, desiring them to take seats in his carriage, they drove away together.

As soon as they arrived at the house, dinner was laid, and Doctor Know-all and his wife seated themselves at the table, and the servants waited upon them. When the first servant placed a dish on the table containing some delicacy, the doctor touched his wife with his elbow, and said in a low voice, 'Grethel, that is the first.'

He only meant the first servant to bring the different courses, as he wished her to notice what a number of servants waited at table in a great lord's house. The man thought, however, that he was speaking of him as the first of the thieves, and, as this was the truth, he was in a dreadful fright, and when he got out into the hall, he said to his companions: 'That doctor knows everything we have been doing; he has just said that I am the first!'

On hearing this the other servants felt almost afraid to go into the dining-hall; but they were obliged to perform their duty, especially as their master was present. Another servant therefore appeared at the second course.

The moment he placed a dish on the table, he heard the doctor say to his wife, 'That is the second!'

The man was as much alarmed as his fellow-servant, and got out of the room as quickly as he could. It was the same with the third, for as each appeared the doctor spoke of him to his wife, and they were all obliged to assist in waiting at table. When the fourth servant brought in a dish and placed it on the table, the nobleman, wishing to prove the cleverness of his visitor, asked him to say what was under the cover.

Now it happened to be a crab, which, of course, the doctor did not know, so he looked at the covered dish, and felt that he was in a great dilemma, from which he could not escape; so he said in a low tone, 'Krebs! Krebs! what will you do?'

But the nobleman only heard the word Krebs,* and he cried eagerly, ' Yes, it is a crab. Ah, I see now that you know everything, and you will be able to tell me where my money is, and who has stolen it.'

The servants were all terribly alarmed, and winked at the doctor to come out to their offices. As soon as he could get away from the table he went out, and they all came around him, owned that five of them had stolen the money, and offered him in their terror money to any amount if he would only not betray them. He promised, on condition that they would show him where they had hidden the money, and they took him to the spot at once.

On this the doctor was quite satisfied, and, returning to the dining-room, seated himself at the table, and said, ' My lord, I will now consult my book, and discover where the money is concealed.'

The fifth servant, who wanted to hear whether the doctor knew any more about them, crept into the hall, and hid himself to listen. Not thinking of a listener, the doctor pulled out his book and turned over leaf after leaf, pretending to find the necessary information. At last, addressing the pretended advice in his book, he exclaimed, ' You are there, but you will have to come out !'

The hidden man, supposing that the doctor spoke to him, sprang out full of terror, crying, ' The man knows everything !'

Doctor Know-all at last took the nobleman to the place where the money was concealed; but he did not tell who had stolen it. So, in addition to the reward offered for the discovery, he received also a good sum from the servants in return for not betraying them, and became a man of great renown.

THE HARE AND THE HEDGEHOG.

It was a beautiful morning, about harvest time, the buckwheat was in flower, the sun shining in the heavens, and the morning breeze waving the golden cornfields, while the lark sung blithely in the clear blue sky, and the bees were buzzing about the flowers. The villagers seemed all alive; many of them were dressed in their best clothes, hastening to the fair.

It was a lovely day, and all nature seemed happy, even to a little hedgehog, who stood at his own door. He had his arms folded, and was singing as merrily as little hedgehogs can do on a pleasant morning. While he thus stood amusing himself, his little wife was washing and dressing the children, and he thought he might as well go and see how the field of turnips was getting on, for, as he and his family fed upon

---

* Krebs is the German for *crab.*

them, they appeared like his own property. No sooner said than done. He shut the house door after him and started off.

He had not gone farther than the little hedge bordering the turnip-field, when he met a hare, who was on his way to inspect the cabbages, which he also considered belonged to him. When the hedgehog saw the hare, he wished him good-morning very pleasantly.

But the hare, who was a grand gentleman in his way, and not very good-tempered, took no notice of the hedgehog's greeting, but said in a most impertinent manner, 'How is it that you are running about the fields so early this morning?'

'I am taking a walk,' said the hedgehog.

'Taking a walk!' cried the hare, with a laugh; 'I don't think your legs are much suited for walking.'

This answer made the hedgehog very angry. He could bear anything but a reference to his bandy legs, so he said, 'You consider your legs are better than mine, I suppose?'

'Well, I rather think they are,' replied the hare.

'I should like to prove it,' said the hedgehog. 'I'll wager anything that if we were to run a race I should beat.'

'That is a capital joke,' cried the hare, 'to think you could beat me with your bandy legs. However, if you wish it, I have no objection to try. What will you bet?'

'A golden Louis d'or and a bottle of wine.'

'Agreed,' said the hare; 'and we may as well begin at once.'

'No, no,' said the hedgehog; 'not in such a hurry as that. I must go home first and get something to eat. In half an hour I will be here again.'

The hare agreed to wait, and away went the hedgehog, thinking to himself, 'The hare trusts in his long legs, but I will conquer him. He thinks himself a very grand gentleman, but he is only a stupid fellow, after all, and he will have to pay for his pride.'

On arriving at home, the hedgehog said to his wife, 'Wife, dress yourself as quickly as possible; you must go to the field with me.'

'What for?' she asked.

'Well, I have made a bet with the hare of a Louis d'or and a bottle of wine, that I will beat him in a race which we are going to run.'

'Why, husband,' cried Mrs. Hedgehog, with a scream, 'what are you thinking of; have you lost your senses?'

'Hold your noise, ma'am,' said the hedgehog, 'and don't interfere with my affairs. What do you know about a man's business? Get ready at once to go with me.'

What could Mrs. Hedgehog say after this? She could only obey and follow her husband, whether she liked it or not. As they walked along together, he said to her, 'Now pay attention to what I say. You see that large field? Well, we are going to race across it. The hare will run in one furrow, and I in another. All you have to do is to hide yourself in the furrow at the opposite end of the field from which we start, and when the hare comes up to you, pop up your head and say, "Here I am."'

As they talked, the hedgehog and his wife reached the place in the field where he wished her to stop, and then went back and found the hare at the starting-place, ready to receive him.

'Do you really mean it?' he asked.

'Yes, indeed,' replied the hedgehog, 'I am quite ready.'

'Then let us start at once,' and each placed himself in his furrow as the hare spoke. The hare counted 'One, two, three,' and started like a whirlwind across the field. The hedgehog, however, only ran a few steps, and then popped down in the furrow and remained still.

When the hare, at full speed, reached the end of the field, the hedgehog's wife raised her head and cried, 'Here I am.'

The hare stood still in wonder, for the wife was so like her husband that he thought it must be him. 'There is something wrong about this,' he thought. 'However, we'll have another try.' So he turned and flew across the field at such a pace that his ears floated behind him.

The hedgehog's wife, however, did not move, and when the hare reached the other end, the husband was there, and cried, 'Here I am.'

The hare was half beside himself with vexation, and he cried, 'One more try, one more.'

'I don't mind,' said the hedgehog. 'I will go on as long as you like.'

Upon this the hare set off running, and actually crossed the field seventy-three times; and at one end the husband said, 'Here am I,' and at the other end the wife said the same. But at the seventy-fourth run the hare's strength came to an end, and he fell to the ground and owned himself beaten.

The hedgehog won the Louis d'or and the bottle of wine, and after calling his wife out of the furrow, they went home together in very good spirits, to enjoy it together; and if they are not dead, they are living still.

The lesson to be learnt from this story is, first, that however grand a person may think himself, he should never laugh at others whom he considers inferior, until he knows what they can do; and, secondly, that when a man chooses a wife, he should take her from the class to which he himself belongs; and if he is a hedgehog she should be one also.

THE THREE TASKS.

THERE once lived a poor maiden, who was young and fair; but she had lost her own mother, and her stepmother did all she could to make her miserable. When she gave her any work to do she made it as hard and heavy as possible, so that it was often almost beyond her strength. She exerted herself to do what was required of her, but the wicked woman's envious heart made her always discontented with what the poor girl did—it was never enough to please her. The more diligent she was, and the more she had to do, the less thanks she received. It seemed always to her as if she were carrying a great burden, which made her life sad and miserable.

One day her stepmother said to her, 'Here are twelve pounds of feathers for you to sort in three different sizes, and if they are not finished by this evening you may expect a sound thrashing. Do you think you are to waste the whole day in idleness?'

After she had gone the poor maiden seated herself by the table; but the tears rolled down her cheeks, for she knew it was impossible for her to finish such a task by the end of the day. She made an attempt, however; but after she had put several feathers together in little heaps, if she happened to sigh, or clasp her hands in her agony, away flew the feathers, and were so scattered that she had to commence her task anew.

At last she placed her elbows on the table, rested her face in her hands, and cried, ' Is there no one in all this earth who will pity me?'

Immediately she heard a soft voice say, ' Be comforted, my child; I am come to help you!'

The maiden looked up, and saw an old woman standing near her. She took the maiden's hand, and said kindly, ' Now tell me what is troubling you?'

She spoke so heartily that the maiden told her all about her unhappy life, and of one burden after another which her stepmother laid upon her, and of the terrible tasks which never would come to an end. ' If I do not finish sorting these feathers by the evening,' she said, ' my stepmother has threatened to beat me; and I know she will keep her word.'

Her tears began to flow as she spoke; but the kind old woman said,

'Be at peace, my child, and go and rest awhile; I will finish your work for you.'

So she made the young girl lie down on a bed in the room, and, worn out with sorrow, she soon fell asleep.

Then the old woman placed herself at the table by the feathers. Ah! how they flew and sorted themselves under the touch of her withered hand! and very soon the whole twelve pounds were finished. When the maiden awoke, there they lay in large snowy heaps, and everything in the room was neat and in order; but the old woman had vanished.

'THEY FLEW AND SORTED THEMSELVES UNDER HER WITHERED HAND.'

The maiden's heart was full of thankfulness, and she sat still till the evening, when her stepmother came into the room.

She was truly astonished when she found the feathers finished. 'See, now,' she said at last, 'what people can do when they are industrious! But why are you sitting there with your hands in your lap? Can you find nothing else to do?' As she left the room she said to herself, 'The creature can do anything; I must give her something more difficult next time.'

On the morrow she called the maiden to her, and said, 'There is a large spoon for you; now go and ladle out the water from the pond that lies near the garden, and if by evening you have not reached the bottom, you know what you have to expect.'

The maiden took the spoon, and saw that it was full of holes; and, even if it had not, it would have been impossible for her to empty the pond with it.

She made an attempt, however; knelt by the water, into which her tears fell, and began to scoop it out. But the good old woman again made her appearance, and, when she saw the cause of her sorrow, she said, ' Be comforted, my child, and go and rest in the shrubbery; I will do your work for you.'

As soon as the old woman was alone she merely touched the water; it immediately rose, like a mist, in the air, and mingled itself with the clouds. Gradually the pond became empty, and when, at sunset, the maiden awoke, the water had disappeared, and she saw only the fish writhing in the mud at the bottom. She at once went to her stepmother, and showed her that she had finished her task.

' You should have finished it long ago,' she said; but she was pale with anger, and determined to think of some still more difficult task for the poor girl.

Next morning she again called, and said:

' To-day I shall expect you to go into the valley, and on the plain build me a beautiful castle, which must be finished by the evening.'

' Oh,' exclaimed the poor maiden in terror, ' how can I ever perform such a great work as this?'

' I will have no excuses,' screamed the stepmother. ' If you can empty a pond with a spoon full of holes, you can build me a castle. I shall expect it to be ready to-day, and if you fail in the slightest thing, whether in kitchen or cellar, you know what is before you.'

She drove the poor girl out as she spoke, and when she reached the valley she found it full of rocks, piled one over the other, and so heavy that, with all her strength, she could not move even the smallest.

She seated herself, and began to weep; yet still hoping for the assistance of the kind old woman, who did not keep her waiting long, but greeted her when she appeared with words of comfort.

' Go and lie down in the shade and sleep,' she said; ' I will build a castle for you, and, when the happy time comes, you can have it yourself.'

As soon as the maiden had gone away, the old woman touched the gray rocks, and immediately they began to move, then to rock together, and presently stand upright, as if they had been walls built by giants. Within these walls the castle rose, as if numberless invisible hands were at work laying stone upon stone. The earth trembled as large halls expanded, and stood near each other in order. The tiles on the roof arranged themselves regularly, and before noon the weathercock, like a golden maiden with flying drapery, stood on the pinnacle of the tower.

The interior of the castle was not finished till evening; and how the old woman managed I cannot say, but the walls were covered with silk and velvet, richly embroidered; and decorated chairs and sofas, marble tables, and other elegant articles, furnished the rooms. Cut-glass chandeliers hung from the ceilings, and sparkled in the light of many lamps. Green parrots sat in golden cages, and foreign birds, who sang sweetly, were in every room. Altogether, the castle was as magnificent as if built for the king himself.

It was after sunset when the maiden awoke, and, seeing the glitter of a thousand lamps, she ran with hasty steps, and, finding the gate open, entered the court. The steps leading to the entrance-hall were covered with red cloth, and the gilded balconies were full of rich and blooming flowers. All was so magnificently beautiful that the maiden stood still with astonishment.

She knew not how long she might have remained standing thus if she had not thought all at once that her stepmother was coming.

'Ah,' said she to herself, 'what joy it would be to live here, and be no longer tormented as I am now!'

She was, however, obliged to go and tell her stepmother that the castle was finished.

'I will just go and see for myself,' she said, and, rising from her seat, she followed the maiden; but, on entering the castle, the brightness and glitter so dazzled her that she was obliged to cover her eyes with her hand. 'You see how easy this is to you,' she said; 'ah, yes, I ought to have given you something still more difficult.'

She went into all the rooms, prying into every corner, to see if she could not find something wrong or defective; but this was impossible.

'I will go downstairs,' she said at last, looking at her stepdaughter maliciously; 'it is necessary for me to examine kitchens and cellars also, and if you have forgotten one single thing, you shall not escape punishment.'

But nothing was wanting: the fire burned on the hearth, the supper was boiling in the saucepan; brooms, brushes, fenders, fire-irons, were in their proper places, and the walls and shelves were covered with brass and copper, glass and china, which glittered in the lamplight:— nothing was wanting, not even the coal-scuttle or the water-can.

'Where are the steps to the cellar?' cried the woman; 'I want to see if the casks are full of wine of the right sort, or it will be bad for you.'

She raised the trap-door as she spoke, and descended the stairs leading to the cellars; but scarcely had she taken two steps, when the heavy door, which was not pushed back far enough, fell to with a dreadful crash. The maiden heard a scream, and followed as quickly as she could to help her unkind stepmother, but having been struck by the door, she had fallen to the bottom of the steps, and there the maiden found her lying dead.

After this the beautiful castle belonged alone to the maiden, who hardly knew, at first, how to understand such good fortune. But after a while servants came to wait upon her, and they found in the drawers and wardrobes beautiful dresses, in which she could array herself. There was also a large chest filled with gold and silver, pearls and precious stones, so that she had not a single wish ungratified.

It was not long before the fame of her beauty and riches got known throughout the world, and the maiden had soon plenty of lovers. But she did not care to accept any of them, till at last a prince, the son of a great king, came to see her. He was the first to touch her heart, and she very soon learnt to love him dearly.

One day, as they sat talking under a linden-tree in the castle garden, the prince said, very sadly, ' My heart's love, I must leave you to get my father's consent to our marriage, but I will not stay away long.'

' Be true to me,' said the maiden, as she took a sorrowful farewell of him.

But when the prince reached home, he found that the king, who did not want him to marry this maiden, had invited many beautiful ladies to his court, and for a time the prince forgot his true bride and the wonderful castle.

One day, while he was riding to the hunt on a beautiful horse, an old woman met him, and asked him for alms. As he drew rein to help her, she said, in a low tone, ' The maiden weeps for her false lover under the linden-tree.'

In a moment the power which had changed his heart towards her was at an end. He turned away and rode quickly to the castle in the valley, which the good fairy had built. When he reached the gates, all looked dark and gloomy, and there, under the linden-tree, stood his forsaken bride, looking sad and mournful. He alighted quickly from his horse, and, advancing towards her, he exclaimed, ' Forgive me, dearest. I am come back, and we will never, never part again !'

No sooner had he uttered these words, than the most brilliant lights shone from the castle windows. Around him on the grass glittered innumerable glowworms. On the steps bloomed lovely flowers, and from the rooms came the song of joyous birds, arrayed in plumage of bright and beautiful colours.

He took the maiden by the hand and led her in. The large hall was full of the castle household, who had assembled, and the priest stood in readiness to marry them. The prince hastened forward, leading the bride who had suffered so much from her stepmother and been so true to her lover ; and she became at last his wife, to the great joy of the castle and its inmates.

THE KING OF THE BIRDS.

In olden times every sound in nature had a sense and significance of some sort. When the hammer of the smith sounded, it was as if it said: 'How I strike! how I strike!' The sound of the plane on the table said, 'I scratch, I scratch.' The rush of the water over the mill-wheel had a meaning, and if the miller was a cheat, it seemed to say sometimes, 'Who cheats? who cheats?' and at others to reply, 'The miller, the miller!' and, when the mill went very fast, 'Stealing six out of eight! stealing six out of eight!'

In these good old days, also, the birds had a language of their own, which everyone could understand, although it sounded only like twittering, screaming, and whistling, and was really music without words. About this time an idea arose among the birds that they would be no longer without a master, and they determined to elect one of their number to be king. One voice only was raised against this proposal; the plover declared that he had lived free, and he would die free. Full of anxiety, he flew about here and there among the birds, crying, 'Don't believe it! don't believe it!' But as no one noticed him, he returned to his lonely home in the marshes, and has never since associated with his own species.

The birds meanwhile were determined to have a general meeting on the subject, so one fine May morning they assembled in great numbers from woods, fields, and meadows. The eagle and the bullfinch, the owl and the crow, the lark and the sparrow, and many more that could be named; even the cuckoo was present, and the lapwing—who is called the cuckoo's clerk, because he lets his note be heard just after him—and a great number of little birds, as well as one without a name who also mixed with the flock.

A hen who, as it happened, had heard nothing of the whole matter wondered greatly at such a large gathering. 'Cluck, cluck, cluck! what are they going to do?' she cackled. But the cock quieted his dear wife, and, telling her not to make such a noise, he explained what the birds were about.

Meanwhile the assembly had decided that the bird who could fly the highest should be chosen as king. A green frog who sat in the bushes, when he heard this, croaked dreadfully, and said there would be many tears shed over that arrangement. The crow, however, said, 'Caw, caw,' for he wished it to be all settled in a friendly manner. They decided to make the experiment of flying the next morning, so that none should be able to say afterwards, 'I could have flown higher had it not been evening, and I was too tired to do any more.'

Next morning, at the appointed signal, the whole flock rose in the air. There was quite a cloud of dust scattered about, and such a rustling noise and flapping of wings—it was as if a dark cloud had passed over the sun. The little birds, however, remained among the branches; they could not attempt such great flights. The large birds kept up for a long time; but none could compete with the eagle, for he went so high that, if they had followed him, the sun would have put out their eyes.

When the eagle saw that the others could not follow him, he thought to himself, 'I need not go any higher; I am sure to be chosen king.'

And the birds beneath him cried out, 'You must be our king; none can fly as high as you do.'

'Excepting I,' cried the little fellow without a name, who had crept unseen among the wing-feathers of the eagle, and mounted with him, and as he was not tired, he flew in the air still higher and higher till he could almost peep into heaven. When he had reached this height, he folded his wings together and sank gradually down to earth, exclaiming in his shrill but delicate voice, 'I am king—I am king!'

'You our king?' cried the birds, in a rage; 'no, no; you have gained your position through trickery and cunning!'

However, they were obliged to make another condition about who should be king, and they decided that it should be he who sunk lowest into the earth after his flight in the air. The goose on this cackled loudly and laid her broad breast on the ground; the cock scratched away quickly to make a hole; the duck, however, got into trouble, for she jumped into an open grave, and sprained her leg so terribly that she was obliged to waddle away to the nearest pond with the cry, 'Rare work, rare work!'

The little bird without a name, however, went in search of a mouse-hole, and as he slipped in, he cried with his shrill voice, 'I am king—I am king!'

'You our king!' cried the other birds, in a rage. 'Do you suppose your cunning tricks can obtain you that honour? So they shut him up and made him a prisoner in the mouse-hole, hoping he might be starved, and the owl was placed sentinel to prevent the little rogue from escaping, however dear his life might be to him.

In the evening, all the birds felt very tired with the great efforts they had made in flying, so they all went home with their wives and children to bed. The owl alone remained by the mouse-hole, staring into it with her great, grave eyes; but at length she also became tired and said to herself, 'I can easily shut one eye, and if I keep the other open the little wretch shall not escape.' She closed one eye, and with the other kept a steadfast look on the mouse-hole.

The little fellow peeped out once or twice, and thought, as the owl appeared asleep, that he could slip away; but the owl saw him, and made such a quick step forward that he darted back in a hurry. A little while after, the owl thought she would rest one eye and open the other, and so keep on changing all night; but when she closed one, she forgot to open the other, and very soon both eyes were shut up, and she was fast asleep.

The little one again peeped out, and saw that now he could easily escape, so he slipped cautiously from the hole and flew away. From that time the owl has never dared to show herself by daylight, lest the other birds should peck off her feathers and pull her to pieces; so she flies about in the night time, and pursues and catches the mice who can make such dangerous holes. And the little bird also keeps out of her way, for he fears she will catch him by the neck and soon make an end of him. He lives in the hedges and builds his nest there, and is constantly crying out, in a piping voice, 'I am king, I am king!' The other birds, therefore, call him in mockery the *hedge-king.**

No one, however, was more pleased at not having to obey the hedge-king than the lark. The moment she caught a sight of the sun, she would rise in the air to a great height, singing, 'Ah, where is that beauty?—that is a beauty!—beauty, beauty!—ah, where is that beauty?'

THE ROBBERS' CAVE.

THERE was once a man and his wife who had only one child, and they lived in a far-away, pleasant valley, quite alone. It happened one day that the mother went into the wood to gather fir twigs, and she took her little son, Hans, with her. It was in the springtime, and the boy,

* *Zaune-könig*, the German for wren and hedge-sparrow.

who was about two years old, ran about the wood and plucked the many-coloured flowers in all the happiness of childhood. Suddenly there sprang out upon them from the bushes two robbers; they seized the mother and the child, and carried them away into the depths of the forests, in which from year to year no human being ever penetrated. In vain the poor woman entreated the robbers to let her and her child go. They had hearts of stone, and would not listen to her prayers and entreaties, but led them both away by force.

After dragging them through dust and thorn bushes for nearly two hours they came to a rock in which there was a door, and the robber knocked. It was very quickly opened, and after passing through a long dark passage they came into a large cave, which was lighted by a fire burning on the hearth. On the sides of the caves hung swords and daggers, and other murderous implements, which glittered in the fire-light, and in the middle stood a black table, at which sat four other robbers gambling, and one of these was the robber chief.

He came forward when he saw the woman, addressed her kindly, and told her to be at peace and without anxiety, for that no one should hurt her in his cave. All he required her to do was to take care of the housekeeping for them, and, if everything was kept in order, her position would not be so bad after all.

Then they gave her something to eat, and pointed to a bed in which she and her child could sleep. The woman remained for many years with the robbers, while Hans grew tall and strong. His mother told him stories, and taught him to read from an old book of chivalry, which she had found in the cave.

When Hans was about nine years old, he made himself a good strong cudgel from a fir branch, and hid it behind his bed. He then went to his mother, and said: 'Dear mother, do tell me, just once, where my father is? I want to see him so much.'

But his mother was silent; she would not tell him, because she feared it would create in him a longing for home, and she knew the wicked robbers would not let him go away from the cave; yet she felt heart-broken to think that Hans could not go to his father.

That night, when the robbers came home from their marauding excursions, Hans fetched his cudgel, and, placing himself before the robber chief, he exclaimed: 'I want to know where my father is, and if you won't tell me I will knock you down!' The chief laughed, and gave Hans such a box on the ear that he rolled under the table like a ball. Hans got up quickly without a word, but he thought to himself, 'I will wait another year before I ask again. I shall manage better next time.'

The year passed away, and Hans prepared himself for another attempt. So he fetched his cudgel, whisked off a little dust from it, and, examining it carefully, said: 'It is a brave, clever little cudgel.'

At night the robbers came home in good spirits, for they brought with them such a large booty that at supper they drank a great deal of wine,

bottle after bottle, till at last their heads began to droop, and their eyes
to be heavy.

Then Hans took up his cudgel, and, standing boldly before them,
asked again where his father was. The chief gave him such a tremendous box on the ear that he rolled quite under the table; but he
was up again in a moment, and struck such rapid blows right and left
amongst them all, which they were too tipsy to resist, that he very
soon had them on the ground, unable to move arm or leg. His mother
stood in a corner watching him, full of wonder at her boy's bravery and
strength.

When his work was finished, he went to his mother and said : 'I
have been in earnest this time, and now I must know where my father
is.'

'Dear Hans,' she replied, 'we will go and search till we find him!'

They took the key of the long passage leading to the door from the
pocket of the chief, and Hans fetched a great flour-sack, into which they
packed gold and silver, and many other beautiful things which they
found, till the bag was full, and then the boy took it on his back.

When they left the cave, the change from darkness almost put out
his eyes; but presently he got used to the daylight and the green wood.
The bright flowers, the song of the birds, and the glorious sun shining in
the sky delighted the boy's heart. He stood looking round him with
astonishment, as if he could not understand it.

But his mother led him away, and for two hours they wandered
about before they could find the road to their cottage. At last they
arrived, fortunately, at the lonely valley, and there it stood before them,
and the father of Hans was sitting at the door.

When he recognised his wife, and heard that Hans was his son, he
wept for joy, for he had long supposed that they were both dead. Hans,
however, although he was only twelve years old, was a head taller than
his father. They went together into the little room; but as soon as
Hans laid the sack on a bench, the walls of the house began to crack.
The bench broke first, and then the floor, so that the heavy sack sank
through into the cellar below.

'Bless me!' cried the father, 'what are you doing, Hans? Why, the
house is falling about our ears!'

'Never mind, father,' said the youth; 'don't let any gray hairs grow
over that trouble. There is in my bag more than enough to pay for
building a new house!'

As it seemed dangerous to remain in the old house, Hans and his
father quickly began to build a new one. Then they had cattle to purchase, and land to buy, and housekeeping to provide, so they had plenty
to do. Hans cultivated the fields, and, when he followed the plough,
and guided it through the ground, the oxen had scarcely any weight to
draw, he was so strong. The next spring Hans asked his father to
keep the money he had brought from the robbers' cave, and said that
all he wanted was a heavy walking-stick to take with him on his travels,

as he intended to visit distant lands. The wished-for walking-stick was soon ready, and Hans quitted his father's house, and journeyed on till he came to a dark woody forest.

Presently he heard a cracking of branches in one of the trees, and, looking up, he saw a great overgrown fellow winding and twisting a cord round a fir-tree, and bending the tree as if it had been a willow twig.

'Hi!' cried Hans, 'what are you about up there?'

'Oh,' replied the man, 'I gathered the twigs yesterday, and now I mean to pull down the whole tree!'

'I like that,' thought Hans; 'he has plenty of strength, I see.' So he called out to him: 'Leave the tree alone, and come with me.'

The man clambered down at this request, and, when he stood by Hans, he was a head taller, although Hans was a big fellow himself.

'You shall be called "Fir-twister,"' said Hans, as they went away together.

After travelling some distance, they heard such violent knocking and hammering, that at every stroke the earth trembled, and, as they walked on, they saw an enormous rock, before which stood a giant striking off large pieces of rock with his fist.

Hans asked him what he was doing, and he replied:

'When I want to sleep at night, the bears and wolves, and all sorts of wild animals, come sniffing and yelping round me, and will not let me even close my eyes; so I am going to make a cave in this rock, that I may lie at night in peace.'

'This fellow will suit me,' thought Hans; 'I may want him.' So he said: 'Leave your house-building and go with me, and you shall be called "Rock-splitter."'

The man was quite willing. So the three rambled on through the wood together, and, wherever they came, the wild animals fled in terror from their path.

One evening they saw before them an old forsaken castle on a rising ground, up which they ascended; and, entering the great hall, they laid themselves down and slept. The next morning Hans went out into the garden, which was quite a wilderness full of thorns and briars, and suddenly from amidst the brushwood a wild boar sprung upon him; but Hans lifted his staff, and with one blow laid him dead at his feet.

Then he took the dead animal on his shoulder, and carried him into the castle. They roasted a portion of the flesh for dinner, and enjoyed themselves, feeling quite content, for they had now sufficient food to last for some time.

After this, they agreed among themselves that two should go ou hunting every day, and each take it in turns to stay at home and cook their meals.

The first day the Fir-twister remained at the old castle, while Hans and the Rock-splitter went to the hunt.

While the Fir-twister was in the kitchen busy at his cooking, there came a little withered-up old man to the castle, and demanded meat.

'Be off, you little scamp!' he cried; 'you will get no meat from me!

To the astonishment of the Fir-twister, the little, insignificant-looking old man sprang upon him, and, before he could prevent him, beat him so terribly with his fist that he fell to the ground and gasped for breath. But the little man did not go away till he had vented his rage fully upon him.

When the two others returned home, the Fir-twister did not tell them of the little man, nor of the dreadful thrashing he had given him. He thought, 'When they remain at home, they must take their chance with the little wretch as well as I,' and the thought gave him great pleasure.

The following day the Rock-splitter remained at home, and the same visitor made his appearance. When the little man found the meat again refused, he attacked the Rock-splitter in the same way, and beat and overpowered him as he had done the other. At last the day came for Hans to stay at home, and though the others knew what he would have to endure, they both remained silent, and thought Hans ought 'to taste the soup' as well as they.

Hans was very busy preparing the dinner in the kitchen, not expecting any visitors. Presently, as he stood skimming the pot at the fire, in walked the little man, and demanded at once a piece of meat.

'The poor little wretch is hungry,' thought Hans; 'I will give him my share, that the others may not come short.' So he offered him a piece of meat.

As soon as the dwarf had devoured it, he asked for more, and the good-natured Hans gave him some a second time, and said: 'That is a beautiful piece, and you must be contented with it.'

But the dwarf asked for a third supply, and, when Hans refused, the wicked little wretch was just going to spring upon him and serve him as he had served the other two, but he was mistaken this time. Hans without much exertion gave him two such severe cuts that he rushed down the steps of the castle in surprise and fright. Hans, in his haste to run after him, fell down and rolled over and over, so that he lost time, and, when he had recovered himself, the dwarf was far away. Hans followed him, however, quickly, and saw him slip into a rocky cave; so, after taking particular notice of the place, he returned home.

The other two, when they reached the castle, were astonished to see Hans quite well and unhurt; but he told them all that had happened, and then they could not any longer be silent about the dwarf's visits, and how he had treated them.

Hans laughed, and said: 'It served you right; why should you have been so greedy with your meat? but still it is too bad to think that such great fellows as you should have been thrashed by a dwarf.'

However, they all determined to punish the little wretch now they knew where to find him. So they took a large basket and a strong cord, and went to the cave in the rocks, into which the dwarf had slipped. They first let Hans down by a rope in a basket, with his club-staff, and, when he reached the ground, he saw a door, which he opened, and in a kind of room sat a most beautiful young lady, more beautiful than Hans had ever seen, and near her stood the dwarf, grinning at him like a baboon.

The poor young lady was bound **with** fetters, and she looked at Hans so sadly, that he was touched with pity for her, and thought: 'I must free her from the power of this wicked dwarf.'

He turned quickly, and with one stroke of his heavy walking-staff the little wretch fell to the ground dead. Immediately the fetters dropped from the maiden, and Hans was enraptured with her beauty.

She told him that she was a king's daughter, who had been stolen from her home by a wicked count, and by him made a prisoner in this rocky cave, with the dwarf to keep guard over her; and terribly he had oppressed and tormented her. Upon hearing this, Hans placed the maiden in the basket, and called to his companions to draw her up. The basket came down again, but Hans did not quite trust his fellow-travellers, 'for,' thought he, 'they have been already false in not telling me of the dwarf's visits, and, who knows? they may have some design against me.'

So he placed his heavy staff in the basket, and it was fortunate for him that he did so; for, when the basket was half-way up, they let go the cord, and if Hans had been really sitting in it he must have been dashed to pieces.

It was, however, still a sad difficulty for him to get out of that deep place, and, ponder as he might, there seemed no way of escape.

'It is very hard,' he said to himself, 'to know that I must stay here and be starved.'

But as he wandered in and out, he came again to the room in which the young lady had been sitting, and saw on the finger of the dead dwarf a ring sparkling and glittering. He drew off the ring, and placed it on his own finger, and, as he turned it round, he suddenly heard a rushing sound over his head. He looked up, and saw a spirit of air hovering over him, who said he was his master, and asked him what his commands were. Hans felt at first quite bewildered; but on saying he wished to be drawn up out of that cave, in a moment he was obeyed, and it appeared to him as if he flew.

When he reached the top none of his companions were to be seen; and on going to the old castle he found it empty. The Fir-twister and the Rock-splitter had gone away, and taken the beautiful lady with them.

Hans directly turned his ring on his finger, and the spirit of the air appeared, and told him that his two companions were on the sea. Hans ran with all his might down to the sea-shore, and was just in time to see at a distance a boat, in which his false companions were rowing away as fast as they could.

In his violent rage, and without a thought, he jumped into the water, still carrying his heavy staff, and attempted to swim after them; but the weight of his staff dragged him down, and he was on the point of sinking, when he thought of the ring.

The moment he turned it around the spirit of the air appeared, and carried him with the speed of lightning to the boat. He sprang in, and with two or three blows of his staff he gave his false companions the reward they deserved, and threw them into the water.

He then rowed away quickly with the terrified princess, whom he had twice rescued; and, on reaching the shore, he at once took her home to her father and mother, who were full of joy at finding her still alive and well. Hans married the beautiful princess, and lived ever after in the greatest happiness.

THE HOUSE IN THE WOOD.

A POOR woodcutter lived with his wife and three daughters in a little hut on the borders of a lonely forest. One morning, when he was going to his work, he said to his wife, 'Send my eldest daughter out into the wood with my dinner at noon. I shall be quite ready for it, and, that she may not lose her way, I will take a bag of millet with me, and strew the seeds on the path.'

As soon as the sun had reached the meridian, and was shining over the wood, the maiden started on her road, with a large jug of soup and some bread for her father's dinner. But the field and hedge sparrows, the larks, the finches, and other birds, had long before picked up the seeds, so that the maiden could not find the track.

Fortunately, she went forward in the right direction; yet the sun went down, and night came on before she could find shelter. The trees rustled in the darkness, the night-owl screamed, and the poor girl was in great fear, when all at once she saw a light twinkling in the distance through the trees. 'There must be people living yonder,' she thought, 'and no doubt they will give me a night's lodging.'

She turned her steps towards the light, and very soon came to a house through the window of which the light shone.

She knocked at the door, and a rough voice cried from within, 'Come in!' She stepped into a narrow dark hall, and tapped at the room door. The same voice cried, 'Come in!' and when the door opened she saw a very old man sitting at a table; his chin rested on his hands, and his white beard fell over it nearly to the ground. Near the stove lay three animals—a cock, a hen, and a speckled cow. The maiden told the old man of her trouble, and asked if she could have a night's lodging. Instead of answering her, the old man turned to the animals, and said :

> ' Little chicks and spotted cow,
> Shall we keep her here or no ?'

The animals made certain sounds which meant that she was to stay. So the old man said : ' You will find plenty of everything here, so go into the kitchen and cook us some supper.'

The maiden found an abundance of all she wanted, and after cooking a dishful of good food she placed it on the table, and, seating herself with the old man, ate a hearty meal, but she never thought of the animals. When she was satisfied she said : ' I am very tired ; where is a bed on which I can sleep ?' In reply came a voice :

> ' You can eat and drink,
> But you cannot think
> Of poor animals such as we ;
> You shall have a bed,
> Just to rest your head,
> But you don't know where it will be.'

The maiden scarcely noticed what the voice said, for the old man told her to go upstairs, where she would find two rooms, with a bed in each ; she was to shake the beds well, and make them both. The young maiden went quickly upstairs, made her own bed, and without thinking of one for the old man, she lay down and went fast asleep. After awhile the old man came up to his room, and, finding his bed not made, shook his head, and, going into the room where the maiden lay sleeping, opened a trap-door in the floor, and let down the bed on which she lay into the cellar beneath.

Meanwhile, the woodcutter returned home in the evening very late, and reproached his wife for having left him the whole day hungry. ' It is not my fault,' she said ; ' I sent the maiden with your dinner at noon, and I suppose she must have lost her way ; she will be back again to-morrow, no doubt.'

Before day, however, the woodcutter was obliged to be off to the forest, and he desired his wife to send his second daughter with his dinner. ' I will carry a bag of linseed with me this time,' he said ; ' as the seeds are larger than the millet, she will see them more easily, and will not be likely to lose her way.'

But at noon, when the maiden went with her father's dinner, the linseed had disappeared ; the birds of the forest, as on the day before, had picked them all up, so that there were none left. She also wandered about all day, and at last found a good supper and a night's lodging in the old man's cottage ; but she also never thought of feeding the animals, or of making the old man's bed, so at night while she slept he opened the trap-door and let her down into the cellar below as he had done her sister. On the third morning, the woodcutter told his wife:

'You must send our youngest child with my dinner to-day; she is always good and obedient; she will not lose her way as her sisters have done ; they wander about like wild bees when they swarm.'

The mother, however, would not listen.

'No,' she said; 'why should I lose my dearest child now that the others are gone?'

'Don't fear,' he said ; 'the maiden will never wander, she is too clever and sensible; besides, I will take a quantity of peas with me and strew them in the way, to show her the right path ; they are so much larger than linseed, and will be sure to remain.'

So, the next day, the mother, with much advice and caution, sent her youngest daughter to the forest. She carried a basket on her arm, but there were no peas to guide her; they were all in the crops of the pigeons, and therefore she knew not which path to take. She was very unhappy, and thought how hungry her poor father would be, and how her mother would fret if she remained away all night. However, in her wanderings after dark, she also saw the light, and came, as her sisters had done, to the house in the wood. She went in and begged for a night's lodging so gently that the man with the white beard said to his animals :

> 'Little chicks and spotted cow,
> Shall we keep her here or no?'

The voice answered, 'Yes,' and presently the maiden went over to the stove where the animals lay, stroked the smooth feathers of the cock and hen with her hand, and rubbed the spotted cow between the horns. When the old man told her to go and cook some supper, she got it ready very quickly, but when she placed the dishes on the table, she said :

'I am not going to feast myself with all these good things while the poor animals have nothing. There will be plenty left for me, and I shall take care of them first.'

Then she went and fetched some barley, which she scattered before the chickens, and a whole armful of sweet hay for the cow.

'Eat that up, you dear animals,' she said, 'and perhaps you are thirsty, so I will bring you some fresh water.'

Then she brought in a large basin of water, and the cock and hen sprung on the brink, dipped in their beaks and lifted their heads in the manner that birds always do drink, while the spotted cow took a long draught. After the animals were fed, the maiden seated herself at the table and ate what the old man had left for her. In a very little while the fowls had their heads behind their wings, and the cow began to blink her eyes, so the maiden said:

'Shall we not go to rest?'

And the old man cried :

> ' Little chicks and spotted cow,
>   Shall we let her sleep here now ?'

And they replied quickly :

> ' Yes, for she is very good,
>   She has brought us drink and food.'

Then the maiden went upstairs, shook both beds, and made them **up,**

THE SPOTTED COW TOOK A LONG DRAUGHT.

and presently the old man came to his room, and when he laid himself on the bed his white beard nearly reached to his feet.

The maiden also said her prayers, and lying down slept peacefully till midnight, when a number of strange noises awoke her.   The corners of the house were creaking and cracking, the doors sprang open and struck against the walls. The rafters groaned, as if their joints were broken and separated; the stairs were turning upside down, and at last there was a crash as if the roof and the walls had fallen in together. Then all was still.

The maiden had been too frightened to move, and all had happened so quickly that she would have had scarcely time to do so. But now, finding she was not hurt, and still in her comfortable bed, she lay quiet and went to sleep again.

But in the morning when the bright sunshine awoke her, what a sight met her eyes! She was lying in a noble room, and everything around her was as splendid as the furniture of a royal palace. The walls were covered with golden flowers on a silken ground. The bed was of ivory, and the covering of red velvet, and on a chair near it stood a pair of slippers embroidered with pearls.

The maiden fancied herself in a dream, but while she wondered three neatly-dressed servants came in, and asked her what they could do for her.

'Nothing,' she replied, 'only go away, and I will get up and cook the old man's breakfast for him, and give those dear animals their food.'

She dressed herself quickly, and went to the old man's room; but what was her astonishment to see lying on the bed a strange man, asleep! While she stood and saw with surprise that he was young and handsome, he woke, raised himself, and said:

'Don't go away; I am a king's son, and a wicked witch changed me into a bearded, gray old man. My castle was changed into the wooden house, and my servants into a cock, a hen, and a spotted cow. The spell was never to be broken unless a maiden came to visit us who had a kind heart, and who was as careful to feed poor animals as human beings, and you are that maiden. And at midnight, while we slept, we were all through you set free; the old wooden house is again a royal castle, and the animals are restored to their former shape as my servants. I will now send them to fetch your father and mother, that they may be present at our marriage, for you are to be my wife.'

'But where are my sisters?' she asked.

'I have shut them up in the cellar,' he replied; 'but to-morrow I will send them to work in the mines till they have learnt that animals require to be fed and kindly treated as well as human beings.'

PRINCESS MALEEN.

THERE was once a king who had only one son, and he fell in love with
the daughter of another mighty king, who was named Princess Maleen.
She was very beautiful, and her father wished her to marry a prince to
whom he had promised her. But they both loved each other so dearly
that they would not be separated, and Princess Maleen told her father
she would not marry anyone else than the son of the neighbouring
king.

On hearing this her father fell into a great rage, and ordered a dark
tower to be built, into which not a sunbeam nor a ray of moonlight
could penetrate. When it was finished, he said to his daughter : ' You
shall be shut up in that tower for seven years, and then I will come
and see if your obstinacy is not cured.'

Provisions to last for the time were stored in the tower, and then the
princess and her maid were led into it, walled up, and cut off at once
from heaven and earth, and there they had to remain in total darkness,
unable to distinguish day from night.

The prince went often to the tower, and called the princess by name,
but no sound could penetrate those thick walls ; and what could she do
but weep and complain?

Time passed on, and by the decrease in the provisions she knew
that the seven years were coming to an end, and she supposed the hour
of her release was at hand ; but no stroke of a hammer was heard, no
stone fell from the walls, and it seemed as if her father had forgotten
her.

Finding no change, and knowing that their provisions would not last
much longer, the position of Princess Maleen and her maid became
very painful, for a terrible death threatened them. ' We must not give
up yet,' said the princess. ' I think we might try to break through the
walls in some way.' She took up the bread-knife as she spoke, and dug
and scraped at the mortar between the stones for a long time, and when
she was tired the maid took her place.

After working very hard they managed to displace one stone, then a
second, and a third, and in three days the first ray of light fell upon
the darkness, and at last there was an opening large enough for them

to look through. The sky was blue, and the fresh air that came into the tower had a sweet fragrance. But how sad everything appeared to the princess! Her father's castle lay in ruins, the towns and villages round it, as far as one could see, were burnt. The fields, far and wide, had been laid waste, and not a living soul could be seen.

They continued to work till the opening in the wall was large enough for anyone to creep through. Then the maid jumped through, and the Princess Maleen quickly followed her. Yet, now that they were free, they knew not which way to wend their steps, for an enemy had evidently destroyed the whole country, driven away the king, and slain all the inhabitants. They wandered on for some time, in hopes of reaching another country; but they found neither a shelter nor a human being to offer them a bit of bread; and so great was their hunger that they were glad to eat stinging-nettle-stalks to quench it.

After wandering about for a long time, they came at last to another land, and there they begged to be taken as servants; but wherever they knocked they were refused, and no one would pity them. At last they arrived at a large town, and went at once to the king's court. But even here they were told to go away, till the cook said she would take one of them to help her in the kitchen; so the Princess Maleen remained to become a second Cinderella.

What was her surprise to find, after a time, that the king in whose castle she now worked as a servant was the father of her former lover, and that he had chosen for his son another bride, who was ugly in countenance and wicked at heart. The marriage was to take place very soon, as the prince was already betrothed to the ugly maiden.

But she hid her great ugliness from every eye, and shut herself up in her own room, only allowing the kitchen-maid to see her, so the Princess Maleen had to wait upon the ugly bride of her own lover.

The day arrived at last in which the bridegroom was to go with his bride to church; but she was so ashamed of her ugliness, and so afraid that the people in the street would point at her and make fun of her, that she sent for Maleen, and said to her: 'I have had a great misfortune, and sprained my foot, therefore I cannot go out into the town to-day; but if you will put on the bridal dress, and take my place, it will be a great honour for you, beyond what you ought to expect.'

But the Princess Maleen replied: 'I wish for no honour that does not rightly belong to me!'

The bride then offered her gold, but it was all in vain, she still refused to go.

At last the ugly maiden got angry, and said: 'If you will not obey me it shall cost you your life, for I have only to say the word, and your head will lie at my feet!'

The Princess Maleen, being known in the castle only as the kitchen-maid, was now obliged to obey. She therefore dressed herself in the bride's clothes, and put on her jewels and ornaments.

When she entered the royal saloon, everyone was astonished at her great beauty, and the king said to his son :

'That is the bride I have chosen for you, and whom you must lead to the church.'

The bridegroom, who had heard that his bride was plain, felt rather surprised, and said to himself :

'She is like my Princess Maleen, and I should believe it was her if I did not know she had been shut up in the tower, and no doubt is dead.'

However, he took her by the hand, and led her to church.

As they sat in the carriage together, he noticed that she looked thoughtful and sad, and he asked her if she was unhappy.

'No,' she replied ; 'but I was thinking of the Princess Maleen.'

The prince did not reply, but he wondered very much that his bride should know that name.

Presently he asked : 'Do you know the Princess Maleen?'

'How should I know her?' she replied.

As they approached the church, he threw round her neck a costly chain of gold, and fastened it with a gold clasp. Then they entered the church, and stood at the altar while the priest joined their hands and married them.

During their ride back to the castle, the princess spoke not one word the whole way, and, when she arrived, she hastened to the chamber of the bride, took off the rich dress and ornaments, and dressed herself in her old gray gown and kirtle. She kept nothing but the gold chain which the prince had given her.

The ugly bride then arrayed herself in the elegant bridal clothes, and, throwing a thick veil over her face, went to join the company at the marriage-feast.

As soon as the guests were departed, the bridegroom said :

'Where is the chain that I gave you at the church-door to-day?'

'What chain?' she answered. 'You gave me no chain.'

'I placed it round your neck myself,' he said, 'and fastened it; therefore, if you know nothing about it, you are not my right bride.'

He pulled the veil from her face as he spoke, and her remarkable ugliness made him start back with surprise and fright, exclaiming :

'Who are you? what do you do here?'

'I am your real bride,' she said, 'the one whom the king, your father, chose for you; but as I feared the people might mock me to-day, I told the kitchen-maid to dress in my clothes, and be proxy for me at the church.'

'Where is that maiden?' he said ; 'I must see her. Go and fetch her here!'

'This shall cost her her life,' she thought, as she went out in a great rage, and said to the servants : 'That kitchen girl is an impostor. Take her out into the court, and cut off her head!'

The servants caught hold of her, and would have dragged her away ; but she screamed so loud for help that the prince heard her voice. He hastened out of his chamber, and ordered that the maiden should be instantly set free. When she came into the light of the lamps, he noticed on her neck the sparkle of the gold ornament he had given her.

'This is the right bride,' he said, 'who went with me to the church;' and he led her away as he spoke.

When they were alone, he said to her: 'On the road to church you mentioned the name of the Princess Maleen, who was once my own beloved bride. If I thought it possible, I should say she now stood before me, for you resemble her in every way.'

'I am the Princess Maleen,' she said. 'I was shut up for seven years in a dark tower. I have suffered hunger and thirst, and sorrow and poverty, and I came to this castle to earn my bread by service. While here, I found it was your home, and that you were going to marry another; and I should have remained silent always if your bride had not sent me with you to the church. It was I whom you married to-day at the altar, and I am your real bride; and, if you still love me, it will be sunshine indeed after all the dark days that are past.'

'I do still love you,' he said, as he took her in his arms and kissed her.

The next day the ugly bride was sent home to her father's house, and from that moment the Princess Maleen and her husband lived in great happiness for the rest of their lives.

The tower in which the princess was enclosed is still standing, and the children play round it, and sometimes in whispers tell each other the story of Princess Maleen.

THE CRYSTAL BALL.

A SORCERESS once had three sons, who loved each other with brotherly affection, but the old woman did not trust them; she thought they would rob her of her power. So she turned the eldest into an eagle, who lived on the top of a rocky mountain, and was often seen whirling round in great circles, or soaring high in the heavens. She changed the second son into a whale, who lived in the deep sea, and at times there would be seen a mighty stream of water rising in the air, which the whale spurted up like a water-spout. Each of the brothers, however, had the privilege of resuming his own natural form for two hours each day.

The third son, who feared that his mother might turn him into a wild beast, such as a bear or a wolf, went away secretly from home. He had heard, also, that in a beautiful castle, called the Castle of the

Golden Sun, lived a beautiful princess, who was under the spell of the sorcerer, and he longed to set her free.

He knew, however, that to do this he must risk his life, for already three-and-twenty young men had met with most terrible deaths in the attempt, and since the last of that number fell a victim, none had dared to venture near the spot. But the young man's heart knew no fear, so he determined to go and seek the Castle of the Golden Sun.

He had been travelling for a long time without finding it, when he came to a great forest, in which he wandered about till he lost his way. All at once he saw in the distance two giants, who beckoned to him with their hands, and when he approached they asked him what he was doing there. He told them he had lost his way.

'Oh,' replied one, 'we can soon show you. We know every corner of the forest; but you must help us in something first. We are both equally strong, and neither can overcome the other, and we have been fighting for a little hat, which is to belong to the one who conquers. Now you little men are as clever as we are, and therefore we will let you decide who is to have it.'

'How can I fight with you for an old hat?' replied the youth.

'Ah,' they replied, 'you call it old; you don't know its value. It is what is called a wishing-hat, and whoever puts it on can wish himself where he will, and in a moment he is there.'

'Give me the hat,' said the young man. 'I will go on a little way, and when I call you must both run a race to overtake me, and whoever reaches me first, to him the hat shall belong.'

The giants agreed, and the youth, taking the hat, put it on and went away; but he was thinking so much of the princess that he forgot the giants and the hat, and continued to go farther and farther without calling them.

Presently he sighed deeply and said, 'Ah, if I were only at the Castle of the Golden Sun.' The words were scarcely out of his mouth when he found himself on a high mountain, and before him stood the Castle of the Golden Sun. He stepped in through the open door, and went from room to room, till he came at last to one in which the princess sat. But how shocked he was when he saw her. She had a complexion as gray as ashes, her face was wrinkled, her eyes dim, and her hair red.

'Are you the king's daughter, whose beauty is so renowned?' he cried.

'Ah,' she replied, 'this is not my own shape. The eyes of mankind can only see me in this hideous form and appearance, for I am under a spell. If, however, you wish to know what I really am, you must look in the mirror, which never allows itself to be mistaken, but represents my image truthfully.'

She gave him, as she spoke, a looking-glass, and he saw in it the representation of a beautiful maiden, as the world once knew her, with the tears of sorrow running down her cheeks.

'Tell me how to set you free,' said the young man. 'I shrink from no danger.'

She replied: 'Whoever can obtain a crystal ball, and hold it before the sorcerer, will destroy his power, and I shall instantly regain my proper form and freedom. But,' she continued, 'so many have already lost their lives in the attempt, and it pains me to think that your young blood should flow, if you venture to encounter such a dangerous undertaking.'

'Nothing shall hinder me,' he replied. 'Only tell me what I am to do.'

'You shall know all,' said the princess. 'Now, listen. You must climb to the top of the mountain upon which this castle stands, and there you will find a wild buffalo, standing by a spring. With him you must fight, and if you are so fortunate as to kill him, a phœnix will rise out of his dead body. This creature you must also destroy, and in it you will find a red-hot egg, and if you break it, instead of a yolk will be seen the crystal ball. But you must be careful not to let the egg fall on the ground. If you do, it will immediately ignite and burn up everything near it. The egg also will melt, and with it the crystal ball, so that all your trouble will be lost.'

The youth, on hearing this, did not delay a moment. He went out and found the buffalo at the spring, snorting and bellowing. The combat, however, did not last long, for, after two or three thrusts with his sword, the animal lay dead at the young man's feet. In a moment there rose a fiery bird from the buffalo's body, who attempted to fly away; but the eagle—the youth's brother who had been changed by the sorceress, and who was flying in the air above their heads—darted swiftly down, drove the bird towards the sea, and so wounded it with its beak that, in her distress, she dropped the egg. It did not fall into the sea, but on a fisherman's little hut, which stood on the shore, and immediately the hut and all around it were in flames. At this moment there rose from the sea an immense stream of water, which fell on the hut and quickly extinguished the fire.

The second brother, the whale, while swimming that way, had also been able to assist the youth, by spirting up the water, as whales do.

No sooner was the fire extinguished, than the young man searched among the embers for the egg, and luckily found it, safe and perfect. It had not melted; but the sudden rush of the cold water had broken the shell, and he could easily remove the crystal ball.

The youth went immediately to the sorcerer, and held the ball before him. 'My power is now destroyed,' he said, 'and you are the king of the Castle of the Golden Sun. You can also restore your brothers to their natural forms whenever you like.'

The young man, on hearing this, hastened to the princess, and on entering her chamber she stood before him in the full blaze of her beauty. Then with joyful hearts they exchanged rings with each other, and swore eternal love.

THE TWELVE WINDOWS.

A KING'S daughter once lived in a castle, which had above its battlements a hall containing twelve windows. She would often ascend to this lofty room, for if she looked out of the windows she could see all over her kingdom. In the first window she could see more clearly than any living being; in the second this power was much increased; in the third her sight could penetrate still farther; and so on, each window excelling the one next it, till at the twelfth she could look out over all the earth, and nothing was hidden from her eyes.

This princess was very proud; she would submit to no one, and was determined in all points to be master. She made it known, however, that she would marry any man who could so completely conceal himself as to make it impossible for her to find him. If, however, anyone attempted to do this and failed, he would have his head cut off and stuck on a pole.

There stood already ninety-seven poles with heads upon them before the castle, and therefore for a long time no one had ventured to make the attempt.

The princess was beginning to feel quite contented, and thought to herself, 'Now I shall remain free for my whole life,' when three brothers appeared before her, and declared that they were ready to try their fortunes in this matter.

She readily agreed to the proposal; but the eldest, who was silly enough to suppose that if he crept into a chalk-pit he would be safe, was quickly discovered by the princess from her first window, and his fate soon decided.

The second brother hid himself in the cellar under the castle; but the princess saw him easily from her first window, and he also was taken out, his head cut off and placed upon the ninety-ninth pole.

After seeing this the youngest brother stepped forward, and begged that he might have a day to consider; and also that the princess would grant him the favour of trying a third time after she had found him twice. If then he failed, he would not expect to save his life. This brother was very handsome, and he begged so earnestly that the princess at length agreed to give him three trials; but she added, 'You will not be fortunate even then.'

On the following morning the young man tried for a long time to think of the safest way to hide himself, but all to no purpose, so he took his gun and went out. Presently he saw a raven on a tree, and pointed his gun at him.

'Don't shoot me,' said the raven; 'some day I shall be able to repay you.'

He turned away on hearing this, and went farther, till he came to a lake, just as a large fish had risen to the surface.

He took aim, but before he could draw the trigger, the fish cried out, 'Don't shoot me; I shall be able to repay your kindness.'

He left the creature to dive in safety, and at a little distance overtook a fox, who was walking lame. He shot, but missed him.

'Oh, dear,' cried the fox, 'do come and pull this thorn out of my foot.'

The young man complied, but after doing so he felt inclined to kill the fox for the sake of his skin and fur.

'Spare my life,' cried the fox; 'I may repay you for it some day.'

The young man granted his request, and as it was now evening he returned home.

On the following day he had to hide himself; but after racking his brains for a long time, he knew not how to set about it. At last he remembered the raven in the forest, so he went to her and said:

'I spared your life yesterday; now tell me how I can hide myself so that the princess may not find me.'

The raven bowed her head, and thought for a long time. At last she croaked, 'I have it!'

Then she fetched one of the eggs from her nest, divided it equally in two parts, then enclosing the young man in the shell, she joined it carefully, placed it in the nest, and sat upon it.

Meanwhile, the princess went to her first window and looked out, but she could discover nothing. She passed on to the second and the third without success, and when she reached the tenth she began to feel very anxious. At last, at the eleventh window, she succeeded. She immediately ordered the raven to be shot, and the eggs to be brought to her. On breaking one the young man knew he was discovered, and reluctantly came out of his strange hiding-place.

'Ah,' she said, 'I promised to let you off the first time, but if you do not manage better in future you will be lost.'

The next day he went to the lake, and cried out to the fish: 'I spared your life yesterday, now tell me how I can conceal myself so that the princess may not find me.'

The fish reflected for a time, and then exclaimed: 'I have it; you will be safe in my stomach!'

So the fish swallowed the young man, and carried him down to the bottom of the sea.

The princess looked through all the windows, but not even in the eleventh could she find him. She was really alarmed now, till at last, in looking from the twelfth window, she discovered his hiding-place.

She then ordered the fish to be caught and killed, and we can understand the poor young man's trouble and fear when he was obliged to come forth from the fish and appear before the princess.

'Two failures have been granted you,' she said, 'but after the next your head will look well on the hundredth pole!'

On the last day he went with a heavy heart to the field, and met the fox.

'You know all the best hiding-places,' he said to him. 'I spared your life yesterday, now advise me where to hide that the princess may not find me.'

'It is a difficult task,' said the fox, putting on a very thoughtful face.

At last he said: 'I know what to do;' and, rising, he led the young man to a spring, and dipping himself in first, he came up changed into a fish-seller, with his market badge. He then told the young man to dive also, and as he rose he was immediately turned into a little sea-mouse, which the merchant put into his basket, and then proceeded at once to the town.

The curious little mouse attracted so much attention that quite a crowd gathered round him.

At length the princess heard of this wonderful creature, and she sent for the merchant; and, on seeing it, offered to purchase it for a large sum of money.

Before he parted with it, he said to the young man: 'Creep quickly into the folds of her hair, and lie still while the princess goes to look for you out of her windows presently.'

In a few moments the time came for the princess to visit her windows, and, desiring the merchant to leave, she went up to the hall. On entering, she stepped from one window to the other, till she came to the twelfth, and, not seeing the young man even from thence, she was overcome with rage and fear, and struck the glass so violently with her hand, that it broke into a thousand pieces, and the whole castle trembled.

On returning to her room, she felt something in her hair. Seizing it hastily, she threw it to the floor, saying:

'Get out of my sight!'

The merchant caught it up, and ran hastily to the spring, where they both dipped themselves, and were restored to their own proper shape.

The young man thanked the fox, and said:

'The raven and the fish are simpletons compared to you; you know successful tricks right well.'

After this the young man went to the castle. The princess, who had already resigned herself to her fate, was ready for him. The marriage was shortly after celebrated with great pomp, and the young husband became lord and master of the whole kingdom.

He never told her how he had succeeded in hiding himself from her the third time, nor who had helped him; so she believed he had done all by his superior knowledge and skill.   She therefore learnt to esteem him, for she thought to herself, 'He can do more than I could with all my windows.'

DISCREET HANS.

HANS'S mother asked, "Whither are you going, Hans?" "To Grethel's," replied he. "Behave well, Hans." "I will take care: good bye, mother." "Good bye, Hans."

Hans came to Grethel. "Good day," said he. "Good day," replied Grethel. "What treasure do you bring to-day?" "I bring nothing. Have you anything to give?" Grethel presented Hans with a needle. "Good bye," said he. "Good bye, Hans." Hans took the needle, stuck it in a load of hay, and walked home behind the waggon.

"Good evening, mother." "Good evening, Hans. Where have you been?" "To Grethel's." "And what have you given her?" "Nothing: she has given me something." "What has Grethel given you?" "A needle," said Hans. "And where have you put it?" "In the load of hay." "Then you have behaved stupidly, Hans; you should put needles on your coat-sleeve." "To behave better, do nothing at all," thought Hans.

"Whither are you going, Hans?" "To Grethel's, mother." "Behave well, Hans." "I will take care: good bye, mother." "Good bye, Hans."

Hans came to Grethel. "Good day," said he. "Good day, Hans. What treasure do you bring?" "I bring nothing. Have you anything to give?" Grethel gave Hans a knife. "Good bye Grethel." "Good bye, Hans." Hans took the knife, put it in his sleeve, and went home.

"Good evening, mother." "Good evening, Hans. Where have you been?" "To Grethel's." "And what did you take to her?" "I took nothing: she has given to me." "And what did she give you?" "A knife," said Hans. "And where have you put it?" "In my sleeve." "Then you have behaved foolishly again, Hans: you should put knives in your pocket." "To behave better, do nothing at all," thought Hans.

"Whither are you going, Hans?" "To Grethel's, mother." "Behave well, Hans." "I will take care: good bye, mother." "Good-bye, Hans."

Hans came to Grethel. "Good day, Grethel." "Good day, Hans. What treasure do you bring?" "I bring nothing. Have you anything to give?" Grethel gave Hans a young goat. "Good bye, Grethel." "Good bye, Hans." Hans took the goat, tied its legs, and put it in his pocket.

Just as he reached home it was suffocated. "Good evening, mother." "Good evening, Hans. Where have you been?" "To Grethel's." "And what did you take to her?" "I took nothing; she

gave to me." "And what did Grethel give you?" "A goat."
"Where did you put it, Hans?" "In my pocket." "There you acted
stupidly, Hans; you should have tied the goat with a rope." "To
behave better, do nothing," thought Hans.

"Whither away, Hans?" "To Grethel's, mother." "Behave well,
Hans." "I'll take care: good bye, mother." "Good bye, Hans."

Hans came to Grethel. "Good day," said he. "Good day, Hans.
What treasure do you bring?" "I bring nothing. Have you
anything to give?" Grethel gave Hans a piece of bacon. "Good bye,
Grethel." "Good bye, Hans." Hans took the bacon, tied it with a
rope, and swung it to and fro so that the dogs came and ate it up.
When he reached home he held the rope in his hand, but there was
nothing on it.

"Good evening, mother," said he. "Good evening, Hans. Where
have you been?" "To Grethel's, mother." "What did you take
there?" "I took nothing: she gave to me." "And what did Grethel
give you?" "A piece of bacon," said Hans. "And where have you
put it?" "I tied it with a rope, swung it about, and the dogs came
and ate it up." "There you acted stupidly, Hans; you should have
carried the bacon on your head." "To behave better, do nothing,"
thought Hans.

"Whither away, Hans?" "To Grethel's, mother." "Behave well,
Hans." "I'll take care: good bye, mother." "Good bye, Hans."

Hans came to Grethel. "Good day," said he. "Good day, Hans.
What treasure do you bring?" "I bring nothing. Have you
anything to give?" Grethel gave Hans a calf. "Good bye," said
Hans. "Good bye." Hans took the calf, set it on his head, and the
calf scratched his face.

"Good evening, mother." "Good evening, Hans. Where have you
been?" "To Grethel's." "What did you take her?" "I took
nothing: she gave to me." "And what did Grethel give you?" "A
calf," said Hans. "And what did you do with it?" "I set it on my
head, and it kicked my face." "Then you acted stupidly, Hans; you
should have led the calf home, and put it in the stall." "To behave
better, do nothing," thought Hans.

"Whither away, Hans?" "To Grethel's, mother." "Behave well,
Hans." "I'll take care: good bye, mother." "Good bye, Hans."

Hans came to Grethel. "Good day," said he. "Good day, Hans.
What treasure do you bring?" "I bring nothing. Have you
anything to give?" Grethel said, "I will go with you, Hans." Hans
tied a rope round Grethel, led her home, put her in the stall, and
made the rope fast; and then he went to his mother.

"Good evening, mother." "Good evening, Hans. Where have you
been?" "To Grethel's." "What did you take her?" "I took
nothing." "What did Grethel give you?" "She gave nothing; she
came with me." "And where have you left her, then?" "I tied her

with a rope, put her in the stall, and threw in some grass.'' ''Then you acted stupidly, Hans; you should have looked at her with friendly eyes.'' ''To behave better, do nothing,'' thought Hans; and then he went into the stall, and made sheep's eyes at Grethel.

And after that Grethel became Hans's wife.

GODFATHER DEATH.

A CERTAIN poor man had twelve children, and was obliged to work day and night to find them bread to eat; but when the thirteenth child was born, he ran out in despair on the highroad to ask the first person he should meet to stand godfather to it.

Presently he met Death striding along on his withered legs, who said, ''Take me for godfather.'' The man asked him who he was, and received for reply, ''I am Death, who make all things equal.'' ''Then,'' answered the man, ''you are the right person—you make no difference between the rich and poor; you shall be godfather to my boy.''

Death replied, ''I will make your child rich and famous; he who has me for a friend can need nought.'' Then the man told him the christening was fixed for the following Sunday, and invited him to come; and at the right time he did appear, and acted very becomingly on the occasion.

When the boy arrived at years of discretion, the godfather came and took him away with him, and leading him into a forest showed him an herb which grew there. ''Now,'' said Death, ''you shall receive your christening gift. I make you a famous physician. Every time you are called to a sick person I will appear to you. If I stand at the head of your patient, you may speak confidently that you can restore him, and if you give him a morsel of that vegetable he will speedily get well, but if I stand at the feet of the sick he is mine, and you may say all medicine is in vain, for the best physician in the world could not cure him. Dare not, however, use the herb against my will, for then it will go ill with you.''

In a very short space of time the youth became the most renowned physician in the world. ''He only wants just to see the sick person, and he knows instantly whether he will live or die,'' said every one to his neighbour; and so it came to pass, that from far and near people came to him, bringing him the sick, and giving him so much money that he soon became a very rich man. Once it happened that the King fell sick, and our Physician was called in to say if recovery were possible. When he came to the bedside, he saw that Death stood at the feet of the King. ''Ah,'' thought he, ''if I might this once cheat Death; he will certainly take offence; but then I am his godchild, and perhaps he will shut his eyes to it,—I will venture.''

So saying he took up the sick man, and turned him round, so that Death stood at the head of the King; then he gave the King some of the herb, and he instantly rose up quite refreshed.

Soon afterwards Death, with an angry and gloomy face, came to the Physician, and pressed him on the arm, saying, ''You have put my light out, but this time I will excuse you, because you are my godchild; however, do not dare to act so again, for it will cost you your life, and I shall come and take you away.''

Soon after this event the daughter of the King fell into a serious illness, and, as she was his only child, he wept day and night until his eyes were almost blinded. He also caused to be made known that whoever saved her life should receive her for a bride, and inherit his crown. When the Physician came to the bedside of the sick, he perceived Death at her feet, and he remembered the warning of his godfather; but the great beauty of the Princess, and the fortune which her husband would receive, so influenced him that he cast all other thoughts to the wind. He would not see that Death cast angry looks at him, and threatened him with his fist; but he raised up his patient, and laid her head where her feet had been. Then he gave her a portion of the wonderful herb, and soon her cheeks regained their colour, and her blood circulated freely.

When Death thus saw his kingdom a second time invaded, and his power mocked, he strode up swiftly to the side of the Physician and said, ''Now is your turn come;'' and he struck him with his icy-cold hand so hard, that the Physician was unable to resist, and was obliged to follow Death to his underground abode. There the Physician saw thousands upon thousands of lamps burning in immeasurable rows, some large, others small, and others yet smaller. Every moment some were extinguished, but others in the same instant blazed out, so that the flames appeared to dance up here and there in continual variation.

''Do you see?'' said Death. ''These are the lamps of men's lives. The larger ones belong to children, the next to those in the flower of their age, and the smallest to the aged and grey-headed. Yet some of the children and youth in the world have but the smallest lamps.''

The Physician begged to be shown his own lamp, and Death pointed to one almost expiring, saying, ''There, that is thine.''

''Ah, my dear godfather,'' exclaimed the Physician, frightened, ''kindle a new one for me; for your love of me do it, that I may enjoy some years of life, marry the Princess, and come to the crown.''

''I cannot,'' answered Death; ''one lamp must be extinguished before another can be lighted.''

"Then place the old one over a new lamp, that its dying fire may kindle a fresh blaze," said the Physician, entreatingly.

Death made as if he would perform his wish, and prepared a large and fresh lamp; but he did it very slowly, in order to revenge himself, and the little flame died before he finished. Then the Physician sank to the earth, and fell for ever into the hands of Death!

THE OLD WITCH.

THERE was once a little girl who was very obstinate and willful, and who never obeyed when her elders spoke to her; and so how could she be happy? One day she said to her parents, "I have heard so much of the old Witch, that I will go and see her. People say she is a wonderful old woman, and has many marvellous things in her house; and I am very curious to see them."

Her parents, however, forbade her going, saying, "The Witch is a wicked old woman, who performs many godless deeds; and if you go near her, you are no longer a child of ours."

The girl, however, would not turn back at her parents' command, but went to the Witch's house. When she arrived there the woman asked her, "Why are you so pale?"

"Ah," replied she, trembling all over, "I have frightened myself so with what I have just seen."

"And what did you see?" inquired the old Witch.

"I saw a black man on your steps."

"That was a collier," replied she.

"Then I saw a grey man."

"That was a sportsman," said the old woman.

"After him I saw a blood-red man."

"That was a butcher," replied the woman.

"But oh, I was most terrified," continued the girl, "when I peeped through your window, and saw not you, but a creature with a fiery head."

"Then you have seen the Witch in her proper dress," said the old woman; "for you I have long waited, and now you shall give me light." So saying, she changed the girl into a block of wood, and then threw it into the fire; and when it was fully alight she sat down on the hearth, warmed herself and said, "Ah, now for once it burns brightly!"

THE FEATHER BIRD.

ONCE upon a time there lived a Sorcerer, who used to take the form
of a beggar, and go begging before the houses, and stealing little
girls, and nobody knew where he took them. One day he appeared
before the house of a man who had three pretty daughters, disguised
as a poor, weak, old cripple, carrying a sack on his back to put all his
alms in. He begged for something to eat, and when the eldest girl
came out and offered him a piece of bread, he only touched her and
she was compelled to jump into his sack. Then he hurried away with
great strides, and carried her through a dark forest to his house, in
which everything was very splendid. There he gave her what she
wished, and told her, "All will be well with you, for you will have
all your heart can desire." This lasted two days, and he then said,
"I must be off and leave you for a short time alone: these are the
house-keeping keys, you can look over everything; but into one room
which this little key unlocks, I forbid you to enter on pain of
death." He gave her also an egg, saying, "Preserve this carefully
for me, and always carry it about with you; for if it be lost, a great
misfortune will happen."

She took the key and the egg and promised all he required; but as
soon as he was gone her curiosity overmastered her, and after she
had looked over the whole house, from attic to cellar, she unlocked
the forbidden door and went in. She was terribly frightened when
she entered the room, for in the middle there stood a large basin,
wherein was some blood. In her terror the egg fell from her hand,
and rolled into the basin; and although she fished it out again
directly, and wiped it, it was of no use, for, scrub and wash all she
might, the blood appeared as fresh as ever. The next day the
Sorcerer came home, and demanded the key and the egg. She handed
them to him with trembling; and he instantly perceived that she had
been into the forbidden chamber. "Have you then dared to enter
that room against my will?" said he; "then now you enter it again
against yours. Your life is forfeited." So saying he drew her in by
the hair and locked her up.

"Now I will fetch the second one," said the Sorcerer to himself:
and, assuming the disguise of a beggar, he went and begged before
the house. Then the second girl brought him a piece of bread, and he
seized her, as the first, and bore her away. It happened to her as it
had to her eldest sister, curiosity led her astray, and on the
Sorcerer's return she was locked up for having opened the forbidden door.

He went now and fetched the third sister; but she was prudent and cunning. As soon as he had given her his directions and had ridden away, she first carefully laid by the egg, and then went and opened the forbidden chamber. Ah, what a scene! She saw her two dear sisters lying there half starved. She raised them, however, and gave them food, and soon they got well and were very happy, and kissed and embraced one another.

On his return the Sorcerer demanded the key and the egg; and when he could find no spot of blood on them, he said to the maiden, "You have withstood temptation; you shall be my bride, and whatever you desire, that will I do."

"Very well," she replied; then first you must take my father and mother a sackful of gold, and you must carry it yourself on your back; in the meantime I will arrange the wedding." Then she ran to her sisters, whom she had concealed in a chamber, and said, "The moment has arrived when I can save you; the Sorcerer himself shall carry you away; and as soon as you arrive at our home, send me help." Then she placed them both in a sack, and covered them over with gold, so that nothing of them could be seen; and then, calling the Sorcerer in, she said, "Now, carry away the sack; but I shall peep through my window, and keep a sharp look-out that you do not rest at all on your journey."

The Sorcerer raised the sack on his shoulder, and went away with it; but it weighed so heavily that the perspiration ran down his face. Presently he wished to rest a minute, but a voice called to him out of the sack, "I am looking through my window, and see that you are stopping: will you go on?" He thought it was his Bride calling to him, so he instantly got up again. A little further he would have rested again; but the same voice called, "I am looking through my window, and see that you are stopping; will you go on again?" And as often as he stopped he heard the same words; and so he was obliged to keep on, until he at last arrived, exhausted and out of breath, with the sack of gold at the house of the father and mother.

Meanwhile, at home the Bride prepared the wedding-feast, and invited the friends of the Sorcerer to come. Then she took a turnip and cut out places for the eyes and teeth, and put a head-dress on it and a crown of flowers, and set it at the topmost window, and left it there peeping down. As soon as all was ready she dipped herself in a cask full of honey, and then ripping up the bed, she rolled herself among the feathers until she looked like a marvellous bird, whom no one could possibly recognise. After this she went out of the house; and on the way some of the wedding-guests met her, and asked her whence she came; and she replied, "I come from the house of the Feather King."

"How does the young Bride?" asked they.

"She has taken herself to the top of the house, and is peeping out of the window."

Soon after the Bridegroom met her as he was slowly travelling back, and asked exactly the same questions as the others, and received the same answers. Then the Bridegroom looked up and saw the decorated turnip, and he thought it was his Bride, and nodded to it and kissed her hand lovingly. But just as he was gone into the house with his guests, the brothers and relations of the Bride, who had been sent to her rescue, arrived. They immediately closed up all the doors of the house, so that no one could escape, and then set fire to it; and the Sorcerer and all his accomplices were burnt to ashes.

THE SIX SWANS.

A KING was once hunting in a large wood, and pursued his game so hotly that none of his courtiers could follow him. But when evening approached he stopped, and looking around him perceived that he had lost himself. He sought a path out of the forest, but could not find one, and presently he saw an old woman with a nodding head, who came up to him. "My good woman," said he to her, "can you not show me the way out of the forest?" "Oh, yes, my lord King," she replied; "I can do that very well, but upon one condition, which, if you do not fulfil, you will never again get out of the wood, but will die of hunger."

"What, then, is this condition?" asked the King.

"I have a daughter," said the old woman, "who is as beautiful as any one you can find in the whole world, and well deserves to be your bride. Now, if you will make her your Queen, I will show you your way out of the wood." In the anxiety of his heart, the King consented, and the old woman led him to her cottage, where the daughter was sitting by the fire. She received the King as if she had expected him, and he saw at once that she was very beautiful, but yet she did not quite please him, for he could not look at her without a secret shuddering. However, after all he took the maiden up on his horse, and the old woman showed him the way, and the King arrived safely at his palace, where the wedding was to be celebrated.

The King had been married once before, and had seven children by his first wife, six boys and a girl, whom he loved above everything else in the world. He became afraid, soon, that the stepmother might not treat them very well, and might even do them some great injury, so he took them away to a lonely castle which stood in the midst of a forest. This castle was so hidden, and the way to it so difficult to discover, that he himself could not have found it if a wise woman had not given him a ball of cotton which had the wonderful property, when he threw it before him, of unrolling itself and

THE
SIX·SWANS

THE·SWANS·CAME·CLOSE·UP·TO·
HER·WITH·RUSHING·WINGS·&·
STOOPED·ROUND·HER·SO·THAT·
SHE·COULD·THROW·THE·SHIRTS·
·OVER·THEM:·

SWAIN. Sc

THE SIX SWANS

showing him the right path. The King went, however, so often to see his dear children, that the Queen noticed his absence, became inquisitive, and wished to know what he went to fetch out of the forest. So she gave his servants a great quantity of money, and they disclosed to her the secret, and also told her of the ball of cotton which alone could show her the way. She had now no peace until she discovered where this ball was concealed, and then she made some fine silken shirts, and, as she had learnt of her mother, she sewed within each one a charm. One day soon after, when the King was gone out hunting, she took the little shirts and went into the forest, and the cotton showed her the path. The children, seeing some one coming in the distance, thought it was their dear father, and ran out towards her full of joy. Then she threw over each of them a shirt, which, as it touched their bodies, changed them into Swans, which flew away over the forest. The Queen then went home quite contented, and thought she was free of her stepchildren; but the little girl had not met her with the brothers, and the Queen did not know of her.

The following day the King went to visit his children, but he found only the maiden. "Where are your brothers?" asked he. "Ah, dear father," she replied, "they are gone away and have left me alone;" and she told him how she had looked out of the window and seen them changed into Swans, which had flown over the forest; and then she showed him the feathers, which they had dropped in the courtyard, and which she had collected together. The King was much grieved, but he did not think that his wife could have done this wicked deed, and, as he feared the girl might also be stolen away, he took her with him. She was, however, so much afraid of the stepmother, that she begged him not to stop more than one night in the castle.

The poor Maiden thought to herself, "This is no longer my place, I will go and seek my brothers;" and when night came she escaped and went quite deep into the wood. She walked all night long and a great part of the next day, until she could go no further from weariness. Just then she saw a rude hut, and walking in she found a room with six little beds, but she dared not get into one, but crept under, and, laying herself upon the hard earth, prepared to pass the night there. Just as the sun was setting, she heard a rustling, and saw six white Swans come flying in at the window. They settled on the ground and began blowing one another until they had blown all their feathers off, and their swan's down stripped off like a shirt. Then the maiden knew them at once for her brothers, and gladly crept out from under the bed, and the brothers were not less glad to see their sister, but their joy was of short duration. "Here you must not stay," said they to her; "this is a robbers' hiding-place; if they should return and find you here, they will murder you.'' ''Can you not protect me, then?'' inquired the sister.

''No,'' they replied; ''for we can only lay aside our swan's feathers for a quarter of an hour each evening, and for that time we regain our human form, but afterwards we resume our changed appearance.''

Their sister then asked them with tears, ''Can you not be restored again?''

''Oh, no,'' replied they; ''the conditions are too difficult. For six long years you must neither speak nor laugh, and during that time you must sew together for us six little shirts of star-flowers, and should there fall a single word from your lips, then all your labour will be vain.'' Just as the brothers finished speaking, the quarter of an hour elapsed, and they all flew out of the window again like Swans.

The little sister, however, made a solemn resolution to rescue her brothers, or die in the attempt; and she left the cottage, and, penetrating deep into the forest, passed the night amid the branches of a tree. The next morning she went out and collected the star-flowers to sew together. She had no one to converse with, and for laughing she had no spirits, so there up in the tree she sat, intent upon her work. After she had passed some time there, it happened that the King of that country was hunting in the forest, and his huntsmen came beneath the tree on which the Maiden sat. They called to her and asked, ''Who art thou?'' But she gave no answer. ''Come down to us,'' continued they; ''we will do thee no harm.'' She simply shook her head, and, when they pressed her further with questions, she threw down to them her gold necklace, hoping therewith to satisfy them. They did not, however, leave her, and she threw down her girdle, but in vain; and even her rich dress did not make them desist. At last the hunter himself climbed the tree and brought down the maiden, and took her before the King. The King asked her, ''Who art thou? What dost thou upon that tree?'' But she did not answer; and then he asked her in all the languages that he knew, but she remained dumb to all, as a fish. Since, however, she was so beautiful, the King's heart was touched, and he conceived for her a strong affection. Then he put around her his cloak, and, placing her before him on his horse, took her to his castle. There he ordered rich clothing to be made for her, and, although her beauty shone as the sunbeams, not a word escaped her. The King placed her by his side at table, and there her dignified mien and manners so won upon him, that he said, ''This Maiden will I marry, and no other in the world;'' and after some days he was united to her.

Now, the King had a wicked stepmother who was discontented with his marriage, and spoke evil of the young Queen. ''Who knows whence the wench comes?'' said she. ''She who cannot speak is not worthy of a King.'' A year after, when the Queen brought her first-born into the world, the old woman took him away. Then she went to the King and complained that the Queen was a murderess. The King, however, would not believe it, and suffered no one to do any injury to his wife, who sat composedly sewing at her shirts and paying attention to nothing else. When a second child was born, the false stepmother used the same deceit, but the King again would not listen to her words, but said, ''She is too pious and good to act so: could she but speak and defend herself, her innocence would come to light.'' But when again, the third time, the old woman stole away the child, and then accused the Queen, who answered not a word to the accusation, the King was obliged to give her up to be tried, and she was condemned to suffer death by fire.

When the time had elapsed, and the sentence was to be carried out, it happened that the very day had come round when her dear brothers should be made free; the six shirts were also ready, all but the last, which yet wanted the left sleeve. As she was led to the scaffold, she placed the shirts upon her arm, and just as she had mounted it, and the fire was about to be kindled, she looked round, and saw six Swans come flying through the air. Her heart leapt for joy as she perceived her deliverers approaching, and soon the Swans, flying towards her, alighted so near that she was enabled to throw over them the shirts, and as soon as she had so done their feathers fell off and the brothers stood up alive and well; but the youngest wanted his left arm, instead of which he had a swan's wing. They embraced and kissed each other, and the Queen, going to the King, who was thunderstruck, began to say, ''Now may I speak, my dear husband, and prove to you that I am innocent and falsely accused;'' and then she told him how the wicked woman had stolen away and hidden her three children. When she had concluded, the King was overcome with joy, and the wicked stepmother was led to the scaffold and bound to the stake and burnt to ashes.

The King and the Queen for ever after lived in peace and prosperity with their six brothers.

THE ALMOND TREE.

Long, long ago, perhaps two thousand years, there was a rich man who had a beautiful and pious wife; and they were very fond of one another, but had no children. Still they wished for some very much, and the wife prayed for them day and night; still they had none.

Before their house was a yard; in it stood an almond tree, under

THE
·ALMOND·TREE·

"KYWITT, KYWITT, KYWITT, I CRY,
OH WHAT A BEAUTIFUL BIRD AM I!"

SWAIN SC

THE ALMOND TREE

which the woman stood once in the winter peeling an apple; and as she peeled the apple she cut her finger, and the blood dropped on to the snow. ''Ah,'' said the woman, with a deep sigh, and she looked at the blood before her, and was very sad; ''had I but a child as red as blood and as white as snow!'' and as she said that, her heart grew light; and it seemed to her as if something would come of her wish. Then she went into the house; and a month passed, the snow disappeared; and two months, then all was green; and three months, then came the flowers out of the ground; and four months, then all the trees in the wood squeezed up against one another, and the green boughs all grew twisted together, and the little birds sang, so that the whole wood resounded, and the blossoms fell from the trees. When the fifth month had gone, and she stood under the almond tree, it smelt so sweet, that her heart leaped for joy, and she could not help falling down on her knees; and when the sixth month had passed, the fruits were large, and she felt very happy; at the end of the seventh month, she snatched the almonds and ate them so greedily, that she was dreadfully ill; then the eighth month passed away, and she called her husband and cried, and said, ''If I die, bury me under the almond tree;'' then she was quite easy, and was glad, till the next month was gone; then she had a child as white as snow, and as red as blood; and when she saw it, she was so delighted that she died.

Then her husband buried her under the almond tree and began to grieve most violently: a little time and he was easier; and when he had sorrowed a little longer he left off; and a little time longer and he took another wife.

With the second wife he had a daughter; but the child by the first wife was a little son, and was as red as blood, and as white as snow. When the woman looked at her daughter, she loved her so much; but then she looked at the little boy, and it seemed to go right through her heart; and it seemed as if he always stood in her way, and then she was always thinking how she could get all the fortune for her daughter; and it was the Evil One who suggested it to her, so that she couldn't bear the sight of the little boy, and poked him about from one corner to another, and buffeted him here, and cuffed him there, so that the poor child was always in fear; and when he came from school he had no peace.

Once the woman had gone into the store-room, and the little daughter came up and said, ''Mother, give me an apple.'' ''Yes, my child,'' said the woman, and gave her a beautiful apple out of the box: the box had a great heavy lid, with a great, sharp iron lock. ''Mother,'' said the little daughter, ''shall not brother have one too?'' That annoyed the woman; but she said, ''Yes, when he comes from school.'' And as she saw out of the window that he was coming, it was just as if the Evil One came over her, and she snatched the apple away from her daughter again, and said, "You shall not have one before your brother!" She threw the apple into the box and shut it. Then the little boy came in at the door; and the Evil One made her say, in a friendly manner, "My son, will you have an apple?" and she looked at him wickedly. "Mother," said the little boy, "How horribly you look! yes, give me an apple." Then she thought she must pacify him. "Come with me," she said, and opened the lid; "reach out an apple;" and as the little boy bent into the box, the Evil One whispered to her—bang! she slammed the lid to, so that his head flew off and fell amongst the red apples. Then in the fright she thought, "Could I get that off my mind!" Then she went up into her room to the chest of drawers, and got out a white cloth from the top drawer, and she set the head on the throat again and tied the handkerchief round, so that nothing could be seen; and placed him outside the door on a chair, and gave him the apple in his hand. After a while little Marline came in the kitchen to her mother, who stood by the fire and had a kettle with hot water before her, which she kept stirring round. "Mother," said little Marline, "brother is sitting outside the door, and looks quite white, and has got an apple in his hand. I asked him to give me the apple, but he didn't answer me; then I was quite frightened." "Go again," said the Mother, "and if he will not answer you, give him a box on the ear." Then Marline went to her brother, and said, "Give me the apple;" but he was silent. Then she gave him a box on the ear, and the head tumbled off, at which she was frightened, and began to cry and sob. Then she ran to her mother, and said, "Oh, mother, I have knocked my brother's head off!" and she cried and cried, and would not be pacified. "Marline," said the Mother, "what have you done? But be quiet, so that nobody may notice it; it can't be helped now; we'll bury him under the almond tree."

Then the mother took the little boy and put him into a box, and put it under the almond tree; but little Marline stood by, and cried and cried, and the tears all fell into the box.

Soon the father came home and sat down to table, and said, "Where is my son?" Then the mother brought in a great big dish of stew; and little Marline cried, and could not leave off. Then said the father again, "Where is my son?" "Oh," said the mother, "he has gone across the country to Mütten; he is going to stop there a bit!"

"What is he doing there? and why did he not say good-bye to me?" "Oh, he wanted to go, and asked me if he might stop there six weeks, he will be taken care of there!" "Ah," said the man, "I feel very sorry; that was not right; he ought to have wished me good-bye." With that he began to eat, and said to Marline, "What are you crying for? your brother will soon come back." "Oh, wife," said he then, "how delicious this tastes; give me some more!" And he ate till all the broth was done.

Little Marline went to her box and took from the bottom drawer
her best silk handkerchief, and carried it outside the door, and cried
bitter tears. Then she laid herself under the almond tree on the
green grass; and when she had laid herself there, all at once she felt
quite light and happy, and cried no more. Then the almond tree
began to move, and the boughs spread out quite wide, and then went
back again; just as when one is very much pleased and claps with
the hands. At the same time a sort of mist rose from the tree; in the
middle of the mist it burned like a fire; and out of the fire there flew
a beautiful bird that sang very sweetly, and flew high up in the air:
and when it had flown away, the almond tree was as it had been
before. Then little Marline was as light and happy as if her brother
were alive still and went into the house to dinner.

The bird flew away and perched upon a Goldsmith's house, and
began to sing,—

> "My mother killed me;
> My father grieved for me;
> My sister, little Marline,
> Wept under the almond tree:
> Kywitt, kywitt, what a beautiful bird am I!"

The Goldsmith sat in his workshop and was making a gold chain
when he heard the bird that sat upon his roof and sang, and it
seemed to him so beautiful. Then he got up, and as he stepped over
the sill of the door he lost one of his slippers; but he went straight
up the middle of the street with one slipper and one sock on. He had
his leather apron on, and in the one hand he had the gold chain, and
in the other the pincers, and the sun shone brightly up the street. He
went and stood and looked at the bird. "Bird," said he then, "how
beautifully you can sing! Sing me that song again." "Nay," said
the Bird, "I don't sing twice for nothing. Give me the gold chain
and I will sing it to you again." "There," said the Goldsmith, "take
the gold chain; now sing me that again." Then the bird came and
took the gold chain in the right claw, and sat before the Goldsmith,
and sang,—

> "My mother killed me;
> My father grieved for me;
> My sister, little Marline,
> Wept under the almond tree:
> Kywitt, kywitt, what a beautiful bird am I!"

Then the bird flew off to a Shoemaker, and perched upon the roof
of his house, and sang,—

> "My mother killed me;
> My father grieved for me;

> My sister, little Marline,
> Wept under the almond tree:
> Kywitt, kywitt, what a beautiful bird am I!''

The Shoemaker heard it, and ran outside the door in his shirt sleeves and looked up at the roof, and was obliged to hold his hand before his eyes to prevent the sun from blinding him. ''Bird,'' said he, ''how beautifully you can sing!'' Then he called in at the door, ''Wife, come out, here's a bird; look at the bird; he just can sing beautifully.'' Then he called his daughter, and children, and apprentices, servant-boy, and maid; and they all came up the street and looked at the bird: oh, how beautiful he was, and he had such red and green feathers, and round about the throat was all like gold, and the eyes sparkled in his head like stars! ''Bird,'' said the Shoemaker, ''now sing me that piece again.'' ''Nay,'' said the Bird, ''I don't sing twice for nothing; you must make me a present of something.'' ''Wife,'' said the man, ''go into the shop; on the top shelf there stands a pair of red shoes, fetch them down.'' The wife went and fetched the shoes. ''There, Bird,'' said the man; ''now sing me that song again.'' Then the bird came and took the shoes in the left claw, and flew up on the roof again, and sang,—

> ''My mother killed me;
> My father grieved for me;
> My sister, little Marline,
> Wept under the almond tree:
> Kywitt, kywitt, what a beautiful bird am I!''

And when he had done singing he flew away. The chain he had in the right claw, and the shoes in the left claw; and he flew far away to a mill; and the mill went clipp-clapp, clipp-clapp, clipp-clapp. And in the mill there sat twenty miller's men; they were shaping a stone, and chipped away, hick-hack, hick-hack, hick-hack; and the mill went clipp-clapp, clipp-clapp, clipp-clapp. Then the bird flew and sat on a lime tree that stood before the mill, and sang,—

> ''My mother killed me;''

then one left off;

> ''My father grieved for me;''

then two more left off and heard it;

> ''My sister,''

then again four left off;

"little Marline,"

now there were only eight chipping away;

"Wept under"

now only five;

"the almond tree."

now only one:

"Kywitt, kywitt, what a beautiful bird am I!"

Then the last left off, when he heard the last word. "Bird," said he, "how beautifully you sing! let me, too, hear that; sing me that again." "Nay," said the Bird, "I don't sing twice for nothing. Give me the millstone and I will sing it again." "Ay," said he, "if it belonged to me alone, you should have it." "Yes," said the others, "if he sings again he shall have it." Then the bird came down, and all the twenty millers caught hold of a pole, and raised the stone up, hu, uh, upp! hu, uh, upp! And the bird stuck his head through the hole, and took it round his neck like a collar, and flew back to the tree, and sang,—

> "My mother killed me;
> My father grieved for me;
> My sister, little Marline,
> Wept under the almond tree:
> Kywitt, kywitt, what a beautiful bird am I!"

And when he had done singing he spread his wings, and had in his right claw the gold chain, in his left the shoes, and round his neck the millstone, and he flew far away to his father's house.

In the room sat the father, the mother, and little Marline, at dinner, and the father said, "Oh, dear, how light and happy I feel!" "Nay," said the mother, "I am all of a tremble, just as if there were going to be a heavy thunderstorm." But little Marline sat and cried and cried, and the bird came flying, and as he perched on the roof the father said, "I feel so cheerful, and the sun shines so deliciously outside, it's exactly as if I were going to see some old acquaintance again." "Nay," said the wife, "I am so frightened, my teeth chatter, and it's like fire in my veins;" and she tore open her stays; but little Marline sat in a corner and cried, and held her plate before her eyes and cried it quite wet. Then the bird perched on the almond tree, and sang,—

          ''My mother killed me;''

Then the mother held her ears and shut her eyes, and would neither see nor hear; but it rumbled in her ears like the most terrible storm, and her eyes burned and twittered like lightning.

          ''My father grieved for me;''

  ''Oh, mother,'' said the man, ''there is a beautiful bird that sings so splendidly; the sun shines so warm, and everything smells all like cinnamon!''

          ''My sister, little Marline,''

Then Marline laid her head on her knees and cried away; but the man said, ''I shall go out, I must see the bird close.'' ''Oh, do not go,'' said the woman; ''it seems as if the whole house shook and were on fire!'' But the man went out and looked at the bird.

          ''Wept under the almond tree:
          Kywitt, kywitt, what a beautiful bird am I!''

And the bird let the gold chain fall, and it fell just round the man's neck, and fitted beautifully. Then he went in and said, ''See what an excellent bird it is; it has given me such a beautiful gold chain, and it looks so splendid.'' But the woman was so frightened that she fell her whole length on the floor, and her cap tumbled off her head. Then the bird sang again,—

          ''My mother killed me;''

  ''Oh, that I were a thousand fathoms under the earth, not to hear that!''

          ''My father grieved for me;''

Then the woman fainted.

          ''My sister, little Marline,''

  ''Ah,'' said Marline, ''I will go out too, and see if the bird will give me something!'' and she went out. Then the bird threw the shoes down.

          ''Wept under the almond tree:
          Kywitt, kywitt, what a beautiful bird am I!''

Then, she was so happy and lively, she put the new red shoes on, and danced and jumped back again. "Oh," said she, "I was so dull when I went out, and now I am so happy. That is a splendid bird : he has given me a pair of red shoes."

"Well," said the woman, and jumped up, and her hair stood on end like flames of fire, "I feel as if the world were coming to an end; I will go out too, and see if it will make me easier." And as she stepped outside the door—bang! the bird threw the millstone on to her head, so that she was completely overwhelmed. The father and little Marline heard it and went out. Then a smoke, and flames, and fire rose from the place, and when that had passed there stood the little brother; and he took his father and little Marline by the hand, and all three embraced one another heartily, and went into the house to dinner.

THE DOG AND THE SPARROW.

THERE was once a Shepherd's Dog, which had a very bad master, who never gave him food enough for his services; and one day, having made up his mind to endure such treatment no longer, the Dog left the man's service and took his way, though with much sorrow. On the road the Dog met a Sparrow, who said, "Brother Dog, why are you so glum?"

The Dog replied, "I am hungry and have nothing to eat."

"Oh," replied the Sparrow, "come with me, and I will soon satisfy you."

So they went together to the town, and, when they came to a butcher's shop, the bird said, "Wait a bit here, I will peck you down a piece of meat;" and flying into the shop, and looking round to see that no one observed her, she pecked and pulled at a joint which hung just over the window till it fell down. The Dog instantly snatched it, and, running into a corner, soon devoured it. When he had done, the Sparrow took him to another shop and pecked down a second piece of meat, and, when the Dog had finished this, the Sparrow asked, "Are you satisfied now, Brother Dog?"

"Yes," he replied, "with flesh; but I have touched no bread at all yet."

So the Sparrow, saying, "That you shall have if you will come with me," led him to a baker's, and pushed down a couple of loaves, and, when the Dog had finished them, she took him to another shop and pushed down more. As soon as these were consumed the

Sparrow asked again if he were satisfied, and the Dog replied, "Yes; and now we'll walk awhile round the town."

Off they started now upon the highroad; but it being very warm weather, they had not walked far, when, as they came to a corner, the Dog said, "I am tired and must go to sleep."

"Very well," replied the Sparrow; "meanwhile I will sit on this twig." So the Dog laid down in the middle of the road and was soon fast asleep.

Presently a Carrier came up the road driving a waggon with three horses, laden with two casks of wine, and as the Sparrow saw that the man did not turn aside, but kept in the middle of the road where the Dog lay, she called out, "Carrier, take care what you do, or I will make you poor!"

But the Carrier, grumbling to himself, "You make me poor, indeed!" cracked his whip and drove the wagon straight on, so that the wheels passed over the Dog and killed him. "You have killed my brother the Dog, and that shall cost you your horses and your cart!"

"Horses and cart, indeed!" said the Carrier; "what harm can you do me?" and he drove on.

Then the Sparrow, hopping under the waggon-covering, pecked at the bunghole of one of the casks until she worked out the cork, so that all the wine ran out without its being perceived by the Carrier; but all at once the man looked behind him and saw the wine dropping from the cart, and, trying the casks, found that one of them was empty. "Ah," cried he, "now I am a poor man!" "Yet not poor enough!" said the Sparrow, and, flying on to the head of one of the horses, she pecked out one of its eyes. When the Carrier saw this he drew out his hatchet and tried to hit the bird, but she flew up, and, instead, he cut his own horse's head, so that it fell down dead. "Ah," cried he, "now I am a poor man!"

"Still not poor enough!" said the Sparrow; and, while the Carrier drove further on with his two horses, she crept again under the covering of the waggon and pecked out the bung of the second cask, so that all the wine dripped out. When the man found this he exclaimed again, "Ah, now I am a poor man!" but the Bird replied, "Not poor enough yet!" and, settling on the head of the second horse, she pecked out its eyes also. Again the driver lifted his axe and made a cut at the Sparrow which flew away, so that the blow fell on his horse and killed it. "Ah, now I am poorer still!" cried the man; but the Bird replied, "Not yet poor enough!" and, perching on the third horse, she pecked out its eyes also. In a terrible passion the driver aimed a blow with his axe as before at the Sparrow, but, unfortunately missing, hit his own horse instead, and so killed his third and last animal. "Ah me! poorer and poorer!" exclaimed the Carrier.

"Not yet poor enough!" reiterated the Sparrow; "now I will make you poor at home;" and so flew away.

The Carrier was forced to leave his waggon in the road, and went home full of rage and passion. "Oh," he said to his wife, "what misfortunes I have had to endure! my wine has all run out, and my horses are all three dead! woe's me!"

"Ah, my husband!" she replied, "and what a wicked bird has come to this house: she has brought with her all the birds in the world, and there they sit among our corn and are eating every ear of it!"

The man stepped out, and, behold, thousands on thousands of birds had alighted upon the ground and had eaten up all the corn, and among them sat the Sparrow. "Ah me, I am poorer than ever!" he cried. "Still not poor enough, Carrier; it shall cost you your life!" replied the Bird, as she flew away.

Thus the Carrier lost all his property, and, now entering the kitchen, he sat down behind the stove and became quite morose and savage. The Sparrow, however, remained outside on the window-sill, calling out, "Carrier, it shall cost you your life!"

At this the man seized his axe and threw it at the Sparrow, but he only cut the window-frame in two, without hurting the bird. Now the Sparrow hopped in, and, perching on the stove, said again, "Carrier, it shall cost you your life!" Blinded with rage and fury he only cut the stove with his axe, and, as the Bird hopped about from one place to another, he pursued her, and hacked through all his furniture, glasses, seats, tables, and lastly, the walls even of his house, without once touching the Bird. However, he at length caught her with his hand, while his wife asked whether she should kill her. "No," said he, "that were too merciful: she shall die much more horribly, for I will eat her." So saying he swallowed her whole, but she began to flutter about in his stomach, and presently came again into his mouth, and called out, "Carrier, it shall cost you your life!"

Thereupon the man handed his wife the axe, saying, "Kill the wretch for me dead in my mouth!" His wife took it and aimed a blow, but, missing her mark, she struck her husband on the head and killed him. Then the Sparrow flew away and was never seen there again.

THE LITTLE FARMER.

THERE was a certain village, wherein several rich farmers were settled, and only one poor one, who was therefore called "The Little Farmer." He had not even a cow, nor money to buy it, though he and his wife would have been only too happy to have had one. One day he said to her, "A good thought has just struck me: our father-in-law, the carver, can make us a calf out of wood and paint it brown, so that it will look like any other; in time, perhaps, it will grow big and become a cow." This proposal pleased his wife, and the carver was instructed accordingly, and he cut out the calf, painted it as it should be, and so made it that its head was bent down as if eating.

When, the next morning, the cows were driven out to pasture, the Farmer called the Shepherd in and said, "See, I have here a little calf, but it is so small that it must as yet be carried." The Shepherd said, "Very well;" and, taking it under his arm, carried it down to the meadow and set it among the grass. All day the calf stood there as if eating, and the Shepherd said, "It will soon grow big and go alone: only see how it is eating!" At evening time, when he wanted to drive his flocks home, he said to the calf, "Since you can stand there to saitsfy your hunger, you must also be able to walk upon your four legs, and I shall not carry you home in my arms." The Little Farmer stood before his house-door waiting for his calf, and as the Shepherd drove his herd through the village he asked after it. The Shepherd replied, "It is still standing there eating: it would not listen and come with me." The Farmer exclaimed, "Eh, what? I must have my calf!" and so they both went together down to the meadow, but some one had stolen the calf, and it was gone. The Shepherd said, "Perhaps it has run away itself;" but the Farmer replied, "Not so—that won't do for me;" and dragging him before the Mayor, he was condemned for his negligence to give the Little Farmer a cow in the place of the lost calf.

Now the Farmer and his wife possessed the long-desired cow, and were very glad; but having no fodder they could give her nothing to eat, so that very soon they were obliged to kill her. The flesh they salted down, and the skin the Little Farmer took to the next town to sell, to buy another calf with what he got for it. On the way he passed a mill, where a raven was sitting with a broken wing, and out of compassion he took the bird up and wrapped it in the skin he was carrying. But the weather being just then very bad, a great storm of wind and rain falling, he was unable to go further, and turning into the mill, begged for shelter. The Miller's wife was at home alone, and said to the Farmer, "Lie down on that straw," and gave him a piece of bread and cheese. The Farmer ate it and lay down, with his skin near him, and the Miller's wife thought he was asleep. Presently in came a man, whom she received very cordially, and invited to sup with her; but the Farmer, when he heard talk of the feast, was vexed that he should have been treated only to bread and cheese. So the woman went down into the cellar and brought up four dishes—roast meat, salad, boiled meat, and wine. As they were sitting down to eat there was a knock outside, and the woman exclaimed, "Oh, gracious! there is my husband!" In a great hurry she stuck the roast meat in the oven, the wine under the pillow, the salad upon the bed, and the boiled meat under it, while her guest stepped into a closet where she kept the linen. This done she let in her husband, and said, "God be praised you are returned again! what weather it is, as if the world were coming to an end!"

The Miller remarked the man lying on the straw, and asked what the fellow did there. His Wife said, "Ah, the poor fellow came in the wind and rain and begged for shelter, so I gave him some bread and cheese and showed him the straw!"

The husband said he had no objection, but bade her bring him quickly something to eat. The wife said, "I have nothing but bread and cheese," and her husband told her with that he should be contented, and asked the Farmer to come and share his meal. The Farmer did not let himself be twice asked, but got up and ate away. Presently the Miller remarked the skin lying upon the ground, in which was the raven, and asked, "What have you there?" The Farmer replied, "I have a truth-teller therein." "Can it tell me the truth too?" inquired the Miller.

"Why not?" said the other; "but he will only say four things, and the fifth he keeps to himself." The Miller was curious, and wished to hear it speak, and the Farmer squeezed the raven's head, so that it squeaked out. The Miller then asked, "What did he say?" and the Farmer replied, "The first thing is, under the pillow lies wine." "That is a rare tell-tale!" cried the Miller, and went and found the wine. "Now again," said he. The Farmer made the raven croak again, and said, "Secondly, he declares there is roast meat in the oven." "That is a good tell-tale!" again cried the Miller, and, opening the oven, he took out the roast meat. Then the Farmer made the raven croak again, and said, "For the third thing, he declares there is salad on the bed."

"That is a good tell-tale!" cried the Miller, and went and found the salad. Then the Farmer made his bird croak once more, and said, "For the fourth thing, he declares there is boiled meat under the bed."

"That is a capital tell-tale!" cried the Miller, while he went and found as it said.

The worthy pair now sat down together at the table, but the Miller's wife felt terribly anxious, and went to bed, taking all the keys with her. The Miller was very anxious to know the fifth thing, but the Man said, "First let us eat quietly these four things, for the other is somewhat dreadful."

After they had finished their meal, the Miller bargained as to how much he should give for the fifth thing, and at last he agreed for three hundred dollars. Then the Farmer once more made the raven croak, and when the Miller asked what it said, he told him, "He declares that in the cupboard where the linen is there is an evil spirit."

The Miller said, "The evil spirit must walk out!" and tried the door, but it was locked, and the woman had to give up the key to the Farmer, who unlocked it. The unbidden guest at once bolted out, and ran out of the house, while the Miller said, "Ah, I saw the black fellow, that was all right!" Soon they went to sleep; but at daybreak the Farmer took his three hundred dollars and made himself scarce.

The Farmer was now quite rich at home, and built himself a fine house, so that his fellows said, "The Little Farmer has certainly found the golden snow, of which he has brought away a basketful;" and they summoned him before the Mayor, that he might be made to say whence his riches came. The man replied, "I have sold my cow's skin in the city for three hundred dollars." And as soon as the others heard this they desired also to make a similar profit. The farmers ran home, killed all their cows, and, taking their skins off, took them to the city to sell them for so good a price. The Mayor, however, said, "My maid must go first;" and when she arrived at the city she went to the merchant, but he gave her only three dollars for her skin. And when the rest came he would not give them so much, saying, "What should I do with all these skins?"

The farmers were much vexed at being outwitted by their poor neighbour, and, bent on revenge, they complained to the Mayor of his deceit. The innocent Little Farmer was condemned to death unanimously, and was to be rolled in a cask full of holes into the sea. He was led away, and a priest sent for who should say for him the mass for the dead. Every one else was obliged to remove to a distance, and when the Farmer looked at the priest he recognised the guest whom he had met at the mill. So he said to him, "I have delivered you out of the cupboard, now deliver me from this cask." Just at that moment the Shepherd passed by with a flock of sheep, and the Farmer, knowing that for a long time the man had desired to be mayor, cried out with all his might, "No, no! I will not do it; if all the world asked me I would not be it! No, I will not!"

When the Shepherd heard this he came up and said, "What are you doing here? What will you not do?"

The Farmer replied, "They will make me mayor if I keep in this cask; but no, I will not be here!"

"Oh," said the Shepherd, "if nothing more is wanting to be mayor I am willing to put myself in the cask!"

"Yes, you will be mayor if you do that," said the Farmer; and, getting out of the cask, the other got in, and the Farmer nailed the lid down again. Now he took the Shepherd's flock and drove it away, while the parson went to the Judge and told him he had said the prayers for the dead. Then they went and rolled the cask down to the water, and while it rolled the Shepherd called out, "Yes, I should like to be mayor!" They thought it was the Little Farmer who spoke; and saying, "Yes, we mean it; only you must first go below there;" and they sent the cask right into the sea.

That done the farmers returned home; and as they came into the village, so came also the Little Farmer, driving a flock of sheep quietly and cheerfully. The sight astounded the others, and they asked, "Whence comest thou? dost thou come out of the water?" "Certainly," answered he; "I sank deeper and deeper till I got to the bottom, where I pushed up the head of the cask, and, getting out, there were beautiful meadows, upon which many lambs were pasturing, and I brought this flock of them up with me."

"Are there any more?" inquired the farmers. "Oh, yes," replied he, "more than you know what to do with!"

Then the farmers agreed that they would go and each fetch up a flock for himself, but the Mayor said, "I must go first." So they went together down to the water, and there happened to be a fine blue sky with plenty of fleecy clouds over it, which were mirrored in the water and looked like little lambs. The farmers called one to another, "Look there! we can see the sheep already on the ground below the water!" and the Mayor, pressing quite forward, said, "I will go first and look about me, and see if it is a good place, and then call you."

So saying, he jumped in, plump, and, as he splashed the water about, the others thought he was calling, "Come along!" and so one after another the whole assemblage plunged in in a grand hurry. Thus was the whole village cleared out, and "the Little Farmer," as their only heir, became a very rich man.

CATHERINE AND FREDERICK.

ONCE upon a time there was a youth named Frederick, and a girl called Catherine, who had married and lived together as a young couple. One day Fred said, "I am now going into the fields, dear Catherine, and by the time I return let there be something hot upon the table, for I shall be hungry, and something to drink too, for I shall be thirsty."

"Very well, dear Fred," said she, "go at once, and I will make all right for you."

As soon, then, as dinner-time approached, she took down a sausage out of the chimney, and putting it in a frying-pan with batter set it over the fire. Soon the sausage began to frizzle and spit while

Catherine stood by holding the handle of the pan and thinking; and among other things she thought that while the sausage was getting ready she might go into the cellar and draw some beer. So she took a can and went down into the cellar to draw the beer, and while it ran into the can, she bethought herself that perhaps the dog might steal the sausage out of the pan, and so up the cellar stairs she ran, but too late, for the rogue had already got the meat in his mouth and was sneaking off. Catherine, however, pursued the dog for a long way over the fields, but the beast was quicker than she, and would not let the sausage go, but bolted off at a great rate. "Off is off!" said Catherine, and turned round, and being very tired and hot, she went home slowly to cool herself. All this while the beer was running out of the cask, for Catherine had forgotten to turn the tap off, and so as soon as the can was full the liquor ran over the floor of the cellar until it was all out. Catherine saw the misfortune at the top of the steps. "My gracious!" she exclaimed, "what shall I do that Fred may not find this out?" She considered for some time till she remembered that a sack of fine malt yet remained from the last brewing, in one corner, which she would fetch down and strew about in the beer. "Yes," said she, "it was spared at the right time to be useful to me now in my necessity;" and down she pulled the sack so hastily that she overturned the can of beer for Fred, and away it mixed with the rest on the floor. "It is all right," said she; "where one is, the other should be;" and she strewed the malt over the whole cellar. When it was done she was quite overjoyed at her work, and said, "How clean and neat it does look to be sure!"

At noontime Fred returned. "Now, wife, what have you ready for me?" said he. "Ah, my dear Fred," she replied, "I would have fried you a sausage, but while I drew the beer the dog stole it out of the pan, and while I hunted the dog the beer all ran out, and as I was about to dry up the beer with the malt, I overturned your can; but be contented, the cellar is quite dry again now."

"Oh, Catherine, Catherine!" said Fred, "you should not have done so! to let the sausage be stolen! and the beer run out! and over all to shoot our best sack of malt!!!"

"Well, Fred," said she, "I did not know that; you should have told me."

But the husband thought to himself, if one's wife acts so, one must look after things one's self. Now, he had collected a tolerable sum of silver dollars, which he changed into gold, and then he told his wife, "Do you see, these are yellow counters, which I will put in a pot and bury in the stable under the cow's stall; but mind that you do not meddle with it, or you will come to some harm."

Catherine promised to mind what he said, but, as soon as Fred was gone, some hawkers came into the village with earthenware for sale, and amongst others they asked her if she would purchase anything.

"Ah good people," said Catherine, "I have no money, and cannot buy anything, but if you can make use of yellow counters I will buy them."

"Yellow counters! ah! why not? let us look at them," said they.

"Go into the stable," she replied, "and dig under the cow's stall, and there you will find the yellow counters. I dare not go myself."

The rogues went at once, and soon dug up the shining gold, which they quickly pocketed, and then they ran off, leaving behind them their pots and dishes in the house. Catherine thought she might as well make use of the new pottery, and since she had no need of anything in the kitchen, she set out each pot on the ground, and then put others on the top of the palings round the house for ornament. When Fred returned, and saw the fresh decorations, he asked Catherine what she had done. "I have bought them, Fred," said she, "with the yellow counters which lay under the cow's stall; but I did not dig them up myself; the pedlars did that."

"Ah, wife, what have you done?" replied Fred, "they were not counters, but bright gold, which was all the property we possessed: you should not have done so."

"Well, dear Fred," replied his wife, "you should have told me so before. I did not know that."

Catherine stood considering for a while, and presently she began, "Come, Fred, we will soon get the gold back again; let us pursue the thieves."

"Well, come along," said Fred; "we will try at all events; but take butter and cheese with you, that we may have something to eat on our journey."

"Yes, Fred," said she, and soon made herself ready; but, her husband being a good walker, she lagged behind. "Ah!" said she, "this is my luck, for when we turn back I shall be a good bit forward." Presently she came to a hill, on both sides of which there were very deep ruts. "Oh, see!" said she, "how the poor earth is torn, flayed, and wounded: it will never be well again all its life!" And out of compassion she took out her butter, and greased the ruts over right and left, so that the wheels might run more easily through them, and, while she stooped in doing this, a cheese rolled out of her pocket and down the mountain. Catherine said when she saw it, "I have already once made the journey up, and I am not coming down after you: another shall run and fetch you." So saying, she took another cheese out of her pocket, and rolled it down; but as it did not return, she thought, "Perhaps they are waiting for a companion, and don't like to come alone;" and down she bowled a third cheese. Still all three stayed, and she said, "I cannot think what was this means; perhaps it is that the third cheese has missed his way: I will send a fourth, that he may call him as he goes by." But this one acted no better than the others, and Catherine became so anxious that she threw down a fifth and a sixth cheese also, and they were the last. For a long time after this she waited, expecting they would come, but when she found they did not she cried out, ''You are nice fellows to send after a dead man! you stop a fine time! but do you think I shall wait for you? Oh, no! I shall go on; you can follow me; you have younger legs than I.''

So saying, Catherine walked on and came up with Fred, who was waiting for her, because he needed something to eat. ''Now,'' said he, ''give me quickly what you brought.'' She handed him the dry bread. ''Where are the butter and cheese?'' cried her husband. ''Oh, Fred, dear,'' she replied, ''with the butter I have smeared the ruts, and the cheeses will soon come, but one ran away, and I sent the others after it to call it back!''

''It was silly of you to do so,'' said Fred, ''to grease the roads with butter, and to roll cheeses down the hill!''

''If you had but told me so,'' said Catherine, vexatiously.

So they ate the dry bread together, and presently Fred said, ''Catherine, did you make things fast at home before you came out?''

''No, Fred,'' said she, ''you did not tell me.''

''Then go back and lock up the house before we go further; bring something to eat with you, and I will stop here for you.''

Back went Catherine, thinking, ''Ah! Fred will like something else to eat. Butter and cheese will not please; I will bring with me a bag of dried apples and a mug of vinegar to drink.'' When she had put these things together she bolted the upper half of the door, but the under door she raised up and carried away on her shoulder, thinking that certainly the house was well protected if she took such good care of the door! Catherine walked along now very leisurely, for said she to herself, ''Fred will have all the longer rest!'' and as soon as she reached him she gave him the door, saying, ''There, Fred, now you have the house door, you can take care of the house yourself.''

''Oh! my goodness,'' exclaimed the husband, ''what a clever wife I have! she has bolted the top door, but brought away the bottom part, where any one can creep through! Now it is too late to go back to the house, but since you brought the door here you may carry it onwards.''

''The door I will willingly carry,'' replied Catherine, ''but the apples and the vinegar will be too heavy, so I shall hang them on the door, and make that carry them!''

Soon after they came into a wood, and looked about for the thieves, but they could not find them, and when it became dark they climbed up into a tree to pass the night. But scarcely had they done this when up came the fellows who carried away what should not go with them, and find things before they are lost. They laid themselves down right under the tree upon which Fred and Catherine were, and making a fire, prepared to share their booty. Then Fred slipped down on the other side, and collected stones, with which he climbed the tree again to beat the thieves with. The stones, however, did them no harm, for the fellows called out, ''Ah! it will soon be morning, for the wind is shaking down the chestnuts.'' All this while Catherine still had the door upon her shoulder, and, as it pressed very heavily, she thought the dried apples were in fault, and said to Fred, ''I must throw down these apples.'' ''No, Catherine,'' said he, ''not now, they might discover us.'' ''Ah, I must though, they are so heavy.''

''Well, then, do it in the hangman's name!'' cried Fred.

As they fell down the rogues said, ''Ah! the birds are pulling off the eaves.''

A little while after Catherine said again, ''Oh! Fred, I must pour out the vinegar, it is so heavy.''

''No, no!'' said he, ''it will discover us.''

''Ah! but I must, Fred, it is very heavy,'' said Catherine.

''Well, then, do it in the hangman's name!'' cried Fred.

So she poured out the vinegar, and as it dropped on them the thieves said, ''Ah! the dew is beginning to fall.''

Not many minutes after Catherine found the door was still quite as heavy, and said again to Fred, ''Now I must throw down this door.''

''No, Catherine,'' said he, ''that would certainly discover us.''

''Ah! Fred, but I must; it presses me so terribly.''

''No, Catherine dear! do hold it fast,'' said Fred.

''There—it is gone!'' said she.

''Then let it go in the hangman's name!'' cried Fred, while it fell crashing through the branches. The rogues below thought the Evil One was descending the tree, and ran off, leaving everything behind them. And early in the morning Fred and his wife descended, and found all their gold under the tree.

As soon as they got home again, Fred said, ''Now, Catherine, you must be very industrious and work hard.''

''Yes, my dear husband,'' said she; ''I will go into the fields to cut corn.'' When she was come into the field she said to herself, ''Shall I eat before I cut, or sleep first before I cut?'' She determined to eat, and soon became so sleepy over her meal, that when she began to cut she knew not what she was doing, and cut off half her clothes, gown, petticoat, and all. When after a long sleep Catherine awoke, she got up half stripped, and said to herself, ''Am I myself! or am I not? Ah! I am not myself.'' By-and-by night came on, and Catherine ran into the village and, knocking at her husband's window, called, ''Fred!''

''What is the matter?'' cried he.

"I want to know if Catherine is in-doors!" said she.

"Yes, yes!" answered Fred, "she is certainly within, fast asleep."

"Then I am at home," said she, and ran away.

Standing outside Catherine found some thieves, wanting to steal, and going up to them she said, "I will help you."

At this the thieves were very glad, not doubting but that she knew where to light on what they sought. But Catherine, stepping in front of the houses, called out, "Good people, what have you that we can steal?" At this the thieves said, "You will do for us with a vengeance!" and they wished they had never come near her; but in order to rid themselves of her they said, "Just before the village the parson has some roots lying in his field; go and fetch some."

Catherine went as she was bid, and began to grub for them, and soon made herself very dirty with the earth. Presently a man came by and saw her, and stood still, for he thought it was the Evil One who was grovelling so among the roots. Away he ran into the village to the parson, and told him the Evil One was in his field, rooting up the turnips. "Ah! heavens!" said the parson, "I have a lame foot, and I cannot go out to exorcise him."

"Then I will carry you a pick-a-back," said the man, and took him up.

Just as they arrived in the field, Catherine got up and drew herself up to her full height.

"Oh! it is the Evil One!" cried the parson, and both he and the man hurried away; and, behold! the parson ran faster with his lame legs, through fear and terror, than the countryman could with his sound legs!

THE ROGUE AND HIS MASTER.

A CERTAIN man, named John, was desirous that his son should learn some trade, and he went into the church to ask the Priest's opinion what would be most desirable. Just then the Clerk was standing near the altar, and he cried out, "The rogue, the rogue!" At these words the man went away, and told his son he must learn to be a rogue, for so the Priest had said. So they set out, and asked one man and another whether he was a rogue, till, at the end of the day, they entered a large forest, and there found a little hut with an old woman in it.

John asked the old woman, "Do you know any man who can teach roguery?" "Here," said the old Woman, "here you may learn, for my son is a master of the art." Then John asked the son whether he

·could teach it perfectly ? and the Rogue replied, ''I will teach your son well; return in four years, and if you know your son then I will not ask any recompense; but if you do not, then you must give me two hundred dollars.''

John now went home, and left his son to learn roguery and witchcraft. When the time was up, the father set out to see his son, considering as he went along by what he should know him. On his way he met a little man, who stopped him, and asked, ''Why are you grieving and looking so mournful?'' ''Oh,'' replied John, ''four years ago I left my son to learn roguery, and the master said, if I returned in that time and knew my son, I should have nothing to pay; but if I did not know him, I must give him two hundred dollars; and, since I have no means of recognising him, I am troubled where to procure the money.''

Then the little man told him to take a basket of bread with him, and when he came to the Rogue's house to put the basket under a hollow tree which stood there, and the little Bird which should peep out would be his son.

John went and did as he was told, and out came a little Bird to peck at the bread. ''Holloa, my son! are you here?'' said John. The son was very glad to hear his father's voice, and said, ''Father, let us go!'' but first the Rogue-master called out, ''The Evil One must have told you where to find your son!''

So the father and son returned home, and on their way they met a coach, and the son said to his father, ''I will change myself into a fine greyhound, and then you can earn some money by me.''

The Lord who was riding in the coach called out, ''Man, will you sell your dog?''

''Yes,'' replied the father.

''How much do you want for him?''

''Thirty dollars,'' was the reply.

''That is too much, my man,'' said the Lord, ''but on account of his very beautiful skin I will buy him of you.''

The bargain concluded, the dog was put inside the coach; but when they had travelled a mile or two the greyhound jumped right out through the glass, and rejoined his father.

After this adventure they went home together, and the following day they went to the next village to market. On their way the son said, ''Father, I will change myself into a Horse, and then you can sell me; but first untie my bridle, and then I can change myself into the form of a man.

The father drove his horse to market, and thither came the Rogue-master and bought him for a hundred dollars, but the father forgot to untie the bridle.

The Rogue rode his horse home, and put him in the stable, and, when the maid came with the corn, the Horse said to her, "Undo my bridle, undo my bridle!"

"Ah, can you speak?" said she, terrified, and untied the horse directly. The Horse thereupon became a sparrow, and flew away out at the door, pursued by the Rogue, who changed himself also into a bird. When they came up with each other, the Rogue changed himself into water, and the other into a fish. But the Rogue could not catch him so, and he changed himself into a cock, but the other instantly became a fox, and bit his master's head off, so that he died.

And he lies there to this very day.

THE FOX AND THE GODMOTHER WOLF.

A CERTAIN She-Wolf had brought a whelp into the world, and invited the Fox to stand godfather, for, said she, "He is a near relative, and possesses a good understanding and much cleverness, so that he can instruct my son, and help him on in the world." The Fox appeared to be very honourable, and said to the Wolf, "My worthy fellow godparent, I thank you much for the honour you show me, and I will so conduct myself that you shall be quite satisfied." At the feast he made himself very sociable and merry; and when it was over he said to the Wolf, "My dear lady, it is our duty to care for the child, and therefore he must have good food, that he may grow strong. I know a sheepfold whence we can easily fetch somewhat."

This speech pleased the Wolf, and she went with the Fox to the farmyard, and there he showed her the place, and said, "You can creep in there unseen, and meanwhile I will go round to the other side, and see if I can pick up a hen."

The Fox, however, did not go as he said, but ran away and stretched himself upon the ground, near the edge of the forest, to rest. The Wolf crept into the stall, where lay a dog, who began to bark, so that the labourers ran in, and surprising the Wolf, poured a panful of burning coals over her skin. At last she escaped, and slipped away out of the stall, and found the Fox lying near the Forest. The Fox made a very wry face, and said, "Ah, my dear godmother, how badly I have fared! The peasants fell upon me, and have nearly broken all my bones, an, if you do not wish me to perish here where I lie, you must carry me away!"

The poor Wolf could scarcely move herself; but yet, out of her great concern for the Fox, she took him upon her back, and carried home, slowly enough, the really strong and unhurt godfather. When they reached home, the Fox cried out to the Wolf, "Farewell, my dear godmother; may you relish your scorching!" and, so saying, he laughed in her face, and quickly bolted off!

THE RABBIT'S BRIDE.

ONCE there was a woman and her daughter who lived in a garden full of fine cabbages, but a Rabbit came in and ate them up. The woman said one day to her daughter, "Go into the garden and hunt that Rabbit."

Mary said to the Rabbit, "There, there little Rabbit! do not eat all the cabbages."

"Come with me, Mary," it said, "and sit upon my bushy tail, and go with me to my bushy house."

Mary would not; and the next day the Rabbit came again, and ate the cabbages, and the woman said to the daughter, "Go into the garden, and hunt the Rabbit."

Mary said to the Rabbit, "THere, there, little Rabbit! do not eat all the cabbages."

"Come with me, then Mary," said the Rabbit; "sit upon my bushy tail, and come with me to my bushy house."

Mary would not; and the third day the Rabbit came again, and ate the cabbages, and the woman said again to her daughter, "Go into the garden, and hunt the Rabbit."

Mary said to the Rabbit, "There, there, little Rabbit! eat not all our cabbages."

"Come with me, then, Mary" said the Rabbit; "sit upon my bushy tail, and come with me to my bushy house."

So Mary this time sat herself upon the Rabbit's tail, and he carried her out to his hut, and said, "Now cook me green lettuces and bran, while I will ask the wedding guests." Soon all the visitors came. (Who, then, were the wedding guests? That I cannot tell you, except as another has told me: they were all Rabbits, and the Crow was there as the parson to marry the bride and bridegroom, and the Fox as the Clerk, and the altar was under a rainbow.)

But Mary was sad, because she was alone; and the little Rabbit came and said, "Get up, get up! the wedding folks are merry and pleased."

Mary said "No," and wept; and the little Rabbit went away, but soon returned, and said, "Get up, get up! the wedding folks are hungry."

The Bride said "No!" again, and still cried. The little Rabbit went away, but soon came back, and said again, "Get up, get up! the wedding folks are waiting for you."

Mary said "No!" again and the little Rabbit went away; but she made a doll of straw with her own clothes, and gave it a red lip, and set it on the kettle with bran, and went home to her mother. Once more came the little Rabbit, and said, "Get up, get up!" and, going towards the doll, he knocked it on the head, so that it fell over on one side.

Then the little Rabbit thought his bride was dead, and went away very sad and sorrowful.

HANS IN LUCK.

Hans had served his master seven years, and at the end of that time he said to him, "Master, since my time is up, I should like to go home to my mother; so give me my wages, if you please."

His Master replied, "You have served me truly and honestly, Hans, and such as your service was, such shall be your reward;" and with these words he gave him a lump of gold as big as his head. Hans thereupon took his handkerchief out of his pocket, and wrapping the gold up in it, threw it over his shoulder and set out on the road towards his native village. As he went along, carefully setting one foot to the ground before the other, a horseman came in sight, trotting gaily and briskly along upon a capital animal. "Ah," said Hans aloud, "what a fine thing that riding is! one is seated, as it were, upon a stool, kicks against no stones, spares one's shoes, and gets along without any trouble!"

The Rider, overhearing Hans making these reflections, stopped and said, "Why, then, do you travel on foot, my fine fellow?"

"Because I am forced," replied Hans, "for I have got a bit of a lump to carry home; it certainly is gold, but then I can't carry my head straight, and it hurts my shoulder."

"If you like we will exchange," said the Rider; "I will give you my horse, and you can give me your lump of gold."

"With all my heart," cried Hans; "but I tell you fairly you undertake a very heavy burden."

The man dismounted, took the gold, and helped Hans on to the horse, and giving him the reins into his hands, said, "Now, when you want to go faster, you must chuckle with your tongue and cry, 'Gee up! gee up!'"

Hans was delighted indeed when he found himself on the top of a horse, and riding along so freely and gaily. After awhile he thought he should like to go rather quicker, and so he cried, "Gee up! gee up!" as the man had told him. The horse soon set off at a hard trot, and before Hans knew what he was about, he was thrown over head and heels into a ditch which divided the fields from the road. The horse, having accomplished this feat, would have bolted off if he had not been stopped by a Peasant who was coming that way, driving a cow before him. Hans soon picked himself up on his legs, but he was terribly put out, and said to the countryman, "That is bad sport, that riding, especially when one mounts such a beast as that, which stumbles and throws one off so as to nearly break one's neck: I will never ride on that animal again. Commend me to your cow: one may walk behind her without any discomfort, and besides one has, every day for certain, milk, butter, and cheese. Ah! what would I not give for such a cow!"

"Well," said the Peasant, "such an advantage you may soon enjoy I will exchange my cow for your horse."

To this Hans consented with a thousand thanks, and the Peasant, swinging himself upon the horse, rode off in a hurry.

Hans now drove his cow off steadily before him, thinking of his lucky bargain in this wise: "I have a bit of bread, and I can, as often as I please, eat with it butter and cheese; and when I am thirsty I can milk my cow and have a draught: and what more can I desire?"

As soon, then, as he came to an inn he halted, and ate with great satisfaction all the bread he had brought with him for his noonday and evening meals, and washed it down with a glass of beer, to buy which he spent his last two farthings. This over, he drove his cow further, but still in the direction of his mother's village. The heat meantime became more and more oppressive as noontime approached, and just then Hans came to a common which was an hour's journey across. Here he got into such a state of heat that his tongue clave to the roof of his mouth, and he thought to himself, "This won't do; I will just milk my cow, and refresh myself." Hans, therefore, tied her to a stump of a tree, and, having no pail, placed his leathern cap below, and set to work, but not a drop of milk could he squeeze out. He had placed himself, too, very awkwardly, and at last the impatient cow gave him such a kick on the head that he tumbled over on the ground, and for a long time knew not where he was. Fortunately, not many hours after, a Butcher passed by, trundling a young pig along upon a wheelbarrow. "What trick is this!" exclaimed he, helping up poor Hans; and Hans told him all that had passed. The Butcher then handed him his flask, and said, "There, take a drink; it will revive you. Your cow might well give no milk: she is an old beast, and worth nothing at the best but for the plough or the butcher!"

"Eh! eh!" said Hans, pulling his hair over his eyes, "who would

HANS IN LUCK

have thought it ? It is all very well when one can kill a beast like that at home, and make a profit of the flesh; but for my part I have no relish for cow's flesh; it's too tough for me! Ah! a young pig like yours is the thing to have; it tastes quite different. And then there are the sausages!"

"Well now, for love of you," said the Butcher, "I will make an exchange, and let you have my pig for your cow."

"Heaven reward you for your kindness!" cried Hans; and giving up the cow, he untied the pig from the barrow, and took into his hand the string with which it was tied.

Hans walked on again, considering how everything had happened just as he wished, and how all his vexations had turned out for the best after all! Presently a Boy overtook him, carrying a fine white goose under his arm, and after they had said "Good day" to each other, Hans began to talk about his luck, and what profitable exchanges he had made. The Boy on his part told him that he was carrying the goose to a christening-feast. "Just lift it," he said to Hans, holding it up by his wings, "just feel how heavy it is; why, it has been fattened up for the last eight weeks, and whoever bites it when it is cooked will have to wipe the grease from each side of his mouth!"

"Yes," said Hans, weighing it with one hand, "it is weighty, but my pig is no trifle either."

While he was speaking the Boy kept looking about on all sides, and shaking his head suspiciously, and at length he broke out, "I am afraid it is not all right about your pig. In the village, through which I have just come, one has been stolen out of the sty of the mayor himself; and I am afraid, very much afraid, you have it now in your hand! They have sent out several people, and it would be a very bad job for you if they found you with the pig; the best thing you can do is to hide it in some dark corner!"

Honest Hans was thunderstruck, and exclaimed, "Ah, Heaven help me in this fresh trouble! you know the neighborhood better than I; do you take my pig and let me have your goose," said he to the boy.

"I shall have to hazard something at that game," replied the Boy, "but still I do not wish to be the cause of your meeting with misfortune;" and so saying, he took the rope into his own hand, and drove the pig off quickly by a side path, while Hans, lightened of his cares, walked on homewards with the goose under his arm. "If I judge rightly," thought he to himself, "I have gained even by this exchange: first there is the good roast; then the quantity of fat which will drip out will make goose broth for a quarter of a year; and then there are the fine white feathers, which when once I have put into my pillow I warrant I shall sleep without rocking. What pleasure my mother will have!"

As he came to the last village on his road there stood a Knife-grinder, with his barrow by the hedge, whirling his wheel round, and singing—

> "Scissors and razors and such-like I grind,
> And gaily my rags are flying behind."

Hans stopped and looked at him, and at last he said, "You appear to have a good business, if I may judge by your merry song?"

"Yes," answered the Grinder, "this business has a golden bottom! A true knife-grinder is a man who as often as he puts his hand into his pocket feels money in it! But what a fine goose you have got; where did you buy it?"

"I did not buy it at all," said Hans, "but took it in exchange for my pig." "And the pig?" "I exchanged for my cow." "And the cow?" "I exchanged a horse for her." "And the horse?" "For him I gave a lump of gold as big as my head." "And the gold?" "That was my wages for a seven years' servitude." "And I see you have known how to benefit yourself each time," said the Grinder; "but, could you now manage that you heard the money rattling in your pocket as you walked, your fortune would be made." "Well! how shall I manage that?" asked Hans.

"You must become a grinder like me; to this trade nothing peculiar belongs but a grindstone, the other necessaries find themselves. Here is one which is a little worn, certainly, and so I will not ask anything more for it than your goose; are you agreeable?"

"How can you ask me?" said Hans; "why, I shall be the luckiest man in the world; having money as often as I dip my hand into my pocket, what have I to care about any longer?"

So saying, he handed over the goose, and received the grindstone in exchange.

"Now," said the Grinder, picking up an ordinary big flint stone which lay near, "now, there you have a capital stone, upon which only beat them long enough and you may straighten all your old nails! Take it, and use it carefully!"

Hans took the stone and walked on with a satisfied heart, his eyes glistening with joy. "I must have been born," said he, "to a heap of luck; everything happens just as I wish, as if I were a Sunday-child."

Soon, however, having been on his legs since daybreak, he began to feel very tired, and was plagued too with hunger, since he had eaten all his provision at once in his joy about the cow bargain. At last he felt quite unable to go farther, and was forced, too, to halt every minute, for the stones encumbered him very much. Just then the thought overcame him, what a good thing it were if he had no need to carry them any longer, and at the same moment he came up to a stream. Here he resolved to rest and refresh himself with a drink, and so that the stones might not hurt him in kneeling he laid them carefully down by his side on the bank. This done, he stopped down to scoop up some water in his hand, and then it happened that he pushed one stone a little too far, so that both presently went plump into the water. Hans, as soon as he saw them sinking to the bottom, jumped up for joy, and then kneeled down and returned thanks, with tears in his eyes, that so mercifully, and without any act on his part, and in so nice a way, he had been delivered from the heavy stones, which alone hindered him from getting on.

"So lucky as I am," exclaimed Hans, "is no other man under the sun!"

Then with a light heart, and free from every burden, he leaped gaily along till he reached his mother's house.

HANS MARRIED.

THERE was once a young country chap called Hans, whose Uncle wanted very much to marry him to a rich wife, so he set him beside the oven and let a good fire be lighted. Then he fetched a jug of milk and a large piece of white bread, and gave Hans a shining newly-coined penny, saying, "Hans, keep this penny safely, and break your white bread into this milk; and mind you stop here, and do not stir from your stool till I return."

"Yes," said Hans, "I will faithfully do all you require."

Then the Uncle went and drew on a pair of old spotted breeches, and, walking to the next village, called on a rich farmer's daughter, and asked her whether she would marry his nephew Hans, assuring her that he was a prudent and clever young man, who could not fail to please her. The girl's covetous father, however, asked, "How is he situated with regard to property? Has he the wherewithal to live?"

"My dear friend," said the Uncle, "my nephew is a warm youth, and has not only a nice penny in hand, but plenty to eat and drink. He can count too, quite as many specks" (meaning money) "as I;" and, as he spoke, he slapped his hand upon his spotted breeches. "Will you," he continued, "take the trouble to go with me, and in an hour's time you shall see everything as I have said?"

The offer appeared so advantageous to the covetous Farmer that he would not let it slip, and therefore said, "If it is so, I have nothing more to say against the wedding."

So the ceremony was performed on an appointed day, and afterwards the young wife wished to go into the fields and view the property of her husband. Hans drew his spotted smock first over his

Sunday clothes, saying to his bride, ''I do not wish to spoil my best things!'' This done, they went together into the fields, and wherever a vine-stock was planted on the road, or the meadows and fields divided, Hans pointed with his finger there, and then laid it on one great spot or another on his smock, and said, ''This spot is mine and thine too, my dear! Do just look at it.'' Hans meant by this, not that his wife should gape at the broad fields, but that she should look at his smock, which was really his own!

''Did you then go to the wedding?'' ''Yes! I was there in full toggery. My head-piece was of snow, and there came the sun and melted it; my clothes were of worsted, and I walked through thorns, so that they were torn off; my shoes were of glass, and I stepped upon a stone, and they cracked and fell to pieces.''

THE DWARFS.

THERE was once upon a time a rich King who had three daughters, who all day long were accustomed to walk in the gardens of their father's palace. The King was a great admirer of every species of tree, but of one in particular it was said that whoever should pluck off a single apple would sink a hundred feet into the ground. Now, when harvest came, the apples on this tree were as red as blood, and the three Princesses went every day under this tree to see if any of the fruit had fallen; but the wind did not blow any down, and the branches were so overloaded that they hung almost on the ground. At last the youngest of the three daughters took such a fancy to the fruit that she said to her sisters, ''Our father loves us so much he will never cause us to disappear underground; he only meant that judgment for strangers;'' and so saying, she plucked an apple, and jumping before her sisters, invited them also to taste it. So the three sisters shared it between them; but as soon as they had eaten it they all sank down below the earth, so far that no bird could scratch them up.

By-and-by, when it became noon, the King wanted his daughters, but they were nowhere to be found, though the servants searched all over the house and gardens. At length, when he could hear nothing about them, the King caused it to be proclaimed throughout the country, that whoever should bring back the Princesses should receive one of them as a bride. Thereupon numbers of young men travelled about on land and sea to find the maidens; for every one was desirous to regain them, they were so amiable and pretty.

Amongst others there went out three young Huntsmen, who, after travelling about eight days, came to a large castle, wherein every room was splendidly furnished; and in one room they found a large table, and on it was spread all manner of delicate food, and everything was still so warm that it smoked; yet nowhere did they hear or see any human being. Here they waited half the day, while the meats still smoked before them, till at length they became very hungry, and, sitting down, they ate what they liked, and afterwards agreed together that one should remain in the castle while the two others sought the Princesses; and, to decide the matter, they drew lots; and it fell to the share of the eldest to stop on the spot. The next day, accordingly, the two younger Brothers took their departure, while the eldest remained in the castle; and about noon a little Dwarf entered, and brought in some pieces of roast meat, which he cut in pieces, and then handed them; and while he held it to the young Huntsman he let one piece fall, and the Dwarf asked him to be good enough to pick it up again. So he bent down to do so, and immediately the Dwarf jumped on him, and caught him by the hair, and beat him roughly. The next day the second brother remained at home, and he fared no better; and, when the two others returned, the eldest asked him how he had passed the day. "Oh! badly enough, I can tell you," he replied; and the two Brothers told each other of what had befallen them; but they said nothing to their youngest Brother, for fear he should refuse to have any part in the matter. So the third day he remained at home, and the Dwarf entered as usual with the meat, and, letting one piece fall, requested the youth to pick it up. But he said to the Dwarf, "What! Can you not pick that up yourself? If you had the trouble of earning your daily bread you would be glad enough, but now you are not worth what you eat!"

This answer made the Dwarf very angry; but the youth gripped hold of him, and gave him such a shake that he exclaimed, "Stop, stop! and let me go, and I will tell you where the King's daughters are."

When the youth heard this he let him drop, and the little mannikin said he was an underground Dwarf, and there were more than a thousand like him; and if any one went with him he could show him where the Princesses were living: that he knew the place, which was a deep well, where no water entered. The Dwarf told him further that he knew his Brothers would not act honourably to him, and therefore, if he would rescue the King's daughters he must go alone, and must take with him a great basket wherein to let himself down, and go armed with his forester's knife; and below he would find three rooms, in each of which would sit a Princess, guarded by dragons with many heads, all of which heads he must cut off. As soon as the Dwarf had said all this he disappeared; and about evening the two Brothers returned, and asked the youngest how he had passed the time. "Oh! very well, indeed," he replied; "and about noon a Dwarf came in, who cut up the meat, and let one piece fall, which he asked me to pick up; but I refused; and, as he flew into a passion, I gave him a shake, and presently he told me where to find the Princesses."

This tale sorely vexed the other Brothers, who turned blue with suppressed rage; but the next morning they all went up the hill, and drew lots who should descend first into the basket. The lot fell, as before, to the eldest, and he went down, taking a bell with him, which when he rang they were to pull him up as fast as they could. So after he had been down a little while he rang his bell furiously; and, as soon as he was drawn up, the second Brother took his place and went down; but he quickly rang to be pulled up again. The turn now came to the youngest Brother, who allowed himself to be let down to the very bottom, and there, getting out of the basket, he marched boldly up to the first door, with his drawn knife in his hand. There he heard the dragons snoring loudly; and, on his carefully opening the door, he saw one of the Princesses sitting within, with the dragon's nine heads in her lap. He raised his knife and cut these heads off; and immediately the Princess jumped up and hugged and kissed him, and fell upon his neck, and then gave him her golden necklace for a reward. Next he went after the second Princess, who had a dragon with seven heads by her side: he also freed her, and then went to the youngest, who was guarded by a four-headed dragon. This beast he also destroyed; and then the three Sisters embraced and kissed him so much that at last he clashed the bell very hard, so that those above might hear. When the basket came down he set each Princess in turns, and let them be drawn up; but, as it descended for him, he remembered the Dwarf's saying that his Brothers would be faithless to him. So he picked up a huge stone, and laid it in the basket, and just as the false Brothers had drawn it half-way up they cut the cord at the top, and the basket with the stone in it fell plump to the bottom. By this means they thought they had rid themselves of their Brother; and they made the three Princesses promise that they would tell their father it was they who had delivered them; and then they went home to the King and demanded the Princesses for their wives. But meanwhile the youngest Brother wandered about sadly in the three chambers, and thought he should have to die there, when all at once he perceived on the walls a flute, and he thought to himself, "Ah! what good can this be here? What is there to make one merry?" He kicked, too, the dragons' heads, saying, "And what good are you to me? you cannot help me!" Up and down, to and fro, many times he walked, so often, indeed, the floor was worn smooth.

By-and-by other thoughts came into his head, and, seizing the flute, he blew a little on it; and, behold, ever so many little Dwarfs instantly appeared! He blew a little longer, and with every note a fresh one came, till at last the room was quite filled with them. Then all of them asked what his wishes were, and he told them that he wanted to be up above on earth again, and in the clear daylight. Immediately each Dwarf seized a hair of his head, and away they flew up the well with him till they landed him at the top. As soon as ever he was safe on his legs again, he set out for the royal palace, and arrived about the time the weddings of the Princesses were to be celebrated. So he hurried up to the room where the King sat with his three daughters; and as soon as he entered they were so overcome that they fainted away. This made the King very angry; and he ordered the new-comer to be put in prison, for he thought he had done his children some injury; but as soon as they recovered themselves they begged their father to set him at liberty. But he asked them their reason; and when they said they dare not tell him, he bade them tell their story to the oven; and meantime he went outside and listened at the door. When the King had heard all, he caused the two traitorous Brothers to be hanged; but he gave his youngest daughter in marriage to the true deliverer.

And to their wedding I went in a pair of glass shoes, and, kicking against the wall, broke them all to pieces.

OLD HILDEBRAND.

ONCE upon a time there lived an old Farmer, and his Daughter with him, whom the Parson of the village, having once seen, took a great fancy to; and he thought he should be very happy if he could manage one day to have a long talk with her alone. To this the Daughter had no objection, and the Parson one day said to her, "Oh! my dear maiden, hear what I have to say: I will tell you how to manage, that we may have a whole day all to ourselves. About the middle of this week do you lie in bed one morning, and tell your father you are very ill, and groan and sigh very badly, and keep that up all the week. Then, on Sunday, when I come to deliver my sermon, I will preach that whoever has at home a sick child, a sick husband, a sick wife, a sick father or mother, a sick sister or brother, or any other relative, and shall make a journey to the Bell Mountain in Wales, such an one's sick child, sick husband or wife, sick father or mother, sick sister or brother, or any other relative, shall become well on the instant!"

"Oh! that I will do for you," said the girl; and thereupon, about the middle of the week, she laid a-bed, and, spite of all her Father brought or did for her, she groaned and sighed till the Sunday, as if she were full of pain. On Sunday the daughter said to her Father, "Oh! I am really so miserably ill, I feel as if I should die; but once before my end I should like to hear the Parson again, and hear the sermon which he will deliver to-day."

"Ah! my child," repied the Farmer, "you must not do that; you would be all the worse for it if you got up. But never mind; I will go to church, and pay great attention to the sermon, and afterwards come and tell you all the Parson said."

"Ah! very well," said the Daughter; "but mind you are very attentive and tell me everything."

So away went the Farmer to church; and after the Parson had chanted and read all the service, he got into the pulpit and began his sermon. In the course of it he said, "If any one here has a sick child, a sick husband or a sick wife, a sick father or mother, a sick brother or a sick sister, or any other relative, and shall go to the Bell Mountain in Wales, such an one's sick child, sick husband or wife, sick father or mother, sick sister or brother, or any other relative, shall regain health immediately; especially if he take with him a cross and some laurel leaves which I will give him after service." Then was nobody quicker than the Farmer in going to the Parson after service for his laurel leaves and cross; and as soon as he had received them, he hurried home; and almost before he got to the door he called out, "Come, my dear daughter, you will soon be well. The Parson has preached to-day that whosoever having a sick child, a sick husband or wife, a sick mother or father, a sick brother or sister, or any other person, shall go to the Bell Mountain, with a cross and laurel leaves given him by the Parson, his sick child, sick husband or wife, sick father or mother, sick sister or brother, or any other relative, shall recover immediately. Now, the laurel leaves and cross I have received from the Parson, and I shall set out immediately on the journey, that you may be the sooner in good health." So saying, he set out; but scarcely had he gone, when the Daughter got up, and very soon afterwards in stepped the Parson. Here we will leave them a bit, while we follow the Farmer in his wanderings. As we have said, he had set out at once, that he might reach the Bell Mountain the quicker; and on his way his Cousin met him, who was an egg-merchant, and was just come home from market, having sold his eggs.

"Good day to you," said the Cousin; "whither are you going?"

"To Wales, Cousin," he replied; "my daughter is very ill; and the Parson said yesterday in his sermon that whoever having at home a sick child, a sick husband or wife, a sick father or a sick mother, a sick brother, sister, or any other relation, should then make a journey to the Bell Mountain in Wales, carrying in his hand some laurel and a cross, blessed and given by the Parson—whoever should to this, then that his sick child, sick mother, or sick father, husband or wife, sick brother or sick sister, or any other relative, would immediately be restored to health. So this laurel and cross I have received from the Priest, and now I am hastening to the mountain."

"But hold, Cousin, stop!" said the other to the Farmer, "are you so simple as to believe that? Why, how do you know that the Parson may not perchance wish to have a comfortable talk with your daughter alone and, therefore has contrived this tale to take you away from home?"

"Mercy on us!" said the Farmer, "if I did but know whether that were true or not!"

"Well, you soon can see," replied the Cousin; "just get into my cart, and I will drive you home, that you may satisfy yourself."

It was soon done; and as they drove nearer to the house they heard the sounds of merriment. There had the Farmer's daughter gathered the best of everything out of the farmyard and garden, and made all manner of savoury dishes, and the Parson was there to partake of them. So the Cousin knocked at the door, and the Maiden inquired who was there.

"It is only me, Cousin," replied he; "will you give me a night's lodging? I have just sold my eggs in the market, and I meant to have got home to-night, but it is so dark already that I dare not go."

"You have come at a very unlucky moment, Cousin," replied the Farmer's Daughter; "but since you are quite alone, you may come in and set yourself down in the chimney-corner."

So the egg-merchant, carrying his basket, in which the Farmer was concealed, came in and sat down where he was bid, while the Parson and the Daughter made themselves very merry together over their meal. Presently the Parson said, "You can sing, I think, my dear; just give us a bit of a song."

"Well," said she, "I could sing once when I was very young; but now I have forgotten how, and it is almost all lost to me."

"Never mind; do just try!" entreated the Parson. So the Farmer's Daughter began :—

> "Oh! well have I sent my father away
> To the mountains in Wales so high!"

and then the Parson joined in,—

> "And there he shall stop for a year and a day;
> And merry the time will pass by."

Presently the Cousin within struck up (but here I must tell you the Farmer's name was Hildebrand),—

> "Hearest thou that, my Hildebrand dear?
> Why sitt'st thou so quiet, so near, so near?"

And directly the Farmer made answer,—

> "Oh! more of your singing I never can stand!
> And out of this basket I must get my hand!"

With these words, he jumped up from the basket, and bundled Parson out of the house.

THE THREE BIRDS.

MANY years ago there lived up among the hills in our country some petty Kings, who every day went out hunting, and had their palaces high above everybody else. One day when one of them had come forth from his castle with his Huntsmen there were three Girls who were tending their cows, and, as they saw the King pass by with his people, the eldest of them, pointing to the King, called out to her companions, "Hilloa! hilloa! if I had any I would have him." Then the two Girls on the other side of the hill exclaimed, each pointing to the two men nearest the King, the one with her right hand, the other with her left, "Hilloa! hilloa! if I had any I would have him." Now these two were the King's Ministers. The King, who heard all that was said, as soon as he returned from the hunt, ordered the three Maidens to be fetched, and asked them what they had meant in the morning by what they said on the mountains. This question, however, they would not answer, and at last the King inquired of the eldest if she would have him for a husband. To this she said yes; and her two Sisters were then asked in marriage by the Ministers, for they were all three beautiful and fair, especially the King's wife, who had flaxen hair.

Now the two Sisters had no children at first, and, as the King had to undertake a long journey, he invited them to come and stay with the Queen. During his absence the Queen bore a child, who had a red forehead, and was, besides, very pretty. The two Sisters, however, agreed together they would throw the child into the mill-pond, and as they did so a little Bird flew up into the air, which sang,—

> "Ready to die
> And for ever to quit
> These lilies and flowers,
> Brave boy, are you fit?"

When the two Sisters heard this they were very much alarmed, and made all the haste they could home. Afterwards, when the King returned, they told him that the Queen had borne a dead child; but the King only replied, ''What God wills I must bear.'' Meanwhile a Fisherman had fished the little Boy up out of the water while it still breathed, and, as his wife had no children of her own, they brought it up. A year after the King again went on a journey, and in his absence another Boy was born, which the two Sisters stole away as before and threw into the water. Just as they did so a Bird flew up as at the first time and sang,—

> ''Ready to die
> And for ever to quit
> These lilies and flowers,
> Little boy, are you fit?''

When the King returned they told the same tale as before about the Queen; but he merely replied, ''What God wills I must bear.'' However, the Fisherman had again luckily rescued the child, whom he brought up with his brother.

Some time passed before the King journeyed again, but during his absence a child was born, and this time it was a little Girl, which the false Sisters also threw into the river, and the little Bird instantly flew up, singing,—

> ''Ready to die
> And for ever to quit
> These lilies and flowers,
> Little maid, are you fit?''

Afterwards, when the King returned, he was told the same tale as before, and this made him so angry that he caused the Queen to be put in prison, where she was kept for many years.

During that time the Children grew up; but when the eldest went out to fish, the other boys would not let him come near, and said, ''Go your own way, you foundling!'' This made him very sad, and he asked the Fisherman who he was, and the Fisherman told him how he had fished him and his brother and sister all out of the water in his net. The eldest boy resolved thereupon that he would go in search of their Father; but the Fisherman was very unwilling to part with him. At length he consented, and the Boy set out, and after travelling for several days came to an immense piece of water, by which stood a Woman fishing.

''Good day, mother,'' said the Boy.

''Thank you, my lad,'' she replied.

''You will sit there a good long time before you catch any fish,'' said the Boy.

"And you will seek a long while before you find your father,"
returned the Woman. "And pray how do you mean to cross this
water?" "Heaven only knows!" he replied; and thereupon the old
Woman took him on her back and carried him across, and there he
searched everywhere, but could never find his Father.

A year after his departure his Brother made up his mind to go in
search of him, and he also, coming to the same great water, found
the old Woman, with whom he held the same conversation, and was
likewise carried across as his Brother had been. The Sister was now
left alone at home, but she became so restless and dispirited at her
brothers' absence that she set out herself in search of them. On her
way she came, as they had done, to the great piece of water, and
found there the same old Woman, to whom she said, "Good day,
mother." "Thank you, my child," was the reply. "God bless your
fishing!" said the Girl. As soon as the old Woman heard this she
became very friendly, and after carrying the maiden across the
water she gave her a staff, and said, "Now, go straight along on this
path, my daughter, and when you come to a great black Dog you
must take care neither to laugh at it nor kick it, but pass it by
quietly. Then you will come to a large castle, upon whose threshold
you must let the staff fall, and then go straight through it to a
fountain on the other side of the castle. This fountain will be in a
stream, wherein stands also a tree, on which there will hang a bird in
a cage, which you must take off. Then take also a glass of water from
the fountain, and return with these the same way exactly as you
came. On the threshold pick up your staff again, and when you pass
the Dog the second time hit it in the face, and then come straight
back to me." The Maiden found everything just as the old Woman
said, and at the back of the castle she found also her two Brothers,
who had been seeking half through the world. So they went together
and came to the place where the black Dog lay, whose face they
knocked, and immediately the Dog became a handsome Prince, and
accompanied them to the great water. There still stood the old
Woman, who was very glad to see them return, and carried them all
across the water. This done, she disappeared, for she was now
released from her labours. The Brothers and Sister, however,
returned to the Fisherman, and all were made happy on seeing each
other again; but the Bird they hung upon the wall in his cage. The
second Brother, however, could not rest at home, and soon he took
his cross-bow and went to the hunt. When he got tired he took out his
flute and played a tune, which the King, who was also hunting,
heard, and coming up to the youth, inquired who had given him
leave to hunt there. "Nobody," he replied.

"To whom do you belong, then?" asked the King.

"I am the Fisherman's son," was the reply.

"But he has no children," said the King.

"If you will not believe me," said the Youth, "come and see."

So the King went to the Fisherman, who told him all that had taken place; and the Bird on the wall began to sing,—

> "The mother sits lonely
> In prison fast kept,
> And these are her children
> Stolen away while she slept,
> By the false-hearted sisters,
> Who, the children to kill,
> In the deep waters threw them,
> By the side of the Mill."

This frightened them all, and the King took the Bird, the Fisherman, and the three Children with him to the castle, and ordered the prison to be opened, and brought his Wife out, who at first was very ill and weak after her long confinement. So her daughter gave her some of the water she had procured at the fountain, and that made her quite well again as soon as she had drunk it. Afterwards the two false Sisters were burnt, and the Daughter of the King married the handsome Prince: and so all were made happy and lived to a good old age.

THE SWEET SOUP.

ONCE upon a time there was a poor but pious little Girl, who lived alone with her mother, and when my story begins they had nothing in the house to eat. So the child went out into the forest, and there she met with an old Woman, who already knew her distress, and who presented her with a pot which had this power:—if one said to it, "Boil, little pot!" it would cook sweet soup; and when one said, "Stop, little pot!" it would immediately cease to boil. The little Girl took the pot home to her mother, and now their poverty and distresses were at an end, for they could have sweet broth as often as they pleased. One day, however, the little girl went out, and in her absence the mother said, "Boil, little pot!" So it began to cook, and she soon ate all she wished; but when she wanted to have the pot stop, she found she did not know the word. Away, therefore, the pot boiled and very quickly was over the edge; and as it boiled and boiled the kitchen presently became full, then the house, and the next house, and soon the whole street. It seemed likely to satisfy all the world, for, though there was the greatest necessity to do so, nobody knew how to stop it. At last, when only a very small cottage of all the village was left unfilled with soup, the child returned, and said at once, "Stop, little pot!" Immediately it ceased to boil; but whoever wishes to enter the village must eat his way through the soup!!!

THE FAITHFUL BEASTS.

THERE was once a Man who had not a great deal of money, but with the little he had he wandered into the wide world. Soon he came to a village where the boys were running together screaming and laughing, and he asked them what was the matter. "Oh!" replied they, "we have got a mouse which we are going to teach to dance: only see what a beautiful sport it is; how it will skip round!" The Man, however, pitied the poor Mouse, and said, "Let it escape, my boys, and I will give you money." So he gave them some coppers, and they let the poor animal loose, which ran as fast as it could into a hole close by. After this the Man went on and came to another village, where the boys had a Monkey, which they forced to dance and tumble, and laughed at without letting the poor thing have any rest. To these also the Man gave money that they might release the Monkey; and by-and-by, coming to a third village, he saw the boys making a Bear in chains dance and stand upright, and if he growled they seemed all the better pleased. This animal's liberty the Man also purchased, and the Bear, very glad to find himself on his four feet again, tramped away.

The Man, however, with these purchases spent all his money, and he found he had not a copper farthing even left in his pocket. So he said to himself, "The King has much in his treasure-chamber which he does not want: of hunger I cannot die; I must take some of this money, and then when I become rich I can replace it." With these thoughts he managed to get into the treasure-chamber and took a little from the heaps, but as he was slipping out he was seized by the King's guards. They said he was a thief, and took him before the justice, who sentenced him, as he had done a criminal act, to be put in a chest on the water. The lid of the chest was full of holes whereby he might obtain air, and, besides, a jug of water and a loaf of bread were put in with him. While he was floating about in great distress of mind, he heard something gnawing and scratching at the lock of his chest, and all at once it gave way and up flew the lid. Then he saw the Mouse and the Monkey and the Bear standing by, and found it was they who had opened the chest because he had helped them; but they did not know how to proceed next, so they held a consultation together. In the meanwhile a white Stone rolled by into the water, in shape like a round egg. "That has come in the very nick of time," said the Bear, "for it is a wonderful stone, which whoever owns he can wish himself in whatever place he desires."

The Man, therefore, picked up the Stone, and as he held it in hand he wished himself in a castle with a garden and stables. Scarcely had he done so when he found himself in a castle with a garden and stables just to his mind, and everything was so beautiful and nice that he could not admire it enough.

After a time some merchants came by that way, and, as they passed, one called to the others, "See what a noble castle stands here, where lately, when we were here before, there was nothing but dreary sand." Their curiosity was therefore aroused, and they entered the castle and inquired of the Man how he had managed to build the place so quickly. "I did not do it," said he, "but my wonderful Stone." "What kind of a stone can it be?" inquired the merchants; and, going in, the Man fetched it and showed it to them. The sight of it pleased them so much that they inquired if it were not for sale, and offered him all their beautiful goods in exchange. The goods took the Man's fancy, and, his heart being fickle and hankering after new things, he suffered himself to be persuaded and thought the beautiful things were worth more than his Stone, so he gave it away to them in exchange. But scarcely had he given it out of his hands when all his fortune vanished, and he found himself again in his floating chest on the water with nothing but his jug of water and loaf of bread. The faithful beasts, the Mouse, Monkey, and Bear, as soon as they saw his misfortune, came again to help him, but they could not manage to unfasten the lock, because it was much stronger than the former one. Thereupon the Bear said, "We must procure the wonderful Stone again, or our work is useless." Now, the merchants had stopped at the castle and lived there constantly, so the three faithful animals went away together, and when they arrived in the neighbourhood the Bear said the Mouse must peep through the keyhole and see what was going on, for since he was small no one would notice him. The Mouse consented and went, but soon returned, saying, "It is useless, I have peeped in, but the Stone hangs on a red riband below the mirror, and above and below sit two great cats with fiery eyes to watch it." Then the others said, "Never mind, go back again and wait till the master goes to bed and falls asleep, then do you slip in through the hole and creep on to the bed, and twitch his nose and bite off one of his whiskers." So the Mouse crept in and did as she was told, and the master, waking up, rubbed his nose in a passion, and exclaimed, "The cats are worth nothing! they let the mice in who bite the very hair off my head!" And, so saying, he hunted them all away, and the Mouse won her game.

The next night, as soon as the master was sound asleep, the Mouse crept in again, and nibbled and gnawed at the riband until it broke in halves, and down fell the Stone, which she then pushed out under the door. But this latter matter was very difficult for the poor Mouse to manage, and she called to the Monkey, who drew it quite out with his long paws. It was an easy matter for him, and he carried the Stone down to the water side accompanied by the others. When they got there the Monkey asked how they were to get at the chest. "Oh," replied the Bear, "that is soon done; I will swim into the water, and you, Monkey, shall sit upon my back, holding fast with your hands while you carry the Stone in your mouth; you, Mouse, can sit in my right ear." They all did as the Bear suggested, and he swam off down the river, but very soon he felt uneasy at the silence, and soon began to chatter, saying, "Do you hear, Mr. Monkey, we are brave fellows, don't you think?" But the Monkey did not answer a word. "Is that manners?" said the Bear again. "Will you not give your comrade an answer? crabbed fellow is he who makes no reply." Then the Monkey could no longer restrain himself, and letting the Stone fall into the water, he cried out, "You stupid fellow, how could I answer you with the Stone in my mouth? Now it is lost, and all through your fault."

"Do not be angry," said the Bear; "we will soon recover it." Thereupon they consulted together, and summoned all the frogs and other creatures living in the water, and said to them, "There is a powerful enemy coming against you; but make haste and procure us the stones as quickly as possible, and we will then build a wall to protect you."

These words frightened the water animals, and they brought up stones on all sides, and at last came a fat old frog waddling along who had the wonderful Stone in her mouth, hanging by a piece of red riband. Then the Bear was glad, and, relieving the frog of his burden, he politely said it was all right, they might go home again now, and so took a short leave. After this the three beasts swam to the Man in the chest, and, breaking the lid in by the aid of stones, they found they had come just in the nick of time, for he had just finished his jug of water and loaf of bread, and was almost starved. However, as soon as the Man had taken the wonderful Stone in his hand he wished himself quite well and back in the castle with the garden and stables. Immediately it was so, and there he and his three faithful beasts dwelt together, happy and contented, to the end of their days.

THE THREE ARMY SURGEONS.

THREE Army Surgeons were once on their travels, confident that they had learnt their profession perfectly; and one day they arrived at an inn where they wished to pass the night. The landlord asked them whence they came and whither they were going; and one of them replied that they were travelling about in search of employment for their talents. "In what do your talents consist?" inquired the landlord. The first said he could cut off his hand, and in the morning put it on again without difficulty; the second said he could take out his eyes, and in the morning replace them without injury; and the third declared he could take out his own heart and put it back again.

"Can you do these things?" said the landlord: "then indeed you are well taught." But they had a salve which healed whatever it touched; and the bottle which contained it they always carried carefully with them. So the one cut off his hand, another took out his eyes, and the third cut out his heart, as they had said, and gave them on a dish to the landlord, who delivered them to the servant to put them by in a cupboard till the morning. Now this servant had a sweetheart on the sly, who was a soldier; and he, coming in, wanted something to eat. As soon as the landlord and the Three Surgeons had gone to bed, the maid opened the cupboard and fetched her lover something; but in her hurry she forgot to shut the door again, and sat down to table with the soldier, and they made themselves merry. While she sat thus, apprehending no misfortune, the cat came slipping in, and, seeing the cupboard door open, snatched the hand, heart, and eyes of the Three Surgeons, and ran away with them. As soon as the Soldier had finished, the maid went to put the dish away in the cupboard, and then perceived that the plate which her master had given into her care was gone. She was terribly frightened and exclaimed, "Oh! what will become of me? the hand is gone, the heart is gone, and the eyes too; how shall I manage in the morning?" "Be quiet," said her sweetheart, "I will help you out of your difficulty; on the gallows outside hangs a thief, whose hand I can cut off; which was it?" "The right," said she, and gave him a sharp knife, with which he went and cut off the right hand of the criminal, and brought it in. Then he caught the cat and took out her eyes; but what was to be done for the heart? "Did you not kill a pig to-day and put the carcass in the cellar?" asked the soldier. "Yes," said the maid. "Then that is just the thing," returned the soldier; "go and fetch the heart from it." The servant did so, and they placed all three on the plate and put them in the cupboard, and then her sweetheart having taken leave, the maid went to bed.

On the morrow when the three Army Surgeons were up, they bade the servant fetch the plate on which lay the hand, heart, and eyes. She brought it from the cupboard, and the first man spread the hand with his salve, and immediately it joined as if it had grown there. The second took up the cat's eyes and placed them in his head, while the third put the pig's heart where his own came from. The landlord meanwhile stood by, wondering at their learning, and saying he would never have believed them had he not seen what they did. Afterwards they paid their bill and went away.

They had not gone far before he with the pig's heart began to run about and snuff in every corner after the manner of swine. The others tried to hold him by the coat, but it was of no use, he would run about among the thickest brush-wood. Th second Surgeon all this while kept rubbing his eyes and could not make out what was amiss. "What have I done?" said he to his comrades. "These are not my eyes, I cannot see; you must lead me, or I shall fall." So they travelled till evening with great trouble to themselves, when they came to another inn. They stepped into the parlour, and there in the corner sat a rich man at a table counting his money. The Surgeon with the thief's hand went up to him and peered at him, and as soon as his back was turned, made a grasp at the gold and took a handful. "For shame, comrade," cried the others; "you must not steal; what are you doing?" "Oh, how can I help myself!" he asked. "My hand is drawn to it, and I must take it whether I will or not!" Soon after this they went to bed, and it was so dark that one could not see his hand before his eyes. All at once the Surgeon with the cat's eyes woke up, and disturbing the others, cried out, "See, see, how the white mice are running about in the room!" The two others thereupon raised their heads, but they could see nothing. "It is evident to me now," said the first Surgeon, "that we have not got our own, we must go back to the landlord who deceived us."

The following morning they rode back to the first inn, and told the landlord they had not received their own things again, for one had got a thief's hand, another a pig's heart, and the third a cat's eyes. The landlord thereupon went to call the servant-maid, but she had escaped out of the backdoor as soon as she saw the Surgeons coming, and did not return. The three now threatened to set fire to the house if the landlord did not give them a large sum of money, and the poor man was compelled to give them all he could scrape together, with which they went away. But although they had enough to last them their lifetime, each would rather have had his own hand, heart, or eyes, than all the money in the world.

THREE LITTLE TALES ABOUT TOADS.

I.

ONCE upon a time there was a little Girl, whose mother gave her every day at noon a little basin of milk and bread, which she used to eat, sitting outside the house in the court. Once when she began to eat, there came a little Toad out of a crack in the wall, which put its head into the milk, and drank some. The Child was pleased with this; and the next day, and every day when she sat there with her basin, and the Toad did not make its appearance, she used to call it thus :—

"Toadie, Toadie, quickly come;
    Hither come, my pet;
And you shall have a little crumb
    And milk before you set!"

At these words the Toad would run and squat itself down to its feast. It showed itself grateful, too, for it always brought the child something out of its secret treasures,—shining stones, pearls, or golden toys, but the Toad would only drink milk, and not touch the bread; so once the Child took its little spoon, and tapped the Toad gently on the head, saying, "Eat some bread, too, pet!" The mother, standing in the kitchen, heard the Child speaking to something, and when she saw it tap the Toad with its spoon she ran out with a faggot of wood and killed the good creature.

From that time a change came over the Child. So long as the Toad had played with it, it had grown strong and hearty, but now its red cheeks vanished, and it became quite thin. Soon the death-bird began to scream in the forest, and the red-breasts collected leaves and twigs for a crown of death; and by-and-by the poor little Child lay on a bier.

II.

An orphan Child was sitting and spinning on the city wall, and saw a Toad come out of an opening beneath the wall. The Child quickly spread out its blue cotton handkerchief near itself, so that the Toad might be obliged to walk over it; and, as the child hoped, rest upon it. As soon as the Toad saw what was done, it turned round, and came again, bringing a little golden crown, which it laid down on the handkerchief, and then returned to its hole. The little Girl took up the crown, which was spun of delicate threads of gold, and glittered in the sun, and put it out of sight; so the Toad, when it came again, could not see it.

Thereupon the poor Toad crept up to the wall, and beat its little head against it, till it lost all its strength, and fell down dead. Now, if the Child had left the crown where it was laid, the Toad would have brought more treasures out of its hole.

III.

"Huhu, huhu!" cried a Toad.

"Come hither," said a Child to it. When the Toad came, the Child asked,—

"Have you seen my sister, Red-stocking, this morning?"

"No, no; not I!" croaked the Toad: "how should I? huhu, huhu!"

And the Toad hopped away.

HANS THE HEDGEHOG.

ONCE upon a time there was a Farmer who had quite enough of money and property to live upon, but rich as he was he lacked one piece of fortune; he had no children. Ofttimes when he went to market with the other farmers they laughed at him and asked why he had no children? At length he flew into a passion, and when he came home he said, "I will have a child, and it shall be a hedgehog." Soon after this speech a child was born to him, which was like a hedgehog in the upper part of its body, and formed as a boy below, and when his wife saw it she was frightened, and cried, "See what you have wished for!" So the man said, "It cannot be helped now, and it must be christened, but we can procure no godfather for it." "We cannot call him anything else than 'Hans the Hedgehog,'" said the wife; and when the priest baptized him he said, "On account of his spikes he can sleep in no common cradle." So behind the stove a little straw was laid, upon which the child slept, and there he kept for eight years, till his father grew tired of him and wished he might die. However, the child did not, but remained in a torpid state, and one day the Farmer resolved to go to a fair which was to be held in the neighboring town. He asked his wife what he should bring home, and she told him "a little piece of meat and a couple of rolls of bread for the housekeeping." Then he asked the servant, and she requested a couple of pots and a pair of stockings. Lastly he asked Hans what he liked, and the child replied, "Bring me, father, a bagpipe." Accordingly, when the Farmer returned home he brought his wife the meat and bread, his servant the pots and stockings, and Hans the Hedgehog the bagpipe. As soon as Hans received his gift he said, "Father, go to the smithy, and let the Cock be bridled, that I may ride away upon it and never return."

The father was glad to be freed from his son, and caused the Cock to be harnessed, and as soon as it was ready Hans the Hedgehog set himself upon it and rode away, taking with him a Boar and an Ass, which he meant to tend in the forest. But in the forest the Cock flew to the top of a lofty tree with him on its back, and there he watched the Boar and Ass for many years until there were many of them, and all the time his father knew nothing of him. While Hans sat on the tree-top he played upon his bagpipe and made beautiful music; and once a King came riding past who had lost his way in the forest, and chanced to hear him. He wondered at the sound, and sent his servants to inquire from whence the music proceeded. They looked about, but saw only a little animal upon a tree which seemed like a cock, and had a hedgehog upon its back which made the music. The King told them to ask why it sat there, and if it knew the way to his kingdom. Then Hans the Hedgehog came down from the tree, and said he would show the way if the King would promise him in writing what first met him in the royal court on his return. The King thought to himself, Hans the Hedgehog understands nothing, and I can write what I please, and so taking pen and ink he wrote something, and when he had done Hans showed him the road, and he arrived happily at home. But his daughter, seeing him at a distance, was so full of joy that she ran to meet her father and kissed him. Then he remembered Hans the Hedgehog, and told her what had happened to him, and how he had promised to a wonderful animal whatever met him first, and how this animal sat upon a cock and played music. However he had written he should not have the first, for Hans the Hedgehog could not read what was written. Thereupon the Princess was glad, and said it was well done, for she could not have been given up to such a creature.

Meanwhile Hans the Hedgehog still tended his flocks and herds and was very merry, sitting up in his tree and blowing his bagpipe. Now it happened that another King came travelling by with his attendants and courtiers, who had also lost himself and knew not how to get home, because the forest was so immense. All at once he heard the music at a distance, and said to his servant, ''Go and see at once what that is.'' So the servant went under the tree and saw the cock perched upon it and the hedgehog on its back, and he asked what he did up there. ''I am watching my flocks and herds; but what is your desire?'' was the reply. The servant said they had lost their way, and could not find their kingdom, if he did not show them the road. Then Hans the Hedgehog climbed down the tree with his cock, and told the old King he would point out the path if he would give to him certainly whatever should meet him first before his royal palace. The King said ''Yes,'' and subscribed to it with his own hand that he should have it. When this was done Hans rode before the King on his cock, and showed him the road, whereby he quickly arrived in safety in his own kingdom. As soon as he approached his

HANS THE HEDGEHOG

court, there was great rejoicing, and his only child, a daughter, who was very beautiful, ran to meet him, embraced and kissed him in her great joy at seeing her dear father return home again. She inquired also where he had stayed so long in the world, and he told her of all his wanderings, and how he had feared he should not get back at all because he had lost his way in such a large forest, where a creature half like a hedgehog and half like a man sat upon a cock in a high tree and made beautiful music. He told her also how this animal had come down from the tree and showed him the road on condition that he gave him whatever first met him in his royal palace on his return home; and she was the first, and that made him grieve. His daughter after a while promised to go with the animal when he came, out of love to her dear father.

Meanwhile Hans the Hedgehog tended his swine, and so many pigs were born that they filled the whole forest. Then Hans would stay no longer in the woods, and sent his father word he should clear all the stables in the village, for he was coming with such great herds that whoever wished might kill from them. At this news the father was grieved, for he thought his son had been dead long since. Soon after, Hans came riding upon his cock, and driving before him his herds into the village to be killed, when there was such a slaughtering and shrieking you might have heard it eight miles off! Hans the Hedgehog did not stay long: he paid another visit to the smithy to have his cock rebridled, then off he started again, while his father rejoiced that he should never see him again.

Hans the Hedgehog rode to the first kingdom we before mentioned, and there the King had ordered that if any one came riding upon a cock, and carrying with him a bagpipe, all should shoot at him, cut at him, and kill him, that he might not enter the castle. When, therefore, Hans the Hedgehog came riding along they pressed round him with bayonets but he flew high up into the air over the gate to the window of the palace and, there alighting, called the King to give him what he had promised or he would kill both him and his daughter. Then the King spoke kindly to his child and begged her to go away, that her life and his might be saved. At last she consented, turning very pale however, and her father gave her a carriage drawn by six white horses, and servants, money and plate besides. She set herself in it, and Hans the Hedgehog by her side, with his cock and bagpipe. Then they took leave and drove away while the King thought he should never see them again; and it happened just as he imagined, for as soon as they had gone a little way out of the city Hans the Hedgehog pulled off the Princess's shawl and pricked her with his quills, saying, "That is your reward for falsehood! go away! I will have nothing to do with you!" With these words he hunted her home, and to her end she was despised.

Hans the Hedgehog rode away next upon his cock with his

bagpipes in his hand to the second kingdom to which he had directed
its King. This King had ordered that, if any one like Hans the
Hedgehog came riding to the gate, the guards should present arms,
admit him freely, shout Viva! and conduct him to the palace. As
soon as the Princess saw the animal coming she was at first
frightened, because it appeared so curious, but as soon as she
recollected her promise she became reconciled. She welcomed Hans
the Hedgehog, and was married to him, and afterwards they dined
at the royal table, sitting side by side, and eating and drinking
together. When evening came on and bedtime, the Princess said she
was afraid of her husband's spikes, but he said she need not fear, he
would do her no harm. Then he told the old King to appoint four
men who should watch before the chamber-door and keep up a great
fire; and when he entered and prepared to go to bed, he would creep
out of his hedgehog skin and lay it down before the bed. When he
had so done, the men must run in, snatch up the skin, and throw it in
the fire, and keep it there till it was quite consumed.

Afterwards, when the clock struck twelve, Hans the Hedgehog
entered his room, stripped off his skin, and laid it down by the bed.
Immediately the four men ran in, snatched it up, and threw it into
the fire, and as soon as it was consumed Hans was freed, and lay in
the bed in a proper human form, but coal-black as if he was burnt.
Thereupon the King sent to his physician, who washed the young
Prince with a precious balsam which made his skin white, so that he
became quite a handsome youth. As soon as the Princess saw this she
jumped for joy; and the following morning they arose gladly, and
were married again in due form and with great feasting; and
afterwards Hans the Hedgehog received the kingdom from the
hands of the old King.

When several years had passed away the young King went with
his bride to his father's house, and told him he was his son. The
Farmer, however, declared he had no children. He had once, he said,
had one who was covered with spikes like a hedgehog, but he had
wandered away into the world. Then the King made himself known
to his father, and showed that he was really his son; and the Farmer
rejoiced greatly, and returned with him to his kingdom.

THE CHILD'S GRAVE.

THERE was once a Mother who had a little Boy, seven years old, so
pretty and good that no one saw him without loving him; and she,
especially, loved him with her whole heart. One day it happened that
he suddenly fell sick, and by-and-by the good God took him to

himself; and the poor Mother was so grieved that she would not be comforted, but cried day and night. Soon after his burial the Child appeared one night in the place where during his lifetime he had been wont to sit and play; and while his Mother wept he wept too, and at daybreak disappeared. When, however, the Mother still lamented his death, and cried without ceasing he appeared again one night in the white shroud in which he was laid in his coffin, and with the garland of flowers round his head. He sat down at the foot of his Mother on the bed, and said to her, "Ah! my Mother, cease to weep, else can I not sleep in my coffin, for my shroud is moistened continually with your tears which fall upon it!"

The Mother thereupon was frightened, and dried her tears: and the next night the Child appeared once more, holding a light in his hand. "See, my dear Mother!" he said, "see, my shroud is dry now, and I can rest in my grave!"

After this the Mother sorrowed no more, but bore her loss with patience and trust in God; while her Child peacefully slept in his narrow grave.

THE TWO KINGS' CHILDREN.

ONCE upon a time there was a King who had a little boy, of whom it was foretold that when he was sixteen years old he would be killed by a stag. Just when he had reached this age, he went out hunting with the royal huntsman, and, during the chase, the Prince wandered away from his companions and soon perceived a fine stag, which he took a fancy to shoot. He pursued it a long way without success, until the stag ran into a little hollow, where it changed itself into a tall, thin man, who said to the Prince, "Now all is well; I have caught you at last; often have I followed you with silent footsteps, but never till this time could I catch you." So saying, the man took the Prince with him, and rowed him over a wide lake, till they came to a royal palace, where they sat down at a table and partook of a meal together. When they had finished, the King said, "I have three daughters, the eldest of whom you must watch this night, sitting from nine o'clock in the evening till morning; and every time the clock strikes, I shall come and call gently, and, if you give me no answers, in the morning you shall die; but, if you reply readily each time, you shall have my daughter to wife."

When the young Prince was led into the chamber he saw a great stone image there, to which the Princess said, "When my father comes at nine, and every hour afterwards, do you give an answer when he speaks instead of the Prince." The stone image nodded its head, at first rapidly, and then gradually slower, till it stopped altogether. The next morning the King told the Prince he had performed his work well, but he could not yet give up his daughter, and he must watch this night the second one, and after that he would consider about giving him his eldest daughter to wife. "Again," said he, "I shall come every hour, and call gently, that you may answer; but if you do not answer, your blood shall flow as a punishment!"

With this they went up to the second daughter's chamber, and there stood a much larger image, which the Princess bade to answer when the King called. The large stone image thereupon nodded its head, as the other had done, first in quick time, and gradually slower, till it stood still. The Prince laid down upon the threshold and went to sleep, with his head resting upon his arm, and the next morning the King said again, "I cannot now give up my daughter, although you have performed what I required; so this night you must watch my youngest child, and then I will consider if you can have my second daughter to wife; again I shall come every hour, and call, and if you reply, well and good; but if not, your blood must flow in satisfaction!"

They ascended to the youngest Princess's room, and there was a much taller and larger image, twice as big as the other two, to which the Princess also said, "Answer, if my father calls." The tall image nodded its head for half-an-hour and then ceased, while the King's son laid down upon the threshold, as before, and went to sleep. The following morning the King said he had certainly watched well, but still he could not give him his daughter till he had first removed a certain huge forest, which, if he had effected by the evening of that day, he would consider the matter. Then he gave him a glass axe, a glass wedge, and a glass mallet, with which the Prince began his work; but at the first stroke the axe broke in halves, and at the first blow both the wedge and the mallet were shivered to pieces. Thereupon he was so troubled, believing that he should be put to death, that he sat down and wept. And, as it was just noonday, the King said to his daughters, "One of you must take him something to eat." "No, no," said the two eldest, "we will not; let the one he watched last wait upon him." So the youngest Princess had to carry the Prince his meal, and when she got to the forest she asked him how he got on. "Alas," said the youth, "everything goes ill!" The Princess pressed him to eat a bit before he went on, but he refused, saying, "No; I must die, and I am resolved I will eat no more." At length he was over-persuaded and did eat what she brought. When he had finished, she made him play at ball with her; and soon he fell asleep from weariness. Then she took her handkerchief, and tied a knot in the end, with which she knocked three times upon the ground, and cried, "Earthmen, come up!" Immediately ever so many little Dwarfs made their appearance, and inquired of the Princess what she wanted. ''In three hours from this time,'' said she, ''this forest must be cleared away, and all the timber piled up in heaps.''

The earthmen collected all their forces and set to work, and in three hours all was completed, and they summoned the Princess to see, who thereupon rapped upon the ground again, crying, ''Earthmen, go home!'' and all disappeared at once. Then she awoke the Prince, who was overjoyed to see what was done; but she bade him not return till it struck six. At that time he came back, and the king inquired if he had done his work. ''Yes,'' answered the Prince, ''I have cleared away the forest.'' Afterwards they sat down to supper, and the King then told the Prince he could not yet give him any of his daughters to wife till he had performed another work. This was to clear out a deep ditch and fill it with water, so that it should look as clear as a mirror, and, besides, be full of all sorts of fish. The next morning accordingly the King gave him a glass spade, and said the ditch must be ready at six o'clock. The Prince began to dig at once, but as soon as he struck the spade into the ground it broke in two, as the hatchet had done the day before. He was sore troubled, for he knew not what to do, and waited till noonday, when the youngest Princess again brought him his dinner, and asked how he got on. ''Alas!'' said he, hiding his face in his hands, ''the same ill-luck has befallen me.'' The Princess tried to comfort him, saying that he would think differently when he had eaten and rested. Still he refused, declaring that he should die, and would eat no more. At last she persuaded him to sit down, and when he had finished he fell asleep, being weary with care. And while he was snoring the Princess took out her handkerchief and rapped on the ground, as before, thrice, while she called, ''Earthmen, come up!'' They appeared at once, and asked her business. ''In three hours from this time you must clear this ditch, and make it as clear as crystal, and, besides, all sorts of fish must be within it.''

The earthmen thereupon collected all their strength, and worked so hard that in two hours it was all ready. When they had done they told the Princess her command was obeyed; and she, rapping thrice on the earth as before, said, ''Return home, then, earthmen!'' They all disappeared at once, and she awoke the Prince, who saw that the ditch was ready. Then the Princess returned home, and bade him not come till six o'clock, at which hour he arrive,d and the King asked him whether the ditch were ready. ''Yes,'' he replied. ''That is well,'' said the King; but at supper he again declared that he could not give up his daughter till he had done another thing. ''What, then, is that?'' asked the Prince. ''There is a great hill,'' replied the King, ''whereon are several crags of rock, which must all be demolished; and, instead thereof, you must build up a fine castle, which must be stronger than one can imagine, and, besides, filled with every necessary appurtenance.'' The following morning the King gave him a glass pickaxe and bore, and told him the work must be ready by six o'clock. At the first stroke with the pickaxe the pieces flew far and wide, and he had only the handle left in his hands, and the bore would make no impression. At these misfortunes he was quite disheartened, and sat down to wait and see if his mistress would assist him. At noonday she came as before, bringing him somewhat to eat, and he ran up to her and told her all his troubles. First she made him eat and go to sleep as before, and then she wrapped thrice as before with her knotted handkerchief on the ground, crying, ''Come up, little earthmen!'' They made their appearance at once, and asked her wishes. And she told them that, in three hours from that time, they must remove all the rocks which were on the hill, and build in their stead a noble castle, finer than any one had ever seen, and filled moreover, with all the necessary appurtenances. The Dwarfs fetched their tools and worked away, and in the three hours they completed everything. They told the Princess when they had finished, and she, rapping on the ground as before three times with her knotted handkerchief, cried, ''Earthmen, go home!'' and immediately they all disappeared. Then she awoke the Prince; and they were merry together as birds in the air, and when six o'clock struck they went home together. The King asked, ''Is that castle ready, too?'' ''Yes,'' was the reply. Afterwards, when they sat down to table, the King said to the Prince, ''I cannot give you my youngest daughter till you have asked her two sisters.'' This speech saddened both the Princess and the Prince, who knew not what to do. But at night he came to her, and they escaped together; but on the way the Princess looked back and saw her father pursuing them. ''Alas!'' she cried, ''what shall we do? my father is behind us, and will overtake us; I will change you into a thorn-bush, and myself into a rose, and always rest in your protection.''

So when the father came to the spot he found only a thorn-bush and a rose, which he was going to pull off, when the thorns pricked his finger, and sent him home again. On his return his wife asked him why he had not brought them with him, and he told her he had followed them till he had lost sight of them, and when he came to the spot he found only a thorn and a rose. ''You should have broken the rose-bud off, and the thorn-bush would have followed of itself!'' exclaimed his wife. Thereupon he went away to fetch the rose, but in the meantime the two had escaped farther away from the field where he left them, and the King was obliged to follow them. The Princess peeped behind her, and, seeing her father coming, cried, ''Ah! now what shall we do? I will transform you into a church, and myself into the parson, and mount in the pulpit to preach.'' So when the

King came to the spot, he found a church and a parson preaching in the pulpit, so he stopped and heard the sermon, and then returned home. The Queen asked if he had brought the fugitive, and he replied no: he had followed them to the spot where he thought they were, and had seen only a church, in the pulpit of which a parson was delivering a sermon. "You should have brought the parson with you," said his wife; "the church must have followed also; but now I must go myself, for it is useless to send you." Just as she was getting near the church, the Princess, peeping round, saw her mother coming, and exclaimed, "This is worse luck than all, for here comes mother; I will change you into a pond and myself into a fish." So when the Queen came to the place she found a large pond, and in the midst of it a fish swimming about and leaping out of the water merrily. The Queen tried to catch the fish, but she could not manage it, and so she drank up the whole pond, but it soon filled again, and she found that she could not succeed. So she turned to go home, but first she gave her daughter three walnuts, and said, "With these you can help yourself if you are in necessity."

The young people journeyed on again, and in about an hour's time they came in sight of the castle where the Prince formerly dwelt, close by which was a village. The Prince, as they approached the place, said to his companion, "Stop here, my dearest, while I go up to the castle and bring down carriages and servants to meet you."

As soon as he arrived at the castle there was great rejoicing at his return, and he told them his bride was waiting for him down in the village below while he went to bring a carriage. The servants soon harnessed the horses, and placed themselves behind the carriage; but the Prince, before he got in, kissed his mother, and as soon as he had done so he forgot all that had happened and all that he was about. The Queen Mother then commanded the horses to be taken out of the carriage and all went back into the house.

Meanwhile the Princess remained below in the village waiting and waiting to be fetched, but nobody came, and by-and-by she hired herself to the miller, whose mill belonged to the castle, and there, by the water, she sat all day long washing linen. One morning the Queen came by the stream while she was taking an airing, and saw the maiden sitting there. "What a fine girl that is!" she exclaimed; "she pleases me well!" but the Queen passed on and thought no more about her. So the maiden remained a long while with the miller, till the time came that the Queen had found a bride from a far distant country for her son. When this bride came a great number of people were invited to celebrate her arrival, and the maiden asked leave of her master to go too. On the wedding-day she opened one of the three nuts her mother had given her, and in it she found a very beautiful dress, which she put on, and went into the church and took a place near the altar. Presently the bride and bridegroom entered and placed themselves before the altar, but, just as the priest was about to bless them, the bride, peeping on one side, saw the maiden with the beautiful dress, and thereupon refused to be married unless she was dressed the same. So all the train had to return home, and the strange lady was asked if she would lend her dress. No! and neither would she sell it for any money; but there was one condition on which she would part with it. This was, that she should be allowed to sleep one night before the door of the Prince's chamber. This was granted; but the servants gave their master a sleeping-draught, so that he did not hear a word of the maiden's plaints, and there she lay all night long endeavouring to remind him how she had cut down the wood for him, filled up the ditch, built the castle, changed him into a thorn-bush, a church, and lastly, a pond, and yet he had forsaken her. But the Prince heard nothing, and the next morning the bride put on the dress, and they went again to church. Then the same events took place as the day before, and the maiden had leave to sleep again in return for her dress. This time the Prince did not take his draught, and he heard all her complaint and was very much troubled. The next morning he went to the maiden and begged her forgiveness for all his forgetfulness. The true bride then drew out and cracked her third nut, and the dress which laid in it was so beautiful, that all the boys and girls ran after, and strewed flowers in the path of the bride. So the Prince and Princess were happily married; but the old Queen and the envious bride were forced to run away.

THE THREE JOURNEYMEN.

THERE were once three Journeymen, who agreed together to travel in company, and always work in the same town. But one season they could find no master to employ them, so that by degrees they became quite ragged, and had nothing to live upon. They asked each other what they should do; and one proposed that they should not stop any longer where they were, but wander about; and when they came to a town where no work was to be had, they should separate, first making an agreement with the landlord of their inn, that he would receive their letters, so that each might know where his companions were. This plan appeared the best they could adopt, and they set out on their travels. On the road a well-dressed man met them, who inquired of them who they were. "We are Journeymen," said they, "in search of work, and hitherto we have been successful; but when we are no longer fortunate we mean to separate."

"There is no necessity for that," said the stranger; "if you only do what I tell you, you shall not want for money or work; for you may even become great lords, and ride in your own carriages."

"If it does not injure our souls and happiness," said one, "we will readily do what you wish."

"No; I have no claim upon you," replied the man; "of that sort, at least."

The other Journeyman, meanwhile, had observed the stranger's feet and when he saw one was a horse's hoof and the other a human foot, he would have nothing to do with the agreement at first. But the Evil One said it was not their souls, but some other man's, which he wanted; and so being reassured, the three Journeymen consented to the agreement. The Evil One then told them that what he desired was, that the first man should answer to every question, "All three of us;" the second, "For money;" and the third should cry, "That is right." This they were to say on all occasions, but any other word they must not speak, on pain of losing all their money again; but so long as they obeyed the instructions, their pockets would always be full of money. For a beginning the Evil One gave them as much as they could carry, and bade them go into such and such a city, and stop at such and such an inn. They entered the appointed place, and the Landlord came towards them and asked if they wished for something to eat. The first man replied, "All three of us." "Yes," said the Landlord, "that is what I mean." "For money," said the second man. "That is understood." "That is right," said the third. "Yes, that *is* right," repeated the Landlord.

Soon a plentiful meal was spread before them, and they were well waited on; and as soon as they had finished the Landlord brought in his bill, and laid it before the three companions. "All three of us," said the first; "For money," said the second; and the third repeated, "That is right." "You are quite right, sirs," said the Landlord, "all three of you must pay; and without the money I cannot entertain you." Thereupon they counted out more money than was asked, and the guests who were looking on said to each other, "These people must be mad!" "Yes; they do not appear quite sane," said the Landlord: but still they remained in his house, speaking no other words than "All three of us. For money; That is right." Nevertheless they saw and knew all that was going on: and one day it chanced that a great merchant came, bringing with him a great deal of money, to the inn. He said to the Landlord, "Take care of my gold, or these three foolish Journeymen may steal it from me." The Landlord did so, and as he carried the saddle-bags into his room he felt that they were heavy with gold. So he put the three Journeymen into a lower room, and the merchant into the best room by himself. At midnight, when the Landlord thought everybody was

asleep, he went, accompanied by his wife, into the rich merchant's chamber, and killed him by a stroke with an axe. The murder committed, they went to bed again; and when daylight came they made a great uproar, for the merchant was found dead, lying in pools of blood. All the inmates of the inn were collected, and the Landlord declared the murder had been committed by the three Journeymen. This the other lodgers confirmed, saying no one else could have done it; and when the three Journeymen were called, and asked if they had done the deed, the first replied, "All three of us;" the second, "For money;" and the third said, "That is right!"

"Now hear them," said the Landlord, "they confess it themselves." Thereupon the three were taken and thrown into prison; and while they lay there they perceived that it was a serious matter for them. But by night the Evil One came, and said to them, "Keep up your courage for one day, and despair not of your fortune, for not a hair of you shall be injured."

The following morning they were taken before the judge, and asked by him, "Are you the murderers?" "All three of us," replied the first. "Why did you kill the merchant?" asked the judge, secondly. "For money," was the reply. "You wretched men," exclaimed the judge, "have you repented of your crime since?" "That is right," said the third Journeyman. Then the judge ordered them to be led away to die, for they had confessed their crime, and were hardened about it.

So the three companions were led away, and the Landlord had to accompany them, being the accuser. Just as they were seized by the hangman and led up to the scaffold, where the executioner stood with a sharp sword, all at once a coach appeared drawn by four blood-red foxes, who went so fast that fire flew out of the stones, while from the window of the coach some one beckoned with a white handkerchief. The executioner said, "There comes a pardon!" and from the coach a voice was heard shouting, "Pardon, pardon!" Presently out of the coach the Evil One stepped, dressed as a distinguished lord, and said to the three prisoners, "You are innocent, you may speak now and state what you saw and heard." Thereupon the first Journeyman said, "We did not kill the merchant, the murderer stands there" (pointing to the Landlord), "and for a proof of this go into his cellar, and you will find many other bodies of those he has destroyed."

The judge, therefore, sent his guards, and they found the cellar as the man described, and the Landlord was consequently taken, and his head was struck off. The Evil One then said to the three Journeymen, "You are free, and will have money all your life, for I have got that for which I bargained."

FERDINAND THE FAITHFUL AND FERDINAND THE UNFAITHFUL.

ONCE upon a time there lived a certain Man and his Wife who as long as they were in prosperous circumstances were blessed with no children, but as soon as poverty came upon them a little boy was born to them. They were now so poor that they could get no one to stand godfather to their child, and the man determined he would go to another town and seek one. On his way he met a poor man, who inquired whither he was going, and he told him he was in search of some one to be sponsor to his son. "Oh!" said the poor man, "you are in distress, and I also! I will be godfather to your child, although I am too poor to give him any gift; go tell your wife and let her come to the church with the child." As soon as they got there the beggar said the name of the boy should be Ferdinand the Faithful; and so he was baptized.

When they came away from the church the beggar said to the Mother, "I cannot go with you because I have nothing to give you, nor you to me; but take this key, and let your husband take care of it till your boy is fourteen years old; and at that age he must go up the hill, and he will there come to a castle to which this key belongs, and whatever is in the castle shall be his."

When the boy reached the age of seven, he was once playing with other children, and they teased him and said he had received no present from his godfather as they had all done. Thereupon the boy went to his father and asked him whether what they said was true. "Oh! no," replied the father, "your godfather left a key for you which unlocks a castle which you will find up the hill." The boy went up, but no castle was to be seen or heard of; but by-and-by, when another seven years had passed, he went up again, and there saw the castle. As soon as he unlocked it he found a horse in a stable, and this so pleased him that he mounted it and rode back to his father, saying, "Now I have got a steed, I will travel."

So he went off, and on the roadside he found a shepherd whom he thought at first of taking with him, but he resolved not to do so, and rode on. But as he passed, the man called, "Ferdinand the Faithful, take me with you." So he went back and took him up behind him. After they had ridden a little way they came to a lake on the shore of which a fish was lying gasping in agony. "Ah! my good fish," cried Ferdinand. "I must help you back into the water;" and, taking it up, he threw it in, and the Fish called out as it fell into the water, "Now since you have assisted me when I was in trouble I will also help you; take this reed pipe, and when you are in need blow

FERDINAND THE FAITHFUL AND FERDINAND THE UNFAITHFUL

thereon, and I will come; and if you chance to fall into the water I will help you out.'' After this Ferdinand rode on, and by-and-by he asked his companion whither he would go. ''To the nearest place; but what is your name?'' ''Ferdinand the Faithful.'' ''Indeed,'' replied the other; ''then your name is like mine, for I am called Ferdinand the Unfaithful.'' So they rode on to the nearest place and stopped at the first inn.

Now, it was unfortunate that Ferdinand the Unfaithful came there, for he knew all manner of evil tricks. There was at this inn a maiden, fair-faced and clear-eyed, who took a liking to Ferdinand the Faithful as soon as he came, because he was handsome and cheerful, and she asked him where he was going. When he had told her he was travelling about, she advised him to stop where he was, for the King needed good servants and couriers, and he was just the sort of man for him. At first he refused to hear about the matter, and said he must go on; so the maiden went herself to the King and said she knew of a good servant. The King bade her bring him before him; and as he had a horse which he said he could not part with on any account, the King made him his courier. As soon then as Ferdinand the Unfaithful heard of this, he asked the maiden if she could not assist him also; and, willing to oblige both, she went to the King and got him a place in the royal household also.

A morning or two after their arrival the King awoke groaning and lamenting that his dear bride was not with him. As soon as Ferdinand the Unfaithful heard this, he went to the King (because all along he had a spite against Ferdinand the Faithful) and advised him to send a messenger after her. ''You have a courier,'' he said; ''why not send him off to fetch her back? and if he does not bring her let his head pay the forfeit?'' Thereupon the King summoned Ferdinand the Faithful, and ordered him on pain of death to bring back his beloved bride from the place where she was.

Ferdinand went into the stable to his favourite horse, and began to groan and weep. ''Oh! what an unlucky man am I!'' The Horse thereupon began to speak, and asked him what was the matter? Ferdinand was astonished to hear the horse speak, and exclaimed, ''What, Schummel, can you talk? Know, then, that I have to fetch the King's bride, and know not where to go.'' Schummel replied, ''Go you to the King, and tell him that if he will give you what you ask, you will fetch his bride; but it must be a shipful of meat and another full of bread, for there are giants across the lake where you must go, who would eat you if you brought no meat, and there are birds also who would peck out your eyes if you took no bread.''

Ferdinand went and told the King, who caused all the butchers to kill and dress meat, and all the bakers to make loaves, with which two ships were filled. As soon as these were ready, Schummel said to

Ferdinand, "Now take me with you in the ship, and set sail, and when we come to the Giants say to them,

> " 'Peace be with you, Giants dear,
> For I have brought you, never fear,
> A good supply of fleshly cheer!'

"And when the Birds come, say,

> " 'Peace be with you, Ravens dear,
> For I have brought you, never fear,
> A good supply of baker's cheer!'

"With these words they will be satisfied, and leave you, and when you come to the castle the Giants will help you; and two of them will go with you to where the Princess sleeps, whom the King wants. You must not awaken her, but the Giants must take her up in her bed, and carry her to the ship."

All this happened precisely as the Horse said, and Ferdinand the Faithful gave the Giants and the Birds what he had brought with him, and thereupon the Giants were satisfied, and brought the Princess to the King. As soon as she came, she said she must have her letters, which were left behind in the castle, and the King ordered Ferdinand the Faithful to fetch them on pain of death.

Ferdinand went again into the stable, and told his horse what duty he had to perform, and Schummel advised him to load the ships as before and sail to the castle. This he did, and the Giants and Birds were satisfied a second time; and when they arrived at the castle, Schummel told Ferdinand where the sleeping chamber of the Princess was, and he went up and fetched the packet of letters. On their way back Ferdinand unluckily dropped the letters into the water, and Schummel said, "Alas! alas! I cannot help you now!" Then Ferdinand bethought himself of his reed pipe, and began to blow it, and presently the Fish which he had formerly saved made its appearance, carrying in its mouth the letters, which it delivered to its preserver. After this they brought home the letters safely to the palace where the wedding was about to be held.

Now, the Queen did not love the King much, because he had a small nose, but she took a great fancy to Ferdinand the Faithful. And once, when all the court was assembled, the Queen said she knew some curious arts. She could cut off a person's head, and put it on again, without doing him any harm. When Ferdinand the Unfaithful heard this, he suggested that she should make the experiment on Ferdinand the Faithful. And so, after a while, she did; and after cutting off his head, put it on again, and it healed up, so that only a red mark was visible round the neck. ''Where did you learn to do that, my child?'' asked the King. ''Oh, I understand it well enough,'' she replied; ''shall I experiment on you?'' The King consented, but when she had cut off his head she would not put it on again; and after the lapse of some time she married Ferdinand the Faithful.

Now he rode again upon his horse Schummel; and one day it told him to ride thrice up the hill; and, as soon as he had done so, the horse was disenchanted and stood up a handsome Prince.

THE BRIGHT SUN BRINGS ON THE DAY.

A TAILOR's journeyman was tramping about the country in search of work, but none could he find; and his poverty became so great that he had not a farthing to spend. Just at that time he met a well-dressed man on the road, and, deaf to the voice of conscience, he went up to him, because he thought he had money, and seizing him cried out, ''Give me your money, or I will take your life!'' ''Spare my life!'' entreated the man, ''for I have no more money than eight farthings.'' But the Tailor said, ''You have money, and I will have it out;'' and he beat the poor man till he was almost dead. But before he expired, the man cried, ''The bright sun brings on the day;'' and died immediately. The Tailor, thereupon, searched the pockets of his victim, and found nothing but the eight farthings which the man had mentioned. So he took up the body and threw it away among the bushes, and then went further in search of work. After he had travelled a long distance, he came to a city, where he was engaged by a Master Tailor, who had a pretty daughter, whom he married and lived with in great happiness. When some years had passed, and the journeyman and his wife had two children, the old father and mother died, and the young people had to keep house for themselves. One morning, as the husband was sitting at the table by the window, his wife brought him his coffee; and, just as he had poured it into the saucer to drink, the bright sun shone in on it at the open window, and danced on the opposite wall in circles. Thereupon the Tailor jumped up and cried, ''It would bring on the day, but it cannot!'' ''Dear husband, what do you mean—what is it?'' asked his wife. ''That I dare not tell you,'' he replied. His wife, however teased him, and spoke so very affectionately to him, saying, she would tell nothing about it, till at last he told her that, many years ago, when he was travelling about for work, and had no money, he had killed a man, whose last words had been, ''The bright sun brings on the day.'' That morning the sun had danced on the wall, but without continuing there, and that had reminded him of the man's words, but he begged his wife to say nothing of the matter to any one. As soon, however, as he had sat down to work, his wife went to her cousin and betrayed the secret to her, making her promise to tell nobody. In three days' time, however, the cousin told some one else, and so it went on till the whole town knew it; and the Tailor was taken before the judge and condemned. Thus, the bright sun brought on the day.

THE IDLE SPINNER.

In a certain village lived a Man and his Wife, who was such a very idle woman that she would do no work at all scarcely; for what her husband gave her to spin she did very slowly, and then would not take the trouble to wind it, so that it lay on the ground ravelled and shackled. Whenever her husband scolded her she was always beforehand with an excuse, and used to say, "Why, how can I wind without a reel? you must go and fetch me one from the wood first." "Well, if that is all," said her husband one day, "if that is all, I will go and find you one." As soon as he said this, the Woman began to be afraid that if he found a piece of wood he would make a reel from it, and she would have to wind up what was ravelled and begin afresh. She therefore considered awhile what she should do, and then the lucky thought came to run into the forest secretly after her husband. She found him in the act of cutting a branch off, for the purpose of trimming it; and so, slipping in among the brushwood where he could not see her, she began to sing—

> "He that cuts a reel shall die,
> And he that winds shall perish."

The Man listened, laid down his axe, and wondered what the voice meant. At last he said, "Ah! well! what should it be? it was nothing but some fancy in my head, about which I need not fear!" So saying, he seized his axe and began again; but the voice sang as before—

> "He that cuts a reel shall die,
> And he that winds shall perish."

The Man stopped again, and began to feel very uncomfortable and frightened; but he soon took courage, and began to chop again. At the same time the voice cried again—

> "He that cuts a reel shall die,
> And he that winds shall perish."

This time he was too frightened to do anything more, and hastily leaving the tree, he set out homewards. Meanwhile his Wife, by a bypath, and by means of great exertion, reached home before him; and when he arrived she looked as innocent as if nothing had happened; and inquired of her husband if he had brought a good reel? "No, no!" he said; "I can see very well that it is of no use; winding won't do!" and then, after telling her all that had happened, he ceased to scold her for her idleness.

But only for a while, for soon the disorder in his house began to vex him again. "Wife, wife!" he said, "it is surely a shame that you leave your thread in that ravel." "Well, do you know what to do?" said she; "since we can get no reel, do you lie down on the floor, and I will stand above you, and then you must throw the thread up to me, and I will send it back to you, and so we will make a skein." "Ah! yes, that will do," said the Man; and they pursued this plan, and as soon as the skein was ready he talked of its being boiled. This aggravated the woman again, and she bethought herself of some new plot, while she consented to do as he proposed. Early in the morning, accordingly, she got up, made a fire, and putting on the kettle, put a lump of tow into it instead of the skein of thread, and left it to soak. This done, she went to her husband, who was still in bed, and said to him, "I have to go out now, but do you get up at once and see after the thread which is in the kettle over the fire; and mind you are very attentive to it, for if by chance the cock should crow before you look at it the thread will all turn to tow."

The husband thereupon got up at once, and stopped for no further directions, but, running as quick as he could into the kitchen, he looked into the kettle, and grew pale with affright; the thread was already changed into tow. After this the poor man was as still as a mouse, for he believed it was his fault that the thread was spoiled; and for the future he dared say nothing about thread and spinning.

But I must confess that after all the Woman was indeed an idle, slovenly wife.

THE THREE BLACK PRINCESSES.

OSTENDIEN was besieged by an enemy, who would not raise the siege unless he received six hundred dollars. So they made it known by the drummers that whoever could get them together should be Burgomaster. There was a poor Fisherman who fished in the sea with his Son, and the enemy came and took his Son prisoner, and gave him six hundred dollars for him. So the father went and gave them to the great men in the town; and the enemy marched off, and the Fisherman became Burgomaster. Then it was cried about that whoever did not say Mr. Burgomaster should be hanged.

The Son got out of the enemy's clutches again, and came to a great forest on a high mountain. The mountain opened, and he went into a great enchanted castle, wherein the chairs, tables, and benches were all hung with black. There came three Princesses, who were dressed all in black, and only had a little bit of white on their faces; they told him not to be afraid, they would not do anything to him, and that he could release them. He said he should be glad enough to do so if he only knew how to set about it. They said that for a whole year he must not speak to them, nor even look at them: whatever he wanted he only had to ask for, and when they might answer him they would do so. When he had been there some time, he said he should like to go and see his father. So they said, "Very well;" and that he should have this bag of gold, and put on those clothes, and must be back again in eight days.

Then he was lifted up, and was in Ostendien directly. He could not find his father any more in the fishing-hut, and asked the people where the poor Fisherman had got to? but they told him he must not say that, or he would come to the gallows. He then arrived at his father's, and said, "Fisherman, how did you come to this?" Then he answered, "You must not say that; for if the great men of the town knew it you would come to the gallows." But he would not leave off, so he was taken to the gallows; and when he got there he said, "Oh, gentlemen, pray give me leave to go to the old fishing-hut!" Then he put on his old smock, and went back to the gentlemen and said, "Do you see now; am I not the son of a poor fisherman? In this dress I earned the daily bread for my father and mother." Then they knew him again, and begged his pardon, and took him home; and he told them all about what had happened to him; that he had got into a great forest on a high mountain; that the mountain had opened, and that he had gone into an enchanted castle, where everything was black, and three Princesses had come, who were all black, except a little bit of white in the face. They had told him not to be afraid, and that he could release them.

Then his Mother said, "That cannot be right; you must take a hallowed kettle with you, and drop some scalding water into their faces."

He went back again and he shuddered from fear, and dropped some water into their faces while they were asleep, and they all turned half white. The three Princesses jumped up, and said, "Accursed dog, our blood shall cry for vengeance! now there is no one born in the world, and no one will be born, who can release us.

We have three brothers locked in seven chains, and they shall tear you to pieces." Then there was a crash through the whole castle, and he jumped out of a window and broke his leg; and the castle sank into the ground again, and the mountain closed, and nobody knew where it had been.

THE SIX SERVANTS.

A LONG time ago lived an old Queen, who was also an enchantress; and her daughter was the most beautiful creature under the sun. But the old woman was ever thinking how to entice men, in order to kill them, and every suitor, therefore, who came was compelled, before he could marry the daughter, to answer a riddle which the Queen proposed, and which was always so puzzling that it could not be solved; and the unfortunate lover was thereupon forced to kneel down and have his head struck off. Many and many a poor youth had been thus destroyed, for the maiden was very pretty; and still another King's son was found who made up his mind to brave the danger. He had heard of the great beauty of the Princess, and he prayed his father to let him go and win her. "Never!" replied the King; "if you go away, you go to die!" At this answer the son felt very ill, and so continued for seven years nigh unto death's door, for no physician could do him any good. At last, when the old King saw all hope was gone, he said to his son, "Go now and try your fortune, for I know not how else to restore you!" As soon as the Prince heard the word he jumped up from his bed, and felt new strength and vigour return to him while he made ready for his journey.

Soon he set off, and as he rode along across a common he saw at a distance something lying on the ground like a bundle of hay; but, as he approached nearer, he discovered that it was a Man who had stretched himself on the earth, and was as big as a little hill! The fellow waited till the Prince came up, and then said to him, rising as he spoke, "If you need any one take me into your service!"

"What shall I do with such an uncouth fellow as you?" asked the Prince.

"That matters not," replied the Man; "were I a thousand times as clumsy, if I can render you a service."

"Very well, perhaps I shall need you," said the Prince; "come with me." So Fatty accompanied his new master, and presently they met with another Man, who was also lying on the ground, with his ear close to the grass. "What are you doing there?" asked the Prince.

"I am listening," he replied.

"And to what are you listening so attentively?" pursued the Prince.

"I am listening to what is going on in the world around," said the Man, "for nothing escapes my hearing; I can even hear the grass growing."

"Tell me, then," said the Prince, "tell me what is passing at the court of the old Queen, who has such a beautiful daughter."

"I hear," replied the Man, "the whistling of the sword which is about to cut off the head of an unsuccessful wooer."

"Follow me, I can find a use for you," said the Prince to the Listener; and so the three now journeyed together. Presently they came to a spot where were lying two feet and part of two legs, but they could not see the continuation of them till they had walked a good stretch further, and then they came to the body, and at length to the head. "Halloa!" cried the Prince, "what a length you are!"

"Oh!" replied Long-Legs, "not so much of that! why, if I stretch my limbs out as far as I can, I am a thousand times as long, and taller than the highest mountain on the earth; but, if you will take me, I am ready to serve you."

The Prince accepted his offer, and, as they went along, they came to a man who had his eyes bandaged up. "Have you blood-shot eyes," inquired the Prince, "that you bind your eyes up in that way?"

"No!" replied the Man; "but I dare not take away the bandage, for whatever I look at splits in two, so powerful is my sight; nevertheless, if I am of use, I will accompany you."

Thereupon the Prince accepted also the services of this Man; and, as they went on, they found another fellow, who, although he was lying on the ground in the scorching heat of the sun, trembled and shivered so that not a limb in his body stood still. "What makes you freeze, when the sun shines like this?" asked the Prince.

"Alas! my nature is quite different from anything else!" replied the Man; "the hotter it is the colder I feel, and the frost penetrates all my bones; while the colder it is the hotter I feel; so that I cannot touch ice for the heat of my body, nor yet go near the fire for fear I should freeze it!"

"You are a wonderful fellow!" said the Prince; come with me, and perhaps I may need you." So the Man followed with the rest; and they came next to a Man who was stretching his neck to such a length that he could see over all the neighbouring hills. "What are you looking at so eagerly?" asked the Prince.

"I have such clear eyes," replied the Man, "that I can see over all the forests, fields, valleys, and hills; in fact, quite round the world."

"Come with me, then," said the Prince, "for I have need of a companion like you."

The Prince now pursued his way with his six servants to the city where the old Queen dwelt. When he arrived he would not tell his name, but told the Witch if she would give him her daughter, he would do all she desired. The old Enchantress was delighted to have such a handsome young man fall into her clutches, and told him she would set him three tasks, and if he performed them all, the Princess should become his wife.

"What is the first, then?" asked the Prince.

"You must fetch for me a ring which I have let fall into the Red Sea," said the Queen. Then the Prince returned home to his servants, and said to them, "The first task is no easy one; it is to fetch a ring out of the Red Sea; but let us consult together."

"I will see where it lies," said he with the clear eyes; and looking down into the water, he continued, "there it hangs on a pointed stone!"

"If I could but see it I would fetch it up," said Long-Arms. "Is that all?" said Fatty, and, lying down on the bank, he held his mouth open to the water, and the stream ran in as if into a pit, till at length the whole sea was as dry as a meadow. Long-Arms, thereupon, bent down a little, and fetched out the ring, to the great joy of the Prince, who carried it to the old Witch. She was mightily astonished, but confessed it was the right ring. "The first task you have performed, happily," she said; "but now comes the second. Do you see those three hundred oxen grazing on the meadows before my palace? all those you must consume, flesh, bones, and skins, and horns; then in my cellar are three hundred casks of wine, which must all be drunk out by you; and if you leave a single hair of any of the oxen, or one drop of the wine, you will lose your life."

"May I invite any guests to the banquet," asked the Prince, "for no dinner is worth having without?" The old woman smiled grimly, but told him he might have one guest for company, but no more.

Thereupon the Prince returned again to his servants, and told them what the task was; and then he invited Fatty to be his guest. He came, and quickly consumed the three hundred oxen, flesh and bones, skin and horns, while he made as if it were only a good breakfast. Next he drank all the wine out of every cask, without so much as using a glass, but draining them all to the very dregs. As soon as the meal was over the Prince went and told the Queen he had performed the second task. She was much astonished, and said no one had ever before got so far as that; but she determined that the Prince should not escape her, for she felt confident he would lose his head about the third task. "This evening," said she, "I will bring my daughter into your room, and you shall hold her round with one arm; but mind you do not fall asleep while you sit there, for at twelve o'clock I shall come, and if my daughter is not with you then you are lost." "This task is easy," thought the Prince to himself; "I shall certainly keep my eyes open." Still he called his servants together, and told them what the old woman had said. "Who knows," said he, "what craftiness may be behind? foresight is necessary; do you keep watch, that nobody passes out of the chamber during the night."

As soon as night came the old Queen brought the Princess to the Prince, and then Long-Arms coiled himself in a circle round the pair, and Fatty placed himself in the doorway, so that not a living soul could enter the room. So there the two sat, and the maiden spoke not a word, but the moon shone through the window upon her face, so that the Prince could see her great beauty. He did nothing but look at her, was full of happiness and love, and felt no weariness at all. This lasted till eleven o'clock, and then the old Witch threw a charm over all, so that they fell fast asleep, and at the same moment the maiden was carried off.

Till a quarter to twelve the three slept soundly, but then the charm lost its strength, and they all awoke again. "Oh, what a terrible misfortune!" cried the Prince as soon as he awoke, "I am lost!" The faithful servants also began to complain; but the Listener said, "Be quiet, and I will hear where she is!" He listened a moment, and then said, "The Princess is sitting three hundred miles from hence, inside a cave, bewailing her fate. You alone can help us, Long-Arms; if you set to the task you will be there in a couple of strides." "Certainly!" said Long-Arms; "but Sharp-Eyes must also go with us to pierce the rock." Then he hoisted Sharp-Eyes upon his back, and in a moment, while one could scarcely turn his hand round, they were before the enchanted rock. Immediately Sharp-Eyes removed his bandage, and, looking round, the rocky cave was shattered into a thousand pieces. Then Long-Arms took the Princess out of the ruins and carried her home first, and, immediately returning for his companion, they were all seated, rejoicing at their fortunate escape, before the clock struck twelve.

As soon as it did strike, the old Enchantress slipped into the room, smiling horribly, for she thought her daughter was safe enough in the rocky cave, and the Prince was hers. But when she perceived her daughter in the arms of the Prince she was terrified, and exclaimed, "Here is one that can do more than I can!" She dared not, however, deny her promise, and the maiden was therefore betrothed to the Prince. But the old Woman whispered in her daughter's ear, "Shame upon you that you listened to common folks, and dared not to choose a husband after your own wishes!"

With these words the proud heart of the Princess was inflamed, and she thought of revenge; and accordingly, the following day, she caused three hundred bundles of faggots to be heaped together, and then said to the Prince, "The three tasks were soon performed; but still I will not marry you until some one shall be found who will sit upon the fire of these faggots and endure it.'' She thought none of his servants would be burnt for their master; and so that, because out of love for her he would himself sit upon the pile, she would be freed from him. But the servants said that Frosty had done nothing as yet, though they all had, and so they placed him on the top of the pile of wood. The fire was immediately kindled, and burnt for three days, until all the wood was consumed; but, when the flames ceased, there stood Frosty in the midst of the ashes, shivering like an aspen-leaf, and declaring that he never before experienced such a frost, and must have perished if it had continued longer.

After this no further excuse could be made, and the beautiful Princess was obliged to take the unknown stranger as her husband. But just as they were going to church the old Queen declared again that she could not bear the shame, and she sent her guards after the wedding-party with orders, at all risks, to bring back her daughter. The Listener, however, had kept his ears open, and he discovered the secret designs of the old Witch. "What shall we do?" asked he of Fatty; but the latter was equal to the occasion, and, spitting behind him once or twice a drop or two of the sea-water which he had formerly drunk, there was formed a great lake, in which the Queen's guards were caught and drowned. The Queen as soon as she saw this catastrophe, despatched her mounted guards; but the Listener heard the rattlings of their trappings, and unbound the eyes of their fellow-servant, whose look, as soon as he directed it upon the approaching enemy, shivered them like glass. The bridal party now passed on undisturbed; and, as soon as the blessing had been pronounced over the new-married pair, the six servants took their leave, saying to their former master, "Your wishes are fulfilled, and you no longer require us; we will, therefore, journey on and seek our fortunes elsewhere.''

Now, about half a mile from the Queen's palace was a village before which a swineherd was tending his drove of pigs; and, as the Prince and Princess passed by it, the former said to his wife, "Do you know who I really am? I am no King's son, but a swineherd, and this man here with the drove is my father; we two must, therefore, get out and assist him!'' So saying, he dismounted with her from the carriage, and they went together into the inn; and he ordered the host to carry away secretly during the night the royal clothes belonging to his wife. Accordingly, when morning came, the poor Princess had nothing to wear; but the hostess gave her an old gown and a pair of old slippers, and of these things made a great favour, telling her that she certainly would not have lent them to her had not her husband begged for them!

The Princess now began really to believe that her husband was a swineherd, and with him she tended the drove, and thought it was a punishment for her pride and ambition. This continued for eight days, and then she could bear it no longer, for her feet were wounded all over. Just at that time two persons came to her, and asked if she knew who her husband was. "Yes, he is a swineherd," she replied, "and is just now gone to drive a little trade with a few ribands and laces."

"Come with us now, and we will take you to him," said the two strangers to the Princess; and they took her into the palace, where her husband stood arrayed in his royal robes in the great hall. She did not, however, recognize him until he fell on her neck, and said to her, "I have suffered so much for you, that it was only right that you should also suffer for me!" and with these words he kissed her lovingly. Soon afterwards their wedding was celebrated with due form, and with so much grandeur that I who tell this story would like to have been there to see!

THE FAIR CATHERINE AND PIF-PAF POLTRIE.

"Good-day, Father Hollenthe. How do you do?" "Very well, I thank you, Pif-paf Poltrie." "May I marry your daughter?" "Oh, yes! if the mother Malcho (Milk-Cow), the brother Hohenstolz (High and Mighty), the sister Kâsetraut (Cheese-maker), and the fair Catherine, are willing, it may be so."

"Where is, then, the mother Malcho?"

"In the stable, milking the cow."

"Good-day, mother Malcho. How do you do?" "Very well, I thank you, Pif-paf Poltrie." "May I marry your daughter?" "Oh, yes, if the father Hollenthe, the brother Hohenstolz, the sister Kâsetraut, and the fair Catherine, are willing, it may be so."

"Where is, then, the brother Hohenstolz?"

"In the yard, chopping up the wood."

"Good-day, brother Hohenstolz. How are you?" "Very well, I thank you, Pif-paf Poltrie." "May I marry your sister?" "Oh, yes! if the father Hollenthe, the mother Malcho, the sister Kâsetraut, and the fair Catherine, are willing, it may be so."

"Where is then, the sister Kâsetraut?"

"In the garden, cutting the cabbages."

"Good-day, sister Kâsetraut. How do you do?" "Very well, I thank you, Pif-paf Poltrie." "May I marry your sister?" "Oh, yes! if the father Hollenthe, the mother Malcho, the brother Hohenstolz, and the fair Catherine, are willing, it may be so."

"Where is, then, the fair Catherine?"

"In her chamber, counting out her pennies."

"Good-day, fair Catherine. How do you do?" "Very well, I thank you, Pif-paf Poltrie." "Will you be my bride?" Oh, yes! if the father Hollenthe, the mother Malcho, the brother Hohenstolz, and the sister Kâsetraut, are willing, so am I."

"How much money have you, fair Catherine?"

"Fourteen pennies in bare money, two and a half farthings owing to me, half a pound of dried apples, a handful of prunes, and a handful of roots; and don't you call that a capital dowry?"

"Pif-paf Poltrie, what trade are you? are you a tailor?" "Better still!" "A shoemaker?" "Better still!" "A ploughman?" "Better still!" "A joiner?" "Better still!" "A smith?" "Better still!" "A miller?" "Better still!" "Perhaps a broom-binder?" "Yes, so am I; now, is not that a pretty trade?"

GOING OUT A-TRAVELLING.

ONCE upon a time there was a poor Woman who had a Son so very fond of travelling that his mother used to say to him, "Where can you ride, when you have no money to take with you?" "I can help myself well," said the Son; "and all day long I will say, 'Not much, not much, not much!'"

So he travelled a whole day and kept saying, "Not much, not much, not much!" By-and-by he came to a Fisherman, to whom he said, "God help you, not much!" When he drew out the net there were very few fish, and taking up a stick he beat the Youth, saying, "Have you never seen me thrash?" "What shall I say, then?" asked the Youth. "A good catch, a good catch, a good catch!"

Thereupon the Youth walked a whole day long, crying, "A good catch!" till he came to a gallows, where they were about to hang up a poor Criminal. "Good morning!" said the Youth, "a good catch, a good catch!" "What do you say, fellow?" said the Criminal, "shall there not be a bad man in the world? is one not enough?" So saying he went up the ladder. "What shall I say, then?" asked the Youth. "You should say, 'God comfort a poor soul!'"

The next day accordingly the Youth walked all day long, repeating "God comfort a poor soul!" Presently he came to a grave, whereby stood a Knacker about to kill an old horse. "Good morning! God comfort the poor soul!" said the Youth. "What do you say, you silly fellow?" said the Knacker, giving the Youth a blow on the ear, so that he could scarce see out of his eyes. "What shall I say, then?" "You should say, 'There lies a carcass in its grave!'"

So all the next day the Youth went on, saying, "There lies a carcass in its grave!"' Presently he met a waggon full of people. "Good morning! there lies a carcass in its grave!" said the Youth. As he spoke the waggon fell into the grave, and the driver, jumping off, gave the Youth a cut with his whip, and drove him home to his Mother.

And all his life long afterwards he never went out a-travelling.

THE MAID OF BRAKEL.

ONCE upon a time a Girl went from Brakel to the St. Anne's chapel under the Hinne mountain; and as she would have liked to have a husband, and thought there was nobody else inside, she began to sing—

> "Oh, holy St. Anne,
> Get me a husband as soon as you can;
> You know him quite well,
> He lives at the Suttmer gate
> Has a round yellow pate,
> You know him quite well."

The Sacristan, however, was standing behind the altar, and heard it all; and he called out in a very gruff voice, "You shan't have him; you shan't have him!"

The girl thought it was the little infant standing by the mother Anne that had called out; so she flew into a passion, and cried, "Pepperlepap, little stupid! hold your noise and let the mother speak!"

KNOIST AND HIS THREE SONS.

BETWEEN Werrol and Soist there lived a man, and his name was Knoist. He had three sons: the one was blind, the other was lame, and the third was stark naked. They once went into the fields, and there they saw a hare. The blind one shot it, the lame one caught it, and the naked one put it into his pocket. Then they came to a mighty big piece of water, on which there were three ships: the one floated, the other sank, and the third had no bottom in it. The one that had no bottom they all three got into. Then they came to a mighty great forest, and there was a great mighty tree: in the tree there was a mighty great chapel, in the chapel there was a wizened old Sacristan and a savage old Priest, and they were dealing out holy water with sticks.

> "Happy is he
> Who from holy water gets free."

THE UNDUTIFUL SON.

ONCE upon a time a man and his wife were sitting before their house-door, with a roast fowl on a table between them, which they were going to eat together. Presently the man saw his old father coming, and he quickly snatched up the fowl and concealed it, because he grudged sharing it, even with his own parent. The old man came, had a draught of water, and then went away again. As soon as he was gone his son went to fetch the roast fowl again; but when he touched it he saw that it was changed into a toad which sprang upon his face and squatted there, and would not go away. When any one tried to take it off, it spat out poison and seemed about to spring in the face, so that at length nobody dared to meddle with it. Now this toad the undutiful son was compelled to feed, lest it should feed on his flesh; and with this companion he moved wearily about from place to place, and had no rest anywhere in this world.

LAZY HARRY.

HARRY was a lazy fellow, and, although he had nothing further to do than to drive his goat daily to the meadow, he sighed continually when he reached home, after his day's work, and would say: "In truth it is a weary life this, and a troublesome job, year after year, to drive a goat into the field every day till the autumn comes. It were better if one could lie down and sleep; but no! one must always be watching lest the goat should injure the young trees, or creep through the hedge into some garden, and so get away. Now how can I obtain quiet and enjoy life?" Once he sat down to collect his thoughts and consider how he should free his shoulders from their burden. For a long time nothing came of his reflections, till all at once it flashed upon him as if a scale had fallen from his eyes. ''I know what I will do,'' he cried; ''I will marry fat Kate; she also has a goat, and she can drive out mine with hers, and so save me the trouble.''

So thinking, Harry got up and set his weary legs in motion to cross over the road (for the distance was no further to the parents of fat Kate) to offer himself as a husband for their industrious and virtuous daughter. The parents did not consider long; ''Like and like agree together,'' thought they, and so consented. Thereupon fat Kate became Harry's wife, and drove out the two goats while her husband passed his time easily, troubling himself about no other labour than his own laziness! Only now and then he went out, because, as he said, he relished the quiet the better afterwards; and if he did not go out he lost all feeling for the rest.

Soon, however, fat Kate became no less lazy. ''Dear Harry,'' said she one day, ''why should we sour our lives without necessity, and harass the best part of our young days? Would it not be better if we gave our two goats, which now disturb us every morning in our best sleep, to our neighbour, and let him give us in return a bee-hive which we can place behind the house in a sunny place, and afterwards need trouble no more about it? The bees need no looking after, and have not to be driven every day into the meadow, for they will fly out and return home of themselves, and collect their honey without any interference on our part!''

''You have spoken like a wise woman,'' replied lazy Harry; ''let us pursue your plan without delay; besides honey both tastes and nourishes better than goats' milk, and can be kept much longer!''

The neighbour willingly gave a bee-hive in exchange for the two goats, and certainly the bees did fly unceasingly from early morning till late in evening in and out of their hive, and filled it too with a store of the choicest honey, so that Harry was able to take out a large jar-full in the autumn.

This jar they placed on a board which was nailed to the wall in their sleeping-room; and as they feared it might be stolen from them, or that the mice might manage to get at it, fat Kate fetched a stout hazelstick and laid it by her bed, so that she could reach it without troubling herself to get up, and drive away by these means the uninvited guests.

Lazy Harry, however, would not leave his bed till noonday; ''He who rises early wastes his possessions,'' he said. One morning when the bright daylight found him still in his bed, and he had just awakened from a long sleep, he said to his wife, ''You women like sweets, and you have been stealing some of the honey; it were better, before you eat it all out, that we barter it away with some one for a

goose.'' ''But not before we have a boy to take care of it,'' replied
the fat Kate. ''Shall I distress myself about the young goose and
waste my strength unnecessarily on their account?''

''Do you think,'' said Harry, ''that a boy will take care of them?
Now-a-days the children don't mind anybody, but act just as they
think proper, because they fancy themselves wiser than their elders;
just like that boy who instead of looking after the cow hunted three
blackbirds.''

''Oh,'' replied Kate, ''he shall catch it if he does not do what I tell
him. I will take a stick and give him no end of blows across the
shoulders. See here, Harry,'' she cried, and caught up the stick
which was laid to keep away the mice. ''See here, I will lay on him
like this.'' But unluckily, in raising the stick she hit the honey-jar,
and threw it down on the bed. The jar was shivered to atoms, and the
beautiful honey flowed all over the ground. ''There lies our goose
and goose boy,'' exclaimed Harry; ''they will not want to be tended
now. But still it is a lucky thing that the jar did not fall upon my
head, so we have good reason to be contented with our fate.'' So
saying, he looked among the broken fragments and discovered one in
which some honey was still left. ''This we will eat,'' said he to his
wife, ''and then rest a while longer after our fright, for what does it
signify if we do lie a little later than usual in bed? the day is long
enough!''

''Yes, yes,'' replied fat Kate, ''the affair has happened at a very
good time. Do you know, the snail was once invited to a wedding, but
he tarried so long on the road, that he arrived at the christening
instead. In front of the house he fell over the step, but all he said
was, Hurrying is no good.''

THE FAMILY SERVANTS.

''WHERE are you going to?'' ''To Walpe.''

''I to Walpe, you to Walpe; so, so, together we go.''

''Have you got a husband? how do you call your husband?''

''Cham.'' ''My husband Cham, your husband Cham; I to Walpe,
you to Walpe; so, so, together we go.''

''Have you got a child? how do you call your child?''

''Grild.'' ''My child Grild, your child Grild; my husband Cham,
your husband Cham: I to Walpe, you to Walpe; so, so, together we
go,''

''Have you got a cradle? how do you call your cradle?''

''Hippodadle.'' ''My cradle Hippodadle, your cradle Hippodadle my child Grild, your child Grild; my husband Cham, your husband Cham; I to Walpe, you to Walpe; so, so, together we go.''

''Have you got a man? how do you call your man?''

''Do-as-well-as-you-can.'' ''My man Do-as-well-as-you-can, your man Do-as-well-as-you-can; my cradle Hippodadle, your cradle Hippodadle; my child Grild, your child Grild; my husband Cham, your husband Cham; I to Walpe, you to Walpe; so, so, together we go.''

THE OLD GRIFFIN.

THERE was once a King, but where he reigned and how he was called I know nothing about. He had no son, only a Daughter, who was always ill, and no doctor could cure her; then it was prophesied to the King, that his Daughter would eat herself well with an apple. So he made it known all over the kingdom, whoever brought his Daughter some apples with which she should eat herself well should marry her and be King. Now, a Peasant, who had three sons, heard of it; and he said to the eldest, ''Go to the garden, take a basketful of those beautiful apples with the red cheeks, and carry them to the court. Perhaps the King's Daughter will be able to eat herself well with them: and then you can marry her and be King.'' The chap did as he was bid, and took to the road. When he had walked a little while he met quite a little Iron Man, who asked him what he had in his basket. So Hele, for that was his name, said, ''Frogs' legs!'' The little man then said, ''Well, so it shall be, and remain;'' and then went on. At last Hele came to the castle, and had it announced that he had got some apples which would cure the Princess if she ate them. At that the King was mightily pleased, and had Hele in court. Oh, dear! when he opened it, instead of apples, he had frogs' legs in the basket, and they were kicking about still. The King got into a great rage, and had him kicked out of the castle. When he got home he told his Father how he had fared. Then the Father sent his next son, whose name was Saeme, but it went just the same with him as with Hele. The little Iron Man met him very soon, and asked him what he had in the basket, and Saeme said, ''Sow thistles;'' and the little Man said, ''Well, so it shall be, and remain.'' When he arrived at the King's castle, and said he had apples with which the King's Daughter could eat herself well, they would not let him in, and told him there had already been one who had made fools of them. But Saeme insisted he had really such apples; they should only let him in. At last they believed him, and took him before the King; but when he opened the basket he had nothing but sow-thistles. That annoyed the King most dreadfully, so that he had Saeme whipped out of the castle. When he got home he told them what had happened to him. Then came the youngest boy, whom they had always called stupid Jack, and asked the Father whether he, too, might go with apples. "Yes," said the Father, "you are just the right sort of fellow; if the clever ones can't succeed, what will you be able to do?" The boy did not believe it. "Well, Father, I will go too." "Get away, you stupid chap!" said the Father; "you must wait till you grow wiser;" and then turned his back upon him; but the boy tugged at his smock-frock behind, and said, "Now Father, I will go too." "Well, just as you like; go—you will be sure to come back," he answered in a spiteful way. The boy was beyond measure delighted, and jumped for joy. "Ay, there! act like a fool! You get stupider from one day to the next," said the Father. That did not affect Jack a bit, who would not be disturbed in his joy. As night soon came on, he thought he would wait the next morning; anyhow, he would not be able to get to court that day. He could not sleep that night in bed, and when he only slumbered a little he dreamed of beautiful maidens, of castles, gold, silver, and all that sort of thing. Early next morning he went his way and soon the Little Man in his iron dress met him and asked him what he had in the basket. "Apples," he answered, "with which the King's Daughter should eat herself well." "Well," said the little Man, "such it shall be, and remain." But at court they would not let Jack in at all; for that there had been two who had said they brought apples, and one had frogs' legs, and the other sow-thistles. But Jack insisted tremendously he had no frogs' legs, but the most beautiful apples that grew in the kingdom. As he spoke so nicely the doorkeeper thought he could not be telling a lie, and let him in; and they did quite right too, for, when Jack uncovered the basket before the King, apples as yellow as gold came tumbling out. The King was delighted, and had some of them taken to his Daughter at once, and waited in anxious expectation until they should bring him word what effect they had. Not long after news was brought him; but what think you it was? It was the Daughter herself! As soon as she had eaten of those apples she had jumped out of bed quite well. What the King's delight was cannot be described.

But now the King would not give Jack his Daughter to marry, and said that he must first make him a boat that would swim better on land than in the water. Jack agreed to the condition and went home and told his adventures. So the Father sent Hele into the wood to make such a boat; he worked away diligently, and whistled the while. At midday, when the sun was at the highest, came the little Iron Man, and asked what he was making, "Wooden bowls," answered he. The little Man answered, "Well, so it shall be, and remain." In the evening Hele thought he had made the boat; but, when he was going to get into it, it turned to wooden bowls. The next day Saeme went into the wood; but he met with exactly the same fate as his brother. On the third day stupid Jack went: he worked very hard, so that the wood resounded all through with his heavy blows, and he sang and whistled besides right merrily. The little man came to him at midday when it was the hottest, and asked him what he was making. "A boat that will swim better on dry land than in the water," he answered, and that when he had done it he should marry the King's Daughter. "Well," said the little Man, "such an one it shall be, and remain." In the evening, when the sun was setting like a ball of gold, Jack made ready his boat and all things belonging to it, and rowed towards the castle; but the boat went as fast as the wind. The King saw it a long way off; but would not give Jack his Daughter yet, and said he must first take a hundred hares out grazing from early morning to late in the evening, and if one were missing he should not have his Daughter. Jack was quite contented, and the next day went out with his herd to the meadow, and kept a sharp look-out that none should stray away. Not many hours had passed when a Maid came from the castle, and said Jack was to give her a hare directly, as some visitors had arrived. But Jack saw through that well enough, and said he would not give her one; the King might treat his visitors to hare-pepper. But the Maid did not believe him, and at last set to scolding. So Jack said that if the King's Daughter came herself he would give her a hare. The Maid told them in the castle, and the King's Daughter did go herself. But in the meantime the little Man had come again to Jack and asked him what he was doing there. Oh, he had got to watch a hundred hares so that none ran away, and then he might marry the King's Daughter, and be King. "Good!" said the little Man, "there's a whistle for you, and when one runs away only just whistle and he will come back again." When the King's Daughter came, Jack gave her a hare into her apron. But when she had got about a hundred steps off, Jack whistled, and the hare jumped out of the cloth, and jump, jump! was back to the herd directly. In the evening the hare-herd whistled again, and looked to see they were all right, and drove them to the castle. The King wondered how Jack had been able to take care of a hundred hares, so that none should run off: but he would not yet give him his Daughter so easily, but said he must first get him a feather from the Old Griffin's tail.

Jack started at once, and marched right briskly on. In the evening he arrived at a castle, where he asked for a night's lodging, for at that time there were no such things as hotels; and the master of the castle greeted him very civilly, and asked him where he was going to. Jack answered, "To the Old Griffin." "Oh, indeed! to the Old Griffin; they say he knows everything, and I have lost the key to an iron money-chest; perhaps you would be good enough to ask him where it is!'' ''Certainly,'' said Jack, ''that I will.'' Early the next morning he started off again on his road, and arrived at another castle, where he again passed the night. When the people learned that he was going to the Old Griffin, they said a daughter was ill in the house; they had already tried every possible remedy, but without effect; would he be kind enough to ask Old Griffin what would cure her? Jack said he would do it with pleasure, and went on again. He arrived at a lake; and, instead of a ferry-boat, there was a big man who had to carry everybody over. The man asked him where he was bound for? ''To the Old Griffin,'' said Jack. ''When you get to him,'' said the Man, ''just ask him why I am obliged to carry everybody over the water.'' ''Yes, to be sure,'' said Jack; ''goodness gracious! yes, willingly!'' The Man then took him up on his shoulder, and carried him over. At last Jack arrived at the Old Griffin's house, and only found the wife at home, not Old Griffin. The woman asked him what he wanted, so he told her he must have a feather from Old Griffin's tail; and that in a castle they had lost the key to the money-chest, and he was to ask the Griffin where it was; and then, in another castle, the daughter was ill, and he was to know what would make her well again; then not far from there was the water, and the man who was obliged to carry everybody over, and he should very much like to know why the man was obliged to carry everybody over. ''But,'' said the Woman, ''look you, my good friend, no Christian can speak with a Griffin; he eats them all up; but, if you like, you can lie there under his bed, and at night, when he is fast asleep, you can reach out and pull a feather out of his tail; and as to those things that you want to know, I will ask him myself.'' Jack was quite satisfied with the arrangement, and got under the bed. In the evening Old Griffin came home, and when he stepped into the room he said, ''Wife, I smell a Christian!'' ''Yes,'' said the Wife, ''there has been one here to-day, but he went away again.'' So Old Griffin said no more. In the middle of the night, when Griffin was snoring away lustily, Jack reached up and pulled a feather out of his tail.

The Griffin jumped up suddenly, and cried, ''Wife, I smell a Christian! and it was just as if someone had been plucking at my tail.'' The Wife said, ''You have no doubt been dreaming. I have told you already that one has been here to-day, but that he went away again. He told me all sorts of things: that in one castle they had lost the key of the money-chest, and could not find it.'' ''Oh the fools!'' exclaimed the Griffin; ''the key lies in the wood-shed, behind the door, under a log of wood.'' ''And, further, he said that in another castle the daughter was ill, and they knew no means to cure her.'' ''Oh, the fools!'' said the Griffin, ''under the cellar stairs a toad has made its nest of her hair, and if she got the hair back again she would be well.'' ''And then, again, he said, at a certain place there was a lake, and a man who was obliged to carry everybody over." "Oh, the fool!" said the Old Griffin, "if he were only to put somebody into the middle he need not carry any more over."

Early next morning the Old Griffin got up and went out, and Jack crept from under the bed with a beautiful feather, having heard what the Griffin had said about the key, the daughter, and the man. The Wife repeated it all to him so that he should not forget, and then he started off towards home. He came to the man at the water first, and he asked him directly what the Griffin had said; but Jack said he must carry him over first, and then he would tell him. So he carried him over; and when they got there Jack told him he had only to put somebody into the middle and then he need carry no more. The man was delighted beyond measure, and told Jack that out of gratitude he should like to carry him over and back once more. But Jack said nay, he would save him the trouble; he was quite contented with him already, and then went on. Then he arrived at the castle where the daughter was ill; he took her on his shoulder, for she was not able to walk, and carried her down the cellar stairs, and then took the toad's nest from under the bottom step, and put it into the daughter's hand, and all at once she jumped off his shoulder, up the stairs before him, strong and well. Now the father and mother were delighted indeed, and made Jack presents of gold and silver, and whatever he wanted, they gave him. When Jack arrived at the other castle he went straight to the wood-shed, and found the key right enough behind the door, under the log of wood, and took it to the master. He was not a little pleased, and gave Jack in return a great deal of gold that was in the box, and all sorts of things besides, such as cows, and sheep, and goats. When Jack returned to the King with all these things, with the money, and gold, and silver, and the cows, sheep, and goats, the King asked him where ever he had come by it all. So Jack said the Old Griffin would give one as much as one liked. The King thought he could find a use for that sort of thing himself, and so started off to the Griffin; but when he got to the water he happened to be the first who arrived there since Jack, and the man put him in the middle and walked off, and the King was drowned.

So Jack married the King's Daughter and became King.

THE OLD BEGGAR WOMAN.

ONCE upon a time there was an old Woman, who begged as you may have seen other old women do; and when anybody gave her anything she would say, "God bless you!" Now this old Beggar

Woman went to a door, and before the fire stood a good-natured lad warming himself; and, as soon as he saw the poor Woman shivering outside, he said to her, "Come and warm yourself." She went in; but going too near the fire, her old rags began to burn before she was aware of it. The youth stood and looked at her; but should he not have extinguished the fire? Certainly; and if he had no water at hand, he should have caused water to flow out of his eyes; and so two charming little streams would have been given!

THE THREE SLUGGARDS.

A CERTAIN King had three Sons, all of whom he loved so much that he did not know which he should name to be King after him. When the day of his death approached, he called them to his bedside, and thus spoke to them: "Dear children, I have something on my mind which I wish to tell you; whichever of you is the laziest, he shall be King when I am dead."

"Then, father, the kingdom belongs to me," said the eldest Son, "for I am so lazy, that if I lie down to sleep, and tears come into my eyes, so that I cannot close them, I yet go to sleep without wiping them away!"

"The Kingdom belongs to me," cried the second Son; "for I am so lazy that when I sit by the fire to warm myself, I allow my boots to scorch before I will draw away my feet."

But the third Son said, "The Kingdom is mine, father, for I am so lazy that were I about to be hanged, and even had I the rope round my neck, and any one should give me a sharp sword to cut it with, I should suffer myself to be swung off before I took the trouble to cut the rope."

As soon as the Father heard this he said to his youngest Son, "You have shown yourself the laziest of all, and you shall be King."

THE HEN-ROOST.

ONCE upon a time there was an Enchanter who collected around him a great crowd of folks, before whom he performed his wonderful tricks. Among other things he caused an old hen to be brought in, which raised a heavy beam for a roosting-place, as though it were as light as a feather. But there was a Girl standing by who had found a four-bladed leaf of shamrock, through which she became so wise that no trick could deceive her, and she saw the pretended beam was nothing but a straw. So she cried out, "Do you not see, you people, that it is no beam, but a straw which the hen is carrying?" Thereupon the enchantment vanished, and the gazers perceiving the truth, hunted the Enchanter away with scorn and ridicule.

Some time afterwards the Girl was to be married, and in a very smart dress she walked in great state over the fields which led to the church. All at once she came to a large swollen stream, over which there was no bridge or plank to cross by. Thereupon the Bride was in distress, but, holding her dress up, she tried to wade through the water. But just as she came about the middle of it a voice, which was that of the Enchanter, cried derisively, "Ah! where are your eyes, that you take this place for water?" At these words her eyes were opened, and she perceived that she stood holding up her dress in the middle of a field of corn-flowers. Then she, in her turn, got laughed at by the spectators; so the Enchanter turned the tables upon her.

LOVE AND SORROW TO SHARE.

ONCE upon a time there was a Tailor so quarrelsome that his poor Wife could never get on with him, although she was both affectionate, pious, and industrious. He was discontented with whatever she did; and would not only mutter and scold, but even knock her about, and beat her. At last the Magistrate was told of his conduct, and the Tailor was summoned and put into prison till he should behave better. For a long time he was kept on bread and water, and at length released, after being admonished to beat his Wife no more, but to live with her in concord, and to share affection and sorrow, as it was fit that married people should do.

For some time all went on well; but soon the Tailor fell into his old habits, and grew more and more discontented and quarrelsome. However, because he dared not beat his Wife, he would pull her hair instead; and one day she escaped from him and rushed out-of-doors. The Tailor pursued her with his yard-measure and shears in his hands, and as he did not gain on her steps he threw the measure and shears at her. The poor woman ran round their court, while her husband continued to throw the shears at her; and if he missed his aim he abused her, and if he hit her he laughed. He kept up this sport so long that the neighbours came to the assistance of his Wife, and he was taken again before the Magistrate and reminded of his promise. "My dear lord," replied the Tailor, "I have kept to what I promised; I have not beaten my Wife, but shared with her affection and sorrow.''

"How can that be?" asked the Judge; "when she has now come a second time with these loud complaints of your conduct!"

"I have not beaten my Wife," reiterated the Tailor; "but all I did was to try and comb out her hair, because she looked so wild. But she ran away from me, and would not hear what I said; so then I pursued her, and in order to remind her of her duty, I threw at her what I chanced to have in my hand; I have also shared with her my love and my sorrow, for as often as I hit her she was made sorry and I was glad; and when I missed her she was glad and I was sorry!"

The Judge, however, was not satisfied with this answer, but sentenced him to a well-earned punishment!

LEAN BETTY.

VERY different from lazy Harry and fat Kate,—who never troubled themselves to disturb their ease,—was lean Betty. She busied herself from morning till night, and gave her husband, tall John, so much to do, that he was as heavily burdened as an ass which carries three sacks. But all was in vain; they had nothing, and they gained nothing, and one night when they went to bed, and could not move their limbs from weariness, they could not sleep for the thoughts that oppressed them. Lean Betty poked her husband in his side, and said to him, "Listen to me, long John! hear what I have thought. Suppose I should find a florin, and some one should give me a second, and then if I borrowed a third, and you gave me a fourth, with these four florins I would buy a young cow."

The husband was pleased with this plan; but he said, "I certainly do not know where I shall get the florin which I am to give you; but, however, supposing you get the money, and can buy a cow with it, you will do well if you follow out your plan. It pleases me to think," he continued, "that if the cow should produce a calf, I could then refresh myself often with a draught of milk!"

"The milk is not for you," returned the wife; "we must let the calf suck, that it may grow big and fat, and then we can sell it for a good price."

"Oh, certainly!" replied the husband; "but still we will take a little milk, for that can make no difference."

"Who ever taught you anything about cows?" said the wife angrily; "it may or may not do harm, but I will not have it done: and, although you may take all the pains you like, you shall not have a drop of milk. Do you think, you lanky John, that because you cannot satisfy yourself, you are going to make away with what it has cost me so much trouble to earn!''

"Hold your tongue, woman!'' exclaimed the husband, ''or I'll give you a box on the ear.''

"What!'' exclaimed she in return; ''what, you will strike me, you whipper-snapper! you sneak! you lazy fellow!'' And, so saying, she tried to catch hold of his hair; but long John, raising himself up, pinioned the thin arms of Betty to her side with one hand, and with the other he kept her head on the pillow, and let her abuse him as she liked, till she fell asleep tired out.

But whether when they awoke they quarrelled again, or went out to look for florins, or found them, I know nothing about!

THE BRIDE-CHOOSING.

THERE was once a young Shepherd who wished to get married; but although he knew three Sisters, each one was as pretty as the others, and the choice was therefore so difficult, that he did not know to which to give the preference. So he asked his Mother's advice; and she told him to invite all three of them to supper, and to place a cheese before them and observe how they cut it. The youth did so; and the first Sister ate her cheese, rind and all; the second cut off the rind so hastily, that she cut with it some of the good cheese and threw it all away; but the third Sister pared the rind off very carefully, neither too much nor too little. The Shepherd thereupon told all this to his Mother, and she said, ''Take the youngest Sister to wife.''

And he did so, and lived contentedly and happily with her all his life long.

THE STOLEN FARTHINGS.

ONCE upon a time a Father sat at table with his wife and children, and with them was a good Friend who had come on a visit. While they sat eating, it struck twelve, and then the Friend saw the door open, and a Child, pale as death, dressed in snow-white garments, come in. It did not look round or speak, but went straight into the next room. Soon it returned and went as silently out at the door again. The second and the third day it happened the same, and then the Friend asked the Father to whom the Child belonged which entered the house every day at noontime. ''I have not seen it, nor do I know to whom it belongs,'' said the Father. So on the following day when the Child came the Friend pointed it out to the Father, but he could not see it, nor the Mother either, nor her children. Then the Friend got up, and, going to the chamber door, opened it a little and peeped in. There he saw the Child sitting on the ground, digging and picking industriously between the crevices of the boards; but as soon as it perceived the stranger it disappeared. The Friend now told the Father what he had seen, and described the child exactly, whereupon the Mother recognised his description, and said, ''Ah! that is my dear Child who died four weeks ago.'' Then they broke up the boards of the room and found beneath them two Farthings which the Child had once received from his Mother to give to a poor man, but he had thought to himself, ''One can buy biscuits with these,'' and so he had kept the Farthings and dropped them between the boards. And on that account he had no rest in his grave, and every mid-day he was compelled to come and seek for the Farthings.

So the parents gave the Farthings to a poor man, and the Child was never once seen again.

THE SOLE.

THE Fishes once grew very discontented because no order was kept in their dominions. None turned aside for the others, but each swam right or left just as it pleased him, sometimes between those who wished to be together, or else pushed them to one side, and the stronger ones gave the weaker blows with their tails, which made them get out of the way as fast as they could, or else devoured them. ''How nice it would be,'' thought the Fishes, ''if we had a king who should exercise the power of judging between us!'' And so at last they assembled together to choose a lord, who should be he who could swim the quickest and render help best to the weaker fishes.

So they laid themselves all in rank and file by the shore, and the Pike gave a signal with his tail, on which they started off. Like an arrow darted away the Pike, closely followed by the Herring, the Gudgeon, the Perch, and the Carp, and the rest. Even the Sole swam among them, hoping to gain the prize.

All at once a cry was heard, ''The Herring is first, the Herring is first!'' ''Who is first?'' asked the flat envious Sole in a vexed tone, ''Who is first?''

Er liebt mich

THE BRIDE-CHOOSING

"The Herring, the Herring!" was the reply.

"The nak-ed Herring, the nak-ed Herring!" said the Sole disdainfully. And since that time the Sole's mouth has become all on one side for a punishment.

THE DURATION OF LIFE.

WHEN the world was first created, it was appointed how many years each creature should exist. So the Ass came and inquired how long he was to live. "Thirty years," he was told, and then he was asked, "Is that sufficient?" "Alas!" replied the Ass, "that is a long time. Think how many wearisome burdens I shall have to carry from morning till night; cornsacks to the mill, that others may eat bread, and I receive nothing but blows and kicks, and yet keep always active and obliging! Take away some of my years, I pray!"

So the Ass was pitied, and a life of only eighteen years appointed to him; whereupon he went gladly away, and the Dog then made his appearance, and asked the same. "How long do you wish to live?" was inquired of him; "Thirty years were too much for the Ass; but perhaps you will be satisfied." "Do you think so?" said the Dog; "remember how much I shall have to run; my feet will not last out; and then when I have lost my voice and cannot bark, and my teeth and cannot bite, what will there be for me to do but to crawl and howl from one corner to another?"

So the Dog's plea was allowed, and twelve years appointed for his age, after which he departed and made room for the Monkey. "You will live thirty years willingly, no doubt," was said to the Monkey; "you need not work like the Ass and the Dog, and therefore will always be well off."

"Alas! it should be so," said the Monkey; "but really it is very different. I must always be making comical faces for people to laugh at; and all the apples they give me to eat turn out sour ones. How often is sadness hidden by a joke! But thirty years I can never endure!"

Thereupon ten years were allowed to him.

Last of all, Man appeared, healthy and vigorous, and requested a time to be appointed to him. "You shall live thirty years," was the reply; "is that enough?" "What a short time!" exclaimed Man; "just when I shall have built myself a house, and lighted a fire upon my own hearth, and just when I shall have planted trees to bear me fruit in their season, and I am thinking of enjoying life, I must die! I pray let my life be lengthened!"

THE DURATION OF LIFE

''The eighteen years of the Ass shall be added.''

''That is not enough!'' said Man.

''You shall have also twelve years of the Dog's life.''

''Still too little!'' replied Man.

''Well, then, you may have the ten years allowed to the Monkey but you must desire no more.''

Man was then obliged to leave, but he was not satisfied.

Thus Man lives seventy years. The first thirty are the days of his manhood, which pass quickly away; he is then healthy and vigorous, works with pleasure, and rejoices in his being. Then follow the eighteen years of the life of the Ass, which bring to him one burden after another; he must work for corn which nourishes others, and abuse and blame become the reward of his labours. Next come the twelve years of the Dog, during which Man has to sit in corners, grumbling because he has no longer any teeth to bite with. And when this time is up, then the ten years of the Monkey bring the close of the scene. Then Man becomes childish and foolish, and does strange things, which make him ridiculous in the eyes of children!

THE BITTERN AND THE HOOPOE.

''WHERE do you find the best pasture for your flocks?'' asked a Master of an old Cowherd.

''Here, Master, where the grass is neither too thick nor too scanty; else it is no use!''

''Why not?'' asked the Master.

''Do you hear that moaning cry out on the meadow?'' asked the cowherd; ''that is the Bittern, who was once a herdsman and the Hoopoe also. I will tell you the tale:—

''The Bittern once kept his flocks on a flourishing green meadow, where flowers grew in great abundance, so that the cows became fat and mettlesome. But the Hoopoe drove his cattle to a high and barren hill, where the wind twisted the sand about, and his cows therefore grew thin and gained no strength. When evening came, and the flocks had to be driven home, the Bittern could not collect his cows, because they were so well fed, and they ran away from him. He called to them, 'Come here, pretty cows!' but in vain, they paid no attention to his words. The Hoopoe, on the contrary, could not get his cows upon their legs, they were become so weary and strengthless. 'Up, up! get up!' he cried; but it was no use, they remained lying on the sand. And so it always happens when one forgets moderation. And to this day, although they no longer keep flocks, the Bittern cries daily, 'Bunt herüm, (here, pretty cow,) and the Hoopoe, 'Up! up! up!'"

MISFORTUNE.

WHEN misfortune pursues any one, it will find him out into whatever corner he may creep, or however far he may flee over the world.

Now, once upon a time, a certain man became so poor, that he had not a single faggot of wood left wherewith to light his fire. So, he went into the forest to fell a tree, but they were all too large and too strong; and he penetrated deeper among them till he found one which he thought would do. Just as he was about to raise his axe he perceived a pack of wolves, coming out of the brushwood, who howled dreadfully as they came nearer. The man threw away his axe, and ran till he came to a bridge. The deep water, however, had rotted the bridge; and so, just as he was about to run over it, it cracked and fell into the water. What was he to do now? If he stopped still, the wolves would overtake him and tear him to pieces; so, in his perplexity, he jumped into the water, but there, because he could not swim, he soon began to sink. By chance a couple of fishermen, who sat on the other bank, saw him; and one of them swam after him and brought him to shore. Then they laid him down beneath an old wall, to dry in the sunshine and regain his strength a bit. But, just as he recovered his senses, and tried to thank the fishermen for their help and to tell his tale, the wall fell upon him and crushed him!

THE OWL.

A COUPLE of hundred years ago, when people were not so wise and crafty as they are now-a-days, a curious circumstance occurred in a certain small town. By chance, one of the large Owls, which folks call Screech-Owls, came from a neighbouring forest, and took up its dwelling in a shed belonging to a citizen of the town, from whence it dared not come out except at night, for fear the other birds should raise a great outcry against it for disturbing their peace. One morning when the Stable-boy went into the shed to fetch some straw, he was frightened so dreadfully on perceiving the Owl, that he ran away, and told his Master that a horrible monster, such as he had never before seen in his lifetime, was sitting in one corner of the shed, and rolled its eyes round as if it would devour everything it could see. "I know you of old," replied his Master; "you have courage enough to chase a blackbird over the fields, but if you see a dead hen lying about, you want a stick laid on you before you will approach it. I must now go myself and see what sort of monster this is."

So saying, the Master set off and walked as bold as possible into the shed and peeped round. But as soon as he saw the curious and hideous creature with his own eyes he went into as great a panic as his servant. He made his escape with a couple of leaps and ran to his neighbours, whom he begged with tears in his eyes to come and assist him against an unknown and dangerous animal, or perhaps the whole town might be endangered if it should make its escape from the shed where it was concealed. Immediately there arose a great outcry and noise in the streets of the town, and the townsmen came armed with spikes, rakes, spades, and hatchets, as if they were going to attack an enemy. At last appeared the Mayor himself at the head of his councillors, and when they were all arranged in the market-place, they made their way to the shed and surrounded it on all sides. Then one of the bravest of the assemblage stepped before the others and entered the shed armed with a pole; but he came out again directly with a shriek, and looking as pale as death he ran off without saying a word. Two others next made the attempt, but they met with no better success; but at last a tall and very strong man, renowned for his deeds of valour, stepped forward and said, "With bare looking at the monster you will never drive him away; some determination must be used; but I see you are all playing the part of old women, and none of you will beard the enemy." So saying, he caused his body armour, his sword, and spear to be brought, and, equipping himself with these, prepared for the attack, while all the others praised his courage, although many of them feared for his life. The two doors of the shed were thrown open, and the warrior perceived the Owl perched in the middle of a large beam which ran across. He caused a ladder to be brought, and when it was fixed ready for him to mount, all called out to him to behave bravely, and reminded him of St. George and the Dragon. He mounted the ladder, and as the Owl saw what his intentions were, and became frightened also by the cries of the people outside, who prevented its exit, it rolled its eyes, ruffled its feathers, snapped its beak, and screeched loudly. "Rush on it! rush on it!" exclaimed the crowd to the valiant Soldier. "If you stood where I do," he said, "you would not be so ready to shout." Then he mounted a stave higher on the ladder; but there he began to tremble, and at length he beat a retreat half fainting!

And now there was no one left who would venture to face the danger. "The monster," said the crowd, "has all but poisoned and wounded to death with his snapping and breathing, our strongest man, and shall we also venture our lives?" Thereupon, they consulted with one another what they should do to prevent ruin from involving the whole town. For a long time nothing satisfactory was proposed, till at last the Mayor hit upon a plan. "My idea is this," he said, "that out of the common purse we purchase and make good to the owner this stable with all it contains, straw, hay, and corn, and then that the whole building, together with the fearful monster therein, be burnt to ashes, and so no one shall lose his life by this occurrence. There is no time to spare, and parsimony in this case would be badly exercised."

All the rest agreed to this proposal, and so the stable was set light to at the four corners, and the poor Owl miserably burnt to death!

THE NAIL.

A TRADESMAN had once transacted a good day's business at a fair, disposed of all his goods, and filled his purse with gold and silver. He prepared afterwards to return, in order to reach home by the evening. So he strapped his portmanteau, with the money in it, upon his horse's back, and rode off. At noon he baited in a small town, and as he was about to set out again, the Stable-boy who brought his horse said to him, "Sir, a nail is wanting in the shoe on the left hind-foot of your animal."

"Let it be wanting," replied the Tradesman; "I am in a hurry and the iron will doubtless hold the six hours I have yet to travel."

Late in the afternoon he had to dismount again, and feed his horse and at this place also the Boy came and told him that a nail was wanting in one of the shoes, and asked him whether he should take the horse to a farrier. "No, no, let it be!" replied the Master; "it will last out the couple of hours that I have now to travel; I am in haste." So saying he rode off; but his horse soon began to limp, and from limping it came to stumbling, and presently the beast fell down and broke its leg. Thereupon the Tradesman had to leave his horse lying on the road to unbuckle the portmanteau, and to walk home with it upon his shoulder, where he arrived at last late at night.

"And all this misfortune," said he to himself, is owing to the want of a nail. More haste the less speed!"

DEATH'S MESSENGERS.

IN olden times a Giant was once wandering up and down a road, when suddenly an unknown man appeared in his path, and cried, "Stop! not a step further." "What, you stripling!" said the Giant, "why, I could crush you between my fingers; will you stand in my way? Who are you who speak so boldly?"

"I am Death," replied the stranger, "whom nobody opposes, and whose commands you must obey."

The Giant, however, refused, and began to wrestle with Death. It was a long and hasty battle, but at length the Giant got the best of it, and knocked Death down with his fist, so that he dropped like a stone. The Giant, thereupon, went his way, leaving Death vanquished and strengthless, so that he could not rise again. "What will be the consequence?" thought Death; "if I lie here in this corner nobody will die in the world, and it will soon get so full of human beings, that they will not be able to stir for one another." Just then, a Young Man came up the road, strong and healthy, singing a song, and looking well about him. As soon as he perceived the helpless beaten one, he went up to him, and compassionately raising him poured a draught of cordial out of his flask down his throat, and waited till strength returned. "Do you know," asked Death, when he had recovered a bit, "do you know who I am, whom you have thus helped on his legs again?"

"No," replied the Youth, "I know you not." "I am Death," he replied; "I spare no one, and can take no excuse from you even. But, to show you that I am not ungrateful, I promise not to take you unawares; but I will send my messengers before I come and fetch you."

"Very well," said the Young Man, "that is a bargain, that I shall know when you are coming, and so long shall be safe from your visit."

With this understanding he pursued his way merrily, and lived in prosperity for some time. But youth and health will not remain for ever; soon came sickness and troubles to the Young Man, so that he complained by day and could get no rest at night. "I shall not die," he said to himself, "for Death must first send his messengers; but I wish these terrible days of illness were over!"

By-and-by he did get well again, and began to live as usual. One day somebody knocked at the window, and looking round he saw Death standing behind him, who said, "Follow me, the hour is come for your departure from the world."

"How so?" exclaimed the Man; "will you break the promise that you made to me to send your messengers before you came yourself? I have seen none.''

''Be silent,'' replied Death; ''have I not sent you one messenger after another?—did not fever come and seize you, shake you, and lay you prostrate?—did not a giddiness oppress your head?—had you not gout in all your limbs?—did not a singing noise injure your ears?—had not you lumbago in your back?—a film over your eyes?—Above all, did not my dear half-brother, Sleep, remind you of me every night when you laid down, as if you were already dead!''

The Man knew not what to reply to all this, and surrendering himself therefore to his fate he followed Death.

MASTER COBBLERSAWL.

MASTER COBBLERSAWL was a small, meagre, but very active man, who had no rest in him. His face, whose only prominent feature was a turned-up nose, was seamed and deadly pale; his hair was grey and rough; his eyes small, but they peered right and left in a piercing way. He observed everything, found fault with everything, knew everything better, and did it better, than any one else, in his own estimation. When he walked in the streets he swung his two arms about in such a hasty fashion, that once he knocked the pail which a girl was carrying so high into the air that the water fell all over him. ''Sheep's-head!'' he exclaimed, shaking himself, ''could you not see that I was following you?'' By trade he was a shoemaker; and when he was at work, he pulled his thread out so hastily, that nobody went near him for fear of his elbows poking into their sides. No comrade remained with him longer than a month, for he had always something to remark upon in the best work. Either the stitches were not even, or one shoe was longer than the other, or one heel higher than the other, or the leather was not drawn sufficiently tight. ''Wait,'' he would say to a young hand, ''wait, and I will show you how one can whiten the skin!'' and so saying he would fetch a strap and lay it across the shoulders of his victim. He called everybody idle and lazy; but still he did not do much for himself, because he could not sit quiet two quarters of an hour together. If his wife got up early in the morning and lighted a fire, he would jump out of bed and run barefoot into the kitchen, crying out, ''Do you want to burn the house down? there is a fire fit for any one to roast an ox at! Wood costs money.''

If the maid, while standing at the washtub, laughed and repeated to herself what she had heard, he would scold her and say, ''There

stands a goose, chattering and forgetting her work with her gossip.''
''Of what use is that fresh soap? shameful waste and a disgraceful
dirtiness, for she wants to spare her hands by not properly rubbing
out the stains!'' So saying, he would jump up and throw down a
whole pailful of water, so as to set the kitchen a-swimming!

Once they were building a new house near him, and he ran to his
window to look on. ''There! they are using that red sandstone again
which never dries,'' he said; ''nobody in that house will be healthy.
And see how quickly the fellows are laying on the stones. The mortar
too is not properly mixed; gravel should be put in, not sand. I expect
the house will fall some day on the heads of the owners.'' So saying,
he sat down again, and did another stitch or so; but soon he sprang
up, and throwing away his apron, ''I will go and speak to those men
myself.'' The carpenters were at work just then. ''How is this?'' he
asked; ''you are not cutting by line. Do you think the beams will lay
straight? no, they will come all away from the joists.'' Then he
snatched an axe out of the hand of one of the carpenters to show him
how he should cut; and just then a waggon laden with clay chanced
to be going past, so Master Cobblersawl threw away the axe, and
cried to the peasant who was with it, ''How inhuman you are! who
would harness young horses to a heavily laden waggon? the poor
beasts will fall down presently.''

The peasant, however, gave him no answer, and so he went back to
his workshop in a passion. Just as he was about to commence again
the job which he had left, his apprentice handed him a shoe. ''What
is this, again?'' exclaimed Master Cobblersawl; ''have I not told
you often and often not to stitch your shoes so wide. Who will buy a
shoe like this with scarce any sole at all to it? I desire that you will
follow my commands to the letter.''

''Yes, master,'' replied the apprentice, ''you may be in the right
to say that the shoe is worth nothing, but it is the very same that you
sewed, and were just now at work upon; for when you ran out you
threw it under the table, and I picked it up. But an angel from
heaven would not convince you that you were wrong.''

A night or two afterwards Master Cobblersawl dreamed that he
was dead and on the way to heaven. When he arrived there and
knocked at the door, the Apostle Peter opened it to see who desired
to enter. ''Ah, is it you, Master Cobblersawl?'' said the Saint, ''I
will let you in, certainly; but I warn you not to interfere with what
you may observe in heaven, or it will be the worse for you.''

''You might have spared yourself the trouble of saying that,''
replied Cobblersawl; ''I know very well how to behave myself; and
here, thank God, there is nothing to blame, as there is on earth.'' So
saying, he stepped in and walked up and down over the wide
expanse of heaven, looking about him right and left, and now and
then shaking his head or muttering to himself. Presently he

perceived two angels carrying a beam, the same which a certain one once had in his own eye when he perceived the mote in his brother's eye. But they were carrying the beam not longways but crossways, and this caused Master Cobblersawl to say to himself, "Did ever anybody see such stupidity?" Still he held his tongue, thinking that after all it was no matter whether the beam were carried straight or not, provided it did not interfere with anybody. Soon afterwards he saw two angels pouring water out of a spring into a tub which was full of holes, so that the water escaped on all sides. They were watering the earth with rain. "Alle Hagel!" exclaimed he suddenly; but recollecting himself, he kept his opinions to himself, and thought, "Perhaps it is mere pastime, and intended for a joke, so that one may do idle things here in heaven as well as upon earth." So he went onwards and saw a waggon stuck fast in a deep rut. "No wonder," said he to the person in charge; "who would have filled it so extravagantly? what have you there?"

"Pious wishes," replied the man; "I could not get with them into the straight road; but fortunately I was able to push along as far as here, and they will not let me stick fast now."

Just then an angel did really come and harnessed horses to the waggon. "Quite right," thought Cobblersawl; "but two horses are not enough to pull the waggon out: there must be four horses at the least." Presently came a second angel, leading two more horses, but he did not harness them before, but behind. Now this was too much for Master Cobblersawl. "Tollpatsch!" he exclaimed aloud, "what are you about? Did anybody ever as long as the world has stood pull a waggon in that way up this road? You think you know better than I in your conceited pride!" and he would have said more, but one of the inhabitants of heaven caught him by the neck and shoved him out of the place with a stern push. Just outside the gate Master Cobblersawl turned his head round, and saw the waggon raised up by four winged horses.

At the same moment he awoke. "Things are certainly somewhat different in heaven to what they are on earth," he said to himself, "and much may therefore be excused; but who could patiently see two horses harnessed behind a waggon and two before? Certainly they had wings, but I did not observe that at first. However, it is a great absurdity that a horse with four good legs must have wings too! But I must get up, or else they will make further mistakes about that house. Still, after all, it is a very lucky thing that I am not dead!"

THE TALE OF SCHLAURAFFENLAND.

I WAS once in Schlauraffenland, which some folks call "Fools' Paradise," and there saw I Rome and the Lateran hanging by a silken thread, a footless man who outran a quick horse, and a sword sharp as a razor which formed a bridge. There I saw, too, a young ass with a silver nose, which was coursing two hares, and a lime tree full of foliage, whereon grew hot pancakes. There, too, I saw a clumsy old goat, which carried on its back a hundred cartloads of grease and sixty cartloads of salt. Is not that enough?

There, also, I saw a plough going without a horse or wheels, and a one-year-old child threw four mill-stones from Ratisbon to Treves, and from Treves away to Strasburg, and a hawk swam over the Rhine without difficulty! There, too, I heard fishes caught with one another's cries, and sweet honey flowed like water out of a deep valley up a high mountain!

There were also two crows which mowed a meadow, and I saw two flies building a bridge, and two doves tearing a wolf; two children who threw down two kids, and two frogs threshing corn with might and main!

There I saw two mice consecrate a bishop; two cats who scratched out a bear's tongue, and a snail who slew two lions. There stood a barber who shaved off his wife's beard, and two sucking children who rocked their mother in a cradle! There I saw two greyhounds dragging a mill out of the water, and an old horse-knacker who said it was all right; and in a stable stood four horses kneading dough with all their strength, and two goats which heated the oven, and a red cow put the bread into the oven. There, also, a cock crowed, "Cock-a-doodle-doo!"

"My tale is over! Cock-a-doodle-doo!"

A PUZZLING TALE.

THREE Women were once changed into flowers, and grew in a field; but one was permitted to go home at night. So one time she said to her Husband, when day was dawning and she was about to return to her companions in the field and become a flower again: "This noontime come and break me off, and then I shall be released and be able to dwell with you in future,"—and thus it happened.

A TALE OF SCHLAURAFFENLAND

But now the question is how the Husband knew his Wife; for all the flowers were alike, and had no difference at all between them. The answer is this: during the night which she passed at home with her Husband, the dew fell upon her two companions which were in the field; and so he knew his Wife, because there was no dew on her flower.

THE POOR BOY IN THE GRAVE.

THERE was once upon a time a poor Lad, whose father and mother were dead, so the Magistrate placed him in the house of a rich Farmer to be fed and brought up. But this Man, and his Wife too, had very bad dispositions; and with all their wealth they were avaricious and mean, and very angry when any one took any of their bread. So the poor Boy, do what he might, received little to eat and many blows.

One day he was set to watch the hen and her chickens, and she ran through a hole in the paling, and a hawk just then flying by, pounced upon her, and carried her off to his roost. The Boy cried, "Thief, thief! stop, thief!" but to what end? the hawk kept his prey, and did not return. The Master hearing the noise came out, and perceived that his hen was gone, which put him in such a rage that he beat the Boy so much that, for a couple of days afterwards, he was unable to stir. Then the poor Lad had to watch the chickens, which was a harder task still, for where one ran the others followed. At last, thinking to make it sure, he tied all the chickens together by a string, so that the hawk could not take one. But what followed? After a couple of days he fell asleep from weariness with watching and with hunger, and then the hawk came and seized one of the chickens; and, because all the others were tied together to that one, he bore them all away and devoured them. Just then the Farmer came home, and perceived the misfortune which had happened, which angered him so much that he beat the Lad so unmercifully, that for several days he could not leave his bed.

When he was on his legs again, the Farmer said to him, "You are so stupid that I can no longer keep you as a watch, and, therefore, you shall be my errand-boy." So saying, he sent him to the Judge, to take him a basket of grapes, and a letter with them. On the way, hunger and thirst plagued the Lad so much that he ate two of the grape bunches. So when he took the basket to the Judge, and the latter had read the letter and counted the grapes, he said, "Two bunches are missing." The Boy then honestly confessed, that, driven by hunger and thirst, he had eaten two bunches; wherefore the Judge wrote a letter to the Farmer, and requested more grapes. These, also, the Boy had to carry, with a letter; and again, urged by great hunger and thirst, he devoured two bunches more. But before he went to the Judge, he took the letter out of the basket, and, laying it under a stone, put the stone over it, so that it could not be seen and betray him. The Judge, however, taxed him with the missing grapes. "Alas!" cried the Boy, "how did you know that? the letter could not tell you, for I had laid it previously under a stone." The Judge was forced to laugh at the simplicity of the Lad, but sent the Farmer a letter, in which he advised him to treat the Boy better, and not allow him to want meat or drink, or he might be taught the difference between justice and injustice.

"I will show you the difference at once!" said the hard-hearted Farmer, when he had read the letter; "if you will eat, you must also work; and if you do anything wrong, you must be recompensed with blows."

The following day he set the poor Boy a hard task, which was to cut a couple of bundles of straw for fodder for the horse. "And," said the Master, in a threatening tone; "I shall be back in five hours, and if the straw is not cut to chaff by that time, I will beat you till you cannot stir a limb."

With this speech the Farmer went to market with his Wife and servant, and left nothing behind for the Boy but a small piece of bread. He sat down at the machine, and began to cut the straw with all his strength, and, as he became hot, he drew off his coat and threw it aside on the straw. Then, in his terror, lest he should not get done in the time, he caught up, without noticing it, his own coat with a heap of straw, and cut it all to shreds. Too late he became aware of this misfortune, which he could not repair, and cried out, "Alas! now it is all up with me. The bad Master has not threatened in vain; when he comes back and sees what I have done, he will beat me to death. I would rather he took my life at once."

Now the Boy had once heard the Farmer's wife say that she had set a jar of poison under her bed, but she had only said so to keep away the sweet-tooths, for, in fact, it contained honey. The Boy, however, drew it out and ate the contents, and when he had done so, he thought to himself, "Ah! people have told me that death is bitter, but it tastes sweetly to me! No wonder that the mistress should so often wish for death." So thinking, he sat down on a stool to die; but instead of growing weaker, he felt really strengthened by the nourishing food. Soon he began to think, "This can be no poison, but I recollect the Farmer once said that in his clothes-chest was a bottle of fly-poison, which will certainly kill me." But this also was no poison, but Hungary wine. The Boy, however, fetched the bottle and drank it out, saying, "This death also tastes sweetly!" Soon the wine began to mount into his head, and to stupify him, so that he thought his death really was at hand. "I feel that I must die," he said; "I will go to the churchyard and seek a grave." He reeled out-of-doors as he spoke, and managed to reach the churchyard, where he dropped into a fresh-opened grave, and at the same time lost all consciousness. Never again in this world did the poor Boy awake. The fumes of the hot wine, noted upon by the cold dews of evening, took away his life, and he remained in the grave wherein he had laid himself.

By-and-by, when the Farmer received the news of the death of his servant, he was frightened, because he feared he might be taken before the Judge, and his terror was so great that he fell to the earth in a swoon. His Wife, who was turning some butter in a pan over the fire, ran to his assistance, and in a moment the grease caught fire and soon communicated with the whole house, which was burnt to ashes in a few hours.

Then the years during which the Farmer and his Wife lived afterwards were spent by them in misery and povery.

THE GIANT AND THE TAILOR.

A CERTAIN Tailor, who was a large boaster but very small performer, took it once into his head to go and look about him in the world. As soon as he could, he left his workshop, and travelled away over hills and valleys, now on this, and now on that; but still onwards. After he had gone some way, he perceived in the distance a steep mountain, and behind it a lofty tower, which rose from the midst of a wild dense forest. "Good gracious!" cried the Tailor, "what is this?" and driven by his curiosity, he went rapidly towards the place. But he opened his mouth and eyes wide enough when he got nearer; for the tower had legs, and sprang in a trice over the steep hill, and stood up a mighty giant before the Tailor. "What are you about here, you puny fly-legs?" asked the Giant in a voice which rumbled on all sides like thunder. "I am trying to earn a piece of bread in this forest," whispered the Tailor.

"Well, then, it is time you entered my service," said the Giant fiercely.

"If it must be so, why not?" said the Tailor, humbly; "but what will you give me?" "What wage shall you have?" repeated the Giant contemptuously; "listen and I will tell you: every year, three hundred and sixty-five days, and one besides, if it be leap-year. Is that right?"

"Quite," said the Tailor; but thought to himself, "one must cut according to his cloth; I will seek to make myself free very soon."

"Go, little rascal, and fetch me a glass of water," cried the Giant. "Why not the whole well, and its spring too?" said the Tailor, but fetched as he was bid. "What! the well and its spring too?" bellowed the Giant, who was rather cowardly and weak, and so began to be afraid, thinking to himself, "This fellow can do more than roast apples; he has a heap of courage. I must take care, or he will be too much of a servant for me!" So, when the Tailor returned with the water, the Giant sent him to fetch a couple of bundles of faggots from the forest, and bring them home. "Why not the whole forest at one stroke, every tree, young and old, knotty and smooth?" asked the Tailor, and went away. "What! the whole forest, and the well, too, and its spring!" murmured the frightened Giant in his beard; and he began to be still more afraid, and believed that the Tailor was too great a man for him, and not fit for his servant. However, when the Tailor returned with his load of faggots, the Giant told him to shoot two or three wild boars for their supper. "Why not rather a thousand at one shot, and the rest afterwards?" cried the boaster. "What, what!" gasped the cowardly giant, terribly frightened. "Oh, well! that is enough for to-day, you may go to sleep now!"

The poor Giant, however, was so very much afraid of the little Tailor, that he could not close his eyes all the night, but tossed about thinking how to get rid of his servant, whom he regarded as an enchanter conspiring against his life. With time comes counsel. The following morning the Giant and the Dwarf went together to a marsh where a great many willow-trees were growing. When they got there the Giant said, "Sit yourself on one of these willow rods, Tailor; on my life I only wish to see if you are in a condition to bend it down."

The boasting Tailor climbed the tree, and perched himself on a bough, and then, holding his breath, he made himself heavy enough thereby to bend the tree down. Soon, however, he had to take breath again, and immediately, having been unfortunate enough to come without his goose in his pocket, the bough flew up, and to the great joy of the Giant, carried with it the Tailor so high into the air that he went out of sight. And whether he has since fallen down again, or is yet flying about in the air, I am unable to tell you satisfactorily.

THE MASTER-THIEF.

An old man and his Wife were, many years ago, sitting one day before their miserable hut, resting for a while from their work. All at once a handsome carriage, drawn by four black steeds, drew up at the door, and out of it stepped a well-dressed Man. The Peasant got up and asked the seeming Lord what he wanted, and how he could serve him. The stranger offering his hand to the Peasant, said, "I desire nothing more than to enjoy a homely repast with you. Cook some potatoes in your usual fashion, and when they are ready I will sit down at your table and eat them."

The Peasant laughed, and replied, "You are some Count, or Prince, or perhaps some Archduke; distinguished Lords like you have often such fancies; but your will shall be done."

The Peasant's Wife thereupon went into the kitchen, and began to wash the potatoes, peel them, and make them into dumplings, as they were used to prepare them. While she thus proceeded with her work, the Peasant invited the Lord to come and look round his garden, which yet yielded a little produce. Now, in the garden he had dug holes, in order to set trees.

"Have you no children to help you in your work?" asked the Stranger.

"No!" replied the Peasant; "but I once had a son, but he wandered out into the world a long while ago. He was a wild youth, and very spirited, and so, instead of learning anything, he was always up to some tricks; at last he ran away from me, and I have heard nothing of him since."

As the Man spoke he took a young tree, and placing it in one of the holes, planted a pole besides it. Then, as he filled in the soil, and pressed it down, he tied the stem at the bottom, middle, and top to the pole, with a straw band.

"But tell me," suddenly said the Stranger, "why you do not bind the crooked, knotty stem, in yon corner, which is almost bent to the ground, likewise to a pole that it may grow straight?"

"My Lord," replied the Peasant, with a laugh, "you talk as you know; one may easily see that you understand nothing of gardening. Yon tree is old and knotted by age, and nobody could make it straight again. Trees should be trained while they are young." "So it is with your son," said the Stranger; "had you trained him when he was young in right ways, he would not have run away; now, he will also grow hardened and knotted."

"Truly, it is long since he went away," replied the old Man, "but perhaps he is changed."

"Would you know him again if he came back?" asked the Stranger abruptly.

"Not by his face, indeed," replied the Peasant; "but he has a mark upon him, a mole upon his shoulder as large as a bean."

At these words the Stranger drew off his coat, and, baring his shoulder, showed his father the mole.

"You are indeed my son," said the old Man, and all his love returned for his child; "but yet, how can you be may son? you have become a great Lord, rolling in riches and abundance; by what path have you arrived at this?"

THE MASTER-THIEF

"Alas! my Father," replied the Son, "the young tree was bound to no pole, and grew crooked; now is it too old to become straight again. How have I gained this, you ask; I have been a Thief. But do not be frightened; I am a Master-Thief. Neither locks nor bolts avail against me; whatever I wish for is mine. Think not that I steal like a common thief; no, I only take from the abundance of the rich. The poor are safe, for I rather give to them than take from them. So also I touch not what I can obtain without craft or skill."

"Alas! my son," replied the old Man, "I can have no pleasure in this; a thief is a thief, whether clever or not, and, I warn you, comes not to any good end." So saying, he led him to his Mother, and when she heard that he was her son she wept for joy, but when she was also told that he had become a thief, two rivers, as it were, of tears flowed from her eyes. At length she said, "He is still my son, although become a Master-Thief, and mine eyes have seen him once more."

The three then sat down to table, and he ate again with his parents the coarse fare which he had not tasted for so long. During the meal the old Peasant said to his son, "If our master, the Count of the castle above there, knew who you were, and what you were doing, he would not, me-thinks, take you in his arms and rock you, as he once did at your christening; he would rather cause you to be hung on the gallows."

"Do not be afraid, my dear Father, he will do nothing to me; I understand my trade too well. To-day even I will go to him."

So when it was evening, the Master-Thief got into his carriage and drove to the castle, where the Count received him with courtesy, because he took him for some noble personage. But when the Stranger disclosed his real character, the Count turned pale, and sat in silence for some time. At last he said, "Since you are my godson, I will forego justice for mercy, and show forbearance to you. But because you profess to be a Master-Thief, I will put your art to the proof, and if then you fail, you must keep your wedding with the hangman's daughter, and the cawing of the rooks shall be the music to celebrate it."

"My lord Count," replied the Master-Thief, "think of three as difficult tasks as you can, and if I do not fulfil my pretentions, do with me as you will."

The Count considered for some minutes, and then said, "For the first task you shall steal out of its stable my favourite horse; for the second you shall take away from my wife and me, when we are asleep, the counterpane under which we lie, without our knowledge, and also the ring off my wife's finger. For the third, and last task, you shall steal out of the church the parson and the clerk. Now mark all this well, for your neck depends upon its due performance."

Thereupon the Master-Thief went to the nearest town, and there purchased the old clothes of a country-wife, and put them on. Then he dyed his face a deep brown, and fashioned wrinkles on it so that nobody could have recognised him. Lastly, he filled a small cask with old Hungary wine, in which he mixed a powerful sleeping drug. Then, laying the cask in a basket which he carried upon his shoulder, he walked with wavering and tottering steps to the castle of the Count. It was quite dark when he arrived there, and so, sitting down upon a stone in the courtyard, he began to cough like an asthmatic old woman, and rubbed his hands together as if they were cold. Now, before the door of the stables, Soldiers were lying round a fire, and one of them remarking the old Woman, called to her to come nearer and warm herself. The seeming old Woman tottered up to the group, and taking her basket from her head, sat down near them. "What have you got in your basket, old Woman?" cried one. "A good taste of wine," she replied; "I maintain myself by trading with it; for some money and your fair words I will give you a glassful." "Come along, then," returned the Soldier; but as soon as he had drunk what was given him, he said, "Ah! this wine is very good; I would rather have two glasses than one!" and so he took a second glass, and then his comrades followed his example.

"Holloa, there!" exclaimed one of the soldiers to another inside in the stable, "here is an old Woman with some wine so good, that it will warm your chest more than all the fire." As he spoke, she carried her cask into the stable, and saw there three Soldiers; one of whom sat on the saddled horse. Another had the bridle in his hand, and a third held on by the tail. The old Woman served out to them the wine as long as it lasted, and then its effects began to show themselves. He who held the bridle let it drop from his hand, and, sinking to the ground, soon began to snore; the other let go the tail and fell asleep, snoring louder than the other; and the soldier who was sitting on the horse bent his head upon its neck, and so fell asleep, and snored like the noise of a smith's bellows. The Soldiers outside, also, had long before fallen asleep, and were lying motionless as stones round their fire. When the Master-Thief saw himself so favoured, he gave to him who held the bridle a rope in his hand, and to the other who held the tail, a wisp of straw; but what to do with him who sat upon the horse's back puzzled him. He could not throw him off, for that would have awakened him, and he would have called for help, so he was obliged to adopt a stratagem. He unbuckled the saddle girths, and knotted fast to the saddle a couple of ropes, which passed through rings in the wall. This done, he drew the sleeping rider, saddle and all, up in the air, and then made the ropes secure to the posts of the stable. He next unchained the horse, but before he led him over the stone floor of the yard, he wrapped his hoofs round with old rags, so that they might not make any noise which could awaken the watchers. Then he led his prize out cautiously, and swinging himself upon his back rode off in haste.

As soon as the day broke, the Master-Thief returned to the castle, mounted on the stolen steed. The Count was up already, and looking out of his window.

"Good morning, sir Count," said the Thief; "here is your horse, which I have luckily taken from his stable. Look around, and see your soldiers lying in the yard fast asleep; and if you go into the stable you will find them equally well occupied there."

The Count was forced to laugh, and said, "Well, for once you have succeeded; but this second time you will not come off so easily. And, I warn you, if you meet me as a Thief, I shall treat you as a thief."

By-and-by night came, and the Countess went to bed, with her wedding-ring held fast in her closed hand. "All the doors are locked and bolted," said the Count, "and I shall keep awake and watch for this Thief, that, if he makes his appearance at the window, I may shoot him."

The Master-Thief, however, went in the dark to the gallows, and cutting down from the rope a poor criminal who had been hung there that day, carried him on his back to the castle. There he placed a ladder up to the sleeping-chamber of the Count, and hoisting the dead man upon his shoulders, began to mount. As soon as he had got so high that the head of the dead man was on a level with the window, the Count, concealed by the curtain, pointed a pistol at it and fired. Immediately the Master-Thief pitched the corpse over, and then, rapidly descending the ladder, concealed himself in a corner. The night was bright, with a clear moonshine, and the Master-Thief plainly saw the Count descend the ladder, and bear the dead man away into the garden, where he began to dig a hole in which to bury him. "Now is the lucky moment! said the Thief to himself; and slipping from his hiding-place, he ran up the ladder, and entered the sleeping-room. "Dear wife," he began, imitating the Count's voice, "the Thief is dead, but he is nevertheless my godson, and more of a rogue than a criminal; I do not wish, therefore, to put his family to shame, for I pity his poor parents. I wish, therfore, before daybreak, to bury him in the garden, that the affair may be kept quiet. Give me the bed-covering, that I may wrap his body in it, and bury him decently."

The Countess gave him the counterpane readily, and as she did so, the Thief continued, "Do you know, I have a fit of magnanimity; give me your ring; since this unfortunate fellow has perilled his life for it, I will bury it with him."

The Countess did not wish to disoblige the Count, and so, drawing off her ring, though unwillingly, she handed it to him. Thereupon the Thief made off with both his prizes, and luckily reached his home before the Count had finished his grave-digging.

You may fancy what a long face the Count pulled the next morning when the Master-Thief brought him the bed-covering and the ring. "Are you a wizard?" he said to him. "Who has fetched you out of the grave, in which I myself laid you, and who has brought you to life again?"

"You did not bury me," replied the Thief, "but a poor criminal from the gallows;" and then he related circumstantially all that had occurred, so that the Count was compelled to believe that he was a clever and crafty fellow.

"But your tasks are not ended yet," said the Count; "you have still the third to do, and if you do not manage that all your former work will be useless."

The Master-Thief laughed, but made no answer; and when night came he went to the village-church with a long sack on his back, a bundle under his arm, and a lantern in his hand. In the sack he had some crabs, and in the bundle some short wax-lights. When he got into the churchyard he stopped and took a crab from his sack, and fixing one of his wax-lights upon its back he placed it on the ground and made it crawl about. Then he took out a second, and a third, and so on, till he had emptied the sack. After that he put on a long black cloak, like a monk's gown, and fastened a grey beard with wax to his chin. Then, being thus completely disguised, he took the sack in which the crabs had been, and, going into the church, proceeded up the chancel. At the same moment the steeple-clock struck twelve, and as soon as the last stroke had rung, the Master-Thief began to cry with a clear, loud voice, "Hear, all you sinners! hear, hear! the end of the world is come, the eternal day is near; hear, hear! Whoever will go to heaven with me, let him creep into this sack. I am Peter, who opens and shuts the gate of heaven. See out there in the churchyard the dead wandering about, collecting their bones together. Come, come, come, and creep into the sack for the world passes away."

His words resounded through the whole village; but the Parson and Clerk, who lived close to the Church, first understood what he said; and when they perceived the lights wandering about in the churchyard, they believed that something uncommon was happening; and went into the church. They listened for a while to the preacher; and at length the Clerk nudged the Parson, and said to him, "It would not be a bad plan if we made use of this opportunity, before the dawning of the eternal day, to get to heaven in an easy way."

"Oh, certainly!" replied the Parson, "that is exactly what I think; if you desire it, we will forthwith enter on the journey."

"Yes!" said the Clerk; "but you have the precedence, Mr. Parson, I will follow you."

So the Parson mounted the chancel steps, and crept into the sack which the Master-Thief held open, closely followed by the Clerk. Immediately the Thief drew the neck of the sack tight, and, swinging it round, dragged it down the steps, and so often as the heads of the poor fellows in it knocked against the floor, he cried to them, "Ah, now we are going over the mountains!" When they were out of the church he dragged them in the same manner through the village, and called the puddles which the sack went into "the clouds." By-and-by they came to the castle, and as he dragged the sack up the steps he named them as those which led to the gate of heaven, and said he, "We shall soon be in the entrance-court now." As soon as he got to the top, he pushed the sack into the dove-cote; and when the doves fluttered about he told the Parson and the Clerk to listen to the angels fluttering their wings. Then he pushed the bolt to and went away.

The next morning the Master-Thief presented himself before the Count, and told him that he had performed the third task, and drawn the Parson and Clerk out of the church. "Where have you left them then?" asked the Count.

"They are lying in a sack in the dove-cote," said the Thief, "and fancy themselves in heaven."

The Count went himself and saw that the Thief had spoken the truth; but he freed the poor men from their imprisonment. After he had done so, he said to the Thief, "You are indeed an arch-thief, and have won your wager. For this time you may escape with a whole skin, but take care to keep away from my provinces; for if you venture again into my power, you shall be elevated on the gallows."

The Master-Thief then took his leave; and after he had said good-bye to his parents, he went away to a distant country, and nobody has seen or heard of him since.

THE ROBBER AND HIS SONS.

ONCE upon a time there lived in a large forest a Robber and his band, who concealed themselves in caves and clefts of rocks; and when any princes, nobles, or rich merchants, passed near them, they started out and robbed them of their money and other property. But in course of time the head Robber grew old; and then he took an aversion to his employment, and repented of the many bad actions he had done. He determined, therefore, to lead a better life, like an honest man, doing good wherever he could. People wondered to see him change so quickly, but they were nevertheless glad of it. Now, he had three Sons, whom, when they had grown up, he called to him, and bade them choose what trade or profession they would be, that they might earn their living honestly. The Sons consulted with one

THE MASTER-THIEF

another, and then answered, ''The apple falls not far from its tree;
we will maintain ourselves as you did, we will become Robbers. A
business whereat we must work from morning till night, and yet
earn a scanty living and little gains, does not please us at all.''

''Alas! my dear children,'' replied the Father, ''why will you not
live quietly, and be content with little? Honest gains last the
longest. Robbery is a wicked and godless trade, which leads to bad
endings; in the riches which you may acquire, you will have no
peace, for that I know from my own experience. I tell you again it
has an evil ending; the jug is taken once too often to the well, and
gets broken; you will be caught at last and hung on the gallows.''

His Sons, however, paid no attention to his warnings, but
remained unconvinced. So the three youths resolved to make a trial,
and because they knew that the Queen had a fine horse of great
value in her stables, they determined to steal it. They were aware
that the horse ate no other fodder than a tender kind of grass, which
grew in a certain marshy wood. Thither they went and cut some of
this grass, which they made into a large bundle, and in the middle
thereof the two elder brothers hid the younger so cleverly, that he
could not be seen. This bundle they carried to the market, and the
Queen's stable-keeper purchased it, caused it to be carried to the
stable of the horse, and there thrown down. As soon as midnight
came, and everybody was fast asleep, the boy made his way out of
the bundle of grass, and, untying the horse, bridled it with its
golden bridle, and laid across it the cloth picked out with gold,
which formed the saddle, and the bells which hung from it he
stopped with wax, that they might not make any sound. This done,
he opened the stable door and rode away in great haste back to his
brothers. The watchmen in the town, however, remarked the thief,
and pursued him; and catching him, together with his brothers, they
took all three prisoners, and carried them off to gaol.

The next morning they were taken before the Queen, and when
she saw how young they were, she made inquiries about their
parentage, and learnt that they were the three sons of an old Robber,
who had changed his mode of life, and was now living an obedient
subject. She caused them to be taken back to prison, and asked the
Father if he would release his Sons. The Old Man said, ''My Sons
are not worthy of a penny being spent to release them.''

''You are a well-known and notable Robber,'' replied the Queen
to him; ''tell me the most remarkable adventure which you have met
with in your life, and I will release your Sons.''

Thus bidden, the old Robber replied, ''My lady Queen, hear my
tale of an occurrence which frightened me more than fire or water.
While travelling about, I learnt that in a wild wooded ravine
between two hills, twenty miles distant from any human habitation,
there dwelt a Giant in possession of an immense treasure of many

thousand pieces of gold and silver. So I selected from my companions as many as a hundred men, and we set out together to the place. It was a long and toilsome road among rocks and precipices, and when we came to the spot, to our great joy we did not find the Giant at home, so we took as much as we could carry of the gold and silver. Just as we were making our way home with this treasure, and fancied ourselves quite safe, we were unawares surrounded and taken prisoners by the Giant, who was accompanied by nine others. They divided us amongst them, each taking ten, and I with nine others fell to the lot of the Giant from whom we had taken the treasure. He bound our hands behind our backs and carried us like sheep to a rocky cave, and when we offered to ransom ourselves with money or property, he replied, 'I do not want your treasures; I shall keep you and devour you, for that is what I reckon upon.' So saying, he felt of us all, and, singling out one, said, 'This is the fattest of you all, and I will make a beginning with him.' Then he struck him down, and putting his flesh in morsels into a kettle full of water, he set it on the fire till it was boiled through, and afterwards made his meal of it. Thus every day he devoured one of us, and because I was the leanest, I was the last. So, when my nine companions were devoured, I bethought myself of a stratagem to escape my turn, and at length I said to the Giant, 'I see you have bad eyes, and suffer with pain in your face; I am a physician, and well experienced in my profession, and therefore if you will spare my life, I will heal your eyes.'

"He promised me my life if I were able to do what I said, and gave me everything that I asked for. I put oil in a vessel and mixed it with sulphur, pitch, salt, arsenic, and other destructive ingredients, and then I put it over the fire, as if I were preparing a plaster for his eyes. As soon then as the oil boiled I caused the Giant to lie down, and I then poured over his eyes, head, and body, the whole contents of the vessel, so that he fully lost his sight, and the whole skin of his body was blistered and burnt. With a fearful howl he jumped up, threw himself then on the ground again, and wallowed here and there, uttering dreadful cries, and roaring like a bull or lion. Then again, springing up in his rage, he caught up a large club which was lying on the ground, and ran all over the cave striking now against the floor and then on the walls, thinking each time to hit me. I could not escape, for the cave was everywhere surrounded with high walls, and the doors were closed with iron bolts. I jumped from one corner to the other, and at last, because I knew not what else to do, I mounted by a ladder to the roof and hung thereon by both hands. There I remained a day and a night, and then, because I could bear it no longer, I climbed down again and mixed with the sheep. There I was obliged to be very active and always run between the Giant's legs with the flock that he might not notice me. At length, I found in one corner of the sheepfold a ram's skin, and managed to draw it on so well that the beast's horns came where my head was. Now the Giant was accustomed when the sheep were going to the meadows to make then run between his legs, by which means he counted them, and also picked out the fattest one, whom he caught and cooked for his dinner. On this occasion I thought I should easily escape by pressing through his legs as the sheep did; but he caught me, and finding me heavy, said, 'You are fat, and shall fill my belly to-day.' I gave one leap and sprang out of his hands, and he caught me again. I escaped a second time, but he caught me again; and seven times I thus alternately eluded and fell into his grasp. Then he flew into a passion and said to me, 'You may run away, and may the wolves devour you, for you have fooled me enough!' As soon as I was outside the cave I threw off the skin which disguised me, and shouted in a mocking tone to him that I had escaped him in spite of all. While I did so he drew a ring from his finger and held it out to me, saying, 'Take this ring as a pledge from me; you have well deserved it. It would not be becoming either, that so crafty and clever a man should go unrewarded by me.' I took the gold ring and put it on my finger, not knowing that it was enchanted, and that it compelled me to utter, whether I wished or not, the words, 'Here I am! here I am!' In consequence of this the Giant was made aware where I was, and pursued me into the forest. But there, because he was blind, he ran every moment against some roots or trunks of trees, and fell down like an immense rock. Each time, however, he quickly raised himself, and, as he had such long legs, and could make such enormous strides, he gained on me very soon, while I still cried, without cessation, 'Here I am! here I am!' I was well aware that the ring was the cause of my exclamations, and I tried to draw it off, but without success. At last, as there was no other resource, I bit off my finger with my own teeth, and, at the same time, I ceased to cry 'Here I am!' and so luckily escaped the Giant. Certainly I thus lost one of my fingers, but I preserved my life by doing so.''

Here the Robber broke off and said to the Queen, "Madam, if it please you, I have told you this adventure to ransom one of my Sons; and now, to liberate the second, I will narrate what further happened to me :—

''As soon as I had escaped from the Giant, I wandered about the wilderness totally unable to tell which way to turn. I climbed to the tops of the firs, and up all the hills, but wherever I looked, far and wide, there was no house, nor field, nor a single trace of a human habitation: the whole country was one terrible wilderness. From mountains, which reached up to heaven, I reached valleys which were only to be compared with abysses. I encountered lions, bears, buffaloes, zebras, poisonous snakes, and fearful reptiles; I saw two wild uncouth men, people with horns and beaks, so frightful, that I shudder even now when I think of them. I hurried on and on, impelled by hunger and thirst, though I feared every minute I should sink with exhaustion. At last, just as the sun was going down, I came to a high mountain, from whence I saw in a deserted valley a column of smoke rising, as it were, from a baker's oven. I ran out as quickly as I could down the mountain in the direction of the smoke, and when I got below I saw three dead men hanging on the bough of a tree. The sight terrified me, for I supposed I had fallen into the power of some other Giant, and I feared for my life. However, taking courage, I went on, and soon came to a cottage whose door stood wide open; and by the fire on the hearth, sat a woman with her child. I entered, greeted her, and asked her why she sat there alone, and where her husband was; I asked, too, if it were far from any human habitation. She told me, in reply, that any country where there were men's dwellings was at a very great distance; and she related, with tears in her eyes how, on the previous night, the wild men of the wood had entered her house and stolen her away with her child from the side of her husband, and carried her to this wilderness. She said, too, that that morning the monsters, before going out, had commanded her to kill and dress her own child, that they might devour it on their return. As soon as I had heard this tale I felt great pity for the poor woman and her child, and resolved to rescue them from their situation. So I ran away to the tree, on which hung the three thieves, and, taking down the middle one, who was the stoutest, carried him into the house. I cut him in pieces and told the woman to give them to the robbers to eat. Her child I concealed in a hollow tree, and then I hid myself behind the house, where I could see when the wild men arrived, and if it were necessary, hasten to the relief of the woman. As soon as the sun set, the three Giants came down from the mountain; they were fearful objects to look at, being similar to apes in their statue and figure. They were dragging behind them a dead body, but I could not see what it was. As soon as they entered the house, they lighted a large fire, and, tearing the body to pieces with their teeth, devoured it uncooked. After that they took the kettle, in which was cooked the flesh of the thief, off the fire, and divided the pieces among them for their supper. As soon as they had done, one of them, who appeared to be the head, asked the woman if what they had eaten were the flesh of her child. She said 'Yes.' And then the monster said, 'I believe that you have concealed your child, and given us to eat one of the thieves off the tree.' So saying, he told his companions to run off and bring him a piece of the flesh of each of the three thieves that he might assure himself they were all there. As soon as I heard this I ran and hung myself by the hands between the two thieves on the rope which had been round the neck of the third. When the monsters came, they cut a piece of flesh from the side of each of us, and I endured the pain without suffering any cry to escape me. I have even now the scar for a witness of the truth of the tale.''

Here the Robber again ceased, and told the Queen that what he had said was intended as a ransom for his second Son, and for the third he would narrate the conclusion of his tale. Then he went on thus :—

''As soon as the wild people had gone away with these three pieces of flesh, I let myself down again and bound up my wound as well as I could with strips of my shirt, but I could not stop the blood, which streamed down me still. I paid no attention to that, however, but kept thinking still how to perform my promise of saving the woman and her child. I hastened back, therefore, to my concealment, and listened to what was passing in the cottage. I could scarcely keep my attention fixed, however, for I felt so much pain from my wound, and, besides, I was quite worn out with hunger and thirst. I observed, nevertheless, the Giant trying the three pieces of flesh which were brought to him, and when he took up the third, which was mine, he exclaimed to his three comrades, 'Run at once and fetch me the middle thief, for his flesh seems to me the best flavoured!' As soon as I heard this I hurried to the gallows and suspended myself again by the rope between the two thieves. Soon the monsters came, and pulling me down, dragged me over the thorns and stones to the house, where they threw me on the floor. Then, sharpening their knives, they prepared to slay and devour me, but just as they were about to begin, there suddenly rolled such a clap of thunder, accompanied by lightning, over the house, that the monsters themselves trembled and paused in their work. The thunder and lightning continued and the rain fell in torrents, while the wind blew as if the whole cottage would be swept away. In the midst of the noise and confusion the monsters fled out of the cottage through the window and roof and left me lying on the ground. The storm lasted for three hours, and then daylight appeared, and soon the sun shone out. I got up, and seeking the woman and her child, we left the ruined hut, and for fourteen days wandered about the wilderness, subsisting on nothing but roots, herbs, and berries, which grew on our path. At length we arrived in a civilised country, and I found the husband and the wife, whose joy you may easily imagine on the return of his wife and child.''

Here the Robber ended his tale, and as soon as he had concluded, the Queen said to him, ''You have atoned for much evil by your restoration of this poor Woman to her husband, and, therefore, I now liberate your three Sons.''

WISE HANS.

How happy is the man, and how well his affairs go on at home, who has a wise boy who listens to every word that is said to him, and then goes and acts according to his own discretion! Such a wise Hans was once sent by his Master to look for a lost cow. He remained a long while absent; but the Master thought, "My trusty Hans spares himself no trouble in his work!" When, however, a still longer time had elapsed, and the Boy did not return, his Master began to fear something had happened, so he made himself ready to go in search of him. He looked about for a long while, and at length found Hans running up and down in a wide field. "Now, my good Hans," cried his Master when he had overtaken him, "have you found the cow which I sent you after?"

"No, Master," he replied, "I have not found the cow, for I have not looked for it."

"What have you been looking for, then, Hans?" asked the Master.

"Something better, and I have found it, too, luckily."

"What is it, Hans?"

"Three Blackbirds," answered the Boy.

"And where are they?" continued his Master.

"One I hear, the second I see, and the third I am hunting," said the Boy.

Take now example by this; do not trouble yourself with your Master's business or his orders; but do rather whatever may please you at the moment, and then you will be reckoned as fine a fellow as this wise Hans.

THE COUNTRYMAN AND THE EVIL SPIRIT.

Once there lived a bold and cunning Countryman, whose tricks are too numerous to be told entire; but one of the best tales is that showing how he managed to over-reach an Evil Spirit and make a fool of him.

It was growing quite dusky one day, when, having ploughed over his fields, he was preparing to return home. Just then he perceived in the middle of his field a heap of red-hot coals, and as he approached it, full of wonder, he observed a little Black Spirit sitting on the top. "You are sitting upon some treasure?" said the Countryman, inquiringly. "Yes, indeed," replied the Spirit; "a treasure containing more gold and silver than you ever saw in your life."

"Then the treasure belongs to me, because it lies on my field," said the Countryman, boldly.

"It shall be thine," replied the Spirit, "if you give me for the next two years half the produce of your land. Of gold I have more than enough, and I wish for some of the fruits of the earth."

To this bargain the Countryman agreed; but first stipulated that to avoid dispute in the division of the produce, what was above ground should belong to the Spirit, and what was beneath the surface to himself. To this, the Spirit readily consented, but the crafty Countryman sowed turnip-seed. So when the harvest time arrived, the Spirit appeared to claim his fruits; but he found nothing but withered yellow stalks, while the Countryman contentedly dug up his turnips. "For once you have got the advantage of me," exclaimed the angry Spirit, "but it shall not happen so again; mine is what grows under the ground, and yours what grows above it." "Very well, I am satisfied," said the Countryman; and when sowing time came round, he put maize seed in the ground instead of turnips. The corn ripened in due course, and then the Spirit appeared to fetch away his crops. Just before he came, the Countryman had cut and carried all his corn, and so when the Evil Spirit arrived he found nothing else but stubble, and thereupon he hurried off in a terrible rage. "So must one toss foxes in blankets!" cried the Countryman when the Evil Spirit was gone, and went and fetched the treasure.

THE EARS OF WHEAT.

AGES upon ages ago, when the angels used to wander on earth, the fruitfulness of the ground was much greater than it is now. Then the Ears of Wheat bore, not fifty or sixty-fold, but four times five-hundred-fold. Then the corn grew from the bottom of the stalk to the top; and so long as the stalk was, so long were the Ears. But as men always do in the midst of their abundance, they forgot the blessing which came from God, and became idle and selfish.

One day a Woman went to a corn-field, and her little Child who accompanied her fell into a puddle and soiled her frock. The Mother tore off a handful of Wheat-ears and cleaned her Daughter's dress with them. Just then an Angel passed by, and saw her. He became very angry, and declared to her that henceforth the Wheat-stalks should no longer produce Ears, for, said he, "You mortals are not worthy of heaven's gifts." The bystanders who heard him, fell on their knees, weeping and praying for him to leave the Wheat-stalks alone, if not for themselves, yet for the poor fowls, who must otherwise perish with hunger. The Angel pitied their distress and granted part of their prayer; and from that day the Ears of Wheat have grown as they do now.

OLD RINKRANK.

THERE was once a King who had a Daughter; and he had a glass mountain built, and said that whoever could run over it without tumbling should have this Daughter for his wife. Then there was one who was so fond of the King's Daughter that he asked the King whether he might not marry her. "Yes," said the King, "if you can run over the mountain without tumbling, then you shall have her." The King's Daughter said she would run over with him, so that she might hold him up if he were going to fall; so they ran over together, but when they got up to the middle the King's Daughter slipped and fell, and the glass mountain opened itself, and she tumbled right into it. Her Sweetheart couldn't see a bit where she had gone through, for the mountain had closed again directly. Then he fretted and cried so much, and the King too was so wretched, that he had the mountain broken down again, thinking he would get his Daughter out again; but they could never find the place where she had tumbled through. In the meantime the King's Daughter had got quite deep into the ground, in a great cave. There, there came to her an old fellow with a tremendous long grey beard, and he told her that if she would be his servant and do all he bade her, she should remain alive; if not he would make away with her. So she did all he told her. In the morning he took his ladder out of his pocket and placed it against the mountain, and climbed up out of it. Then he pulled the ladder up after him. She had then to cook his dinner, to make his bed, and to do all his work; and when he came home again he always brought great heaps of gold and silver with him.

Now, when she had been many years with him, and had already grown quite old, he called her Mother Mansrot, and she had to call him Old Rinkrank. One day, when he was out again, she made his bed, and washed his dishes, and then she shut up all the doors and windows quite close; but there was a little loophole, through which the light shone into the house, and that she left open. When Old

Rinkrank came home again he knocked at his door, and called out, "Open the door for me." "Nay, Old Rinkrank," said she; "I shan't open the door." Then he said:

"Here stand I, poor Rinkrank,
Upon my seventeen long shanks;
Mother Mansrot, wash my dishes!"

"I have already washed your dishes," said she. Then he said again:

"Here stand I, poor Rinkrank,
Upon my seventeen long shanks;
Mother Mansrot, make my bed!"

"I have already made your bed," said she. Then he said again:

"Here stand I, poor Rinkrank,
Upon my seventeen long shanks;
Mother Mansrot, open the door!"

Then he ran all round about the house, and saw that the little loop hole was open, so he thought, "I will just look in there, to see what she is about that she won't open the door for me." So he went and tried to look in, but he couldn't get his head through on account of his long beard; so he poked his beard through the loophole first, and when he had got it quite through Mother Mansrot ran up, and fastened the trapdoor with a band which she had tied to it, and so the beard was fastened in quite tight. Then he began to scream most miserably, it hurt him so; and he begged and prayed she would let him loose; but she said not before he gave her the ladder on which he climbed out of the mountain. Then, whether he willed or not, he was obliged to say where the ladder was. So she tied a very long band to the trap-door, and placed the ladder against the mountain, and climbed up out of it; and when she was at the top she pulled the trap-door open. She went then to her father and narrated all that had happened to her. The King was greatly rejoiced; and her Sweetheart was there still; so they went and dug up the mountain, and found Old Rinkrank with all his gold and silver. Then the King had Old Rinkrank killed, and took home all his silver and gold. And the King's Daughter married her old Sweetheart, and they lived right merrily in splendour and happiness.

THE BOOTS MADE OF BUFFALO LEATHER.

A Soldier who is afraid of nothing, cares for nothing. Now such an one had received his discharge, and because he had learnt no trade, he could earn no money; and so he wandered about hither and thither, begging alms of good people. Over his shoulders hung an old weatherproof cloak, and he had still left a pair of buffalo leather boots. One day, thus equipped, he went on walking through the fields without attending to the guide-posts, and at last he came to an immense forest. He did not know where he was, but he saw a man sitting upon the trunk of a tree, who was well dressed in a green huntsman's coat. The Soldier held out his hand to him, and then laying himself down on the grass, stretched out his legs. "I see you have a pair of fine shining boots on," said he to the Huntsman; "but if you had to walk about as much as I, they would not last you very long. Look at mine! they are made of buffalo leather, and although they have served me a long time, they would still go through thick and thin." The Huntsman made no answer; and after a while the Soldier got up and said, "I can stop here no longer; hunger urges me forward; but pray, Brother Thin-Boots, where does this path lead to!" "I do not know myself," replied the Huntsman; "I have lost myself in this forest." "Then you are in the same plight as I," returned the Soldier; "like and like please one another; we will remain together and seek the way." The Huntsman only laughed, but they set out together, and kept on till nightfall. "We shall not get out of this forest to-night," exclaimed the Soldier at last; "but I can see a light glimmering in the distance, where they will give us something to eat." It was a stone cottage, and when they knocked at the door, an old Woman opened it. "We are seeking a night's lodging," said the Soldier to her, "and some fodder for our stomachs, for mine is as empty as my purse."

"You cannot stop here," answered the old Woman; "this is a robber's house, and you will be wise if you go away before they return, or you will be lost."

"It cannot be worse," said the Soldier; "for two days I have not eaten a morsel; and so it is all one to me whether I perish in this house or out in the forest. I shall come in and risk it!"

The Huntsman did not wish to follow, but the Soldier, drawing his arm within his own, drew him in, saying, "Come, comrade, we will suffer together!"

The old Woman pitied them, and told them to creep behind the stove, and then when the robbers were satisfied and slept, she would give them something to eat. Scarcely had they hid snugly in the corner, than in came the twelve robbers; and placing themselves round the table, demanded their supper with harsh language. The old Woman soon brought in an immense dish of baked meat, and the robbers prepared to fall to. Soon the smell of the savoury mess ascended the Soldier's nose, and he said to the Huntsman, "I can hold out no longer I must sit down at the table and take a share!" "You will lose your life!" whispered the Huntsman, holding him fast by the arm. The Soldier began to cough loudly, and as soon as the robbers heard this, they threw aside their knives and forks, and rising hastily from the table discovered the pair behind the stove. "Aha, you rascals!" they called; "what are you sitting there in that corner for? Are you sent as spies? Just wait a bit, and you shall learn how to fly on a bare branch!" "Oh! have some manners, if you please!" returned the Soldier; "give us something to eat first, and afterwards you shall do what you like with us!" The robbers were astonished to hear such bold words, and the Captain said, "Good! I see you are not afraid; eat you shall, but afterwards you shall die." "We shall see!" muttered the Soldier; and sitting down at the table, he began to cut and eat in earnest. "Brother Thin-Boots," he exclaimed to the Huntsman, "come and eat; you are hungry as well as I, and a better joint than this you could not have at home." The Huntsman, however, refused; and the robbers looking at the Soldier, said to one another, "This fellow makes no ceremony." When he had done eating, he asked for something to drink, saying, "Well! the meat was good enough; now let us have a good draught of wine." The Captain happened to be in a good humour, and so he told the old Woman to fetch a bottle of the very best wine out of the cellar. When it was brought, the Soldier drew out the cork so that it made a great noise; and then going to the Huntsman he whispered to him, "Pay attention, my brother, and you shall see a grand wonder; I will now drink the health of the whole company!" So saying, he swung the bottle over the heads of the robbers, at the same time shouting out, "You shall all live, but with your mouths open and your right hands uplifted!" Scarcely were the words out of his mouth, than the robbers all sat motionless as if they were made of stone, their mouths open and their right arms stretched out. "I see," said the Huntsman to the Soldier, "you can play any other trick you please; but, come now, let us go home." "Oh no, Brother Thin-Shoes!" replied the Soldier, "that were too early to march away; we have beaten the enemy and now we must take the booty. Come now, eat and drink what you like." So they stopped there three days, and every day the old Woman had to fetch up fresh wine. The fourth day the Soldier said to his companion, "It is time now to break the spell, but that we may have a short march the old Woman shall show us the nearest road."

As soon as they arrived at the town the Soldier went to his old comrades, and told them that he had found in the forest a nest of thieves, and if they wished he would show them where. They agreed to go, and the Soldier persuaded the Huntsman to accompany him again, and see how the robbers behaved when they were caught. So first he placed the soldiers round the robbers in a circle, and then drinking a draught of wine out of the bottle, he swung it over them and exclaimed, "You shall all live." In a moment they had the power of motion again, but they were soon thrown down and bound hand and foot with ropes. Then they were thrown like sacks upon a waggon, and the Soldier bade his comrades drive it away to the prison. But the Huntsman, taking aside one of the soldiers, gave him a commission and sent him off to the town. They walked on, and by-and-by, as they approached the town, the Soldier perceived an immense crowd of men rushing out at the gates, hurrahing loudly and waving green branches of trees in the air. He soon saw that it was the body-guards of the King who were approaching them; and turning to the Huntsman he asked, "What does this mean?" "Do you not know," he replied, "that the King has been absent from his kingdom for a length of time? To-day he returns, and these are coming out to meet him." "But where is the King? I do not see him," said the Soldier. "Here he is," answered the Huntsman; "I am the King, and I caused my return to be proclaimed." With these words he opened his hunting-coat and showed his royal dress. The Soldier was frightened, and falling on his knees he begged the King's pardon for having treated him so unceremoniously, and called him by such names. The King, however, holding out his hand, said to him, "You are a brave Soldier, and have saved my life; you shall suffer poverty no longer; I will care for you, and if at any time you want a piece of meat as good as we had in the forest, come to my palace and dine with me. But before you drink healths you must ask my permission."

THE GOLDEN KEY.

ONE winter, when a deep snow was lying on the ground, a poor Boy had to go out in a sledge to fetch wood. As soon as he had collected together a sufficient quantity, he thought that before he returned home he would make a fire to warm himself at, because his limbs were so frozen. So sweeping the snow away, he made a clear space, and presently found a small gold key. As soon as he picked it up, he began to think that where there was a key there must also be a lock; and digging in the earth he found a small iron chest. "I hope the key will fit," thought he to himself; "there are certainly great treasures in this box!" He looked all over it, but could not find any key hole; till at last he did discover one, which was, however, so small, that it could scarcely be seen. He tried the key, and behold! it fitted exactly. Then he turned it once round, and now we must wait until he has quite unlocked it, and lifted the lid up, and then we shall learn what wonderful treasures were in the chest!

THE TAILOR IN OLYMPUS.

ONE glorious day in summer, Jupiter determined to spend the day in the Elysian fields, and extending his royal favour to all the gods and goddesses, took them with him to enjoy the excursion, leaving only Mercury in Olympus. The thunderer left strict orders with him, "that, during their absence, he should admit nobody," so Mercury stood sentry at the gate. After a time, a knock was heard. Mercury asked who was there, and what was wanted. "I am a poor honest tailor," replied a small voice, "and beg you to admit me." "Honest, indeed!" said Mercury; "yes, like an unhanged thief, have you not continually made cabbage of the cloth entrusted to you. You will not come in here! The king has forbidden me to let anybody in while he is away." "Pray be merciful," entreated the tailor, "scraps that fall under the shop-board cannot be considered stolen, and indeed are not worth mentioning. See! I limp, and my feet are blistered from the long journey, it is impossible for me to turn back; let me in and I will do all your work—nurse the children and carry them about, clear up their litters, and mend the clothes they tear." Mercury allowed himself to be persuaded, thinking, perhaps, that he might depute the tailor to execute some of his numerous duties, so he opened the gate just enough to permit the tailor with his spare figure to slip through. But he was obliged to go into a corner behind the door, and remain there quiet, lest when Jove returned he should discover him, and be angry. The tailor consented; but when Mercury went out of the door for a moment, he arose, took advantage of the opportunity, and pried into every corner of Olympus. He came at last to a place where there were many beautiful chairs placed in a semicircle, and in the midst a magnificent golden armchair, set with precious stones; it was more elevated than the rest, and before it stood a golden footstool. This was Jupiter's throne, which he occupied when at home, and from which he could observe all that mortals did upon earth. The tailor stood for a while and admired the armchair, which pleased him more than all the rest; then, not being able to restrain the inclination, he placed himself in it, which enabled him to see all that was taking place on earth. He saw an ugly old woman washing linen at a brook, and observed her lay two veils aside. This made the tailor so angry, that he seized the golden footstool and flung it with all his strength at the old thief's head, and it fell to the earth; but discovering that he had no means of restoring it again to its place, he slipped out of the chair, and back to his place behind the door, as if he had never stirred from the spot.

In the evening, Jupiter and all the train of divinities came back, and no discovery of the little tailor took place; but when the king of the gods took possession of his chair, in order to repose himself, the footstool was not to be found. Mercury was called, and he was asked where the stool was, but he could not tell. Jove then further inquired if anybody had been allowed to enter. "I know of no one," replied Mercury, "except a lame tailor, who is still behind the door." The tailor was produced, and then asked if he could account for the disappearance of the stool; if he had taken it away, and where it was. "Great Jove," replied he, in dismay at the discovery of the act, "I threw it at a thievish old woman, who made me angry because she stole two veils she had been entrusted to wash." "Oh! you rogue," replied Jove, "if I were to punish as you punish, how long do you think I should be able to carry it on? I should have been long ago without chairs, stools, benches, or even a stick of furniture, all would have been cast down upon the offenders? However, you cannot stay here, but must depart the way you came, and then look to yourself. None can punish here save I, the mighty Jove." Mercury conducted the tailor through the gate of Olympus; and his feet being blistered, and his shoes full of holes, he took a staff in his hand, and went on a pilgrimage to St. Martin's Well.

THE DEVIL'S SOOTY BROTHER.

A DISBANDED soldier had nothing to live on, and did not know how to get on. So he went out into the forest, and when he had walked for a short time, he met a little man who was, however, the Devil. The little man said to him, "What ails you, you seem so very sorrowful?" Then the soldier said, "I am hungry, but have no money." The Devil said, "If you will hire yourself to me, and be my serving-man, you shall have enough for all your life. You shall serve me for seven years, and after that you shall again be free. But one thing I must tell you, and that is, you must not wash, comb, or trim yourself, or cut your hair or nails, or wipe the water from your eyes.'' The soldier said, ''All right, if there is no help for it,'' and went off with the little man, who straightaway led him down into hell. Then he told him what he had to do, he was to poke the fire under the kettles wherein the hell-broth was stewing, keep the house clean, drive all the sweepings behind the doors, and see that everything was in order, but if he once peeped into the kettles, it would go ill with him. The soldier said, ''Good, I will take care.'' And then the old Devil went out again on his wanderings, and the soldier entered upon his new duties, made the fire, and swept the dirt well behind the doors, just as he had been bidden. When the old Devil came back again, he looked to see if all had been done, appeared satisfied, and went forth a second time. The soldier now took a good look on every side; the kettles were standing all round hell with a mighty fire below them, and inside they were boiling and sputtering. He would have given anything to look inside them, if the Devil had not so particularly forbidden him: at last, he could no longer restrain himself, slightly raised the lid of the first kettle, and peeped in, and there he saw his former corporal shut in. ''Aha, old bird!'' said he. ''Do I meet you here? You once had me in your power, now I have you,'' and he quickly let the lid fall, poked the fire, and added a fresh log. After that, he went to the second kettle, raised its lid also a little, and peeped in; his former ensign was inside that. ''Aha, old bird, so I find you here! you once had me in your power, now I have you.'' He closed the lid again, and fetched yet another log to make it really hot. Then he wanted to see who might be shut up in the third kettle—it was actually a general. ''Aha, old bird, do I meet you here? Once you had me in your power, now I have you,'' and he fetched the bellows and made hell-fire flare well up under him. So he did his work seven years in hell, did not wash, comb, or trim himself, or cut his hair or nails, or wash the water out of his eyes, and the seven years seemed so short to him that he thought he had only been half a year. Now when the time had fully gone by, the Devil came and said, ''Well Hans, what have you done?'' ''I have poked the fire under the kettles, and I have swept all the dirt well behind the doors.''

''But you have peeped into the kettles as well; it is lucky for you that you added fresh logs to them, or else your life would have been forfeited; now that your time is up, will you go home again?'' ''Yes,'' said the soldier, ''I should very much like to see what my father is doing at home.'' The Devil said, ''In order that you may receive the wages you have earned, go and fill your knapsack full of the sweepings, and take it home with you. You must also go unwashed and uncombed, with long hair on your head and beard, and with uncut nails and dim eyes, and when you are asked whence you come, you must say, ''From hell,'' and when you are asked who you are, you are to say, "The Devil's sooty brother, and my King as well." The soldier held his peace, and did as the Devil bade him, but he was not at all satisfied with his wages. Then as soon as he was up in the forest again, he took his knapsack from his back, to empty it, but on opening it, the sweepings had become pure gold. "I should never have expected that," said he, and was well pleased, and entered the town. The landlord was standing in front of the inn, and when he saw the soldier approaching, he was terrified, because Hans looked so horrible, worse than a scare-crow. He called to him and asked, "Whence comest thou?" "From hell." "Who art thou?" "The Devil's sooty brother, and my King as well." Then the host would not let him enter, but when Hans showed him the gold, he came and unlatched the door himself. Hans then ordered the best room and attendance, ate, and drank his fill, but neither washed nor combed himself as the Devil had bidden him, and at last lay down to sleep. But the knapsack full of gold remained before the eyes of the landlord, and left him no peace, and during the night he crept in and stole it away. Next morning, however, when Hans got up and wanted to pay the landlord and travel further, behold, his knapsack was gone! But he soon composed himself and thought, "Thou hast been unfortunate from no fault of thine own," and straightway went back again to hell, complained of his misfortune to the old Devil, and begged for his help. The Devil said, "Seat yourself, I will wash, comb, and trim you, cut your hair and nails, and wash your eyes for you," and when he had done with him, he gave him the knapsack back again full of sweepings, and said, "Go and tell the landlord that he must return you your money, or else I will come and fetch him, and he shall poke the fire in your place." Hans went up and said to the landlord, "Thou hast stolen my money; if thou dost not return it, thou shalt go down to hell in my place, and wilt look as horrible as I." Then the landlord gave him the money, and more besides, only begging him to keep it secret, and Hans was now a rich man.

He set out on his way home to his father, bought himself a shabby smock-frock to wear, and strolled about making music, for he had learned to do that while he was with the Devil in hell. There was, however, an old King in that country, before whom he had to play, and the King was so delighted with his playing, that he promised him his eldest daughter in marriage. But when she heard that she was to be married to a common fellow in a smock-frock, she said, "Rather than do it, I would go into the deepest water," and then the King gave him the youngest, who was quite willing to do it to please her father, and thus the Devil's sooty brother got the King's daughter, and when the aged King died, the whole kingdom likewise.

THE WILLFUL CHILD.

ONCE upon a time there was a child who was willful, and would not do what her mother wished. For this reason God had no pleasure in her, and let her become ill, and no doctor could do her any good, and in a short time she lay on her death-bed. When she had been lowered into her grave, and the earth was spread over her, all at once her arm came out again, and stretched upwards, and when they had put it in and spread fresh earth over it, it was all to no purpose, for the arm always came out again. Then the mother herself was obliged to go to the grave, and strike the arm with a rod, and when she had done that, it was drawn in, and then at last the child had rest beneath the ground.

THE OLD MAN MADE YOUNG AGAIN.

IN the time when our Lord still walked this earth, he and St. Peter stopped one evening at a smith's and received free quarters. Then it came to pass that a poor beggar, hardly pressed by age and infirmity, came to this house and begged alms of the smith. St. Peter had compassion on him and said, "Lord and master, if it please thee, cure his torments that he may be able to win his own bread." The Lord said kindly, "Smith, lend me thy forge, and put on some coals for me, and then I will make this ailing old man young again." The smith was quite willing, and St. Peter blew the bellows, and when the coal fire sparkled up large and high our Lord took the little old man, pushed him in the forge in the midst of the red-hot fire, so that he glowed like a rose-bush, and praised God with a loud voice. After that the Lord went to the quenching tub, put the glowing little man into it so that the water closed over him, and after he had carefully cooled him, gave him his blessing, when behold the little man sprang nimbly out, looking fresh, straight, healthy, and as if he were but twenty. The smith, who had watched everything closely and attentively, invited them all to supper. He, however, had an old half-blind crooked mother-in-law who went to the youth, and with great earnestness asked if the fire had burnt him much. He answered that he had never felt more comfortable, and that he had sat in the red heat as if he had been in cool dew. The youth's words echoed in the ears of the old woman all night long, and early next morning, when the Lord had gone on his way again and had heartily thanked the smith, the latter thought he might make his old mother-in-law young again likewise, as he had watched everything so carefully, and it lay in the province of his trade. So he called to ask her if she, too, would like to go bounding about like a girl of eighteen. She said, "With all my heart, as the youth has come out of it so well." So the smith made a great fire, and thrust the old woman into it, and she writhed about this way and that, and uttered terrible cries of murder. "Sit still; why are thou screaming and jumping about so?" cried he, and as he spoke he blew the bellows again until all her rags were burnt. The old woman cried without ceasing, and the smith thought to himself, "I have not quite the right art," and took her out and threw her into the cooling-tub. Then she screamed so loudly that the smith's wife upstairs and her daughter-in-law heard, and they both ran downstairs, and saw the old woman lying in a heap in the quenching-tub, howling and screaming, with her face wrinkled and shrivelled and all out of shape. Thereupon the two, who were both with child, were so terrified that that very night two boys were born who were not made like men but apes, and they ran into the woods, and from them sprang the race of apes.

THE LORD'S ANIMALS AND THE DEVIL'S.

THE Lord God had created all animals, and had chosen out the wolf to be his dog, but he had forgotten the goat. Then the Devil made ready and began to create also, and created goats with fine long tails. Now when they went to pasture, they generally remained caught in the hedges by their tails, then the Devil had to go there and disentangle them, with a great deal of trouble. This enraged him at last, and he went and bit off the tail of every goat, as may be seen to this day by the stump. Then he let them go to pasture alone, but it came to pass that the Lord God perceived how at one time they gnawed away at a fruitful tree, at another injured the noble vines, or destroyed other tender plants. This distressed him, so that in his goodness and mercy he summoned his wolves, who soon tore in pieces the goats that went there. When the devil observed this, he went before the Lord and said, "Thy creatures have destroyed mine." The Lord answered, "Why didst thou create things to do harm?" The Devil said, "I was compelled to do it: inasmuch as my thoughts run on evil, what I create can have no other nature, and thou must pay me heavy damages." "I will pay thee as soon as the oak leaves fall; come then, thy money will then be ready counted out." When the oak-leaves had fallen, the Devil came and demanded what was due to him. But the Lord said, "In the church of Constantinople stands a tall oak-tree which still has all its leaves." With raging and curses, the Devil departed, and went to seek the oak, wandered in the wilderness for six months before he found it, and when he returned, all the oaks had in the meantime covered themselves again with green leaves. Then he had to forfeit his indemnity, and in his rage he put out the eyes of all the remaining goats, and put his own in instead.

This is why all goats have devil's eyes, and their tails bitten off, and why he likes to assume their shape.

THE PEASANT IN HEAVEN.

ONCE on a time a poor pious peasant died, and arrived before the gate of heaven. At the same time a very rich, rich lord came there who also wanted to get into heaven. Then Saint Peter came with the key, and opened the door, and let the great man in, but apparently did not see the peasant, and shut the door again. And now the peasant outside, heard how the great man was received in heaven with all kinds of rejoicing, and how they were making music, and singing within. At length all became quiet again, and Saint Peter came and opened the gate of heaven, and let the peasant in. The peasant, however, expected that they would make music and sing when he went in also, but all remained quite quiet; he was received with great affection, it is true, and the angels came to meet him, but no one sang. Then the peasant asked Saint Peter how it was that they did not sing for him as they had done when the rich man went in, and said that it seemed to him that there in heaven things were done with just as much partiality as on earth. Then said Saint Peter, "By no means, thou art just as dear to us as any one else, and wilt enjoy every heavenly delight that the rich man enjoys, but poor fellows like thee come to heaven every day, but a rich man like this does not come more than once in a hundred years!"

EVE'S VARIOUS CHILDREN.

WHEN Adam and Eve were driven out of Paradise, they were compelled to build a house for themselves on unfruitful ground, and eat their bread in the sweat of their brow. Adam dug up the land,

and Eve spun. Every year Eve brought a child into the world; but the children were unlike each other, some pretty, and some ugly. After a considerable time had gone by, God sent an angel to them, to announce that he was coming to inspect their household. Eve, delighted that the Lord should be so gracious, cleaned her house diligently, decked it with flowers, and strewed reeds on the floor. Then she brought in her children, but only the beautiful ones. She washed and bathed them, combed their hair, put clean raiment on them, and cautioned them to conduct themselves decorously and modestly in the presence of the Lord. They were to bow down before him civilly, hold out their hands, and to answer his questions modestly and sensibly. The ugly children were, however, not to let themselves be seen. One hid himself beneath the hay, another under the roof, a third in the straw, the fourth in the stove, the fifth in the cellar, the sixth under a tub, the seventh beneath the wine-cask, the eighth under an old fur cloak, the ninth and tenth beneath the cloth out of which she always made their clothes, and the eleventh and twelfth under the leather out of which she cut their shoes. She had scarcely got ready, before there was a knock at the house-door. Adam looked through a chink, and saw that it was the Lord. Adam opened the door respectfully, and the Heavenly Father entered. There, in a row, stood the pretty children, and bowed before him, held out their hands, and knelt down. The Lord, however, began to bless them, laid his hands on the first, and said, "Thou shalt be a powerful King;" and to the second, "Thou a prince," to the third, "Thou a count," to the fourth, "Thou a knight," to the fifth, "Thou a nobleman," to the sixth, "Thou a burgher," to the seventh, "Thou a merchant," to the eighth, "Thou a learned man." He bestowed upon them also all his richest blessings. When Eve saw that the Lord was so mild and gracious, she thought, "I will bring hither my ill-favoured children also, it may be that he will bestow his blessing on them likewise." So she ran and brought them out of the hay, the straw, the stove, and wherever else she had concealed them. Then came the whole coarse, dirty, shabby, sooty band. The Lord smiled, looked at them all, and said, "I will bless these also." He laid his hands on the first, and said to him, "Thou shalt be a peasant," to the second, "Thou a fisherman," to the third, "Thou a smith," to the fourth, "Thou a tanner," to the fifth, "Thou a weaver," to the sixth, "Thou a shoemaker," to the seventh, "Thou a tailor," to the eighth, "Thou a potter," to the ninth, "Thou a waggoner," to the tenth, "Thou a sailor," to the eleventh, "Thou an errand-boy," to the twelfth, "Thou a scullion all the days of thy life."

When Eve had heard all this she said, "Lord, how unequally thou dividest thy gifts! After all they are all of them my children, whom I have brought into the world, thy favours should be given to all alike." But God answered, "Eve, thou dost not understand. It is right and necessary that the entire world should be supplied from thy children; if they were all princes and lords, who would grow corn, thresh it, grind and bake it? Who would be blacksmiths, weavers, carpenters, masons, labourers, tailors and seamstresses? Each shall have his own place, so that one shall support the other, and all shall be fed like the limbs of one body." Then Eve answered, "Ah, Lord, forgive me, I was too quick in speaking to thee. Have thy divine will with my children."

THE CRUMBS ON THE TABLE.

A COUNTRYMAN one day said to his little puppies, "Come into the parlour and enjoy yourselves, and pick up the bread-crumbs on the table; your mistress has gone out to pay some visits." Then the little dogs said, "No, no, we will not go. If the mistress gets to know it, she will beat us." The countryman said, "She will know nothing about it. Do come; after all, she never gives you anything good." Then the little dogs again said, "Nay, nay, we must let it alone; we must not go." But the countryman let them have no peace until at last they went, and got on the table, and ate up the bread-crumbs with all their might. But at that very moment the mistress came, and seized the stick in great haste, and beat them and treated them very hardly. And when they were outside the house, the little dogs said to the countryman, "Dost, dost, dost, dost, dost thou see?" Then the countryman laughed and said, "Didn't, didn't, didn't you expect it?" So they just had to run away.

THE MOON.

IN days gone by there was a land where the nights were always dark, and the sky spread over it like a black cloth, for there the moon never rose, and no star shone in the obscurity. At the creation of the world, the light at night had been sufficient. Three young fellows once went out of this country on a travelling expedition, and arrived in another kingdom, where, in the evening when the sun had disappeared behind the mountains, a shining globe was placed on an oak tree, which shed a soft light far and wide. By means of this, everything could very well be seen and distinguished, even though it was not so brilliant as the sun. The travellers stopped and asked a countryman who was driving past with his cart, what kind of a light that was. "That is the moon," answered he; "our mayor bought it for three thalers, and fastened it to the oak tree. He has to pour oil into it daily, and to keep it clean, so that it may always burn clearly. He receives a thaler a week from us for doing it."

When the countryman had driven away, one of them said, "We could make some use of this lamp, we have an oak tree at home, which is just as big as this, and we could hang it on that. What a pleasure it would be not to have to feel about at night in the darkness!" "I'll tell you what we'll do," said the second; "we will fetch a cart and horses and carry away the moon. The people here may buy themselves another." "I'm a good climber," said the third, "I will bring it down." The fourth brought a cart and horses, and the third climbed the tree, bored a hole in the moon, passsd a rope through it, and let it down. When the shining ball lay in the cart, they covered it over with a cloth, that no one might observe the theft. They conveyed it safely into their own country, and placed it on a high oak. Old and young rejoiced, when the new lamp let its light shine over the whole land, and bedrooms and sitting-rooms were filled with it. The dwarfs came forth from their caves in the rocks, and the tiny elves in their little red coats danced in rings on the meadows.

The four took care that the moon was provided with oil, cleaned the wick, and received their weekly thaler, but they became old men, and when one of them grew ill, and saw that he was about to die, he appointed that one quarter of the moon, should, as his property, be laid in the grave with him. When he died, the mayor climbed up the tree, and cut off a quarter with the hedge shears, and this was placed in his coffin. The light of the moon decreased, but still not visibly. When the second died, the second quarter was buried with him, and the light diminished. It grew weaker still after the death of the third, who likewise took his part of it away with him; and when the fourth was borne to his grave, the old state of darkness recommenced, and whenever the people went out at night without their lanterns they knocked their heads together.

When, however, the pieces of the moon had united themselves together again in the world below, where darkness had always prevailed, it came to pass that the dead became restless and awoke from their sleep. They were astonished when they were able to see again; the moonlight was quite sufficient for them, for their eyes had become so weak that they could not have borne the brilliance of the sun. They rose up and were merry, and fell into their former ways of living. Some of them went to the play and to dance, others hastened to the public-houses, where they asked for wine, got drunk, brawled, quarrelled, and at last took up cudgels, and belaboured each other. The noise became greater and greater, and at last reached even to heaven.

Saint Peter who guards the gate of heaven thought the lower world had broken out in revolt and gathered together the heavenly troops, which are to drive back the Evil One when he and his associates storm the abode of the blessed. As these, however, did not come, he got on his horse and rode through the gate of heaven, down into the world below. There he reduced the dead to subjection, bade them lie down in their graves again, took the moon away with him, and hung it up in heaven.

THE LYING TALE.

I WILL tell you something. I saw two roast hens flying; they flew quickly, and had their heads to the sky and their tails to the ground! I saw an anvil and a mill-stone swimming over the Rhine, but slowly and lightly, and a frog sat and ate a plough-share at Whitsuntide on the ice. There were three fellows wished to catch a hare, and went upon crutches and stilts; the one was deaf, the second blind, and the third dumb, and the fourth could not stir a foot. Do you wish to know how that happened? The blind man saw the hare coursing over the fields, the dumb man called to the lame one, and he caught the hare by the neck.

There were some fellows who wished to sail on dry land, and they spread the sail, and were carried over the meadows; but when they attempted to get up a high mountain they were miserably drowned. A crab was hunting a hare, and high upon the roof lay a cow which had climbed there. In this land flies are as big as goats.

Pray open the window that these lies may escape.

THE CHILDREN'S LEGENDS.

THE LEGEND OF SAINT JOSEPH IN THE FOREST.

THERE was once upon a time a Mother who had three Daughters, the eldest of whom was stupid and bad-tempered; the second, however, was much better, though she, too, had her faults; but the youngest was a pious, good child. The Mother was odd in her tastes, for she loved the eldest the most, and could not endure her youngest Daughter; and therefore she often sent the poor girl out into the forest, where she hoped to be rid of her, hoping that she would wander about so as to lose herself. Her guardian angel however, (and such an one watches over every good child), did not forsake her, but led her always along the right road. Once the angel seemed to have forsaken her, and the Child wandered on by herself. She walked on till evening, and then saw a light burning in the distance. She went up to it, and found a little cottage, and knocking at the door it opened, and she came to a second door, where she knocked again. An old man, with a snowwhite beard and a venerable countenance, opened it, and he was no other than St. Joseph. In a friendly voice he said, "Come in, dear Child; sit down on my stool by the fire and warm yourself; I will fetch you some clear water if you are thirsty, but I have nothing for you to eat but a couple of roots, and those you must scrape and cook for yourself." With these words St. Joseph handed her the roots, and, carefully peeling them, she took up a small saucepan and put them in. Then she added to them some water and the bread which her Mother had given her, and put them over the fire till they were boiled down to a soup. When it was done, St. Joseph said, "I am so hungry, give me some of your broth to eat." This the Girl very willingly did, and gave him more than she took for herself. Still, however, with God's blessing, she had quite sufficient. As soon as they had finished their supper, St. Joseph said, "It is time now to go to bed, but as I have only one bed, do you lie down in that, and I will make my bed of straw." "No, no," she replied; "keep you your own bed, the straw is tender enough for me." St. Joseph, however, would carry her to the bed, and there laying her down, she went to sleep as soon as she had said her prayers. The next morning, when she awoke, she would have said, "Good morning!" to St. Joseph, but she could nowhere see him. She arose and looked for him, but she could not find him in any corner; and while she searched she perceived hanging behind the door a sack full of money, on which it was written that it was for the Maiden who had slept there that night. She took the sack, and jumping merrily along under its weight, took it to her Mother, who was obliged for once to be satisfied with her youngest Daughter.

The following day the second Daughter also took a fancy to go into the forest, and her Mother gave her a much larger pancake and a piece of bread. It happened to her the same as it had done to her Sister. Towards evening she came to the cottage where St. Joseph lived, and he told her to make herself some soup. As soon as it was ready he said as before, "I pray you give me some of that to eat, for I am so hungry." The child told him to eat with her; and when afterwards he proposed to give her his bed and lie himself on the straw, she said to him, "Share the bed with me, there is room enough for us both!" But St. Joseph laid her down in the bed by herself and slept on the straw, and by the next morning, when she awoke, he had disappeared. Behind the door she found a small bag of gold, as long as her hand, and on it was written that it was for the Maiden who had slept there that night. She took the bag and hastened home to her Mother, but she kept secretly two pieces of gold for herself.

Now, the eldest Sister became covetous, and the next morning she prepared to go to the forest. Her Mother gave her several pancakes, as many as she liked, and not only bread, but cheese. About evening she arrived, like her Sisters, at the cottage of St. Joseph, and found him there. She was also bidden to cook her soup, and when it was ready St. Joseph said, "I am so hungry, give me some of your soup to eat." But the Maiden replied, "Wait until I am satisfied, and then what I leave you shall have." So she went on eating till she had nearly finished, and St. Joseph had only the scrapings of the basin. The good old man, however, offered her his bed, and said he would lie on the straw, and this kindness she took as if it were her due, and she let the Saint lie down on his hard couch. The next morning, when she awoke, he had disappeared, but she cared nothing about that, and thought only of the bag of gold, which she expected to find behind the door. She certainly did see something lying there, but because she could not exactly tell what it was, she bent herself down

Einsiedels
Abendlied.

THE LEGEND OF SAINT JOSEPH IN THE FOREST

so that her nose touched it. It stuck to her nose, and when she stood up and looked at herself she found to her terror that it was a second nose growing from the first! She began to howl and shriek, but to what purpose? she could not help seeing her nose, because it was so long. She ran out of the house with a loud cry, and ran on till she met St. Joseph, and as soon as she saw him she fell down on her knees and begged him to take away the second nose. Out of pity for her, he did at last remove it and gave her two pennies. As soon as she reached home her Mother met her at the door, and asked her what she had received. She told a lie, and answered, "A great sack full of money, but I lost it on the way." "Lost it!" repeated the Mother, "then let us look for it again;" and catching her Daughter's hand, she dragged her back to search. At first she wept and would not go, but at length she consented, and on they went. At every step they took snakes and lizards started up, so many that they could not guard them off; and soon one stuck its fang into the breast of the Daughter and she fell dead; and then another pierced the foot of the Mother because she had not brought her Child up better.

HUMILITY AND POVERTY LEAD TO HEAVEN.

ONCE upon a time there was a King's Son, who went into the fields sad and thoughtful. He looked up at the sky, which was so beautifully blue and clear, and said with a sigh, "Ah! how happy must they be who are in heaven." At the same moment he perceived a grey old Man, who was walking the same way, and he asked him the question how he could go to heaven. "Through humility and poverty," answered the old Man, "Put on my old clothes, and wander about the world for seven years to learn what misery is: take no money with you, but when you are hungry, beg a piece of bread of charitable people, and thus you will approach gradually the gate of heaven."

Thus advised, the Prince drew off his fine clothing, and putting on instead the Beggar's rags, he went forth into the world, and endured much misery. He took only the scantiest meals, spoke never a word, but prayed daily to God, to take him, if he pleased, to heaven. When seven years had passed, he returned to his father's house, but nobody recognised him. He told the servants to go and tell his parents that he was returned; but the servants would not believe him, and only laughed at his pretensions. "Then go and tell my brothers," said he, "that they may come to me, for I should like to see them once again." This request they also refused; but at length one went and told the King's children, but they troubled not their heads about it. Then he wrote a letter to his mother, and depicted all his misery, but said nothing about his being her son. The Queen, pitying his misfortune, caused a place to be made for him below the staircase, and there two servants daily had to bring him food. But one of them was wicked at heart, and asked, "What shall the Beggar do with good food?" and so he kept it for himself, or gave it to the dogs, while he took the poor weak, half-starved Prince nothing but water. The other servant, however, was honest, and took him daily what he received for him. It was only a little, but still enough to sustain life for a long while; and with it he was quite content, though he grew weaker and weaker. But when his illness increased, he desired to receive the last rites of the church, and while the service was performing, all at once every bell in the city and the country round tolled. As soon as the service was over, the Priest went to the poor Beggar, and found him lying dead, holding in one hand a rose, and in the other a lily; and near him lay a paper, whereon was written his history.

And after he was buried, there grew on one side of his grave a rose, and on the other side a lily.

THE THREE GREEN TWIGS.

ONCE upon a time there lived a Hermit at the foot of a mountain near the forest, who spent his time in prayer and good works, and each evening he carried up the hill a pail of water as an act of penitence. Many a beast refreshed himself from this pail, and many a flower also was revived, for on the height blew continually a hot wind, which dried the air and the earth. The wild fowls also, who avoided human beings, would circle down near the water and dip their long beaks into it. And because the Hermit was so pious, unseen an Angel always accompanied him up the hill, counting his steps, and bringing him, when the work was done, a meal, like as was done to that Prophet who, at God's command, was fed by the ravens. Thus the Hermit grew older and more pious every day; and once it happened that as he ascended the hill, he saw at a distance a poor sinner led to the gallows. As he looked he said, "Now is he judged rightly!" and as soon as he had so said the Angel left him and brought him no food that evening. He grew frightened, and tried in his heart to think how he had offended God; but he could remember nothing. He ceased to eat or drink, and throwing himself on the earth, prayed all day and night long. Once, as he was bitterly weeping in the forest, he heard a little Bird singing clearly and beautifully, and the sound so disturbed him that he exclaimed, "Alas! you sing merrily, because you are happy; but I would that you could tell me wherein I have offended God that I might do penance, and so my heart become glad again!" Presently the Bird spoke, "You did wrong because you condemned a poor criminal whom you saw led to the gallows, and therefore was God angry, because to him alone belongs the right of judgment. Still, if you are penitent and confess your sins, God will yet pardon you." At the moment the Bird finished speaking the Angel stood once more beside the Hermit, and giving a withered branch, said to him, "You shall carry this till Three Green Twigs spring from it; and at night when you sleep you must always place it beneath your head. Your bread you must beg from door to door, and you must not remain in any house more than one night. This is the penance which God imposes on you."

So the hermit took the dry branch and went back to the world which he had not seen for so long. He ate and drank nothing but what was given to him at the door of charitable people, although at many houses his prayer was refused, and many a door was shut against him, and thus he often passed whole days without a crumb of bread. One day he had thus passed, door after door was shut against him, and nobody would give him anything, or shelter him for the night; so he went into the wood and found a tumble-down cottage, in which an old Woman was sitting. He went in and said to her, "Pray shelter me this night, my good Woman." She replied, "No, I dare not, even if I would; I have three sons, wild and wicked, who, if they come home from their plundering and find you here, will kill us both." "Let me stop, nevertheless," entreated the Hermit: "they will do nothing to either you or me." So the old Woman took compassion on him and bade him sit down. He laid himself down in a corner with the dry branch under his head, and when the old Woman observed this she inquired the reason, and he told her that he carried it as a penance, and was forced to use it every night for his pillow. "I have offended God," he said, "because when I saw a poor criminal led to the gallows, I said that justice was done to him." The old Woman began to weep bitterly as he finished his tale, and exclaimed, "Alas! if God so punishes for a single word, how will he judge my sons when they appear before him!"

At midnight the Robbers came home shouting and laughing. They lighted a fire, and as the blaze lit up the cottage they saw the old Man lying in one corner. In a rage they started up and asked their Mother, "Who is this man? Have we not forbidden you ever to allow any one to enter our house?"

"Let him be, he is only a poor sinner doing penance for his sins,"

THE THREE GREEN TWIGS

pleaded the Mother. "What has he done?" asked the Robbers; and, turning to the old Man, they said, "Tell us your crimes." So the Hermit lifted himself up, and related how he had sinned by saying a few words, for which God was very angry with him, and had made him do penance. As he finished his tale the hearts of the Three Brothers were powerfully affected, and they were so frightened with the remembrance of their daily lives that they began to repent with heartfelt sorrow. Meanwhile, the old Hermit having thus turned the three sinners from their evil ways, laid down to sleep. In the morning he was found dead, and from the dry branch which formed his pillow Three Green Twigs had burst forth.

And by this it was known that God had fully pardoned him.

THE OLD WIDOW.

In a certain large town there once lived an Old Widow, who sat every evening alone in her room, thinking how, one by one, she had lost and buried her husband, her two sons, and all her relations and friends, so that now she was quite alone in the world. Her heart grew very sorrowful with these thoughts; but the loss of her two sons troubled her the most, and she wept for them very bitterly. She sat quite still, lost in thought, and all at once she heard the bell ringing for early prayers in the church. She wondered how she could have passed all the night in sorrowing; but lighting her lantern she went to the church. As she entered she saw it was already lit up: but not as usual with tapers, but a glimmering light shone through the whole building. It was already filled with worshippers, and every seat was occupied, so that when the Poor Widow went to her accustomed place, she found it already filled. As she looked round at the people, she perceived that they were her deceased relations, who sat there in their old every-day dresses; but with pale countenances. They neither spoke nor sang, but a gentle whisper and hum floated through the church. Presently an Aunt of the Poor Widow got up and said to her, "Look towards the altar, and you will see your two sons." She looked and saw her two children, the one hanging on the gallows, and the other broken on the wheel. "See," continued the Aunt, "thus would it have happened to them, had life been given to them, instead of their being mercifully taken by God when they were innocent children." With trembling steps the Old Widow went home, and on her knees thanked God that he had dealt so much better with her than her heart had imagined. But on the third day she laid down on her bed and died.

THE ROSE.

THERE was once a poor Woman who had two Children, and the youngest went every day into the forest to fetch wood. Once, when it had strayed far away looking for branches, a little, but strong and healthy Child came to it and helped it to pick up wood, and carried the bundles up to the house; but then in less than a moment he was gone. The Child told its mother of this; but she would not believe it. At last the Child brought home a Rose, and told its mother that the beautiful Child had given it, and had said that when the Rose was in full bloom then he would come again. The Mother put the Rose into water. One morning the Child did not get out of bed, and the mother went to it and found it dead; but it lay looking quite happy and pleased, and the Rose that morning was in full bloom.

THE TWELVE APOSTLES.

THREE hundred years before the birth of the Lord Christ, there lived a mother who had twelve sons, but was so poor and needy that she no longer knew how she was to keep them alive at all. She prayed to God daily that he would grant that all her sons might be on the earth with the Redeemer who was promised. When her necessity became still greater she sent one of them after the other out into the world to seek bread for her. The eldest was called Peter, and he went out and had already walked a long way, a whole day's journey, when he came into a great forest. He sought for a way out, but could find none, and went farther and farther astray, and at the same time felt such great hunger that he could scarcely stand. At length he became so weak that he was forced to lie down, and he believed death to be at hand. Suddenly there stood beside him a small boy who shone with brightness, and was as beautiful and kind as an angel. The child smote his little hands together, until Peter was forced to look up and saw him. Then the child said, "Why art thou sitting there in such trouble?" "Alas!" answered Peter, "I am going about the world seeking bread, that I may yet see the dear Saviour who is promised, that is my greatest desire." The child said, "Come with me, and thy wish shall be fulfilled." He took poor Peter by the hand, and led him between some cliffs to a great cavern. When they entered it, everything was shining with gold, silver, and crystal, and in the midst of it twelve cradles were standing side by side. Then said the little angel, "Lie down in the first, and sleep a while, I will rock thee." Peter did so, and the angel sang to him and rocked him until he was asleep. And when he was asleep, the second brother came also, guided thither by his guardian angel, and he was rocked to sleep like the first, and thus came the others, one after the other, until all twelve lay there sleeping in the golden cradles. They slept, however, three hundred years, until the night when the Saviour of the world was born. Then they awoke, and were with him on earth, and were called the twelve apostles.

GOD'S FOOD.

THERE were once upon a time two sisters, one of whom had no children and was rich, and the other had five and was a widow, and so poor that she no longer had food enough to satisfy herself and her children. In her need, therefore, she went to her sister, and said, "My children and I are suffering the greatest hunger; thou art rich, give me a mouthful of bread." The very rich sister was as hard as a stone, and said, "I myself have nothing in the house," and drove away the poor creature with harsh words. After some time the husband of the rich sister came home, and was just going to cut himself a piece of bread, but when he made the first cut into the loaf, out flowed red blood. When the woman saw that she was terrified and told him what had occurred. He hurried away to help the widow and her children, but when he entered her room, he found her praying. She had her two youngest children in her arms, and the three eldest were lying dead. He offered her food, but she answered, "For earthly food have we no longer any desire. God has already satisfied the hunger of three of us, and he will hearken to our supplications likewise." Scarcely had she uttered these words than the two little ones drew their last breath, whereupon her heart broke, and she sank down dead.

OUR LADY'S LITTLE GLASS.

ONCE upon a time a waggoner's cart which was heavily laden with wine had stuck so fast that in spite of all that he could do, he could not get it to move again. Then it chanced that Our Lady just happened to come by that way, and when she perceived the poor man's distress, she said to him, "I am tired and thirsty, give me a glass of wine, and I will set they cart free for thee." "Willingly," answered the waggoner, "but I have no glass in which I can give thee the wine." Then Our Lady plucked a little white flower with red stripes, called field bindweed, which looks very like a glass, and gave it to the waggoner. He filled it with wine, and then Our Lady drank it, and in the self-same instant the cart was set free, and the waggoner could drive onwards. The little flower is still always called Our Lady's Little Glass.

THE HEAVENLY WEDDING.

A POOR peasant-boy one day heard the priest say in church that whosoever desired to enter into the kingdom of heaven must always go straight onward. So he set out, and walked continually straight onward over hill and valley without ever turning aside. At length his way led him into a great town, and into the midst of a church, where just at that time God's service was being performed. Now when he beheld all the magnificence of this, he thought he had reached heaven, sat down, and rejoiced with his whole heart. When the service was over, and the clerk bade him go out, he replied, "No, I will not go out again, I am glad to be in heaven at last." So the clerk went to the priest, and told him that there was a child in the church who would not go out again, because he believed he was in heaven. The priest said, "If he believes that, we will leave him inside." So he went to him, and asked if he had any inclination to work. "Yes," the little fellow replied, "I am accustomed to work, but I will not go out of heaven again." So he stayed in the church, and when he saw how the people came and knelt and prayed to Our Lady with the blessed child Jesus which was carved in wood, he thought "that is the good God," and said, "Dear God, how thin you are! The people must certainly let you starve; but every day I will give you half my dinner." From this time forth, he every day took half his dinner to the image, and the image began to enjoy the food. When a few weeks had gone by, people remarked that the image was growing larger and stout and strong, and wondered much. The priest also could not understand it, but stayed in the church, and followed the little boy about, and then he saw how he shared his food with the Virgin Mary, and how she accepted it.

After some time the boy became ill, and for eight days could not leave his bed; but as soon as he could get up again, the first thing he did was to take his food to Our Lady. The priest followed him, and heard him say, "Dear God, do not take it amiss that I have not brought you anything for such a long time, for I have been ill and could not get up." Then the image answered him and said, "I have seen thy good-will, and that is enough for me. Next Sunday thou shalt go with me to the wedding." The boy rejoiced at this, and repeated it to the priest, who begged him to go and ask the image if he, too, might be permitted to go. "No," answered the image, "thou alone." The priest wished to prepare him first, and give him the holy communion and the child was willing, and next Sunday, when the host came to him, he fell down and died, and was at the eternal wedding.

THE HAZEL-BRANCH.

ONE afternoon the Christ-child had laid himself in his cradle-bed and had fallen asleep. Then his mother came to him, looked at him full of gladness, and said, "Hast thou laid thyself down to sleep, my child? Sleep sweetly, and in the meantime I will go into the wood, and fetch thee a handful of strawberries, for I know that thou wilt be pleased with them when thou awakest." In the wood outside, she found a spot with the most beautiful strawberries; but as she was stooping down to gather one, an adder sprang up out of the grass. She was alarmed, left the strawberries where they were, and hastened away. The adder darted after her; but Our Lady, as you can readily understand, knew what it was best to do. She hid herself behind a hazel-bush, and stood there until the adder had crept away again. Then she gathered the strawberries, and as she set out on her way home she said, "As the hazel-bush has been my protection this time, it shall in future protect others also." Therefore, from the most remote times, a green hazel-branch has been the safest protection against adders, snakes, and everything else which creeps on the earth.